THE GOLDEN NOTEBOOK

The powerful and absorbing novel
that raised the consciousness
of a generation

"Doris Lessing writes about her own sex with the
unrelenting intensity of Simone de Beauvoir, and
about sex itself with the frankness and detail of
John O'Hara."
—*Washington Post*

"A long and complex novel which draws on all
the talents and insights of this gifted woman. It
is no ordinary work of fiction . . . The technique,
in a word, is brilliant, and in itself places Doris
Lessing in the forefront of present British women
novelists."
—John Barkham, *Saturday Review Syndicate*

"England's brilliant Doris Lessing looks deeply
into the problem of a sensitive and disillusioned
modern woman . . . Seldom are the troubled re-
cesses of a soul probed as ruthlessly as Mrs.
Lessing has done here . . . It is a rewarding book,
an unusually perceptive one."
—*Milwaukee Journal*

"This exciting writer has tried much, has aimed
high, has paraded a dazzling galaxy of gifts."
—*Baltimore Sun*

ABOUT THE AUTHOR

DORIS LESSING is one of the leading writers in the world today. She was born in 1919, grew up in Southern Rhodesia, and settled in England in 1949. In the subsequent years she wrote numerous books, including *Going Home* and *African Stories*—magnificent portraits of the loved and hated land of youth—*The Grass Is Singing, The Habit of Loving, In Pursuit of the English, A Man and Two Women,* and *The Four-Gated City.* Her most recent works are *The Temptation of Jack Orkney* and *The Summer Before the Dark.* Mrs. Lessing is best known for her pioneering novel, *THE GOLDEN NOTEBOOK,* and for the intelligence and passion with which she writes about women like herself and about their involvement in various centers of tension in the contemporary world.

THE GOLDEN NOTEBOOK

DORIS LESSING

With a new Introduction
by the author

BANTAM BOOKS
TORONTO · NEW YORK · LONDON

THE GOLDEN NOTEBOOK
*A Bantam Book / published by arrangement with
Simon & Schuster, Inc.*

PRINTING HISTORY
Simon & Schuster edition published June 1962
2nd printing .... October 1962
3rd printing .... March 1973

Bantam edition / September 1973

2nd printing .... April 1974	5th printing .... March 1976
3rd printing .... October 1974	6th printing .... August 1977
4th printing .... July 1975	7th printing .... March 1979
8th printing ...... December 1979	
9th printing	

Back cover courtesy of Jill Krementz

ISBN 0-553-13675-5

Published simultaneously in the United States and Canada

*Bantam Books are published by Bantam Books, Inc. Its trade-
mark, consisting of the words "Bantam Books" and the por-
trayal of a bantam, is Registered in U.S. Patent and Trademark
Office and in other countries. Marca Registrada. Bantam
Books, Inc., 666 Fifth Avenue, New York, New York 10019.*

PRINTED IN THE UNITED STATES OF AMERICA

Contents

Introduction   vii

FREE WOMEN: 1   *Anna meets her friend Molly in the summer of 1957 after a separation*   3

    THE NOTEBOOKS   55

FREE WOMEN: 2   *Two visits, some telephone calls and a tragedy*   257

    THE NOTEBOOKS   282

FREE WOMEN: 3   *Tommy adjusts himself to being blind while the older people try to help him*   371

    THE NOTEBOOKS   410

FREE WOMEN: 4   *Anna and Molly influence Tommy, for the better. Marion leaves Richard. Anna does not feel herself*   507

    THE NOTEBOOKS   524

THE GOLDEN NOTEBOOK   611

FREE WOMEN: 5   *Molly gets married and Anna has an affair*   647

Contents

Introduction

BEYOND ...

EXPERIMENTS ...

TELEWOMEN ...

FIRST WORDS ...

MEN, WOMEN ...

Introduction

The shape of this novel is as follows:

There is a skeleton, or frame, called *Free Women*, which is a conventional short novel, about 60,000 words long, and which could stand by itself. But it is divided into five sections and separated by stages of the four Notebooks, Black, Red, Yellow and Blue. The Notebooks are kept by Anna Wulf, a central character of *Free Women*. She keeps four, and not one because, as she recognises, she has to separate things off from each other, out of fear of chaos, of formlessness—of breakdown. Pressures, inner and outer, end the Notebooks; a heavy black line is drawn across the page of one after another. But now that they are finished, from their fragments can come something new, *The Golden Notebook*.

Throughout the Notebooks people have discussed, theorised, dogmatised, labelled, compartmented- sometimes in voices so general and representative of the time that they are anonymous, you could put names to them like those in the old Morality Plays, Mr. Dogma and Mr. I-am-Free-Because-I-Belong-Nowhere. Miss I-Must-Have-Love-and-Happiness and Mrs. I-Have-to-be-Good-At-Everything-I do, Mr. Where-is-a-Real-Woman? and Miss Where-is-a-Real-Man?, Mr. I'm-Mad-Because-They-Say-I-Am, and Miss Life-through-Experiencing-Everything, Mr. I-make-Revolution-and-Therefore-I-Am, and Mr. and Mrs. If-We-Deal-Very-Well-with-This-Small-Problem-Then-Perhaps-We-Can-Forget-W -Daren't-Look-at-The-Big-Ones. But they have also reflected each other, been aspects of each other, given birth to each other's thoughts and behaviour—*are* each other, form wholes. In the inner Golden Notebook, things have come together, the divisions have broken down, there is formlessness with the end of fragmentation—the triumph of the second theme, which is that of unity. Anna and Saul Green the American "break down". They are crazy, lunatic, mad—what you will. They "break down" into each other, into other people, break through the false patterns they have made of their pasts, the patterns and formulas they have made to shore up themselves and each other, dissolve. They hear each other's thoughts, recognise each other in themselves. Saul Green, the man who has been envious and destructive of Anna, now supports her, advises her, gives her the theme for her next book, *Free Women*—an ironical title, which begins: "The two women were alone in the London flat." And Anna, who has been jealous of Saul to the point of insanity, possessive and demanding, gives Saul the pretty new notebook, *The Golden Notebook*, which she has previously refused to do, gives him the theme for his next book, writing in it the first sentence: "On a dry hillside in Algeria a soldier watched the moonlight glinting on his rifle." In the inner Golden Notebook, which is written by both of them, you can no longer distinguish between what is Saul and what is Anna, and between them and the other people in the book.

This theme of "breakdown", that sometimes when people "crack up" it is a way of self-healing, of the inner self's dismissing false dichotomies and divisions, has of course been written about by other people, as well as by me, since then. But this is where, apart from the odd short story, I first wrote about it. Here it is rougher, more close to experience, before experience has shaped itself into thought and pattern—more valuable perhaps because it is rawer material.

But nobody so much as noticed this central theme, because the book was instantly belittled, by friendly reviewers as well as by hostile ones, as being about the sex war, or was claimed by women as a useful weapon in the sex war.

I have been in a false position ever since, for the last thing I have wanted to do was to refuse to support women.

To get the subject of Women's Liberation over with—I support it, of course, because women are second-class citizens, as they are saying energetically and competently in many countries. It can be said that they are succeeding, if only to the extent they are being seriously listened to. All kinds of people previously hostile or indifferent say: "I support their aims but I don't like their shrill voices and their nasty ill-mannered ways." This is an inevitable and easily recognisable stage in every revolutionary movement: reformers must expect to be disowned by those who are only too happy to enjoy what has been won for them. I don't think that Women's Liberation will change much though—not because there is anything wrong with their aims, but because it is already clear that the whole world is being shaken into a new pattern by the cataclysms we are living through: probably by the time we are through, if we do get through at all, the aims of Women's Liberation will look very small and quaint.

But this novel was not a trumpet for Women's Liberation. It described many female emotions of aggression, hostility, resentment. It put them into print. Apparently what many women were thinking, feeling, experiencing, came as a great surprise. Instantly a lot of very ancient weapons were unleashed, the main ones, as usual, being on the theme of "She is unfeminine", "She is a man-hater." This particular reflex seems indestructible. Men—and many women—said that the suffragettes were defeminised, masculine, brutalised. There is no record I have read of any society anywhere when women demanded more than nature offers them that does not also describe this reaction from men—and some women. A lot of women were angry about *The Golden Notebook*. What women will say to other women, grumbling in their kitchens and complaining and gossiping or what they make clear in their masochism, is often the last thing they will say aloud—a man may overhear. Women are the cowards they are because they have been semi-slaves for so long. The number of women prepared to stand up for what they really think, feel, experience with a man they are in love with is still small. Most women will still run like little dogs with stones thrown at them when a man says: You are unfeminine, aggressive, you are unmanning me. It is my belief that any woman who marries or takes seriously in any way at all a man who uses this threat, deserves everything she gets. For such a man is a bully, does not know anything about the world he lives in, or about its history—men and women have taken infinite numbers of roles in the past, and do now, in different societies. So he is ignorant, or fearful about being out of step—a coward. . . . I write all these remarks with exactly the same feeling as if I were writing a letter to post into the distant past: I am so sure that everything we now take for granted is going to be utterly swept away in the next decade.

(So why write novels? Indeed, why! I suppose we have to go on living *as if*. . .)

Some books are not read in the right way because they have skipped a stage of opinion, assume a crystallisation of information in society which has not yet taken place. This book was written as if the attitudes that have been created by the Women's Liberation movements already existed. It came out first ten years ago, in 1962. If it were coming out now for the first time it might be read, and not merely reacted to: things have changed very fast. Certain hypocrisies have gone. For instance, ten, or even five years ago—it has been a sexually contumacious time—novels and plays were being plentifully written by men furiously critical of women—particularly from the States but also in this country—portrayed as bullies and betrayers, but particularly as underminers and sappers. But these attitudes in male writers were taken for granted, accepted as sound philosophical bases, as quite normal, certainly not as womanhating, aggressive or neurotic. It still goes on, of course—but things are better, there is no doubt of it.

I was so immersed in writing this book, that I didn't think about how it might be received. I was involved not merely because it was hard to write—keeping the plan of it in my head I wrote it from start to end, consecutively, and it was difficult —but because of what I was learning as I wrote. Perhaps giving oneself a tight structure, making limitations for oneself, squeezes out new substance where you least expect it. All sorts of ideas and experiences I didn't recognise as mine emerged when writing. The actual time of writing, then, and not only the experiences that had gone into the writing, was really traumatic: it changed me. Emerging from this crystallising process, handing the manuscript to publisher and friends, I learned that I had written a tract about the sex war, and fast discovered that nothing I said then could change that diagnosis.

Yet the essence of the book, the organisation of it, everything in it, says implicitly and explicitly, that we must not divide things off, must not compartmentalise.

"Bound. Free. Good. Bad. Yes. No. Capitalism. Socialism. Sex. Love. . . ." says Anna, in *Free Women*, stating a theme— shouting it, announcing a motif with drums and fanfares . . . or so I imagined. Just as I believed that in a book called *The Golden Notebook* the inner section called the Golden Notebook might be presumed to be a central point, to carry the weight of the thing, to make a statement.

But no.

Other themes went into the making of this book, which was a crucial time for me: thoughts and themes I had been holding in my mind for years came together.

One was that it was not possible to find a novel which described the intellectual and moral climate of a hundred years ago, in the middle of the last century, in Britain, in the way Tolstoy did it for Russia, Stendhal for France. (At this point it is necessary to make the obligatory disclaimers.) To read

The Red and the Black, and *Lucien Leuwen* is to know that
France as if one were living there, to read *Anna Karenina*
is to know that Russia. But a very useful Victorian novel
never got itself written. Hardy tells us what it was like to be
poor, to have an imagination larger than the possibilities of a
very narrow time, to be a victim. George Eliot is good as far
as she goes. But I think the penalty she paid for being a Victorian woman was that she had to be shown to be a good
woman even when she wasn't according to the hypocrisies of
the time—there is a great deal she does not understand because she is moral. Meredith, that astonishingly underrated
writer is perhaps nearest. Trollope tried the subject but lacked
the scope. There isn't one novel that has the vigour and conflict of ideas in action that is in a good biography of William
Morris.

Of course this attempt on my part assumed that that filter
which is a woman's way of looking at life has the same validity
as the filter which is a man's way . . . setting that problem
aside, or rather, not even considering it, I decided that to
give the ideological "feel" of our mid-century, it would have
to be set among socialists and marxists, because it has been
inside the various chapters of socialism that the great debates
of our time have gone on; the movements, the wars, the
revolutions, have been seen by their participants as movements
of various kinds of socialism, or Marxism, in advance, con-
tainment, or retreat. (I think we should at least concede the
possibility that people looking back on our time may see it
not at all as we do—just as we, looking back on the English,
the French, or even the Russian Revolutions see them differently from the people living then.) But "Marxism", and its
various offshoots, has fermented ideas everywhere, and so
fast and energetically that, once "way out" it has already been
absorbed, has become part of ordinary thinking. Ideas that
were confined to the far left thirty or forty years ago had per-
vaded the left generally twenty years ago, and have provided
the commonplaces of conventional social thought from right
to left for the last ten years. Something so thoroughly absorbed is finished as a force—but it was dominant, and in a
novel of the sort I was trying to do, had to be central.

Another thought that I had played with for a long time was
that a main character should be some sort of an artist, but
with a "block." This was because the theme of the artist has
been dominant in art for some time—the painter, writer,
musician, as exemplar. Every major writer has used it, and

most minor ones. Those archetypes, the artist and his mirror-image the businessman, have straddled our culture, one shown as a boorish insensitive, the other as a creator all excesses of sensibility and suffering and a towering egotism which has to be forgiven because of his products—in exactly the same way, of course, as the businessman has to be forgiven for the sake of his. We get used to what we have, and forget that the artist-as-exemplar is a new theme. Heroes a hundred years ago weren't often artists. They were soldiers and empire builders and explorers and clergymen and politicians—too bad about women who had scarcely succeeded in becoming Florence Nightingale yet. Only oddballs and eccentrics wanted to be artists, and had to fight for it. But to use this theme of our time "the artist", "the writer", I decided it would have to be developed by giving the creature a block and discussing the reasons for the block. These would have to be linked with the disparity between the overwhelming problems of war, famine, poverty, and the tiny individual who was trying to mirror them. But what was intolerable, what really could not be borne any longer, was this monstrously isolated, monstrously narcissistic, pedestalled paragon. It seems that in their own way the young have seen this and changed it, creating a culture of their own in which hundreds of thousands of people make films, assist in making films, make newspapers of all sorts, make music, paint pictures, write books, take photographs. They have abolished that isolated, creative, sensitive figure—by copying him in hundreds of thousands. A trend has reached an extreme, its conclusion, and so there will be a reaction of some sort, as always happens.

The theme of "the artist" had to relate to another, subjectivity. When I began writing there was pressure on writers not to be "subjective". This pressure began inside communist movements, as a development of the social literary criticism developed in Russia in the nineteenth century, by a group of remarkable talents, of whom Belinsky was the best known, using the arts and particularly literature in the battle against Csarism and oppression. It spread fast everywhere, finding an echo as late as the Fifties, in this country, with the theme of "commitment." It is still potent in communist countries. "Bothering about your stupid personal concerns when Rome is burning" is how it tends to get itself expressed, on the level of ordinary life—and was hard to withstand, coming from one's nearest and dearest, and from people doing everything one respected most: like, for instance, trying to fight colour prejudice in Southern Africa. Yet all the time novels, stories, art of every sort, became more and more personal. In the Blue Notebook, Anna writes of lectures she has been giving: " 'Art during the Middle Ages was communal, unindividual; it came out of a group consciousness. It was without the driving painful individuality of the art of the bourgeois era. And one day we will leave behind the driving egotism of individual art. We will return to an art which will express not man's self-divisions and separateness from his fellows but his responsibility for his fellows and his brotherhood. Art from the West becomes more and more a shriek of torment recording pain. Pain is becoming our deepest reality . . ." I have been saying something like this. About three months ago, in the middle of this lecture, I began to stammer and couldn't finish . . .'

Anna's stammer was because she was evading something. Once a pressure or a current has started, there is no way of avoiding it: there was no way of *not* being intensely subjective: it was, if you like, the writer's task for that time. You couldn't ignore it: you couldn't write a book about the building of a bridge or a dam and not develop the mind and feelings of the people who built it. (You think this is a caricature?— Not at all. This *either/or* is at the heart of literary criticism in communist countries at this moment.) At last I understood that the way over, or through this dilemma, the unease at writing about "petty personal problems" was to recognise that nothing is personal, in the sense that it is uniquely one's own. Writing about oneself, one is writing about others, since your problems, pains, pleasures, emotions—and your extraordinary and remarkable ideas—can't be yours alone. The way to deal with the problem of "subjectivity", that shocking business of being preoccupied with the tiny individual who is at the same time caught up in such an explosion of terrible and marvellous possibilities, is to see him as a microcosm and in this way to break through the personal, the subjective, making the personal general, as indeed life always does, transforming a private experience—or so you think of it when still a child, "*I* am falling in love", "*I* am feeling this or that emotion, or thinking that or the other thought"—into something much larger: growing up is after all only the understanding that one's unique and incredible experience is what everyone shares.

Another idea was that if the book were shaped in the right way it would make its own comment about the conventional novel: the debate about the novel has been going on since the novel was born, and is not, as one would imagine from reading contemporary academics, something recent. To put the short novel *Free Women* as a summary and condensation of all that mass of material, was to say something about the conventional novel, another way of describing the dissatisfaction of a writer when something is finished: "How little I have managed to say of the truth, how little I have caught of all that complexity; how can this small neat thing be true when what I experienced was so rough and apparently formless and unshaped."

But my major aim was to shape a book which would make its own comment, a wordless statement: to talk through the way it was shaped.

As I have said, this was not noticed.

One reason for this is that the book is more in the European tradition than the English tradition of the novel. Or rather, in the English tradition as viewed at the moment. The English novel after all does include *Clarissa* and *Tristam Shandy*, *The Tragic Comedians*—and Joseph Conrad.

But there is no doubt that to attempt a novel of ideas is to give oneself a handicap: the parochialism of our culture is intense. For instance, decade after decade bright young men and women emerge from their universities able to say proudly: "Of course I know nothing about German literature." It is the mode. The Victorians knew everything about German literature, but were able with a clear conscience not to know much about the French.

As for the rest—well, it is no accident that I got intelligent criticism from people who were, or who had been, marxists. They saw what I was trying to do. This is because Marxism looks at things as a whole and in relation to each other—or tries to, but its limitations are not the point for the moment. A person who has been influenced by Marxism takes it for granted that an event in Siberia will affect one in Botswana. I think it is possible that Marxism was the first attempt, for our time, outside the formal religions, at a world-mind, a world ethic. It went wrong, could not prevent itself from dividing and subdividing, like all the other religions, into smaller and smaller chapels, sects and creeds. But it was an attempt.

This business of seeing what I was trying to do—it brings me to the critics, and the danger of evoking a yawn. This sad bickering between writers and critics, playwrights and critics: the public have got so used to it they think, as of quarrelling children: "Ah yes, dear little things, they are at it again." Or: "You writers get all that praise, or if not praise, at least all that attention—so why are you so perennially wounded?"

And the public are quite right. For reasons I won't go into here, early and valuable experiences in my writing life gave me a sense of perspective about critics and reviewers; but over this novel, *The Golden Notebook*, I lost it: I thought that for the most part the criticism was too silly to be true. Recovering balance, I understood the problem. It is that writers are looking in the critics for an *alter ego*, that other self more intelligent than oneself who has seen what one is reaching for, and who judges you only by whether you have matched up to your aim or not. I have never yet met a writer who, faced at last with that rare being, a real critic, doesn't lose all paranoia and become gratefully attentive—he has found what he thinks he needs. But what he, the writer, is asking is impossible. Why should he expect this extraordinary being, the perfect critic (who does occasionally exist), why should there be anyone else who comprehends what he is trying to do? After all, there is only one person spinning that particular cocoon, only one person whose business it is to spin it.

It is not possible for reviewers and critics to provide what they purport to provide—and for which writers so ridiculously and childishly yearn.

This is because the critics are not educated for it; their training is in the opposite direction.

It starts when the child is as young as five or six, when he arrives at school. It starts with marks, rewards, "places", "streams", stars—and still in many places, stripes. This horse-race mentality, the victor and loser way of thinking, leads to "Writer X is, is not, a few paces ahead of Writer Y. Writer Y has fallen behind. In his last book Writer Z has shown himself as better than Writer A." From the very beginning the child is trained to think in this way: always in terms of comparison, of success, and of failure. It is a weeding-out system: the weaker get discouraged and fall out; a system designed to produce a few winners who are always in competition with each other. It is my belief—though this is not the place to develop this—that the talents every child has, regardless of his official "I.Q.", could stay with him through life, to enrich him and everybody else, if these talents were not regarded as commodities with a value in the success-stakes.

The other thing taught from the start is to distrust one's own judgement. Children are taught submission to authority, how to search for other people's opinions and decisions, and how to quote and comply.

As in the political sphere, the child is taught that he is

free, a democrat, with a free will and a free mind, lives in a free country, makes his own decisions. At the same time he is a prisoner of the assumptions and dogmas of his time, which he does not question, because he has never been told they exist. By the time a young person has reached the age when he has to choose (we still take it for granted that a choice is inevitable) between the arts and the sciences, he often chooses the arts because he feels that here is humanity, freedom, choice. He does not know that he is already moulded by a system: he does not know that the choice itself is the result of a false dichotomy rooted in the heart of our culture. Those who do sense this, and who don't wish to subject themselves to further moulding, tend to leave, in a half-unconscious, instinctive attempt to find work where they won't be divided against themselves. With all our institutions, from the police force to academia, from medicine to politics, we give little attention to the people who leave—that process of elimination that goes on all the time and which excludes, very early, those likely to be original and reforming, leaving those attracted to a thing because that is what they are already like. A young policeman leaves the Force saying he doesn't like what he has to do. A young teacher leaves teaching, her idealism snubbed. This social mechanism goes almost unnoticed—yet it is as powerful as any in keeping our institutions rigid and oppressive.

These children who have spent years inside the training system become critics and reviewers, and cannot give what the author, the artist, so foolishly looks for—imaginative and original judgement. What they can do, and what they do very well, is to tell the writer how the book or play accords with current patterns of feeling and thinking—the climate of opinion. They are like litmus paper. They are wind gauges —invaluable. They are the most sensitive of barometers of public opinion. You can see changes of mood and opinion here sooner than anywhere except in the political field—it is because these are people whose whole education has been just that—to look outside themselves for their opinions, to adapt themselves to authority figures, to "received opinion"— a marvellously revealing phrase.

It may be that there is no other way of educating people. Possibly, but I don't believe it. In the meantime it would be a help at least to describe things properly, to call things by their right names. Ideally, what should be said to every child, repeatedly, throughout his or her school life is something like this:

"You are in the process of being indoctrinated. We have not yet evolved a system of education that is not a system of indoctrination. We are sorry, but it is the best we can do. What you are being taught here is an amalgam of current prejudice and the choices of this particular culture. The slightest look at history will show how impermanent these must be. You are being taught by people who have been able to accommodate themselves to a regime of thought laid down by their predecessors. It is a self-perpetuating system. Those of you who are more robust and individual than others, will be encouraged to leave and find ways of educating yourself— educating your own judgement. Those that stay must remember, always and all the time, that they are being moulded and patterned to fit into the narrow and particular needs of this particular society."

Like every other writer I get letters all the time from young people who are about to write theses and essays about my books in various countries—but particularly in the United States. They all say: "Please give me a list of the articles about your work, the critics who have written about you, the authorities." They also ask for a thousand details of total irrelevance, but which they have been taught to consider important, amounting to a dossier, like an immigration department's.

These requests I answer as follows: "Dear Student. You are mad. Why spend months and years writing thousands of words about one book, or even one writer, when there are hundreds of books waiting to be read. You don't see that you are the victim of a pernicious system. And if you have yourself chosen my work as your subject, and if you do have to write a thesis —and believe me I am very grateful that what I've written is being found useful by you—then why don't you read what I have written and make up your own mind about what you think, testing it against your own life, your own experience. Never mind about Professors White and Black."

"Dear Writer"—they reply. "But I have to know what the authorities say, because if I don't quote them, my professor won't give me any marks."

This is an international system, absolutely identical from the Urals to Yugoslavia, from Minnesota to Manchester.

The point is, we are all so used to it, we no longer see how bad it is.

I am not used to it, because I left school when I was four-teen. There was a time I was sorry about this, and believed I had missed out on something valuable. Now I am grateful for a lucky escape. After the publication of *The Golden Note-book*, I made it my business to find out something about the literary machinery, to examine the process which made a critic, or a reviewer. I looked at innumerable examination pa-pers—and couldn't believe my eyes; sat in on classes for teaching literature, and couldn't believe my ears.

You might be saying: That is an exaggerated reaction, and you have no right to it, because you say you have never been part of the system. But I think it is not at all exaggerated, and that the reaction of someone from outside is valuable simply because it is fresh and not biased by allegiance to a particular education.

But after this investigation, I had no difficulty in answering my own questions: Why are they so parochial, so personal, so small-minded? Why do they always atomise, and belittle, why are they so fascinated by detail, and uninterested in the whole? Why is their interpretation of the word *critic* always to find fault? Why are they always seeing writers as in conflict with each other, rather than complementing each other . . . simple, this is how they are trained to think. That valuable person who understands what you are doing, what you are aiming for, and can give you advice and real criticism, is nearly always someone right outside the literary machine, even outside the university system; it may be a student just begin-ning, and still in love with literature, or perhaps it may be a thoughtful person who reads a great deal, following his own instinct.

I say to these students who have to spend a year, two years, writing theses about one book: "There is only one way to read, which is to browse in libraries and bookshops, picking up books that attract you, reading only those. dropping them when they bore you, skipping the parts that drag—and never, never reading anything because you feel you ought, or because it is part of a trend or a movement. Remember that the book which bores you when you are twenty or thirty will open doors for you when you are forty or fifty—and vice versa. Don't read a book out of its right time for you. Remember that for all the books we have in print, are as many that have never reached print, have never been written down—even now, in this age of compulsive reverence for the written word, his-tory, even social ethic, are taught by means of stories, and the people who have been conditioned into thinking only in terms of what is written—and unfortunately nearly all the products of our educational system can do no more than this —are missing what is before their eyes. For instance, the real history of Africa is still in the custody of black storytellers and wise men, black historians, medicine men: it is a verbal history, still kept safe from the white man and his predations. Everywhere, if you keep your mind open, you will find the truth in words *not* written down. So never let the printed page be your master. Above all, you should know that the fact that you have to spend one year, or two years, on one book, or one author means that you are badly taught—you should have been taught to read your way from one sympathy to another, you should be learning to follow your own intuitive feeling about what you need: that is what you should have been developing, not the way to quote from other people."

But unfortunately it is nearly always too late.

It did look for a while as if the recent student rebellions might change things, as if their impatience with the dead stuff they are taught might be strong enough to substitute something more fresh and useful. But it seems as if the rebellion is over. Sad. During the lively time in the States, I had letters with accounts of how classes of students had refused their syllabuses, and were bringing to class their own choice of books, those that they had found relevant to their lives. The classes were emotional, sometimes violent, angry, exciting, sizzling with life. Of course this only happened with teachers who were sympathetic, and prepared to stand with the students against authority—prepared for the consequences. There are teachers who know that the way they have to teach is bad and boring—luckily there are still enough, with a bit of luck, to overthrow what is wrong, even if the students themselves have lost impetus.

Meanwhile there is a country where . . .

Thirty or forty years ago, a critic made a private list of writers and poets which he, personally, considered made up what was valuable in literature, dismissing all others. This list he defended lengthily in print, for The List instantly became a subject for much debate. Millions of words were written for and against—schools and sects, for and against, came into being. The argument, all these years later, still continues . . . no one finds this state of affairs sad or ridiculous. . .

Where there are critical books of immense complexity and learning, dealing, but often at second- or thirdhand, with original work—novels, plays, stories. The people who write these books form a stratum in universities across the world—they are an international phenomenon, the top layer of literary academia. Their lives are spent in criticising, and in criticising each other's criticism. They at least regard this activity as more important than the original work. It is possible for literary students to spend more time reading criticism and criticism of criticism than they spend reading poetry, novels, biography, stories. A great many people regard this state of affairs as quite normal, and not sad and ridiculous. . . .

Where I recently read an essay about Antony and Cleopatra by a boy shortly to take A levels. It was full of originality and excitement about the play, the feeling that any real teaching about literature aims to produce. The essay was returned by the teacher like this: I cannot mark this essay, you haven't quoted from the authorities. Few teachers would regard this as sad and ridiculous. . .

Where people who consider themselves educated, and indeed as superior to and more refined than ordinary non-reading people, will come up to a writer and congratulate him or her on getting a good review somewhere—but will not consider it necessary to read the book in question, or ever to think that what they are interested in is success. . .

Where when a book comes out on a certain subject, let's say star-gazing, instantly a dozen colleges, societies, television programmes, write to the author asking him to come and speak about star-gazing. The last thing it occurs to them to do is to read the book. This behaviour is considered quite normal, and not ridiculous at all. . .

Where a young man or woman, reviewer or critic, who has not read more of a writer's work than the book in front of him, will write patronisingly, or as if rather bored with the whole business, or as if considering how many marks to give an essay, about the writer in question—who might have written fifteen books, and have been writing for twenty or thirty years—giving the said writer instruction on what to write next, and how. No one thinks this is absurd, certainly not the young person, critic or reviewer, who has been taught to patronise and itemise everyone for years, from Shakespeare downwards.

Where a Professor of Archeology can write of a South American tribe which has advanced knowledge of plants, and of medicine and of psychological methods: "The astonishing thing is that these people have no written language . . ." And no one thinks him absurd.

Where, on the occasion of a centenary of Shelley, in the same week and in three different literary periodicals, three young men, of identical education, from our identical universities, can write critical pieces about Shelley, damning him with the faintest possible praise, and in identically the same tone, as if they were doing Shelley a great favour to mention him at all —and no one seems to think that such a thing can indicate that there is something seriously wrong with our literary system.

Finally . . . this novel continues to be, for its author, a most instructive experience. For instance. Ten years after I wrote it, I can get, in one week, three letters about it, from three intelligent, well-informed, concerned people, who have taken the trouble to sit down and write to me. One might be in Johannesburg, one in San Francisco, one in Budapest. And here I sit, in London, reading them, at the same time, or one after another—as always, grateful to the writers, and delighted that what I've written can stimulate, illuminate—or even annoy. But one letter is entirely about the sex war, about man's inhumanity to woman, and woman's inhumanity to man, and the writer has produced pages and pages all about nothing else, for she—but not always a she—can't see anything else in the book.

The second is about politics, probably from an old Red like myself, and he or she writes many pages about politics, and never mentions any other theme.

These two letters used, when the book was as it were young, to be the most common.

The third letter, once rare but now catching up on the others, is written by a man or a woman who can see nothing in it but the theme of mental illness.

But it is the same book.

And naturally these incidents bring up again questions of what people see when they read a book, and why one person sees one pattern and nothing at all of another pattern, and how odd it is to have, as author, such a clear picture of a book, that is seen so very differently by its readers.

And from this kind of thought has emerged a new conclusion: which is that it is not only childish of a writer to want readers to see what he sees, to understand the shape and aim of a novel as he sees it—his wanting this means that he has not understood a most fundamental point. Which is that the book is alive and potent and fructifying and able to promote thought and discussion *only* when its plan and shape and intention are not understood, because that moment of seeing the shape and plan and intention is also the moment when there isn't anything more to be got out of it.

And when a book's pattern and the shape of its inner life is as plain to the reader as it is to the author—then perhaps it is time to throw the book aside, as having had its day, and start again on something new.

Doris Lessing
June 1971

■ FREE WOMEN: 1 ■

▪ FREE WOMEN: 1 ▪

*Anna meets her friend Molly in the
summer of 1957 after a separation*

THE two women were alone in the London flat.
    'The point is,' said Anna, as her friend came back from
the telephone on the landing, 'the point is, that as far as
I can see, everything's cracking up.'

Molly was a woman much on the telephone. When it rang
she had just enquired: 'Well, what's the gossip?' Now she
said, 'That's Richard, and he's coming over. It seems today's
his only free moment for the next month. Or so he insists.'

'Well I'm not leaving,' said Anna.

'No, you stay just where you are.'

Molly considered her own appearance—she was wearing
trousers and a sweater, both the worse for wear. 'He'll have
to take me as I come,' she concluded, and sat down by the
window. 'He wouldn't say what it's about—another crisis
with Marion, I suppose.'

'Didn't he write to you?' asked Anna, cautious.

'Both he and Marion wrote—ever such *bonhomous* letters.
Odd, isn't it?'

This *odd, isn't it?* was the characteristic note of the intimate conversations they designated gossip. But having struck
the note, Molly swerved off with: 'It's no use talking now,
because he's coming right over, he says.'

'He'll probably go when he sees me here,' said Anna,
cheerfully, but slightly aggressive. Molly glanced at her,
keenly, and said: 'Oh, but why?'

It had always been understood that Anna and Richard
disliked each other; and before Anna had always left when
Richard was expected. Now Molly said: 'Actually I think he

3

rather likes you, in his heart of hearts. The point is, he's committed to liking me, on principle—he's such a fool he's always got to either like or dislike someone, so all the dislike he won't admit he has for me gets pushed off on to you.'

'It's a pleasure,' said Anna. 'But do you know something? I discovered while you were away that for a lot of people you and I are practically interchangeable.'

'You've only just understood *that*?' said Molly, triumphant as always when Anna came up with—as far as she was concerned—facts that were self-evident.

In this relationship a balance had been struck early on: Molly was altogether more worldly-wise than Anna who, for her part, had a superiority of talent.

Anna held her own private views. Now she smiled, admitting that she had been very slow.

'When we're so different in every way,' said Molly, 'it's odd. I suppose because we both live the same kind of life—not getting married and so on. That's all they see.'

'Free women,' said Anna, wryly. She added, with an anger new to Molly, so that she earned another quick scrutinising glance from her friend: 'They still define us in terms of relationships with men, even the best of them.'

'Well, *we* do, don't we?' said Molly, rather tart. 'Well, it's awfully hard not to,' she amended, hastily, because of the look of surprise Anna now gave her. There was a short pause, during which the women did not look at each other but reflected that a year apart was a long time, even for an old friendship.

Molly said at last, sighing: 'Free. Do you know, when I was away, I was thinking about us, and I've decided that we're a completely new type of woman. We must be, surely?'

'There's nothing new under the sun,' said Anna, in an attempt at a German accent. Molly, irritated—she spoke half a dozen languages well—said: 'There's nothing new under the sun,' in a perfect reproduction of a shrewd old woman's voice, German accented.

Anna grimaced, acknowledging failure. She could not learn languages, and was too self-conscious ever to become somebody else: for a moment Molly had even looked like Mother

4

Sugar, otherwise Mrs Marks, to whom both had gone for psycho-analysis. The reservations both had felt about the solemn and painful ritual were expressed by the pet name, 'Mother Sugar'; which, as time passed, became a name for much more than a person, and indicated a whole way of looking at life—traditional, rooted, conservative, in spite of its scandalous familiarity with everything amoral. *In spite of*—that was how Anna and Molly, discussing the ritual, had felt it; recently Anna had been feeling more and more it was *because of*; and this was one of the things she was looking forward to discussing with her friend.

But now Molly, reacting as she had often done in the past, to the slightest suggestion of a criticism from Anna of Mother Sugar, said quickly: 'All the same, she was wonderful, and I was in much too bad a shape to criticise.'

'Mother Sugar used to say, "You're Electra," or "You're Antigone," and that was the end, as far as she was concerned,' said Anna.

'Well, not quite the end,' said Molly, wryly insisting on the painful probing hours both had spent.

'Yes,' said Anna, unexpectedly insisting, so that Molly, for the third time, looked at her curiously. 'Yes. Oh I'm not saying she didn't do me all the good in the world. I'm sure I'd never have coped with what I've had to cope with without her. But all the same ... I remember quite clearly one afternoon, sitting there—the big room, and the discreet wall lights, and the Buddha and the pictures and the statues.'

'*Well?*' said Molly, now very critical.

Anna, in the face of this unspoken but clear determination not to discuss it, said: 'I've been thinking about it all during the last few months ... no I'd like to talk about it with you. After all, we both went through it, and with the same person ...'

'*Well?*'

Anna persisted: 'I remember that afternoon, knowing I'd never go back. It was all that damned art all over the place.'

Molly drew in her breath, sharp. She said, quickly: 'I don't know what you mean.' As Anna did not reply, she said,

5

accusing: 'And have you written anything since I've been away?'

'No.'

'I keep telling you,' said Molly, her voice shrill, 'I'll never forgive you if you throw that talent away. I mean it. I've done it, and I can't stand watching you—I've messed with painting and dancing and acting and scribbling, and now ... you're so talented, Anna. *Why?* I simply don't understand.'

'How can I ever say why, when you're always so bitter and accusing?'

Molly even had tears in her eyes, which were fastened in the most painful reproach on her friend. She brought out with difficulty: 'At the back of my mind I always thought, well, I'll get married, so it doesn't matter my wasting all the talents I was born with. Until recently I was even dreaming about having more children—yes I know it's idiotic but it's true. And now I'm forty and Tommy's grown up. But the point is, if you're not writing simply because you're thinking about getting married ...'

'But we both want to get married,' said Anna, making it humorous; the tone restored reserve to the conversation; she had understood, with pain, that she was not, after all, going to be able to discuss certain subjects with Molly.

Molly smiled, drily, gave her friend an acute, bitter look, and said: 'All right, but you'll be sorry later.'

'*Sorry*,' said Anna, laughing, out of surprise. 'Molly, why is it you'll never believe other people have the disabilities you have?'

'You were lucky enough to be given one talent, and not four.'

'Perhaps my one talent has had as much pressure on it as your four?'

'I can't talk to you in this mood. Shall I make you some tea while we're waiting for Richard?'

'I'd rather have beer or something.' She added, provocative: 'I've been thinking I might very well take to drink later on.'

Molly said, in the older sister's tone Anna had invited: 'You shouldn't make jokes, Anna. Not when you see what it

6

does to people—look at Marion. I wonder if she's been drinking while I was away?'

'I can tell you. She has—yes, she came to see me several times.'

'She came to see *you?*'

'That's what I was leading up to, when I said you and I seem to be interchangeable.'

Molly tended to be possessive—she showed resentment, as Anna had known she would, as she said: 'I suppose you're going to say Richard came to see you too?' Anna nodded; and Molly said, briskly, 'I'll get us some beer.' She returned from the kitchen with two long cold-beaded glasses, and said: 'Well you'd better tell me all about it before Richard comes, hadn't you?'

Richard was Molly's husband; or rather, he had been her husband. Molly was the product of what she referred to as 'one of those 'twenties marriages.' Her mother and father had both glittered, but briefly, in the intellectual and bohemian circles that had spun around the great central lights of Huxley, Lawrence, Joyce, etc. Her childhood had been disastrous, since this marriage only lasted a few months. She had married, at the age of eighteen, the son of a friend of her father's. She knew now she had married out of a need for security and even respectability. The boy Tommy was a product of this marriage. Richard at twenty had already been on the way to becoming the very solid businessman he had since proved himself: and Molly and he had stood their incompatibility for not much more than a year. He had then married Marion, and there were three boys. Tommy had remained with Molly. Richard and she, once the business of the divorce was over, became friends again. Later, Marion became her friend. This, then, was the situation to which Molly often referred as: 'It's all very odd, isn't it?'

'Richard came to see me about Tommy,' said Anna.

'What? Why?'

'Oh—idiotic! He asked me if I thought it was good for Tommy to spend so much time brooding. I said I thought it was good for everyone to brood, if by that he meant, think-

7

ing; and that since Tommy was twenty and grown up it was not for us to interfere anyway.'

'Well it isn't good for him,' said Molly.

'He asked me if I thought it would be good for Tommy to go off on some trip or other to Germany—a business trip, with him. I told him to ask Tommy, not me. Of course Tommy said no.'

'Of course. Well I'm sorry Tommy didn't go.'

'But the real reason he came, I think, was because of Marion. But Marion had just been to see me, and had a prior claim so to speak. So I wouldn't discuss Marion at all. I think it's likely he's coming to discuss Marion with you.'

Molly was watching Anna closely. 'How many times did Richard come?'

'About five or six times.'

After a silence, Molly let her anger spurt out with: 'It's very odd he seems to expect me almost to control Marion. Why me? Or you? Well, perhaps you'd better go after all. It's going to be difficult if all sorts of complications have been going on while my back was turned.'

Anna said firmly: 'No, Molly. I didn't ask Richard to come and see me. I didn't ask Marion to come and see me. After all, it's not your fault or mine that we seem to play the same role for people. I said what you would have said—at least, I think so.'

There was a note of humorous, even childish pleading in this. But it was deliberate. Molly, the older sister, smiled and said: 'Well, all right.' She continued to observe Anna narrowly; and Anna was careful to appear unaware of it. She did not want to tell Molly what had happened between her and Richard now; not until she could tell her the whole story of the last miserable year.

'Is Marion drinking badly?'

'Yes, I think she is.'

'And she told you all about it?'

'Yes. In detail. And what's odd is, I swear she talked as if I were you—even making slips of the tongue, calling me Molly and so on.'

8

'Well I don't *know*,' said Molly. 'Who would ever have thought? And you and I are different as chalk and cheese.'

'Perhaps not so different,' said Anna, drily; but Molly laughed in disbelief.

She was a tallish woman, and big-boned, but she appeared slight, and even boyish. This was because of how she did her hair, which was a rough, streaky gold, cut like a boy's; and because of her clothes, for which she had a great natural talent. She took pleasure in the various guises she could use: for instance, being a hoyden in lean trousers and sweaters, and then a siren, her large green eyes made-up, her cheekbones prominent, wearing a dress which made the most of her full breasts.

This was one of the private games she played with life, which Anna envied her; yet in moments of self-rebuke she would tell Anna she was ashamed of herself, she so much enjoyed the different roles: 'It's as if I were really different— don't you see? I even feel a different person. And there's something spiteful in it—that man, you know, I told you about him last week—he saw me the first time in my old slacks and my sloppy old jersey, and then I rolled into the restaurant, nothing less than a *femme fatale*, and he didn't know how to have me, he couldn't say a word all evening, and I enjoyed it. Well, Anna?'

'But you do enjoy it,' Anna would say, laughing.

But Anna was small, thin, dark, brittle, with large black always-on-guard eyes, and a fluffy haircut. She was, on the whole, satisfied with herself, but she was always the same. She envied Molly's capacity to project her own changes of mood. Anna wore neat, delicate clothes, which tended to be either prim, or perhaps a little odd; and relied upon her delicate white hands, and her small, pointed white face to make an impression. But she was shy, unable to assert herself, and, she was convinced, easily overlooked.

When the two women went out together, Anna deliberately effaced herself and played to the dramatic Molly. When they were alone, she tended to take the lead. But this had by no means been true at the beginning of their friendship. Molly, abrupt, straightforward, tactless, had frankly domineered Anna. Slowly, and the offices of Mother Sugar had had a good deal to do with it, Anna learned to stand up for herself. Even now there were moments when she should challenge Molly when she did not. She admitted to herself she was a coward; she would always give in rather than have fights or scenes. A quarrel would lay Anna low for days, whereas Molly thrived on them. She would burst into exuberant tears, say unforgivable things, and have forgotten all about it half a day later. Meanwhile Anna would be limply recovering in her flat.

That they were both 'insecure' and 'unrooted,' words which dated from the era of Mother Sugar, they both freely acknowledged. But Anna had recently been learning to use these words in a different way, not as something to be apologised for, but as flags or banners for an attitude that amounted to a different philosophy. She had enjoyed fantasies of saying to Molly: We've had the wrong attitude to the whole thing, and it's Mother Sugar's fault—what is this security and balance that's supposed to be so good? What's wrong with living emotionally from hand-to-mouth in a world that's changing as fast as it is?

But now, sitting with Molly talking, as they had so many hundreds of times before, Anna was saying to herself: Why do I always have this awful need to make other people see things as I do? It's childish, why should they? What it amounts to is that I'm scared of being alone in what I feel.

The room they sat in was on the first floor, overlooking a narrow side street, whose windows had flower boxes and painted shutters, and whose pavements were decorated with three basking cats, a pekinese and the milk-cart, late because it was Sunday. The milkman had white shirt-sleeves, rolled up; and his son, a boy of sixteen, was sliding the gleaming white bottles from a wire basket on to the doorsteps. When he reached under their window, the man looked up and nodded. Molly said: 'Yesterday he came in for coffee. Full of triumph, he was. His son's got a scholarship and Mr Gates wanted me to know it. I said to him, getting in before he could, "My son's had all these advantages, and all that education, and look at him, he doesn't know what to do with

10

himself. And yours hasn't had a penny spent on him and he's got a scholarship." "That's right," he said, "that's the way of it." Then I thought, well I'm damned if I'll sit here, taking it, so I said: "Mr Gates, your son's up into the middle-class now, with us lot, and you won't be speaking the same language. You know that, don't you?" "It's the way of the world," he says. I said, "It's not the way of the world at all, it's the way of this damned class-ridden country." He's one of those bloody working class tories, Mr Gates is, and he said: "It's the way of the world, Miss Jacobs, you say your son doesn't see his way forward? That's a sad thing." And off he went on his milk-round, and I went upstairs and there was Tommy sitting on his bed, just sitting. He's probably sitting there now, if he's in. The Gates boy, he's all of a piece, he's going out for what he wants. But Tommy—since I came back three days ago, that's all he's done, sat on his bed and thought.'

'Oh Molly, don't worry so much. He'll turn out all right.' They were leaning over the sill, watching Mr Gates and his son. A short, brisk, tough little man, and his son was tall, tough, and good-looking. The women watched how the boy, returning with an empty basket, swung out a filled one from the back of the milk-cart, receiving instructions from his father with a smile and a nod. There was perfect understanding *there*; and the two women, both of them bringing up children without men, exchanged a grimacing envious smile.

'The point is,' said Anna, 'neither of us were prepared to get married simply to give our children fathers. So now we must take the consequences. If there are any. Why should there be?'

'It's all very well for you,' said Molly, sour. 'You never worry about anything, you just let things slide.'

Anna braced herself—almost did not reply, and then with an effort said: 'I don't agree, we try to have things both ways. We've always refused to live by the book and the rule; but then why start worrying because the world doesn't treat us by rule? That's what it amounts to.'

'There you are,' said Molly, antagonistic; 'but I'm not a theoretical type. You always do that—faced with something you start making up theories. I'm simply worried about Tommy.'

Now Anna could not reply: her friend's tone was too strong. She returned to her survey of the street. Mr Gates and his boy were turning the corner out of sight, pulling the red milk-cart behind them. At the opposite end of the street was a new interest: a man pushing a hand-cart. 'Fresh country strawberries,' he was shouting. 'Picked fresh this morning, morning-picked country strawberries . . .'

Molly glanced at Anna, who nodded, grinning like a small girl. (She was disagreeably conscious that the little-girl smile was designed to soften Molly's criticism of her.) 'I'll get some for Richard too,' said Molly, and ran out of the room, picking up her handbag from a chair.

Anna continued to lean over the sill, in a warm space of sunlight, watching Molly, who was already in energetic conversation with the strawberry seller. Molly was laughing and gesticulating, and the man shook his head and disagreed, while he poured the heavy red fruit on to his scales.

'Well you've no overhead costs,' Anna heard, 'so why should we pay just what we would in the shops?'

'They don't sell morning-fresh strawberries in the shops, miss, not like these.'

'Oh go on,' said Molly, as she disappeared with her white bowl of red fruit. 'Sharks, that's what you are!'

The strawberry man, young, yellow, lean and deprived, lifted a snarling face to the window where Molly had already inserted herself. Seeing the two women together he said, as he fumbled with his glittering scales, 'Overhead costs, what do you know about it?'

'Then come up and have some coffee and tell us,' said Molly, her face vivid with challenge.

At which he lowered his face and said to the street floor: 'Some people have to work, if others haven't.'

'Oh go on,' said Molly, 'don't be such a sourpuss. Come up and eat some of your strawberries. On me.'

He didn't know how to take her. He stood, frowning, his young face uncertain under an over-long slope of greasy fairish hair. 'I'm not that sort, if you are,' he remarked, at last, off-stage, as it were.

'So much the worse for you,' said Molly, leaving the window, laughing at Anna in a way which refused to be guilty.

But Anna leaned out, confirmed her view of what had happened by a look at the man's dogged, resentful shoulders, and said in a low voice: 'You hurt his feelings.'

'Oh hell,' said Molly, shrugging. 'It's coming back to England again—everybody so shut up, taking offence, I feel like breaking out and shouting and screaming whenever I set foot on this frozen soil. I feel locked up the moment I breathe our sacred air.'

'All the same,' said Anna, 'he thinks you were laughing at him.'

Another customer had slopped out of the opposite house; a woman in Sunday comfort, slacks, loose shirt, and a yellow scarf around her head. The strawberry man served her, non-committal. Before he lifted the handles to propel the cart onwards, he looked up again at the window, and seeing only Anna, her small sharp chin buried in her forearm, her black eyes fixed on him, smiling, he said with grudging good-humour: 'Overhead costs, *she* says ...' and snorted lightly with disgust. He had forgiven them.

He moved off up the street behind the mounds of softly red, sun-glistening fruit, shouting: 'Morning-fresh strawberries, picked this morning!' Then his voice was absorbed into the din of traffic from the big street a couple of hundred yards down.

Anna turned and found Molly setting bowls of the fruit, loaded with cream, on the sill. 'I've decided not to waste any on Richard,' said Molly, 'he never enjoys anything anyway. More beer?'

'With strawberries, wine, obviously,' said Anna greedily; and moved the spoon about among the fruit, feeling its soft sliding resistance, and the slipperiness of the cream under a gritty crust of sugar. Molly swiftly filled glasses with wine and set them on the white sill. The sunlight crystallised beside each glass on the white paint in quivering lozenges of crimson

13

and yellow light, and the two women sat in the sunlight, sighing with pleasure and stretching their legs in the thin warmth, looking at the colours of the fruit in the bright bowls and at the red wine.

But now the door-bell rang, and both instinctively gathered themselves into more tidy postures. Molly leaned out of the window again, shouted: 'Mind your head!' and threw down the door-key, wrapped in an old scarf.

They watched Richard lean down to pick up the key, without even a glance upwards, though he must know that at least Molly was there. 'He hates me doing that,' she said. 'Isn't it odd? After all these years? And his way of showing is simply to pretend it didn't happen.'

Richard came into the room. He looked younger than his middle age, being well-tanned after an early summer holiday in Italy. He wore a tight yellow sports shirt, and new light trousers: every Sunday of his year, summer or winter, Richard Portmain wore clothes that claimed him for the open air. He was a member of various suitable golf and tennis clubs, but never played unless for business reasons. He had had a cottage in the country for years; but sent his family to it alone, unless it was advisable to entertain business friends for a week-end. He was by every instinct urban. He spent his week-ends dropping from one club, one pub, one bar, to the next. He was a shortish, dark, compact man, almost fleshy. His round face, attractive when he smiled, was obstinate to the point of sullenness when he was not smiling. His whole solid person—head poked out forward, eyes unblinking, had this look of dogged determination. He now impatiently handed Molly the key, that was loosely bundled inside her scarlet scarf. She took it and began trickling the soft material through her solid white fingers, remarking: 'Just off for a healthy day in the country, Richard?'

Having braced himself for just such a jibe, he now stiffly smiled, and peered into the dazzle of sunlight around the white window. When he distinguished Anna, he involuntarily frowned, nodded stiffly, and sat down hastily across the room from both of them, saying: 'I didn't know you had a visitor, Molly.'

'Anna isn't a visitor,' said Molly.

She deliberately waited until Richard had had the full benefit of the sight of them, indolently displayed in the sunshine, heads turned towards him in benevolent enquiry, and offered: 'Wine, Richard? Beer? Coffee? Or a nice cup of tea perhaps?'

'If you've got a Scotch, I wouldn't mind.'

'Beside you,' said Molly.

But having made what he clearly felt to be a masculine point, he didn't move. 'I came to discuss Tommy.' He glanced at Anna, who was licking up the last of her strawberries.

'But you've already discussed all this with Anna, so I hear, so now we can all three discuss it.'

'So Anna's told you . . .'

'Nothing,' said Molly. 'This is the first time we've had a chance to see each other.'

'So I'm interrupting your first heart to heart,' said Richard, with a genuine effort towards jovial tolerance. He sounded pompous, however, and both women looked amusedly uncomfortable, in response to it.

Richard abruptly got up.

'Going already?' enquired Molly.

'I'm going to call Tommy.' He had already filled his lungs to let out the peremptory yell they both expected, when Molly interrupted with: 'Richard, don't shout at him. He's not a little boy any longer. Besides I don't think he's in.'

'Of course he's in.'

'How do you know?'

'Because he's looking out of the window upstairs. I'm surprised you don't even know whether your son is in or not.'

'Why? I don't keep a tab on him.'

'That's all very well, but where has that got you?'

The two now faced each other, serious with open hostility. Replying to his: Where has that got you? Molly said: 'I'm not going to argue about how he should have been brought up. Let's wait until your three have grown up before we score points.'

'I haven't come to discuss my three.'

15

'Why not? We've discussed them hundreds of times. And I suppose you have with Anna too.'

There was now a pause while both controlled their anger, surprised and alarmed it was already so strong. The history of these two was as follows: They had met in 1935. Molly was deeply involved with the cause of Republican Spain. Richard was also. (But, as Molly would remark, on those occasions when he spoke of this as a regrettable lapse into political exoticism on his part: Who wasn't in those days?) The Portmains, a rich family, precipitously assuming this to be a proof of permanent communist leanings, had cut off his allowance. (As Molly put it: My dear, cut him off without a penny! Naturally Richard was delighted. They had never taken him seriously before. He instantly took out a party card on the strength of it.) Richard who had a talent for nothing but making money, as yet undiscovered, was kept by Molly for two years, while he prepared himself to be a writer. (Molly; but of course only years later: Can you imagine anything more banal? But of course Richard has to be commonplace in everything. Everyone was going to be a great writer, but everyone! Do you know the really deadly skeleton in the communist closet—the really awful truth? It's that every one of the old party war horses—you know, people you'd imagine had never had a thought of anything but the party for years, everyone has that old manuscript or wad of poems tucked away. Everyone was going to be the Gorki or the Mayakovski of our time. Isn't it terrifying? Isn't it pathetic? Every one of them, failed artists. I'm sure it's significant of something, if only one knew *what*.) Molly was still keeping Richard for months after she left him, out of a kind of contempt. His revulsion against left-wing politics, which was sudden, coincided with his decision that Molly was immoral, sloppy and bohemian. Luckily for her, however, he had already contracted a liaison with some girl which, though short, was public enough to prevent him from divorcing her and gaining custody of Tommy, which he was threatening to do. He was then readmitted into the bosom of the Portmain family, and accepted what Molly referred to, with amiable contempt, as 'a job in the city.' She had no idea, even now, just how powerful a man Richard had become by that act of deciding to inherit a position. Richard then married Marion, a very young, warm, pleasant, quiet girl, daughter of a moderately distinguished family. They had three sons.

Meanwhile Molly, talented in so many directions, danced a little—but she really did not have the build for a ballerina; did a song and dance act in a revue—decided it was too frivolous; took drawing lessons, gave them up when the war started when she worked as a journalist; gave up journalism to work in one of the cultural outworks of the communist party; left for the same reason everyone of her type did—she could not stand the deadly boredom of it; became a minor actress, and had reconciled herself, after much unhappiness, to the fact that she was essentially a dilettante. Her source of self-respect was that she had not—as she put it—given up and crawled into safety somewhere. Into a safe marriage.

And her secret source of uneasiness was Tommy, over whom she had fought a years-long battle with Richard. He was particularly disapproving because she had gone away for a year, leaving the boy in her house, to care for himself.

He now said, resentful: 'I've seen a good deal of Tommy during the last year, when you left him alone . . .'

She interrupted with: 'I keep explaining, or trying to—I thought it all out and decided it would be good for him to be left. Why do you always talk as if he were a child? He was over nineteen, and I left him in a comfortable house, with money, and everything organised.'

'Why don't you admit you had a whale of a good time junketting all over Europe, without Tommy to tie you?'

'Of course I had a good time, why shouldn't I?'

Richard laughed, loudly and unpleasantly, and Molly said, impatient, 'Oh for God's sake, of course I was glad to be free for the first time since I had a baby. Why not? And what about you—you have Marion, the good little woman, tied hand and foot to the boys while you do as you like—and there's another thing. I keep trying to explain and you never listen. I don't want him to grow up one of these damned mother-ridden Englishmen. I wanted him to break free of me. Yes, don't laugh, but it wasn't good, the two of us together in this house, always so close and knowing everything the other one did.'

Richard grimaced with annoyance and said, 'Yes, I know your little theories on this point.'

At which Anna came in with: 'It's not only Molly—all the women I know—I mean, the real women, worry that their sons are going to grow up like ... they've got good reason to worry.'

At this Richard turned hostile eyes on Anna; and Molly watched the two of them sharply.

'Like *what*, Anna?'

'I would say,' said Anna, deliberately sweet, 'just a trifle unhappy about their sex lives? Or would you say that's putting it too strongly, hmmmm?'

Richard flushed, a dark ugly flush, and turned back to Molly saying to her: 'All right, I'm not saying you deliberately did something you shouldn't.'

'Thank you.'

'But what the hell's wrong with the boy? He never passed an exam decently, he wouldn't go to Oxford, and now he sits around, brooding and ...'

Both Anna and Molly laughed out at the word brooding.

'The boy worries me,' said Richard. 'He really does.'

'He worries me,' said Molly reasonably. 'And that's what we're going to discuss, isn't it?'

'I keep offering him things. I invite him to all kinds of things where he'd meet people who'd do him good.'

Molly laughed again.

'All right, laugh and sneer. But things being as they are, we can't afford to laugh.'

'When you said, do him good, I imagined good emotionally. I always forget you're such a pompous little snob.'

'Words don't hurt anyone,' said Richard, with unexpected dignity. 'Call me names if you like. You've lived one way, I've lived another. All I'm saying is, I'm in a position to offer that boy—well anything he liked. And he's simply not interested. If he were doing anything constructive with your lot, it'd be different.'

'You always talk as if I try to put Tommy against you.'

18

'Of course you do.'

'If you mean, that I've always said what I thought about the way you live, your values, your success game, that sort of thing, of course I have. Why should I be expected to shut up about everything I believe in? But I've always said, there's your father, you must get to know that world, it exists, after all.'

'Big of you.'

'Molly's always urging him to see more of you,' said Anna. 'I know she has. And so have I.'

Richard nodded impatiently, suggesting that what they *said* was unimportant.

'You're so stupid about children, Richard. They don't like being split,' said Molly. 'Look at the people he knows with me—artists, writers, actors and so on.'

'And politicians. Don't forget the comrades.'

'Well why not? He'll grow up knowing something about the world he lives in, which is more than you can say about your three—Eton and Oxford, it's going to be, for all of them. Tommy knows all kinds. He won't see the world in terms of the little fishpond of the upper class.'

Anna said: 'You're not going to get anywhere if you two go on like this.' She sounded angry; she tried to right it with a joke: 'What it amounts to is, you two should never have married, but you did, or at least you shouldn't have had a child, but you did—' Her voice sounded angry again, and again she softened it, saying, 'Do you realise you two have been saying the same things over and over for years? Why don't you accept that you'll never agree about anything and be done with it?'

'How can we be done with it when there's Tommy to consider,' said Richard, irritably, very loud.

'Do you have to shout?' said Anna. 'How do you know he hasn't heard every word? That's probably what's wrong with him. He must feel such a bone of contention.'

Molly promptly went to the door, opened it, listened. 'Nonsense, I can hear him typing upstairs.' She came back saying 'Anna you make me tired when you get English and tight-lipped.'

'I hate loud voices.'

'Well I'm Jewish and I like them.'

Richard again visibly suffered. 'Yes—and you call yourself Miss Jacobs. Miss. In the interests of your right to independence and your own identity—whatever *that* might mean. But Tommy has Miss Jacobs for a mother.'

'It's not the miss you object to,' said Molly cheerfully. 'It's the Jacobs. Yes it is. You always were anti-Semitic.'

'Oh hell,' said Richard, impatient.

'Tell me, how many Jews do you number among your personal friends?'

'According to you I don't have personal friends, I only have business friends.'

'Except your girl-friends of course. I've noticed with interest that three of your women since me have been Jewish.'

'For God's sake,' said Anna. 'I'm going home.' And she actually got off the window-sill. Molly laughed, got up and pushed her down again. 'You've got to stay. Be chairman, we obviously need one.'

'Very well,' said Anna, determined. 'I will. So stop wrangling. What's it all about, anyway? The fact is, we all agree, we all give the same advice, don't we?'

'Do we?' said Richard.

'Yes. Molly thinks you should offer Tommy a job in one of your things.' Like Molly, Anna spoke with automatic contempt of Richard's world, and he grinned in irritation.

'One of my things? And you agree, Molly?'

'If you'd give me a chance to say so, yes.'

'There we are,' said Anna. 'No grounds even for argument.'

Richard now poured himself a whisky, looking humorously patient; and Molly waited, humorously patient.

'So it's all settled?' said Richard.

'Obviously not,' said Anna. 'Because Tommy has to agree.'

'So we're back where we started. Molly, may I know why you aren't against your precious son being mixed up with the hosts of mammon?'

'Because I've brought him up in such a way that—he's a good person. He's all right.'

'So he can't be corrupted by me?' Richard spoke with controlled anger, smiling. 'And may I ask where you get your extraordinary assurance about your values—they've taken quite a knock in the last two years, haven't they?'

The two women exchanged glances, which said: He was bound to say it, let's get it over with.

'It hasn't occurred to you that the real trouble with Tommy is that he's been surrounded half his life with communists or so-called communists—most of the people he's known have been mixed up in one way and another. And now they're all leaving the party, or have left—don't you think it might have had some effect?'

'Well, obviously,' said Molly.

'Obviously,' said Richard, grinning in irritation. 'Just like that—but what price your precious values—Tommy's been brought up on the beauty and freedom of the glorious Soviet fatherland.'

'I'm not discussing politics with you, Richard.'

'No,' said Anna, 'of course you shouldn't discuss politics.'

'Why not, when it's relevant?'

'Because you don't discuss them,' said Molly. 'You simply use slogans out of the newspapers.'

'Well can I put it this way? Two years ago you and Anna were rushing out at meetings and organising everything in sight . . .'

'I wasn't, anyhow,' said Anna.

'Don't quibble. Molly certainly was. And now what? Russia's in the doghouse and what price the comrades now? Most of them having nervous breakdowns or making a lot of money, as far as I can make out.'

'The point is,' said Anna, 'that socialism is in the doldrums in this country . . .'

'And everywhere else.'

'All right. If you're saying that one of Tommy's troubles is that he was brought up a socialist and it's not an easy time to be a socialist—well of course we agree.'

'The royal we. The socialist we. Or just the we of Anna and Molly?'

'Socialist, for the purposes of this argument,' said Anna.

'And yet in the last two years you've made an about-turn.'

'No we haven't. It's a question of a way of looking at life.'

'You want me to believe that the way you look at life, which is a sort of anarchy, as far as I can make out, is socialist?'

Anna glanced at Molly; Molly ever-so-slightly shook her head, but Richard saw it, and said, 'No discussion in front of the children, is that it? What astounds me is your fantastic arrogance. Where do you get it from, Molly? What are you? At the moment you've got a part in a masterpiece called *The Wings of Cupid*.'

'We minor actresses don't choose our plays. Besides, I've been bumming around for a year, not earning, and I'm broke.'

'So your assurance comes from the bumming round? It certainly can't come from the work you do.'

'I call a halt,' said Anna. 'I'm chairman—this discussion is closed. We're talking about Tommy.'

Molly ignored Anna, and attacked. 'What you say about me may or may not be true. But where do you get *your* arrogance from? I don't want Tommy to be a businessman. You are hardly an advertisement for the life. Anyone can be a businessman, why, you've often said so to me. Oh come off it Richard, how often have you dropped in to see me and sat there saying how empty and stupid your life is?'

Anna made a quick warning movement, and Molly said, shrugging, 'All right, I'm not tactful. Why should I be? Richard says my life isn't up to much, well I agree with him, but what's his? Your poor Marion, treated like a housewife or a hostess, but never as a human being. Your boys, being put through the upper-class mill simply because you want it, given no choice. Your stupid little affairs. Why am I supposed to be impressed?'

'I see that you two have after all discussed me,' said Richard, giving Anna a look of open hostility.

'No we haven't,' said Anna. 'Or nothing we haven't said for years. We're discussing Tommy. He came to see me and I told him he should go and see you, Richard, and see if he couldn't do one of those expert jobs, not business, it's stupid

22

to be just business, but something constructive, like the United Nations or Unesco. He could get in through you, couldn't he?'

'Yes, he could.'

'What did he say, Anna?' asked Molly.

'He said he wanted to be left alone to think. And why not? He's twenty. Why shouldn't he think and experiment with life, if that's what he wants? Why should we bully him?'

'The trouble with Tommy is he's never been bullied,' said Richard.

'Thank you,' said Molly.

'He's never had any direction. Molly's simply left him alone as if he was an adult, always. What sort of sense do you suppose it makes to a child—freedom, make-up-your-own-mind, I'm-not-going-to-put-any-pressure-on-you; and at the same time, the comrades, discipline, self-sacrifice, and kow-towing to authority . . .'

'What you have to do is this,' said Molly. 'Find a place in one of your things that isn't just share-pushing or promoting or money-making. See if you can't find something constructive. Then show it to Tommy and let him decide.'

Richard, his face red with anger over his too-yellow, too-tight shirt, held a glass of whisky between two hands, turning it round and round, looking down into it. 'Thanks,' he said at last, 'I will.' He spoke with such a stubborn confidence in the quality of what he was going to offer his son, that Anna and Molly again raised their eyebrows at each other, conveying that the whole conversation had been wasted, as usual. Richard intercepted this glance, and said: 'You two are so extraordinarily naïve.'

'About business?' said Molly, with her loud jolly laugh.

'About big business,' said Anna quietly, amused, who had been surprised, during her conversations with Richard, to discover the extent of his power. This had not caused his image to enlarge, for her; rather he had seemed to shrink, against a background of international money. And she had loved Molly the more for her total lack of respect for this man who had been her husband, and who was in fact one of the financial powers of the country.

23

'Ohhh,' groaned Molly, impatient.

'Very big business,' said Anna laughing, trying to make Molly meet this, but the actress shrugged it off, with her characteristic big shrug of the shoulders, her white hands spreading out, palms out, until they came to rest on her knees.

'I'll impress her with it later,' said Anna to Richard. 'Or at least try to.'

'What is all this?' asked Molly.

'It's no good,' said Richard, sarcastic, grudging, resentful. 'Do you know that in all these years she's never been interested enough even to ask?'

'You've paid Tommy's school fees, and that's all I ever wanted from you.'

'You've been putting Richard across to everyone for years as a sort of—well an enterprising little businessman, like a jumped-up grocer,' said Anna. 'And it turns out that all the time he's a tycoon. But really. A big shot. One of the people we have to hate—on principle,' Anna added laughing.

'Really?' said Molly, interested, regarding her former husband with mild surprise that this ordinary and—as far as she was concerned—not very intelligent man could be anything at all.

Anna recognised the look—it was what she felt—and laughed.

'Good God,' said Richard, 'talking to you two, it's like talking to a couple of savages.'

'Why?' said Molly. 'Should we be impressed? You aren't even self-made. You just inherited it.'

'What does it matter? It's the thing that matters. It may be a bad system, I'm not even going to argue—not that I could with either of you, you are both as ignorant as monkeys about economics, but it's what runs this country.'

'Well of course,' said Molly. Her hands still lay, palms upward, on her knees. She now brought them together in her lap, in an unconscious mimicry of the gesture of a child waiting for a lesson.

'But why despise it?' Richard, who had obviously been

24

meaning to go on, stopped, looking at those meekly mocking hands. 'Oh Jesus!' he said, giving up.

'But we don't. It's too—anonymous—to despise. We despise . . .' Molly cut off the word *you*, and as if in guilt at a lapse in manners, let her hands lose their pose of silent impertinence. She put them quickly out of sight behind her. Anna, watching, thought amusedly: If I said to Molly, you stopped Richard talking simply by making fun of him with your hands, she wouldn't know what I meant. How wonderful to be able to do that, how lucky she is . . .

'Yes I know you despise me, but why? You're a half-successful actress, and Anna once wrote a book?'

Molly's hands instinctively lifted themselves from beside her, and fingers touching, negligent, on Molly's knee, said: Oh what a bore you are Richard. Richard looked at them, and frowned.

'That's got nothing to do with it,' said Molly.

'Indeed.'

'It's because we haven't given in,' said Molly, seriously.

'To what?'

'If you don't know we can't tell you.'

Richard was on the point of exploding out of his chair—Anna could see his thigh muscles tense and quiver. To prevent a row she said quickly, drawing his fire: 'That's the point, you talk and talk, but you're so far away from—what's real, you never understand anything.'

She succeeded. Richard turned his body towards her, leaning forward so that she was confronted with his warm smooth brown arms, lightly covered with golden hair, his exposed brown neck, his brownish-red hot face. She shrank back slightly with an unconscious look of distaste, as he said: 'Well Anna, I've had the privilege of getting to know you better than I did before, and I can't say you impress me with knowing what you want, what you think or how you should go about things.'

Anna, conscious that she was colouring, met his eyes with an effort, and drawled deliberately: 'Or perhaps what it is you don't like is that I do know what I want, have always been prepared to experiment, never pretend to myself the

25

second rate is more than it is, and know when to refuse. Hmmmm?'

Molly, looking quickly from one to the other, let out her breath, made an exclamation with her hands, by dropping them apart, emphatically, on to her knees, and unconsciously nodded—partly because she had confirmed a suspicion and partly because she approved of Anna's rudeness. She said, 'Hey, what is this?' drawling it out arrogantly, so that Richard turned from Anna to her. 'If you're attacking us for the way we live again, all I can say is, the less you say the better, what with your private life the way it is.'

'I preserve the forms,' said Richard, with such a readiness to conform to what they both expected of him, that they both, at the same moment, let out peals of laughter.

'Yes darling, we know you do,' said Molly. 'Well, how's Marion? I'd love to know.'

For the third time Richard said, 'I see you've discussed it,' and Anna said: 'I told Molly you had been to see me. I told her what I didn't tell you—that Marion had been to see me.'

'Well, let's have it,' said Molly.

'Why,' said Anna, as if Richard were not present, 'Richard is worried because Marion is such a problem to him.'

'That's nothing new,' said Molly, in the same tone.

Richard sat still, looking at the women in turn. They waited; ready to leave it, ready for him to get up and go, ready for him to justify himself. But he said nothing. He seemed fascinated by the spectacle of these two, flashingly hostile to him, a laughing unit of condemnation. He even nodded, as if to say: Well, go on.

Molly said: 'As we all know, Richard married beneath him—oh, not socially of course, he was careful not to do that, but quote, she's a nice ordinary woman unquote, though luckily with all those lords and ladies scattered around in the collateral branches of the family tree, so useful I've no doubt for the letter-heads of companies.'

At this Anna let out a snort of laughter—the lords and ladies being so irrelevant to the sort of money Richard controlled. But Molly ignored the interruption and went on: 'Of course practically all the men one knows are married to

26

nice ordinary dreary women. So sad for them. As it happens, Marion is a good person, not stupid at all, but she's been married for fifteen years to a man who makes her feel stupid ...'

'What would they do, these men, without their stupid wives,' sighed out Anna.

'Oh, I simply can't think. When I really want to depress myself, I think of all the brilliant men I know, married to their stupid wives. Enough to break your heart, it really is. So there is stupid ordinary Marion. And of course Richard was faithful to her just as long as most men are, that is, until she went into the nursing home for her first baby.'

'Why do you have to go so far back?' exclaimed Richard involuntarily, as if this had been a serious conversation, and again both women broke into fits of laughter.

Molly broke it, and said seriously, but impatiently, 'Oh hell Richard, why talk like an idiot? You do nothing else but feel sorry for yourself because Marion is your Achilles heel, and you say why go so far back?' She snapped at him, deadly serious, accusing: 'When Marion went into the nursing home.'

'It was thirteen years ago,' said Richard, aggrieved.

'You came straight over to me. You seemed to think I'd fall into bed with you, you were even all wounded in your masculine pride because I wouldn't. Remember? Now we *free women* know that the moment the wives of our men friends go into the nursing home, dear Tom, Dick and Harry come straight over, they always want to sleep with one of their wives' friends, God knows why, a fascinating psychological fact among so many, but it's a fact. I wasn't having any, so I don't know who you went to ...'

'How do you know I went to anyone?'

'Because Marion knows. Such a pity how these things get round. And you've had a succession of girls ever since, and Marion has known about them all, since you have to confess your sins to her. There wouldn't be much fun in it, would there, if you didn't?'

Richard made a movement as if to get up and go—Anna again saw his thigh muscles tense, and relax. But he changed

27

his mind and sat still. There was a curious little smile pursing his mouth. He looked like a man determined to smile under the whip.

'In the meantime Marion brought up three children. She was very unhappy. From time to time you let it drop that perhaps it wouldn't be so bad if she got herself a lover—even things up a bit. You even suggested she was such a middle-class woman, so tediously conventional . . .' Molly paused at this, grinning at Richard. 'You are really such a pompous little hypocrite,' she said, in an almost friendly voice. Friendly with a sort of contempt. And again Richard moved his limbs uncomfortably, and said, as if hypnotised, 'Go on.' Then, seeing that this was rather asking for it, he said hastily: 'I'm interested to hear how you'd put it.'

'But surely not surprised?' said Molly. 'I can't remember ever concealing what I thought of how you treated Marion. You neglected her except for the first year. When the children were small she never saw you. Except when she had to entertain your business friends and organise posh dinner parties and all that nonsense. But nothing for herself. Then a man did get interested in her, and she was naïve enough to think you wouldn't mind—after all, you had said often enough, why don't you get yourself a lover, when she complained of your girls. And so she had an affair and all hell let loose. You couldn't stand it, and started threatening. Then he wanted to marry her *and* take the three children, yes, he cared for her that much. But no. Suddenly you got all moral, rampaging like an Old Testament prophet.'

'He was too young for her, it wouldn't have lasted.'

'You mean, she might have been unhappy with him? You were worried about her being unhappy?' said Molly, laughing contemptuously. 'No, your vanity was hurt. You worked really hard to make her in love with you again, it was all jealous scenes and love and kisses until that moment she broke it off with him finally. And the moment you had her safe, you lost interest and went back to the secretaries on the fancy divan in your beautiful big business office. And you think it's so unjust that Marion is unhappy and makes scenes and drinks more than is good for her. Or perhaps I should

28

say, more than is good for the wife of a man in your position. Well, Anna, is there anything new since I left a year ago?'

Richard said angrily: 'There's no need to make bad theatre of it.' Now that Anna was coming in, and it was no longer a battle with his former wife, he was angry.

'Richard came to ask me if I thought it was justified for him to send Marion away to some home or something. Because she was such a bad influence on the children.'

Molly drew in her breath. 'You *didn't*, Richard?'

'No. But I don't see why it's so terrible. She was drinking heavily about that time and it's bad for the boys. Paul—he's thirteen now, after all, found her one night when he got up for a drink of water, he found her unconscious on the floor, tight.'

'You were really thinking of sending her away?' Molly's voice had gone blank, empty even of condemnation.

'All right, Molly, all right. But what would you do? And you needn't worry—your lieutenant here was as shocked as you are, Anna made me feel as guilty as you like.' He was half-laughing again, though ruefully. 'And actually, when I leave you I ask myself if I really do deserve such total disapproval? You exaggerate so, Molly. You talk as if I'm some sort of Bluebeard. I've had half a dozen unimportant affairs. So do most of the men I know who have been married any length of time. Their wives don't take to drink.'

'Perhaps it would have been better if you had in fact chosen a stupid and insensitive woman?' suggested Molly. 'Or you shouldn't have always let her know what you were doing? Stupid! She's a thousand times better than you are.'

'It goes without saying,' said Richard. 'You always take it for granted that women are better than men. But that doesn't help me much. Now look here Molly, Marion trusts you. Please see her as soon as you can, and talk to her.'

'Saying what?'

'I don't know. I don't care. Anything. Call me names if you like, but see if you can stop her drinking.'

Molly sighed, histrionically, and sat looking at him, a look of half-compassionate contempt around her mouth.

'Well I really don't know,' she said at last. 'It is really all very odd. Richard why don't you do something? Why don't you try to make her feel you like her, at least? Take her for a holiday or something?'

'I did take her with me to Italy.' In spite of himself, his voice was full of resentment at the fact he had had to.

'Richard,' said both women together.

'She doesn't enjoy my company,' said Richard. 'She watched me all the time—I can see her watching me all the time, for me to look at some woman, waiting for me to hang myself. I can't stand it.'

'Did she drink while you were on holiday?'

'No, but . . .'

'There you are then,' said Molly, spreading out her flashing white hands, which said, What more is there to say?

'Look here Molly, she didn't drink because it was a kind of contest, don't you see that? Almost a bargain—I won't drink if you don't look at girls. It drove me nearly around the bend. And after all, men have certain practical difficulties— I'm sure you two emancipated females will take this in your stride, but I can't make it with a woman who's watching me like a jailor . . . getting into bed with Marion after one of those lovely holiday afternoons was like an I'll-dare-you-to-prove-yourself contest. In short, I couldn't get a hard on with Marion. Is that clear enough for you? And we've been back for a week. So far she's all right. I've been home every evening, like a dutiful husband, and we sit and are polite with each other. She's careful not to ask me what I've been doing or who I've been seeing. And I'm careful not to watch the level in the whisky bottle. But when she's not in the room I look at the bottle, and I can hear her brain ticking over, *he must have been with some woman because he doesn't want me.* It's hell, it really is. Well all right,' he cried, leaning forward, desperate with sincerity, 'all right Molly. But you can't have it both ways. You two go on about marriage, well you may be right. You probably are. I haven't seen a marriage yet that came anywhere near what it's supposed to be. All right. But you're careful to keep out of it. It's a hell of an institution, I agree. But I'm involved in it, and you're preaching from some pretty safe sidelines.'

Anna looked at Molly, very dry. Molly raised her brows and sighed.

'And now what?' said Richard, good humoured.

'We are thinking of the safety of the sidelines,' said Anna, meeting his good humour.

'Come off it,' said Molly. 'Have you got any idea of the sort of punishment women like us take?'

'Well,' said Richard, 'I don't know about that, and frankly, it's your own funeral, why should I care? But I know there's one problem you haven't got—it's a purely physical one. How to get an erection with a woman you've been married to fifteen years?'

He said this with an air of camaraderie, as if offering his last card, all the chips down.

Anna remarked, after a pause, 'Perhaps it might be easier if you had ever got into the habit of it?'

And Molly came in with: 'Physical you say? Physical? It's emotional. You started sleeping around early in your marriage because you had an emotional problem, it's nothing to do with physical.'

'No? Easy for women.'

'No, it's not easy for women. But at least we've got more sense than to use words like physical and emotional as if they didn't connect.'

Richard threw himself back in his chair and laughed. 'All right,' he said at last. 'I'm in the wrong. Of course. All right. I might have known. But I want to ask you two something, do you really think it's all my fault? I'm the villain as far as you are concerned. But why?'

'You should have loved her,' said Anna, simply.

'Yes,' said Molly.

'Good Lord,' said Richard, at a loss. 'Good Lord. Well I give up. After all I've said—and it hasn't been easy mind you . . .' he said this almost threatening, and went red as both women rocked off into fresh peals of laughter. 'No it's not easy to talk frankly about sex to women.'

'I can't imagine why not, it's hardly a great new revelation, what you've said,' said Molly.

'You're such a ... such a pompous ass,' said Anna. 'You bring out all this stuff, as if it were the last revelation from some kind of oracle. I bet you talk about sex when you're alone with a popsy. So why put on this club-man's act just because there are two of us?'

Molly said quickly: 'We still haven't decided about Tommy.'

There was a movement outside the door, which Anna and Molly heard, but Richard did not. He said, 'All right Anna, I bow to your sophistication. There's no more to be said. Right. Now I want you two superior women to arrange something. I want Tommy to come and stay with me and Marion. If he'll condescend to. Or doesn't he like Marion?'

Molly lowered her voice and said, looking at the door, 'You needn't worry. When Marion comes to see me, Tommy and she talk for hours and hours.'

There was another sound, like a cough, or something being knocked. The three sat silent as the door opened and Tommy came in.

It was not possible to guess whether he had heard anything or not. He greeted his father first, carefully: 'Hullo, father,' nodded at Anna, his eyes lowered against a possible reminder from her that the last time they met he had opened himself to her sympathetic curiosity, and offered his mother a friendly but ironic smile. Then he turned his back on them, to arrange for himself some strawberries remaining in the white bowl, and with his back still turned enquired: 'And how *is* Marion?'

So he had heard. Anna thought that she could believe him capable of standing outside the door to listen. Yes, she could imagine him listening with precisely the same detached ironic smile with which he had greeted his mother.

Richard, disconcerted, did not reply, and Tommy insisted: 'How is Marion?'

'Fine,' said Richard, heartily. 'Very well indeed.'

'Good. Because when I met her for a cup of coffee yesterday she seemed in a pretty bad way.'

Molly raised swift eyebrows towards Richard, Anna made a small grimace, and Richard positively glared at both of them, saying the whole situation was their fault.

Tommy, continuing not to meet their eyes, and indicating with every line of his body that they underestimated his comprehension of their situations and the implacability of his judgement on them, sat down, and slowly ate strawberries. He looked like his father. That is to say he was a closely-welded, round youth, dark, like his father, with not a trace of Molly's dash and vivacity. But unlike Richard, whose tenacious obstinacy was open, smouldering in his dark eyes and displayed in every impatient efficient movement, Tommy had a look of being buttoned in, a prisoner of his own nature. He was wearing, this morning, a scarlet sweat shirt and loose blue jeans, but would have looked better in a sober business suit. Every movement he ever made, every word he said, seemed in slow motion. Molly had used to complain, humorously, of course, that he sounded like someone who had taken an oath to count ten before he spoke. And she had complained, humorously, one summer when he had grown a beard, that he looked as if he had glued the rakish beard on to his solemn face. She had continued to make these loud, jolly complaints until Tommy had remarked: 'Yes, I know you'd rather I looked like you—been attractive I mean. But it's bad luck, I've got your character, and it should have been the other way around—well surely, if I'd had your looks and my father's character—well, his staying power, at any rate, it would have been better?'—he had persisted with it, doggedly, as he did when trying to make her see a point that she was being wilfully obtuse about. Molly had worried about this for some days, even ringing Anna up: 'Isn't it awful, Anna? Who would have believed it? You think something for years, and come to terms with it, and then suddenly, they come out with something and you see they've been thinking it too?'

'But surely you wouldn't want him to be like Richard?'

'No, but he's right about the staying power. And the way he came out with it—it's bad luck I've got your character, he said.'

Tommy ate his strawberries until there were none left,

33

berry after berry. He did not speak, and neither did they. They sat watching him eat, as if he had willed them to do this. He ate carefully. His mouth moved in the act of eating as it did in the act of speaking, every word separate, each berry whole and separate. And he frowned steadily, his soft dark brows knitted, like a small boy's over lessons. His lips even made small preliminary movements before a mouthful, like an old person's. Or like a blind man, thought Anna, recognising the movement; once she had sat opposite a blind man on the train. So had his mouth been set, rather full and controlled, a soft, self-absorbed pout. And so had his eyes been, like Tommy's even when he was looking at someone: as if turned inwards on himself. Though of course he was blind. Anna felt a small rising hysteria, as she had sitting opposite the blind man, looking at the sightless eyes that seemed as if they were clouded with introspection. And she knew that Richard and Molly felt the same; they were frowning and making restless nervous movements. He's bullying us all, thought Anna, annoyed; he's bullying us horribly. And again she imagined how he had stood outside the door, listening, probably for a long time; she was by now unfairly convinced of it, and disliking the boy, because of how he was willing them to sit and wait for his pleasure.

Anna was just forcing herself, against a most extraordinary prohibition, emanating from Tommy, to say something, to break the silence, when Tommy laid down his plate, and the spoon neatly across it, and said calmly: 'You three have been discussing me again.'

'Of course not,' said Richard, hearty and convincing.

'Of course,' said Molly.

Tommy allowed them both a tolerant smile, and said: 'You've come about a job in one of your companies. Well I did think it over, as you suggested, but I think if you don't mind I'll turn it down.'

'Oh Tommy,' said Molly, in despair.

'You're being inconsistent, mother,' said Tommy, looking towards her, but not at her. He had this way of directing his gaze towards someone, but maintaining an inward-seeming stare. His face was heavy, almost stupid-looking, with the

34

effort he was making to give everyone their due. 'You know it's not just a question of taking a job, is it? It means I've got to live like them.' Richard shifted his legs and let out an explosive breath, but Tommy continued: 'I don't mean any criticism, father.'

'If it's not a criticism, what is it?' said Richard, laughing angrily.

'Not a criticism, just a value judgement,' said Molly, triumphant.

'Ah, *hell*,' said Richard.

Tommy ignored them, and continued to address the part of the room in which his mother was sitting.

'The thing is, for better or for worse, you've brought me up to believe in certain things, and now you say I might just as well go and take a job in Portmain's. Why?'

'You mean,' said Molly, bitter with self-reproach, 'Why don't I offer you something better?'

'Perhaps there isn't anything better. It's not your fault— I'm not suggesting it is.' This was said with a soft, deadly finality, so that Molly frankly and loudly sighed, shrugged, and spread out her hands.

'I wouldn't mind being like your lot, it's not that. I've been around listening to your friends for years and years now, you all of you seem to be in such a mess, or think you are even if you're not,' he said, knitting his brows, and bringing out every phrase after careful thought. 'I don't mind that, but it was an accident for you, you didn't say to yourselves at some point: I am going to be a certain kind of person. I mean, I think that for both you and Anna there was a moment when you said, and you were even surprised, Oh, so I'm that kind of person, am I?'

Anna and Molly smiled at each other, and at him, acknowledging it was true.

'Well then,' said Richard jauntily. 'That's settled. If you don't want to be like Anna and Molly, there's the alternative.'

'No,' said Tommy. 'I haven't explained myself, if you can say that. No.'

'But you've got to do something,' cried Molly, not at all humorous, but sounding sharp and frightened.

'You don't,' said Tommy, as if it were self-evident.

'But you've just said you didn't want to be like us,' said Molly.

'It's not that I wouldn't want to be, but I don't think I could.' Now he turned to his father, in patient explanation. 'The thing about mother and Anna is this; one doesn't say, Anna Wulf the writer, or Molly Jacobs the actress—or only if you don't know them. They aren't—what I mean is—they aren't what they *do*; but if I start working with you, then I'll be what I do. Don't you see that?'

'Frankly, no.'

'What I mean is, I'd rather be . . .' he floundered, and was silent a moment, moving his lips together, frowning. 'I've been thinking about it because I knew I'd have to explain it to you.' He said this patiently, quite prepared to meet his parents' unjust demands. 'People like Anna or Molly and that lot, they're not just one thing, but several things. And you know they could change and be something different. I don't mean their characters would change, but they haven't set into a mould. You know if something happened in the world, or there was a change of some kind, a revolution or something . . .' He waited, a moment, patiently, for Richard's sharply irritated indrawn breath over the word revolution, to be expelled, and went on: 'they'd be something different if they had to be. But you'll never be different, father. You'll always have to live the way you do now. Well I don't want that for myself,' he concluded, allowing his lips to set, pouting, over his finished explanation.

'You're going to be very unhappy,' said Molly, almost moaning it.

'Yes, that's another thing,' said Tommy. 'The last time we discussed everything, you ended by saying, "Oh, but you're going to be unhappy." As if it's the worst thing to be. But if it comes to unhappiness, I wouldn't call either you or Anna happy people, but at least you're much happier than my father. Let alone Marion.' He added the last softly, in direct accusation of his father.

36

Richard said, hotly, 'Why don't you hear my side of the story, as well as Marion's?'

Tommy ignored this, and went on: 'I know I must sound ridiculous. I knew before I even started I was going to sound naïve.'

'Of course you're naïve,' said Richard.

'You're not naïve,' said Anna.

'When I finished talking to you last time, Anna, I came home and I thought, Well, Anna must think I'm terribly naïve.'

'No, I didn't. That's not the point. What you don't seem to understand is, we'd like you to do better than we have done.'

'Why should I?'

'Well perhaps we might still change and be better,' said Anna, with deference towards youth. Hearing the appeal in her own voice she laughed and said, 'Good Lord, Tommy, don't you realise how judged you make us feel?'

For the first time Tommy showed a touch of humour. He really looked at them, first at her, and then at his mother, smiling. 'You forget that I've listened to you two talk all my life. I know about you, don't I? I do think that you are both rather childish sometimes, but I prefer that to . . .' He did not look at his father, but left it.

'It's a pity you've never given me a chance to talk,' said Richard, but with self-pity; and Tommy reacted by a quick, dogged withdrawal away from him. He said to Anna and Molly, 'I'd rather be a failure, like you, than succeed and all that sort of thing. But I'm not saying I'm choosing failure. I mean, one doesn't choose failure, does one? I know what I don't want, but not what I do want.'

'One or two practical questions,' said Richard, while Anna and Molly wryly looked at the word failure, used by this boy in exactly the same sense they would have used it. All the same, neither had applied it themselves—or not so pat and final, at least.

'What are you going to live on?' said Richard.

Molly was angry. She did not want Tommy flushed out of the safe period of contemplation she was offering him by the fire of Richard's ridicule.

37

But Tommy said: 'If mother doesn't mind, I don't mind living off her for a bit. After all, I hardly spend anything. But if I have to earn money, I can always be a teacher.'

'Which you'll find a much more straitened way of life than what I'm offering you,' said Richard.

Tommy was embarrassed. 'I don't think you really understood what I'm trying to say. Perhaps I didn't say it right.'

'You're going to become some sort of a coffee-bar bum,' said Richard.

'No. I don't see that. You only say that because you only like people who have a lot of money.'

Now the three adults were silent. Molly and Anna because the boy could be trusted to stand up for himself; Richard because he was afraid of unleashing his anger. After a time Tommy remarked: 'Perhaps I might try to be a writer.'

Richard let out a groan. Molly said nothing, with an effort. But Anna exclaimed: 'Oh Tommy, and after all that good advice I gave you.'

He met her with affection, but stubbornly: 'You forget Anna, I don't have your complicated ideas about writing.'

'What complicated ideas?' asked Molly, sharply.

Tommy said to Anna: 'I've been thinking about all the things you said.'

'What things?' demanded Molly.

Anna said: 'Tommy, you're frightening to know. One says something, and you take it all up so seriously.'

'But you *were* serious?'

Anna suppressed an impulse to turn it off with a joke, and said: 'Yes, I was serious.'

'Yes, I know you were. So I thought about what you said. There was something arrogant in it.'

'Arrogant?'

'Yes, I think so. Both the times I came to see you, you talked, and when I put together all the things you said, it sounds to me like arrogance. Like a kind of contempt.'

The other two, Molly and Richard, were now sitting back, smiling, lighting cigarettes, being excluded, exchanging looks.

But Anna, remembering the sincerity of this boy's appeal

38

to her, had decided to jettison even her old friend Molly, for the time being at least.

'If it sounded like contempt, then I don't think I can have explained it right.'

'Yes. Because it means you haven't got confidence in people. I think you're afraid.'

'What of?' asked Anna. She felt very exposed, particularly before Richard, and her throat was dry and painful.

'Of loneliness. Yes I know that sounds funny, for you, because of course you choose to be alone rather than to get married for the sake of not being lonely. But I mean something different. You're afraid of writing what you think about life, because you might find yourself in an exposed position, you might expose yourself, you might be alone.'

'Oh,' said Anna, bleakly. 'Do you think so?'

'Yes. Or if you're not afraid, then it's contempt. When we talked about politics, you said the thing you'd learned from being a communist was that the most terrible thing of all was when political leaders didn't tell the truth. You said that one small lie could spread into a marsh of lies and poison everything—do you remember? You talked about it for a long time ... well then. You said that about politics. But you've got whole books you've written for yourself which no one ever sees. You said you believed that all over the world there were books in drawers, that people were writing for themselves—and even in countries where it isn't dangerous to write the truth. Do you remember, Anna? Well, that's a sort of contempt.' He had been looking, not at her, but directing towards her an earnest, dark, self-probing stare. Now he saw her flushed, stricken face, but he recovered himself, and said hesitantly: 'Anna you were saying what you really thought, weren't you?'

'Yes.'

'But Anna, you surely didn't expect me not to think about what you said?'

Anna closed her eyes a moment, smiling painfully. 'I suppose I underestimated—how much you'd take me seriously.'

'That's the same thing. It's the same thing as the writing. Why shouldn't I take you seriously?'

'I didn't know Anna was writing at all, these days,' said Molly, coming in firmly.

'I don't,' said Anna, quickly.

'There you are,' said Tommy. 'Why do you say that?'

'I remember telling you that I'd been afflicted with an awful feeling of disgust, of futility. Perhaps I don't like spreading those emotions.'

'If Anna's been filling you full of disgust for the literary career,' said Richard, laughing, 'then I won't quarrel with her for once.'

It was a note so false that Tommy simply ignored him, which he did by politely controlling his embarrassment and going straight on: 'If you feel disgust, then you feel disgust. Why pretend not? But the point is, you were talking about responsibility. That's what I feel too—people aren't taking responsibility for each other. You said the socialists had ceased to be a moral force, for the time, at least, because they wouldn't take moral responsibility. Except for a few people. You said that, didn't you—well then. But you write and write in notebooks, saying what you think about life, but you lock them up, and that's not being responsible.'

'A very great number of people would say that it was irresponsible to spread disgust. Or anarchy. Or a feeling of confusion.' Anna said this half-laughing, plaintive, rueful, trying to make him meet her on this note.

And he reacted immediately, by closing up, sitting back, showing she had failed him. She, like everyone else—so his patient, stubborn pose suggested, was bound to disappoint him. He retreated into himself, saying: 'Anyway, that's what I came down to say. I'd like to go on doing nothing for a month or two. After all it's costing much less than going to university as you wanted.'

'Money's not the point,' said Molly.

'You'll find that money is the point,' said Richard. 'When you change your mind, ring me up.'

'I'll ring you up in any case,' said Tommy, giving his father his due.

'Thanks,' said Richard, short and bitter. He stood for a

moment, grinning angrily at the two women. 'I'll drop in one of these days, Molly.'

'Any time,' said Molly, with sweetness.

He nodded coldly at Anna, laid his hand briefly on his son's shoulder, which was unresponsive, and went out. At once Tommy got up, and said: 'I'll go up to my room.' He walked out, his head poked forward, a hand fumbling at the door-knob, the door opened just far enough to take his width: he seemed to squeeze himself out of the room; and they heard his regular, thumping footsteps up the stairs.

'*Well*,' said Molly.

'Well,' said Anna, prepared to be challenged.

'It seems a lot of things have been going on while I was away.'

'For one thing, it seems I said things to Tommy I shouldn't.'

'Or not enough.'

Anna said with an effort: 'Yes I know you want me to talk about artistic problems and so on. But for me it's not like that ...' Molly merely waited, looking sceptical, and even bitter. 'If I saw it in terms of an artistic problem, then it'd be easy, wouldn't it? We could have ever such intelligent chats about the modern novel.' Anna's voice was full of irritation, and she tried smiling to soften it.

'What's in those diaries then?'

'They aren't diaries.'

'Whatever they are.'

'Chaos, that's the point.'

Anna sat watching Molly's thick white fingers twist together and lock. The hands were saying: Why do you hurt me like this?—but if you insist then I'll endure it.

'If you wrote one novel, I don't see why you shouldn't write another,' said Molly, and Anna began to laugh, irresistibly, while her friend's eyes filled with sudden tears.

'I wasn't laughing at you.'

'You simply don't understand,' said Molly, determinedly muffling the tears. 'It's always meant so much to me that you should produce something, even if I didn't.'

Anna nearly said, stubbornly, 'But I'm not an extension of

you,' but knew it was something she might have said to her mother, so stopped herself. Anna could remember her mother very little; she had died so early; but at moments like these, she was able to form for herself the image of somebody strong and dominating, whom Anna had had to fight.

'You get so angry over certain subjects I don't know how to begin,' said Anna.

'Yes, I'm angry. I'm angry. I'm angry about all the people I know who fritter themselves away. It's not only you. It's lots of people.'

'While you were away something happened that interested me. Remember Basil Ryan—the painter, I mean.'

'Of course. I used to know him.'

'Well there was an announcement in the paper, he said he'd never paint again. He said, it was because the world is so chaotic art is irrelevant.' There was a silence, until Anna appealed: 'Doesn't that mean anything to you?'

'No. And certainly not from you. After all, you aren't someone who writes little novels about the emotions. You write about what's real.'

Anna almost laughed again, and then said soberly, 'Do you realise how many of the things we say are just echoes? That remark you've just made is an echo from communist party criticism—at its worst moments, moreover. God knows what that remark means, I don't. I never did. If marxism means anything, it means that a little novel about the emotions should reflect "what's real" since the emotions are a function and a product of a society ...' She stopped, because of Molly's expression. 'Don't look like that Molly. You said you wanted me to talk about it, so I am. And there's something else. Fascinating, if it wasn't so depressing. Here we are, 1957, waters under bridges, etc. And suddenly in England, we have a phenomenon in the arts I'm damned if I'd foreseen—a whole lot of people, who've never had anything to do with the Party, suddenly standing up, and exclaiming, just as if they had just thought it out for themselves, that little novels or plays about the emotions don't reflect reality. The reality, it would surprise you to hear, is economics, or machine guns mowing people down who object to the new order.'

'Just because I can't express myself, I think it's unfair,' said Molly quickly.

'Anyway, I only wrote one novel.'

'Yes, and what are you going to do when the money from that stops coming in? You were lucky over that one, but it's going to stop some time.'

Anna held herself quiet, with effort. What Molly had said was pure spite: she was saying, I'm glad that you are going to be subjected to the pressures the rest of us have to face. Anna thought, I wish I hadn't become so conscious of everything, every little nuance. Once I wouldn't have noticed: now every conversation, every encounter with a person seems like crossing a mined field; and why can't I accept that one's closest friends at moments stick a knife in, deep, between the ribs?

She almost said, drily: You'll be glad to hear the money's only trickling in and I'll have to get a job soon. But she said, cheerfully, replying to the surface of Molly's words: 'Yes, I think I'll be short of money very soon, and I'll have to get a job.'

'And you haven't done anything while I was away.'

'I've certainly done a lot of complicated living.' Molly looked sceptical again, so Anna gave up. She said, humorous, light, plaintive: 'It's been a bad year. For one thing, I nearly had an affair with Richard.'

'So it would seem. It must have been a bad year for you even to think of Richard.'

'You know, there's a very interesting state of anarchy up there. You'd be surprised—why haven't you ever talked to Richard about his work, it's so odd.'

'You mean, you were interested in him because he's so rich?'

'Oh, *Molly*. Obviously not. No. I told you, everything's cracking up. That lot up there, they don't believe in anything. They remind me of the white people in Central Africa—they used to say: "Well of course, the blacks will drive us into the sea in fifty years' time." They used to say it cheerfully. In other words, "We know that what we are doing is wrong." But it's turned out to be a good deal shorter than fifty years.'

'But about Richard.'

'Well he took me out to a posh dinner. It was an occasion. He had just bought a controlling interest in all the aluminium saucepans, or pot-cleaners, or aircraft propellers in Europe— something like that. There were four tycoons and four popsies. I was one of the popsies. I sat there and looked at those faces around the table. Good God, it was terrifying. I reverted to my most primitive communist phase—you remember, when one thinks all one has to do is to shoot the bastards— that is, before one learned their opposite numbers are just as irresponsible. I looked at those faces, I just sat and looked at those faces.'

'But that's what we've always said,' said Molly. 'So what's new?'

'It did rather bring it all home. And then the way they treat their women—all quite unconscious, of course. My God, we might have moments of feeling bad about our lives, but how lucky we are, our lot are at least half civilised.'

'But about Richard.'

'Oh yes. Well. It wasn't important. He was just an incident. But he brought me home all in his new Jaguar. I gave him coffee. He was all ready. I sat there and thought, Well he's no worse than some of the morons I've slept with.'

'Anna, what has got into you?'

'You mean you've never felt that awful moral exhaustion, what the hell does it matter?'

'It's the way you talk. It's new.'

'I daresay. But it occurred to me—if we lead what is known as free lives, that is, lives like men, why shouldn't we use the same language?'

'Because we aren't the same. That is the point.'

Anna laughed. 'Men. Women. Bound. Free. Good. Bad. Yes. No. Capitalism. Socialism. Sex. Love . . .'

'Anna, what happened with Richard?'

'Nothing. You're making too much of it. I sat drinking coffee and looking at that stupid face of his and I was thinking, If I was a man I'd go to bed, quite likely simply

44

because I thought he was stupid—if he were a woman, I mean. And then I was so bored, so bored, so bored. Then he felt my boredom and decided to reclaim me. So he stood up and said: Oh well I suppose I'd better be getting home to 16 Plane Avenue, or whatever it is. Expecting me to say, Oh no, I can't bear you to leave. You know, the poor married man, bound to wife and kiddies. They all do it. Please be sorry for me, I have to get home to 16 Plane Avenue and the dreary labour-saving house in the suburbs. He said it once. He said it three times—just as if he didn't live there, weren't married to her, as if it had nothing to do with him. The little house at 16 Plane Avenue and the missus.'

'As a matter of accuracy, a bloody great mansion with two maids and three cars at Richmond.'

'You must admit he radiates an atmosphere of the suburbs. Odd. But they all do—I mean those tycoons, they all did. One could positively see the labour-saving devices and the kiddies all in their slumber-wear, coming down to kiss daddy good night. Bloody complacent swine they all are.'

'You are talking like a whore,' said Molly; then looked conscious, smiling, because she was surprised she had used the word.

'Oddly enough it's only by the greatest effort of will I don't feel like one. They put so much effort—oh unconsciously, of course, and that's where they win, every time, into making one feel it. Well. Anyway. I said, "Good night, Richard, I'm so sleepy, and thank you so much for showing me all that high life." He stood there wondering if he shouldn't say, Oh dear, I've got to go home to my dreary wife, for the fourth time. He was wondering why that unimaginative woman Anna was so unsympathetic to him. Then I could see him thinking, of course, she's nothing but an intellectual, what a pity I didn't take one of my other girls. So then I waited—you know, for that moment, when they have to pay one back? He said: "Anna, you should take more care of yourself, you're looking ten years older than you should, you are getting positively wizened." So I said, "But Richard, if I'd said to you, Oh yes, do come into bed, at this very moment you'd be saying how

beautiful I was. Surely the truth lies somewhere in between?"
. . .'

Molly was holding a cushion to her breasts, and hugging it and laughing.

'So he said: "But Anna, when you invited me up to coffee you surely must have known what it meant. I'm a very virile man," he said, "and I either have a relationship with a woman or I don't." So then I got tired of him, and said, "Oh do go away Richard, you're an awful bore . . ." so you can understand that there were bound to be—is the word I'm looking for *tensions*—between me and Richard today.'

Molly stopped laughing and said: 'All the same, you and Richard, you must be mad.'

'Yes,' said Anna, completely serious. 'Yes, Molly, I think I've been not far off it.'

But at this Molly got up, and said quickly: 'I'm going to make lunch.' The look she gave Anna was guilty and contrite. Anna got up too, and said 'Then I'll come into the kitchen for a moment.'

'You can tell me the gossip.'

'Ohhh,' said Anna yawning, very casual. 'Come to think of it, what can I tell you that's new? Everything's the same. But exactly.'

'In a year? The Twentieth Congress. Hungary. Suez. And doubtless the natural progression of the human heart from one thing to another? No change?'

The small kitchen was white, crammed with order, glistening from the surfaces of ranked coloured cups, plates, dishes; and from drops of steam condensing on the walls and ceiling. The windows were misted. The oven seemed to leap and heave with the energy of the heat inside it. Molly flung up the window and a hot smell of roasting meat rushed out over damp roofs and soiled back yards, as a waiting ball of sunlight leaped neatly over the sill and curled itself on the floor.

'England,' said Molly. 'England. Coming back this time was worse than usual. I felt the energy going out of me even on the boat. I walked into the shops yesterday and I looked at the nice, decent faces, everyone so kind, and so decent and

46

so bloody dull.' She stared briefly out of the window, and then determinedly turned her back on it.

'We'd better accept the fact that we and everybody we know's likely to spend their lives grumbling about England. We are living in it, however.'

'I'm going to leave again soon. I'd go tomorrow if it wasn't for Tommy. Yesterday I was down rehearsing at the theatre. Every man in the cast is a queer but one, and he's sixteen. So what am I doing here? All the time I was away, everything came naturally, the men treat you like women, you feel good, I never remembered my age, I never thought about sex. I had a couple of nice gay affairs, nothing tormented, everything easy. But as soon as you set foot here, you have to tighten your belt, and remember, Now be careful, these men are Englishmen. Except for the rare exception. And you get all self-conscious and sex-conscious. How can a country so full of screwed up people be any good?'

'You'll have settled down in a week or two.'

'I don't want to settle down. I can feel resignation creeping up already. And this house. It ought to be painted again. I simply don't want to start—painting and putting up curtains. Why is everything such hard work here? It isn't in Europe. One sleeps a couple of hours a night and is happy. Here, one sleeps and makes an effort . . .'

'Yes, yes,' said Anna, laughing. 'Well, I'm sure we'll be making the same speech to each other for years, every time we come back from somewhere.'

The house shook as a train went past, close, underground. 'And you ought to do something about that ceiling,' added Anna, looking up at it. The house, laid open by a bomb towards the end of the war, had stood empty for two years, receiving wind and rain through all its rooms. It had been patched up again. When the trains passed, grains of substance could be heard trickling behind clean surfaces of paint. The ceiling had a crack across it.

'Oh hell,' said Molly. 'I can't face it. But I suppose I shall. Why is it, it's only in this country everybody one knows seems to put a good face on things, everyone is bravely carrying a burden.' Tears were smudging her eyes, and she blinked them away and turned back to her oven.

'Because this is the country we know. The other countries are the places we don't think in.'

'That's not altogether true and you know it. Well. You'd better be quick with the news. I'm going to serve lunch in a minute.' It was now Molly's turn to exude an atmosphere of being alone, of not having been met. Her hands, pathetic and stoical, reproached Anna. As for Anna she was thinking: If I join in now, in a what's-wrong-with-men session, then I won't go home, I'll stay for lunch and all afternoon, and Molly and I will feel warm and friendly, all barriers gone. And when we part, there'll be a sudden resentment, a rancour—because after all, our real loyalties are always to men, and not to women . . . Anna nearly sat down, ready to submerge herself. But she did not. She thought: I want to be done with it all, finished with the men vs. women business, all the complaints and the reproaches and the betrayals. Besides, it's dishonest. We've chosen to live a certain way, knowing the penalties, or if we didn't we know now, so why whine and complain . . . and besides, if I'm not careful, Molly and I will descend into a kind of twin old-maidhood, where we sit around saying to each other, Do you remember how that man, what-was-his-name said that insensitive thing, it must have been in 1947 . . .

'Well, let's have it,' said Molly, very brisk, to Anna, who had stood silent for some time now.

'Yes. You don't want to hear about the comrades, I take it?'

'In France and Italy the intellectuals talk day and night about the Twentieth Congress and Hungary, the perspectives of and the lessons of and mistakes to be learned from.'

'In that case, since it's the same here, though thank God people are getting bored with it, I'll skip it.'

'Good.'

'But I think I'll mention three of the comrades—oh, only in passing,' added Anna hastily, as Molly grimaced. 'Three fine sons of the working class and trade union officials.'

'Who?'

48

'Tom Winters, Len Colhoun, Bob Fowler.'

'I knew them, of course,' said Molly quickly. She always knew, or had known, everyone. 'Well?'

'Just before the Congress, when there was all that disquiet in our circles, what with this plot and that, and Yugoslavia, etc., it so happened that I met them, in connection with what they naturally referred to as cultural matters. With condescension. At that time I and similar types were spending a lot of time fighting inside the Party—a naïve lot we were, trying to persuade people it was much better to admit that things stank in Russia than to deny it. Well. I suddenly got letters from all three of them—independently, of course, they didn't know, any of them, the others had written. Very stern, they were. Any rumours to the effect that there was any dirty work in Moscow or ever had been or that Father Stalin had ever put a foot wrong were spread by enemies of the working class.'

Molly laughed, but from politeness; the nerve had been touched too often.

'No, that isn't the point. The point is, these letters were interchangeable. Discounting handwriting of course.'

'Quite a lot to discount.'

'To amuse myself, I typed out all three letters—long ones at that, and put them side by side. In phraseology, style, tone, they were identical. You couldn't possibly have said, this letter was written by Tom, or that one by Len.'

Molly said resentfully: 'For that notebook or whatever it is you and Tommy have a secret about?'

'No. To find out something. But I haven't finished.'

'Oh all right, I won't press you.'

'Then came the Congress and almost instantly I got three more letters. All hysterical, self-accusatory, full of guilt, self-abasement.'

'You typed them out again?'

'Yes. And put them side by side. They might have been written by the same person. *Don't you see?*'

'No. What are you trying to prove?'

'Well, surely the thought follows—what stereotype am I? What anonymous whole am I part of?'

49

'Does it? It doesn't for me.' Molly was saying: 'If you choose to make a nonentity of yourself, do, but don't stick that label on me.'

Disappointed, because this discovery and the ideas that had followed from it were what she had been most looking forward to talking over with Molly, Anna said quickly: 'Oh all right. It struck me as interesting. And that's about all—there was a period of what may be described as confusion, and some left the Party. Or *everyone* left the Party—meaning those whose psychological time was up. Then suddenly, and in the same week—and that's what's so extraordinary Molly . . .' In spite of herself, Anna was appealing to Molly again—'In the same week, I got three more letters. Purged of doubt, stern and full of purpose. It was the week after Hungary. In other words, the whip had been cracked, and the waverers jumped to heel. Those three letters were identical too—I'm not talking about the actual words, of course,' said Anna impatiently, as Molly looked deliberately sceptical. 'I mean the style, the phrases, the way words were linked together. And those intermediary letters, the hysterical self-abasing letters, might never have been written. In fact I'm sure Tom, Len and Bob have suppressed the memory that they ever wrote them.'

'But you kept them?'

'Well I'm not going to use them in a court of law, if that's what you mean.'

Molly stood slowly wiping glasses on a pink and mauve striped cloth, and holding each one up to the light before setting it down. 'Well I'm so sick of it all I don't think I want ever to bother with it again.'

'But Molly, we can't do that, surely? We were communists or near-communists or whatever you like for years and years. We can't suddenly say, Oh well, I'm bored.'

'The funny thing is I'm bored. Yes I know it's odd. Two or three years ago I felt guilty if I didn't spend all my free time organising something or other. Now I don't feel at all guilty if I simply do my job and laze around for the rest. I don't care any more, Anna. I simply don't.'

'It's not a question of feeling guilty. It's a question of thinking out what it all means.'

Molly did not reply, so Anna went on quickly: 'Would you like to hear about the Colony?'

The Colony was the name they gave to a group of Americans, all living in London for political reasons.

'Oh God no. I'm sick of them too. No, I'd like to know what happened to Nelson, I'm fond of him.'

'He's writing the American masterpiece. He left his wife. Because she was neurotic. Got himself a girl. Very nice one. Decided she was neurotic. Went back to his wife. Decided she was neurotic. Left her. Has got himself another girl who so far hasn't become neurotic.'

'And the others?'

'In one way and another, ditto, ditto, ditto.'

'Well let's skip them. I met the American colony in Rome. Bloody miserable lot they are.'

'Yes. Who else?'

'Your friend Mr Mathlong—you know, the African?'

'Of course I know. Well he's currently in prison so I suppose by this time next year he'll be Prime Minister.'

Molly laughed.

'And there's your friend de Silva.'

'He *was* my friend,' said Molly laughing again, but resisting Anna's already critical tone.

'Then the facts are as follows. He went back to Ceylon with his wife—if you remember she didn't want to go. He wrote to me because he had written to you and got no reply. He wrote that Ceylon is marvellous and full of poetry and that his wife was expecting another child.'

'But she didn't want another child.'

Suddenly Anna and Molly both laughed; they were suddenly in harmony.

'Then he wrote to say he missed London and all its cultural freedoms.'

'Then I suppose we can expect him any moment.'

'He came back. A couple of months ago. He's abandoned his wife, apparently. She's much too good for him, he says,

51

weeping big tears, but not too big, because after all she is stuck with two kids in Ceylon and no money, so he's safe.'

'You've seen him?'

'Yes.' But Anna found herself unable to tell Molly what had happened. What would be the use? They'd end up, as she had sworn they would not, spending the afternoon in the dry bitter exchange that came so easily to them.

'And how about you Anna?'

And now, for the first time, Molly had asked in a way which Anna could reply to, and she said at once:

'Michael came to see me. About a month ago.' She had lived with Michael for five years. This affair had broken up three years ago, against her will.

'How was it?'

'Oh, in some ways, as if nothing had happened.'

'Of course, when you know each other so well.'

'But he was behaving—how shall I put it? I was a dear old friend, you know. He drove me to some place I wanted to go. He was talking about a colleague of his. He said, "Do you remember Dick?" Odd, don't you think, that he couldn't remember if I remembered Dick, since we saw a lot of him then. Dick's got a job in Ghana he said. He took his wife. His mistress wanted to go too, said Michael. Very difficult these mistresses are, said Michael, and then he laughed. Quite genuinely, you know, the debonair touch. That was what was painful. Then he looked embarrassed, because he remembered that I had been his mistress, and went red and guilty.'

Molly said nothing. She watched Anna closely.

'That's all, I suppose.'

'A lot of swine they all are,' said Molly cheerfully, deliberately striking the note that would make Anna laugh.

'Molly,' said Anna painfully, in appeal.

'What? It's no good going on about it, is it?'

'Well, I've been thinking. You know, it's possible we made a mistake.'

'What? Only one?'

But Anna would not laugh. 'No. It's serious. Both of us are dedicated to the proposition that we're tough—no listen, I'm serious. I mean—a marriage breaks up, well, we say, our

52

marriage was a failure, too bad. A man ditches us—too bad we say, it's not important. We bring up kids without men—nothing to it, we say, we can cope. We spend years in the communist party and then we say, Well, well, we made a mistake, too bad.'

'What are you trying to say,' said Molly, very cautious, and at a great distance from Anna.

'Well don't you think it's at least possible, just possible that things can happen to us so bad that we don't ever get over them? Because when I really face it I don't think I've really got over Michael. I think it's done for me. Oh I know, what I am supposed to say is, Well, well, he's ditched me—what's five years after all, on with the next thing.'

'But it has to be, on with the next thing.'

'Why do our lot never admit failure? Never. It might be better for us if we did. And it's not only love and men. Why can't we say something like this—we are people, because of the accident of how we were situated in history, who were so powerfully part—but only in our imaginations, and that's the point—with the great dream, that now we have to admit that the great dream has faded and the truth is something else—that we'll never be any use. After all Molly, it's not much loss is it, a few people, a few people of a certain type, saying that they've had it, they're finished. Why not? It's almost arrogant not to be able to.'

'Oh Anna! All this is simply because of Michael. And probably he'll come in again one of these days and you'll pick up where you left off. And if he doesn't, what are you complaining of? You've got your writing.'

'Good Lord,' said Anna softly. 'Good Lord.' Then after a moment, she forced the safe tone back: 'Yes, it's all very odd ... well, I must be rushing home.'

'I thought you said Janet was staying with a friend?'

'Yes, but I've got things to do.'

They kissed, briskly. That they had not been able to meet each other was communicated by a small, tender, even humorous squeeze of the hand. Anna went out into the street to walk home. She lived a few minutes' walk away, in Earls Court. Before she turned into the street she lived in she automatically cut out the sight of it. She did not live in the street, or even in the building, but in the flat; and she would not let the sight return to her eyes until her front door was shut behind her.

The rooms were on two floors at the top of the house, five large rooms, two down and three up. Michael had persuaded Anna, four years before, to move into her own flat. It was bad for her, he had said, to live in Molly's house, always under the wing of the big sister. When she had complained she could not afford it, he had told her to let a room. She had moved, imagining he would share this life with her; but he had left her shortly afterwards. For a time she had continued to live in the pattern he had set for her. There were two students in one big room, her daughter in another, and her own bedroom and living-room were organised for two people—herself and Michael. One of the students left, but she did not bother to replace him. She took a revulsion against her bedroom, which had been planned for Michael to share, and moved down to the living-room, where she slept and attended to her notebooks. Upstairs still lived the student, a youth from Wales. Sometimes Anna thought that it could be said she was sharing a flat with a young man; but he was a homosexual, and there was no tension in the arrangement. They hardly saw one another. Anna attended to her own life while Janet was at school, a couple of blocks away; and when Janet was home, devoted herself to her. An old woman came in once a week to clean the place. Money trickled in irregularly from her only novel, *Frontiers of War*, once a best-seller, which still earned just enough for her to live on. The flat was attractive, white painted, with bright floors. The balustrades and bannisters of the stairs made white patterns against red paper.

This was the framework of Anna's life. But it was only alone, in the big room, that she was herself. It was an oblong room, recessed to take a narrow bed. Around the bed were stacked books, papers, a telephone. There were three tall windows in the outer wall. At one end of the room, near the fireplace, was a desk with a typewriter, at which she dealt with letters, and the book reviews and articles she sometimes, but infrequently, wrote. At the other end was a long trestle table, painted black. A drawer held the four notebooks. The top of this table was always kept clear. The walls and ceiling of the room were white, but shabbied by the dark air of London. The floor was painted black. The bed had a black cover. The long curtains were a dull red.

Anna now passed slowly from one to another of the three windows, examining the thin and discoloured sunshine that failed to reach the pavements which were the floor of the rift between high Victorian houses. She covered the windows over, listening with pleasure to the intimate sliding sound of the curtain runners in their deep grooves, and to the soft swish, swish, swish of the heavy silk meeting and folding together. She switched the light on over the trestle table, so that the glossy black shone, mirroring a red gleam from the near curtain. She laid the four notebooks out, one after another, side by side.

She used an old-fashioned music stool for this occupation, and she now spun it high, almost as high as the table itself, and sat, looking down at the four notebooks as if she were a general on the top of a mountain, watching her armies deploy in the valley below.

THE NOTEBOOKS

[The four notebooks were identical, about eighteen inches square, with shiny covers, like the texture of a cheap watered silk. But the colours distinguished them—black, red, yellow and blue. When the covers were laid back, exposing the four first pages, it seemed that order had not immediately imposed itself. In each, the first page or two showed broken scribblings and half-sentences. Then a title appeared, as if Anna had, almost automatically, divided herself into four, and then, from the nature of what she had written, named these

55

divisions. And this is what had happened. The first book, the black notebook, began with doodlings, scattered musical symbols, treble signs that shifted into the £ sign and back again; then a complicated design of interlocking circles, then words:]

> black
> > dark, it is so dark
> > it is dark
> > > there is a kind of darkness here

[And then, in a changed startled writing:]

Every time I sit down to write, and let my mind go easy, the words, It is so dark, or something to do with darkness. Terror. The terror of this city. Fear of being alone. Only one thing stops me from jumping up and screaming or running to the telephone to ring somebody, it is to deliberately think myself back into that hot light . . . white light light closed eyes, the red light hot on the eyeballs. The rough pulsing heat of a granite boulder. My palm flat on it, moving over the lichens. The grain of the lichens. Tiny, like minute animals' ears, a warm rough silk on my palm, dragging insistently at the pores of my skin. And hot. The smell of the sun on hot rock. Dry and hot, and the silk of dust on my cheek, smelling of sun, the sun. Letters from the agent about the novel. Every time one of them arrives I want to laugh—the laughter of disgust. Bad laughter, the laughter of helplessness, a self-punishment. Unreal letters, when I think of a slope of hot pored granite, my cheeks against hot rock, the red light on my eyelids. Lunch with the agent. Unreal—the novel is more and more a sort of creature with its own life. *Frontiers of War* now has nothing to do with me, it is a property of other people. Agent said it should be a film. Said no. She was patient—her job to be.

[A date was scribbled here—1951.]

(1952) Had lunch with film man. Discussed cast for

Frontiers. So incredible wanted to laugh. I said no. Found myself being persuaded into it. Got up quickly and cut it short, even caught myself seeing the words *Frontiers of War* up outside a cinema. Though of course he wanted to call it *Forbidden Love.*

(1953) Spent all morning trying to remember myself back into sitting under the trees in the vlei near Mashopi. Failed.

[Here appeared the title or heading of the notebook:]

THE DARK

[The pages were divided down the middle by a neat black line, and the subdivisions headed:]

Source	*Money*

[Under the left word were fragments of sentences, scenes remembered, letters from friends in Central Africa gummed to the page. On the other side, a record of transactions to do with *Frontiers of War,* money received from translations, etc., accounts of business interviews and so on.

After a few pages the entries on the left ceased. For three years the black notebook had in it nothing but business and practical entries which appeared to have absorbed the memories of physical Africa. The entries on the left began again opposite a typed manifesto-like sheet gummed to the page, which was a synopsis of *Frontiers of War,* now changed to *Forbidden Love,* written by Anna with her tongue in her cheek, and approved by the synopsis desk in her agent's office:]

Dashing young Peter Carey, his brilliant scholastic career at Oxford broken by World War II, is posted to Central Africa with the sky-blue-uniformed youth of the R.A.F. to be trained as a pilot. Idealistic and inflammable, young Peter is shocked by the go-getting, colour-ridden small-town society he finds, falls in with the local group of high-living lefts, who exploit his naïve young radicalism. During the week they

57

clamour about the injustices meted out to the blacks; weekends they live it up in a lush out-of-town hotel run by John-Bull-type landlord Boothby and his comely wife, whose pretty teen-age daughter falls in love with Peter. He encourages her, with all the thoughtlessness of youth; while Mrs Boothby, neglected by her hard-drinking money-loving husband, conceives a powerful but secret passion for the good-looking youth. Peter, disgusted by the leftists' weekend orgies, secretly makes contact with the local African agitators, whose leader is the cook at the hotel. He falls in love with the cook's young wife, neglected by her politics-mad husband, but this love defies the taboos and mores of the white settler society. Mistress Boothby surprises them in a romantic rendezvous; and in her jealous rage informs the authorities of the local R.A.F. camp, who promise her Peter will be posted away from the Colony. She tells her daughter, unaware of her unconscious motive, which is to humiliate the untouched young girl whom Peter has preferred to herself and who becomes ill because of the insult to her white-girl's pride and announces she will leave home in a scene where the mother, frantic, screams: 'You couldn't even attract him. He preferred the dirty black girl to you.' The cook, informed by Mrs Boothby of his young wife's treachery, throws her off, telling her to return to her family. But the girl, proudly defiant, goes instead to the nearest town, to take the easy way out as a woman of the streets. Heart-broken Peter, all his illusions in shreds, spends his last night in the Colony drunk, and by chance encounters his dark love in some shabby shebeen. They spend their last night together in each other's arms, in the only place where white and black may meet, in the brothel by the sullied waters of the town's river. Their innocent and pure love, broken by the harsh inhuman laws of this country and by the jealousies of the corrupt, will know no future. They talk pathetically of meeting in England when the war is over, but both know this to be a brave lie. In the morning Peter says good-bye to the group of local 'progressives'; his contempt for them clear in his grave young eyes. Meanwhile his dark young love is lurking at the other end of the platform in a group of her own people. As the train steams out she waves; he does not see her; his eyes already reflect thought of the death that awaits him—Ace Pilot that he is!—and she returns to the streets of the dark town, on the arm of another man, laughing brazenly to hide her sad humiliation.

[Opposite this was written:]

The man at the synopsis desk was pleased by this; began discussing how to make the story 'less upsetting' to the moneybags—for instance, the heroine should not be a faithless wife, which would make her unsympathetic, but the daughter of the cook. I said I had written it in parody whereupon, after a moment's annoyance, he laughed. I watched his face put on that mask of bluff, goodnatured tolerance which is the mask of corruption in this particular time (for instance, Comrade X, on the murder of three British communists in Stalin's prisons, looked exactly like this when he said: Well, but we've never made enough allowance for human nature) and he said: 'Well, Miss Wulf, you're learning that when you're eating with the devil the spoon has got to be not only a long one, but made of asbestos—it's a perfectly good synopsis and written in their terms.' When I persisted, he kept his temper and enquired, oh very tolerantly, smiling indefatigably, whether I didn't agree that in spite of all the deficiencies of the industry, good films got made. 'And even films with a good progressive message Miss Wulf?' He was delighted at finding a phrase guaranteed to pull me in, and showed it; his look was both self-congratulatory and full of cynical cruelty. I came home, conscious of a feeling of disgust so much more powerful than usual that I sat down and made myself read the novel for the first time since it was published. As if it had been written by someone else. If I had been asked to review it in 1951, when it came out, this is what I should have said:

'A first novel which shows a genuine minor talent. The novelty of its setting: a station in the Rhodesian veld with its atmosphere of rootless money-driving white settlers against a background of sullen dispossessed Africans; the novelty of its story, a love affair between a young Englishman thrown into the Colony because of the war and a half-primitive black woman, obscures the fact that this is an unoriginal theme, scantily developed. The simplicity of Anna Wulf's style is her strength; but it is too soon to say whether this is the conscious simplicity of artistic control, or the often deceptive sharpness of form which is sometimes arbitrarily achieved by allowing the shape of a novel to be dictated by a strong emotion.'

But from 1954 on:

'The spate of novels with an African setting continues. *Frontiers of War* is competently told, with a considerable vigour of insight into the more melodramatic sexual relationships. But there is surely very little new to be said about the black-white conflict. The area of colour-bar hatreds and cruelties has become the best documented in our fiction. The most interesting questions raised by this new report from the racial frontiers is: why, when the oppressions and tensions of white-settled Africa have existed more or less in their present form for decades, is it only in the late forties and fifties that they exploded into artistic form. If we knew the answer we would understand more of the relations between society and the talent it creates, between art and the tensions that feed it. Anna Wulf's novel has been sprung by little more than a warm-hearted indignation against injustice: good, but no longer enough . . .'

During that period of three months when I wrote reviews, reading ten or more books a week, I made a discovery: that the interest with which I read these books had nothing to do with what I feel when I read—let's say—Thomas Mann, the last of the writers in the old sense, who used the novel for philosophical statements about life. The point is, that the function of the novel seems to be changing; it has become an outpost of journalism; we read novels for information about areas of life we don't know—Nigeria, South Africa, the American army, a coal-mining village, coteries in Chelsea, etc. We read *to find out what is going on*. One novel in five hundred or a thousand has the quality a novel should have to make it a novel—the quality of philosophy. I find that I read with the *same kind of curiosity* most novels, and a book of reportage. Most novels, if they are successful at all, are original in the sense that they report the existence of an area of society, a type of person, not yet admitted to the general literate consciousness. The novel has become a function of the fragmented society, the fragmented consciousness. Human beings are so divided, are becoming more and more divided, *and more subdivided in themselves,* reflecting the world, that they reach out desperately, not knowing they do it, for information about other groups inside their own country, let alone about groups in other countries. It is a blind grasping out for their own wholeness, and the novel-report is a means towards it. Inside this country, Britain, the middle-class has no knowledge of the lives of the working-people, and vice-versa; and reports and articles and novels are sold across the frontiers, are read as if savage tribes were being investigated. Those fishermen in Scotland were a different species from the coalminers I stayed with in Yorkshire; and both come from a different world than the housing estate outside London.

Yet I am incapable of writing the only kind of novel which interests me: a book powered with an intellectual or moral passion strong enough to create order, to create a new way of looking at life. It is because I am too diffused. I have decided never to write another novel. I have fifty 'subjects' I could write about; and they would be competent enough. If there is one thing we can be sure of, it is that competent and informative novels will continue to pour from the publishing houses. I have only one, and the least important of the qualities necessary to write at all, and that is curiosity. It is the curiosity of the journalist. I suffer torments of dissatisfaction and incompletion because of my inability to enter those areas of life my way of living, education, sex, politics, class bar me from. It is the malady of some of the best people of this time; some can stand the pressure of it; others crack under it; it is a new sensibility, a half-unconscious attempt towards a new imaginative comprehension. But it is fatal to

61

art. I am interested only in stretching myself, on living as fully as I can. When I said that to Mother Sugar she replied with the small nod of satisfaction people use for these resounding truths, that the artist writes out of an incapacity to live. I remember the nausea I felt when she said it; I feel the reluctance of disgust now when I write it: it is because this business about art and the artist has become so debased, the property of every sloppy-minded amateur that any person with a real connection with the arts wants to run a hundred miles at the sight of the small satisfied nod, the complacent smile. And besides, when a truth has been explored so thoroughly—this one has been the subject matter of art for this century, when it has become such a monster of a cliché, one begins to wonder, is it so finally true? And one begins to think of the phrases 'incapacity to live,' 'the artist,' etc., letting them echo and thin in one's mind, fighting the sense of disgust and the staleness, as I tried to fight it that day sitting before Mother Sugar. But extraordinary how this old stuff issued so fresh and magisterial from the lips of psychoanalysis. Mother Sugar, who is nothing if not a cultivated woman, a European soaked in art, uttered commonplaces in her capacity as witch-doctor she would have been ashamed of if she were with friends and not in the consulting room. One level for life, another for the couch. I couldn't stand it; that is, ultimately, what I couldn't stand. Because it means one level of morality for life, and another for the sick. I know very well from what level in my self that novel, *Frontiers of War,* came from. I knew when I wrote it. I hated it then and I hate it now. Because that area in myself had become so powerful it threatened to swallow everything else, I went off to the witch-doctor, my soul in my hands. Yet the healer herself, when the word Art cropped up, smiled complacently; that sacred animal the artist justifies everything, everything he does is justified. The complacent smile, the tolerant nod, is not even confined to the cultivated healers, or the professors; it's the property of the money-changers, the little jackals of the press, the enemy. When a film mogul wants to buy an artist—and the real reason why he seeks out the original talent and the spark of creativity is because he wants to destroy it, unconsciously that's what he wants, to justify himself by destroying the real thing—he calls the victim an artist. You are an artist, of course ... and the victim more often than not, smirks, and swallows his disgust.

The real reason why so many artists now take to politics, 'commitment' and so on is that they are rushing into a discipline, any discipline at all, which will save them from the poison of the word 'artist' used by the enemy.

I remember very clearly the moment in which that novel was born. The pulse beat, violently; afterwards, when I knew I would write, I worked out what I could write. The 'subject' was almost immaterial. Yet now what interests me is precisely this—why did I not write an account of what had happened, instead of shaping a 'story' which had nothing to do with the material that fuelled it. Of course, the straight, simple, formless account would not have been a 'novel,' and would not have got published, but I was genuinely not interested in 'being a writer' or even in making money. I am not talking now of that game writers play with themselves when writing, the psychological game—that written incident came from that real incident, that character was transposed from that one in life, this relationship was the psychological twin of that. I am simply asking myself: Why a story at all—not that it was a bad story, or untrue, or that it debased anything. Why not, simply, the truth?

I feel sick when I look at the parody synopsis, at the letters from the film company; yet I know that what made the film company so excited about the possibilities of that novel as a film was precisely what made it successful as a novel. The novel is 'about' a colour problem. I said nothing in it that wasn't true. But the emotion it came out of was something frightening, the unhealthy, feverish illicit excitement of wartime, a lying nostalgia, a longing for licence, for freedom, for the jungle, for formlessness. It is so clear to me that I can't read that novel now without feeling ashamed, as if I were in a street naked. Yet no one else seems to see it. Not one of the reviewers saw it. Not one of my cultivated and literary friends saw it. It is an immoral novel because that terrible lying nostalgia lights every sentence. And I know that in order to write another, to write those fifty reports on society which I have the material to write, I would have to deliberately whip up in myself that same emotion. And it would be that emotion which would make those fifty books novels and not reportage.

When I think back to that time, those weekends spent at the Mashopi Hotel, with that group of people, I have to first switch something off in me; now, writing about it, I have to switch it off, or 'a story' would begin to emerge, a novel, and not the truth. It is like remembering a particularly intense love affair, or a sexual obsession. And it is extraordinary how, as the nostalgia deepens, the excitement 'stories' begin to form, to breed like cells under a microscope. And yet it is so powerful, that nostalgia, that I can only write this, a few sentences at a time. Nothing is more powerful than this nihilism, an angry readiness to throw everything overboard, a willingness, a longing to become part of dissolution. This emotion is one of the strongest reasons why wars continue. And the people who read *Frontiers of War* will have had fed in them this emotion, even though they were not conscious of it. That is why I am ashamed, and why I feel continually as if I had committed a crime.

The group was composed of people thrown together by chance, and who knew they would not meet again as soon as this particular phase of the war was over. They all knew and acknowledged with the utmost frankness that they had nothing in common.

Whatever fervours, beliefs, and awful necessities the war created in other parts of the world, it was characterised in ours, right from the start, by double-feeling. It was immediately evident that for us war was going to be a very fine thing. This wasn't a complicated thing that needed to be explained by experts. Material prosperity hit Central and South Africa tangibly; there was suddenly a great deal more money for everyone, and this was true even of the Africans, even in an economy designed to see that they had the minimum necessary to keep them alive and working. Nor were there any serious shortages of commodities to buy with the money. Not serious enough at least to interfere with the enjoyment of life. Local manufacturers began to make what had been imported before, thus proving in another way that war has two faces—it was such a torpid, slovenly economy, based as it was on the most inefficient and backward labour force, that it needed some sort of jolt from outside. The war was such a jolt.

There was another reason for cynicism—because people began to be cynical, when they were tired of being ashamed, as they were, to start with. This war was presented to us as a crusade against the evil doctrines of Hitler, against racialism, etc., yet the whole of that enormous land-mass, about half the total area of Africa, was conducted on precisely Hitler's assumption—that some human beings are better than others because of their race. The mass of the Africans up and down the continent were sardonically amused at the sight of their white masters crusading off to fight the racialist devil—those Africans with any education at all. They enjoyed the sight of the white baases so eager to go off and fight on any available battle-front against a creed they would all die to defend on their own soil. Right through the war, the correspondence columns of the papers were crammed with arguments about whether it was safe to put so much as a pop-gun into the hands of any African soldier since he was likely to turn it against his white masters, or to use this useful knowledge later. It was decided, quite rightly, that it was not safe.

Here were two good reasons why the war had for us, from the very beginnings, its enjoyable ironies.

(I am again falling into the wrong tone—and yet I hate that tone, and yet we all lived inside it for months and years, and it did us all, I am sure, a great deal of damage. It was self-punishing, a locking of feeling, an inability or a refusal to fit conflicting things together to make a whole; so that one can live inside it, no matter how terrible. The refusal means one can neither change nor destroy; the refusal means ultimately either death or impoverishment of the individual.)

I will try to put down the facts merely. For the general population the war had two phases. The first when things were going badly and defeat was possible; this phase ended, finally, at Stalingrad. The second phase was simply sticking it out until victory.

For us, and I mean by us the left and the liberals associated with the left, the war had three phases. The first was when Russia disowned the war. This locked the loyalties of us all—the half hundred or hundred people whose emotional spring was a faith in the Soviet Union. This period ended when Hitler attacked Russia. Immediately there was a burst of energy.

People are too emotional about communism, or rather, about their own communist parties, to think about a subject that one day will be a subject for sociologists. That is, the social activities that go on as a direct or indirect result of the existence of a communist party. People or groups of people who don't even know it have been inspired, or animated, or given a new push into life because of the communist party, and this is true of all countries where there has been even a tiny communist party. In our own small town, a year after Russia entered the war, and the left had recovered because of it, there had come into existence (apart from the direct activities of the party which is not what I am talking about) a small orchestra, readers' circles, two dramatic groups, a film society, an amateur survey of the conditions of urban African children which, when it was published, stirred the white conscience and was the beginning of a long-overdue sense of guilt, and half a dozen discussion groups of African problems. For the first time in its existence there was something like a cultural life in that town. And it was enjoyed by hundreds of people who knew of the communists only as a group of people to hate. And of course a good many of these phenonema were disapproved of by the communists themselves, then at their most energetic and dogmatic. Yet the communists had inspired them because a dedicated faith in humanity spreads ripples in all directions.

For us, then (and this was true of all the cities up and down our part of Africa), a period of intense activity began. This phase, one of jubilant confidence, ended some time in 1944, well before the end of the war. This change was not due to an outside event, like a change in the Soviet Union's 'line'; but was internal, and self-developing, and, looking back, I can see its beginning almost from the first day of the establishment of the 'communist' group. Of course all the discussion clubs, groups, etc., died when the Cold War began and any sort of interest in China and the Soviet Union became suspect instead of fashionable. (The purely cultural organisations like orchestras, drama groups and so on continued.) But when 'left' or 'progressive' or 'communist' feeling— whichever word is right, and at this distance it's hard to say—was at its height in our town, the inner group of people who had initiated it were already falling into inertia, or bewilderment or at best worked out of a sense of duty. At the time, of course, no one understood it; but it was inevitable. It is now obvious that inherent in the structure of a communist party or group is a self-dividing principle. Any communist party anywhere exists and perhaps even flourishes by this process of discarding individuals or groups; not because of personal merits or demerits, but according to how they accord with the inner dynamism of the party at any given moment. Nothing happened in our small, amateur and indeed ludicrous group that hadn't happened right back with the Iskra group in London at the beginning of the century, at the start of organised communism. If we had known anything at all about the history of our own movement we would have been saved from the cynicism, the frustration, the bewilderment—but that isn't what I want to say now. In our case, the inner logic of 'centralism' made the process of disintegration inevitable because we had no links at all with what African movements there were—that was before the birth of any Nationalist movement, before any kind of trade union. There were then a few Africans who met secretly under the noses of the police but they didn't trust us, because we were white. One or two came to ask our advice on technical questions but we never knew what was really in their minds. The situation was that a group of highly militant white politicos, equipped with every kind of information about organising revolutionary movements were operating in a vacuum because the black masses hadn't begun to stir, and wouldn't for another few years. And this was true of the communist party

67

in South Africa too. The battles and conflicts and debates inside our group which might have driven it into growth, had we not been an alien body, without roots, destroyed us very fast. Inside a year our group was split, equipped with sub-groups, traitors, and a loyal hard core whose personnel, save for one or two men, kept changing. Because we did not understand the process, it sapped our emotional energy. But while I know that the process of self-destruction began almost at birth, I can't quite pinpoint that moment when the tone of our talk and behaviour changed. We were working as hard, but it was to the accompaniment of a steadily deepening cynicism. And our jokes, outside the formal meetings, were contrary to what we said, and thought we believed in. It is from that period of my life that I know how to watch the jokes people make. A slightly malicious tone, a cynical edge to a voice, can have developed inside ten years into a cancer that has destroyed a whole personality. I've seen it often, and in many other places than political or communist organisations.

The group I want to write about became a group after a terrible fight in 'the party.' (I have to put it in inverted commas because it was never officially constituted, more a kind of emotional entity.) It split in two, and over something not very important—so unimportant I can't even remember what it was, only the horrified wonder we all felt that so much hatred and bitterness could have been caused by a minor question of organisation. The two groups agreed to continue to work together—so much sanity remained to us; but we had different policies. I want to laugh out of a kind of despair even now—it was all so irrelevant, the truth was the group was like a group of exiles, with exiles' fevered bitterness over trifles. And we were all—twenty or so of us, exiles; because our ideas were so far in advance of the country's development. Yes, now I remember that the quarrel was because one half of the organisation complained that certain members were not 'rooted in the country.' We split on these lines.

And now for our small sub-group. There were three men from the aircamps, who had known each other first at Oxford—Paul, Jimmy and Ted. Then George Hounslow, who worked on the roads. Then Willi Rodde, the refugee from Germany. Myself. Maryrose who had actually been born in the country. I was the odd man out in this group because I was the only one who was free. Free in the sense that I had chosen to come to the Colony in the first place and could leave it when I liked. And why did I not leave it? I hated the place, and had done so since I first came to it in 1939 to marry and become a tobacco farmer's wife. I met Steven in London the year before, when he was on holiday. The day after I arrived on the farm I knew I liked Steven but could never stand the life. But instead of returning to London I went into the city and became a secretary. For years my life seems to have consisted of activities I began to do provisionally, temporarily, with half a heart, and which I then stayed with. For instance I became 'a communist' because the left people were the only people in the town with any kind of moral energy, the only people who took it for granted that the colour bar was monstrous. And yet there were always two personalities in me, the 'communist' and Anna, and Anna judged the communist all the time. And vice-versa. Some kind of lethargy I suppose. I knew the war was coming and it would be hard to get a passage home, yet I stayed. Yet I did not enjoy the life, I don't enjoy pleasure, but I went to sundowner parties and dances and I played tennis and enjoyed the sun. It seems such a long time ago that I can't *feel* myself doing any of these things. I can't 'remember' what it was like to be Mr Campbell's secretary or to dance every night, etc. It happened to someone else. I can see myself though, but even that wasn't true until I found an old photograph the other day which showed a small, thin, brittle black-and-white girl, almost doll-like. I was more sophisticated than the colonial girls of course; but far less experienced—in a colony people have far more room to do as they like. Girls can do things there that I'd have to fight to do in England. My sophistication was literary and social. Compared with a girl like Maryrose, for all her apparent fragility and vulnerability, I was a baby. The photograph shows me standing on the Club steps, holding a racket. I look amused and critical; it's a sharp little face. I never acquired that admirable Colonial quality—good humour. (Why is it admirable? Yet I enjoy it.) But I can't remember what I felt, except that I repeated to myself every day, even after the war began, that now I must book my passage home. About then I met Willi Rodde and got involved with politics. Not for the first time. I was too young of course to have been involved with Spain, but friends had been; so communism and the left was nothing new to me. I did not like Willi. He did not like me. Yet we began to live together, or as much as is possible in a small town where everyone knows what you do. We had rooms in the same hotel and shared meals. We were together for nearly three years. Yet we neither liked nor understood each other. We did not even enjoy sleeping together. Of course then I was inexperienced, having slept only with Steven, and that briefly. But even then I knew, as Willi knew, that we were incompatible. Having learned about sex since, I know that the word incompatible means something very real. It doesn't mean, not being in love, or not being in sympathy, or not being patient, or being ignorant. Two people can be sexually incompatible who are perfectly happy in bed with other people, as if the very chemical structures of their bodies were hostile. Well, Willi and I understood this so well that our vanity wasn't involved. Our emotions were, about this point only. We had a kind of pity for each other; we were both afflicted permanently with a feeling of sad helplessness because we were unable to make each other happy in this way. But nothing stopped us from choosing other partners. We did not. That I did not isn't surprising, because of that quality in me I call lethargy, or curiosity, which always keeps me in the situation long after I should leave it. Weakness? Until I wrote that word I never thought of it as applying to me. But I suppose it does. Willi, however, was not weak. On the contrary he was the most ruthless person I have ever known.

Having written that, I am astounded. What do I mean? He was capable of great kindness. And now I remember that all those years ago, I discovered that no matter what adjective I applied to Willi, I could always use the opposite. Yes. I have looked in my old papers. I find a list, headed *Willi*:

Ruthless	Kind
Cold	Warm
Sentimental	Realistic

And so on, down the page; and underneath I wrote: 'From the process of writing these words about Willi I have discovered I know nothing about him. About someone one understands, one doesn't have to make lists of words.'

But really what I discovered, though I didn't know it then, was that in describing any personality all these words are meaningless. To describe a person one says: 'Willi, sitting stiffly at the head of the table, allowed his round spectacles to glitter at the people watching him and said, formally, but with a gruff clumsy humour. . . .' Something like that. But the point is, and it is the point that obsesses me (and how odd this obsession should be showing itself, so long ago, in helpless lists of opposing words, not knowing what it would develop into), once I say that words like good/bad, strong/weak, are irrelevant, I am accepting amorality, and I do accept it the moment I start to write 'a story,' 'a novel,' because I simply don't care. All I care about is that I should describe Willi and Maryrose so that a reader can feel their reality. And after twenty years of living in and around the left, which means twenty years' preoccupation with this question of morality in art, that is all I am left with. So what I am saying is, in fact, that the human personality, that unique flame, is so sacred to me, that everything else becomes unimportant? Is that what I am saying? And if so, what does it mean?

But to return to Willi. He was the emotional centre of our sub-group, and had been, before the split, the centre of the big group—another strong man, similar to Willi, was now leading the other sub-group. Willi was centre because of his absolute certainty that he was right. He was a master of dialectic; could be very subtle and intelligent in diagnosing a social problem, could be, even in the next sentence, stupidly dogmatic. As time went on, he became steadily more heavy-minded. Yet the odd thing was that people continued to re-volve around him, people much subtler than he, even when they knew he was talking nonsense. Even when we had reached the stage when we could laugh, in front of him and at him, and at some monstrous bit of logic-chopping, we continued to revolve around and depend on him. It is terrifying that this can be true.

For instance, when he first imposed himself and we ac-cepted him, he told us that he had been a member of the underground working against Hitler. There was even some fantastic story about his having killed three S.S. men and secretly buried them and then escaped to the frontier and away to England. We believed it, of course. Why not? But even after Sam Kettner came up from Johannesburg, who had known him for years, and told us that Willi had never been anything more in Germany than a liberal, had never joined any anti-Hitler group, and had only left Germany when his age-group became eligible for the army, it was as if we believed it. Because we thought him capable of it? Well, I'm sure he was. Because, in short, a man is as good as his fantasies?

But I don't want to write Willi's history—it was common enough for that time. He was a refugee from sophisticated Europe stuck for the duration of the war in a backwater. It is his character I want to describe—if I can. Well, the most remarkable thing about him was how he would sit down to work out everything that might conceivably happen to him in the next ten years, and then make plans in advance. There is nothing that most people find harder to understand than that a man can continuously scheme to meet all the contingencies that might occur five years ahead. The word used for this is opportunism. But very few people are genuinely opportunists. It takes not only clarity of mind about oneself, which is fairly common; but a stubborn and driving energy, which is rare. For instance, for the five years of the war Willi drank beer (which he hated) every Saturday morning with a C.I.D. man (whom he despised) because he had worked out that this particular man was likely to have become a senior official by the time Willi needed him. And he was right, because when the war ended, it was this man who pulled strings for Willi to get his naturalisation through long before any of the other refugees got theirs. And therefore Willi was free to leave the Colony a couple of years before they were. At it turned out he decided not to live in England, but to return to Berlin; but had he chosen England, then he would have needed British nationality—and so on. Everything he did had this quality of careful calculated planning. Yet it was so blatant that nobody believed it about him. We thought, for example, that he really liked the C.I.D. man as a person, but was ashamed of admitting he liked a 'class enemy.' And when Willi used to say: 'But he will be useful to me,' we would laugh affectionately as at a weakness that made him more human.

For, of course, we thought him inhuman. He played the role of commissar, the communist intellectual leader. Yet he was the most middle-class person I have known. I mean by this that in every instinct he was for order, correctness and conservation of what existed. I remember Jimmy laughing at him and saying that if he headed a successful revolution on Wednesday, by Thursday he would have appointed a Ministry of Conventional Morality. At which Willi said he was a socialist and not an anarchist.

He had no sympathy for the emotionally weak or deprived or for the misfits. He despised people who allowed their lives to be disturbed by personal emotion. Which didn't mean he wasn't capable of spending whole nights giving good advice to someone in trouble; but the advice tended to leave the sufferer feeling he was inadequate and unworthy.

Willi had had the most conventional upper-middle-class upbringing imaginable. Berlin in the late twenties and thirties; an atmosphere which he called decadent, but of which he had been very much a part; a little conventional homosexuality at the age of thirteen; being seduced by the maid when he was fourteen; then parties, fast cars, cabaret singers; a sentimental attempt to reform a prostitute about which he was now sentimentally cynical; an aristocratic contempt for Hitler, and always plenty of money.

He was—even in this Colony and when he was earning a few pounds a week, perfectly dressed; elegant in a suit made

73

for ten shillings by an Indian tailor. He was of middle height, lean, stooped a little; wore a cap of absolutely smooth gleaming black hair which was rapidly receding; had a high pale forehead, extremely cold greenish eyes usually invisible behind steadily focused spectacles, and a prominent and authoritarian nose. He would listen patiently while people spoke, his lenses flashing, and then take off the glasses, exposing his eyes, which were at first weak and blinking from the adjustment, then suddenly narrowed and critical, and speak with a simplicity of arrogance that took everyone's breath away. That was Wilhelm Rodde, the professional revolutionary who later (after failing to get the good well-paid job in a London firm he had counted on) went to East Germany (remarking with his usual brutal frankness: I'm told they are living very well there, with cars and chauffeurs) and became an official with a good deal of power. And I am sure he is an extremely efficient official. I am sure he is humane, when it is possible. But I remember him at Mashopi; I remember us all at Mashopi—for now all those years of nights of talk and activity, when we were political beings, seem to me far less revealing of what we were than at Mashopi. Though of course, as I've said, that is true only because we were politically in a vacuum, without a chance of expressing ourselves in political responsibility.

The three men from the camp were united by nothing but the uniform, although they had been friends at Oxford. They acknowledged that the end of the war would be the end of their intimacy. They would sometimes even acknowledge their lack of real liking for each other, in the light, hard, self-mocking voice which was common to us all during that particular phase—to all, that is, save Willi, whose concession to the tone or style of that time was to allow freedom to others. It was his way of participating in anarchy. At Oxford these three had been homosexuals. When I write the word down and look at it, I realise its power to disturb. When I remember the three, how they were, their characters, there is no shock, or moment of disturbance. But at the word *homosexual,* written—well, I have to combat dislike and disquiet. Extraordinary. I qualify the word by saying that already, only eighteen months later, they were making jokes about 'our homosexual phase,' and jibing at themselves for doing something simply because it had been fashionable. They had been in a loose group of about twenty, all vaguely left-wing, vaguely literary, all having affairs with each other in every kind of sexual combination. And again, put like that, it becomes too emphatic. It was the early part of the war; they were waiting to be called up; it was clear in retrospect that they were deliberately creating a mood of irresponsibility as a sort of social protest and sex was part of it.

The most striking of the three, but only because of his quality of charm, was Paul Blackenhurst. He was the young man I used in *Frontiers of War* for the character of 'gallant young pilot' full of enthusiasm and idealism. In fact he was without any sort of enthusiasm, but he gave the impression of it, because of his lively appreciation of any moral or social anomaly. His real coldness was hidden by charm, and a certain grace in everything he did. He was a tall youth, well-built, solid, yet alert and light in his movements. His face was round, his eyes very round and very blue, his skin extraordinarily white and clear, but lightly freckled over the bridge of a charming nose. He had a soft thick shock of hair always falling forward on his forehead. In the sunlight it was a full light gold, in the shade a warm golden brown. The very clear eyebrows were of the same soft glistening brightness. He confronted everyone he met with an intensely serious, politely enquiring, positively deferential bright-blue beam from his eyes, even stooping slightly in his attempt to convey his earnest appreciation. His voice, at first meeting, was a low charming deferential murmur. Very few failed to succumb to this delightful young man so full (though of course against his will) of the pathos of that uniform. It took most people a long time to discover that he was mocking them. I've seen women, and even men, when the meaning of one of his cruelly quiet drawling statements came home to them, go literally pale with the shock of it; and stare at him incredulous that such open-faced candour could go with such deliberate rudeness. He was, in fact, extremely like Willi, but only in the quality of his arrogance. It was an upper-class arrogance. He was English, upper-middle-class, extremely intelligent. His parents were gentry; his father, Sir something or other. He had that absolute assurance of nerve and body that comes from being bred in a well-set-up conventional family without any money worries. The 'family'—and, of course, he spoke of it with mockery, were spread all over the upper reaches of English society. He would say, drawling: 'Ten years ago I'd have claimed that England belongs to me and I know it! Of course, the war'll do away with all that, won't it?' And his smile would convey that he believed in nothing of the sort, and hoped we were too intelligent to believe it. It was arranged that when the war was over, he would go into the City. He spoke of that, too, with mockery. 'If I marry well,' he'd say, only the corners of his attractive mouth showing amusement, 'I'll be a captain of industry. I have intelligence and the education and the background—all I need is the money. If I don't marry well I'll be a lieutenant— much more fun, of course, to be under orders, and much less responsibility.' But we all knew he would be a colonel at least. But what is extraordinary is that this sort of talk went on when the 'communist' group was at its most confident. One personality for the committee room; another for the café afterwards. And this is not as frivolous as it sounds; because if Paul had been caught up in a political movement that could have used his talents, he would have stayed with it; exactly as Willi, failing to reach his fashionable business consultant-ship (which he was born for) became a communist administrator. No, looking back I see that the anomalies and cynicisms of that time were only reflections of what was possible.

Meanwhile he made jokes about 'the system.' He had no belief in it, that goes without saying, his mocking at it was genuine. But in his character of future lieutenant, he'd raise a clear blue gaze to Willi and drawl: 'I'm using my time usefully, wouldn't you say? By observing the comrades? I'll have a flying start over my rival lieutenants, won't I? Yes, I'll understand the enemy. Probably you, dear Willi. Yes.' At which Willi would give a small grudging appreciative smile.

Once he even said: 'It's all very well for you, you've got something to go back to. I'm a refugee.'

They enjoyed each other's company. Although Paul would have died rather than admit (in his role as future officer-in-industry) a serious interest in anything, he was fascinated by history, because of his intellectual pleasure in paradox—that is what history meant to him. And Willi shared this passion—for history, not for the paradoxical ... I remember him saying to Paul: 'It's only a real dilettante who could see history as a series of improbabilities,' and Paul, replying: 'But my dear Willi, I'm a member of a dying class, and you'd be the first to appreciate that I can't afford any other attitude?' Paul, shut into the officers' mess with men who for the most part he considered morons, missed serious conversation, though of course he would never have said so; and I daresay the reason he attached himself to us in the first place was because we offered it. Another reason was that he was in love with me. But then we were all, at various times, in love with each other. It was, as Paul would explain, 'obligatory in the times we live in to be in love with as many people as possible.' He did not say this because he felt he would be killed. He did not believe for a moment he would be killed. He had worked out his chances mathematically; they were much better now than earlier, during the Battle of Britain. He was going to fly bombers, less dangerous than fighter planes. And besides, some uncle of his attached to the senior levels of the Air Force had made enquiries and determined (or perhaps arranged) that Paul would be posted, not to England, but to India, where the casualties were comparatively light. I think that Paul was truly 'without nerves.' In other words, his nerves, well cushioned since birth by security, were not in the habit of signalling messages of doom. They told me—the men who flew with him—that he was always cool, confident, accurate, a born pilot.

In this he was different from Jimmy McGrath, also a good pilot, who suffered a hell of fear. Jimmy used to come into the hotel after a day's flying and say he was sick with nerves. He'd admit he hadn't slept for nights with anxiety. He would confide in me, gloomily, that he had a premonition he would be killed tomorrow. And he would ring me up from the camp the day after to say his premonition had been justified because in fact he had 'nearly pranged his kite,' and it was sheer luck he wasn't dead. His training was a continual torment to him.

Yet Jimmy flew bombers, and apparently very well, over Germany right through the last phase of the war, when we were systematically laying the German cities in ruins. He flew continuously for over a year, and he survived.

Paul was killed the last day before he left the Colony. He had been posted to India, so his uncle was right. His last evening was spent with us at a party. Usually he controlled his drinking, even when pretending to drink wild with the rest of us. That night he drank himself blind, and had to be put into a bath in the hotel by Jimmy and Willi and brought around. He went back to camp as the sun was coming up to say good-bye to his friends there. He was standing on the airstrip, so Jimmy told me later, still half-conscious with alcohol, the rising sun in his eyes—though of course, being Paul, he would not have shown the state he was in. A plane came in to land, and stopped a few paces away. Paul turned, his eyes dazzling with the sunrise, and walked straight into the propeller, which must have been an almost invisible sheen of light. His legs were cut off just below the crutch and he died at once.

Jimmy was also middle-class; but Scotch, not English. There was nothing Scots about him, except when he got drunk, when he became sentimental about ancient English atrocities, like Glencoe. His voice was an elaborately affected Oxford drawl. This accent is hard enough to take in England, but in a Colony it is ludicrous. Jimmy knew it, and would emphasise it deliberately to annoy people he didn't like. For us, whom he did like, he would make apologies. 'But after all,' he would say, 'I know it's silly, but this expensive voice will be my bread and butter after the war.' And so Jimmy, like Paul, refused—at least on one level of his personality— to believe in the future of the socialism he professed. His family was altogether less impressive than Paul's. Or rather, he belonged to a decaying branch of a family. His father was an unsatisfactory retired Indian Colonel—unsatisfactory, as Jimmy emphasised, because, 'He isn't the real thing. He likes Indians and goes in for humanity and Buddhism—I *ask* you!' He was drinking himself to death, so Jimmy said; but I think this was put in simply to round off the picture; because he would also show us poems written by the old man; and he was probably secretly very proud of him. He was an only child, born when his mother, whom he adored, was already over forty. Jimmy was the same physical type as Paul—at first glance. A hundred yards off, they were recognisably of the same human tribe, hardly to be distinguished. But close to, their resemblances emphasised their total difference of fibre. Jimmy's flesh was heavy, almost lumpish; he carried himself heavily; his hands were large but podgy, like a child's hands. His features, of the same carved clear whiteness as Paul's, with the same blue eyes, lacked grace, and his gaze was pathetic and full of a childish appeal to be liked. His hair was pale and lightless, and fell about in greasy strands. His face, as he took pleasure in pointing out, was a decadent face. It was over-full, over-ripe, almost flaccid. He was not ambitious, and wanted no more than to be a Professor of History at some university, which he has since become. Unlike the others he was truly homosexual, though he wished he wasn't. He was in love with Paul whom he despised and who was irritated by him. Much later he married a woman fifteen years older than himself. Last year he wrote me a letter in which he described this marriage—it was obviously written when he was drunk and posted, so to speak, into the past. They slept together, with little pleasure on her side, and none on his—'though I did put my mind to it, I do assure you!'—for a few weeks. Then she got pregnant, and that was the end of sex between them. In short, a not uncommon English marriage. His wife, it appears, has no suspicion he is not a normal man. He is quite dependent on her and if she died I suspect he'd commit suicide, or retreat into drink.

Ted Brown was the most original. A boy from a large working-class family, he had won scholarships all his life and finally to Oxford. He was the only genuine socialist of the three—I mean socialist in his instincts, in his nature. Willi used to complain that Ted behaved 'as if he lived in a full-blown communist society or as if he'd been brought up in some damned kibbutz.' Ted would look at him, genuinely puzzled: he could not understand why that should be a criticism. Then he'd shrug and choose to forget Willi in some new enthusiasm. He was a lively, slight, lank, black-shock-haired, hazel-eyed, energetic young man, always without money—he gave it away; with his clothes in a mess—he had no time for them, or gave them away; without time for himself, for he gave that away to everyone. He had a passion for music, about which he had taught himself a good deal, for literature, and for his fellow human beings whom he saw as victims with himself of a gigantic and almost cosmic conspiracy to deprive them of their true natures. Which of course were beautiful, generous, and good. He sometimes said he preferred being homosexual. This meant that he had a succession of protégés. The truth was he couldn't stand that other young men of his class hadn't had his advantages. He would seek out some bright mechanic in the camp; or, at the public meetings in town some youth who seemed to be there out of real interest and not because he had nothing better to do; seize hold of him, make him read, instruct him in music, explain to him that life was a glorious adventure, and come to us exclaiming that 'when one finds a butterfly under a stone one has to rescue it.' He was always rushing into the hotel with some raw, bemused young man, demanding that we should jointly 'take him on.' We always did. During the two years he was in the Colony, Ted rescued a dozen butterflies, all of whom had an amused and affectionate respect for him. He was collectively in love with them. He changed their lives. After the war, in England, he kept in touch, made them study, directed them into the Labour Party—by then he was no longer a communist; and saw to it that they did not, as he put it, hibernate. He married, very romantically and against every kind of opposition, a German girl, has three children, and teaches English at a school for backward children. He was a competent pilot, but it was typical of him that he deliberately made himself fail the final tests, because he was at the time wrestling with the soul of a young ox from Manchester who refused to be musical and insisted on preferring football to literature. Ted explained to us that it was more important to rescue a human being from darkness than to add another pilot to the war effort, fascism or no fascism. So he stayed on the ground, was sent back to England, and served in the coal-mines, which experience permanently affected his lungs. Ironically enough the young man for whom he did this was the only one he failed with.

When ejected from the coal-mine as unfit, he somehow got himself to Germany in the role of an educator. His German wife is very good for him, being practical and competent and a good nurse. Ted now needs looking after. He complains bitterly that the state of his lungs forces him to 'hibernate.'

Even Ted was affected by the prevailing mood. He could not endure the wranglings and bitterness inside the party group, and the split when it came was the last straw. 'I'm obviously not a communist,' he said to Willi, sombrely, with bitterness, 'because all this hair-splitting seems to me nonsense.' 'No, you obviously are not,' replied Willi, 'I was wondering how long it'd take you to see it.' Above all Ted was disquieted because the logic of the previous polemics had led him into the sub-group led by Willi. He thought the leader of the other group, a corporal from an aircamp and an old Marxist, 'a dried-up bureaucrat,' but he preferred him as a human being to Willi. Yet he was committed to Willi . . . which leads me to something I've not before thought about. I keep writing the word group. Which is a collection of people. Which one associates with a collective relationship—and it is true we met day after day for months, for hours every day. But looking back, looking back to really remember what happened, it is not at all like that. For instance I don't think Ted and Willi ever really talked together—they jibed at each other occasionally. No, there was one time they made contact and that was in a flaming quarrel. It was on the verandah of the hotel at Mashopi, and while I can't remember what the quarrel was about I remember Ted shouting: 'You're the sort of man who'd shoot fifty people before breakfast and then eat six courses. No, you'd order someone else to shoot them, that's what you'd do.' And Willi in reply:

'Yes, if it were necessary I would . . .' And so on, for an hour or more, and all this while the ox-wagons rolled by in the white dust of the sand-veld, the trains rocked by on the way from the Indian Ocean to the capital, while the farmers drank in their khaki in the bar, and groups of Africans, in search of work, hung about under the jacaranda tree, hour after hour, waiting patiently for the moment when Mr Boothby, the big boss, would have time to come and interview them.

And the others? Paul and Willi together, talking about history—interminably. Jimmy in argument with Paul—usually about history; but in fact what Jimmy was saying, over and over again, was that Paul was frivolous, cold, heartless. But Paul and Ted had no connection with each other, they did not even quarrel. As for me, I played the role of 'the leader's girl friend'—a sort of cement, an ancient role indeed. And of course if any of my relationships with these people had had any depth, I would have been disruptive and not conciliatory. And there was Maryrose, who was the unattainable beauty. And so what was this group? What held it together? I think it was the implacable dislike and fascination for each other of Paul and Willi, who were so much alike, and bound to such different futures.

Yes. Willi, with his guttural, so-correct English, and Paul, with his exquisite, cool enunciation—the two voices, hour after hour, at night, in the Gainsborough hotel. That is what I remember most clearly of the group during the period before we went to Mashopi and everything changed.

The Gainsborough hotel was really a boarding-house; a place people lived in for long stretches. The boarding-houses of the town were mostly converted private houses, more comfortable certainly, but uncomfortably genteel. I stayed in one for a week and left: the contrast between the raw Colonialism of the city, and the primness of the boarding-house full of English middle-class who might never have left England, was more than I could stand. The Gainsborough hotel was newly-built, a large, rattling, ugly place full of refugees, clerks, secretaries, and married people who couldn't find a house or a flat; the town was jostling full because of the war, and rents were soaring.

It was typical of Willi that he had not been in the hotel a week before he had special privileges, and this in spite of being a German, and technically an enemy alien. Other German refugees pretended to be Austrians, or kept out of the way, but Willi's name in the hotel register was Dr Wilhelm Karl Gottlieb Rodde, ex-Berlin, 1939. Just like that. Mrs James who ran the hotel was in awe of him. He had taken care to let her know his mother was a countess. In fact she was. She believed him to be a medical doctor, and he had not troubled to let her know what the word Doctor meant in Europe. 'It's not my fault she's stupid,' he said, when we criticised him for it. He gave her free advice about the law, patronised her, was rude when he did not get what he wanted and in short had her running around after him, as he said himself, 'like a frightened little dog.' She was the widow of a miner who had died in a fall of rock on the Rand; a woman of fifty, obese, harried, sweating and incompetent. She fed us stews, pumpkin and potatoes. Her African servants cheated her. Until Willi told her how to run the place, which he did without being asked, at the end of the first week he was there, she lost money. After his instructions she made a great deal—she was a rich woman by the time Willi left the hotel: with investments chosen by him in property all over the city.

I had the room next to Willi. We ate at the same table. Our friends dropped in day and night. For us, the enormous ugly dining-room which closed finally at eight (dinner from seven to eight) was opened even after midnight. Or we made ourselves tea in the kitchens, and at the most Mrs James might come down in her dressing-gown, smiling placatorily, to ask us to lower our voices. It was against the rules to have people in our rooms after nine o'clock at night; but we ran study classes in our rooms till four or five in the morning several nights a week. We did as we liked, while Mrs James got rich, and Willi told her she was a silly goose without any business sense.

She would say: 'Yes, Mr Rodde,' and giggle and sit coyly on his bed to smoke a cigarette. Like a schoolgirl. I remember Paul saying: 'Do you really think it's right for a socialist to get what he wants by making a fool of an old woman?' 'I'm earning her a lot of money.' 'I was talking about sex,' said Paul, and Willi said: 'I don't know what you mean.' He didn't. Men are far more unconscious than women about using their sex in this way; far less honest.

So the Gainsborough hotel was for us an extension of Left Club and the Party group; and associated, for us, with hard work.

We went to the Mashopi hotel for the first time on an impulse. It was Paul who directed us to it. He was flying somewhere in the area; the aircraft was grounded because of a sudden storm; and he returned with his instructor by car, stopping off in the Mashopi hotel for lunch. He came into the Gainsborough that night in high spirits, to share his good humour with us. 'You'd never believe it—slammed right down in the middle of the bush, all surrounded by kopjes and savages and general exotica, the Mashopi hotel, and a bar with darts and a shove-halfpenny board, and steak and kidney pie served with the thermometer at ninety, and in addition to everything, Mr and Mrs Boothby—and they're the spitting bloody image of the Gatsbys—remember? The couple who ran the pub at Aylesbury? The Boothbys might never have set a foot outside England. And I swear he's an ex-sergeant-major. Couldn't be anything else.'

'Then she's an ex-barmaid,' said Jimmy, 'and they've got a comely daughter they want to marry off. Remember Paul, how that poor bloody girl couldn't keep her eyes off you in Aylesbury?'

'Of course you Colonials wouldn't appreciate the exquisite incongruity of it,' said Ted. For the purposes of such jokes, Willi and I were Colonials.

'Ex-sergeant-majors who might never have left England run half the hotels and bars in the country,' I said. 'As you might have discovered if you were ever able to tear yourselves away from the Gainsborough.'

For the purposes of jokes like these, Ted, Jimmy and Paul despised the Colony so much they knew nothing about it. But of course, they were extremely well-informed.

It was about seven in the evening, and dinner at the Gainsborough was imminent. Fried pumpkin, stewed beef, stewed fruit.

'Let's go down and have a look at the place,' said Ted. 'Now. We can have a pint and be back to catch the bus to camp.' He made the suggestion with his usual enthusiasm; as if the Mashopi hotel was certain to turn out the most beautiful experience life had yet offered us.

We looked at Willi. There was a meeting that night, run by the Left Club, then at its zenith. We were all expected to be there. We had never, not once, defected from duty. But Willi agreed, casually, as if there were nothing remarkable in it: 'That's something we could very well do. Mrs James' pumpkin can be eaten by someone else for this one night.'

Willi ran a cheap fifth-hand car. We all five of us got into it and drove down to Mashopi, about sixty miles away. I remember it was a clear but oppressive night—the stars thick and low, with the heavy glitter of approaching thunder. We drove between kopjes that were piles of granite boulders, characteristic of that part of the country. The boulders were charged with heat and electricity, so that blasts of hot air, like soft fists, came on to our faces as we passed the kopjes.

We reached the Mashopi hotel about eight-thirty, and found the bar blazing with light and packed with the local farmers. It was a small bright place, shining from polished wood, and the polished black cement floor. As Paul had said, there was a well-used darts board and a shove-halfpenny. And behind the bar stood Mr Boothby, six feet tall, portly, his stomach protruding, his back straight as a wall, his heavy face with its network of liquor-swollen veins dominated by a pair of cool, shrewd prominent eyes. He remembered Paul from midday and enquired how the repairs to the aircraft were progressing. It had not been damaged; but Paul began on a long story how a wing had been struck by lightning and he had descended to the tree-tops by parachute, his instructor clutched under his arm—so manifestly untrue, that Mr Boothby looked uneasy from the first word. And yet Paul told it with such earnest, deferential grace that until he concluded, 'Mine is not to reason why; mine is but to fly and

85

die'—wiping away a mock-gallant tear, that Mr Boothby let out a small reluctant grunt of laughter and suggested a drink. Paul had expected the drink to be on the house—a reward for a hero, so to speak; but Mr Boothby held out his hand for the money with a long narrowed stare, as if to say: 'Yes, I know it's not a joke, and you'd have made a fool of me if you could.' Paul paid with good grace and continued the conversation. He came over to us, beaming, a few minutes later to say that Mr Boothby had been a sergeant in the B.S.A. Police; that he had married his wife on leave in England, and she had worked behind the bar in a pub; that they had a daughter aged eighteen, and they had been running this hotel for eleven years. 'And very admirably too, if I may say so,' we had heard Paul say. 'I very much enjoyed my lunch today.'

'But it's nine o'clock,' said Paul, 'and the dining-room is closing, and mine host didn't offer to feed us. So I've failed. We shall starve. Forgive me my failure.'

'I'll see what I can do,' said Willi. He went over to Mr Boothby, ordered whisky, and within five minutes had succeeded in getting the dining-room opened, especially for us. I don't know how he did it. To begin with, he was such a bizarre note in this bar full of sun-burned khaki-clad farmers and their dowdy wives that the eyes of everyone had been returning to him, again and again, ever since he came in. He was wearing an elegant cream shantung suit, and his hair shone black under the strident lights, and his face was pale and urbane. He said, in his over-correct English, so unmistakably German, that he and his good friends had travelled all the way from town to taste the Mashopi food they had heard so much about, and he was sure that Mr Boothby would not disappoint him. He spoke with exactly the same arrogant hidden cruelty that Paul had used in telling the story about the parachute descent, and Mr Boothby stood silent, staring coldly at Willi, his great red hands unmoving on the bar-counter. Willi then calmly took out his wallet and produced a pound note. I don't suppose anyone had dared to tip Mr Boothby for years. Mr Boothby did not at once reply. He slowly and deliberately turned his head and his eyes became more prominent still as he narrowed them on the monetary possibilities of Paul, Ted and Jimmy, all standing with large tankards in their hands. He then remarked: 'I'll see what my wife can do,' and left the bar, leaving Willi's pound note on the counter. Willi was meant to take it back; but he left it there, and came over to us. 'There is no difficulty,' he announced.

Paul had already engaged the attention of the daughter of a farmer. She was about sixteen, pretty, pudgy, wearing a flounced flowered muslin dress. Paul was standing in front of her, his tankard poised high in one hand, and he was remarking in his light pleasant voice: 'I've been wanting to tell you ever since I came into this bar, that I haven't seen a dress like yours since I was at Ascot three years ago.' The girl was hypnotised by him. She was blushing. But I think that in a moment she would have understood he was being insolent. But now Willi laid his hand on Paul's arm and said: 'Come on. All that will do later.'

We went out onto the verandah. Across the road stood gum-trees, their leaves glistening with moonlight. A train stood hissing out steam and water onto the rails. Ted said in a low passionate voice: 'Paul you're the best argument I've ever known for shooting the entire upper-class to be rid of the lot of you.' I instantly agreed. This was by no means the first time this had happened. About a week before Paul's arrogance had made Ted so angry he had gone off, white and sick-looking, saying he would never speak to Paul again. 'Or Willi—you are two of a kind.' It had taken hours of persuasion on my part and Maryrose's to bring back Ted into the fold. Yet now Paul said, lightly: 'She's never heard of Ascot and when she finds out she'll be flattered,' and all Ted said was, after a long pause: 'No, she won't. She won't.' And then a silence, while we watched the rippling silver leaves, and then: 'What the hell. You'll never understand it as long as you live, either of you and I don't *care*.' The *I don't care* was in a tone I had never heard from Ted, almost frivolous. And he laughed. I had never heard him laugh like that. I felt bad, at sea—because Ted and I had always been allies in this battle, and now I was deserted.

The main block of the hotel stood directly by the main road, and consisted of the bar and the dining-room with the kitchens behind it. There was a verandah along the front supported by wooden pillars, up which plants grew. We sat on benches in silence, yawning, suddenly exhausted and very hungry. Soon Mrs Boothby, summoned from her own house by her husband, let us into the dining-room and shut the doors again so that travellers might not come in and demand food. This was one of the Colony's main roads, and always full of cars. Mrs Boothby was a large, full-bodied woman, very plain, with a highly-coloured face and tightly-crimped colourless hair. She wore tight corsets, and her buttocks shelved out abruptly, and her bosom was high like a shelf in front. She was pleasant, kindly, anxious to oblige, but dignified. She apologised, that as we were so late, she could not serve a full dinner, but she would do her best. Then, with a nod and a good night, she left us to the waiter, who was sulky at being kept in so long after his proper hours. We ate plates of good thick roast beef, roast potatoes, carrots. And afterwards, apple pie and cream and the local cheese. It was English pub food, cooked with care. The big dining-room was silent. All the tables gleamed with readiness for tomorrow's breakfast. The windows and doors were hung with heavy floral linen. Headlights from the passing cars continually lightened the linen, obliterating the pattern, so that the reds and blues of the flowers glowed out very bright when the dazzle of light had swept on and up the road towards the city. We were all sleepy and not very talkative. But I felt better after a while, because Paul and Willi, as usual, were treating the waiter as a servant, ordering him about and making demands, and suddenly Ted came to himself, and began talking to the man as a human being—and with even more warmth than usual, so I could see he was ashamed of his moment on the verandah. While Ted made enquiries about the man's family, his work, his life, offering information about himself, Paul and Willi simply ate, as always on these occasions. They had made their position clear long ago. 'Do you imagine, Ted, that if you are kind to servants you are going to advance the cause of socialism?' 'Yes,' Ted had said. 'Then I can't help you,' Willi had said, with a shrug, meaning there was no hope for him. Jimmy was demanding more to drink. He was already drunk; he got drunk more quickly than anyone I've known. Soon Mr Boothby came in and said that as travellers we were entitled to drink—making it plain why we had been allowed to eat so late in the first place. But instead of the hard drinks he wanted us to order, we asked for wine, and he brought us chilled white Cape wine. It was very good wine; and we did not want to drink the raw Cape brandy Mr Boothby brought us but we did drink it, and then some more wine. And then Willi announced that we were all coming down next week-end, and could Mr Boothby arrange rooms for us. Mr Boothby said it was no trouble at all—offering us a bill that we had difficulty in raising the money to settle.

Willi had not asked any of us if we were free to spend the week-end in Mashopi, but it seemed a good idea. We drove back through the now chilly moonlight, the mist lying cold and white along the valleys, and it was very late and we were all rather tight. Jimmy was unconscious. When we got into town it was too late for the three men to get back to camp; so they took my room at the Gainsborough, and I went into Willi's. On such occasions they used to get up very early, about four, and walk to the edge of the little town, and wait for a lift that would take them out to the camp where they all had to start flying about six, when the sun rose.

And so the next week-end we all went down to Mashopi. Willi and myself. Maryrose. Ted, Paul and Jimmy. It was late on Friday night, because we had a party discussion on the 'line.' As usual it was how to draw the African masses into militant action. The discussion was acrimonious in any case because of the official split—which did not prevent us from considering ourselves a unit for this particular evening. There were about twenty people, and the end of it was that while we all agreed the existing 'line' was 'correct'—we also agreed we weren't getting anywhere.

When we got into the car without suitcases or kitbags, we were all silent. We were silent all the way out of the suburbs. Then the argument about the 'line' began again—between

Paul and Willi. They said nothing that hadn't been said at length, in the meeting, but we all listened, hoping, I suppose, for some fresh idea that would lead us out of the tangle we were in. The 'line' was simple and admirable. In a colour-dominated society like this, it was clearly the duty of socialists to combat racialism. Therefore, 'the way forward' must be through a combination of progressive white and black vanguards. Who were destined to be the white vanguard? Obviously, the trade unions. And who the black vanguard? Clearly, the black trade unions. At the moment there were no black trade unions, for they were illegal and the black masses were not developed yet for illegal action. And the white trade unions, jealous of their privileges, were more hostile to the Africans than any other section of the white population. So our picture of what ought to happen, must happen in fact, because it was a first principle that the proletariat was to lead the way to freedom, was not reflected anywhere in reality. Yet the first principle was too sacred to question. Black nationalism was, in our circles (and this was true of the South African communist party), a right-wing deviation, to be fought. The first principle, based as it was on the soundest humanist ideas, filled us full of the most satisfactory moral feelings.

I see I am falling into the self-punishing, cynical tone again. Yet how comforting this tone is, like a sort of poultice on a wound. Because it is certainly a wound—I, like thousands of others can't remember our time in or near 'The Party' without a terrible dry anguish. Yet that pain is like the dangerous pain of nostalgia, its first cousin and just as deadly. I'll go on with this when I can write it straight, not in that tone.

I remember Maryrose put an end to the argument by remarking: 'But you aren't saying anything that you didn't say earlier.' That stopped it. She often did this, she had a capacity for silencing us all. Yet the men patronised her, they thought nothing of her capacity for political thought. It was because she could not, or would not, use the jargon. But she grasped points quickly and put them in simple terms. There is

90

a type of mind, like Willi's, that can only accept ideas if they are put in the language he would use himself.

Now she said: 'There must be something wrong somewhere, because if not, we wouldn't have to spend hours and hours discussing it like this.' She spoke with confidence; but now that the men did not reply—and she felt their tolerance of her, she grew uneasy and appealed: 'I'm not saying it right, but you see what I mean ...' Because she had appealed, the men were restored, and Willi said benevolently: 'Of course you say it right. Anyone as beautiful as you can't say it wrong.'

She was sitting near me, and she turned her head in the dark of the car to smile at me. We exchanged that smile very often. 'I'm going to sleep,' she said, and put her head on my shoulder and went off to sleep like a little cat.

We were all very tired. I don't think people who have never been part of a left movement understand how hard the dedicated socialists do work, day in and day out; year in, year out. After all, we all earned our livings, and the men in the camps, at least the men actually being trained, were under continuous nervous stress. Every evening we were organising meetings, discussion groups, debates. We all read a great deal. More often than not we were up till four or five in the morning. In addition to this we were all curers of souls. Ted took to extremes an attitude we all had, that anyone in any sort of trouble was our responsibility. And part of our duty was to explain to anyone with any kind of a spark that life was a glorious adventure. Looking back I should imagine that of all the appallingly hard work we did, the only part of it that achieved anything was this personal proselytising. I doubt whether any of the people we took on will forget the sheer exuberance of our conviction in the gloriousness of life, for if we didn't have it by temperament we had it on principle. All kinds of incidents come back—for instance Willi, who after some days of wondering what to do for a woman who was unhappy because her husband was unfaithful to her, decided to offer her the *Golden Bough* because, 'when one is personally unhappy the correct course is to take a historical view of the matter.' She returned the book, apologetically, saying it was above her head and that in any case she had decided to leave her husband because she had decided he was more trouble than he was worth. But she wrote to Willi regularly when she left our town, polite, touching, grateful letters. I remember the terrible words: 'I'll never forget that you were kind enough to take an interest in me.' (They didn't strike me at the time, though.)

We had all been living at this pitch for over two years—I think it's possible we were all slightly mad out of sheer exhaustion.

Ted began to sing, to keep himself awake; and Paul, in a completely different voice from the one he had used in the discussion with Willi, started on a whimsical fantasy about what would happen in an imaginary white-settled Colony when the Africans revolted. (This was nearly a decade before Kenya and the Mau Mau.) Paul described how 'two men and a half' (Willi protested against the reference to Dostoievsky, whom he considered a reactionary writer) worked for twenty years to bring the local savages to a realisation of their position as a vanguard. Suddenly a half-educated demagogue who had spent six months at the London School of Economics created a mass movement overnight, on the slogan: 'Out with the Whites.' The two-men-and-a-half, responsible politicians, were shocked by this, but it was too late—the demagogue denounced them as being in the pay of the whites. The whites, in a panic, put the demagogue and the two-men-and-a-half into prison on some trumped-up charge; and, left leaderless, the black masses took to the forests and the kopjes and became guerrilla fighters. 'As the black regiments were slowly defeated by the white regiments, dozens of nice clean-minded highly educated boys like us, brought all the way out from England to maintain law and order, slowly succumbed to black magic, and the witch-doctors. This nasty un-Christian behaviour very properly alienated all right-minded people away from the black cause, and the nice clean boys like us, in a fury of moral condemnation, beat them up, tortured them, and hanged them. Law and order won. The whites let the two-men-and-a-half out of prison, but hanged the demagogue. A minimum of democratic rights were announced for the black populace but the two-men-and-a-half, etc., etc., etc.'

We, none of us, said anything to this flight of fancy. It was so far from our prognostications. Besides, we were shocked at his tone. (Of course, now I recognise it as frustrated idealism—now I write the word in connection with Paul it surprises me. It's the first time I've believed he was capable of it.) He went on: 'There is another possibility. Suppose that the black armies win? There's only one thing an intelligent nationalist leader can do, and that is to strengthen nationalist feeling and develop industry. Has it occurred to us, comrades, that it will be our duty, as progressives, to support nationalist states whose business it will be to develop all those capitalist unegalitarian ethics we hate so much? Well, has it? Because I see it, yes, I can see it in my crystal ball—but we are going to have to support it all. Oh, yes, yes, because there'll be no alternative.'

'You need a drink,' Willi remarked at this point.

The bars were all closed by this time in the road-side hotels, so Paul went to sleep. Maryrose was asleep. Jimmy was asleep. Ted remained awake beside Willi in the front seat, whistling some aria or other. I don't think he had been listening to Paul—when he whistled bits of music or sang it was always a sign of disapproval.

Long afterwards, I remember thinking that in all those years of endless analytical discussion only once did we come anywhere near the truth (far enough off as it was) and that was when Paul spoke in a spirit of angry parody.

When we reached the hotel it was all dark. A sleepy servant waited on the verandah to take us to our rooms. The bedroom block was built a couple of hundred yards from the dining-room and bar block, on a slope at the back. There were twenty rooms under a single roof, built back to back, verandahs on either side, ten rooms to a verandah. The rooms were cool and pleasant in spite of having no cross ventilation. There were electric fans and large windows. Four rooms had been allotted to us. Jimmy went in with Ted, I with Willi; and Maryrose and Paul had a room each. This arrangement was afterwards confirmed; or rather, since the

Boothbys never said anything, Willi and I always shared a room at the Mashopi hotel. We, none of us, woke until long after breakfast. The bar was open and we drank a little, mostly in silence, and had lunch, almost in silence, remarking from time to time how odd it was we should feel so tired. The lunches at the hotel were always excellent, quantities of cold meats and every imaginable kind of salad and fruit. We all went to sleep again. The sun was already going down when Willi and I woke and had to wake the others. And we were in bed again half an hour after dinner was over. And the next day, Sunday, was almost at bad. That first week-end was, in fact, the most pleasant we spent there. We all were in a tranquillity of extreme fatigue. We hardly drank, and Mr Boothby was disappointed in us. Willi was particularly silent. I think it was that week-end that he decided to withdraw from politics, or at least as far as he could, and devote himself to study. As for Paul, he was being genuinely simple and pleasant with everyone, particularly Mrs Boothby, who had taken a fancy to him.

We drove back to town very late on the Sunday because we did not want to leave the Mashopi hotel. We sat on the verandah drinking beer before we left, the hotel dark behind us. The moonlight was so strong we could see the grains of white sand glittering individually where it had been flung across the tarmac by the ox-wagon wheels. The heavy-hanging, pointed leaves of the gum-trees shone like tiny spears. I remember Ted saying: 'Look at us all sitting here, with not a word to say. It's a dangerous place, Mashopi. We'll come here, week-end after week-end and hibernate in all this beer and moonlight and good food. Where will it all end, I ask you?'

We did not return for a month. We had all understood how tired we were, and I think we were frightened what might happen if we let the tension of tiredness snap. It was a month of very hard work. Paul, Jimmy and Ted were finishing their training and flew every day. The weather was good. There was a great deal of peripheral political activity like lectures, study groups and survey work. But 'the Party' only met once. The other sub-group had lost five members. It is interesting that on the one occasion we all met we fought bitterly until nearly morning; but for the rest of the month we were meeting personally all the time, and with good feeling, to discuss details of the peripheral work we were responsible for. Meanwhile our group continued to meet in the Gainsborough. We made jokes about the Mashopi hotel and its sinister relaxing influence. We used it as a symbol for every sort of luxury, decadence and weak-mindedness. Our friends who had not been there, but who knew it was an ordinary road-side hotel, said we were mad. A month after our first visit there was a long week-end, from Thursday night to the following Wednesday—in the Colony they took their holidays seriously; and we made up a party to go again. It consisted of the original six and Ted's new protégé, Stanley Lett from Manchester, for whose sake he later failed himself as a pilot. And Johnny, a jazz pianist, Stanley's friend. We also arranged that George Hounslow should meet us there. We got ourselves there by car and by train and by the time the bar closed on the Thursday night it was clear that this week-end would be very different from the last.

The hotel was full of people for the long week-end. Mrs Boothby had opened an annexe of an extra dozen rooms. There were to be two big dances, one public and one private, and already there was an air of pleasant dislocation of ordinary life. When our party sat down to dinner very late, a waiter was decorating the corners of the dining-room with coloured paper and strings of light bulbs; and we were served with an especial ice pudding made for the following night. And there was an emissary from Mrs Boothby to ask if the 'airforce boys' would mind helping her decorate the big room tomorrow. The messenger was June Boothby, and it was clear she had come out of curiosity to see the boys in question, probably because her mother had talked of them. But it was equally clear she was not impressed. A good many Colonial girls took one look at the boys from England and dismissed them forever as sissy and wet and soft. June was such a girl. That evening she stayed just long enough to deliver the message and to hear Paul's over-polite delight in accepting 'on behalf of the airforce' her mother's kind invitation. She went out again at once. Paul and Willi made a few jokes about the marriageable daughter, but it was in the spirit of their jest about 'Mr and Mrs Boothby, the publican and his wife.' For the rest of that week-end and the succeeding week-ends they ignored her. They apparently considered her so plain that they refrained from mentioning her out of a sense of pity, or perhaps even—though neither of these men showed much sign of this emotion generally—a sense of chivalry. She was a tall, big-bodied girl, with great red clumsy arms and legs. Her face was high-coloured, like her mother's; she had the same colourless hair prinked around her full clumsy-featured face. She had not one feature or attribute with charm. But she did have a sulky bursting prowling sort of energy, because she was in that state so many young girls go through—a state of sexual obsession that can be like a sort of trance. When I was fifteen, still living in Baker Street with my father, I spent some months in that state, so that now I can't walk through that area without remembering, half amused, half embarrassed, an emotional condition which was so strong it had the power to absorb into it pavements, houses, shop windows. What was interesting about June was this: surely nature should have arranged matters so that the men she met must be aware of what afflicted her. Not at all. That first evening Maryrose and I involuntarily exchanged glances and nearly laughed out loud from recognition and amused pity. We did not, because we also understood that the so obvious fact was not obvious to the men and we wanted to protect her from their laughter. All the women in the place were aware of June. I remember sitting one morning on the verandah with Mrs Lattimer, the pretty red-haired woman who flirted with young Stanley Lett, and June came into sight prowling blindly under the gum-trees by the railway lines. It was like watching a sleepwalker. She would take half a dozen steps, staring across the valley at the piled blue mountains, lift her hands to her hair, so that her body, tightly outlined in bright red cotton, showed every straining line and the sweat patches dark under the armpits—then drop her arms, her fists clenched at her sides. She would stand motionless, then walk on again, pause, seem to dream, kick at the cinders with the toe of high white sandal, and so on, slowly, till she was out of sight beyond the sun-glittering gum-trees. Mrs Lattimore let out a deep rich sigh, laughed her weak indulgent laugh, and said: 'My God, I wouldn't be a girl again for a million pounds. My God, to go through all that again, not for a million million.' And Maryrose and I agreed. Yet, although to us every appearance of this girl was so powerfully embarrassing, the men did not see it and we took care not to betray her. There is a female chivalry, woman for woman, as strong as any other kind of loyalty. Or perhaps it was we didn't want brought home to us the deficiencies of imagination of our own men.

June spent most of her time on the verandah of the Boothby house which was a couple of hundred yards to one side of the hotel. It was built on ten-foot-deep foundations away from the ants. Its verandah was deep and cool, white-painted, and had creepers and flowers everywhere. It was extraordinarily bright and pretty, and here June lay on an old cretonne-covered sofa listening to the portable gramophone, hour after hour, inwardly fashioning the man who would be permitted to deliver her from her sleep-walking state. And a few weeks later the image had become strong enough to create the man. Maryrose and I were sitting on the hotel verandah when a lorry stopped on its way down East, and out got a great lout of a youth with massive red legs and sun-heated arms the size of ox-thighs. June came prowling down the gravelled path from her father's house, kicking at the gravel with her sharp sandals. A pebble scattered to his feet as he walked to the bar. He stopped and gazed at her. Then, looking repeatedly over his shoulder, with a blank, almost hypnotised glance, he entered the bar. June followed. Mr Boothby was serving Jimmy and Paul with gins-and-tonic and talking about England. He took no notice of his daughter, who sat in a corner and posed herself, looking dreamily out past Maryrose and myself into the hot morning dust and glitter. The youth took his beer and sat along the bench about a yard from her. Half an hour later, when he climbed back into his lorry, June was with him. Maryrose and I suddenly and at the same moment burst into fits of helpless laughter and we only stopped ourselves when Paul and Jimmy looked out of the bar to find out what the joke was. A month later June and the boy were officially engaged, and it was only then that everyone became aware that she was a quiet, pleasant and sensible girl. The look of drugged torpor had gone completely from her. It was only then that we realised how irritated Mrs Boothby had been because of her daughter's state. There was something over-gay, over-relieved in the way she accepted her help in the hotel, became friends with her again, discussed plans for the wedding. It was almost as if she had felt guilty at how irritated she had been. And perhaps this long irritation was the part cause of her later losing her temper and behaving so unjustly.

Shortly after June had left us on that first night, Mrs Boothby came in. Willi asked her to sit down and join us. Paul hastened to add his invitation. Both spoke in what seemed to the rest of us an exaggeratedly, offensively polite way. Yet the last time she had been with Paul, on the week-end we had all been so tired, he had been simple and without arrogance, talking to her about his father and mother, about 'home.' Though of course his England and hers were two different countries.

The joke among us was that Mrs Boothby had a weakness for Paul. We, none of us, really believed it; if we had we wouldn't have joked—or I hope very much that we wouldn't. For at this early stage we liked her very much. But Mrs Boothby was certainly fascinated by Paul. Yet she was also fascinated by Willi. And precisely because of the quality we hated in them both—the rudeness, the arrogance that underlay their cool good manners.

It was from Willi I learned how many women like to be bullied. It was humiliating and I used to fight against accepting it as true. But I've seen it over and over again. If there was a woman the rest of us found difficult, whom we humoured, whom we made allowances for, Willi would say: 'You just don't know anything, what she needs is a damned good hiding.' (The 'good hiding' was a Colonial phrase, usually used by the whites thus: 'What that kaffir needs is a damned good hiding'—but Willi had appropriated it for general use.) I remember Maryrose's mother, a dominating neurotic woman who had sapped all the vitality out of the girl, a woman of about fifty, as vigorous and fussy as an old hen. For Maryrose's sake we were polite, we accepted her when she came bustling after her daughter into the Gainsborough. When she was there Maryrose sank into a state of listless irritation, a nervous exhaustion. She knew she ought to fight her mother, but did not have the moral energy. This woman, whom we were prepared to be bored by, to humour, Willi cured in half a dozen words. She had come into the Gainsborough one evening and found us all sitting around the deserted dining-room talking. She said loudly: 'So there you all are as usual. You ought to be in bed.' And she was just about to sit down and join us, when Willi, without raising his voice, but letting those spectacles of his glitter at her, said: 'Mrs Fowler.' 'Yes, Willi? Is that you again?' 'Mrs Fowler, why do you come here chasing after Maryrose and making such a nuisance of yourself?' She gasped, coloured, but remained standing by the chair she had been about to sit down in, staring at him. 'Yes,' said Willi, calmly. 'You are an old nuisance. You can sit down if you like, but you must keep quiet and not talk nonsense.' Maryrose turned quite white with fright and with pain on behalf of her mother. But Mrs Fowler, after a moment's silence, gave a short flustered laugh and sat down and kept perfectly quiet. And after that, if she came into the Gainsborough she always behaved with Willi like a well-brought-up small girl in the presence of a bullying father. And it was not only Mrs Fowler and the woman who owned the Gainsborough.

Now it was Mrs Boothby, who was not at all the bully who seeks a bully stronger than herself. Nor was she insensitive about intruding herself. And yet, even after she must have understood with her nerves, if not her intelligence—she was not an intelligent woman—that she was being bullied, she would come back again and again for more. She did not succumb into flustered satisfaction at having been 'given a hiding,' like Mrs Fowler, or get coy and girlish like Mrs James at the Gainsborough; she would listen patiently, and argue back, engage herself so to speak with the surface of

99

the talk, ignoring the underlying insolence, and in this way she sometimes even shamed Willi and Paul back into courtesy. But in private I am sure she must sometimes have flushed up, clenching her fists, and muttering: 'Yes, I'd like to hit them. Yes, I should have hit him when he said that.'

That evening Paul almost at once started on one of his favourite games—parodying the Colonial clichés to the point where the Colonial in question must become aware he or she was being made fun of. And Willi joined in.

'Your cook has, of course, been with you for years—would you like a cigarette?'

'Thank you, my dear, but I don't smoke. Yes, he's a good boy, I must say that for him, he's always been very loyal.'

'He's almost one of the family, I should think?'

'Yes, I think of him like that. And he's very fond of us, I'm sure. We've always treated him fair.'

'Perhaps not so much as a friend as a child?' (This was Willi.) 'Because they are nothing but great big children.'

'Yes, that's true. They're just children when you really understand them. They like to be treated the way you'd treat a child—firm, but right. Mr Boothby and I believe in treating the blacks fair. It's only right.'

'But on the other hand, you mustn't let them take advantage of you,' said Paul. 'Because if you do, they lose all respect.'

'I'm glad to hear you say that, Paul, because most of you English boys have all kinds of fancy ideas about the kaffirs. But it's true. They have to know there's a line they must never step over.' And so on and so on and so on.

It wasn't until Paul said—he was sitting in his favourite pose—tankard poised, his blue eyes fixed winningly on hers: 'And, of course, there's centuries of evolution between them and us, they're nothing but baboons really,' that she blushed and looked away. Baboons was a word already too crude for the Colony, although even five years before it was acceptable, and even in the newspaper leaders. (Just as the word *kaffirs* would have become, in its turn, too crude in ten years' time.) Mrs Boothby could not believe that an 'educated young man from one of the best colleges in England' would use the word baboons. But when she again looked at Paul, her honest red face prepared for hurt, there he sat, his cherubic smile just as winningly attentive as it had been a month ago when he had been, undeniably, nothing more than a rather homesick boy glad to be mothered a little. She sighed abruptly, and got up, saying politely: 'And now if you'll excuse me I'll go and get the old man's supper. Mr Boothby likes a late snack—he never gets time for his dinner, serving in the bar all evening.' She wished us good night, giving Willi, then Paul, a long, rather hurt, earnest inspection. She left us.

Paul put back his head and laughed and said: 'They're incredible, they're fantastic, they are simply not true.'

'Aborigines,' said Willi, laughing. Aborigines was his word for the white people of the Colony.

Maryrose said quietly: 'I don't see the point of that, Paul. It's just making fools of people.'

'Dear Maryrose. Dear beautiful Maryrose,' said Paul, chuckling into his beer.

Maryrose was beautiful. She was a tiny slender girl, with waves of honey-coloured hair and great brown eyes. She had appeared on magazine covers in the Cape, had been a dress model for a while. She was entirely without vanity. She smiled patiently and insisted in her slow good-humoured way: 'Yes, Paul. After all, I've been brought up here. I understand Mrs Boothby. I was like that too until people like you explained I was wrong. You won't change her by making fun of her. You just hurt her feelings.'

Paul again gave his deep chuckle, and insisted: 'Maryrose, Maryrose, you're too good to be true too.'

But later that evening she did succeed in making him ashamed.

George Hounslow, a roads man, lived a hundred miles or so down the line in a small town with his wife, three children, and the four old parents. He was arriving at midnight in his lorry. He proposed to spend the evenings of the week-end with us, attending to his work along the main road in the daytime. We left the dining-room and went off to sit under the bunch of gum-trees near the railway line to wait for George. Under the trees was a rough wooden table and some wooden benches. Mr Boothby sent down a dozen bottles of chilled Cape white wine. We were all mildly tight by then. The hotel was in darkness. Soon the lights in the Boothbys' house went out. There was a small light from the station building and a small gleam of lights from the bedroom block up the rise several hundreds of yards off. Sitting under the gum-trees with the cold moonlight sifting over us through the branches, and the night wind lifting and laying the dust at our feet, we might have been in the middle of the veld. The hotel had been absorbed into the wild landscape of granite-bouldered kopjes, trees, moonlight. Miles away the main road crossed a rise, a thin gleam of pale light between banks of black trees. The dry oily scent of the gum-trees, the dry irritating smell of dust, the cold smell of wine, added to our intoxication.

Jimmy fell asleep, slumped against Paul, who had his arm around him. I was half-asleep, against Willi's shoulder. Stanley Lett and Johnnie, the pianist, sat side by side watching the rest of us with an amiable curiosity. They made no secret of the fact, now or at any other time, that we, not they, were on sufferance, and this on the clearly expressed grounds that they were working-class, would remain working-class, but they had no objection to observing at first-hand, because of the happy accidents of war, the behaviour of a group of intellectuals. It was Stanley who used the word, and he refused to drop it. Johnnie, the pianist, never talked. He did not use words, ever. He always sat near Stanley, allying himself in silence with him.

Ted had already begun to suffer because of Stanley, the 'butterfly under a stone,' who refused to see himself as in need of rescue. To console himself he sat by Maryrose and put his arm around her. Maryrose smiled good-humouredly, and remained in the circle of his arm, but as if she detached herself from him and every other man. Very many as it were professionally pretty girls have this gift of allowing themselves to be touched, kissed, held, as if this were a fee they have to pay to Providence for being born beautiful. There is a tolerant smile which goes with a submission to the hands of men, like a yawn or a patient sigh. But there was more to it, in Maryrose's case.

'Maryrose,' said Ted, bluffly, looking down at the gleaming little head at rest on his shoulder, 'why don't you love any of us, why don't you let any of us love you?'

Maryrose merely smiled, and even in this broken light, branch-and-leaf-stippled, her brown eyes showed enormous and shone softly.

'Maryrose has a broken heart,' observed Willi above my head.

'Broken hearts belong to old-fashioned novels,' said Paul. 'They don't go with the time we live in.'

'On the contrary,' said Ted. 'There are more broken hearts than there have ever been, just because of the times we live in. In fact I'm sure any heart we are ever likely to meet is so cracked and jarred and split it's just a mass of scar tissue.'

Maryrose smiled up at Ted, shyly, but gratefully, and said seriously: 'Yes, of course that's true.'

Maryrose had had a brother whom she deeply loved. They were close by temperament, but more important, they had the tenderest of bonds because of their impossible, bullying, embarrassing mother against whom they supported each other. This brother had been killed in North Africa the previous year. It happened that Maryrose was in the Cape at the time doing modelling. She was, of course, much in demand because of how she looked. One of the young men looked like her brother. We had seen a photograph of him—a slight, fair-moustached, aggressive young man. She fell instantly in love with him. She said to us—and I remember the sense of shock we felt, as we always did with her, because of her absolute but casual honesty: 'Yes, I know I fell in love with him because he looked like my brother, but what's wrong with that?' She was always asking, or stating: 'What's wrong with that?' and we could never think of an answer. But the young man was like her brother only in looks, and while he was happy to have an affair with Maryrose he did not want to marry her.

'It may be true,' said Willi, 'but it's very silly. Do you

know what's going to happen to you, Maryrose, unless you watch out? You're going to make a cult of this boy-friend of yours, and the longer you do that the unhappier you'll be. You'll keep off all the nice boys you could marry, and eventually you'll marry someone for the sake of marrying, and you'll be one of these dissatisfied matrons we see all around us.'

In parenthesis I must say that this is exactly what happened to Maryrose. For another few years she continued to be delectably pretty, allowed herself to be courted while she maintained her sweet smile that was like a yawn, sat patiently inside the circle of this man's arm or that; and finally and very suddenly married a middle-aged man who already had three children. She did not love him. Her heart had gone dead when her brother was crushed into pulp by a tank.

'So what do you think I should do?' she enquired, with her terrible amiability, across a patch of moonlight, to Willi.

'You should go to bed with one of us. As soon as possible. There's no better cure for an infatuation than that,' said Willi, in the brutally good-humoured voice he used when speaking out of his role as sophisticated Berliner. Ted grimaced, and removed his arm, making it clear that he was not prepared to ally himself with such cynicism, and that if he went to bed with Maryrose it would be out of the purest romanticism. Well, of course it would have been.

'Anyway,' observed Maryrose, 'I don't see the point. I keep thinking about my brother.'

'I've never known anyone be so completely frank about incest,' said Paul. He meant it as a kind of joke, but Maryrose replied, quite seriously, 'Yes, I know it was incest. But the funny thing is, I never thought of it as incest at the time. You see, my brother and I loved each other.'

We were shocked again. I felt Willi's shoulder stiffen, and I remember thinking that only a few moments before he had been the decadent European; but the idea that Maryrose had slept with her brother plunged him back into his real nature, which was puritanical.

There was a silence, then Maryrose observed: 'Yes, I can see why you are shocked. But I think about it often these days. We didn't do any harm, did we? And so I don't see what was wrong with it.'

Silence again. Then Paul plunged in, gaily: 'If it doesn't make any difference to you, why don't you go to bed with me, Maryrose? How do you know, you might be cured?'

Paul still sat upright, supporting the lolling child-like weight of Jimmy against him. He supported Jimmy tolerantly, just as Maryrose had allowed Ted to put his arm around her. Paul and Maryrose played the same roles in the group, from the opposite sides of the sex barrier.

Maryrose said calmly: 'If my boy-friend in the Cape couldn't really make me forget my brother, why should you?'

Paul said: 'What is the nature of the obstacle that prevents you from marrying this swain of yours?'

Maryrose said: 'He comes from a good Cape family, and his parents won't let me marry him, because I'm not good enough.'

Paul allowed himself his deep attractive chuckle. I'm not saying he cultivated this chuckle, but he certainly knew it was one of his attractions. 'A good family,' he said derisively. 'A good family from the Cape. It's rich, it really is.'

This was not as snobbish as it sounds. Paul's snobbishness was expressed indirectly, in jokes, or in a play on words. Actually he was indulging his ruling passion, the enjoyment of incongruity. And I'm not in a position to criticise, for I daresay the real reason I stayed in the Colony long after there was any need was because such places allow opportunity for this type of enjoyment. Paul was inviting us all to be amused, as he had when he had discovered Mr and Mrs Boothby, John and Mary Bull in person, running the Mashopi Hotel.

But Maryrose said quietly: 'I suppose it must seem funny to you, since you are used to good families in England, and of course I can see that's different from a good family in the Cape. But it comes to the same thing for me, doesn't it?'

Paul maintained a whimsical expression which concealed the beginnings of discomfort. He even, as if to prove her attack on him was unjust, instinctively moved so that Jimmy's head fell more comfortably on his shoulder, in an effort to show a capacity for tenderness.

'If I slept with you, Paul,' stated Maryrose, 'I daresay I'd get fond of you. But you're the same as he is—my boy-friend from the Cape. You'd never marry me, I wouldn't be good enough. You have no heart.'

Willi laughed gruffly. Ted said: 'That fixes you, Paul.' Paul did not speak. In moving Jimmy a moment before the young man's body had slipped so that Paul now had to sit supporting his head and shoulders across his knees. Paul cradled Jimmy like a baby; and for the rest of the evening he watched Maryrose with a quiet and rueful smile. And after that he always spoke to her gently, trying to woo her out of her contempt for him. But he did not succeed.

At about midnight, the glare of a lorry's headlights swallowed the moonlight, and swung off the main road to come to rest in a patch of empty sand by the railway lines. It was a big lorry, loaded with gear; and a small caravan was hitched on behind it. This caravan was George Hounslow's home when he was superintending work along the roads. George jumped down from the driver's seat and came over to us, greeted by a full glass of wine held out to him by Ted. He drank it down, standing, saying in between gulps: 'Drunken sots, oafs, sodden sods, sitting here swilling.' I remember the smell of the wine, cool and sharp, as Ted tilted another bottle to refill the glass; the wine splashed over and hissed on the dust. The dust smelled heavy and sweet, as if it had rained.

George came to kiss me. 'Beautiful Anna, beautiful Anna—but I can't have you because of this bloody man Willi.' Then he ousted Ted, kissing Maryrose on her averted cheek, and said: 'All the beautiful women there are in the world, and we only have two of them here, it makes me want to cry.' The men laughed, and Maryrose smiled at me. I smiled back. Her smile was full of a sudden pain, and so I realised that mine was also. Then she looked uncomfortable, at having betrayed herself, and we quickly looked away from each other, from the exposed moment. I don't think either of us would have cared to analyse the pain we felt. And now George sat forward, holding a glass brimming with wine, and said: 'Sods and comrades, stop lolling about, the moment has come to tell me the news.'

We stirred, became animated, forgot our sleepiness. We listened while Willi gave George information about the political situation in town. George was an extremely serious man. And he had a deep reverence for Willi—for Willi's brain. He was convinced of his own stupidity. He was convinced, and very likely had been all his life, of his general inadequacy and also of his ugliness.

In fact he was rather good-looking, or at least women always responded to him, even when they were not aware of it. Mrs Lattimore, for instance, the pretty red-head, who often exclaimed how repulsive she thought him, but could never take her eyes off him. He was quite tall, but looked shorter, because of his broad shoulders, which he carried stooped forward. His body narrowed fast from the broad shoulders to his flanks. He had a bull-like set to him, all his movements were stubborn, and abrupt with the subdued controlled irritation of power kept in leash and unwillingly so. It was because of his family life which was difficult. At home he was, and had had to be for many years, patient, self-sacrificing, disciplined. By nature I would say he was none of these things. Perhaps this was the reason for his need to run himself down, for his lack of belief in himself. He was a man who could have been much bigger than his life had given him room to be. He knew this, I think; and because he secretly felt guilty at being frustrated by his family circumstances, his self-denigration was a way of punishing himself. I don't know . . . or perhaps he punished himself in this way for his continual unfaithfulness to his wife? One has to be much older than I was then to understand George's relationship with his wife. He had a fierce loyal compassion for her, the compassion of one victim for another.

He was one of the most lovable people I have ever known. He was certainly the funniest. He was spontaneously irresistibly funny. I've seen him keep a room full of people laughing helplessly from the time the bar closed until the sun rose. We lay about on the beds and on the floor laughing so that we couldn't move. Yet next day, remembering the jokes, they weren't particularly funny. Yet we were sick laughing—it was partly because of his face, which was handsome, but copy-book handsome, almost dull in its regularity, so that one expected him to talk to rule; but I think mostly because he had a very long narrow upper lip, which gave a look of wooden and almost stupid obstinacy to his face. Then out came the sad, self-punishing, irresistible stream of talk, and he watched us rolling with laughter, yet never laughed with his victims, but watched with positive astonishment, as if he were thinking: Well I can't be as hopeless as I think I am if I can make all these clever people laugh like this.

He was about forty. That is, twelve years older than the oldest of us, Willi. We would never have thought of it, but he couldn't forget it. He was a man who would always watch each year slide past as if jewels were slipping one by one through his fingers into the sea. This was because of his feeling for women. His other passion was politics. Not the least of his burdens was that he had been brought up by parents who came from slap in the middle of the old socialist tradition in Britain—a nineteenth-century socialism—rationalist, practical, above all, religiously anti-religious. And such an upbringing was not calculated to make him fit in with the people of the Colony. He was an isolated and lonely man, living in a tiny, backward, isolated town. We, this group of people so much younger than he, were the first real friends he had in years. We all loved him. But I don't believe for a moment he knew it, or would allow himself to know it. His humility was too strong. In particular, his humility in relation to Willi. I remember once, exasperated because of the way he would sit, expressing reverence for Willi with every part of him, while Willi laid down the law about something or other, I said: 'For God's sake George, you're such a nice man, and I can't stand seeing you lick the boots of a man like Willi.'

'But if I had Willi's brain,' he replied and it was typical of him he didn't enquire how I could make such remarks about a man with whom, after all, I was living—'if I had his brain I'd be the happiest man in the world.' And then his upper lip narrowed in self-mockery: 'What do you mean *nice*? I'm a sod, you know I am. I tell you the things I do and then you say I'm nice.' He was referring to what he told Willi and me, but no one else, about his relations with women.

I've thought about that often since. I mean, about the word nice. Perhaps I mean good. Of course they mean nothing, when you start to think about them. A good man, one says; a good woman; a nice man, a nice woman. Only in talk of course, these are not words you'd use in a novel. I'd be careful not to use them.

Yet of that group, I will say simply, without further analysis, that George was a good person, and that Willi was not. That Maryrose and Jimmy and Ted and Johnnie the pianist were good people, and that Paul and Stanley Lett were not. And furthermore, I'd bet that ten people picked at random off the street to meet them, or invited to sit in that party under the eucalyptus trees that night, would instantly agree with this classification—would, if I used the word *good*, simply like that, know what I meant.

And thinking about this, which I have done so much, I discover that I come around, by a back door, to another of the things that obsess me. I mean, of course, this question of 'personality.' Heaven knows we are never allowed to forget that the 'personality' doesn't exist any more. It's the theme of half the novels written, the theme of the sociologists and all the other -ologists. We're told so often that human personality has disintegrated into nothing under pressure of all our knowledge that I've even been believing it. Yet when I look back to that group under the trees, and re-create them in my memory, suddenly I know it's nonsense. Suppose I were to meet Maryrose now, all these years later, she'd make some gesture, or turn her eyes in such a way, and there she'd be, Maryrose, and indestructible. Or suppose she 'broke down,' or became mad. She would break down into her components, and the gesture, the movement of the eyes would remain, even though some connection had gone. And so all this talk, this anti-humanist bullying, about the evaporation of the personality becomes meaningless for me at that point when I manufacture enough emotional energy inside myself to create in memory some human being I've known. I sit down, and remember the smell of the dust and the moonlight, and see Ted handing a glass of wine to George, and George's over-grateful response to the gesture. Or I see, as in a slow-motion film, Maryrose turn her head, with her terrifyingly patient smile ... I've written the word film. Yes. The moments I remember all have the absolute assurance of a smile, a look, a gesture, in a painting or a film. Am I saying then that the certainty I'm clinging to belongs to the visual arts, and not to the novel, not to the novel at all, which has been claimed by the disintegration and the collapse? What business has a novelist to cling to the memory of a smile or a look, knowing so well the complexities behind them? Yet if I did not, I'd never be able to set a word down on paper; just as I used to keep myself from going crazy in this cold northern city by deliberately making myself remember the quality of hot sun-light on my skin.

And so I'll write again that George was a good man. And that I could not stand seeing him turn into an awkward schoolboy when he listened to Willi ... that evening he received the facts about the troubles in the left groups in town with humility, and a nod which said that he would think about them privately, and at length—because of course he was too stupid to make up his mind about anything without hours and hours of thought, even though the rest of us were so clever we didn't need it.

We, all of us, considered that Willi had been cavalier in his analysis; he had spoken as if he had been in committee, had conveyed nothing of our new disquiet, the new tone of disbelief and mockery.

And Paul, repudiating Willi, now chose to tell George, in his own way, of the truth. He began a dialogue with Ted. I remember watching Ted and wondering if he would respond to the light, whimsical challenge. Ted hesitated, looked uncomfortable, but joined in. And because it was not his character, it was against his deep beliefs, there was an exaggerated wild quality to his talk that jarred us more than listening to Paul.

Paul had begun by describing a committee meeting with 'two-men-and-a-half' deciding the whole fate of the African continent 'without, of course, any reference to the Africans themselves.' (This was, of course, treachery—to admit, in front of outsiders like Stanley Lett and Johnnie the pianist that we could have any doubts about our beliefs. George looked dubiously at the pair, decided that they must have joined us, because otherwise we'd never be so irresponsible, and gave a smile of pleasure because we had two new recruits.) And now Paul described how the two-men-and-a-half, finding themselves in Mashopi, would go about 'guiding Mashopi towards a correct line of action.'

'I would say that the hotel would be a convenient place to start, wouldn't you, Ted?'

'Near the bar, Paul, all modern conveniences.' (Ted was not much of a drinker, and George frowned at him, bewildered, as he spoke.)

'The trouble is, that it's not exactly a centre of the developing industrial proletariat. Of course, one could, and in fact we probably should, say the same of the whole country?'

'Very true, Paul. But on the other hand the district is plentifully equipped with backward and half-starving farm labourers.'

'Who only need a guiding hand from the said proletariat if only they existed.'

'Ah, but I have it. There are five poor bloody blacks working on the railway line here, all in rags and misery. Surely they'd do?'

'So all we have to do is to persuade them towards a correct understanding of their class position, and we'll have the whole district in a revolutionary uproar before we can say Left-wing Communism, an Infantile Disorder.'

George looked at Willi, waiting for him to protest. But that morning Willi had said to me that he intended to devote all his time to study, he had no further time for 'all these playboys and girls looking for husbands.' It was so easily that he dismissed the people he had taken seriously enough to work with for years.

George was now deeply uneasy; he had sensed the pith of our belief was no longer in us, and this meant that his loneliness was confirmed. Now he spoke across Paul and Ted to Johnnie the pianist.

'They're talking a lot of cock, aren't they mate?'

Johnnie nodded agreement—not to the words, I think he seldom listened to words, he only sensed if people were friendly to him or not.

'What's your name? I haven't run across you before, have I?'

'Johnnie.'

'You're from the Midlands?'

'Manchester.'

'You two are members?'

Johnnie shook his head; George's jaw slowly dropped, then he passed his hand quickly across his eyes and sat slumped, in silence. Meanwhile Johnnie and Stanley remained side by side, observing. They were drinking beer. Now George, in a sudden desperate attempt to break down the barriers, leaped up and poised a wine bottle. 'Not much left, but have some,' he said to Stanley.

'Don't care for it,' said Stanley. 'Beer's for us.' And he patted his pockets and the front of his tunic, where beer bottles stuck out at all angles. Stanley's great genius was to unfailingly 'organise' supplies of beer for Johnnie and himself. Even when the Colony ran dry, which it did from time to time, Stanley would appear with crates of the stuff, which he had stored away in caches all over the city, and which he sold at a profit while the drought lasted.

'You're right,' said George. 'But we poor bloody Colonials have had our stomachs adjusted to Cape hogwash since we were weaned.' George loved wine. But even this gauge of amity had no softening effect on the couple. 'Don't you think these two ought to have their bottoms smacked?' George enquired, indicating Ted and Paul. (Paul smiled; Ted looked ashamed.)

'Don't care for all that stuff myself,' said Stanley. At first George thought he was still referring to the wine; but when he realised it was politics that were meant, he glanced sharply at Willi, for guidance. But Willi had sunk his head into his shoulders and was humming to himself. I knew he was suffering from homesickness. Willi had no ear, could not sing, but when he was remembering Berlin, he would tunelessly hum, over and over again, one of the tunes from Brecht's *Threepenny Opera*.

> Oh the *shark* has
> Wicked *teeth* dear
> And he *keeps* them
> Shining white . . .

Years later it was a popular song, but I first heard it in Mashopi, from Willi; and I remember the sharp feeling of dislocation it gave me to hear the pop-song in London, after Willi's sad nostalgic humming of what he told us was 'A song we used to sing when I was a child—a man called Brecht, I wonder what happened to him, he was very good once.'

'What's going on, mates?' George demanded, after a long silence full of discomfort.

'I would say that a certain amount of demoralisation is setting in,' said Paul deliberately.

'Oh *no*,' said Ted, but checked himself and sat frowning. Then he jumped up and said: 'I'm going to bed.'

'We're all going to bed,' said Paul. 'So wait a minute.'

'I want my bed. I'm proper sleepy,' said Johnnie, a longer statement than we had yet heard from him. He got up unsteadily, and poised himself with a hand on Stanley's shoulder. It appeared that he had been thinking things over and now saw the necessity for some kind of a statement. 'It's like this,' he said to George. 'I came down to th'otel because I'm a mate of Stanley's. He said they've got a piano and a bit of a dance Saturday nights. But I don't go for the politics. You're George Hounslow. I've heard them talk of you. Pleased to meet you.' He held out his hand, and George shook it warmly.

Stanley and Johnnie wandered off into the moonlight towards the bedroom block, and Ted got up and said: 'And me too, and I'll never come back here again.'

'Oh, don't be so dramatic,' said Paul coldly. The sudden

113

coldness surprised Ted, who gazed around at us all, vaguely, hurt and embarrassed. But he sat down again.

'What the hell are those two chaps doing with us?' demanded George roughly. It was the roughness of unhappiness. 'Nice chaps I'm sure, but what are we doing talking about our problems in front of them?'

Willi still did not respond. The thin mournful humming went on, a couple of inches above my ear: 'Oh the *shark* has, wicked *teeth* dear . . .'

Paul said, deliberate and nonchalant to Ted: 'I think we've incorrectly assessed the class situation of Mashopi. We've overlooked the obvious key man. Here he is under our noses all the time—Mrs Boothby's cook.'

'What the hell do you mean, the cook?' demanded George— much too roughly. He was standing up, aggressive and hurt, and he kept swilling his wine around his glass, so that it sloshed off into the dust. We all thought his belligerence was due, simply, to surprise at our mood. We hadn't seen him for some weeks. I think we were all measuring the depth of the change in us, because it was the first time we had seen ourselves reflected, so to speak, in our own eyes of so short a time ago. And because we felt guilty we resented George— resented him enough to want to hurt him. I remember very clearly, sitting there, looking at George's honest angry face, and saying to myself, Good Lord! I think he's ugly—I think he's ridiculous, I can't remember feeling that before. And then understanding why I felt like this. But, of course, it was only afterwards that we really came to understand the real cause of George's reaction to Paul's mentioning the cook.

'Obviously the cook,' said Paul deliberately, spurred on by his new desire to provoke and hurt George. 'He can read. He can write. He has ideas—Mrs Boothby complains of it. Ergo, he is an intellectual. Of course he'll have to be shot later when ideas become a hindrance, but he'll have served his purpose. After all, we'll be shot with him.'

I remember George's long puzzled look at Willi. Then how he examined Ted, who had his head back, his chin pointed up towards the boughs, as he inspected the stars glinting through the leaves. Then his worried stare at Jimmy who was still a sodden corpse in Paul's arms.

Ted said briskly: 'I've had enough. We'll escort you to your caravan, George, and leave you.' It was a gesture of reconciliation and friendship, but George said sharply: 'No.' Because he reacted like that Paul immediately got up, dislodging Jimmy who collapsed on the bench, and said with cool insistence. 'Of course we'll take you to your bed.'

'No,' said George again. He sounded frightened. Then, hearing his own voice, he altered it. 'You silly buggers. You drunken sots, you'll trip all over the railway lines.'

'I said,' remarked Paul casually, 'that we'll come and tuck you in.' He swayed as he stood, but steadied himself. Paul, like Willi, could drink heavily and hardly show it. But he was drunk by now.

'No,' said George. 'I said no. Didn't you hear me?'

And now Jimmy came to himself, staggering up off the bench, and hooking on to Paul for steadiness. The two young men swayed a moment, then went off in a rush towards the railway lines and George's caravan.

'Come back,' shouted George. 'Silly idiots. Drunken fools. Clods.' They were now yards away, balancing their bodies on fumbling legs. The shadows from the long sprawling legs cut sharp and black across the glittering sand almost to where George stood. They looked like small jerky marionettes, descending long black ladders. George stared, frowned, then swore deeply and violently and ran after them. Meanwhile the rest of us made tolerant grimaces at each other—What's wrong with George? George reached the two, grabbed their shoulders, spun them around to face him. Jimmy fell. There was a stretch of rough gravel by the lines and he slipped on the loose stones. Paul remained upright, stiff with the effort of keeping his balance. George was down in the dirt with Jimmy, trying to get him up again, trying to lift the heavy body in its thick felt-like case of uniform. 'You silly sod,' he was saying, roughly tender to the drunken boy. 'I told you to come back, didn't I? Well didn't I?' And he almost shook him with exasperation, though he checked himself, even while he was trying, and with the tenderest compassion, to raise him.

By this time the rest of us had run down and stood by the others on the track. Jimmy was lying on his back, eyes closed. He had cut his forehead on the gravel, and the blood poured black across his white face. He looked asleep. His lank hair had for once achieved grace, and lay across his forehead in a full springing wave. The individual hairs gleamed.

'Oh hell,' said George, full of despair.

'Then why make such a fuss?' said Ted. 'We were only going to take you to your lorry.'

Willi cleared his throat. It was always a rasping, rather clumsy sound. He did this frequently. It was never from nervousness, but sometimes as a tactful warning, and sometimes the statement: I know something you don't. I recognised that this time it meant the second, and he was saying that the reason why George didn't want anyone near his caravan was because there was a woman in it. Willi would never betray a confidence, even indirectly, when sober, so that meant he was drunk. To cover the indiscretion I whispered to Maryrose: 'We keep forgetting that George is older than us, we must seem like a pack of kids to him.' I spoke loudly enough for the others to hear. And George heard and gave me a wry grateful smile over his shoulder. But we still couldn't move Jimmy. There we all stood, looking down at him. It was now long after midnight, and the heat had gone from the soil, and the moon was low over the mountains behind us. I remember wondering how it was that Jimmy, who when in his senses could never seem anything but graceless and pathetic, had just this once, when he was lying drunk in a patch of dirty gravel, managed to appear both dignified and moving, with the black wound on his forehead. And I was simultaneously wondering who the woman could be—which of the tough farmers' wives, or marriageable daughters, or hotel guests we had drunk with in the bar that evening had crept down to George's caravan, trying to make herself invisible in the water-clear moonlight. I remember envying her. I remember loving George for just that moment with a sharp painful love, while I called myself all kinds of a fool. For I had turned him down often enough. At that time

116

in my life, for reasons I didn't understand until later, I didn't let myself be chosen by men who really wanted me.

At last we managed to get Jimmy on his feet. It took all of us, tugging and pulling. And we supported and pushed him up between the gum-trees and the long path between the flowerbeds to the hotel room. There he instantly rolled over, asleep, and stayed asleep while we sponged his cut. It was deep and full of gravel, and took a long time to stop the blood. Paul said he would stay up and watch beside Jimmy, 'though I hate myself in the role of a bloody Florence Nightingale.' No sooner had he sat down, however, than he fell asleep, and in the end it was Maryrose who sat up and watched beside both of them until morning. Ted departed to his room with a brief, almost angry good night. (Yet in the morning he would have swung over into a mood of self-mockery and cynicism. He was to spend months altering sharply between a guilty gravity and an increasingly bitter cynicism—later he was to say that this was the time in his life he was most ashamed of.) Willi, George and myself stood on the steps in the now dimming moonlight. 'Thanks,' said George. He looked hard and close into my face and then Willi's, hesitated, and did not say what he had been going to. Instead he added the gruffly obligatory jest: 'Do the same for you some time.' And he strode off down towards the lorry near the railway lines, while Willi murmured: 'He looks just like a man with an assignation.' He was back in his sophisticated role, drawling it, with a knowing smile. But I was envying the unknown woman too much to respond, and we went to sleep in silence. And we would have slept, very likely, until midday, if we had not been woken by the three airforce men, bringing in our trays. Jimmy had a bandage around his head, and looked ill. Ted was wildly and improbably gay, and Paul was radiating charm as he announced: 'We've already started undermining the cook, because he allowed us to cook your breakfast, darling Anna, and as an additional but necessary chore, Willi's.' He slid the tray before me with an air. 'The cook's at work on all the good things for tonight. Do you like what we've brought you?'

They had brought food enough for us all, and we feasted

on paw-paw and avocado pear, and bacon and eggs and hot fresh bread and coffee. The windows were open and the sunlight was hot outside, and wind coming into the room was warm and smelling of flowers. Paul and Ted sat on my bed and we flirted; and Jimmy sat on Willi's and was humble about being drunk the night before. But it was already late, and the bar was open, and we soon got dressed and walked down together through the flowerbeds that filled all the sunlight with the dry spicy-smelling tang of wilting and over-heated petals, to the bar. The verandahs of the hotel were full of people drinking, the bar was full, and the party, as Paul announced, waving his tankard, had begun.

But Willi had withdrawn himself. For one thing, he did not approve of such bohemianism as collective bedroom break-fasts. 'If we were married,' he had complained, 'it might be all right.' I laughed at him, and he said: 'Yes. Laugh. But there's sense in the old rules. They kept people out of trouble.' He was annoyed because I laughed, and said that a woman in my position needed extra dignity of behaviour. 'What position?'—I was suddenly very angry, because of the trapped feeling women get at such moments. 'Yes, Anna, but things are different for men and for women. They always have been and they very likely always will be.' 'Always have been?'—inviting him to remember his history. 'For as long as it matters.' 'Matters to you—not to me.' But we had had this quarrel before; we knew all the phrases either was likely to use—the weakness of women, the property sense of men, women in antiquity, etc., etc., etc., *ad nauseam*. We knew it was a clash of temperament so profound that no words could make any difference to either of us—the truth was that we shocked each other in our deepest feelings and instincts all the time. So the future professional revolutionary gave me a stiff nod and settled himself on the hotel verandah with his Russian grammars. But he would not be left alone to study for long, for George was already striding up through the gum-trees, looking very serious.

Paul greeted me with: 'Anna, come and see the lovely things in the kitchen.' He put his arm around me, and I knew Willi had seen, as I had intended him to, and we walked

118

through the stone-floored passages to the kitchen, which was a large low room at the back of the hotel. The tables were loaded with food, and draped with netting against the flies. Mrs Boothby was there with the cook, and clearly wondering how she had put herself into the position that we were such favoured guests we could wander in and out of the kitchen at will. Paul at once greeted the cook and enquired after his family. Mrs Boothby didn't like this of course; this was the reason for Paul's doing it at all. Both the cook and his white employer responded to Paul in the same way—watchful, puzzled, slightly distrustful. For the cook was confused. Not the least of the results of having hundreds and thousands of airforce men in the Colony for five years was that a number of Africans had it brought home to them that it was possible —well, among other things, that a white man could treat a black man as a human being. Mrs Boothby's cook knew the familiarity of the feudal relationship; he knew the crude brutality of the newer impersonal relationship. But he was now discussing his children with Paul on equal terms. There was a slight hesitation before each of his remarks, the hesitation of disuse, but the man's natural dignity, usually ignored, carried him quickly into the manner of someone in conversation with an equal. Mrs Boothby listened for a few minutes, then cut it short by saying: 'If you really want to be of help, Paul, you and Anna can go into the big room and do some decorating.' She spoke in a tone which was meant to tell Paul that she had understood he had been making fun of her the night before. 'Certainly,' Paul said. 'With pleasure.' But he made a point of continuing his talk with the cook for a while. This man was unusually good-looking—a strong, well-set middle-aged man with a lively face and eyes; a great many of the Africans in this part of the Colony were poor specimens physically from ill-feeding and disease; but this one lived at the back of the Boothbys' house in a small cottage with his wife and five children. This was of course against the law, which laid down that black people should not live on white men's soil. The cottage was poor enough, but twenty times better than the usual African hut. There were flowers and vegetables around it, and chickens and guinea-fowl. I should imagine that he was very well content with his service at the Mashopi hotel.

When Paul and I left the kitchen he greeted us as was customary: ''Morning, Nkos. 'Morning, Nkosikaas'—that is, Good morning Chief and Chieftainess.

'Christ,' said Paul, with irritation and anger, when we were outside the kitchen. And then, in the whimsical cool tone of his self-preservation: 'But it's strange I should mind at all. After all, it has pleased God to call me into the station of life which will so clearly suit my tastes and talents, so why should I care? But all the same . . .'

We walked up to the big room through the hot sunlight, the dust warm and fragrant under our shoes. His arm was around me again and now I was pleased to have it there for other reasons than that Willi was watching. I remember feeling the intimate pressure of his arm in the small of my back, and thinking that, living in a group as we did, these quick flares of attraction could flare and die in a moment, leaving behind them tenderness, unfulfilled curiosity, a slightly wry and not unpleasant pain of loss; and I thought that perhaps it was above all the tender pain of unfulfilled possibilities that bound us. Under a big jacaranda tree that grew beside the big room, out of sight of Willi, Paul turned me around towards him and smiled down at me, and the sweet pain shot through me again and again. 'Anna,' he said, or chanted. 'Anna, beautiful Anna, absurd Anna, mad Anna, our consolation in this wilderness, Anna of the tolerantly amused black eyes.' We smiled at each other, with the sun stabbing down at us through the thick green lace of the tree in sharp gold needles. What he said then was a kind of revelation. Because I was permanently confused, dissatisfied, unhappy, tormented by inadequacy, driven by wanting towards every kind of impossible future, the attitude of mind described by 'tolerantly amused eyes' was years away from me. I don't think I really saw people then, except as appendages to my needs. It's only now, looking back, that I understand, but at the time I lived in a brilliantly lit haze, shifting and flickering according to my changing desires. Of course, that is only a description of being young. But it was Paul who, alone among us, had 'amused eyes' and as we went into the big room hand in hand, I was looking at him and wondering if it were possible that such a self-possessed youth could conceivably be as unhappy and tormented as I was; and if it were true that I had, like him, 'amused eyes'—what on earth could that mean? I fell all of a sudden into an acute irritable depression, as in those days I did very often, and from one second to the next, and I left Paul and went by myself into the bay of a window.

I think that was the most pleasant room I have been in in all my life. The Boothbys had built it because there was no public hall at this station, and they were always having to clear their dining-room for dances or political meetings. But they had built it from good-nature, as a gift to the district, and not for profit.

It was as large as a big hall, but it looked like a living-room, with walls of polished red brick and a floor of dark red cement. The pillars—there were eight great pillars supporting the deep thatched roof—were of unpolished reddish-orange brick. The fireplaces at either end were both large enough to roast an ox. The wood of the rafters was thorn, and had a slightly bitter tang, whose flavour changed according to whether the air was dry or damp. At one end was a grand piano on a small platform, and at the other a radiogram with a stack of records. Each side had a dozen windows, one set showing the piled granite boulders behind the station, and the other miles across country to the blue mountains.

Johnnie was playing the piano at the far end, with Stanley Lett and Ted beside him. He was oblivious of both. His shoulders and feet tapped and shrugged to the jazz, his rather puffy white face blank as he stared away to the mountains. Stanley did not mind that Johnnie was indifferent to him: Johnnie was his meal-ticket, his invitation to parties where Johnnie played, his passport to a good time. He made no secret of why he was with Johnnie—he was the frankest of petty crooks. In return he saw that Johnnie had plenty of 'organised' cigarettes, beer and girls, all for nothing. I said he was a crook, but this is nonsense of course. He was a man who had understood from the beginning that there is one law for the rich and one for the poor. This was purely theoretical knowledge for me until I actually lived in a working-class area in London. That was when I understood Stanley Lett. He had the profoundest instinctive contempt for the law; contempt, in short, for the State about which we talked so much. I suppose that was why Ted was intrigued with him? He used to say: 'But he's so intelligent!'—the inference being that if the intelligence were used, he could be harnessed to the cause. And I suppose Ted wasn't so far wrong. There is a type of trade union official like Stanley: tough, controlled, efficient, unscrupulous. I never saw Stanley out of a shrewd control of himself, used as a weapon to get everything he could out of a world he took for granted was organised for the profit of others. He was frightening. He certainly frightened me, with his big hard bulk, hard clear features, and cold analytical grey eyes. And why did he tolerate the fervent and idealistic Ted? Not, I think, for what he could get out of him. He was genuinely touched that Ted, 'a scholarship boy,' was still concerned about his class. At the same time he thought him mad. He would say: 'Look, mate, you've been lucky, got more brains than most of us. You use your chances and don't go mucking about. The workers don't give a muck for anyone but themselves. You know it's true. I know it's true.' 'But Stan,' Ted harangued him, his eyes flashing, his black hair in agitated motion all over his head: 'Stan if enough of us cared for the others, we could change it all—don't you see?' Stanley even read the books Ted gave him, and returned them saying: 'I've got nothing against it. Good luck to you, that's all I can say.'

On this morning Stanley had stacked the top of the piano with ranks of beer mugs. In a corner was a packing case stacked with bottles. The air around the piano was thick with smoke, lit with stray gleams of reflected sunlight. The three men were isolated from the room in a haze of sun-lanced smoke. Johnnie played, played, played, quite oblivious. Stanley drank and smoked and kept an eye on the girls coming in who might do for himself or Johnnie. And Ted alternatively yearned after the political soul of Stanley and the musical soul of Johnnie. As I've said, Ted had taught himself music, but he could not play. He would hum snatches from Prokoviev, Mozart, Bach, his face agonised with impotent desire, forcing Johnnie to play. Johnnie played anything by ear, he played the airs as Ted hummed them, while his left hand hovered impatiently just above the keys. The moment the hypnotic pressure of Ted's concentration relaxed, the left hand broke into syncopation, and then both hands were furious in a rage of jazz, while Ted smiled and nodded and sighed, and tried to catch Stanley's eye in rueful amusement. But Stanley's returning smile was for mateyness only, he had no ear at all.

These three stayed at the piano all day.

There were about a dozen people in the hall but it was so large it looked empty. Maryrose and Jimmy were hanging paper garlands from the dark rafters, standing on chairs and assisted by about a dozen aircraftsmen who had come down from town by train having heard that Stanley and Johnnie were there. June Boothby was on a window sill, watching out of her private dream. When invited to help with the work she slowly shook her head and turned it to stare out of the window at the mountains. Paul stood to one side of the working group for a while, then came over to join me on my window sill, having commandeered some of Stanley's beer.

'Isn't that a sad sight, dear Anna?' said Paul, indicating the group of young men with Maryrose. 'There they are, every one positively hang-dog with sex frustration, and there she is, beautiful as the day, and with not a thought for anyone but her dead brother. And there's Jimmy, shoulder to shoulder with her, and he has no thought for anyone in the world but me. From time to time I tell myself I should go to bed with him, because why not? It would make him so happy. But the truth is, I'm reluctantly coming to the conclusion that not only I am not a homosexual, but that I never was. Because who do I yearn for, stretched on my lonely pillow? Do I yearn for Ted? Or even for Jimmy? Or for any of the gallant young heroes with whom I am so constantly surrounded? Not at all. I yearn for Maryrose. And I yearn for you. Preferably not both together of course.'

George Hounslow came into the hall and went straight over to Maryrose. She was still on her chair, supported by her gallants. They gave way in all directions as he approached. Suddenly something frightening happened. George's approach to women was clumsy, over-humble, and he might even stammer. (But his stammer always sounded as if he were doing it on purpose.) Meanwhile his deep-set brown eyes would be fixed on the women with an almost bullying intentness. And yet his manner would remain humble, apologetic. Women got flustered or angry, or laughed nervously. He was a sensualist of course. I mean, a real sensualist, not a man who played the role of one, as so many do, for one reason or another. He was a man who really, very much, needed women. I say this because there aren't many men left who do. I mean civilised men, the affectionate non-sexual men of our civilisation. George needed a woman to submit to him, he needed a woman to be under his spell physically. And men can no longer dominate women in this way without feeling guilty about it. Or very few of them. When George looked at a woman he was imagining her as she would be when he had fucked her into insensibility. And he was afraid it would show in his eyes. I did not understand this then, I did not understand why I got confused when he looked at me. But I've met a few men like him since, all with the same clumsy impatient humility, and with the same hidden arrogant power.

George was standing below Maryrose who had her arms raised. Her shining hair was down over her shoulders, and she wore a sleeveless yellow dress. Her arms and legs were a smooth gold-brown. The airforce men were almost stupefied with her. And George, for a moment, had the same look of stunned immobility. George said something. She let her arms drop, stepped slowly down off the chair and now stood below him, looking up. He said something else. I remember the look on his face—chin poked forward aggressively, eyes intent, and a stupidly abased expression. Maryrose lifted her fist and jabbed it up at his face. As hard as she could—his face jerked back and he even staggered a step. Then, without looking at him, she climbed back on her chair and continued to hang garlands. Jimmy was smiling at George with an eager embarrassment, as if he were responsible for the blow. George came over to us, and he was again the willing clown, and Maryrose's swains were back in their poses of helpless adoration.

'Well,' said Paul. 'I'm very impressed. If Maryrose would hit me like that, I'd believe I was getting somewhere.'

But George's eyes were full of tears. 'I'm an idiot,' he said. 'A dolt. Why should a beautiful girl like Maryrose look at me at all?'

'Why indeed?' said Paul.

'I believe my nose is bleeding,' said George, so as to have an excuse to blow it. Then he smiled. 'I'm in trouble all around,' he said. 'And that bastard Willi is too busy with his bloody Russian to be interested.'

'We're all in trouble,' said Paul. He was radiating a calm physical well-being, and George said: 'I hate young men of twenty. What sort of trouble could you conceivably be in?'

'It's a hard case,' said Paul. 'First, I'm twenty. That means I'm very nervous and ill-at-ease with women. Second, I'm twenty. I have all my life before me, and frankly the prospect often appals me. Thirdly, I'm twenty, and I'm in love with Anna and my heart is breaking.'

George gave me a quick look to see if this were true, and I shrugged. George drank down a full tankard of beer without stopping, and said: 'Anyway I've no right to care whether anyone's in love with anyone. I'm a sod and a bastard. Well, that would be bearable, but I'm also a practising socialist. And I'm a swine. How can a swine be a socialist, that's what I want to know?' He was joking, but his eyes were full of tears again, and his body was clenched and tense with misery.

Paul turned his head with his characteristic indolent charm, and let his wide blue eyes rest on George. I could positively hear him thinking: Oh, Lord, here's some real trouble, I don't even want to hear about it ... he let himself slide to the floor, gave me the warmest and tenderest of smiles, and said: 'Darling Anna, I love you more than my life, but I'm going to help Maryrose.' His eyes said: Get rid of this gloomy idiot and I'll come back. George scarcely noticed him going.

'Anna,' said George. 'Anna, I don't know what to do.' And I felt just as Paul had: I don't want to be involved with real trouble. I wanted to be off with the group hanging garlands, for now that Paul had become a member of it, it was suddenly gay. They were beginning to dance. Paul and Maryrose, even June Boothby, because there were more men than girls, and people were drifting up from the hotel, drawn by the dance music.

'Let's get out,' said George. 'All this youth and jollity. It depresses me unutterably. Besides, if you come too, your man will talk. It's him I want to talk to.'

'Thanks,' I said, without much grace. But I went with him to the hotel verandah which was rapidly losing its occupants to the dance room. Willi patiently laid down his grammar, and said: 'I suppose it's too much to expect, to be allowed to work in peace.'

We sat down, the three of us, our legs stretched into the sun, the rest of our bodies in the shade. The beer in our long glasses was light and golden and had spangles of sunlight in it. Then George began talking. What he was saying was so serious, but he spoke with a self-mocking jocularity, so that everything seemed ugly and jarring, and all the time the pulse of music came from the dance room and I wanted to be' there.

The facts were these. I've said his family life was difficult. It was intolerable. He had a wife and two sons and a daughter. He supported his wife's parents and his own. I've been in that little house. It was intolerable even to visit. The young couple, or rather, the middle-aged couple who supported it, were squeezed out of any real life together by the four old people and the three children. His wife worked hard all day and so did he. The four old ones were all, in various ways, invalids and needed special care and diets and so on. In that living-room in the evening, the four played cards interminably, with much bickering and elderly petulance; they played for hours, in the centre of the room, and the children did their homework where they could, and George and his wife went to bed early, more often than not from sheer exhaustion, apart from the fact their bedroom was the only place they could have some privacy. That was the home. And then half the week George was off along the roads, sometimes working hundreds of miles away on the other side of the country. He loved his wife, and she loved him, but he felt permanently guilty because managing that household would by itself have been hard work for any woman, let alone having to work as a secretary as well. None of them had had a holiday in years, and they were all permanently short of money, and miserable bickering went on about sixpences and shillings.

Meanwhile, George had his affairs. And he liked African women particularly. About five years before he was in Mashopi for the night and had been very much taken with the wife of the Boothbys' cook. This woman had become his mistress. 'If you can use such a word,' said Willi, but George insisted, and without any consciousness of humour: 'Well why not? Surely if one doesn't like the colour bar, she's entitled to the proper word, as a measure of respect, so to speak.'

George often travelled through Mashopi. Last year he had seen the group of children and one of them was lighter than the others and looked like George. He had asked the woman, and she had said yes, she believed it was his child. She was not making an issue of it.

'Well?' said Willi, 'what's the problem?'

I remember George's look of sheer, miserable incredulity. 'But Willi—you stupid clod, there's my child, I'm responsible for it living in that slum back there.'

'Well?' said Willi again.

'I'm a socialist,' said George. 'And as far as it's possible in this hellhole I try to be a socialist and fight the colour bar. Well? I stand on platforms and make speeches—oh, very tactfully of course, saying that the colour bar is not in the best interests of all concerned, and gentle Jesus meek and mild wouldn't have approved, because it's more than my job is worth to say it's inhuman and stinkingly immoral and the whites are damned to eternity for it. And now I propose to

127

behave just like every other stinking white sot who sleeps with a black woman and adds another half-caste to the Colony's quota.'

'She hasn't asked you to do anything about it,' said Willi.

'But that isn't the point.' George sank his face on his flat palms, and I saw the wetness creep between his fingers. 'It's eating me up,' he said. 'I've known about it this last year and it's driving me crazy.'

'Which isn't going to help matters much,' said Willi, and George dropped his hands sharply, showing his tear-smeared face and looked at him.

'Anna?' appealed George, looking at me. I was in the most extraordinary tumult of emotion. First, I was jealous of the woman. Last night I had been wishing I was her, but it was an impersonal emotion. Now I knew who it was, and I was astounded to find I was hating George and condemning him—just as I had resented him last night when he made me feel guilty. And then, and this was worse, I was surprised to find I resented the fact the woman was black. I had imagined myself free of any such emotion, but it seemed I was not, and I was ashamed and angry—with myself, and with George. But it was more than that. Being so young, twenty-three or four, I suffered, like so many 'emancipated' girls, from a terror of being trapped and tamed by domesticity. George's house, where he and his wife were trapped without hope of release, save through the deaths of four old people, represented to me the ultimate horror. It frightened me so that I even had nightmares about it. And yet—this man, George, the trapped one, the man who had put that unfortunate woman, his wife, in a cage, also represented for me, and I knew it, a powerful sexuality from which I fled inwardly, but then inevitably turned towards. I knew by instinct that if I went to bed with George I'd learn a sexuality that I hadn't come anywhere near yet. And with all these attitudes and emotions conflicting in me, I still liked him, indeed loved him, quite simply, as a human being. I sat there on the verandah, unable to speak for a while, knowing that my face was flushed and my hands trembling. And I listened to the music and the singing from the big room up the hill and I

128

felt as if George were excluding me by the pressure of his unhappiness from something unbelievably sweet and lovely. At that time it seemed I spent half my life believing I was being excluded from this beautiful thing; and yet I knew with my intelligence that it was nonsense—that Maryrose, for instance, envied me because she believed Willi and I had everything she wanted—she believed we were two people who loved each other.

Willi had been looking at me, and now he said: 'Anna is shocked because the woman is black.'

'That's part of it,' I said. 'I'm surprised that I do feel like that though.'

'I'm surprised you admit it,' said Willi, coldly, and his spectacles flashed.

'I'm surprised you don't,' said George to Willi. 'Come off it. You're such a bloody hypocrite.' And Willi lifted his grammars and set them ready on his knee.

'What's the alternative, have you an intelligent suggestion?' enquired Willi. 'Don't tell me. Being George, you believe it's your duty to take the child into your house. That means the four old people will be shocked into their graves, apart from the fact no one will ever speak to them again. The three children will be ostracised at school. Your wife will lose her job. You will lose your job. Nine people will be ruined. And what good will that do your son, George? May I ask?'

'And so that's the end of it all?' I asked.

'Yes, it is,' said Willi. He wore his usual expression at such moments, obstinate and patient, and his mouth was set.

'I could make it a test case,' said George.

'A test case of what?'

'All this bloody hypocrisy.'

'Why use the word to me—you've just called me a hypocrite.' George looked humble, and Willi said: 'Who'd pay the price of your noble gesture? You've got eight people dependent on you?'

'My wife isn't dependent on me. I'm dependent on her. Emotionally that is. Do you imagine I don't know it?'

'Do you want me to put the facts again?' said Willi, over-patient, and glancing at his text-books. Both George and

I knew that because he had been called a hypocrite he would never soften now, but George went on: 'Willi, isn't there anything at all? Surely, it can't be finished, just like that?'

'Do you want me to say that it's unfair or immoral or something helpful like that?'

'Yes,' said George, after a pause, dropping his chin on his chest. 'Yes, I suppose that's what I want. Because what's worse is that if you think I've stopped sleeping with her, I haven't. There might be another little Hounslow in the Boothby kitchen any day. Of course, I'm more careful than I was.'

'That's your affair,' said Willi.

'You are an inhuman swine,' said George after a pause.

'Thank you,' said Willi. 'But there's nothing to be done, is there? You agree, don't you?'

'That boy's going to grow up there among the pumpkins and the chickens and be a farm labourer or a half-arsed clerk, and my other three are going to get through to university and out of this bloody country if I have to kill myself paying for it.'

'What is the point?' said Willi. 'Your blood? Your sacred sperm, or what?'

Both George and I were shocked. Willi saw it with a tightening of his face, and it remained angry as George said: 'No, it's the responsibility. It's the gap between what I believe in and what I do.'

Willi shrugged and we were silent. Through the heavy midday hush came the sound of Johnnie's drumming fingers.

George looked at me again, and I rallied myself to fight Willi. Looking back I want to laugh—because I automatically chose to argue in literary terms, just as he automatically answered in political terms. But at the time it didn't seem extraordinary. And it didn't seem extraordinary to George either, who sat nodding as I spoke.

'Look,' I said. 'In the nineteenth century literature was full of this. It was a sort of moral touchstone. Like Resurrection, for instance. But now you just shrug your shoulders and it doesn't matter?'

'I haven't noticed that I shrugged,' said Willi. 'But perhaps it is true that the moral dilemma of a society is no longer crystallised by the fact of an illegitimate child?'

'Why not?' I asked.

'Why not?' said George, very fierce.

'Well, would you really say the problem of the African in this country is summed up by the Boothbys' cook's white cuckoo?'

'You put things so prettily' said George angrily. (And yet he would continue to come to Willi humbly for advice, and revere him, and write to him self-abasing letters for years after he left the Colony.) Now he stared out into the sunlight, blinking away tears, and then he said: 'I'm going to get my glass filled.' He went off to the bar.

Willi lifted his text-book, and said without looking at me: 'Yes, I know. But I'm not impressed by your reproachful eyes. You'd give him the same advice, wouldn't you? Full of ohs and ahs, but the same advice.'

'What it amounts to is that everything is so terrible that we've got calloused because of it and we don't really care.'

'May I suggest you stick to certain basic principles—such as abolishing what is wrong, changing what is wrong? Instead of sitting around crying about it?'

'And in the meantime?'

'In the meantime I'm going to study and you will go off and let George weep on your shoulder and be very sorry for him, which will achieve precisely nothing.'

I left him and walked slowly back up to the big room. George was leaning against the wall, a glass in his hand, eyes closed. I knew I should go to him, but I didn't. I went into the big room. Maryrose was sitting by herself at a window and I joined her. She had been crying.

I said: 'This seems to be a day for everyone to cry.'

'Not you,' said Maryrose. This meant that I was too happy with Willi to need to cry, so I sat down by her and said: 'What's wrong?'

'I was sitting here and watching them dance and I began thinking. Only a few months ago we believed that the world was going to change and everything was going to be beautiful and now we know it won't.'

'Do we?' I said, with a kind of terror.

'Why should it?' she asked, simply. I didn't have the moral energy to fight it, and after a pause she said: 'What did George want you for? I suppose he said I was a bitch for hitting him?'

'Can you imagine George saying anyone is a bitch for hitting him? Well why did you?'

'I was crying about that too. Because of course the real reason I hit him was because I know someone like George could make me forget my brother.'

'Well perhaps you should let someone like George have a try?'

'Perhaps I should,' she said. She gave me a small, old smile, which said so clearly: What a baby you are!—that I said angrily: 'But if you know something, why don't you do something about it?'

Again the small smile, and she said: 'No one will ever love me like my brother did. He really loved me. George would make love to me. And that wouldn't be the same thing, would it? But what's wrong with saying: I've had the best thing already and I'll never have it again, instead of just having sex. What's wrong with it?'

'When you say, what's wrong with it, like that, then I never know what answer to make, even though I know there's something wrong.'

'What, then?' She sounded really curious, and I said, even more angry: 'You just don't try, you don't try. You just give up.'

'It's all very well for you,' she said, meaning Willi again, and now I couldn't say anything. It was my turn to want to cry, and she saw it, and said out of her infinite superiority in suffering: 'Don't cry, Anna, there's never any point. Well I'm going to get washed for lunch.' And she went off. All the young men were now singing, around the piano, so I left the room too, and went to where I had seen George leaning. I clambered through nettles and blackjacks, because he had moved further around to the back, and was standing staring through a grove of paw-paw trees at the little shack where the cook lived with his wife and his children. There were a couple of brown children squatting in the dust among the chickens.

I noticed that George's very sleek arm was trembling as he tried to light a cigarette, and he failed, and threw it impatiently away, unlit, and he remarked calmly: 'No, my bye-blow is not present.'

A gong rang down at the hotel for lunch.

'We'd better go in,' I said.

'Stay here with me a minute.' He put his hand on my shoulder, and the heat of it burned through my dress. The gong stopped sending out its long metallic waves of sound, and the piano stopped inside. Silence, and a dove cooed from the jacaranda tree. George put his hand on my breast, and he said: 'Anna, I could take you to bed now—and then Marie, that's my black girl, and then go back to my wife tonight and have her, and be happy with all three of you. Do you understand that, Anna?'

'No,' I said, angry. And yet his hand on my breast made me understand it.

'Don't you?' he said, ironic. 'No?'

'No,' I insisted, lying on behalf of all women, and thinking of his wife, who made me feel caged.

He shut his eyes. His black eyelashes made tiny rainbows as they trembled on his brown cheek. He said, without opening his eyes: 'Sometimes I look at myself from the outside. George Hounslow, respected citizen, eccentric of course, with his socialism, but that's cancelled out by his devotion to all the aged parents and his charming wife and three children. And beside me I can see a whacking great gorilla swinging its arms and grinning. I can see the gorilla so clearly I'm surprised no one else can.' He let his hand fall off my breast so that I was able to breathe steadily again and I said: 'Willi's right. You can't do anything about it so you must stop tormenting yourself.' His eyes were still shut. I didn't know I was going to say what I did, but his eyes flew open and he backed away, so it was some sort of telepathy. I said: 'And you can't commit suicide.'

'Why not?' he asked curiously.

'For the same reason you can't take the child into your house. You've got nine people to worry about.'

'Anna, I've been wondering if I'd take the child into my house if I had—let's say, only two people to worry about?'

I didn't know what to say. After a moment he put his arm around me and walked me through the blackjacks and the nettles saying: 'Come down with me to the hotel and keep the gorilla off.' And now, of course, I was perversely annoyed that I had refused the gorilla and was in the role of sexless sister, and I sat by Paul at lunch and not by George. After lunch we all slept for a long time, and began to drink early. Although the dance that night was private, for 'the associated farmers of Mashopi and District,' by the time the farmers and their wives arrived in their big cars the dancing room was already full of people dancing. All of us, and a lot more airforce down from the city, and Johnnie was playing the piano and the regular pianist, who was not a tenth as good as Johnnie, had gone very willingly off to the bar. The master of ceremonies for the evening formalised matters by making a hasty and not very sincere speech about welcoming the boys in blue, and we all danced until Johnnie got tired, which was about five in the morning. Afterwards we stood about in groups under a clear cold star-frosted sky, and the moon made sharp black shadows around us. We all had our arms about each other and we were singing. The scent of the flowers was clear and cool again in the reviving night air, and they stood up fresh and strong. Paul was with me, we had been dancing together all evening. Willi was with Maryrose— he had been dancing with her. And Jimmy, who was very drunk, was stumbling around by himself. He had cut himself again somehow and was bleeding from a small wound over his eyes. And that was the end of our first full day, and it set the pattern for all the rest. The big 'general' dance next night was attended by all the same people, and the Boothbys' bar did well, the Boothbys' cook was overworked, and presumably his wife had assignations with George. Who was painfully, fruitlessly attentive to Maryrose.

On that second evening Stanley Lett began his attentions to Mrs Lattimer, the red-head, which ended in—but I was going to say disaster. That word is ridiculous. Because what is so painful about that time is that nothing was disastrous. It was all wrong, ugly, unhappy and coloured with cynicism, but nothing was tragic, there were no moments that could change anything or anybody. From time to time the emotional lightning flashed and showed a landscape of private misery, and then—we went on dancing. Stanley Lett's affair with Mrs Lattimer only led to an incident that I suppose must have happened a dozen times in her marriage.

She was a woman of about forty-five, rather plump, with the most exquisite hands and slender legs. She had a delicate white skin, and enormous soft periwinkle blue eyes, the hazy, tender, short-sighted, almost purple blue eyes that look at life through a mist of tears. But in her case it was alcohol as well. Her husband was a big bad-tempered commercial type who was a steady brutal drinker. He began drinking when the bar opened and drank all day, getting steadily more morose. Whereas drinking made her soft and sighing and tearful. I never, not once, heard him say anything to her that wasn't brutal. It appeared she didn't notice, or had given up caring. They had no children, but she was inseparable from her dog, the most beautiful red setter, the colour of her hair, with eyes as yearning and tearful as hers. They sat together on the hotel verandah, the red-haired woman and her feathery red dog, and received homage and supplies of drinks from the other guests. The three used to come to the hotel every week-end. Well, Stanley Lett was fascinated by her. She had no side, he said. She was a real good sort, he said. That second night of dancing she was squired by Stanley while her husband drank in the bar until it closed, when he stood swaying by the piano until at last Stanley gave him a final finishing-off drink, so that he stumbled off to bed, leaving his wife dancing. It seemed he did not care what she did. She spent her time with us, or with Stanley, who had 'organised' for Johnnie a woman on a farm two miles off whose husband had gone to the war. The four were having, as they repeatedly said, a fine good time. We danced in the big room; and Johnnie played, with the farmer's wife, a big high-coloured blonde from Johannesburg, sitting beside him. Ted had temporarily given up the battle for Stanley's soul. As he said himself, sex had proved too strong for him. All that long week-end—it was nearly a week, we drank and danced with the sound of Johnnie's piano perpetually in our ears.

And when we got back to town we knew that, as Paul remarked, our holiday had not done us much good. Only one person had maintained any sort of self-discipline and that was Willi, who worked steadily a good part of every day with his grammars. Though even he had succumbed a little—to Maryrose. It had been agreed that we should all go back to Mashopi. We went, I think, about two week-ends later. This was different from the general holiday—the hotel was empty save for ourselves, the Lattimers and their dog and the Boothbys. We were greeted by the Boothbys with much civility. It was clear that we had been discussed, that our proprietary ways with the hotel were much disapproved of, but that we spent too much money to be discouraged. I don't remember much of that week-end, or the four or five week-ends which succeeded it—at intervals of some weeks. We did not go down every week-end.

It must have been about six or eight months after our first visit that the crisis, if it can be called a crisis, occurred. It was the last time we went to Mashopi. We were the same people as before: George and Willi and Maryrose and myself; Ted, Paul and Jimmy. Stanley Lett and Johnnie were now part of another group with Mrs Lattimer and her dog and the farmer's wife. Sometimes Ted joined them, and sat silent, very much out of it, to return shortly afterwards to us, where he sat equally silent, smiling to himself. It was a new smile for him, wry, bitter, and self-judging. Sitting under the gum-trees we would hear Mrs Lattimer's lazy musical voice from the verandah: 'Stan-boy, get me a drink? What about a cigarette for me, Stan-boy? Son, come here and talk to me.' And he called her Mrs Lattimer, but sometimes, forgetting, Myra, at which she would droop her black Irish eyelashes at him. He was about twenty-two or twenty-three; there were twenty years between them, and they very much enjoyed publicly playing the mother-and-son roles, with the sexuality

136

so strong between them that we would look around apprehensively when Mrs Lattimer came near.

Looking back at those week-ends they seem like beads on a string, two big glittering ones to start with, then a succession of small unimportant ones, then another brilliant one to end. But that is just the lazy memory, because as soon as I start to think about the last week-end, I realise that there must have been incidents during the intervening week-ends that led up to it. But I can't remember, it's all gone. And I get exasperated, trying to remember—it's like wrestling with an obstinate other-self who insists on its own kind of privacy. Yet it's all there in my brain if only I could get at it. I am appalled at how much I didn't notice, living inside the subjective highly-coloured mist. How do I know that what I 'remember' was what was important? What I remember was chosen by Anna, of twenty years ago. I don't know what this Anna of now would choose. Because the experience with Mother Sugar and the experiments with the notebooks have sharpened my objectivity to the point where (but this kind of observation belongs to the blue notebook, not this one). At any rate, although it seems now that the final week-end exploded into all kinds of dramas without any previous warning, of course this is not possible.

For instance, Paul's friendship with Jackson must have become quite highly developed to provoke Mrs Boothby as it did. I can remember the moment when she ordered Paul finally out of the kitchen—it must have been the week-end before the last. Paul and I were in the kitchen talking to Jackson. Mrs Boothby came in and said: 'You know it's against the rules for hotel guests to come into the kitchen.' I remember quite clearly the feeling of shock, as at an unfairness, like children feel when grown-ups are being arbitrary. So that means we must have been running in and out of the kitchen all that time without protest from her. Paul punished her by taking her at her word. He would wait at the back door of the kitchen until the time Jackson was due to go off after lunch, and then ostentatiously walk with him across to the wire fence that enclosed Jackson's cottage, talking with his hand on the man's arm and shoulder. And this contact between black and white flesh was deliberate, to provoke any white person that might be watching. We didn't go near the kitchen again. And because we were in a mood of high childishness we would giggle and talk of Mrs Boothby like children talking about a headmistress. It seems extraordinary to me that we were capable of being so childish, and that we didn't care that we were hurting her. She had become 'an aborigine' because she resented Paul's friendship with Jackson. Yet we knew quite well there wasn't a white person in the Colony who wouldn't have resented it, and in our political roles we were capable of infinite patience and understanding in explaining to some white person why their racial attitudes were inhuman.

I remember something else—Ted reasoning with Stanley Lett about Mrs Lattimer. Ted said that Mr Lattimer was getting jealous and with good reason. Stanley was good-naturedly derisive: Mr Lattimer treated his wife like dirt, he said, and deserved what he got. But the derision was really for Ted, for it was he who was jealous, and of Stanley. Stanley did not care that Ted was hurt. And why should he? When anyone is wooed on one level for the sake of another it is always resented. Always. Of course, Ted was primarily in pursuit of the 'butterfly under the stone' and his romantic emotions were well under control. But they were there all right, and Ted deserved that moment, which occurred more than once, when Stanley smiled his hard-lipped knowing smile, his cold eyes narrowed, and said: 'Come off it, mate. You know that's not my cup of tea.' And yet Ted had been offering a book, or an evening listening to music. Stanley had become openly contemptuous of Ted. And Ted, instead of telling him to go to hell, allowed it. Ted was one of the most scrupulous people I've known, yet he would go off on 'organising expeditions' with Stanley, to get beer or filch food. Afterwards he would tell us he had only gone in order to get an opportunity to explain to Stanley that this was not, 'as he would come to see in time,' the right way to live. But then he would give us a quick, ashamed glance, and turn his face away, smiling his new bitterly self-hating smile.

And then there was the affair of George's son. All the

group knew about it. Yet George was by nature a discreet man and I'm sure during that year he was tormenting himself he had mentioned it to no one. Neither Willi nor I told anyone. Yet we all knew. I suppose that one night when we were half-drunk, George made some reference that he imagined was unintelligible. Soon we were joking about it in the way we now made joking despairing references to the political situation in the country. I remember that one evening George made us laugh until we were helpless with a fantasy about how one day his son would come to his house demanding work as a houseboy. He, George, would not recognise him, but some mystical link, etc., would draw him to the poor child. He would be given work in the kitchen and his sensitivity of nature and innate intelligence, 'all inherited from me of course,' would soon endear him to the whole household. In no time he would be picking up the cards the four old people dropped at the card-table and providing a tender undemanding friendship for the three children—'his half-siblings.' For instance, he would prove invaluable as a ball-boy when they played tennis. At last his patient servitude would be rewarded. Light would flash on George suddenly, one day, at the moment when the boy was handing him his shoes, 'very well-polished, of course.' 'Baas, is there anything more I can do?' 'My son!' 'Father. At last!' And so on and so on.

That night we saw George sitting by himself under the trees, head in his hands, motionless, a despondent heavy shadow among the moving shadows of the glittering spear-like leaves. We went down to sit with him, but there was nothing that anyone could say.

On that last week-end there was to be another big dance, and we arrived by car and by train, at various times through the Friday, and met in the big room. When Willi and I arrived Johnnie was already at the piano with his red-faced blonde beside him; Stanley was dancing with Mrs Lattimer, and George was talking to Maryrose. Willi went straight over and ousted George, and Paul came over to claim me. Our relationship had remained the same, tender and half-mocking and full of promise. Outside observers might have, and probably did, think the link-up was Willi and Maryrose, Paul and myself. Though at moments they might have thought it was George and myself and Paul and Maryrose. Of course the reason why these romantic, adolescent relationships were possible was because of my relationship with Willi which was, as I've said, almost a sexual. If there is a couple in the centre of a group with a real full sexual relationship it acts like a catalyst for the others, and often, indeed, destroys the group altogether. I've seen many such groups since, political and unpolitical, and one can always judge the relationship of the central couple (because there is always a central couple) by the relationships of the couples around them.

On that Friday there was trouble within an hour of our arrival. June Boothby came up to the big room to ask Paul and myself to come to the hotel kitchen and help her with food for the dinner that evening, because Jackson was busy with the party food for tomorrow. June had by then become engaged to her young man and had been released from her trance. Paul and I went with her. Jackson was mixing fruit and cream for an ice-pudding, and Paul at once began talking to him. They were discussing England, to Jackson such a remote and magical place that he would listen for hours to the simplest details about it—the underground system, for instance, or the buses, or Parliament. June and I stood together and made salads for the hotel evening meal. She was impatient to be free for her young man, who was expected at any moment. Mrs Boothby came in, looked at Paul and Jackson, and said: 'I thought I told you I wouldn't have you in the kitchen?'

'Oh, Mom,' said June impatiently, 'I asked them. Why don't you get another cook, it's too much work for Jackson.'

'Jackson's been doing the work for fifteen years, and there's never been trouble till now.'

'Oh, Mom, there's no trouble. But since the war and all the airforce boys all the time, there's more work. I don't mind helping out, and neither does Paul and Anna.'

'You'll do as I tell you, June,' said her mother.

'Oh, Mom,' said June, annoyed but still good-natured. She grimaced at me: Don't take any notice. Mrs Boothby saw her, and said: 'You're getting above yourself my girl. Since when have you given orders in the kitchen?'

June lost her temper and walked straight out of the room.

Mrs Boothby, breathing heavily, her plain, always high-coloured face even redder than usual, looked in distress at Paul. If Paul had made some gentle remark, done anything at all to mollify her, she would have collapsed into her real good-nature at once. But he did as he had done before: nodded at me to go with him, and went calmly out of the back door saying to Jackson: 'I'll see you later when you've finished work. If you ever do finish work.' I said to Mrs Boothby: 'We wouldn't have come if June hadn't asked us.' But she wasn't interested in appeals from me and made no reply. So I went back to the big room and danced with Paul.

All this time we had been making jokes that Mrs Boothby was in love with Paul. Perhaps she was, a little. But she was a very simple woman and a hard-working one. Very hard-working since the war, and the hotel which had once been a place for travellers to stop the night had become a week-end resort. It must have been a strain for her. And then there was June who had been transformed in the last few weeks from a sulking adolescent into a young woman with a future. Looking back I think it was June's marriage that was at the bottom of her mother's unhappiness. June must have been her only emotional outlet. Mr Boothby was always behind the bar counter, and he was the kind of drinker that is hardest of all to live with. Men who drink heavily in bouts are nothing compared to the men who 'carry their drink well'—who carry a load of drink every day, every week, year in and year out. These steady hard-drinkers are very bad for their wives. Mrs Boothby had lost June, who was going to live three hundred miles away. Nothing: no distance for the Colony, but she had lost her for all that. And perhaps she had been affected by the wartime restlessness. A woman who must have resigned herself, years ago, to not being a woman at all, she had watched for weeks now, Mrs Lattimer who was the same age as herself, being courted by Stanley Lett. Perhaps she did have secret dreams about Paul. I don't know. But looking back I see Mrs Boothby as a lonely pathetic figure. But I didn't think so then. I saw her as a stupid 'aborigine.' Oh, Lord, it's painful thinking of the people one has been cruel to. And she would have been made happy by so little—if we had invited her to come and drink with us sometimes, or talked to her. But we were locked in our group and we made stupid jokes and laughed at her. I can remember her face as Paul and I left the kitchen. She was gazing after Paul—hurt, bewildered; her eyes seemed frantic with incomprehension. And her sharp high voice to Jackson: 'You're getting very cheeky Jackson. Why are you getting so cheeky?'

It was the rule that Jackson should have three to five off every afternoon, but like a good feudal servant, when things were busy, he waived this right. This afternoon it was not until about five that we saw him leave the kitchen and walk slowly towards his house. Paul said: 'Anna dear, I would not love you so much if I didn't love Jackson more. And by now it's a question of principle . . .' And he left me and walked down to meet Jackson. The two stood talking together by the fence, and Mrs Boothby watched them from her kitchen window. George had joined me when Paul left. George looked at Jackson and said: 'The father of my child.'

'Oh, stop it,' I said, 'it doesn't do any good.'

'Do you realise Anna what a farce it all is? I can't even give that child of mine money? Do you realise how utterly bloodily *bizarre*—Jackson earns five quid a month. Admittedly, burdened down by children and the senile as I am, five quid a month is a lot to me—but if I gave Marie five pounds, just to get that poor kid some decent clothes, it would be so much money for them that . . . she told me, food for the Jackson family costs ten shillings a week. They live on pumpkin and mealiemeal and scraps from the kitchen.'

'Doesn't Jackson even suspect?'

'Marie thinks not. I asked her. Do you know what she said: "He's a good husband to me," she said. "He's kind to me and all my children" . . . do you know Anna, when she said that, I've never in all my life felt such a sod.'

'You're still sleeping with her?'

'Yes. Do you know, Anna, I love that woman, I love that woman so much that . . .'

After a while we saw Mrs Boothby come out of the kitchen and walk towards Paul and Jackson. Jackson went into his shack, and Mrs Boothby, rigid with lonely anger, went to her house. Paul came in to us and told us she had said to Jackson: 'I don't give you time off to talk cheeky with white men who ought to know better.' Paul was too angry to be flippant. He said: 'My God, Anna, my God. My God.' Then, slowly recovering, he swung me off to dance again and said: 'What really interests me is that there are people, like you for instance, who genuinely believe that the world can be changed.'

We spent the evening dancing and drinking. We all went to bed very late. Willi and I went to bed in a bad temper with each other. He was angry because George had been pouring out his troubles again and he was bored with George. He said to me: 'You and Paul seem to be getting on very well.' He could have said that any time during the last six months. I replied: 'And it's equally true that you and Maryrose are.' We were already in our twin beds on either side of the room. He had some book on the development of early German socialism in his hand. He sat there, all his intelligence concentrated behind his gleaming spectacles, wondering if it was worth while to quarrel. I think he decided it would only turn into our familiar argument about George . . . 'sloppy sentimentality' *vs* 'dogmatic bureaucracy.' Or perhaps—for he was a man incredibly ignorant about his motives—he believed that he resented my relationship with Paul. And perhaps he did. Challenged then, I replied: 'Maryrose.' Challenged now, I would say that every woman believes in her heart that if her man does not satisfy her she has a right to go to another. That is her first and strongest thought, regardless of how she might soften it later out of pity or expediency. But Willi and I were not together because of sex. And so? I write this and think how strong must have been that argumentative battling quality between us that even now I instinctively and out of sheer habit assess it in terms of rights or wrongs. Stupid. It's always stupid.

We didn't quarrel that night. After a moment he began his lonely humming: Oh the shark has, wicked teeth dear ... and he picked up his book and read and I went to sleep.

Next day bad temper prickled through the hotel. June Boothby had gone to a dance with her fiancé, and had not returned until morning. Mr Boothby had shouted at his daughter when she came in and Mrs Boothby had wept. The row with Jackson had permeated through the staff. The waiters were sullen with us all at lunch. Jackson went off at three o'clock according to the letter of the law, leaving Mrs Boothby to do the food for the dance, and June would not help her mother because of how she had been spoken to the day before. And neither would we. We heard June shouting: 'If you weren't so mean you'd get another assistant cook, instead of making a martyr of yourself for the sake of five pounds a month.' Mrs Boothby had red eyes, and again her face had the look of frantic disorganised emotion, and she followed June around, protesting. Because, of course, she was not mean. Five pounds was nothing to the Boothbys; and I suppose the reason why she didn't get an extra cook was because she didn't mind working twice as hard and thought there was no reason why Jackson shouldn't as well.

She went off to her house to lie down. Stanley Lett was with Mrs Lattimer on the verandah. The hotel tea was served at four by a waiter, but Mrs Lattimer had a headache and wanted black coffee. I suppose there must have been some trouble with her husband, but we had come to take his complaisance so much for granted we didn't think of that until later. Stanley Lett went to the kitchen to ask the waiter to make coffee but the coffee was locked up, and Jackson, trusted family retainer, had the keys of the store cupboard. Stanley Lett went off to Jackson's cottage to borrow the keys. I don't think it occurred to him that this was tactless, in the circumstances. He was simply, as was his nature, 'organising' supplies. Jackson, who liked Stanley because he associated the R.A.F. with human treatment, came down from his cottage to open the cupboard and make black coffee for Mrs Lattimer. Mrs Boothby must have been seen all this from her bedroom windows, for now she came down and told Jackson that if he ever did such a thing again he would get the sack. Stanley tried to soothe her but it was no use, she was like a possessed woman, and her husband had to take her off to lie down again.

George came to Willi and me and said: 'Do you realise what it would mean if Jackson got the sack? The whole family would be sunk.'

'You mean you would,' said Willi.

'No, you silly clot, for once I'm thinking of them. This is their home. Jackson'd never find another place where he could have his family with him. He'd have to get a job somewhere and the family would have to go back to Nyasaland.'

'Very likely,' said Willi. 'They'd be in the same position as the other Africans, instead of being in the minority of half of one per cent—if it's as much as that.'

The bar opened soon after, and George went off to drink. He had Jimmy with him. It seems I've forgotten the most important thing of all—Jimmy's having upset Mrs Boothby. This had happened the week-end before. Jimmy in the presence of Mrs Boothby had put his arms around Paul and kissed him. He was drunk at the time. Mrs Boothby, an unsophisticated woman, was terribly shocked. I tried to explain to her that the virile conventions or assumptions of the Colony were not those of England, but afterwards she could not look at Jimmy without disgust. She had not minded the fact that he was regularly drunk, that he was unshaven and looked really unpleasant with the two half-healed scars showing through yellow stubble, that he slumped about in an unbuttoned uncollared uniform. All that was all right; it was all right for real men to drink and not to shave and to disregard their looks. She had even been rather maternal and gentle with him. But the word 'homosexual' put him outside her pale. 'I suppose he's what they call a homosexual,' she said, using the word as if it, too, were poisoned.

Jimmy and George got themselves drunk in the bar and by the time the dance started they were maudlin and affectionate. The big room was full when they came in. Jimmy and George danced together, George parodying the thing,

145

but Jimmy looking childishly happy. Once round the room—but it was enough. Mrs Boothby was already there, looking like a seal in a black satin dress, her face flaming with distress. She went over to the couple and told them to take their disgusting behaviour somewhere else. No one else had even noticed the incident, and George told her not to be a silly bitch, and began dancing with June Boothby. Jimmy stood open-mouthed and helpless, very much the small boy who has been smacked and doesn't know what for. Then he wandered off into the night by himself.

Paul and I danced. Willi and Maryrose danced. Stanley and Mrs Lattimer danced. Mr Lattimer was in the bar and George kept leaving us to pay visits to his caravan.

We were all more noisy and derisive about everything than we had ever been. I think we all knew it was our last week-end. Yet no decision had been made about not coming again; just as no formal decision had been made about coming in the first place. There was a feeling of loss; for one thing Paul and Jimmy were due to be posted soon.

It was nearly midnight when Paul remarked that Jimmy had been gone a long time. We searched through the crowd in the big room, and no one had seen him. Paul and I went to look for him and met George at the door. Outside the night was damp and clouded. In that part of the country there is often two or three days' break in the regularly clear weather we took for granted, while a very fine rain or mist blows softly, like the small soft rain of Ireland. So it was now, and groups and couples stood cooling off, but it was too dark to see their faces, and we wandered among them trying to distinguish Jimmy by his shape. The bar had closed by then and he was not on the hotel verandah or in the dining-room. We began to worry, for more than once we had had to rescue him from a flowerbed or under the gum-trees, hopelessly drunk. We searched through the bedrooms. We searched slowly through the gardens, stumbling over bushes and plants, not finding him. We were standing at the back of the main hotel building, wondering where to look next, when the lights went on in the kitchen half a dozen paces in front of us. Jackson came into the kitchen, slowly, alone. He did not know he was being watched. I had never seen him other than polite and on guard; but now he was both angry and troubled—I remember looking at that face and thinking I had never really seen it before. His face changed—he was looking at something on the floor. We pressed forward to see, and there was Jimmy lying asleep or drunk or both on the floor of the kitchen. Jackson bent down to raise him and, as he did so, Mrs Boothby came in behind Jackson. Jimmy awoke, saw Jackson and lifted his arms like a newly roused child and put them around Jackson's neck. The black man said: 'Baas Jimmy, Baas Jimmy, you must go to bed. You must not be here.' And Jimmy said: 'You love me Jackson, don't you, you love me, none of the others love me.'

Mrs Boothby was so shocked that she let herself slump against the wall, and her face was a greyish colour. By then we three were in the kitchen, lifting Jimmy up and away from his clinging grip around Jackson's neck.

Mrs Boothby said: 'Jackson, you leave tomorrow.'

Jackson said: 'Missus, what have I done?'

Mrs Boothby said: 'Get out. Go away. Take your dirty family and yourself away from here. Tomorrow, or I'll get the police to you.'

Jackson looked at us, his eyebrows knotting and unknotting, puckers of uncomprehending pain tightening the skin of his face and releasing it, so that his face seemed to clench and unclench. Of course, he had no idea at all why Mrs Boothby was so upset.

He said slowly: 'Missus, I've worked for you fifteen years.'

George said: 'I'll speak to her, Jackson.' George had never before previously addressed a direct word to Jackson. He felt too guilty before him.

And now Jackson turned his eyes slowly towards George and blinked slowly, like someone who has been hit. And George stayed quiet, waiting. Then Jackson said: '*You* don't want us to leave, baas?'

I don't know how much that meant. Perhaps Jackson had known about his wife all the time. It certainly sounded like it then. But George shut his eyes a moment, then stammered out something, and it sounded ludicrous, like an idiot talking. Then he stumbled out of the kitchen.

We half lifted, half pushed Jimmy out of the kitchen, and we said: 'Good night, Jackson, thank you for trying to help Baas Jimmy.' But he did not answer.

We put Jimmy to bed, Paul and I. As we came down from the bedroom block through the wet dark, we heard George talking to Willi a dozen paces away. Willi was saying: 'Quite so.' And 'Obviously.' And 'Very likely.' And George was getting more and more vehement and incoherent.

Paul said in a low voice: 'Oh, my God, Anna, come with me, now.'

'I can't,' I said.

'I might leave the country any day now. I might never see you again.'

'You know I can't.'

Without replying he walked off into the dark, and I was just going after him when Willi came up. We were close to our bedroom, and we went into it. Willi said: 'It's the best thing that can have happened. Jackson and family will leave and George will come to his senses.'

'This means, almost for certain, that the family will have to split up. Jackson won't have his family with him again.'

Willi said: 'That's just like you. Jackson's been lucky enough to have his family. Most of them can't. And now he'll be like the others. That's all. Have you been weeping and wailing because of all the others without their families?'

'No, I've been supporting policies that should put an end to the whole bloody business.'

'Quite. And quite right.'

'But I happen to know Jackson and his family. Sometimes I can't believe you mean the things you say.'

'Of course you can't. Sentimentalists can never believe in anything but their own emotions.'

'And it's not going to make any difference to George. Because the tragedy of George is not Marie but George. When she goes there'll be someone else.'

'It might teach him a lesson,' said Willi, and his face was ugly as he said it.

I left Willi in the bedroom and stood on the verandah. The mist had thinned to show a faint diffused cold light from a half-obscured sky. Paul was standing a few paces off looking at me. And suddenly all the intoxication and the anger and misery rose in me like a bomb bursting and I didn't care about anything except being with Paul. I ran down to him and he caught my hand and without a word we both ran, without knowing where we were running or why. We ran along the main road east, slipping and stumbling on the wet puddling tarmac, and swerved off on to a rough grass track that led somewhere, but we didn't know where. We ran along it, through sandy puddles we never saw, through the faint mist that had come down again. Dark wet trees loomed up on either side, and fell behind and we ran on. Our breath went, and we stumbled off the track into the veld. It was covered with a low invisible leafy growth. We ran a few paces, and fell side by side in each other's arms in the wet leaves while the rain fell slowly down, and over us low dark clouds sped across the sky, and the moon gleamed out and went, struggling with the dark, so that we were in the dark again. We began to tremble so hard that we laughed; our teeth were clattering together. I was wearing a thin crepe dance dress and nothing else. Paul took off his uniform jacket and put it round me, and we lay down again. Our flesh together was hot, and everything else was wet and cold. Paul, maintaining his poise even now, remarked: 'I've never done this before, darling Anna. Isn't it clever of me to choose an experienced woman like you?' Which made me laugh again. We were neither of us at all clever, we were too happy. Hours later the light grew clear above us and the distant sound of Johnnie's piano at the hotel stopped, and looking up we saw the clouds had swept away and the stars were out. We got up, and remembering where the sound of the piano had come from we walked in what we thought was the direction of the hotel. We walked, stumbling, through scrub and grass, our hands hot together, and the tears and the wet from the grass ran down our faces. We could not find the hotel: the wind must have been blowing the sound of the dance music off course. In the dark we scrambled and climbed and finally we found ourselves on the top of a small kopje. And there was a complete silent blackness for miles around under a grey glitter of stars. We sat together on a wet ledge of granite with our arms around each other, waiting for the light to come. We were so wet and cold and tired we did not talk. We sat cheek to cold cheek and waited.

I have never, in all my life, been so desperately and wildly and painfully happy as I was then. It was so strong I couldn't believe it. I remember saying to myself, This is it, this is being happy, and at the same time I was appalled because it had come out of so much ugliness and unhappiness. And all the time, down our cold faces, pressed together, the hot tears were running.

A long time later, a red glow came up into the dark in front of us, and the landscape fell away from it, silent, grey, exquisite. The hotel, unfamiliar from this height, appeared half a mile away, and not where we expected it. It was all dark, not a light anywhere. And now we could see that the rock we sat on was at the mouth of a small cave, and the flat rock wall at its back was covered with Bushman paintings. They were fresh and glowing even in this faint light, but badly chipped. All this part of the country was covered with these paintings, but most were ruined because white oafs threw stones at them, not knowing their value. Paul looked at the little coloured figures of men and animals all cracked and scarred and said: 'A fitting commentary to it all, dear Anna, though I'd be hard put to it to find the right words to explain why, in my present state.' He kissed me, for the last time, and we slowly climbed down through the tangles of sodden grass and leaves. My crepe dress had shrunk in the wet and was above my knees, and this made us laugh, because I could only take tiny steps in it. We walked very slowly along a track to the hotel, and then up to the bedroom block, and there on the verandah sat Mrs Lattimer, crying. The door into the bedroom behind her was half-open, and Mr Lattimer sat on the floor by the door. He was still drunk, and he was saying in a methodical, careful, drunken voice: 'You whore. You ugly whore. You barren bitch.' This had happened before, obviously. She lifted her ruin of a face to us, pulling at her lovely red hair with both hands, the tears dropping off her chin. Her dog crouched beside her, whining softly, its head in her lap, and the red feathery tail swept apologetically back and forth across the floor. Mr Lattimer took no notice of us at all. His red ugly eyes were fixed on his wife: 'You lazy barren whore. You street girl. You dirty bitch.'

Paul left me, and I went into the bedroom. It was dark and stuffy.

Willi said: 'Where have you been?'

I said: 'You know where.'

'Come here.'

I went over to him, and he gripped my wrist and brought me down beside him. I remember lying there and hating him and wondering why the only time I could remember him making love to me with any conviction was when he knew I had just made love to someone else.

That incident finished Willi and me. We never forgave each other for it. We never mentioned it again, but it was always there. And so a 'sexless' relationship was ended finally, by sex.

Next day was Sunday and we assembled just before lunch under the trees by the railway lines. George had been sitting there by himself. He looked old and sad and finished. Jackson had taken his wife and his children and vanished in the night; they were now walking north to Nyasaland. The cottage or shack which had seemed so full of life had been emptied and made derelict overnight. It looked a broken-down little place, standing there empty beyond the paw-paw trees. But Jackson had been in too much of a hurry to take his chickens. There were some guinea-fowl, and some great red laying hens, and a handful of the wiry little birds called kaffir fowls, and a beautiful young cockerel in glistening brown and black feathers, black tail feathers iridescent in the sunlight, scratching at the dirt with his white young claws and crowing loudly. 'That's me,' said George to me, looking at the cockerel, and joking to save his life.

Back in the hotel for lunch, Mrs Boothby came to apologise to Jimmy. She was hurried and nervous, and her eyes were red, but although she could not even look at him without showing distaste, she was genuine enough. Jimmy accepted the apology with eager gratitude. He did not remember what had happened the night before and we never told him. He thought she was apologising for the incident on the dance floor with George.

Paul said: 'And what about Jackson?'

She said: 'Gone and good riddance.' She said it in a heavy uneven voice, that had an incredulous wondering sound to it. Obviously she was wondering what on earth could have happened to make her dismiss so lightly the faithful family servant of fifteen years. 'There are plenty of others glad to get his job,' she said.

We decided to leave the hotel that afternoon, and we never went back. A few days later Paul was killed and Jimmy went off to fly his bombers over Germany. Ted shortly got himself failed as a pilot and Stanley Lett told him he was a fool. Johnnie the pianist continued to play at parties and remained our inarticulate, interested, detached friend.

George tracked down, through the native commissioners, the whereabouts of Jackson. He had taken his family to Nyasaland, left them there, and was now cook at a private house in the city. Sometimes George sent the family money, hoping it would be believed it came from the Boothbys who, he claimed, might be feeling remorse. But why should they? Nothing had happened, as far as they were concerned, that they should be ashamed of.

And that was the end of it all.

That was the material that made *Frontiers of War*. Of course, the two 'stories' have nothing at all in common. I remember very clearly the moment I knew I would write it. I was standing on the steps of the bedroom block of the Mashopi hotel with a cold hard glittering moonlight all around me. Down beyond the eucalyptus trees on the railway lines a goods train had come in and was standing and hissing and clattering off clouds of white steam. Near the train was George's parked lorry, and behind it the caravan, a brown painted box of a thing that looked like a flimsy packing case. George was in the caravan at that moment with Marie—I had just seen her creep down and climb in. The wet cooling flowerbeds smelt strongly of growth. From the dance room came the drumming of Johnnie's piano. Behind me I could hear the voices of Paul and Jimmy talking to Willi, and Paul's sudden young laugh. I was filled with such a dangerous delicious intoxication that I could have walked straight off the steps into the air, climbing on the strength of my own drunkenness into the stars. And the intoxication, as I knew even then, was the recklessness of infinite possibility, of danger, the secret ugly frightening pulse of war itself, of the death that we all wanted, for each other and for ourselves.

[A date, some months later.]

I read this over today, for the first time since I wrote it. It's full of nostalgia, every word loaded with it, although at the time I wrote it I thought I was being 'objective.' Nostalgia for what? I don't know. Because I'd rather die than have to live through any of that again. And the 'Anna' of that time is like an enemy, or like an old friend one has known too well and doesn't want to see.

[The second notebook, the red one, had been begun without any hesitations at all. The British Communist Party was written across the first page, underlined twice, and the date, Jan. 3rd, 1950, set underneath:]

Last week, Molly came up at midnight to say that the Party members had been circulated with a form, asking for their history as members, and there was a section asking them to detail their 'doubts and confusions.' Molly said she had begun to write this, expecting to write a few sentences, had found herself writing 'a whole thesis—dozens of bloody pages.' She seemed upset with herself. 'What is it I want—a confessional? Anyway, since I've written it, I'm going to send it in.' I told her she was mad. I said: 'Supposing the British Communist Party ever gets into power, that document will be in the files, and if they want evidence to hang you, they've got it—thousands of times over.' She gave me her small, almost sour smile—the smile she uses when I say things like this. Molly is not an innocent communist. She said: 'You're very cynical.' I said: 'You know it's the truth. Or could be.' She said: 'If you think in that way, why are you talking of joining the Party?' I said: 'Why do you stay in it, when you think in that way too?' She smiled again, the sourness gone, ironically, and nodded. Sat a while, thinking and smoking. 'It's all very odd, Anna, isn't it?' And in the morning she said: 'I took your advice, I tore it up.'

On the same day I had a telephone call from Comrade John saying that he had heard I was joining the Party, and that 'Comrade Bill'—responsible for culture—would like to interview me. 'You don't have to see him of course, if you don't feel like it,' said John hastily, 'but he said he would be interested to meet the first intellectual prepared to join the Party since the cold war started.' The sardonic quality of this appealed to me and I said I'd see Comrade Bill. This although I had not, in fact, finally decided to join. One reason not to, that I hate joining anything, which seems to me contemptible. The second reason, that my attitudes towards communism are such that I won't be able to say anything I believe to be true to any comrade I know, is surely decisive? It seems not however, for in spite of the fact that I've been telling myself for months I couldn't possibly join an organisation that seems to me dishonest, I've caught myself over and over again on the verge of the decision to join. And always at the same moments—there are two of them. The first, whenever I meet, for some reason, writers, publishers, etc.— the literary world. It is a world so prissy, maiden-auntish; so class-bound; or if it's the commercial side, so blatant, that any contact with it sets me thinking of joining the Party. The other moment is when I see Molly, just rushing off to organise something, full of life and enthusiasm, or when I come up the stairs, and I hear voices from the kitchen—I go in. The atmosphere of friendliness, of people working for a common end. But that's not enough. I'll see their Comrade Bill tomorrow and tell him that I'm by temperament 'A fellow traveller,' and I'll stay outside.

The next day.

154

Interview at King Street, a warren of little offices behind a façade of iron-protected glass. Had not really noticed the place before though I've been past it often enough. The protected glass gave me two feelings—one of fear; the world of violence. The other, a feeling of protectiveness—the need to protect an organisation that people throw stones at. I went up the narrow stairs thinking of the first feeling: how many people have joined the British C.P. because, in England, it is difficult to remember the realities of power, of violence; the C.P. represents to them the realities of naked power that are cloaked in England itself? Comrade Bill turned out to be a very young man, Jewish, spectacled, intelligent, working-class. His attitude towards me brisk and wary, his voice cool, brisk, tinged with contempt. I was interested that, at the contempt, which he was not aware he was showing, I felt in myself the beginnings of a need to apologise, almost a need to stammer. Interview very efficient; he had been told I was ready to join, and although I went to tell him I would not, I found myself accepting the situation. I felt (probably because of his attitude of contempt), well, he's right, they're getting on with the job, and I sit around dithering with my conscience. (Though, of course, I don't think he's right.) Before I left, he remarked, out of the blue, 'In five years' time, I suppose you'll be writing articles in the capitalist press exposing us as monsters, just like all the rest.' He meant, of course, by 'all the rest'—intellectuals. Because of the myth in the Party that it's the intellectuals who drift in and out, when the truth is the turnover is the same in all the classes and groups. I was angry. I was also, and that disarmed me, hurt. I said to him: 'It's lucky that I'm an old hand. If I were a raw recruit I might be disillusioned by your attitude.' He gave me a long, cool, shrewd look which said: Well, of course I wouldn't have made that remark if you hadn't been an old hand. This both pleased me—being back in the fold, so to speak, already entitled to the elaborate ironies and complicities of the initiated; and made me suddenly exhausted. I'd forgotten of course, having been out of the atmosphere so long, the tight, defensive, sarcastic atmosphere of the inner circles. But at the moments when I've wanted to join it's been with a full understanding of the nature of the inner circles. All the communists I know—that is, the ones of any intelligence, have the same attitude towards 'the centre'—that the Party has been saddled with a group of dead bureaucrats who run it, and that the real work gets done in spite of the centre. Comrade John's remark for instance, when I first told him I might join: 'You're mad. They hate and despise writers who join the Party. They only respect those who don't.' 'They' being the centre. It was a joke of course, but fairly typical. On the underground, read the evening newspaper. Attack on Soviet Union. What they said about it seemed to me true enough, but the tone—malicious, gloating, triumphant, sickened me, and I felt glad I had joined the Party. Came home to find Molly. She was out, and I spent some hours despondent, wondering why I had joined. She came in and I told her, and said: 'The funny thing is I was going to say I wouldn't join but I did.' She gave her small sourish smile (and this smile is only for politics, never for anything else, there is nothing sour in her nature), 'I joined in spite of myself too.' She had never given any hint of this before, was always such a loyalist, that I must have looked surprised. She said: 'Well now you're in, I'll tell you.' Meaning that to an outsider the truth could not be told. 'I've been around Party circles so long that . . .' But even now she couldn't say straight out 'that I knew too much to want to join.' She smiled, or grimaced instead. 'I began working in the Peace thing, because I believed in it. All the rest were members. One day that bitch Ellen asked me why I wasn't a member. I was flippant about it—a mistake, she was angry. A couple of days later she told me there was a rumour I was an agent, because I wasn't a member. I suppose she started the rumour. The funny thing is, obviously if I was an agent I'd have joined—but I was so upset, I went off and signed on the dotted line . . .' She sat smoking and looking unhappy. Then said again: 'All very odd, isn't it?' And went off to bed.

5th Feb., 1950

It's as I foresaw, the only discussions I have about politics where I say what I think is with people who have been in the

Party and have now left. Their attitude towards me frankly tolerant—a minor aberration, that I joined.

19th August, 1951

Had lunch with John, the first time since I joined the Party. Began talking as I do with my ex-party friends, frank acknowledgement of what is going on in Soviet Union. John went into automatic defence of the Soviet Union, very irritating. Yet this evening had dinner with Joyce, *New Statesman* circles, and she started to attack Soviet Union. Instantly I found myself doing the automatic-defence-of-Soviet-Union act, which I can't stand when other people do it. She went on; I went on. For her, she was in the presence of a communist so she started on certain clichés. I returned them. Twice tried to break the thing, start on a different level, failed—the atmosphere prickling with hostility. This evening Michael dropped in. I told him about this incident with Joyce. Remarked that although she was an old friend, we probably wouldn't meet again. Although I had changed my mental attitudes about nothing, the fact I had become a Party member, made me, for her, an embodiment of something she had to have certain attitudes towards. And I responded in kind. At which Michael said: 'Well, what did you expect?' He was speaking in his role of East European exile, ex-revolutionary, toughened by real political experience, to me in my role as 'political innocent.' And I replied in that role, producing all sorts of liberal inanities. Fascinating—the roles we play, the way we play parts.

15th Sept., 1951

The case of Jack Briggs. Journalist on *Times*. Left it at outbreak of war. At that time, unpolitical. Worked during the war for British intelligence. During this time influenced by communists he met, moved steadily to the left. After the war refused several highly-paid jobs on the conservative newspapers, worked for low salary on left paper. Or—leftish; for when he wanted to write an article on China, that pillar of the left, Rex, put him in a position where he had to resign. No money. At this point, regarded as a communist in the newspaper world, and therefore unemployable, his name comes up in the Hungarian Trial, as British agent conspiring to overthrow communism. Met him by accident, he was desperately depressed—a whispering campaign around the Party and near-party circles, that he was and had been 'A capitalist spy.' Treated with suspicion by his friends. A meeting of the writers' group. We discussed this, decided to approach Bill, to put an end to this revolting campaign. John and I saw Bill, said it was obviously untrue Jack Briggs could ever be an agent, demanded he should do something. Bill affable, pleasant. Said he would 'make enquiries,' let us know. We let the 'enquiries' pass; knowing this meant a discussion higher up the Party. No word from Bill. Weeks passed. Usual technique of Party officials—let things slide, in moments of difficulty. We went to see Bill again. Extremely affable. Said he could do nothing. Why not? 'Well in matters of this case when there might be doubt . . .' John and I angry, demanded of Bill if he, personally, thought it was conceivable Jack could ever have been an agent. Bill hesitated, began on a long, manifestly insincere rationalisation, about how it was possible that anyone could be an agent 'including me.' With a bright, friendly smile. John and I left, depressed, angry—and with ourselves. We made a point of seeing Jack Briggs personally, and insisting that others did, but the rumours and spiteful gossip continue. Jack Briggs in acute depression, and also completely isolated, from right and left. To add to the irony, three months after his row with Rex about the article on China, which Rex said was 'communist in tone,' the respectable papers began publishing articles in the same tone, whereupon Rex, the brave man, found it the right time to publish an article on China. He invited Jack Briggs to write it. Jack, in an inverted, bitter mood, would not.

This story, with variations more or less melodramatic, is the story of the communist or near-communist intellectual in this particular time.

3rd Jan., 1952
I write very little in this notebook. Why? I see that

everything I write is critical of the Party. Yet I am still in it. Molly too.

• •

Three of Michael's friends hanged yesterday in Prague. He spent the evening talking to me—or rather to himself. He was explaining, first, why it was impossible that these men could be traitors to communism. Then he explained, with much political subtlety, why it was impossible that the Party should frame and hang innocent people; and that these three had perhaps got themselves, without meaning to, into 'objectively' anti-revolutionary positions. He talked on and on and on until finally I said we should go to bed. All night he cried in his sleep. I kept jerking awake to find him whimpering, the tears wetting the pillow. In the morning I told him that he had been crying. He was angry—with himself. He went off to work looking an old man, his face lined and grey, giving me an absent nod—he was so far away, locked in his miserable self-questioning. Meanwhile I help with a petition for the Rosenbergs. Impossible to get people to sign it, except party and near-party intellectuals. (Not like France. The atmosphere of this country has changed dramatically in the last two or three years, tight, suspicious, frightened. It would take very little to send it off balance into our version of McCarthyism.) I am asked, even by people in the Party, let alone the 'respectable' intellectuals, why do I petition on behalf of the Rosenbergs but not on behalf of the people framed in Prague? I find it impossible to reply rationally, except that someone has to organise an appeal for the Rosenbergs. I am disgusted—with myself, with the people who won't sign for the Rosenbergs; I seem to live in an atmosphere of suspicious disgust. Molly began crying this evening, quite out of the blue—she was sitting on my bed, chatting about her day, then she began crying. In a still, helpless way. It reminded me of something, could not think of what, but of course it was Maryrose, suddenly letting the tears slide down her face sitting in the big room at Mashopi, saying: 'We believed everything was going to be beautiful and now we know it

159

won't.' Molly cried like that. Newspapers all over my floor, about the Rosenbergs, about the things in Eastern Europe.

•   •

The Rosenbergs electrocuted. Felt sick all night. This morning I woke asking myself: why should I feel like this about the Rosenbergs, and only feel helpless and depressed about the frame-ups in communist countries? The answer an ironical one. I feel responsible for what happens in the West, but not at all for what happens over there. And yet I am in the Party. I said something like this to Molly, and she replied, very brisk and efficient (she's in the middle of a hard organising job), 'All right, I know, but I'm busy.'

•   •

Koestler. Something he said sticks in my mind—that any communist in the West who stayed in the Party after a certain date did so on the basis of a private myth. Something like that. So I demand of myself, what is my private myth? That while most of the criticisms of the Soviet Union are true, there must be a body of people biding their time there, waiting to reverse the present process back to real socialism. I had not formulated it so clearly before. Of course there is no Party member I could say this to, though it's the sort of discussion I have with ex-party people. Suppose that all the Party people I know have similarly incommunicable private myths, all different? I asked Molly. She snapped: 'What are you reading that swine Koestler for?' This remark is so far from her usual level of talk, political or otherwise, I was surprised, tried to discuss it with her. But she's very busy. When she's on an organising job (she is doing a big exhibition of art from Eastern Europe) she's too immersed in it to be interested. She's in another role altogether. It occurred to me today, that when I talk to Molly about politics, I never know what person is going to reply—the dry, wise, ironical political woman, or the Party fanatic who sounds, literally, quite maniacal. And I have these two personalities myself. For instance, met Editor Rex in the street. That was last week. After the greetings were exchanged, I saw a spiteful, critical look coming on to his face, and I knew it was going to be a crack about the Party. And I knew if he made one, I'd defend it. I couldn't bear to hear him, being spiteful, or myself, being stupid. So I made an excuse and left him. The trouble is, what you don't realise when you join the Party, soon you meet no one but communists or people who have been communists who can talk without that awful dilettantish spite. One becomes isolated. That's why I shall leave the Party, of course.

●　　●

I see that I wrote yesterday, I would leave the Party. I wonder when, and on what issue?

●　　●

Had dinner with John. We meet rarely—always on the verge of political disagreement. At the end of the dinner, he said: 'The reason why we don't leave the Party is that we can't bear to say good-bye to our ideals for a better world.' Trite enough. And interesting because it implies he believes, and that I must, only the communist party can better the world. Yet we neither of us believe any such thing. But above all, this remark struck me because it contradicted everything he had been saying previously. (I had been arguing that the Prague affair was obviously a frame-up and he was saying that while the Party made 'mistakes' it was incapable of being so deliberately cynical.) I came home thinking that somewhere at the back of my mind when I joined the Party was a need for wholeness, for an end to the split, divided, unsatisfactory way we all live. Yet joining the Party intensified the split—not the business of belonging to an organisation whose every tenet, on paper, anyway, contradicts the ideas of the society we live in; but something much deeper than that. Or at any rate, more difficult to understand. I tried to think about it, my brain kept swimming into blankness, I got confused and exhausted. Michael came in, very late. I told him what I was trying to think out. After all, he's a witch-doctor, a soul-curer. He looked at me, very dry and ironic, and remarked: 'My dear Anna, the human soul, sitting in a kitchen, or for that matter, in a double bed, is quite complicated enough, we don't understand the first thing about it. Yet you're sitting there worrying because you can't make sense of the human soul in the middle of a world revolution?' And so I left it, and I was glad to, but I was nevertheless feeling guilty because I was so happy not to think about it.

●　　　●

I went to visit Berlin with Michael. He in search of old friends, dispersed in the war, might be anywhere. 'Dead, I expect,' he said in his new tone of voice, which is flat with a determination not to feel. Dates from the Prague trial, this voice. East Berlin terrifying place, bleak, grey, ruinous, but above all the atmosphere, the lack of freedom like an invisible poison continually spreading everywhere. The most significant incident this one: Michael ran into some people he knew from before the war. They greeted him with hostility—so that Michael, having run forward, to attract their attention, saw their hostile faces and shrank into himself. It was because they knew he had been friendly with the hanged men in Prague, or three of them, they were traitors, so that meant he was a traitor too. He tried, very quiet and courteous, to talk. They were like a group of dogs, or animals, facing outward, pressing against each other for support against fear. I've never experienced anything like that, the fear and hate on their faces. One of them, a woman with flaming angry eyes, said: 'What are you doing, *comrade*, wearing that expensive suit?' Michael's clothes are always off the peg, he spends nothing on clothes. He said: 'But Irene, it's the cheapest suit I could buy in London.' Her face snapped shut into suspicion, she glanced at her companions, then a sort of triumph. She said: 'Why do you come here, spreading that capitalist poison? We know you are in rags and there are no consumer goods.' Michael was at first stunned, then he said, still with irony, that even Lenin had understood the possibility that a newly-established communist society might suffer from a shortage of consumer goods. Whereas England which, 'as I think you know, Irene,' is a very solid capitalist society, is quite well-equipped with consumer goods. She gave a sort of grimace of fury, or hatred. Then she turned on her heel and went off, and her companions went with her. All Michael said was: 'That used to be an intelligent woman.' Later he made jokes about it, sounding tired and depressed. He said for instance: 'Imagine Anna, that all those heroic communists have died to create a society where Comrade Irene can spit at me for wearing a very slightly better suit than her husband has.'

•   •

Stalin died today. Molly and I sat in the kitchen, upset. I kept saying, 'We are being inconsistent, we ought to be pleased. We've been saying for months he ought to be dead.' She said: 'Oh, I don't know, Anna, perhaps he never knew about all the terrible things that were happening.' Then she laughed and said: 'The real reason we're upset is that we're scared stiff. Better the evils we know.' 'Well, things can't be worse.' 'Why not? We all of us seem to have this belief that things are going to get better. Why should they? Sometimes I think we're moving into a new ice age of tyranny and terror, why not? Who's to stop it—us?' When Michael came in later, I told him what Molly had said—about Stalin's not knowing; because I thought how odd it was we all have this need for the great man, and create him over and over again in the face of all the evidence. Michael looked tired and grim. To my surprise he said: 'Well, it might be true, mightn't it? That's the point—anything might be true anywhere, there's never any way of really knowing the truth about anything. Anything is possible—everything's so crazy, anything at all's possible.'

His face looked disintegrated and flushed as he said this. His voice toneless, as it is these days. Later he said: 'Well, we are pleased he is dead. But when I was young and politically active, he was a great man for me. He was a great man for all of us.' Then he tried to laugh, and he said: 'After all, there's nothing wrong, in itself, in wanting there to be great men in the world.' Then he put his hand over his eyes in a new gesture, shielding his eyes, as if the light hurt him. He said: 'I've got a headache, let's go to bed, shall we?' In bed we didn't make love, we lay quietly side by side, not talking. He was crying in his sleep; I had to wake him out of a bad dream.

•　　•　　•

By-election. North London. Candidates—Conservative, Labour, Communist. A Labour seat, but with a reduced majority from the previous election. As usual, long discussions in C.P. circles about whether it is right to split the Labour vote. I've been in on several of them. These discussions have the same pattern. No, we don't want to split the vote; it's essential to have Labour in, rather than a Tory. But on the other hand, if we believe in C.P. policy, we must try to get our candidate in. Yet we know there's no hope of getting a C.P. candidate in. This impasse remains until emissary from Centre comes in to say that it's wrong to see the C.P. as a kind of ginger group, that's just defeatism, we have to fight the election as if we were convinced we were going to win it. (But we know we aren't going to win it.) So the fighting speech by the man from Centre, while it inspires everyone to work hard, does not resolve the basic dilemma. On the three occasions I watched this happen, the doubts and confusions were solved by—*a joke*. Oh yes, very important in politics, that joke. This joke made by the man from Centre himself: It's all right, comrades, we are going to lose our deposit, we aren't going to win enough votes to split the Labour vote. Much relieved laughter, and the meeting splits up. This joke, completely contradicting everything in official policy, in fact sums up how everyone feels. I went up to canvass, three afternoons. Campaign H.Q. in the house of a comrade living in the area; campaign organised by the ubiquitous Bill, who lives in the constituency. A dozen or so housewives, free to canvass in the afternoons—the men come in at night. Everyone knew each other, the atmosphere I find so wonderful—of people working together for a common end. Bill, a brilliant organiser, everything worked out to the last detail. Cups of tea and discussion about how things were going before we went out to canvass. This is a working-class area. 'Strong support for the Party around here,' said one woman, with pride. Am given two dozen cards, with the names of people who have already been canvassed, marked 'doubtful.' My job to see them again, and talk them into voting for the C.P. As I leave the campaign H.Q., discussion about the right way to dress for canvassing—most of these women much better dressed than the women of the area. 'I don't think it's right to dress differently than usual,' says one woman, 'it's a kind of cheating.' 'Yes, but if you turn up at the door too posh, they get on the defensive.' Comrade Bill, laughing and good-natured—the same energetic good nature as Molly, when she's absorbed in detailed work, says: 'What matters is to get results.' The two women chide him for being dishonest. 'We've got to be honest in everything we do, because otherwise they won't trust us.' The names I am given are of people scattered over a wide area of working streets. A very ugly area of uniform, small, poor houses. A main station half a mile away, shedding thick smoke all around. Dark clouds, low and thick, and the smoke drifting up to join them. The first house has a cracked fading door. Mrs C., in a sagging wool dress and apron, a worn-down woman. She has two small boys, well-dressed and kept. I say I am from the C.P.; she nods. I say: 'I understand you are undecided whether to vote for us?' She says: 'I've got nothing against you.' She's not hostile, but polite. She says: 'The lady who came last week left a book.' (A pamphlet.) Finally she says: 'But we've always voted Labour, dear.' I mark the card Labour, crossing out the Doubtful, and go on. The next, a Cypriot. This house even poorer, a young man looking harassed, a pretty dark girl, a new baby. Scarcely any furniture. New in England. It emerges that the point they are 'doubtful' about is whether they are entitled to the vote at all. I explain that they are. Both very good-natured, but wanting me to leave, the baby is crying, an atmosphere of pressure and harassment. The man says he doesn't mind the communists but he doesn't like the Russians. My feeling is they won't trouble to vote, but I leave the card 'doubtful' and go on to the next. A well-kept house, with a crowd of teddy-boys outside. Wolf-whistles and friendly jibes as I arrive. I disturb the housewife, who is pregnant and has been lying down. Before letting me in, she complains to her son that he said he was going to the shops for her. He says he will go later: a nice-looking, tough, well-dressed boy of sixteen or so—all the children in the area well-dressed, even when their parents are not. 'What do you want?' she says to me. 'I'm from the C.P.'—and explain. She says: 'Yes, we've had you before.' Polite, but indifferent. After a discussion during which it's hard to get her to agree or disagree with anything, she says her husband has always voted Labour, and she does what her husband says. As I leave she shouts at her son, but he drifts off with a group of his friends, grinning. She yells at him. But this scene has a feeling of good nature about it: she doesn't really expect him to go shopping for her, but shouts at him on principle, while he expects her to shout at him, and doesn't really mind. At the next house, the woman at once and eagerly offers a cup of tea, says she likes elections, 'people keep dropping in for a bit of a talk.' In short, she's lonely. She talks on and on about her personal problems on a dragging, listless harassed note. (Of the houses I visited this was the one which seemed to me to contain the real trouble, real misery.) She said she had three small children, was bored, wanted to go back to work, her husband wouldn't let her. She talked and talked and talked, obsessively, I was there nearly three hours, couldn't leave. When I finally asked her if she was voting for the C.P., she said: 'Yes, if you like dear'—which I'm sure she had said to all the canvassers. She added that her husband always voted Labour. I changed the 'doubtful' to Labour, and went on. At about ten that night I went back, with all the cards but three changed to Labour, and handed them in to Comrade Bill. I said: 'We have some pretty optimistic canvassers.' He flicked the cards over, without comment, replaced them in their boxes, and remarked loudly for the benefit of other canvassers coming in: 'There's real support for our policy, we'll get our candidate in yet.' I canvassed three afternoons in all, the other two not 'doubtfuls' but going into houses for the first time. Found two C.P. voters, both Party members, the rest all Labour. Five lonely women going mad quietly by themselves, in spite of husband and children or rather because of them. The quality they all had: self-doubt. A guilt because they were not happy. The phrase they all used: 'There must be something wrong with me.' Back in the campaign H.Q. I mentioned these women to the woman in charge for the afternoon. She said: 'Yes, whenever I go canvassing, I get the heeby-jeebies. This country's full of women going mad all by themselves.' A pause, then she added, with a slight aggressiveness, the other side of the self-doubt, the guilt shown by the women I'd talked to: 'Well, I used to be the same until I joined the Party and got myself a purpose in life.' I've been thinking about this—the truth is, these women interest me much more than the election campaign. Election Day: Labour in, reduced majority. Communist candidate loses deposit. *Joke.* (In campaign H.Q. Maker of joke, Comrade Bill.) 'If we'd got another two thousand votes, the Labour majority would have been on a knife-edge. Every cloud has a silver lining.'

• •

Jean Barker. Wife of minor Party official. Aged thirty-four. Small, dark, plump. Rather plain. Husband patronises her. She wears, permanently, a look of strained, enquiring good-nature. Comes around collecting Party dues. A born talker, never stops talking, but the most interesting kind of talker there is, she never knows what she is going to say until it is out of her mouth, so that she is continually blushing, catching herself up short, explaining just what it is she has meant, or laughing nervously. Or she stops with a puzzled frown in the middle of a sentence, as if to say: 'Surely I don't think *that*?' So while she talks she has the appearance of someone listening. She has started a novel, says she hasn't got time to finish it. I have not yet met one Party member, anywhere, who has not written, half-written, or is planning to write a novel, short stories, or a play. I find this an extraordinary fact, though I don't understand it. Because of her verbal incontinence, which shocks people, or makes them laugh, she is developing the personality of a clown, or a licensed humourist. She has no sense of humour at all. But when she hears some remark she makes pretend that surprises her, she knows from experience that people will laugh, or be upset, so she laughs herself, in a puzzled nervous way, then hurries on. She has three children. She and her husband very ambitious for them, goad them through school, to get scholarships. Children carefully educated in the Party 'line,' conditions in Russia, etc. They have the defensive closed-in look with strangers of people knowing themselves to be in a minority. With communists, they tend to show off their Party know-how, while their parents look on, proud.

Jean works as a manager of a canteen. Long hours. Keeps her flat and her children and herself very well. Secretary of local Party branch. She is dissatisfied with herself. 'I'm not doing enough, I mean the Party's not enough, I get fed up, just paper work, like an office, doesn't mean anything.' Laughs, nervously. 'George—' (her husband) 'says that's the incorrect attitude, but I don't see why I should always have to bow down. I mean, they're wrong often enough, aren't they?' Laughs. 'I decided to do something worthwhile for a change.' Laughs. 'I mean, something different. After all, even the leading comrades are talking about sectarianism aren't they ... well of course the leading comrades should be the *first* to say it ...' Laughs. 'Though that's not what seems to happen ... anyway, I decided to do something useful for a change.' Laughs. 'I mean, something different. So now I have a class of backward children on Saturday afternoons. I used to be a teacher you know. I coach them. No, not Party children, just ordinary children.' Laughs. 'Fifteen of them. It's hard work. George says I'd be better occupied making Party members, but I wanted to do something really useful ...' And so on. The Communist Party is largely composed of people who aren't really political at all, but who have a powerful sense of service. And then there are those who are lonely, and the Party is their family. The poet, Paul, who got drunk last week and said he was sick and disgusted with the Party, but he joined it in 1935, and if he left it, he'd be leaving 'his whole life.'

[The yellow notebook looked like the manuscript of a novel, for it was called *The Shadow of the Third*. It certainly began like a novel:]

Julia's voice came loud up the stairs: 'Ella, aren't you going to the party? Are you going to use the bath? If not, I will.' Ella did not answer. For one thing, she was sitting on her son's bed, waiting for him to drop off to sleep. For another, she had decided not to go to the party, and did not want to argue with Julia. Soon she made a cautious movement off the bed, but at once Michael's eyes opened, and he said: 'What party? Are you going to it?' 'No,' she said, 'go to sleep.' His eyes sealed themselves, the lashes quivered and lay still. Even asleep he was formidable, a square-built, tough four-year-old. In the shaded light his sandy hair, his lashes, even a tiny down on his bare forearm gleamed gold. His skin was brown and faintly glistening from the summer. Ella quietly turned off the lights—waited; went to the door— waited; slipped out—waited. No sound. Julia came brisk up the stairs, enquiring in her jolly off-hand voice: 'Well, are you going?' 'Shhhh, Michael's just off to sleep.' Julia lowered her voice and said: 'Go and have your bath now. I want to wallow in peace when you're gone.' 'But I said I'm not going,' said Ella, slightly irritable.

'Why not?' said Julia, going into the large room of the flat. There were two rooms and a kitchen, all rather small and low-ceilinged, being right under the roof. This was Julia's house, and Ella lived in it, with her son Michael, in these three rooms. The larger room had a recessed bed, books, some prints. It was bright and light, rather ordinary, or anonymous. Ella had not attempted to impose her own taste on it. Some inhibition stopped her: this was Julia's house, Julia's furniture; somewhere in the future lay her own taste.

It was something like this that she felt. But she enjoyed living here and had no plans for moving out. Ella went after Julia and said: 'I don't feel like it.' 'You never feel like it,' said Julia. She was squatting in an armchair sizes too big for the room, smoking. Julia was plump, stocky, vital, energetic, Jewish. She was an actress. She had never made much of being an actress. She played small parts, competently. They were, as she complained, of two kinds: 'Stock working-class comic, and stock working-class pathetic.' She was beginning to work for television. She was deeply dissatisfied with herself.

When she said: 'You never feel like it,' it was a complaint partly against Ella, and partly against herself. She always felt like going out, could never refuse an invitation. She would say that even when she despised some role she was playing, hated the play, and wished she had nothing to do with it, she nevertheless enjoyed what she called 'flaunting her personality around.' She loved rehearsals, theatre shop and small talk and malice.

Ella worked for a woman's magazine. She had done articles on dress and cosmetics, and of the getting-and-keeping-a-man kind, for three years, hating the work. She was not good at it. She would have been sacked if she had not been a friend of the woman editor. Recently she had been doing work she liked much better. The magazine had introduced a medical column. It was written by a doctor. But every week several hundred letters came in and half of them had nothing to do with medicine, and were of such a personal nature that they had to be answered privately. Ella handled these letters. Also she had written half a dozen short stories which she herself described satirically as 'sensitive and feminine,' and which both she and Julia said were the kind of stories they most disliked. And she had written part of a novel. In short, on the face of it there was no reason for Julia to envy Ella. But she did.

The party tonight was at the house of the doctor under whom Ella worked. It was a long way out, in North London. Ella was lazy. It was always an effort for her to move herself. And if Julia had not come up, she would have gone to bed and read.

'You say,' said Julia, 'that you want to get married again, but how will you ever, if you never meet anybody?'

'That's what I can't stand,' said Ella, with sudden energy. 'I'm on the market again, so I have to go off to parties.'

'It's no good taking that attitude—that's how everything is run, isn't it?'

'I suppose so.'

Ella, wishing Julia would go, sat on the edge of the bed (at the moment a divan and covered with soft-green-woven stuff), and smoked with her. She imagined she was hiding what she felt, but in fact she was frowning and fidgety. 'After all,' said Julia, 'you never meet anyone but those awful phonies in your office.' She added, 'Besides your decree was absolute last week.'

Ella suddenly laughed, and after a moment Julia laughed with her, and they felt at once friendly to each other.

Julia's last remark had struck a familiar note. They both considered themselves very normal, not to say conventional women. Women, that is to say, with conventional emotional reactions. The fact that their lives never seemed to run on the usual tracks was because, so they felt, or might even say, they never met men who were capable of seeing what they really were. As things were, they were regarded by women with a mixture of envy and hostility, and by men with emotions which—so they complained—were depressingly banal. Their friends saw them as women who positively disdained ordinary morality. Julia was the only person who would have believed Ella if she had said that for the whole of the time while she was waiting for the divorce she had been careful to limit her own reactions to any man (or rather, they limited themselves) who showed an attraction for her. Ella was now free. Her husband had married the day after the divorce was final. Ella was indifferent to this. It had been a sad marriage; no worse than many, certainly; but then Ella would have felt a traitor to her own self had she remained in a compromise marriage. For outsiders, the story went that Ella's husband George had left her for somebody else. She resented the pity she earned on this account, but did nothing to put things right, because of all sorts of complicated pride. And besides, what did it matter what people thought?

She had the child, her self-respect, a future. She could not imagine this future without a man. Therefore, and of course she agreed that Julia was right to be so practical, she ought to be going to parties and accepting invitations. Instead she was sleeping too much and was depressed.

'And besides, if I go, I'll have to argue with Dr West, and it does no good.' Ella meant that she believed Dr West was limiting his usefulness, not from lack of conscientiousness, but from lack of imagination. Any query which he could not answer by advice as to the right hospitals, medicine, treatment, he handed over to Ella.

'I know, they are absolutely awful.' By *they*, Julia meant the world of officials, bureaucrats, people in any kind of office. *They*, for Julia, were by definition middle-class—Julia was a communist, though she had never joined the Party, and besides she had working-class parents.

'Look at this,' said Ella excitedly, pulling a folded blue paper from her handbag. It was a letter, on cheap writing paper, and it read: 'Dear Dr Allsop. I feel I must write to you in my desperation. I get my rheumatism in my neck and head. You advise other sufferers kindly in your column. Please advise me. My rheumatism began when my husband passed over on the 9th March, 1950, at 3 in the afternoon at the Hospital. Now I am getting frightened, because I am alone in my flat, and what might happen if my rheumatism attacked all over and then I could not move for help. Looking forward to your kind attention, yours faithfully. (Mrs) Dorothy Brown.'

'What did he say?'

'He said he had been engaged to write a medical column, not to run an out-patients for neurotics.'

'I can hear him,' said Julia, who had met Dr West once and recognised him as the enemy at first glance.

'There are hundreds and thousands of people, all over the country, simmering away in misery and no one cares.'

'No one cares a damn,' said Julia. She stubbed out her

172

cigarette and said, apparently giving up her struggle to get Ella to the party, 'I'm going to have my bath.' And she went downstairs with a cheerful clatter, singing.

Ella did not at once move. She was thinking: If I go, I'll have to iron something to wear. She almost got up to examine her clothes, but frowned and thought: If I'm thinking of what to wear, that means that I really want to go? How odd. Perhaps I do want to go? After all, I'm always doing this, saying I won't do something, then I change my mind. The point is, my mind is probably already made up. But which way? I don't change my mind. I suddenly find myself doing something when I've said I wouldn't. Yes. And now I've no idea at all what I've decided.

A few minutes later she was concentrating on her novel, which was half-finished. The theme of this book was a suicide. The death of a young man who had not known he was going to commit suicide until the moment of death, when he understood that he had in fact been preparing for it, and in great detail, for months. The point of the novel would be the contrast between the surface of his life, which was orderly and planned, yet without any long-term objective, and an underlying motif which had reference only to the suicide, which would lead up to the suicide. His plans for his future were all vague and impossible, in contrast with the sharp practicality of his present life. The undercurrent of despair or madness or illogicalness would lead on to, or rather, refer back from, the impossible fantasies of a distant future. So the real continuity of the novel would be in the at first scarcely noticed substratum of despair, the growth of the unknown intention to commit suicide. The moment of death would also be the moment when the real continuity of his life would be understood—a continuity not of order, discipline, practicality, commonsense, but of unreality. It would be understood at the moment of death that the link between the dark need for death, and death, itself, had been the wild, crazy fantasies of a beautiful life; and that the commonsense and the order had been (not as it had seemed earlier in the story) symptoms of sanity, but intimations of madness.

The idea for this novel had come to Ella at a moment

when she found herself getting dressed to go out to dine with people after she had told herself she did not want to go out. She said to herself, rather surprised at the thought: This is precisely how I would commit suicide. I would find myself just about to jump out of an open window or turning on the gas in a small closed-in room, and I would say to myself, without any emotion, but rather with the sense of suddenly understanding something I should have understood long before: Good Lord! So that's what I've been meaning to do. That's been it all the time! And I wonder how many people commit suicide in precisely this way? It is always imagined as some desperate mood, or a moment of crisis. Yet for many it must happen just like that—they find themselves putting their papers in order, writing farewell letters, even ringing up their friends, in a cheerful, friendly way, almost with a feeling of curiosity ... they must find themselves packing newspapers under the door, against window-frames, quite calmly and efficiently, remarking to themselves, quite detached: Well, well! How very interesting. How extraordinary I didn't understand what it was all about before!

Ella found this novel difficult. Not for technical reasons. On the contrary, she could imagine the young man very clearly. She knew how he lived, what all his habits were. It was as if the story were already written somewhere inside herself, and she was transcribing it. The trouble was, she was ashamed of it. She had not told Julia about it. She knew her friend would say something like: 'That's a very negative subject, isn't it?' Or: 'That's not going to point the way forward ...' Or some other judgment from the current communist armoury. Ella used to laugh at Julia for these phrases, yet at the bottom of her heart it seemed that she agreed with her, for she could not see what good it would do anyone to read a novel of this kind. Yet she was writing it. And besides being surprised and ashamed of its subject, she was sometimes frightened. She had even thought: Perhaps I've made a secret decision to commit suicide that I know nothing about? (But she did not believe this to be true.) And she continued to write the novel, making excuses such as: 'Well, there's no need to get it published, I'll just write it for myself.' And in speaking of it to friends, she would joke: 'But everyone I know is writing a novel.' Which was more or less true. In fact her attitude towards this work was the same as someone with a passion for sweet-eating, indulged in solitude, or some other private pastime, like acting out scenes with an invisible alter ego, or carrying on conversation with one's image in the looking-glass.

Ella had taken a dress out of the cupboard and set out the ironing-board, before she said: So, I'm going to the party after all, am I? I wonder at what point I decided that? While she ironed the dress, she continued to think about her novel, or rather to bring into the light a little more of what was already there, waiting, in the darkness. She had put the dress on and was looking at herself in the long glass before she finally left the young man to himself, and concentrated on what she was doing. She was dissatisfied with her appearance. She had never very much liked the dress. She had plenty of clothes in her cupboard, but did not much like any of them. And so it was with her face and hair. Her hair was not right, it never was. And yet she had everything to make her really attractive. She was small, and small-boned. Her features were good, in a small, pointed face. Julia kept saying: 'If you did yourself up properly you'd be like one of those piquant French girls, ever so sexy, you're that type.' Yet Ella always failed. Her dress tonight was a simple black wool which had looked as if it ought to be 'ever so sexy' but it was not. At least, not on Ella. And she wore her hair tied back. She looked pale, almost severe.

'But I don't care about the people I'm going to meet,' she thought, turning away from the glass. 'So it doesn't matter. I'd try harder for a party I really wanted to go to.'

Her son was asleep. She shouted to Julia outside the bathroom door: 'I'm going after all.' To which Julia replied with a calm triumphant chuckle: 'I thought you would.' Ella was slightly annoyed at the triumph, but said: 'I'll be back early.' To which Julia did not reply directly. She said: 'I'll keep my bedroom door open for Michael. Good night.'

To reach Dr West's house meant half an hour on the underground, changing once, and then a short trip by bus.

One reason why Ella was always reluctant to drag herself out of Julia's house was because the city frightened her. To move, mile after mile, through the weight of ugliness that is London in its faceless peripheral wastes made her angry; then the anger ebbed out, leaving fear. At the bus-stop, waiting for her bus, she changed her mind and decided to walk, to punish herself for her cowardice. She would walk the mile to the house, and face what she hated. Ahead of her the street of grey mean little houses crawled endlessly. The grey light of a late summer's evening lowered a damp sky. For miles in all directions, this ugliness, this meanness. This was London— endless streets of such houses. It was hard to bear, the sheer physical weight of the knowledge because—where was the force that could shift the ugliness? And in every street, she thought, people like the woman whose letter was in her handbag. These streets were ruled by fear and ignorance, and ignorance and meanness had built them. This was the city she lived in, and she was part of it, and responsible for it . . . Ella walked fast, alone in the street, hearing her heels ring behind her. She was watching the curtains at the windows. At this end, the street was working-class, one could tell by the curtains, of lace and flowered stuffs. These were the people who wrote in the terrible unanswerable letters she had to deal with. But now things suddenly changed, because the curtains at the windows changed—here was a sheen of peacock blue. It was a painter's house. He had moved into the cheap house and made it beautiful. And other profession- al people had moved in after him. Here were a small knot of people different from the others in the area. They could not communicate with the people further down the street, who could not, and probably would not, enter these houses at all. Here was Dr West's house—he knew the first-comer, the painter, and had bought the house almost opposite. He had said: 'Just in time, the values are rising already.' The garden was untidy. He was a busy doctor with three children and his wife helped him with his practice. No time for gardens. (The gardens further down the street had been mostly well- tended.) From this world, thought Ella, came no letters to the oracles of the women's magazines. The door opened in on the brisk, kindly face of Mrs West. She said: 'So here you are at last,' and took Ella's coat. The hall was pretty and clean and practical—Mrs West's world. She said: 'My husband tells me you've been having another brush with him over his lunatic fringe. It's good of you to take so much trouble over these people.' 'It's my job,' said Ella. 'I'm paid for it.' Mrs West smiled, with a kindly tolerance. She resented Ella. Not because she worked with her husband—no, this was too crude an emotion for Mrs West. Ella had not understood Mrs West's resentment until one day she had used the phrase: You career girls. It was a phrase so discordant, like 'lunatic fringe' and 'these people' that Ella had been unable to reply to it. And now Mrs West had made a point of letting her know that her husband discussed his work with her, establishing wifely rights. In the past, Ella had said to herself: But she's a nice woman, in spite of everything. Now, angry, she said: She's not a nice woman. These people are all dead and damned, with their disinfecting phrases, *lunatic fringe* and *career girls*. I don't like her and I'm not going to pretend I do . . . She followed Mrs West into the living-room, which held faces she knew. The woman for whom she worked at the magazine, for instance. She was also middle-aged, but smart and well-dressed, with bright curling grey hair. She was a professional woman, her appearance part of her job, unlike Mrs West, who was pleasant to look at, but not at all smart. Her name was Patricia Brent, and the name was also part of her profession—Mrs Patricia Brent, editress. Ella went to sit by Patricia, who said: 'Dr West's been telling us you've been quarrelling with him over his letters.' Ella looked swiftly around, and saw people smiling expectantly. The incident had been served up as party fare, and she was expected to play along with it a little, then allow the thing to be dropped. But there must not be any real discussion, or discordance. Ella said smiling: 'Hardly quarrelling.' She added, on a carefully plaintive-humorous note, which was what they were waiting for: 'But it's very depressing, after all, these people you can't do anything for.' She saw she had used the phrase, these people, and was angry and dispirited. I shouldn't have come, she thought. These people (meaning, this time, the Wests and what they stood for) only tolerate you if you're like them.

'Ah, but that's the point,' said Dr West. He said it briskly. He was an altogether brisk, competent man. He added, teasing Ella: 'Unless the whole system's changed of course. Our Ella's a revolutionary without knowing it.' 'I imagined,' said Ella, 'that we all wanted the system changed.' But that was altogether the wrong note. Dr West involuntarily frowned, then smiled. 'But of course we do,' he said. 'And the sooner the better.' The Wests voted for the Labour Party. That Dr West was 'Labour' was a matter of pride to Patricia Brent, who was a Tory. Her tolerance was thus proved. Ella had no politics, but she was also important to Patricia, for the ironical reason that she made no secret of the contempt she felt for the magazine. She shared an office with Patricia. The atmosphere of this office, and all the others connected with the magazine, had the same atmosphere, the atmosphere of the magazine—coy, little-womanish, snobbish. And all the women working there seemed to acquire the same tone, despite themselves, even Patricia herself, who was not at all like this. For Patricia was kind, hearty, direct, full of a battling self-respect. Yet in the office she would say things quite out of character, and Ella, afraid for herself, criticised her for it. Then she went on to say that while they were both in a position where they had to earn their livings, they didn't have to lie to themselves about what they had to do. She had expected, even half-wished, that Patricia would tell her to leave. Instead she had been taken out to an expensive lunch where Patricia defended herself. It turned out that for her this job was a defeat. She had been fashion editress of one of the big smart woman's magazines, but apparently had not been considered up to it. It was a magazine with a fashionable cultural gloss, and it was necessary to have an editress with a nose for what was fashionable in the arts. Patricia had no feeling at all for the cultural band-waggon, which, as far as Ella was concerned, was a point in her favour, but the proprietor of this particular group of woman's magazines had shifted Patricia over to *Women at Home,* which was angled towards working-class women, and had not even a pretence of cultural tone. Patricia was now well-suited for her work, and it was this which secretly chagrined her. She had wistfully enjoyed the atmosphere of the other magazine which had fashionable authors and artists associated with it. She was the daughter of a county family, rich but philistine; her childhood had been well supported by servants, and it was this, an early contact with 'the lower-classes'—she referred to them as such, inside the office, coyly; outside, unself-consciously—that gave her her shrewd direct understanding of what to serve her readers.

Far from giving Ella the sack, she had developed the same wistful respect for her that she had for the glossy magazine she had had to leave. She would casually remark that she had working for her someone who was a 'highbrow'—someone whose stories had been published in the 'highbrow papers.'

And she had a far warmer, more human understanding of the letters which came into the office than Dr West.

She now protected Ella by saying: 'I agree with Ella. Whenever I take a look at her weekly dose of misery, I don't know how she does it. It depresses me so I can't even eat. And believe me, when my appetite goes, things are serious.'

Now everybody laughed, and Ella smiled gratefully at Patricia who nodded, as if to say: 'It's all right, we weren't criticising you.'

Now the talk began again and Ella was free to look around her. The living-room was large. A wall had been broken down. In the other, identical little houses of the street, two minute ground-floor rooms served as kitchen—full of people and used to live in, and parlour, used for company. This room was the entire ground-floor of the house, and a staircase led up to the bedrooms. It was bright, with a good many different colours—sharp blocks of contrasting colour, dark green, and bright pink and yellow. Mrs West had no taste, and the room didn't come off. In five years' time, Ella thought, the houses down the street will have walls in solid bright colours, and curtains and cushions in tune. We are pushing this phase of taste on them—in *Women at Home,* for instance. And this room will be—what?

Whatever is the next thing, I suppose ... but I ought to be more sociable, this is a party, after all ...

Looking around again she saw it was not a party, but an association of people who were there because the Wests had said: 'It's time we asked some people around,' and they had come saying: 'I suppose we've got to go over to the Wests.'

I wish I hadn't come, Ella thought, and there's all that long way back again. At this point a man left his seat across the room and came to sit by her. Her first impression was of a lean young man's face, and a keen, nervously critical smile which, as he talked, introducing himself (his name was Paul Tanner and he was a doctor) had moments of sweetness, as it were against his will, or without his knowledge. She realised she was smiling back, acknowledging these moments of warmth, and so she looked more closely at him. Of course, she had been mistaken, he was not as young as she had thought. His rather rough black hair was thinning at the crown, and his very white, slightly freckled skin was incised sharply around his eyes. These were blue, deep, rather beautiful; eyes both combative and serious, with a gleam in them of uncertainty. A nerve-hung face, she decided, and saw that his body was tensed as he talked, which he did well, but in a self-watchful way. His self-consciousness had her reacting away from him, whereas only a moment ago she had been responding to the unconscious warmth of his smile.

These were her first reactions to the man she was later to love so deeply. Afterwards he would complain, half-bitter, half-humorous: 'You didn't love me at all, to begin with. You should have loved me at first sight. If just once in my life a woman would take one look at me and fall in love, but they never do.' Later still, he would develop the theme, consciously humorous now, because of the emotional language: 'The face is the soul. How can a man trust a woman who falls in love with him only after they have made love? You did not love *me* at all.' And he would maintain a bitter, humorous laugh, while Ella exclaimed: 'How can you separate love-making off from everything else? It doesn't make sense.'

Her attention was going away from him. She was aware

she was beginning to fidget, and that he knew it. Also that he minded: he was attracted to her. His face was too intent on keeping her; she felt that somewhere in all this was pride, a sexual pride which would be offended if she did not respond, and this made her feel a sudden desire to escape. This complex of emotions, all much too sudden and violent for comfort, made Ella think of her husband George. She had married George almost out of exhaustion, after he had courted her violently for a year. She had known she shouldn't marry him. Yet she did; she did not have the will to break with him. Shortly after the marriage she had become sexually repelled by him, a feeling she was unable to control or hide. This redoubled his craving for her, which made her dislike him the more—he even seemed to get some thrill or satisfaction out of her repulsion for him. They were apparently in some hopeless psychological deadlock. Then, to pique her, he had slept with another woman and told her about it. Belatedly she had found the courage to break with him that she lacked before: she took her stand, dishonestly, in desperation, on the fact he had broken faith with her. This was not her moral code, and the fact she was using conventional arguments, repeating endlessly because she was a coward, that he had been unfaithful to her, made her despise herself. The last few weeks with George were a nightmare of self-contempt and hysteria, until at last she left his house, to put an end to it, to put a distance between herself and the man who suffocated her, imprisoned her, apparently took away her will. He then married the woman he had made use of to bring Ella back to him. Much to Ella's relief.

She was in the habit, when depressed, to worry interminably over her behaviour during this marriage. She made many sophisticated psychological remarks about it; she denigrated both herself and him; felt wearied and soiled by the whole experience, and worse, secretly feared that she might be doomed, by some flaw in herself, to some unavoidable repetition of the experience with another man.

But after she had been with Paul Tanner for only a short time, she would say, with the utmost simplicity: 'Of course, I never loved George.' As if there were nothing more to be said about it. And as far as she was concerned, there was nothing more to be said. Nor did it worry her at all that all the complicated psychological attitudes were hardly on the same level as: 'Of course I never loved him,' with its corollary that: 'I love Paul.'

Meanwhile she was restless to get away from him and felt trapped—not by him, by the possibilities of her past resurrecting itself in him.

He said: 'What was the case that sparked off your argument with West?' He was trying to keep her. She said: 'Oh, you're a doctor too, they're all cases, of course.' She had sounded shrill and aggressive, and now she made herself smile and said: 'I'm sorry. But the work worries me more than it should, I suppose.' 'I know,' he said. Dr West would never have said: 'I know,' and instantly Ella warmed to him. The frigidity of her manner, which she was unconscious of, and which she could never lose except with people she knew well, melted away at once. She fished in her handbag for the letter, and saw him smile quizzically at the disorder she revealed. He took the letter, smiling. He sat with it in his hand, unopened, looking at her with appreciation, as if welcoming her, her real self, now open to him. Then he read the letter and again sat holding it, this time opened out. 'What could poor West do? Did you want him to prescribe ointments?' 'No, no, of course not.' 'She's probably been pestering her own doctor three times a week ever since—' he consulted the letter, '—the 9th of March, 1950. The poor man's been prescribing every ointment he can think of.' 'Yes, I know,' she said. 'I've got to answer it tomorrow morning. And about a hundred more.' She held out her hand for the letter. 'What are you going to say to her?' 'What can I say? The thing is, there are thousands and thousands, probably millions of them.' The word millions sounded childish, and she looked intently at him, trying to convey her vision of a sagging, dark weight of ignorance and misery. He handed her the letter and said: 'But what are you going to say?' 'I can't say anything she really needs. Because what she wanted, of course, was for Dr Allsop himself to descend on her, and rescue her, like a knight on a white horse.' 'Of course.'

'That's the trouble. I can't say, Dear Mrs Brown, you haven't got rheumatism, you're lonely and neglected, and you're inventing symptoms to make a claim on the world so that someone will pay attention to you. Well, can I?' 'You can say all that, tactfully. She probably knows it herself. You could tell her to make an effort to meet people, join some organisation, something like that.' 'It's arrogant, me telling her what to do.' 'She's written for help, so it's arrogant not to.' 'Some organisation, you say! But that's not what she wants. She doesn't want something impersonal. She's been married for years and now she feels as if half of herself's torn away.'

At this he regarded her gravely for some moments, and she did not know what he was thinking. At last he said: 'Well, I expect you're right. But you could suggest she write to a marriage bureau.' He laughed at the look of distaste that showed on her face, and went on: 'Yes, but you'd be surprised how many good marriages I've organised myself, through marriage bureaux.'

'You sound like—a sort of psychiatric social worker,' she said, and as soon as the words were out, she knew what the reply would be. Dr West, the sound general practitioner, with no patience for 'frills,' made jokes about his colleague, 'the witch-doctor,' to whom he sent patients in serious mental trouble. This, then, was 'the witch-doctor.'

Paul Tanner was saying, with reluctance: 'That's what I am, in a sense.' She knew the reluctance was because he did not want from her the obvious response. What the response was she knew because she had felt a leap inside herself of relief and interest, an uneasy interest because he was a witch-doctor, possessed of all sorts of knowledge about her. She said quickly: 'Oh, I'm not going to tell you my troubles.' After a pause during which, she knew, he was looking for the words which would discourage her from doing so, he said: 'And I never give advice at parties.'

'Except to widow Brown,' she said.

He smiled, and remarked: 'You're middle-class, aren't you?' It was definitely a judgement. Ella was hurt. 'By origin,' she said. He said: 'I'm working-class, so perhaps I know rather more about widow Brown than you do.'

At this point Patricia Brent came over, and took him away to talk to some member of her staff. Ella realised that they had made an absorbed couple, in a party not designed for couples. Patricia's manner had said that they had drawn attention. So Ella was rather annoyed. Paul did not want to go. He gave her a look that was urgent, and appealing, yet also hard. Yes, thought Ella, a hard look, like a nod of command that she should stay where she was until he was free to come back to her. And she reacted away from him again.

It was time to go home. She had only been at the Wests an hour, but she wanted to get away. Paul Tanner was now sitting between Patricia and a young woman. Ella could not hear what was being said but both the women wore expressions of half-excited, half-furtive interest, which meant they were talking, obliquely or directly, about Dr Tanner's profession, and as it illuminated themselves, while he maintained a courteous but stiff smile. He's not going to get free of them for hours, Ella thought; and she got up and made her excuses to Mrs West, who was annoyed with her for leaving so soon. She nodded at Dr West, whom she would meet tomorrow over a pile of letters, and smiled at Paul, whose blue eyes swung up, very blue and startled, at the news that she was leaving. She went into the hall to put on her coat, and he came out, hurriedly, behind her, offering to take her home. His manner was now off-hand, almost rude, because he had not wanted to be forced into such a public pursuit. Ella said: 'It's probably out of your way.' He said: 'Where do you live?' and when she told him, said firmly it was not out of his way at all. He had a small English car. He drove it fast and well. The London of the car-owner and taxi-user is a very different city from that of the tube and bus-user. Ella was thinking that the miles of grey squalor she had travelled through were now a hazy and luminous city blossoming with lights; and that it had no power to frighten her. Meanwhile, Paul Tanner darted at her sharp enquiring glances and asked brief practical questions about her life. She told him, meaning to challenge his pigeon-holing of her, that she had served throughout the war in a canteen for factory women, and had lived in the same hostel. That after the war she had contracted tuberculosis, but not badly, and had spent six months on her back in a sanatorium. This was the experience that had changed her life, changed her much more deeply than the war years with the factory women. Her mother had died when she was very young, and her father, a silent, hard-bitten man, an ex-army officer from India, had brought her up. 'If you could call it a bringing-up—I was left to myself, and I'm grateful for it,' she said, laughing. And she had been married, briefly and unhappily. To each of these bits of information, Paul Tanner nodded; and Ella saw him sitting behind a desk, nodding at the replies to a patient's answers to questions. 'They say you write novels,' he said, as he slid the car to a standstill outside Julia's house. 'I don't write novels,' she said, annoyed as at an invasion of privacy, and immediately got out of the car. He quickly got out of his side and reached the door at the same time she did. They hesitated. But she wanted to go inside, away from the intentness of his pursuit of her. He said brusquely: 'Will you come for a drive with me tomorrow afternoon?' As an after-thought, he gave a hasty glance at the sky, which was heavily clouded, and said: 'It looks as if it will be fine.' At this she laughed, and out of the good feeling engendered by the laugh, said she would. His face cleared into relief—more, triumph. He's won a kind of victory, she thought, rather chilled. Then, after another hesitation, he shook hands with her, nodded, and went off to his car, saying he would pick her up at two o'clock. She went indoors through the dark hall, up dark stairs, through the silent house. A light showed under Julia's door. It was very early, after all. She called: 'I'm back, Julia,' and Julia's full clear voice said: 'Come in and talk.' Julia had a large comfortable bedroom, and she lay on massed pillows in a large double bed, reading. She wore pyjamas, the sleeves rolled up to the elbows. She looked good-natured, shrewd and very inquisitive. 'Well, how was it?' 'Boring,' said Ella, making this a criticism of Julia for forcing her to go—by her invisible strength of will. 'I was brought home by a psychiatrist,' she added, using the word deliberately, to see appear on Julia's face the look she had felt on her own, and seen on the faces of Patricia and the young woman. When she saw it, she felt ashamed and sorry she had said it—as if she had deliberately committed an act of aggression towards Julia. Which I have, she thought. 'And I don't think I like him,' she added, relapsing into childishness, playing with the scent bottles on Julia's dressing-table. She rubbed scent into the flesh of her wrists, watching Julia's face in the looking-glass, which was now again sceptical, patient and shrewd. She thought: Well, of course Julia's a sort of mother-image, but do I have to play up to it all the time?—And besides, most of the time I feel maternal towards Julia, I have a need to protect her, though I don't know from what. 'Why don't you like him?' enquired Julia. This was serious, and Ella would now have to think seriously. Instead she said: 'Thanks for looking after Michael,' and went upstairs to bed, giving Julia a small, apologetic smile as she went.

Next day sunlight was settled over London, and the trees in the streets seemed not to be part of the weight of the buildings, and of pavements, but an extension of fields and grass and country. Ella's indecision about the drive that afternoon swung into pleasure as she imagined sunshine on grass; and she understood, from the sudden flight upwards of her spirits, that she must recently have been more depressed than she had realised. She found herself singing as she cooked the child's lunch. It was because she was remembering Paul's voice. At the time she had not been conscious of Paul's voice, but now she heard it—a warm voice, a little rough where the edges of an uneducated accent remained. (She was listening, as she thought of him, rather than looking at him.) And she was listening, not to the words he had used, but to tones in which she was now distinguishing delicacy, irony, and compassion.

Julia was taking Michael off for the afternoon to visit friends, and she left early, as soon as lunch was over, so that the little boy would not know his mother was going for a drive without him. 'You look very pleased with yourself, after all,' said Julia. Ella said: 'Well, I haven't been out of

London for months. Besides, this business of not having a man around doesn't suit me.' 'Who does it suit?' retorted Julia. 'But I don't think any man is better than none.' And having planted this small dart, she departed with the child, in good humour.

Paul was late, and from the way he apologised, almost perfunctorily, she understood he was a man often late, and from temperament, not only because he was a busy doctor with many pressures on him. On the whole she was pleased he was late. One look at his face, that again had the cloud of nervous irritability settled on it, reminded her that last night she had not liked him. Besides, being late meant that he didn't really care for her, and that eased a small tension of panic that related to George, and not to Paul. (She knew this herself.) But as soon as they were in the car and heading out of London, she was aware that he was again sending small nervous glances towards her; she felt determination in him. But he was talking and she was listening to his voice, and it was every bit as pleasant as she remembered it. She listened, and looked out of the window, and laughed. He was telling how he came to be late. Some misunderstanding between himself and the group of doctors he worked with at his hospital, 'No one actually said anything aloud, but the upper-middle-classes communicate with each other in inaudible squeaks, like bats. It puts people of my background at a terrible disadvantage.' 'You're the only working-class doctor there?' 'No, not in the hospital, just in that section. And they never let you forget it. They're not even conscious of doing it.' This was good-humoured, humorous. It was also bitter. But the bitterness was from old habit, and had no sting in it.

This afternoon it was easy to talk, as if the barrier between them had been silently dissolved in the night. They left the ugly trailing fringes of London behind, sunlight lay about them, and Ella's spirits rose so sharply that she felt intoxicated. Besides, she knew that this man would be her lover, she knew it from the pleasure his voice gave her, and she was full of a secret delight. His glances at her now were smiling, almost indulgent, and like Julia he remarked: 'You look very pleased with yourself.' 'Yes, it's getting out of

187

London.' 'You hate it so much?' 'Oh, no, I like it, I mean, I like the way I live in it. But I hate—this.' And she pointed out of the window. The hedges and trees had again been swallowed by a small village. Nothing left here of the old England, it was new and ugly. They drove through the main shopping street, and the names on the shops were the same as they had driven past repeatedly, all the way out of London.

'Why?'

'Well, obviously, it's so ugly.' He was looking curiously into her face. After a while he remarked: 'People live in it.' She shrugged. 'Do you hate them as well?' Ella felt resentful: it occurred to her that for years, anyone she was likely to meet would have understood without explanation why she hated 'all this'; and to ask her if she 'hated them as well,' meaning ordinary people, was off the point. Yet after thinking it over, she said, defiant: 'In a way, yes. I hate what they put up with. It ought to be swept away—all of it.' And she made a wide sweeping movement with her hand, brushing away the great dark weight of London, and the thousand ugly towns, and the myriad small cramped lives of England.

'But it's not going to be, you know,' he said, with a small smiling obstinacy. 'It's going to go on—and there'll be more chain shops, and television aerials, and respectable people. That's what you mean, isn't it?'

'Of course. But you just accept it. Why do you take it all for granted?'

'It's the time we live in. And things are better than they were.'

'Better!' she exclaimed, involuntarily, but checked herself. For she understood she was setting against the word *better* a personal vision that dated from her stay in hospital, a vision of some dark, impersonal destructive force that worked at the roots of life and that expressed itself in war and cruelty and violence. Which had nothing to do with what they argued. 'You mean,' she said, 'better in the sense of no unemployment and no one being hungry?'

'Strangely enough, yes, that's what I do mean.' He said it in such a way that it put a barrier between them—he was from the working-people, and she was not, and he was of the initiated. So she kept silence until he insisted: 'Things are much better, much much better. How can you not see it? I remember . . .' And he stopped—this time, not because (as Ella put it) he was 'bullying' her, from superior knowledge, but from the painfulness of what he remembered.

So she tried again: 'I can't understand how anyone can see what's happening to this country and not hate it. On the surface everything's fine—all quiet and tame and suburban. But underneath it's poisonous. It's full of hatred and envy and people being lonely.'

'That's true of everything, everywhere. It's true of any place that has reached a certain standard of living.'

'That doesn't make it any better.'

'Anything's better than a certain kind of fear.'

'You mean, real poverty. And you mean, of course, that I'm not equipped to understand that at all.'

At this he glanced at her quickly, in surprise at her persistence—and, as Ella felt, out of a certain respect for it. There was no trace in that glance of a man assessing a woman for her sexual potentialities, and she felt more at ease.

'So you'd like to put a giant bulldozer over it all, over all England?'

'Yes.'

'Leaving just a few cathedrals and old buildings and a pretty village or two?' 'Yes.' 'And then you'd bring the people back into fine new cities, each one an architect's dream, and tell everyone to like it or lump it.' 'Yes.' 'Or perhaps you'd like a merrie England, beer, skittles, and the girls in long homespun dresses?'

She said, angry: 'Of course not! I hate all the William Morris stuff. But you're being dishonest. Look at you—I'm sure you've spent most of your energy simply getting through the class barrier. There can't be any connection at all between how you live now and the way your parents lived. You must be a stranger to them. You must be split into two parts. That's what this country is like. You know it is. Well I hate it, I hate all that. I hate a country so split up that—I didn't

189

know anything about it until the war and I lived with all those women.'

'*Well*,' he said at last, 'they were right last night—you're a revolutionary after all.'

'No, I'm not. Those words don't mean anything to me. I'm not interested in politics at all.'

At which he laughed, but said, with an affection that touched her: 'If you had your way, building the new Jerusalem, it would be like killing a plant by suddenly moving it into the wrong soil. There's a continuity, some kind of invisible logic to what happens. You'd kill the spirit of people if you had your way.'

'A continuity isn't necessarily right, just because it's a continuity.'

'Yes, Ella, it is. It is. Believe me, it is.'

This was so personal, that it was her turn to glance, surprised, at him, and decide to say nothing. He is saying, she thought, that the split in himself is so painful that sometimes he wonders if it was worth it . . . and she turned away to look out of the window again. They were passing through another village. This was better than the last: there was an old centre, of mellow rooted houses, warm in the sunshine. But around the centre, ugly new houses and even in the main square, a Woolworth's, indistinguishable from all the others, and a fake Tudor pub. There would be a string of such villages, one after another. Ella said: 'Let's get away from the villages, where there isn't anything at all.'

This time his look at her, which she noted, but did not understand until afterwards, was frankly startled. He did not say anything for a time, but when a small road appeared, wandering off through deep sun-lit trees, he turned off into it. He asked: 'Where's your father living?'

'Oh,' she said, 'I see what you're getting at. Well he's not like that at all.'

'Like what? I didn't say anything.'

'No, but you imply it all the time. He's ex-Indian army. But he isn't like the caricatures. He got unfit for the army and was in the administration for a time. And he's not like that either.'

'So what is he like?'

She laughed. The sound held affection which was spontaneous and genuine, and a bitterness which she did not know was there. 'He bought an old house when he left India. It's in Cornwall. It's small and isolated. It's very pretty. Old—you know. He's an isolated man, he always has been. He reads a lot. He knows a lot about philosophy and religion—like Buddha, for instance.'

'Does he like you?'

'*Like* me?' The question was startling to Ella. Not once had she asked herself whether her father liked her. She turned to Paul in a flash of recognition, laughing: 'What a question. But you know, I don't know?' And added, in a small voice: 'No, come to think of it, and I never have, I don't believe he does, not really.'

'Of course he does,' said Paul over-hastily, clearly regretting he had asked.

'There's no of course about it,' and Ella sat silent, thinking. She knew that Paul's glances at her were guilty and affectionate, and she liked him very much for his concern for her.

She tried to explain: 'When I go home for week-ends, he's pleased to see me—I can see that. He never complains that I don't go more often though. But when I'm there it doesn't seem to make any difference to him. He has a routine. An old woman does the house. The meals are just so. He has a few things to eat he always has, like red beef and steak and eggs. He drinks one gin before lunch, and two or three whiskys after dinner. He goes for a long walk every morning after breakfast. He gardens in the afternoon. He reads every night until very late. When I'm there, it's all just the same. He doesn't even talk to me.' She laughed again. 'It's what you said earlier—I'm not on the wavelength, he has one very close friend, a colonel, and they look alike, both lean and leathery with fierce eyebrows, and they communicate in high, inaudible squeaks. They sometimes sit opposite each other for hours and never say a word, just drink whisky, or they sometimes make short references to India. And when my father is alone, I think he communicates with God or Buddha or somebody. But not with me. Usually if I say something, he sounds embarrassed, or talks about something else.' Ella fell silent thinking that was the longest speech she had made to him, and it was odd it should be so, since she seldom spoke of her father, or even thought of him. Paul did not take it up, but instead asked abruptly: 'How's this?' The rough track had come to an end in a small hedged-in field. 'Oh,' said Ella. 'Yes. This morning I was hoping you'd take me to a small field, just like this.' She got quickly out of the car, just conscious of his startled glance; but she did not remember it until later, when she was searching her memory to find out how he had felt about her that day.

She wandered for a time through the grasses, fingering them, smelling them, and letting the sun fall on her face. When she drifted back to him, he had spread a rug on the grass and was sitting on it, waiting. His look of waiting destroyed the ease that had been created in her by the small freedom of the sun-lit field, and set up a tension. She thought, as she flung herself down, he's set on something, good Lord, is he going to make love to me so soon? Oh, no, he wouldn't, not yet. All the same, she lay near him, and was happy, and was content to let things take their course.

Later—and not so much later, he would say, teasing her, that she had brought him here because she had decided she wanted him to make love to her, that she had planned it. And she always got furiously indignant, and then as he persisted, set cold towards him. And then she would forget it. And then he came back to it, and because she knew it was important to him, the little recurring wrangle left a poisoned spot which spread. It was not true. In the car she had known he would be her lover, because of the quality of his voice, which she trusted. But at some time, it didn't matter when. He would know the right time, she felt. And so if the right time was then, that first afternoon alone, it must be right. 'And what do you suppose I would have done if you hadn't made love to me?' she would ask, later, curious and hostile. 'You'd have been bad-tempered,' he replied, laughing but with a curious undertone of regret. And the regret, which was genuine, drew her to him, as if they were fellow-victims of some cruelty in life neither could help.

'But you arranged it all,' she would say. 'You even brought out a rug for the purpose. I suppose you always take a rug in the car for afternoon jaunts, just in case.'

'Of course, nothing like a nice warm rug on the grass.'

At which she would laugh. And later still she would think, chilled: 'I suppose he had taken other women to that field, it was probably just a habit of his.'

Yet at the time she was perfectly happy. The weight of the city was off her, and the scent of the grasses and the sun delicious. Then she became aware of his half-ironical smile and sat up, on the defensive. He began to talk, consciously ironical, about her husband. She told him what he wanted to know, briefly, since she had offered the facts last night. And then she told him, also briefly, about the child; but this time she was cursory because she felt guilty because she was here, in the sun, and Michael would have enjoyed the drive and the warm field.

She understood that Paul had said something about his wife. It took some moments for this to sink in. He also said he had two children. She felt a shock, but did not let it disturb her confidence in the moment. The way he spoke of his wife, which was hurried and almost irritable, told Ella he did not love her. She was using the word 'love' already, and with a naivety quite foreign to her normal way of analysing relationships. She even imagined he must be separated from his wife, if he could speak of her so casually.

He made love to her. Ella thought, 'Well he's right, it is the right moment, here, where it's beautiful.' Her body held too many memories of her husband for her to lack tensions. But soon she gave herself up, and in confidence, because their bodies understood each other. (But it was only later, she would use a phrase like 'our bodies understood each other.' At the time, she was thinking: *We* understand each other.) Yet once, opening her eyes, she saw his face, and it held a hard, almost ugly look. And she shut her eyes not to see it, and was happy in the movements of love. Afterwards, she saw his face turned away, and the hard look again. She

193

instinctively moved away from him, but his hand on her belly held her down. He said, half-teasing: 'You're much too thin.' She laughed, without hurt, because the way his hand lay on her flesh told her he liked her as she was. And she liked herself, naked. It was a frail, slight body, with sharp edges to the shoulders and the knees, but her breasts and stomach glistened white, and her small feet were delicate and white. Often she had wanted to be different, had longed to be larger, fuller, rounder, 'more of a woman,' but the way his hand touched her cancelled all that and she was happy. He kept his hand's soft pressure on her vulnerable stomach for some moments, then suddenly withdrew it and began to dress. She, feeling abandoned, began to dress also. She was suddenly unaccountably close to tears, and her body again seemed too thin and light. He asked: 'How long since you slept with a man?'

She was confused, wondering: George, he means? But he didn't count, I didn't love him. I hated him touching me. 'I don't know,' she said, and as she spoke understood he meant that she had slept with him out of hunger. Her face began to burn and she got quickly up off the rug, turning her face away, and then said, in a voice which sounded ugly to herself: 'Not since last week. I picked up a man at a party and brought him home with me.' She was looking for words from her memories of the girls at the canteen, during the war. She found them, and said: 'A nice piece of flesh, he was.' She got into the car, slamming the door. He threw the rug into the back of the car, got hastily in, and began the business of reversing the car back and forth so as to get it facing out of the field.

'You make a habit of it, then?' he enquired. His voice was sober, detached. She thought that whereas a moment ago he was asking on his own account, as a man; now he was again talking 'like a man behind a desk.' She was thinking that she only wanted the drive home to be over so that she could go home and cry. The love-making was now linked in her mind with memories of her husband, and the shrinking of her body from George's, because she was shrinking away in spirit from this new man.

'Do you make a habit of it?' he asked again.

'Of what?' She laughed. 'Oh, I see.' And she looked at him incredulously, as if he were mad. At the moment he seemed to her slightly mad, his face tense with suspicion. He was not at all, now, the 'man behind a desk,' but a man hostile to her. Now she was quite set against him, and she laughed angrily, and said: 'You're very stupid after all.'

They did not speak again until they reached the main road, and joined the stream of traffic slowly congealed along the way back to the city. Then he remarked, in a different voice, companionable, a peace-offering: 'I'm not in a position to criticise, after all. My love life could hardly be described as exemplary.'

'I hope you found me a satisfactory diversion.'

He looked puzzled. He seemed stupid to her because he was not understanding. She could see him framing words and then discarding them. And so she gave him no chance to talk. She felt as if she had been dealt, deliberately, one after the other, blows which were aimed at some place just below her breasts. She was almost gasping at the pain of these blows. Her lips were trembling, but she would rather have died than cry in front of him. She turned her face aside, watching a country-side now falling into shadow and cold, and began to talk herself. She could, when she set herself to it, be hard, malicious, amusing. She entertained him with sophisticated gossip about the magazine office, the affairs of Patricia Brent, etc. etc., while she despised him for accepting this counterfeit of herself. She talked on and on, while he was silent; and when they reached Julia's house, she got fast out of the car, and was in the doorway before he could follow her. She was fumbling with the key in the lock when he came up behind her and said: 'Would your friend Julia put your son to bed tonight? We could go to a play if you'd like it. No, a film, it's Sunday.' She positively gasped with surprise: 'But I'm not going to see you again, surely you don't expect me to?'

He took her shoulders with his hands from behind and said: 'But, why not? You liked me, it's no good pretending you didn't.' To this, Ella had no answer, it was not her language. And she could not remember, now, how happy she had been with him in the field. She said: 'I'm not seeing you again.'

'Why not?'

She furiously wriggled her shoulders free, put the key in the door, turned it, and said: 'I haven't slept with anyone at all for a long time. Not since an affair I had for a week, two years ago. It was a lovely affair . . .' She saw him wince and felt pleasure because she was hurting him, and because she was lying, it had not been a lovely affair. But, telling the truth now, and accusing him with every atom of her flesh, she said: 'He was an American. He never made me feel bad, not once. He wasn't at all good in bed, I'm sure that's one of your phrases, isn't it? But he didn't despise me.'

'Why are you telling me this?'

'You're so stupid,' she said, in a gay scornful voice. And she felt a hard bitter gaiety rise in her, destructive of him and of herself. 'You talk about my husband. Well what's he got to do with it? As far as I'm concerned I never slept with him at all . . .' He laughed, incredulously and bitterly, but she went on: 'I hated sleeping with him. It didn't count. And you say, how long is it since you slept with another man? Surely it's all perfectly simple. You're a psychiatrist, you say, a soul-doctor, and you don't understand the simplest things about anyone.'

With which she went into Julia's house, and shut the door, and put her face to the wall and began to cry. From the feeling of the house she knew it was still empty. The bell rang, almost in her ear: Paul trying to make her open the door. But she left the sound of the bell behind, and went up through the dark well of the house to the bright little flat at the top, slowly, crying. And now the telephone rang. She knew it was Paul, in the telephone box across the street. She let it ring, because she was crying. It stopped and started again. She looked at the compact, impersonal black curves of the instrument and hated it; she swallowed her tears, steadied her voice and answered. It was Julia. Julia said she wanted to stay to supper with her friends; she would bring the child home with her later and put him to bed, and if Ella wanted to go out she could. 'What's the matter with you?' came Julia's voice, full and calm as usual, across two miles of streets. 'I'm crying.' 'I can hear you are, what for?' 'Oh, these bloody men, I hate them all.' 'Oh well, if it's like that, but better go off to the pictures then, it'll cheer you up.' Immediately Ella felt better, the incident was less important, and she laughed.

When the telephone rang half-an-hour later, she answered it, not thinking of Paul. But it was he. He had waited in his car, he said, to telephone again. He wanted to talk to her. 'I don't see what we'll achieve by it,' said Ella, sounding cool and humorous. And he, sounding humorous and quizzical, said: 'Come to the pictures, and we won't talk.' So she went. She met him with ease. This was because she had told herself she would not make love with him again. It was all finished. Her going out with him was because it seemed melodramatic not to. And because his voice on the telephone had no connection at all with the hardness of his face above her in the field. And because they now would return to their relationship in the car driving away from London. His attitude to having had her in the field had simply cancelled it out. It hadn't happened, if that was the way he felt about it!

Later he would say: 'When I telephoned you, after you had flounced indoors—you just came, you just needed persuading.' And he laughed. She hated the tone of the laugh. At such moments he would put on a rueful, and self-consciously rueful, rake's smile, playing the part of a rake so that he could laugh at himself. Yet he was having it both ways, Ella felt, for his complaint was genuine. And so at such moments she would first smile with him, at his parody of the rake; and then quickly change the subject. It was as if he had a personality at these moments not his. She was convinced it was not his. It was on a level that not only had nothing to do with the simplicity and ease of their being together; but betrayed it so completely that she had no alternative but to ignore it. Otherwise she would have had to break with him.

They did not go to the pictures, but to a coffee bar. Again he told stories about his work at the hospital. He had two posts, at two different hospitals. At one he was a consultant psychiatrist. At the other he was doing a reorganising job. As he put it: 'I'm trying to change a snake-pit into something more civilised. And who do I have to fight? The public? Not at all, it's the old-fashioned doctors . . .' His stories had two themes. One the stuffed-shirt pomposity of the middle level of the medical establishment. Ella realised that all his criticisms were from the simplest class viewpoint; implicit in what he said, though he didn't say it, was that stupidity and lack of imagination were middle-class characteristics, and that his attitude, progressive and liberating, was because he was working-class. Which of course was how Julia talked; and how Ella herself criticised Dr West. And yet several times she found herself stiffening in resentment, as if it were she who was being criticised; and when this happened she fell back on her memories of the years in the canteen, and thought that if she had not had that experience she would not be able now to see the upper class of this country, from beneath, through the eyes of the factory girls, like so many bizarre fish viewed through the glass bottom of an aquarium. Paul's second theme was the reverse side of the first, and marked by a change of his whole personality when he touched on it. Telling his critical stories he was full of a delighted malicious irony. But talking of his patients he was serious. His attitude was the same as hers to the 'Mrs Browns' —they were already referring to her petitioners in this collective way. He spoke of them with an extraordinary delicacy of kindness, and with an angry compassion. The anger was for their helplessness.

She liked him so much now that for her it was as if the episode in the field had not happened. He took her home and came into the hall after her, still talking. They went up the stairs, and Ella was thinking: I suppose we'll have some coffee and then he'll go. She was quite genuine in this. And yet, when he again made love to her, she again thought: Yes, it's right, because we've been so close together all evening. Afterwards, when he complained: 'Of course you knew I'd make love to you again,' she would reply: 'Of course I didn't. And if you hadn't it wouldn't have mattered.' At which he would either reply: 'Oh, what a hypocrite!' Or: 'Then you've no right to be so unconscious of your motives.'

Being with Paul Tanner, that night, was the deepest experience Ella had with a man; so different from anything she had known before that everything in the past became irrelevant. This feeling was so final, that when, towards early morning, Paul asked: 'What does Julia think about this sort of thing?' Ella replied vaguely: 'What sort of thing?'

'Last week, for instance. You said you brought a man home from a party.'

'You're mad,' she said, laughing comfortably. They lay in the dark. She turned her head to see his face; a dark line of cheek showed against the light from the window; there was something remote and lonely about it, and she thought: He's got into the same mood he was in earlier. But this time it did not disturb her, for the simplicity of the warm touch of his thigh against hers made the remoteness of his face irrelevant.

'But what does Julia say?'

'What about?'

'What will she say in the morning?'

'Why should she say anything at all?'

'I see,' he said briefly; and got up and added: 'I'll have to go home and shave and get a clean shirt.'

That week he came to her every night, late, when Michael was asleep. And he left early every morning, to 'pick up a clean shirt.'

Ella was completely happy. She drifted along on a soft tide of not-thinking. When Paul made a remark from 'his negative personality,' she was so sure of her emotions that she replied: 'Oh, you're so stupid, I told you, you don't understand anything.' (The word negative was Julia's, used after a glimpse of Paul on the stairs: 'There's something bitter and negative about that face.') She was thinking that soon he would marry her. Or perhaps not soon. It would be at the right time, and he would know when that was. His marriage must be no marriage at all, if he could stay with her, night after night, going home at dawn, 'for a clean shirt.'

On the following Sunday, a week after their first excursion

into the country, Julia again took the little boy off to friends, and this time Paul took Ella to Kew. They lay on the grass behind a hedge of sheltering rhododendrons, trees above them, the sun sifting over them. They held hands. 'You see,' said Paul, with his small rake's grimace, 'we're like an old married couple already—we know we're going to make love in bed tonight, so now we just hold hands.'

'But what's the matter with it?' asked Ella, amused.

He was leaning over, looking into her face. She smiled up at him. She knew that he loved her. She felt a perfect trust in him. 'What's the matter with it?' he said with a sort of humorous desperation. 'It's terrible. Here you and I are . . .' *How* they were was reflected in his face and eyes, which were warm on her face—'and look what it would be like if we were married.' Ella felt herself go cold. She thought, Surely he's not saying that as a man does, warning a woman? He's not so cheap, surely? She saw an old bitterness on his face, and thought: No, he's not, thank God, he's carrying on some conversation with himself. And the light inside her was relit. She said: 'But you aren't married at all. You can't call that being married. You never see her.'

'We got married when we were both twenty. There should be a law against it,' he added, with the same desperate humour, kissing her. He said, with his mouth on her throat: 'You're very wise not to get married, Ella. Be sensible and stay that way.'

Ella smiled. She was thinking: And so I was wrong after all. That's exactly what he's doing, saying: You can expect just so much from me. She felt completely rejected. And he still lay with his hands on her arms, and she could feel the warmth of them right through her body, and his eyes, warm and full of love for her, were a few inches above hers. He was smiling.

That night in bed, making love to him was a mechanical thing, she went through the motions of response. It was a different experience from the other nights. It seemed he did not know it; and they lay afterwards as usual close in each other's arms. She was chilled and full of dismay.

The day after she had a conversation with Julia, who had

been silent all this time about Paul's staying the nights. 'He's married,' she said. 'He's been married thirteen years. It's a marriage so that it doesn't matter if he doesn't go home at nights. Two children.' Julia made a non-committal grimace and waited. 'The thing is, I'm not sure at all . . . and there's Michael.'

'What's his attitude to Michael?'

'He's only seen him once, for a moment. He comes in late—well you know that. And he's gone by the time Michael wakes up. To pick up a clean shirt from home.' At which Julia laughed, and Ella laughed with her.

'An extraordinary woman she must be,' said Julia. 'Does he talk about her?'

'He said, they got married too young. And then he went off to the wars, and when he came back, he felt a stranger to her. And as far as I can make out, he's done nothing but have love affairs ever since.'

'It doesn't sound too good,' said Julia. 'What do you feel for him?' At the moment, Ella felt nothing but a cold hurt despair. For the life of her she could not reconcile their happiness and what she called his cynicism. She was in something like a panic. Julia was examining her, shrewdly. 'I thought, the first time I saw him, he's got such a tight miserable face.' 'He's not at all miserable,' said Ella quickly. Then, seeing her instinctive and unreasoning defence of him, she laughed at herself and said: 'I mean, yes, there is that in him, a sort of bitterness. But there's his work and he likes it. He rushes from hospital to hospital, and tells marvellous stories about it all, and then the way he talks about his patients—he really cares. And then with me, at night, and he never seems to need to sleep.' Ella blushed, conscious that she was boasting. 'Well, it's true,' she said, watching Julia's smile. 'And then off he rushes in the morning, after practically no sleep, to pick up a shirt and presumably have a nice little chat with his wife about this and that. Energy. Energy is not being miserable. Or even bitter, if it comes to that. The two things aren't connected.'

'Oh, well,' said Julia. 'In that case you'd better wait and see what happens, hadn't you?'

That night Paul was humorous and very tender. It's as if he's apologising, Ella thought. Her pain melted. In the morning she found herself restored to happiness. He said, as he dressed: 'I can't see you tonight, Ella.' She said, without fear: 'Well, that's all right.' But he went on, laughing: 'After all, I've got to see my children sometime.' It sounded as if he were accusing her of having deliberately kept him from them. 'But I haven't stopped you,' said Ella. 'Oh, yes you have, you have,' he said, half-singing it. He kissed her lightly, laughing, on the forehead. That's how he kissed his other women, she thought, when he left them for good. Yes. He didn't care about them, and he laughed and kissed them on the forehead. And suddenly a picture came into her mind, at which she stared, astonished. She saw him putting money on to a mantelpiece. But he was not—that she knew, the sort of man who would pay a woman. Yet she could see him, clearly, putting money on a mantelpiece. Yes. It was somewhere implicit in his attitude. And to her, Ella, but what's that got to do with all these hours we've been together, when every look and move he's made told me he loved me? (For the fact that Paul had told her, again and again, that he loved her, meant nothing, or rather would have meant nothing if it had not been confirmed by how he touched her, and the warmth of his voice.) And now, leaving, he remarked, with his small bitter grimace: 'And so you'll be free tonight, Ella.' 'What do you mean, free?' 'Oh ... for your other boy-friends; you've been neglecting them, haven't you?'

She went to the office, after leaving the child at his nursery school, feeling as if cold had got into her bones, into her backbone. She was shivering slightly. Yet it was a warm day. For some days she had not been in connection with Patricia, she had been too absorbed in her happiness. Now she easily came close to the older woman again. Patricia had been married for eleven years; and her husband had left her for a younger woman. Her attitude towards men was a gallant, good-natured, wisecracking cynicism. This jarred on Ella; it was something foreign to her. Patricia was in her fifties, lived alone, and had a grown-up daughter. She was, Ella knew, a courageous woman. But Ella did not like to think too closely about Patricia; to identify with her, even in sympathy, meant she might be cutting off some possibility for herself. Or so she felt. Today Patricia made some dry comment about a male colleague who was separating from his wife, and Ella snapped at her. Later she came back into the room, and apologised, for Patricia was hurt. Ella always felt at a disadvantage with the older woman. She did not care for her as much as she knew Patricia did for her. She knew she was some sort of symbol for Patricia, a symbol perhaps of her own youth? (But Ella would not think about that, it was dangerous.) Now she made a point of staying with Patricia and talking and making jokes, and saw, with dismay, tears in her employer's eyes. She saw, very sharply, a plump, kindly, smart, middle-aged woman, with clothes from the fashion magazines that were like a uniform, and her gallant mop of tinted greying curls; and her eyes—hard for her work, and soft for Ella. While she was with Patricia, she was telephoned by the editor of one of the magazines that had published a story of hers. He asked if she were free to lunch. She said she was, listening in her mind to the word *free*. For the last ten days she had not felt free. Now she felt, not free, but disconnected, or as if she floated on someone else's will— Paul's. This editor had wanted to sleep with her, and Ella had rejected him. Now she thought that very likely she would sleep with him. Why not? What difference did it all make? This editor was an intelligent, attractive man, but the idea of his touching her repelled her. He had not one spark of that instinctive warmth for a woman, liking for a woman, which was what she felt in Paul. And that was why she would sleep with him; she could not possibly have let a man touch her now, whom she found attractive. But it seemed Paul did not care one way or the other; he made jokes about the 'man she had taken home from the party,' almost as if he liked her for it. Very well, then; very well—if that's what he wanted, she didn't care at all. And she took herself off to lunch, carefully made-up, in a mood of sick defiance of the whole world.

The lunch was as usual—expensive; and she liked good food. He was amusing; and she liked his talk. She was eased into her usual intellectual rapport with him, and meanwhile

203

watched him and thought it was inconceivable that she could make love with him. Yet why not? She liked him, didn't she? Well then? And love? But love was a mirage, and the property of the women's magazines; one certainly couldn't use the word love in connection with a man who didn't care whether one slept with other men or not. But if I'm going to sleep with this man, I'd better do something about it. She did not know how to; she had rejected him so often he took the rejection for granted. When lunch was over, and they were on the pavement, Ella was suddenly released: what nonsense, of course she wasn't going to sleep with him, now she would go back to the office and that would be that. Then she saw a couple of prostitutes in a doorway, and she remembered her picture of Paul that morning; and when the editor said: 'Ella, I do so wish that . . .' she interrupted with a smile and said: 'Then take me home. No, to your place, not to mine.' For she could not have borne to have any man but Paul in her own bed now. This man was married, and he took her to his bachelor flat. His home was in the country, he was careful to keep his wife and children there, and he used this flat for adventures like these. All the time she was naked with this man, Ella was thinking of Paul. He must be mad. What am I doing with a madman? He really imagines I could sleep with another man when I'm with him? He can't possibly believe it. Meanwhile, she was being as nice as she could be to this intelligent comrade of her intellectual lunches. He was having difficulties, and Ella knew this was because she did not really want him, and so it was her fault, though he was blaming himself. And so she set herself to please, thinking there was no reason for him to feel bad, simply because she was committing the crime of sleeping with a man she did not care tuppence for . . . and when it was all over, she simply discounted the whole incident. It had meant nothing at all. She was left, however, vulnerable, quivering with the need to cry, and desperately unhappy. She was yearning, in fact, towards Paul. Who rang her next day to say that he couldn't come that night either. And now Ella's need for Paul was so great that she told herself it didn't matter in the slightest, of course he had to work, or to go home to his children.

The next evening they met full of defences on either side. A few minutes later they had all vanished, and they were together again. Some time that night he remarked: 'Odd isn't it, it really is true that if you love a woman sleeping with another woman means nothing.' At the time she did not hear this—somewhere in her a mechanism had started to work which would prevent her hearing him when he made remarks that might make her unhappy. But she heard it next day, the words suddenly came back into her mind and she listened to them. So during those two nights he had been experimenting with someone else, and had had the same experience as she. So now she was full of confidence again, and of trust in him. Then he began to question her about what she had done during those two days. She said she had had lunch with an editor who had published one of her stories. 'I've read one of your stories. It was rather good.' He said this with pain, as if he had rather the story were bad. 'Well, why shouldn't it be good?' she asked. 'I suppose that was your husband, George?' 'Partly, not altogether.' 'And this editor?' For a moment she thought of saying: 'I've had the same experience you've had.' Then she thought: If he's capable of being upset by things that never happened, what would he say if I told him I did sleep with that man? Though I didn't, it didn't count, it was not the same thing at all.

Afterwards Ella judged that their 'being together' (she never used the word affair) started from that moment—when they had both tested their responses to other people and found that what they felt for each other made other people irrelevant. That was the only time she was to be unfaithful to Paul, though she did not feel it mattered. Yet she was miserable she had done it because it became a sort of crystallisation of all his later accusations of her. After that he came to her nearly every night, and when he could not come she knew it was not because he did not want to. He would come in late, because of his work, and because of the child. He helped her with her letters from 'Mrs Brown,' and this was a very great pleasure to her, working together over these people for whom she could sometimes do something.

205

She did not think of his wife at all. At least, not at the beginning.

Her only worry, at the beginning, was Michael. The little boy had loved his own father, now married again and living in America. It was natural for the child to turn with affection to this new man. But Paul would stiffen when Michael put his arms around him, or when he rushed at him in welcome. Ella watched how he instinctively stiffened, half-laughed, and then his mind (the mind of the soul-doctor, considering how best to deal with the situation) started to work. He would gently put down Michael's arms, and talk to him gently, as if he were grown-up. And Michael responded. It hurt Ella to see how the little boy, denied this masculine affection, would respond by being grown-up, serious, answering serious questions. A spontaneity of affection had been cut off in him. He kept it for her, warm and responsive in touch and in speech, but for Paul, for the men's world, he had a responsible, calm, thoughtful response. Sometimes Ella panicked a little: I'm doing Michael harm, he is going to be harmed. He'll never again have a natural warm response to a man. And then she would think: But I don't really believe it. It must be good for him that I'm happy, it must be good for him that I'm a real woman at last. And so Ella did not worry for long, her instincts told her not to. She let herself go into Paul's love for her, and did not think. Whenever she found herself looking at this relationship from the outside, as other people might see it, she felt frightened and cynical. So she did not. She lived from day to day, and did not look ahead.

•   •

Five years.

If I were to write this novel, the main theme, or motif, would be buried, at first, and only slowly take over. The motif of Paul's wife—the third. At first Ella does not think about her. Then she has to make a conscious effort not to think about her. This is when she knows her attitude towards this unknown woman is despicable: she feels triumph over her, pleasure that she has taken Paul from her. When Ella first becomes conscious of this emotion she is so appalled and ashamed that she buries it, fast. Yet the shadow of the third grows again, and it becomes impossible for Ella not to think. She thinks a great deal about the invisible woman to whom Paul returns (and to whom he will always return), and it is now not out of triumph, but envy. She envies her. She slowly, involuntarily, builds up a picture in her mind of a serene, calm, unjealous, unenvious, undemanding woman, full of resources of happiness inside herself, self-sufficient, yet always ready to give happiness when it is asked for. It occurs to Ella (but much later, about three years on) that this is a remarkable image to have developed, since it does not correspond to anything at all Paul says about his wife. So where does the picture come from? Slowly Ella understands that this is what she would like to be herself, this imagined woman is her own shadow, everything she is not. Because by now she knows, and is frightened of, her utter dependence on Paul. Every fibre of herself is woven with him, and she cannot imagine living without him. The mere idea of being without him causes a black cold fear to enclose her, so she does not think of it. And she is clinging, so she comes to realise, to this image of the other woman, the third, as a sort of safety or protection for herself.

The second motif is in fact part of the first, though this would not be apparent until the end of the novel—Paul's jealousy. The jealousy increases, and is linked with the rhythm of his slow withdrawal. He accuses her, half-laughing, half-serious, of sleeping with other men. In a café he accuses her of making eyes at a man she has not even noticed. To begin with, she laughs at him. Later she grows bitter, but always suppresses bitterness, it is too dangerous. Then, as she comes to understand the image she has created of the other serene, etc., woman, she wonders about Paul's jealousy, and comes to think—not from bitterness, but to understand it, what it really means. It occurs to her that Paul's shadow, his imagined third, is a self-hating rake, free, casual, heartless. (This is the role he sometimes plays, self-mockingly, with her.) So what it means is, that in coming together with Ella, in a serious relationship, the rake in

207

himself has been banished, pushed aside, and now stands in the wings of his personality, temporarily unused, waiting to return. And Ella now sees, side by side with the wise, serene, calm woman, her shadow, the shape of this compulsive self-hating womaniser. These two discordant figures move side by side, keeping pace with Ella and Paul. And there comes a moment (but right at the end of the novel, its culmination) when Ella thinks: Paul's shadow-figure, the man he sees everywhere, even in a man I haven't even noticed, is this almost musical-comedy libertine. So that means that Paul with me is using his 'positive' self. (Julia's phrase.) With me he is good. But I have as a shadow a good woman, grown-up and strong and un-asking. Which means that I am using with him my 'negative' self. So this bitterness I feel growing in me, against him, is a mockery of the truth. In fact, he's better than I am, in this relationship. These invisible figures that keep us company all the time prove it.

Subsidiary motifs. Her novel. He asks what she is writing and she tells him. Reluctantly, because his voice is always full of distrust when he mentions her writing. She says: 'It's a novel about suicide.'

'And what do you know about suicide?'

'Nothing, I'm just writing it.' (To Julia she makes bitter jokes about Jane Austen hiding her novels under the blotting paper when people come into the room; quotes Stendhal's dictum that any woman under fifty who writes, should do so under a pseudonym.)

During the next few days he tells her stories about his patients who are suicidal. It takes her a long time to understand he is doing this because he thinks she is too naïve and ignorant to write about suicide. (And she even agrees with him.) He is instructing her. She begins to hide her work from him. She says she doesn't care about 'being a writer, she just wants to write the book, to see what will happen.' This makes no sense to him, it seems, and soon he begins to complain that she is using his professional knowledge to get facts for the novel.

The motif of Julia. Paul dislikes Ella's relationship with Julia. He sees it as a pact against him, and makes professional jokes about the Lesbian aspects of this friendship. At which Ella says that in that case, his friendships with men are homosexual? But he says she has no sense of humour. At first Ella's instinct is to sacrifice Julia for Paul; but later their friendship does change, it becomes critical of Paul. The conversations between the two women are sophisticated, full of critical insight, implicitly critical of men. Yet Ella does not feel this is disloyalty to Paul, because these conversations come from a different world; the world of sophisticated insight has nothing to do with her feeling for Paul.

The motif of Ella's maternal love for Michael. She is always fighting to get Paul to be a father to the child and always failing. And Paul says: 'You'll come to be glad yet, you'll see I was right.' Which can only mean: When I've left you, you'll be glad I didn't form close ties with your son. And so Ella chooses not to hear it.

The motif of Paul's attitude to his profession. He is split on this. He takes his work for his patients seriously, but makes fun of the jargon he uses. He will tell a story about a patient, full of subtlety and depth, but using the language of literature and of emotion. Then he will judge the same anecdote in psychoanalytical terms, giving it a different dimension. And then, five minutes later, he will be making the most intelligent and ironical fun of the terms he has just used as yardsticks to judge the literary standards, the emotional truths. And at each moment, in each personality—literary, psychoanalytical, the man who distrusts all systems of thought that consider themselves final—he will be serious and expect Ella to accept him, fully for that moment; and he resents it when she attempts to link these personalities in him.

Their life together becomes full of phrases, and symbols. 'Mrs Brown' means his patients and her women who ask for help.

'Your literary lunches,' is his phrase for her infidelities, used sometimes humourously, sometimes seriously.

'Your treatise on suicide.' Her novel, his attitude to it.

And another phrase which becomes more and more important, though when he uses it first she does not understand how deep an attitude in him it reflects. 'We are both boulder-pushers.' This is his phrase for what he sees as his own failure. His fight to get out of his poor background, to win scholarships, to get the highest medical degrees, came out of an ambition to be a creative scientist. But he knows now he will never be this original scientist. And this defect has been partly caused by what is best in him, his abiding, tireless compassion for the poor, the ignorant, the sick. He has always, at a point when he should have chosen the library or the laboratory, chosen the weak instead. He will never now be a discoverer or a blazer of new paths. He has become a man who fights a middle-class, reactionary medical superintendent who wants to keep his wards locked and his patients in straitjackets. 'You and I, Ella, we are the failures. We spend our lives fighting to get people very slightly more stupid than ourselves to accept truths that the great men have always known. They have known for thousands of years that to lock a sick person into solitary confinement makes him worse. They have known for thousands of years that a poor man who is frightened of his landlord and of the police is a slave. They have known it. We know it. But do the great enlightened mass of the British people know it? No. It is our task, Ella, yours and mine, to tell them. Because the great men are too great to be bothered. They are already discovering how to colonise Venus and to irrigate the moon. That is what is important for our time. You and I are the boulder-pushers. All our lives, you and I, we'll put all our energies, all our talents, into pushing a great boulder up a mountain. The boulder is the truth that the great men know by instinct, and the mountain is the stupidity of mankind. We push the boulder. I sometimes wish I had died before I got this job I wanted so much—I thought of it as something creative. How do I spend my time? Telling Dr Shackerly, a frightened little man from Birmingham who bullies his wife because he doesn't know how to love a woman, that he must open the doors of his hospital, that he must not keep poor sick people shut in a cell lined with buttoned white leather in the dark, and that straitjackets are stupid. That is how I spend my days. And treating illness that is caused by a society so stupid

210

that ... And you, Ella. You tell the wives of workmen who are all just as good as their masters to use the styles and furnishings made fashionable by businessmen who use snobbery to make money. And you tell poor women who are slaves of everyone's stupidity to go out and join a social club or to take up a healthful hobby of some kind, to take their minds off the fact they are unloved. And if the healthful hobby doesn't work, and why should it, they end up in my Out-patients ... I wish I had died, Ella. I wish I had died. No, of course you don't understand that, I can see from your face you don't ...'

Death again. Death come out of her novel and into her life. And yet death in the form of energy, for this man works like a madman, out of a furious angry compassion, this man who says he wishes he were dead never rests from work for the helpless.

•   •

It is as if this novel were already written and I were reading it. And now I see it whole I see another theme, of which I was not conscious when I began it. The theme is, naivety. From the moment Ella meets Paul and loves him, from the moment she uses the word love, there is the birth of naivety.

And so now, looking back at my relationship with Michael (I used the name of my real lover for Ella's fictitious son with the small over-eager smile with which a patient offers an analyst evidence he has been waiting for but which the patient is convinced is irrelevant), I see above all my naivety. Any intelligent person could have foreseen the end of this affair from its beginning. And yet I, Anna, like Ella with Paul, refused to see it. Paul gave birth to Ella, the naïve Ella. He destroyed in her the knowing, doubting, sophisticated Ella and again and again he put her intelligence to sleep, and with her willing connivance, so that she floated darkly on her love for him, on her naivety, which is another word for a spontaneous creative faith. And when his own distrust of himself destroyed this woman-in-love, so that she began thinking, she would fight to return to naivety.

Now, when I am drawn to a man, I can assess the depth of a possible relationship with him by the degree to which the naïve Anna is re-created in me.

Sometimes when I, Anna, look back, I want to laugh out loud. It is the appalled, envious laughter of knowledge at innocence. I would be incapable now of such trust. I, Anna, would never begin an affair with Paul. Or Michael. Or rather, I would begin an affair, just that, knowing exactly what would happen; I would begin a deliberately barren, limited relationship.

What Ella lost during those five years was the power to create through naivety.

●　　●

The end of the affair. Though that was not the word that Ella used then. She used it afterwards, and with bitterness.

Ella first understands that Paul is withdrawing from her at the moment when she realises he is not helping her with the letters. He says: 'What's the use? I deal with widow Brown all day at the hospital. I can't do any good, not really. I help one here and there. Ultimately the boulder-pushers don't really help anything. We imagine we do. Psychiatry and welfare work, it's putting poultices on unnecessary misery.'

'But Paul, you know you help them.'

'All the time I'm thinking, we are all obsolete. What sort of a doctor is it who sees his patients as symptoms of a world sickness?'

'If it were true you really feel like that, you wouldn't work so hard.'

He hesitated, then delivered this blow: 'But Ella, you're my mistress, not my wife. Why do you want me to share all the serious business of life with you?'

Ella was angry. 'Every night you lie in my bed and tell me everything. I am your wife.' As she said it, she knew she was signing the warrant for the end. It seemed a terrible cowardice that she had not said it before. He reacted with a small offended laugh, a gesture of withdrawal.

●　　●

Ella finishes her novel and it is accepted for publication. She knows it is a quite good novel, nothing very startling. If she were to read it she would report that it was a small, honest novel. But Paul reads it and reacts with elaborate sarcasm.

He says: 'Well, we men might just as well resign from life.'

She is frightened, and says: 'What do you mean?' Yet she laughs, because of the dramatic way he says it, parodying himself.

Now he drops his self-parody and says with great seriousness: 'My dear Ella, don't you know what the great revolution of our time is? The Russian revolution, the Chinese revolution—they're nothing at all. The real revolution is, women against men.'

'But Paul, that doesn't mean anything to me.'

'I saw a film last week, I went by myself, I didn't take you, that was a film for a man by himself.'

'What film?'

'Did you know that a woman can now have children without a man?'

'But what on earth for?'

'You can apply ice to a woman's ovaries, for instance. She can have a child. Men are no longer necessary to humanity.'

At once Ella laughs, and with confidence. 'But what woman in her senses would want ice applied to her ovaries instead of a man?'

Paul laughs too. 'For all that Ella, and joking apart, it's a sign of the times.'

At which Ella cries out: 'My God, Paul, if at any time during the last five years you'd asked me to have a baby, I'd have been so happy.'

The instinctive, startled movement of withdrawal from her. Then the deliberate careful answer, laughing: 'But, Ella, it's the principle of the thing. Men are no longer necessary.'

'Oh, principles,' says Ella, laughing. 'You're mad. I always said you were.'

At which he says, soberly: 'Well, maybe you're right. You are very sane, Ella. You always were. You say I'm mad. I know it. I get madder and madder. Sometimes I wonder why they don't lock me up instead of my patients. And you get saner and saner. It's your strength. You'll have ice applied to your ovaries yet.'

At which she cries out, so hurt that she doesn't care any longer how she sounds to him: 'You *are* mad. Let me tell you I'd rather die than have a child like that. Don't you know that ever since I've known you I've wanted to have your child? Ever since I've known you everything has been so joyful that ...' She sees his face, which instinctively rejects what she has just said. 'Well, all right then. But supposing that is why you'll ultimately turn out to be unnecessary— because you haven't got any faith in what you are ...' His face is now startled and sad, but she is in full flood and doesn't care. 'You've never understood one simple thing—it's so simple and ordinary that I don't know why you don't understand. Everything with you has been happy and easy and joyful, and you talk about women putting ice on their ovaries. Ice. Ovaries. What does it mean? Well, if you want to sign yourselves off the face of the earth then do it, I don't care.' At which he says, opening his arms. 'Ella. Ella! Come here.' She goes to him, he holds her, but in a moment he teases her: 'But you see, I was right—when it comes to the point you openly admit it, you'd push us all off the edge of the earth and laugh.'

•   •

Sex. The difficulty of writing about sex, for women, is that sex is best when not thought about, not analysed. Women deliberately choose not to think about technical sex. They get irritable when men talk technically, it's out of self-preservation: they want to preserve the spontaneous emotion that is essential for their satisfaction.

Sex is essentially emotional for women. How many times has that been written? And yet there's always a point even with the most perceptive and intelligent man, when a woman looks at him across a gulf: he hasn't understood; she suddenly feels alone; hastens to forget the moment, because if she doesn't she would have to think. Julia, myself and Bob sitting

214

in her kitchen gossiping. Bob telling a story about the break-up of a marriage. He says: 'The trouble was sex. Poor bastard, he's got a prick the size of a needle.' Julia: 'I always thought she didn't love him.' Bob, thinking she hadn't heard: 'No, it's always worried him stiff, he's just got a small one.' Julia: 'But she never did love him, anyone could see that just by looking at them together.' Bob, a bit impatient now: 'It's not their fault, poor idiots, nature was against the whole thing from the start.' Julia: 'Of course it's her fault. She should never have married him if she didn't love him.' Bob, irritated because of her stupidity, begins a long technical explanation, while she looks at me, sighs, smiles, and shrugs. A few minutes later, as he persists, she cuts him off short with a bad-tempered joke, won't let him go on.

As for me, Anna, it was a remarkable fact that until I sat down to write about it, I had never analysed how sex was between myself and Michael. Yet there was a perfectly clear development during the five years, which shows in my memory like a curving line on a graph.

When Ella first made love with Paul, during the first few months, what set the seal on the fact she loved him, and made it possible for her to use the word, was that she immediately experienced orgasm. Vaginal orgasm that is. And she could not have experienced it if she had not loved him. It is the orgasm that is created by the man's need for a woman, and his confidence in that need.

As time went on, he began to use mechanical means. (I look at the word mechanical—a man wouldn't use it.) Paul began to rely on manipulating her externally, on giving Ella clitoral orgasms. Very exciting. Yet there was always a part of her that resented it. Because she felt that the fact he wanted to was an expression of his instinctive desire not to commit himself to her. She felt that without knowing it or being conscious of it (though perhaps he was conscious of it) he was afraid of the emotion. A vaginal orgasm is emotion and nothing else, felt as emotion and expressed in sensations that are indistinguishable from emotion. The vaginal orgasm is a dissolving in a vague, dark generalised sensation like being swirled in a warm whirlpool. There are several differ-

215

ent sorts of clitoral orgasms, and they are more powerful (that is a male word) than the vaginal orgasm. There can be a thousand thrills, sensations, etc., but there is only one real female orgasm and that is when a man, from the whole of his need and desire, takes a woman and wants all her response. Everything else is a substitute and a fake, and the most inexperienced woman feels this instinctively. Ella had never experienced clitoral orgasm before Paul, and she told him so, and he was delighted. 'Well, you are a virgin in something, Ella, at least.' But when she told him she had never experienced what she insisted on calling 'a real orgasm' to anything like the same depth before him, he involuntarily frowned, and remarked: 'Do you know that there are eminent physiologists who say women have no physical basis for vaginal orgasm?' 'Then they don't know much, do they?' And so, as time went on, the emphasis shifted in their love-making from the real orgasm to the clitoral orgasm, and there came a point when Ella realised (and quickly refused to think about it) that she was no longer having real orgasms. That was just before the end, when Paul left her. In short, she knew emotionally what the truth was when her mind would not admit it.

It was just before the end, too, that Paul told her something which (since in bed he preferred her having clitoral orgasm) she simply shrugged away as another symptom of this man's divided personality—since the tone of the story, his way of telling it, contradicted what she in fact was experiencing with him.

'Something happened at the hospital today that would have amused you,' he said. They were sitting in the dark parked car outside Julia's. She slid across to be near him, and he put his arm around her. She could feel his body shaking with laughter. 'As you know, our august hospital gives lectures every fortnight for the benefit of the staff. Yesterday it was announced that Professor Bloodrot would lecture us on the orgasm in the female swan.' Ella instinctively moved away, and he pulled her back, and said: 'I knew you were going to do that. Sit still and listen. The hall was full—I don't have to tell you. The professor stood up, all six foot three of him,

216

like a buckled foot-rule, with his little white beard wagging, and said he had conclusively proved that female swans do not have an orgasm. He would use this useful scientific discovery as a basis for a short discussion on the nature of the female orgasm in general.' Ella laughed. 'Yes, and I knew you would laugh at just that point. But I haven't finished. It was noticeable that at this point there was a disturbance in the hall. People were getting up to leave. The venerable professor, looking annoyed, said that he trusted that this subject would not be found offensive to anyone. After all, research into sexuality, as distinct from superstition about sex, was being conducted in all hospitals of this type throughout the world. But still, people were leaving. Who was leaving? All the women. There were about fifty men, and about fifteen women. And every one of those lady doctors had got up and were going out as if they had been given an order. Our professor was very put out. He stuck out his little beard in front of him, and said that he was surprised his lady colleagues, for whom he had such a respect, were capable of such prudery. But it was no use, there wasn't a woman in sight. At which our professor cleared his throat and announced he would continue his lecture, despite the deplorable attitude of the female doctors. It was his opinion, he said, based on his researches into the nature of the female swan, that there was no physiological basis for a vaginal orgasm in women ... no, don't move away, Ella, really women are most extraordinarily predictable. I was sitting next to Dr Penworthy, father of five, and he whispered to me that it was very strange—usually the professor's wife, being a lady of great public-mindedness, was present at her husband's little talks, but she had not come that day. At this point I committed an act of disloyalty to my sex. I followed the women out of the hall. They had all vanished. Very strange, not a woman in sight. But at last I found my old friend Stephanie, drinking coffee in the canteen. I sat down beside her. She was definitely very withdrawn from me. I said: "Stephanie, why have you all left our great professor's definitive lecture on sex?" She smiled at me very hostile and with great sweetness and said: "But my dear Paul, women of any sense know better, after

217

all these centuries, than to interrupt when men start telling them how they feel about sex." It took me half an hour's hard work and three cups of coffee to make my friend Stephanie like me again.' He was laughing again, holding her inside his arm. He turned to look at her face, and said: 'Yes. Well don't be angry with me too, just because I am the same sex as the professor—that's what I said to Stephanie too.' Ella's anger dissolved and she laughed with him. She was thinking: Tonight he'll come up with me. Whereas until recently he had spent nearly every night with her, now he went home two or three nights a week. He said, apparently at random: 'Ella, you're the least jealous woman I've ever known.' Ella felt a sudden chill, then panic, then the protective mechanism worked fast: She simply did not hear what he had said, and asked: 'Are you coming up with me?' He said: 'I'd decided not to. But if I had really decided I wouldn't be sitting here, would I?' They went upstairs, holding hands. He remarked: 'I wonder how you and Stephanie would get on?' She thought that his look at her was strange, 'as if he's testing something.' Again the small panic, while she thought, he talks a great deal about Stephanie these days, I wonder if ... Then her mind went dim, and she said: 'I've got some supper ready if you'd like it.'

They ate, and he looked over at her and said: 'And you're such a good cook too. What am I going to do with you, Ella?'

'What you are doing now,' she said.

He was watching her, with a look of desperate, despairing humour that she saw very often now. 'And I've not succeeded in changing you in the slightest. Not even your clothes or the way you do your hair.'

This was a recurrent battle between them. He would move her hair this way and that about her head, pull the stuff of her dress into a different line, and say: 'Ella, why do you insist on looking like a rather severe school-mistress? God knows, you're not remotely like that.' He would bring her a blouse cut low, or show her a dress in a shop window, and say: 'Why don't you buy a dress like that?'

But Ella continued to wear her black hair tied back, and

refused the startling clothes he liked. At the back of her mind was the thought: He complains now that I'm not satisfied with him and I want another man. What would he think if I started to wear sexy clothes? If I made myself very glamorous he'd not be able to bear it. It's bad enough as it is.

She once said, laughing at him: 'But Paul, you bought me that red blouse. It's cut to show the top of my breasts. But when I put it on, you came into the room, and came right over and buttoned it up—you did it instinctively.'

Tonight he came over to her and untied her hair and let it fall loose. Gazing close into her face, frowning, he teased out fronds of hair over her forehead, and arranged it around her neck. She allowed him to do as he liked, remaining quiet under the warmth of his hands, smiling at him. Suddenly she thought: He's comparing me with someone, he's not seeing me at all. She moved away from him, quickly, and he said: 'Ella, you could be a really beautiful woman if you would let yourself be.'

She said: 'So you don't think I'm beautiful then?'

He half-groaned, half-laughed, and pulled her down on to the bed. 'Obviously not,' he said. 'Well then,' she said, smiling and confident.

It was that night that he remarked, almost casually, that he had been offered a job in Nigeria, and was thinking of going. Ella heard him, but almost absentmindedly; accepting the off-hand tone he imposed on the situation. Then she realised a pit of dismay had opened in her stomach and that something final was happening. Yet she insisted on thinking, Well it will solve everything. I can go with him. There's nothing to keep me here. Michael could go to some kind of school there. And what have I here to keep me?

It was true. Lying in the darkness, inside Paul's arms, she thought that those arms had slowly, over the years, shut out everyone else. She went out very little, because she did not enjoy going out by herself, and because she had accepted, very early on, that to go out together into company meant more trouble than it was worth. Either Paul was jealous, or he said he was odd-man-out among her literary friends. At which Ella would say: 'They aren't friends, they are ac-

'quaintances.' She had no vital connection with anyone but her son, Paul, and Julia. Julia would keep, it was a friendship for life. So now she said: 'I can come with you, can't I?' He hesitated, and said, laughing: 'But you don't want to give up all your exciting literary goings-on in London?' She told him he was quite crazy, and began making plans to go.

One day she went with him to his home. His wife and children were away on holiday. It was after a film they had just seen together, and he had said he wanted to pick up a clean shirt. He pulled his car up outside a small house, in a row of identical houses in a suburb off to the north of Shepherd's Bush. Children's toys lay abandoned over a small patch of neat garden.

'I keep telling Muriel about the kids,' he said, irritated. 'They really can't leave their things lying about like this.'

This was the moment that she understood this was his home.

'Well, come in a moment,' he said. She did not want to go inside, but she followed him. The hall had a conventional flowered wallpaper and a dark sideboard and a strip of pretty carpet. For some reason it comforted Ella. The living-room came from a different epoch of taste: it had three different wallpapers and discordant curtains and cushions. Evidently it had just been done up; it still had the look of being on show. It was depressing, and Ella followed Paul into the kitchen on his search for the clean shirt, on this occasion a medical journal he needed. The kitchen was the used room of the house, and was shabby. But one wall had been covered with red wallpaper, so it seemed that this room, too, was in the process of being transformed. On the kitchen table were stacked dozens of copies of *Women at Home*. Ella felt she had been delivered a direct blow; but told herself that after all she worked for this nasty snobbish magazine, and what right had she to sneer at people who read it? She told herself that she knew no one who was absorbed heart and soul in the work they did; everyone seemed to work reluctantly, or with cynicism, or with a divided mind, so she was no worse than everyone else. But it was no use; there was a small television set in a corner of the kitchen, and she imagined the wife sitting here, night after night, reading *Women at Home* or looking at the television set and listening for the children upstairs. Paul saw her standing there, fingering the magazines and examining the room, and remarked, with his familiar grim humour: 'This is her house, Ella. To do as she likes in. It's surely the least I can do.'

'Yes, it's the least.' 'Yes. It must be upstairs,' and Paul left the kitchen and started upstairs, saying over his shoulder: 'Well come up, then?' She wondered: Is he showing me his home in order to demonstrate something? Because he wants to tell me something? He doesn't know I hate being here?

But she again obediently followed him up and into the bedroom. This room was different again, and had evidently been exactly as it was now for a long time. It had twin beds, on either side of a neat little table on which was a big framed photograph of Paul. The colours were green and orange and black, with a great many restless zebra stripes—the 'jazz' era in furnishing, twenty-five years after its birth. Paul had found his magazine, which was on the bedside table, and was ready to leave again. Ella said: 'One of these days I'll get a letter, handed on by Dr West. "Dear Dr Allsop. Please tell me what to do. Lately I can't sleep at nights. I've been drinking hot milk before going to bed and trying to keep a relaxed mind, but it doesn't help. Please advise me, Muriel Tanner. P.S. I forgot to mention, my husband wakes me early, about six o'clock, coming in from working late at the hospital. Sometimes he doesn't come home all week. I get low in my spirits. This has been going on five years now."'

Paul listened, with a sober, sad face. 'It's been no secret to you,' he said at last, 'that I'm not exactly proud of myself as a husband.'

'For God's sake, why don't you put an end to it then?'

'What!' he exclaimed, half-laughing already, and back in his role as a rake, 'abandon the poor woman with two children?'

'She might get herself a man who cared for her. Don't tell me you'd mind if she did. Surely you don't like the idea of her living like this?'

He answered seriously: 'I've told you, she's a very simple

221

woman. You always assume other people are like you. Well they aren't. She likes watching television and reading *Women at Home* and sticking bits of wallpaper on the walls. And she's a good mother.'

'And she doesn't mind not having a man?'

'For all I know she has, I've never enquired,' he said, laughing again.

'Oh well, I don't know!' said Ella, completely dispirited, following him downstairs again. She left the discordant little house thankfully, as if escaping from a trap; and she looked down the street and thought that probably they were all like this, all in fragments, not one of them a whole, reflecting a whole life, a whole human being; or, for that matter, a whole family. 'What you don't like,' said Paul, as they drove off, 'is that Muriel might be happy living like this.'

'How can she be?'

'I asked her some time ago, if she'd like to leave me. She could go back to her parents, if she wanted. She said no. Besides, she'd be lost without me.'

'Good Lord!' said Ella, disgusted and afraid.

'It's true, I'm a sort of father, she depends on me completely.'

'But she never sees you.'

'I'm nothing if not efficient,' he said, shortly. 'When I go home I deal with everything. The gas heaters, and the electricity bill and where to buy a cheap carpet, and what to do about the children's school. Everything.' When she did not reply he insisted: 'I've told you before, you're a snob, Ella. You can't stand the fact that maybe it's how she likes to live.'

'No, I can't. And I don't believe it. No woman in the world wants to live without love.'

'You're such a perfectionist. You're an absolutist. You measure everything against some kind of ideal that exists in your head, and if it doesn't come up to your beautiful notions then you condemn it out of hand. Or you pretend to yourself that it's beautiful even when it isn't.'

Ella thought: He means us; and Paul was already going on: 'For instance—Muriel might just as well say of you:

Why on earth does she put up with being my husband's mistress, what security is there in that? And it's not respectable.'

'Oh, security!'

'Oh, quite so. You say, scornfully, Oh, security! Oh, respectability! But Muriel wouldn't. They're very important to her. They're very important to most people.'

It occurred to Ella that he sounded angry and even hurt. It occurred to her that he identified himself with his wife (and yet all his tastes, when he was with her, Ella, were different) and that security and respectability were important to him also.

She was silent, thinking: If he really likes living like that, or at least, needs it, it would explain why he's always dissatisfied with me. The other side of the sober respectable little wife is the smart, gay, sexy mistress. Perhaps he really would like it if I were unfaithful to him and wore tarty clothes. Well I won't. This is what I am, and if he doesn't like it he can lump it.

Later that evening he said, laughing, but aggressive: 'It would do you good, Ella, to be like other women.'

'What do you mean?'

'Waiting at home, the wife, trying to keep your man against the other woman. Instead of having a lover at your feet.'

'Oh, is that where you are?' she said, ironically. 'But why do you see marriage as a kind of fight? I don't see it as a battle.'

'You don't!' he said, ironical in his turn. And after a pause: 'You've just written a novel about suicide.'

'What's that got to do with it?'

'All that intelligent insight . . .' He checked himself and sat looking at her, rueful and critical and—Ella thought, condemning. They were up in her little room, high under the roof, the child sleeping next door, the remains of the meal she had cooked on the low table between them, as they had been a thousand times. He turned a glass of wine between his fingers and said, in pain: 'I don't know how I'd have got through the last months without you.' 'What's happened particularly the last few months?' 'Nothing. That's the point. It all goes on and on. Well, in Nigeria I won't be patching up old sores, wounds on a mangy lion. That's my work, putting ointment on the wounds of an old animal that hasn't the vitality any more to heal itself. At least in Africa I'll be working for something new and growing.'

He went to Nigeria with unexpected suddenness. Unexpected, at least, to Ella. They were still talking of it as something that would happen in the future when he came in to say he was leaving next day. The plans for how she would join him were necessarily vague, until he knew the conditions there. She saw him off at the airport, as if she would be meeting him again in a few weeks. Yet after he had kissed her good-bye, he turned with a small bitter nod and a twisted smile, a sort of a painful grimace of his whole body, and suddenly Ella felt the tears running down her face, and she was cold with loss in every nerve. She was unable to stop crying, to prevent the cold that made her shiver, steadily, for days afterwards. She wrote letters, and made plans, but it was from inside a shadow that slowly deepened over her. He wrote once, saying it was impossible to say definitely yet how she and Michael could come out to join him; and then there was silence.

One afternoon she was working with Dr West, over a pile of the usual letters, and he remarked: 'I had a letter from Paul Tanner yesterday.'

'Did you?' Dr West, so far as she knew, did not know of her relationship with Paul.

'Sounds as if he's liking it out there, so I suppose he'll take his family out.' He carefully clipped some letters together for his own pile, and went on: 'Just as well he went, I gather. He told me just before he left he'd got himself involved with a pretty flighty piece. Heavily involved, it sounded. She didn't sound much good to me.'

Ella made herself breathe normally, examined Dr West, and decided that this was just casual gossip about a mutual friend, and not meant to wound her. She took up a letter he had handed her, which began: 'Dear Dr Allsop, I'm writing to you about my little boy who is walking in his sleep ...'

224

and said: 'Dr West, surely this is your province?' For this amiable battle had continued, unchanged, for all the years they had worked together. 'No, Ella, it is not. If a child walks in its sleep, it's no good my prescribing medicines, and you'd be the first to blame me if I did. Tell the woman to go to the clinic and suggest tactfully that it's her fault and not the child's. Well, I don't have to tell you what to say.' He took up another letter and said: 'I told Tanner to stay out of England as long as possible. These things are not always easy to break off. The young lady was pestering him to marry her. A not-so-young lady, actually. That was the trouble. I suppose she'd got tired of a gay life and wanted to settle down.'

Ella made herself not-think about this conversation until she had completed the division of letters with Dr West. Well, I've been naïve, she decided at last. I suppost he was having an affair with Stephanie at the hospital. At least, he never mentioned anyone but Stephanie, he was always talking about her. But he never spoke of her in that tone, 'flighty piece.' No that's the Wests' language, they use idiotic phrases like flighty piece and getting tired of a gay life. How extraordinarily common these respectable middle-class people are.

Meanwhile she was deeply depressed; and the shadow that she had been fighting off since Paul had left engulfed her completely. She thought about Paul's wife: she must have felt like this, this complete rejection, when Paul lost interest in her. Well at least she, Ella, had had the advantage of being too stupid to realise that Paul was having an affair with Stephanie. But perhaps Muriel had also chosen to be stupid— had chosen to believe that Paul spent so many nights at the hospital?

Ella had a dream which was unpleasant and disturbing. She was in the ugly little house, with its little rooms that were all different from each other. She was Paul's wife, and only by an effort of will could she prevent the house disintegrating, and flying off in all directions because of the conflict between the rooms. She decided she must furnish the whole house again, in one style, hers. But as soon as she hung new curtains or painted a room out, Muriel's room was re-created. Ella was like a ghost in this house and she realised it would hold together, somehow, as long as Muriel's spirit was in it and it was holding together precisely because every room belonged to a different epoch, a different spirit. And Ella saw herself standing in the kitchen, her hand on the pile of *Women at Home*; she was a 'sexy piece' (she could hear the words being said, by Dr West) with a tight coloured skirt and a very tight jersey and her hair was cut fashionably. And Ella realised that Muriel was not there after all, she had gone to Nigeria to join Paul, and Ella was waiting in the house until Paul came back.

When Ella woke after this dream she was crying. It occurred to her, for the first time, that the woman from whom Paul had had to separate himself, for whom he had gone to Nigeria, because he had at all costs to separate himself from her, was herself. She was the flighty piece.

She understood also that Dr West had spoken deliberately, perhaps because of some phrase in Paul's letter to him; it was a warning from the respectable world of Dr West, protecting one of its members, to Ella.

Strangely enough, the shock was enough, for a while at least, to break the power of the depressive mood that had held her for months now in its dark grip. She swung over into a mood of bitter, angry defiance. She told Julia that Paul had 'ditched her,' and that she had been a fool not to see it before (and Julia's silence said she agreed with Ella completely). She said that she had no intention of sitting around and crying about it.

Without knowing that she had been unconsciously planning to do this, she went out and bought herself new clothes. They were not the 'sexy' clothes Paul had urged on her, but they were different from any clothes she had worn before, and fitted her new personality, which was rather hard, casual, and indifferent—or at least, so she believed. And she had her hair cut, so it was in a soft provocative shape around her small pointed face. And she decided to leave Julia's house. It was the house she had lived in with Paul, and she could no longer stand it.

Very cool, clear and efficient, she found herself a new flat and settled into it. It was a large flat, much too large for the child and herself. It was only after she had settled in it she understood the extra space was for a man. For Paul, in fact, and she was still living as if he were returning to her.

Then she heard, quite by chance, that Paul had returned to England for leave and had been here already for two weeks. On the night of the day she heard this news, she found herself dressed and made-up, her hair carefully done, standing at the window looking down into the street, and waiting for him. She waited until long after midnight, thinking: His work at the hospital might easily keep him as late as this, I mustn't go to bed too early, because he'll see the lights are out, and not come up, for fear of waking me.

She stood there, night after night. She could see herself standing there, and said to herself: This is madness. This is being mad. Being mad is not being able to stop yourself doing something that you know to be irrational. Because you know Paul will not come. And yet she continued to dress herself and to stand for hours at the window, waiting, every night. And, standing there and looking at herself, she could see how this madness was linked with the madness that had prevented her from seeing how the affair would inevitably end, the naivety that had made her so happy. Yes, the stupid faith and naivety and trust had led, quite logically, into her standing at the window waiting for a man whom she knew, quite well, would never come to her again.

After some weeks, she heard from Dr West, apparently casually, though with a hidden triumphant malice, that Paul had gone back to Nigeria again. 'His wife wouldn't go with him,' said Dr West. 'She doesn't want to uproot herself. Perfectly happy where she is, apparently.'

• •

The trouble with this story is that it is written in terms of analysis of the laws of dissolution of the relationship between Paul and Ella. I don't see any other way to write it. As soon as one has lived through something, it falls into a pattern. And the pattern of an affair, even one that has lasted five years and has been as close as a marriage, is seen in terms of

227

what ends it. That is why all this is untrue. Because while living through something one doesn't think like that at all.

Supposing I were to write it like this: two full days, in every detail, one at the beginning of the affair, and one towards the end? No, because I would still be instinctively isolating and emphasising the factors that destroyed the affair. It is that which would give the thing its shape. Otherwise it would be chaos, because these two days, separated by many months in time, would have no shadow over them, but would be records of a simple unthinking happiness with perhaps a couple of jarring moments (which in fact would be reflections of the approaching end but would not be felt like that at the time) but moments swallowed in the happiness.

Literature is analysis after the event.

The form of that other piece, about what happened in Mashopi, is nostalgia. There is no nostalgia in this piece, about Paul and Ella, but the form is a kind of pain.

To show a woman loving a man one should show her cooking a meal for him or opening a bottle of wine for the meal, while she waits for his ring at the door. Or waking in the morning before he does to see his face change from the calm of sleep into a smile of welcome. Yes. To be repeated a thousand times. But that isn't literature. Probably better as a film. Yes, the physical quality of life, that's living, and not the analysis afterwards, or the moments of discord or premonition. A shot in a film: Ella slowly peeling an orange, handing Paul yellow segments of the fruit, which he takes, one after another, thoughtfully, frowning: he is thinking of something else.

[The blue notebook began with a sentence:]

'Tommy appeared to be accusing his mother.'

[Then Anna had written:]

I came upstairs from the scene between Tommy and Molly and instantly began to turn it into a short story. It struck me that my doing this—turning everything into fiction—must be

228

an evasion. Why not write down, simply, what happened between Molly and her son today? Why do I never write down, simply, what happens? Why don't I keep a diary? Obviously, my changing everything into fiction is simply a means of concealing something from myself. Today it was so clear: sitting listening to Molly and Tommy at war, very disturbed by it; then coming straight upstairs and beginning to write a story without even planning to do it. I shall keep a diary.

Jan. 7th, 1950

Tommy was seventeen this week. Molly has never put pressure on him to make up his mind about his future. In fact, recently she told him to stop worrying and to go off to France for a few weeks to 'broaden his mind.' (This phrase irritated him when she used it.) Today he came into the kitchen on purpose to quarrel—both Molly and I knew it as soon as he walked in. He has been in a mood of hostility to Molly for some time. This started after his first visit to his father's house. (At the time we didn't realise how deeply the visit affected him.) It was then he began to criticise his mother for being a communist and 'bohemian.' Molly laughed it off, and said that country houses full of landed gentry and money were fun to visit but he was damned lucky not to have to live that life. He paid a second visit a few weeks later, and returned to his mother over-polite, full of hostility. At which point I intervened: told him, which Molly was too proud to do, about the history of Molly and his father—the way he bullied her financially to make her go back to him, then the threats to tell her employers she was a communist, etc., so that she might lose her job—the whole long ugly story. Tommy at first didn't believe me; no one could be more charming than Richard over a long week-end, I should imagine. Then he believed me, but it didn't help. Molly suggested he should go down to his father's for the summer in order (as she put it to me) that the glamour should have time to wear off. He went. For six weeks. Country house. Charming conventional wife. Three delightful little girls. Richard at home for week-ends, bringing business

229

guests, etc. The local gentry. Molly's prescription worked like a charm. Tommy announced that 'week-ends were long enough.' She was delighted. But too soon. Today's quarrel like a scene from a play. He came in, ostensibly on the grounds that he had to decide about his National Service: he was clearly expecting Molly to say he should be a conscientious objector. Molly would, of course, like him to be; but said it was his decision. He began by arguing that he should do his National Service. This became an attack on her way of life, her politics, her friends—everything she is. There they sat, on either side of the kitchen table, Tommy's dark obstinate muzzled face pointed at her, she sitting all loose and at ease, half her attention on the food cooking for lunch, continually rushing off to the telephone on Party business—he patiently, angrily, waiting through each telephone call until she came back. And at the end of the long fight, he had talked himself into a decision that he should be a conscientious objector; and now his attack on her was linked with this position—the militarism of the Soviet Union, etc. When he went upstairs, announcing, as if this came naturally from what went before, that he intended to marry very young and have a large family, Molly let herself go limp into exhaustion and then began to cry. I came upstairs to give Janet her lunch. Disturbed. Because Molly and Richard make me think of Janet's father. As far as I am concerned this was a highly neurotic stupid involvement of no importance. No amount of repeating phrases like: the father of my child, can make me feel different about it. One day Janet is going to say: 'My mother was married to my father for a year, then they divorced.' And when she is older and I've told her the truth: 'My mother lived with my father for three years; then they decided to have a baby and married so I should not be illegitimate, then divorced.' But these words will have no connection with anything that I feel to be true. Whenever I think about Max, I am overcome with helplessness. I remember the feeling of helplessness made me write about him before. (Willi in the black notebook.) But the moment the baby was born, the silly empty marriage seemed to be cancelled out. I remember thinking, when I first saw Janet:

Well, what does it matter, love, marriage, happiness, etc. Here's this marvellous baby. But Janet won't understand that. Tommy doesn't. If Tommy could feel that, he'd stop resenting Molly for leaving his father. I seem to remember starting a diary once before, before Janet was born. I'll look for it. Yes, here is the entry I vaguely remembered.

9th October, 1946

I came in last night from work into that horrible hotel room. Max lying on the bed, silent. I sat on the divan. He came over, put his head in my lap and his arms around my waist. I could feel his despair. He said: 'Anna, we have nothing to say to each other, why not?' 'Because we aren't the same kind of person.' 'What does that mean, the same kind of person?' he asked, injecting the automatic irony into his voice—a sort of willed, protective, ironic drawl. I felt chilled, thinking, perhaps it doesn't mean anything, but I held tight on to the future, and said: 'But surely it means something, being the same kind of person?' Then he said: 'Come to bed.' In bed, he put his hand on my breast and I felt sexual revulsion and said: 'What's the use, we aren't any good for each other and never have been?' So we went to sleep. Towards morning, the young married couple in the next room made love. The walls were so thin in that hotel we could hear everything. Listening to them made me unhappy; I've never been so unhappy. Max woke and said: 'What's the matter?' I said: 'You see, it's possible to be happy, and we should both hold on to that.' It was very hot. The sun was rising, and the couple next door were laughing. There was a faint warm stain of pink light on the wall from the sun. Max lay beside me, and his body was hot and unhappy. The birds were singing, very loud, then the sun got too hot and quenched them. Suddenly. One minute they were making a shrill lively discordant noise, then silence. The couple were talking and laughing and then their baby woke and began to cry. Max said: 'Perhaps we should have a baby?' I said: 'You mean, having a baby would bring us together?' I said it irritably, and hated myself for saying it; but his sentimentality grated on me. He looked obstinate, and repeated: 'We

231

should have a baby.' Then I suddenly thought: Why not? We can't leave the Colony for months yet. We haven't the money. Let's have a baby—I'm always living as if something wonderful is going to crystalise some time in the future. Let's make something happen now . . . and so I turned to him and we made love. That was the morning Janet was conceived. We married the following week in the registry office. A year later, we separated. But this man never touched me at all, never got close to me. But there's Janet . . . I think I shall go to a psycho-analyst.

January 10th, 1950

Saw Mrs Marks today. After the preliminaries, she said: 'Why are you here?' I said: 'Because I've had experiences that should have touched me and they haven't.' She was waiting for more, so I said: 'For instance, the son of my friend Molly—last week he decided to become a conscientious objector, but he might just as well have decided not to be. That's something I recognise in myself.' 'What?' 'I watch people—they decide to be this thing or that. But it's as if it's a sort of dance—they might just as well do the opposite with equal conviction.' She hesitated, then asked: 'You have written a novel?' 'Yes.' 'Are you writing another?' 'No, I shall never write another.' She nodded. I already knew that nod, and I said: 'I'm not here because I'm suffering from a writer's block.' She nodded again and I said: 'You'll have to believe that if . . .' This hesitation was awkward and full of aggression and I said with a smile I knew to be aggressive: '. . . if we're going to get on.' She smiled, drily. Then: 'Why don't you want to write another book?' 'Because I no longer believe in art.' 'So you don't believe in art?'—isolating the words, and holding them up for me to examine. 'No.' 'So.'

Jan. 14th, 1950

I dream a great deal. The dream: I am in a concert hall. A doll-like audience in evening dress. A grand-piano. Myself, dressed absurdly in Edwardian satin, and a choker of pearls, like Queen Mary, seated at the piano. I am unable to play a note. The audience waits. The dream is stylised, like a scene

232

in a play or an old illustration. I tell Mrs Marks this dream, and she asks: 'What is it about?' I reply: 'About lack of feeling.' And she gives her small wise smile which conducts our sessions like a conductor's baton. Dream: Wartime in Central Africa. A cheap dance-hall. Everyone drunk, and dancing close for sex. I wait at the side of the dance-floor. A smooth doll-like man approaches me. I recognise Max. (But he has a literary quality from what I wrote in the notebook about Willi.) I walk into his arms, doll-like, freeze, can't move. Once again the dream has a grotesque quality. It's like a caricature. Mrs Marks asks: 'What is that dream about?' 'The same thing, lack of feeling. I was frigid with Max.' 'So you are frightened about being frigid?' 'No, because he was the only man I have been frigid with.' She nods. Suddenly I start to worry: Shall I be frigid again?

Jan. 19th, 1950

This morning I was in my room under the roof. Through the wall a baby was crying, I was reminded of that hotel room in Africa, where the baby would wake us crying in the morning, then he would be fed and start gurgling and making happy noises while his parents made love. Janet was playing on the floor with her bricks. Last night Michael asked me to drive with him and I said I couldn't because Molly was going out, so I couldn't leave Janet. He said, ironically: 'Well, the cares of motherhood must ever come before lovers.' Because of the cold irony, I reacted against him. And this morning I felt enclosed by the repetitive quality—the baby crying next door, and my hostility to Michael. (Remembering my hostility towards Max.) Then a feeling of unreality—couldn't remember where I was—here, in London, or there, in Africa, in that other building, where the baby cried through the wall. Janet looked up from the floor and said: 'Come and play, mummy.' I couldn't move. I forced myself up out of the chair after a while and sat on the floor beside the little girl. I looked at her, and thought: That's my child, my flesh and blood. But I couldn't feel it. She said again: 'Play, mummy.' I moved wooden bricks for a house, but like a machine. Making myself perform every movement. I could see myself

233

sitting on the floor, the picture of a 'young mother playing with her little girl.' Like a film shot, or a photograph. I told Mrs Marks about this and she said: 'So?' I said: 'It's the same as the dreams, only suddenly in real life.' She waited, and I said: 'It was because I felt hostility towards Michael— and that froze everything.' 'You are sleeping with him?' 'Yes.' She waited and I said, smiling: 'No, I'm not frigid.' She nodded. A waiting nod. I didn't know what she was expecting me to say. She prompted: 'Your little girl asked you to come and play?' I didn't understand. She said: 'To play. To come and play. You couldn't play.' Then I was angry, understanding. For the last few days I've been brought again and again, and so skilfully, to the same point; and every time I've been angry; and always my anger is made to seem a defence against the truth. I said: 'No, that dream was not about art. It was not.' And trying to joke: 'Who dreamed that dream, you or I?' But she wouldn't laugh at the joke: 'My dear, you wrote that book, you are an artist.' She said the word artist with a gentle, understanding, reverent smile. 'Mrs Marks, you must believe me, I don't care if I never write another word.' 'You don't care,' she said, meaning me to hear behind the *don't care* my words: Lack of feeling. 'Yes,' I insisted, 'I don't care.' 'My dear, I became a psychotherapist because I once believed myself to be an artist. I treat a great many artists. How many people have sat where you are sitting, because they are blocked, deep in themselves, unable to create any longer.' 'But I am not one of them.' 'Describe yourself.' 'How?' 'Describe yourself as if you were describing someone else.' 'Anna Wulf is a small dark thin spiky woman, over-critical and on the defensive. She is thirty-three years old. She was married for a year to a man she didn't care for and has a small daughter. She is a communist.' She smiled. I said: 'No good?' 'Try again: for one thing, Anna Wulf wrote a novel which was praised by the critics and did so well she is still in fact living on the money it earned.' I was full of hostility. 'Very well: Anna Wulf is sitting in a chair in front of a soul-doctor. She is there because she cannot deeply feel about anything. She is frozen. She has a great many friends and acquaintances. People are pleased to see her. But she

234

only cares about one person in the world, her daughter, Janet.' 'Why is she frozen?' 'She is afraid.' 'What of?' 'Of death.' She nodded, and I broke in across the game and said: 'No, not of my death. It seems to me that ever since I can remember anything the real thing that has been happening in the world was death and destruction. It seems to me it is stronger than life.' 'Why are you a communist?' 'At least they believe in something.' 'Why do you say *they*, when you are a member of the Communist Party?' 'If I could say *we*, really meaning it, I wouldn't be here, would I?' 'So you don't care, really, about your comrades?' 'I get on easily with everyone, if that's what you mean?' 'No, that's not what I mean.' 'I told you, the only person I really care about, really, is my daughter. And that's egotism.' 'You don't care about your friend, Molly?' 'I'm fond of her.' 'And you don't care about your man, Michael?' 'Supposing he dropped me tomorrow, how long would I remember that—I like sleeping with him?' 'You've known him how long—three weeks? Why should he drop you?' I couldn't think of a reply, in fact I was surprised I had said it at all. Our time was up. I said good-bye and as I went out she said: 'My dear, you must remember the artist has a sacred trust.' I could not help laughing. 'Why do you laugh?' 'Doesn't it strike you as funny—art is sacred, a majestic chord in C Major?' 'I will see you the day after tomorrow as usual, my dear.'

January 31st, 1950

I took dozens of dreams to Mrs Marks today—all dreamed over the last three days. They all had the same quality of false art, caricature, illustration, parody. All the dreams were in marvellous fresh vivid colour, that gave me great pleasure. She said: 'You are dreaming a great deal.' I said: 'As soon as I close my eyes.' She: 'And what are all these dreams about?' I smile, before she can; at which she looks at me sternly, ready to take a strong line. But I say: 'I want to ask you something. Half those dreams were nightmares, I was in real terror, sweating when I woke up. And yet I enjoyed every minute of them. I enjoy dreaming. I look forward to sleep because I am going to dream. I wake myself up in the night, again and again, to enjoy the knowledge of my dreaming. In the morning I feel as happy as if I've built cities in my sleep. Well? But yesterday I met a woman who has been in psycho-analysis for ten years—an American naturally.' Here Mrs Marks smiled. 'This woman told me with a sort of bright sterilised smile that her dreams were more important to her than her life, more real to her than anything that happened in the day-time with her child and her husband.' Mrs Marks smiled. 'Yes, I know what you are going to say. And it's true—she told me she once believed herself to be a writer. But then I've never met anyone anywhere or any class, colour or creed, who hasn't at some time believed themselves to be writers, painters, dancers or something. And that is probably a more interesting fact than anything else we've discussed in this room—after all a hundred years ago it would never have crossed most people's minds to be artists. They recognised the station in life it had pleased God to call them to. *But*—isn't there something wrong with the fact that my sleep is more satisfying, exciting, enjoyable than anything that happens to me awake? I don't want to become like that American woman.' A silence, her conducting smile. 'Yes, I know you want me to say that all my creativity is going into my dreams.' 'Well, isn't it true?' 'Mrs Marks, I'm going to ask if we can ignore my dreams for a time.' She says drily: 'You come to me, a psychotherapist, and ask if we can ignore your dreams?' 'Isn't it possible at least that my dreaming so enjoy-ably is an escape away from feeling.' She sits quiet thinking. Oh, she is a most intelligent wise old woman. She makes a small gesture, asking me to be quiet while she thinks whether this is sensible or not. And in the meantime I look at the room we are sitting in. It is tall, long, darkened, quietened. It has flowers everywhere. The walls are covered with repro-ductions of masterpieces and there are statues. It is almost like an art gallery. It is a dedicated room. It gives me pleas-ure, like an art gallery. The point is, that nothing in my life corresponds with anything in this room—my life has always been crude, unfinished, raw, tentative; and so have the lives of the people I have known well. It occurred to me, looking at this room, that the raw unfinished quality in my life was precisely what was valuable in it and I should hold fast to it. She came out of her brief meditation and said: 'Very well, my dear. We'll leave your dreams for a while, and you will bring me your waking fantasies.'

On that day, the last entry, I stopped dreaming as if a magic wand had been waved. 'Any dreams?' she asks casually, to find out if I'm ready to forget my absurd evasion of her. We discuss the nuances of my feeling for Michael. We are happy together most of the time, then suddenly I have feelings of hatred and resentment for him. But always for the same reasons: when he makes some crack about the fact I have written a book—he resents it, makes fun of my being 'an authoress'; when he is ironical about Janet, that I put being a mother before loving him; and when he warns me he does not intend to marry me. He always makes this warning after he has said he loves me and I am the most important thing in his life. I get hurt and angry. I said to him, angrily: 'Surely that's a warning one need only make once,' then he teased me out of my bad temper. But that night I was frigid with him for the first time. When I told Mrs Marks, she said: 'Once I treated a woman for three years for frigidity. She was living with a man she loved. But she never in all those three years had an orgasm. On the day they married she had an orgasm for the first time.' Having told me this she nodded, emphatically, as if to say: There you are, you see! I laughed, and said: 'Mrs Marks, do you realise what a pillar of reaction you are?' She said, smiling: 'And what does that word mean, my dear?' 'It means a great deal to me,' I said. 'And yet on the night after your man says he won't marry you, you are frigid?' 'But he has said it or implied it other times and I haven't been frigid.' I was conscious of dishonesty, so I admitted: 'It's true my response in bed is in relation to how he accepts me.' 'Of course, you are a real woman.' She uses this word, a woman, a real woman, exactly as he does artist, a true artist. An absolute. When she said, 'you are a real woman,' I began to laugh, helplessly, and after a while she laughed too. Then she said, why are you laughing and I told

237

her. She was on the point of using the occasion to bring in the word 'art'—which neither of us has mentioned since I stopped dreaming. But instead she said: 'Why do you never mention your politics to me?'

I thought it out, and said: 'About the C.P.—I swing from fear and hatred of it to a desperate clinging to it. Out of a need to protect it and look after it—do you understand that?' She nodded, so I went on: 'And Janet—I can resent her existence violently because she prevents me doing so many things I want to do, and love her at the same time. And Molly. I can hate her one hour for her bossiness and protectiveness and love her the next. And Michael—it's the same thing. So we can obviously confine ourselves to one of my relationships and be dealing with my whole personality?' Here she smiled, drily. 'Very well,' she said, 'let's confine ourselves to Michael.'

15th March, 1950

I went to Mrs Marks and said that while I was happier with Michael than I have ever been in my life, something was happening that I did not understand. I would go to sleep in his arms, dissolved and happy, and wake in the morning hating and resenting him. At which she said: 'Well, my dear, so perhaps it is time you started dreaming again?' I laughed, and she waited for me to stop laughing, so I said, 'You always win.' Last night I began to dream again as if I had been ordered to dream.

27th March, 1950

I am crying in my sleep. All I can remember when I wake is that I have been crying. When I told Mrs Marks, she said: 'The tears we shed in our sleep are the only genuine tears we shed in our lives. The waking tears are self-pity.' I said: 'That's very poetic, but I can't believe you mean it.' 'And why not?' 'Because when I go to sleep knowing I am going to cry, there's pleasure in it.' She smiles; I wait for it—but by now she is not going to help me. 'You aren't going to suggest,' I say, ironical, 'that I am a masochist?' She nods: of

course. 'There's pleasure in pain,' I say, sounding the trumpet
for her. She nods. I say: 'Mrs Marks, that sad nostalgic pain
that makes me cry is the same emotion I wrote that damned
book out of.' She sits up, straight, shocked. Because I could
describe a book, art, that noble activity, as damned. I say:
'All you've done is to bring me, step by step, to the subjective
knowledge of what I knew before anyway, that the root of
that book was poisoned.' She says: 'All self-knowledge is
knowing, on deeper and deeper levels, what one knew before.' I say: 'But that isn't good enough.' She nods and sits
thinking. I know something is coming but I don't know what.
Then she says: 'Do you keep a diary?' 'Off and on.' 'Do you
write in it what happens here?' 'Sometimes.' She nods. And I
know what is in her mind. It is that the process, writing a
diary, is the beginning of what she thinks of as unfreezing,
the releasing of the 'block' that stops me writing. I felt so
angry, so resentful, that I couldn't say anything. I felt as if, in
mentioning the diary, in making it part of her process, so to
speak, she was robbing me of it.

[At this point the diary stopped, as a personal document.
It continued in the form of newspaper cuttings, carefully
pasted in and dated.]

March, 50

The modeller calls this the 'H-Bomb Style,' explaining that
the 'H' is for peroxide of hydrogen, used for colouring. The
hair is dressed to rise in waves as from a bomb-burst, at the
nape of the neck. *Daily Telegraph*

July 13th, 50

There were cheers in Congress today when Mr Lloyd
Bentsen, Democrat, urged that President Truman should tell
the North Koreans to withdraw within a week or their towns
would be atom-bombed. *Express*

July 29th, 50

Britain's decision to spend £100 millions more on Defence

239

means, as Mr Attlee has made clear, that hoped-for improvements in living standards and social services must be postponed. *New Statesman*

Aug. 3, 50

America is to go right ahead with the H Bomb, expected to be hundreds of times more powerful than the atom bombs. *Express*

Aug. 5th, 50

Basing its conclusions on the lessons of Hiroshima and Nagasaki as to the range of blast, heat-flash, radiation, etc., it assumes that one atom bomb might kill 50,000 people in a British built-up area. But, leaving out the Hydrogen Bomb, it is surely unsafe to assume that . . . *New Statesman*

24th Nov., 50

MACARTHUR PUTS IN 100,000 TROOPS IN AN OFFENSIVE TO END THE WAR IN KOREA. *Express*

9th Dec., 50

KOREA PEACE TALKS OFFERED BUT ALLIES WOULD NOT APPEASE. *Express*

16th Dec., 50

U.S. 'IN GRAVE DANGER.' Emergency call today. President Truman tonight told Americans that the U.S. is in 'grave danger' created by the rulers of the Soviet Union.

13th Jan., 51

Truman yesterday set vast targets for the U.S. Defence effort involving sacrifices for all Americans. *Express*

12th March, 51

A-BOMBS BY EISENHOWER. I would use them at once

if I thought it would bring sufficient destruction to the enemy. *Express*

April 6th, 51

WOMAN ATOM SPY TO DIE. Husband too sent to Electric Chair. Judge: You Caused Korea.

May 2nd

KOREA: 371 KILLED, WOUNDED OR MISSING.

9th June, 51

The U.S. Supreme Court has sustained the conviction of the eleven leaders of the American Communist Party for conspiracy to teach the violent overthrow of the Government. The sentences of five years in prison and individual fines of $10,000 will now be enforced. *Statesman*

16th June, 51

Sir: *The Los Angeles Times* of June 2, states: 'In Korea it is estimated that some 2 million civilians, the greater part of them children, have been killed or have died of exposure since the start of the war. More than ten million are homeless and destitute.' Dong Sung Kim, special envoy of the Republic of Korea, reported June 1st here: 'In just one night, there were 156 villages burned. The villages were in the path of an enemy advance. So, of course, the U.N. planes had to destroy them. And all the old people and children who were still there because they were unable to heed the evacuation orders were killed.' *New Statesman*

13th July, 51

Truce Talks Held Up—because the Reds refuse to allow 20 Allied reporters and photographers into Kaesong. *Express*

July 16th

10,000 in oil-land riots. Troops use tear-gas. *Express*

July 28th

Rearmament has up till now brought no sacrifice to the American people. On the contrary, consumption is still rising.
New Statesman

1st Sept., 51

The technique of quick-freezing germ-cells and keeping them indefinitely can mean a complete change in the significance of time. At present it applies to the male sperm, but it might also be adapted to the female ovum. A man alive in 1951 and a woman alive in 2,051 might be 'mated' in 2,251 to produce a child by a pre-natal foster-mother. *Statesman*

Oct. 17, 51

MOSLEM WORLD FLARES. More troops for Suez. *Express*

Oct. 20

ARMY SEALS OFF EGYPT. *Express*

16th Nov., 51

12,790 Allied war prisoners and 250,000 South Korean civilians have been murdered by Reds in Korea. *Express*

24th Nov., 51

Within the lifetime of some of our children the world's population may be expected to reach 4,000 millions. How shall we work the miracle of feeding the 4,000 millions?
Statesman

24th Nov., 51

No one knows how many people were executed, imprisoned, sent to labour camps or died during months of interrogation in the great Soviet purge of 1937–39, nor whether a million or twenty million people are engaged in forced labour in Russia today. *Statesman*

Dec. 13th, 51

RUSSIA BUILDS A-BOMBER. Fastest in the World.
Express

1st Dec., 51

The U.S. is riding the greatest boom in history. Though its spending on armaments and on overseas economic aid alone is now larger than the entire pre-war Federal Budget. *Statesman*

29th Dec., 51

This was the first peace-time year in British history when we had eleven divisions overseas and consumed ten per cent of our national income in armaments. *Statesman*

29th Dec., 51

There are signs that McCarthy and his friends may at last have gone too far in the United States. *Statesman*

12th Jan, 1952

When President Truman told the world, early in 1950, that the U.S. would accelerate efforts to produce the H-bomb—which would have, according to the scientists, an explosive effect 1,000 times greater than the Hiroshima bomb, or equal to twenty million tons of T.N.T.—Albert Einstein pointed out quietly that there 'emerges, more and more distinctly, the spectre of general annihilation.' *Statesman*

1st March, 1952

Just as hundreds of thousands of innocent people were condemned as witches in the Middle Ages, so multitudes of Communists and Russian patriots were purged for mythical counter-revolutionary activities. Indeed, it was precisely because there was nothing to uncover that the arrests reached such fantastic proportions (by a most ingenious method, Mr

243

Weissberg calculates that eight million innocent people probably passed through the prisons between 1936 and 1939).

Statesman

22nd March, 1952

The charge that the United Nations are using bacteriological warfare in Korea cannot be dismissed merely because it would be insane. *Statesman*

April 15th, 52

Roumanian Communist Government has ordered mass deportation of 'unproductive people' from Bucharest. They number 200,000 or one-fifth of the city. *Express*

28th June, 52

It is impossible to establish the number of Americans who have had their passports restricted or denied, but known cases reveal that a wide range of individuals of different backgrounds, beliefs and political persuasions have been affected. The list includes . . . *Statesman*

5th July, 52

Most important of all, the effect of the American witch-hunt is to produce a general level of conformity, a new orthodoxy from which a man dissents at his economic peril.

Statesman

2nd Sept., 52

The Home Secretary said that although grave damage must be caused by an accurately delivered atom bomb, it is sometimes wildly exaggerated. *Express*

I am well aware that you cannot carry out a revolution with rosewater; my query was whether, in order to defeat the danger of war from Formosa, it was necessary to execute a million and a half, or whether to disarm them might not have been adequate. *Statesman*

Dec. 13th, 1952

JAPANESE DEMAND ARMS. *Express*

Dec. 13th

Title II of the McCarran Act specifically provides for the establishment of so-called detention centres. Far from *directing* the creation of such centres, the law *authorises* the Attorney-General of the U.S. to apprehend and detain 'in such places of detention as may be prescribed by him ... all persons as to whom there is reasonable ground to believe that such persons probably will engage in or probably will conspire with others to engage in acts of espionage and sabotage.'

Oct. 3rd, 52

OUR BOMB GOES OFF. First British atomic weapon exploded successfully. *Express*

11th Oct., 52

MAU MAU SLASH COLONEL. *Express*

23rd Oct., 52

BIRCH THEM. Lord Goddard, Chief Justice. *Express*

25th Oct., 52

Colonel Robert Scott, Commanding Officer of the American Air Base at Furstenfeldbruck: 'The preliminary treaty between America and Germany has been signed. I earnestly hope that your fatherland will soon stand as a full-fledged member of the N.A.T.O. forces ... I impatiently wait with you for the day when we will stand shoulder to shoulder as friends and brothers to resist the threat of Communism. I hope and pray that the moment will soon come when either I or some other American commander will turn this fine Air Base over to some German Wing Commander with the beginning of Germany's new Luftwaffe.' *Statesman*

17th Nov., 52

U.S. TRIES OUT H. BOMB. *Express*

1st Nov., 52

Korea: Total casualties since the truce talks started including civilians, will soon be getting close to the number of prisoners whose status has become the main obstacle to the truce. *Statesman*

27th Nov., 52

Kenya's Government announced tonight that as collective punishment for the murder of Commander Jack Meiklejohn last Saturday, 750 men and 2,200 women and children have been evacuated from their homes. *Express*

8th Nov.

In recent years it has been fashionable to denounce the critics of McCarthyism as dyspetic 'anti-Americans.' *Statesman*

22nd Nov., 52

It is only two years since President Truman gave the word 'Go' on the H-Bomb programme. Forthwith a billion-dollar plant was put under construction at Savannah River, South Carolina, to produce tritium (triple-atom-hydrogen); by the end of 1951, the B-bomb industry had become an industrial undertaking comparable only with U.S. Steel and General Motors. *Statesman*

22nd Nov., 52

But the first shot of the present campaign was fired—most conveniently to coincide with the hectic climax of a Republican election campaign which had made all possible capital out of Alger Hiss's 'contamination' of the State Department— by the Republican Senator, Alexander Wiley, of Wisconsin in his disclosure that he had demanded an investigation of the 'extensive infiltration' of the U.N. Secretariat by American Communists ... Then the Senate Sub-Committee on Internal Security proceeded to cross-examine its first twelve victims in the new drive, all of them high officials ... yet the refusal of the 12 witnesses to testify about any Communist affiliations did not save them from ... But the witch-hunting Senators were clearly out for bigger fry than the twelve against whom the only evidence of subversion and espionage adduced was their silence. *Statesman*

Nov. 29th, 52

The Czech Sabotage Trial, though it follows the standard pattern of political justice in the People's Democracies, is of unusual interest. In the first place, Czechoslovakia was the only country in the Eastern Bloc which possessed a deeply rooted democratic way of life, including full civil liberties and an independent judiciary. *Statesman*

Dec. 3rd, 52

DARTMOOR MAN FLOGGED. Thug gets 12 lashes with the Cat. *Express*

Dec. 17th, 1952

11 COMMUNIST LEADERS HANGED IN PRAGUE. Capitalist Spies Claims Czech Government.

29th Dec., 1952

A new £10,000 atom factory designed to double Britain's output of atomic weapons. *Express*

13th January, 53

SOVIET MURDER-PLOT SHOCK. Moscow radio accused early today a group of Terrorist Jewish doctors of trying to assassinate Russian leaders—including some of the top Soviet military men and an atomic scientist. *Express*

6th March, 1953

STALIN DIES. *Express*

23rd March, 1953

2,500 MAU MAU ARRESTS. *Express*

23rd March, 1953

AMNESTY IN RUSSIA FOR PRISONERS. *Express*

1st April, 1953

WHAT COULD PEACE IN KOREA MEAN TO YOU?
Express

7th May, 1953

PEACE HOPES RISING IN KOREA. *Express*

8th May, 1953

America is discussing possible United Nations action 'to curb Communist aggression in S.E. Asia.' And she is sending large quantities of planes, tanks and ammunition to Indo-China. *Express*

13th May

ATROCITIES IN EGYPT. *Express*

18th July, 1953

BERLIN NIGHT BATTLE. 15,000 People of East Berlin were fighting a division of Soviet tanks and infantry in the dark streets early this morning. *Express*

6th July

REVOLT IN ROUMANIA. *Express*

10th July, 53

BERIA TRIED AND SHOT. *Express*

27th July, 1953

KOREAN CEASE-FIRE. *Express*

7th August, 1953

MASS P.O.W. RIOT. Mass rioting by 12,000 North Korean p.o.w. was put down by U.N. guards using tear-gas and small arms fire. *Express*

20th Aug., 1953

300 dead in coup. Persia. *Express*

19th Feb., 1954

Britain has A-bomb stock-pile now. *Express*

27th March, 1954

2nd H-BOMB IS DELAYED—Isles still too hot from blast No. 1. *Express*

30th March

2nd H-BOMB EXPLODED. *Express*

[And now the personal entries began again.]

2nd April, 1954

I realised today that I was beginning to withdraw from what Mrs Marks calls my 'experience' with her; and because of something she said; she must have known it for some time. She said: 'You must remember that the end of an analysis does not mean the end of the experience itself.' 'You mean, the yeast goes on working?' She smiled and nodded.

4th April, 1954

I had the bad dream again—I was menaced by the anarchic principle, this time in the shape of an inhuman sort of dwarf. In the dream was Mrs Marks, very large and powerful; like a kind of amiable witch. She heard the dream out, and said: 'When you are on your own, and you are threatened, you must summon the good witch to your aid.' 'You,' I said. 'No, you, embodied in what you have made of me.' So the thing is over, then. It was as if she had said: Now you are on your own. For she spoke casually, indifferently almost, like someone turning away. I admired the skill of this; it was as if, on leave-taking, she were handing me something— a flowering branch, perhaps, or a talisman against evil.

7th April, 1954

She asked me if I had kept notes of the 'experience.' Now she has never, not once, in the last three years mentioned the diary; so she must have known by instinct I had not kept notes. I said: 'No.' 'You have kept no record at all?' 'No. I have a very good memory, though.' A silence. 'So the diary you started has remained empty?' 'No, I stuck in cuttings from newspapers.' 'What kind of cuttings?' 'Just things that struck me—events that seemed important.' She gave me the quizzical look, which said: Well, I'm waiting for the definition. I said: 'I glanced over them the other day: what I've got is a record of war, murder, chaos, misery.' 'And that seems to you the truth about the last few years?' 'Doesn't it seem to you to be the truth?' She looked at me—ironical. She was saying without words that our 'experience' has been creative and fructifying, and that I am dishonest in saying what I did. I said: 'Very well then; the newspaper cuttings were to keep things in proportion. I've spent three years, more, wrestling with my precious soul, and meanwhile . . .' 'Meanwhile what?' 'It's just a matter of luck that I haven't been tortured, murdered, starved to death, or died in a prison.' She looked patiently ironical, and I said. 'Surely you must see that what happens here, in this room, doesn't only link one with what you call creativity. It links one with ... but I don't know what to call it.' 'I'm glad you aren't going to use the word destruction.' 'All right, everything has two faces, etc., but for all that, whenever anything happens anywhere that is terrible, I dream about it, as if I were involved in it personally.' 'You have been cutting all the bad things out of the newspapers and sticking them in your diary of this experience, as an instruction to yourself of how to dream?' 'But Mrs Marks, what's wrong with that?' We have reached this particular deadlock so often, neither of us try to break it. She sat smiling at me, dry and patient. I faced her, challenging her.

9th April, 1954

She said to me today as I was leaving: 'And now my dear, when are you going to start writing again?' I might have said, of course, that all this time I've been scribbling off and on in the notebooks but that is not what she meant. I said: 'Very likely never.' She made an impatient, almost irritable gesture; she looked vexed, like a housewife whose plans have gone wrong—the gesture was genuine, not one of the smiles, or nods, or shakes of the head, or impatient clicks of the tongue that she uses to conduct a session. 'Why can't you understand that,' I said, really wanting to make her understand, 'that I can't pick up a newspaper without what's in it seeming so overwhelmingly terrible that nothing I could write would seem to have any point at all?' 'Then you shouldn't read the newspapers.' I laughed. After a while she smiled with me.

15th April, 1954

I have had several dreams, all to do with Michael's leaving me. It was from my dreams that I knew he soon would; he soon will. In my sleep I watch these scenes of parting. Without emotion. In my life I am desperately, vividly unhappy; asleep I am unmoved. Mrs Marks asked me today: 'If I were to ask you to say in a phrase what you have learned from me, what would you reply?' 'That you have taught me to cry,' I said, not without dryness. She smiled, accepting the dryness. 'And so?' 'And I'm a hundred times more vulnerable than I was.' 'And so? Is that all?' 'You mean, I am also a hundred times stronger? I don't know. I don't know at all. I hope so.' 'I know,' she said, with emphasis. 'You are very much stronger. And you will write of this experience.' A quick firm nod; then she said: 'You will see. In a few months' time, perhaps a few years' time.' I shrugged. We made an appointment for next week; it will be the last appointment.

23rd April

I had a dream for my last appointment. I took it to Mrs Marks. I dreamed I held a kind of casket in my hands, and inside it was something very precious. I was walking up a long room, like an art gallery or a lecture hall, full of dead pictures and statues. (When I used the word dead, Mrs Marks smiled, ironically.) There was a small crowd of people waiting at the end of the hall on a kind of platform. They were waiting for me to hand them the casket. I was incredibly happy that at last I could give them this precious object. But when I handed it over, I saw suddenly they were all businessmen, brokers, something like that. They did not open the box, but started handing me large sums of money. I began to cry. I shouted: 'Open the box, open the box,' but they couldn't hear me, or wouldn't listen. Suddenly I saw they were all characters in some film or play, and that I had written it, and was ashamed of it. It all turned into farce, flickering and grotesque, I was a character in my own play. I opened the box and forced them to look. But instead of a beautiful thing, which I thought would be there, there was a mass of fragments, and pieces. Not a whole thing, broken into fragments, but bits and pieces from everywhere, all over the world—I recognised a lump of red earth that I knew came from Africa, and then a bit of metal that came off a gun from Indo-China, and then everything was horrible, bits of flesh from people killed in the Korean War and a communist party badge off someone who died in a Soviet prison. This, looking at the mass of ugly fragments, was so painful that I couldn't look, and I shut the box. But the group of businessmen or money-people hadn't noticed. They took the box from me and opened it. I turned away so as not to see, but they were delighted. At last I looked and I saw that there was something in the box. It was a small green crocodile with a winking sardonic snout. I thought it was the image of a crocodile, made of jade, or emeralds, then I saw it was alive, for large frozen tears rolled down its cheeks and turned into diamonds. I laughed out loud when I saw how I had cheated the businessmen and I woke up. Mrs Marks listened to this dream without comment, she seemed uninterested. We said good-bye with affection, but she has already turned away, inwardly, as I have. She said I must 'drop in to see her' if I needed her. I thought, how can I need you when you have bequeathed to me your image; I know perfectly well I shall dream of that large maternal witch every time I am in trouble. (Mrs Marks is a very small wiry, energetic woman, yet I have always dreamed of her as large and powerful.) I went out of that darkened, solemn room in which I have spent so many hours half-in, half-out, of fantasy and dream, the room which is like a shrine to art, and I reached the cold ugly pavement. I saw myself in a shop window: a small, rather pale, dry, spiky woman, and there was a wry look on my face which I recognised as the grin on the snout of that malicious little green crocodile in the crystal casket of my dream.

FREE WOMEN: 2

■ FREE WOMEN: 2 ■

Two visits, some telephone calls and a tragedy

THE telephone rang just as Anna was tiptoeing from
the child's room. Janet started up again, and said on a
satisfied grumbling note: 'That's Molly, I expect, and you'll
be talking for hours and hours.' 'Shhhh,' said Anna; and went
to the telephone thinking: For children like Janet the fabric
of security is woven, not of grandparents, cousins, a settled
home; but that friends telephone every day, and certain
words are spoken.

'Janet is just going to sleep and she sends her love,' she
said loudly into the instrument; and Molly replied, playing
her part: 'Send my love to Janet and say she must go to sleep
at once.'

'Molly says you must go to sleep, she says good night,' said
Anna loudly into the darkened room. Janet said: 'How can I
go to sleep when now you two are going to talk for hours
and hours?' The quality of the silence from Janet's room,
however, told Anna that the child was going to sleep, satisfied; and she lowered her voice and said: 'All right. How
are you?'

Molly said, over-casual: 'Anna, is Tommy with you?'

'No, why should he be?'

'Oh, I just wondered . . . If he knew I was worrying he'd
be furious, of course.'

For the last month, Molly's daily bulletins from the house
half a mile away had consisted of nothing but Tommy; who
was sitting hour after hour in his room, alone, not moving,
apparently not even thinking.

Now Molly abandoned the topic of her son, and gave
Anna a long, humorous, grumbling account of the dinner she

257

had had the night before with some old flame from America. Anna listened, hearing the under-current of hysteria in her friend's voice, waiting for her to conclude: 'Well anyway, I looked at that pompous middle-aged slob sitting there, and I thought of what he used to be like—well, I expect he was thinking, what a pity Molly's turned out the way she has—but why do I criticise everyone so? There isn't anyone good enough for me ever? And it isn't even as if I can compare present offerings with some beautiful past experience, because I can't remember ever being really satisfied, I've never said: Yes, this is it. But I've been remembering Sam for years ever so nostalgically, as the best of the bunch, and even wondering why I was such a fool to turn him down, and today I was remembering how much he bored me even then—what are you going to do when Janet is asleep? Are you going out?'

'No. I'm staying in.'

'I've got to dash to the theatre. I'm late as it is. Anna would you telephone Tommy here, in about an hour—make some excuse or other.'

'What's worrying you?'

'Tommy went down to Richard's office this afternoon. Yes, I know, you could have knocked me down with a feather. Richard rang me and said: "I insist Tommy comes to see me at once." So I said to Tommy: "Your father insists you go to see him at once." Tommy said, "all right mother," and got up and went. Just like that. To humour me. I got the feeling if I'd said, Jump out of the window, he'd have jumped.'

'Has Richard said anything?'

'He rang about three hours ago, ever so sarcastic and superior, saying I didn't understand Tommy. I said I was glad he did, at least. But he said Tommy had just left. But he hasn't come home. I went up to Tommy's room and he's got half a dozen books on psychology from the library on his bed. He's been reading them all at once from the look of it ... I must rush, Anna, it takes me half an hour to make up for this part—bloody stupid play, why did I ever say I'd be in it? Well, good night.'

Ten minutes later Anna was standing by her trestle table, preparing to work on her blue notebook, when Molly rang again. 'I've just had a call from Marion. Can you believe it?—Tommy went down to see her. He must have taken the first train after leaving Richard's office. He stayed twenty minutes and then left again. Marion said he was very quiet. And he hasn't been there for ages. Anna, don't you think it's odd?'

'He was very quiet?'

'Well, Marion was drunk again. Of course Richard hadn't come. He's never home before midnight these days—there's that girl in his office. Marion went on and on about it. She was probably going on and on to Tommy too. She was talking about you—she's got it in for you all right. So I suppose Richard must have told her he had been having a thing with you.'

'But we didn't.'

'Have you seen him again?'

'No. Nor Marion either.'

The two women stood by their respective telephones, silent; if they had been in the same room they would have exchanged wry glances or smiles. Suddenly Anna heard: 'I'm terrified, Anna. Something awful is happening, I'm sure of it. Oh God, I don't know what to do, and I must rush—I'll have to take a taxi now. Good-bye.'

Usually, at the sound of feet on the stairs, Anna removed herself from the part of the big room where she would be forced into an unnecessary exchange of greetings with the young man from Wales. This time she looked sharply around and only just prevented an exclamation of relief as the footsteps turned out to be Tommy's. His smile acknowledged her, her room, the pencil in her hand, and her spread notebooks, as a scene he had expected to see. But having smiled, his dark eyes focused inwards again, and his face set solemn. Anna had instinctively reached for the telephone, and checked herself, thinking she should make an excuse to go upstairs and telephone from there. But Tommy said: 'I suppose you are thinking you must telephone my mother?' 'Yes. She has just rung me.' 'Then go upstairs if you want, I don't mind.' This was kindly, to set her at ease. 'No, I'll ring from here.' 'I suppose she's been snooping in my room and she's upset because of all those madness books.'

At the word madness, Anna felt her face tighten in shock; saw Tommy notice it; then exclaimed, with energy: 'Tommy, sit down. I've got to talk to you. But first I must ring Molly.' Tommy showed no surprise at her sudden decisiveness.

He sat down, arranged himself neatly, legs together, arms before him on the chair-arms, and watched Anna as she telephoned. But Molly had already left. Anna sat on her bed, frowning with annoyance: she had become convinced that Tommy was enjoying frightening them all. Tommy remarked: 'Anna, your bed's just like a coffin.' Anna saw herself, small, pale, neat, wearing black trousers and a black shirt, squatting cross-legged on the narrow black-draped bed. 'Then it's like a coffin,' she said; but she got off the bed and sat opposite him in a chair. His eyes were now moving, slow and careful, from object to object around the room, giving Anna exactly the same allowance of attention as chair, books, fireplace, a picture.

'I hear you went to see your father?'

'Yes.'

'What did he want you for?'

'You were going to say, If you don't mind my asking—' he said. Then he giggled. The giggle was new—harsh, uncontrolled, and malicious. At the sound Anna felt rise in her a wave of panic. She even felt a desire to giggle herself. She calmed herself, thinking: He hasn't been here five minutes, but his hysteria's infecting me already. Be careful.

She said, smiling: 'I was going to say it, but I stopped myself.'

'What's the point of that? I know you and my mother discuss me all the time. You're worried about me.' Again he was calmly but triumphantly malicious. Anna had never associated malice or spite with Tommy; and she felt as if there were a stranger in her room. He even looked strange, for his blunt dark obstinate face was twisted into a mask of smiling spite: he was looking upwards at her from slitted spiteful eyes and smiling.

'What did your father want?'

'He said that one of the firms *his* firm controls is building a dam in Ghana. He said would I like to go out and take a job looking after the Africans—welfare work.'

'You said no?'

'I said I didn't see the point—I mean, the point of them is being cheap labour for him. So even if I did make them a bit healthier and feed them better and that kind of thing, or even get schools for the children, it wouldn't be the point at all. So he said another of his company's companies is doing some engineering job in North Canada, and he offered me a welfare job there.'

He waited, looking at Anna. The malicious stranger had vanished from the room; Tommy was himself, frowning, thoughtful, puzzled. He said unexpectedly: 'You know, he's not stupid at all.'

'I don't think we've said he is.'

Tommy smiled patiently, saying: You're dishonest. He said aloud: 'When I said I didn't want those jobs he asked why, and I told him, and he said, I reacted like that because of the influence of the communist party.'

Anna laughed: I told you so; and said: 'He means your mother and me.'

Tommy waited for her to have finished saying what he had expected her to say, and said: 'There you are. That's not what he meant. No wonder you all think each other stupid; you expect each other to be. When I see my father and my mother together, I don't recognise them, they're so stupid. And you too, when you are with Richard.'

'Well what did he mean, then?'

'He said that what I replied to his offers summed up the real influence of the communist parties on the West. He said that anyone who has been, or is, in the C.P., or who has had anything to do with it is a megalomaniac. He said that if he was Chief of Police trying to root out communists somewhere, he'd ask one question: Would you go to an undeveloped country and run a country clinic for fifty people? All the Reds would answer: 'No, because what's the point of improving the health of fifty people when the basic organisation of society is unchanged.' He leaned forward, confronting her, and insisted: 'Well, Anna?' She smiled and nodded: All right; but it was not enough. She said: 'No, that's not stupid at all.'

'No.' He leaned back, relieved. But having rescued his father, so to speak, from Molly's and Anna's scorn, he now paid them their due: 'But I said to him, that test wouldn't rule you or my mother out, because both of you would go to that clinic, wouldn't you?' It was important to him that she should say yes; but Anna insisted on honesty, for her own sake. 'Yes, I would, but he's right. That's exactly how I'd feel.'

'But you'd go?'

'Yes.'

'I wonder if you would? Because I don't think I would. I mean, I'm not taking either of these jobs so that proves it. And I haven't even been a communist—I've just seen you and my mother and your friends at it, and it's influenced me. I'm suffering from a paralysis of the will.'

'Richard used the words, paralysis of the will?' said Anna, disbelieving.

'No. It's what he meant. I found the words in one of the madness books. What he actually said was, the result of the communist countries on Europe is that people can't be bothered. Because everyone's got used to the idea of whole countries changing completely in about three years—like China or Russia. And if they can't see a complete change ahead, they can't be bothered . . . do you think that's true?'

'It's partly true. It's true of people who have been inside the communist myth.'

'Not so long ago you were a communist and now you use words like communist myth.'

'Sometimes I get the impression you blame me and your mother and the rest of us for not still being communists.'

Tommy lowered his head, sat frowning. 'Well I remember when you used to be so active, rushing around doing things. You don't now.'

'Any activity being better than none?'

He raised his head and said sharply, accusing: 'You know what I mean.'

'Yes of course I do.'

'Do you know what I said to my father? I said if I went out to do his dishonest welfare work I'd start organising revolutionary groups among the workers. He wasn't angry at all. He said revolutions were a primary risk of big business these days and he'd be careful to take out an insurance policy against the revolution I'd stir up.' Anna said nothing and Tommy said: 'It was a joke, do you see?'

'Yes, I see.'

'But I told him not to lose any sleep on my account. Because I wouldn't organise revolutions. Twenty years ago I would. But not now. Because now we know what happens to revolutionary groups—we'd be murdering each other inside five years.'

'Not necessarily.'

Tommy's look at her said: You're dishonest. He said: 'I remember about two years ago, you and my mother were talking. You said to my mother, If we'd been unlucky enough to be communists in Russia or Hungary or somewhere, one of us would very likely have shot the other as a traitor. That was a joke too.'

Anna said: 'Tommy, your mother and I have both led somewhat complicated lives, and we've done a lot of things. You can't expect us to be full of youthful certainties and slogans and battle-cries. We're both of us getting on for being middle-aged.' Anna heard herself make these remarks with a certain amount of wry surprise, even dislike. She was saying to herself: I sound like a tired old liberal. She decided, however, to stand by them, and looked at Tommy to find him very critically looking at her. He said: 'You mean, I've no right to make middle-aged remarks at my age? Well, Anna, I feel middle-aged. Now what do you have to say?' The malicious stranger had come back, and was sitting in front of her, his eyes full of spite.

She said quickly: 'Tommy, tell me something: how would you sum up your interview with your father?'

Tommy sighed and became himself. 'Whenever I go to his office I am surprised. I remember the first time—I'd always seen him in our house, and once or twice at Marion's. Well,

263

I'd always thought him very—ordinary, you know? Common-place. Dull. Like you and my mother do. Well, the first time I saw him in his office I felt confused—I know you're going to say it's the power he has, all that money. But it was more than that. He suddenly didn't seem ordinary and second-rate.'

Anna sat silent, thinking: What is he getting at? What am I failing to see?

He said: 'Oh I know what you're thinking, you're thinking Tommy is ordinary and second-rate himself.'

Anna blushed: she had, in the past, thought that of Tom-my. He saw her blush and smiled malignantly. He said: 'Ordinary people aren't necessarily stupid, Anna. I know quite well what I am. And that's why I am confused when I'm in my father's office, watching him being a sort of tycoon. Because I'd do that well too. But I couldn't, ever, because I'd do it with a divided mind—because of you and my mother. The difference between my father and me is that I know I'm commonplace and he doesn't. I know quite well that people like you and my mother are a hundred times better than he is—even though you're such failures and in such a mess. But I'm sorry I know it. You mustn't tell my mother this, but I'm very sorry my father didn't bring me up—if he had I'd have been very happy to inherit his shoes.'

Anna could not prevent herself giving him a sharp glance—she suspected he had said this so that she should in fact tell Molly what he had said, so as to hurt her. But on his face was the patient, earnest, inward-looking stare of his intro-spection. Anna could feel, however, a wave of hysteria rise in herself; and knew it reflected his; and searched wildly for words which could check him. She saw him turn his heavy head on the pivot of his thick short neck and look at her notebooks lying exposed on the trestle; and thought: Good Lord, I hope he hasn't come here to talk about them? About me? She said quickly: 'I think you're making your father out to be much more simple than he is. I don't think he has an undivided mind: he once said being a big businessman these days was like being a rather superior office boy. And you forget that in the 'thirties he had a spell of being a communist, and he was even a bit of a bohemian for a while.'

'And his way of remembering that now is to have affairs with his secretaries—that's his way of persuading himself he's not just an ordinary respectable cog in the middle-class wheel.' This came out shrill and revengeful, and Anna thought: That's what he has come to talk about. She felt relief.

Tommy said: 'After I went to my father's office this afternoon I went down to see Marion. I just wanted to see her. I usually see her in our house. She was drunk, and those kids were pretending not to notice it. She was talking about my father and his secretary and they were pretending not to know what she was talking about.' Now he waited for her to say something, leaning forward, his eyes slitted in accusation. When she did not speak, he said: 'Well, why don't you say what you think? I know you despise my father. It's because he's not a good man.'

At the word good, Anna involuntarily laughed, and saw his frown. She said: 'I'm sorry, but it's not a word I use.'

'Why not? It's what you mean. My father's ruined Marion and he's ruining those children. Well, isn't he? Well, you're not going to say it's Marion's fault?'

'Tommy, I don't know what to say—you come here, and I know you want me to say things that make sense. But I simply don't know . . .'

Tommy's pale sweating face was deadly earnest, and his eyes shone with sincerity. But with something else—in them was a gleam of the spiteful satisfaction; he was convicting her of failing him; and pleased that she was failing him. Again he turned his head and looked at the notebooks. Now, thought Anna; now I must say what he wants to hear. But before she could think, he had got up and walked over to the notebooks. Anna tensed herself and sat quiet; she could not endure that anyone should see those notebooks and yet she felt that Tommy had a right to see them: but she could not have explained why. He stood with his back to her, looking down at the notebooks. Then he turned his head and said: 'Why do you have four notebooks?'

265

'I don't know.'

'You must know.'

'I didn't ever say to myself: I'm going to keep four notebooks, it just happened.'

'Why not one notebook?'

She thought a while and said: 'Perhaps because it would be such a—scramble. Such a mess.'

'Why shouldn't it be a mess?'

Anna was trying for just the right words to offer him when Janet's voice sounded from upstairs: 'Mummy?'

'Yes? I thought you were asleep.'

'I was asleep. I'm thirsty. Who are you talking to?'

'Tommy. Do you want him to come up and say good night?'

'Yes. And I want some water.'

Tommy quietly turned himself and went out; Anna heard him running water from the tap in the kitchen, and then plodding up the stairs. Meanwhile she was in an extraordinary tumult of sensations; as if every particle and cell of her body had been touched with some irritant. Tommy's presence in the room and the necessity to think of how to face him had kept her more or less Anna, more or less herself. But now she hardly recognised herself. She wanted to laugh, to cry, even to scream; she wanted to hurt some object by taking hold of it and shaking and shaking until—this object was of course Tommy. She told herself that his state of mind had infected her; that she was being invaded by his emotions; marvelled that what appeared in his face as gleams of spite and hatred appeared in his voice briefly as shrillness or hardness—should be the outward signs of such a violent inward storm; and suddenly understood that her palms and her armpits were cold and wet. She was afraid. All her various and conflicting sensations amounted to this: she was terrified. It surely wasn't possible that she was physically frightened of Tommy? So frightened and yet she had sent him upstairs to talk to her child? But no, she was not in the least frightened for Janet. She could hear the two voices upstairs in cheerful exchange. Then a laugh—Janet's. Then the slow determined steps and Tommy came back. He said at once: 'What do you think Janet will be when she grows up?' His face was pale and obstinate, but no more; and Anna felt easier. He stood by the trestle table, one hand on it, and Anna said: 'I don't know. She's only eleven.'

'Don't you worry about it?'

'No. Children keep changing. How do I know what she'll want later on?'

His mouth pouted forward in a critical smile, and she said: 'Why, have I said something stupid again?'

'It's the way you say it. Your attitude.'

'I'm sorry.' But in spite of herself, this sounded aggrieved, certainly irritated; and Tommy very briefly smiled with satisfaction. 'Do you ever think about Janet's father?'

This shock reached Anna's diaphragm; she felt it tighten. She said, however: 'No, hardly ever.' He stared at her; and she went on: 'You want me to say what I really feel, don't you? You sounded just then like Mother Sugar. She would say to me things like: He's the father of your child. Or: He was your husband. But it didn't mean anything to me. What's troubling you—that your mother didn't really care for Richard? Well she was much more involved with Richard than I ever was with Max Wulf.' He was standing straight, very pale, and his stare was all inwards; Anna doubted whether he saw her at all. It appeared however that he was listening, so she went on: 'I understand what it means: having a child by the man you love. But I didn't understand it until I loved a man. I wanted to have a child by Michael. But the fact is, I had a child by a man I didn't love . . .' She trailed off, wondering if he were listening. His eyes were directed at the wall at a point some feet away. He turned his dark abstracted gaze towards her, and said in a tone of feeble sarcasm she had never heard from him: 'Go on, Anna. It's a great revelation to me, hearing an experienced person talk of their emotions.' His eyes, however, were deadly serious, so she swallowed the annoyance that the sarcasm had released in her, and went on: 'It seems to me like this. It's not a terrible thing I mean, it may be terrible, but it's not damaging, it's not poisoning, to do without something one wants. It's not bad to say: My work is not what I really want, I'm capable of doing something bigger. Or I'm a person who needs love, and I'm doing without it. What's terrible is to pretend that the second-rate is first-rate. To pretend that you don't need love when you do; or you like your work when you know quite well you're capable of better. It would be very bad if I said, out of guilt or something: I loved Janet's father, when I know quite well I didn't. Or for your mother to say: I loved Richard. Or I'm doing work I love . . .' Anna stopped. Tommy had nodded. She could not make out whether he was pleased with what she had said, or whether it was a thought so obvious he didn't want to hear it said. He turned back to the notebooks, and opened the blue-covered one. Anna saw his shoulders heave in sarcastic laughter, designed to provoke her.

'Well?'

He read out: 'March 12, 1956. Janet is suddenly aggressive and difficult. Altogether a difficult phase.'

'Well?'

'I remember your once saying to my mother, how's Tommy? My mother's voice is not exactly designed for confidences. She said in a ringing whisper: Oh, he's in a difficult phase.'

'Perhaps you were.'

'A phase—it was one night when you were having supper with my mother in the kitchen. I lay in bed and listened, you were laughing and talking. I came down the stairs to get a glass of water. I was unhappy just then, worrying about everything. I couldn't do my school-work and I was frightened at night. Of course the glass of water was just a pretence. I wanted to be in the kitchen—because of the way you two laughed. I wanted to be near the laughter. I didn't want either of you to know I was scared. Outside the door I heard you say: How's Tommy, and my mother said, He's in a difficult phase.'

'Well?' Anna was in a trough of exhaustion: she was thinking of Janet. Janet had just woken up and asked for a glass of water. Was Tommy meaning to say to her that Janet was unhappy?

'It cancelled me out,' said Tommy sullenly. 'All through

268

my childhood I kept reaching something that seemed new and important. I kept gaining victories. That night I had won a victory—being able to come down the dark stairs pretending that nothing was wrong. I was clinging on to something, a feeling of who I really was. Then my mother says, just a phase. In other words, what I felt just then didn't matter, it was a product of glands or something, and it would pass.'

Anna said nothing; she was worrying about Janet. Yet the child seemed friendly, cheerful, and she was doing well at school. She very seldom woke at night and had never said anything about being afraid of the dark.

Tommy was saying: 'I suppose you and my mother have been saying that I am in a difficult phase?'

'I don't think we've said it. But I expect we've implied it,' said Anna wryly.

'What I feel now doesn't matter at all? But at what point am I entitled to say to myself, what I am feeling now is valid? After all, Anna—' Here Tommy turned to face her: 'one can't go through one's whole life in phases. There must be a goal somewhere.' His eyes gleamed out hatred; and it was with difficulty that Anna said: 'If you're suggesting that I've reached a goal, and I'm judging you from some superior point, then it's not true.'

'Phases,' he insisted. 'Stages. Growing pains.'

'But I think that's how women see—people. Certainly their own children. In the first place, there's always been nine months of not knowing whether the baby would be a girl or a boy. Sometimes I wonder what Janet would have been like if she'd been born a boy. Don't you *see*? And then babies go through one stage after another, and then they are children. When a woman looks at a child she sees all the things he's been at the same time. When I look at Janet sometimes I see her as a small baby and I *feel* her inside my belly and I see her as various sizes of small girl, all at the same time.' Tommy's stare was accusing and sarcastic, but she persisted: 'That's how women see things. Everything in a sort of continuous creative stream—well, isn't it natural we should?'

'But we're not individuals for you at all. We are simply temporary shapes of something. *Phases*.' And he laughed, angrily. Anna thought that this was the first time he had really laughed, and was encouraged. For a while they were both silent, while he fingered the notebooks, half turned away from her, and she watched him, trying to calm herself, trying to breathe deeply and remain quiet and steady. But her palms were still wet; the thought kept coming into her mind: it's as if I were fighting something, fighting some invisible enemy. She could almost *see* the enemy—something evil, she was sure of it; an almost tangible shape of malice and destruction, that stood between her and Tommy, trying to destroy them both.

She said at last: 'I know what you've come here for. You've come so that I can tell you what we are alive for. But you know in advance what I'm likely to say, because you know me so well. So that means you've come here already knowing what I'm going to say—to confirm something.' She added in a low voice, not meaning to say it: 'That's why I'm so frightened.' It was an appeal; Tommy gave her a quick glance; it was an acknowledgement that she was right to be afraid.

He said stubbornly: 'You're going to tell me that in a month's time I'll feel differently. Suppose I don't? Well tell me Anna—what are we alive for?' Now he was shaking with silent triumphant laughter, his back turned.

'We're a sort of latter-day stoic,' said Anna. 'Our kind of people.'

'You're including me in your kind of people? Thank you Anna.'

'Perhaps your trouble is, you have too many choices.' The set of his shoulders said that he was listening, so she went on: 'Through your father you can reach a half dozen different countries and almost any kind of work. Your mother and I could get you a dozen different sorts of job in the theatre or in publishing. Or you could spend five years or so pleasantly bumming about—your mother or I would pay for you, even if your father wouldn't.'

'A hundred things to do, but only one thing to be,' he said, obstinately. 'But perhaps I don't feel myself worthy of such a

270

wealth of opportunity? And perhaps I'm not a stoic, Anna—have you met Reggie Gates?'

'The milkman's son? No, but your mother has told me.'

'Of course she has. I can almost hear her. The point is, and I'm sure she's made it, he hasn't any choice at all. He's got a scholarship, and if he fails to make the exam, he'll spend his life delivering milk with his father. But if he passes, and he will, he'll be up in the middle-class with us. He hasn't got a hundred opportunities. He's got just one. But he really knows what he wants. He's not suffering from paralysis of the will.'

'You're envying Reggie Gates for his handicaps?'

'Yes. And do you know, he's a Tory. He thinks that people who complain about the system are barmy. I went to a football game with him last week. I wish I were him.' Now he laughed again; but this time Anna felt chilled by the sound. He went on: 'Do you remember Tony?'

'Yes,' said Anna, remembering one of his school friends, who had surprised everyone by deciding to be a conscientious objector. He had worked in a coal mine for two years instead of going into the army, very much annoying his respectable family.

'Tony became a socialist three weeks ago.'

Anna laughed but Tommy said: 'No, that's the point. Do you remember when he became a conscientious objector? It was just to annoy his parents. You know that's true Anna.'

'Yes, but he went through with it, didn't he?'

'I knew Tony very well. I know it was almost—a sort of joke. He even told me once he wasn't even sure he was right. But he wasn't going to let his parents have the laugh on him—that was exactly what he said.'

'All the same,' Anna insisted, 'it couldn't have been easy—two years, doing that sort of work, and he stuck it out.'

'That's not good enough, Anna. And that's exactly how he became a socialist. You know that group of new socialists—mostly Oxford types? They are going to start a magazine, *The Left Review*, or something. Well I've met them. They shout slogans and behave like a lot of . . .'

'Tommy, that's stupid.'

'No it isn't. The only reason they're doing it is, no one can join the communist party now, it's a sort of substitute. They use that awful jargon—well I've heard you and my mother laughing about the jargon so why is it all right for them to use it? Because they're young, I suppose you are going to say, but it's not good enough. And I'll tell you something. In five years time Tony will have a fine job on the National Coal Board or something like that. He'll be a Labour M.P. perhaps. He'll be making speeches about left this and socialist that—' Tommy had become shrill again, he was out of breath.

'He might also be doing a very useful job,' said Anna.

'He doesn't really believe in it. It's an attitude he's taken up. And he's got a girl—he's going to marry her. A sociologist. She's one of that crowd too. They rush around sticking up posters and shouting slogans.'

'You sound as if you envy him.'

'Don't patronise me, Anna. You're patronising me.'

'I didn't mean to. I don't think I was.'

'Yes you are. I know quite well if you were discussing Tony with my mother you'd be saying something different. And if you could see that girl—I can just hear what you'd be saying. She's a sort of mother-figure. Why aren't you honest with me Anna?' This last phrase he positively shrieked at her; his face was distorted. He glared at her, then turned quickly, and as if he had needed this flare of anger to give him courage, he began examining her notebooks, his back set in stubborn opposition to the possibility of her preventing him.

Anna sat still, terribly exposed, forcing herself into immobility. She was suffering, remembering the intimacy of what she had written. And he read on and on, in a stubborn fever, while she simply sat there. Then she felt herself go into a kind of stupor of exhaustion, and thought vaguely: Well, what does it matter? If this is what he needs, then what does it matter what I feel?

Some time later, perhaps as long as an hour, he asked: 'Why do you write things in different kinds of hand-writing? And you bracket bits off? You give importance to one kind of feeling and not to others? How do you decide what's important and what isn't?'

272

'I don't know.'

'That isn't good enough. You know it isn't. Here you've got an entry, it was when you were still living in our house. "I stood looking down out of the window. The street seemed miles down. Suddenly I felt as if I'd flung myself out of the window. I could see myself lying on the pavement. Then I seemed to be standing by the body on the pavement. I was two people. Blood and brains were scattered everywhere. I knelt down and began licking up the blood and the brains." '

He looked at her, accusing, and Anna was silent. 'When you had written that, you put heavy brackets around it. And then you wrote: "I went to the shop and bought a pound and a half of tomatoes, half a pound of cheese, a pot of cherry jam, and a quarter of tea. Then I made a tomato salad and took Janet to the park for a walk." '

'Well?'

'That was the same day. Why did you put brackets round the first bit, about licking up the blood and the brains?'

'We all have mad flashes about being dead on the pavement, or cannibalism, or committing suicide or something.'

'They aren't important?'

'No.'

'The tomatoes and the quarter of tea is what is important?'

'Yes.'

'What makes you decide that the madness and the cruelty isn't just as strong as the—getting on with living?'

'It's not just that. I'm not bracketing off the madness and the cruelty—it's something else.'

'What?' He insisted on an answer, and Anna, out of her depths of exhaustion, looked for one.

'It's a different kind of sensibility. Don't you see? In a day when I buy food and cook it and look after Janet and work, there's a flash of madness—when I write it down it looks dramatic and awful. It's just because I write it down. But the real things that happened in that day were the ordinary things.'

'Then why write it down at all? Do you realise the whole of this notebook, the blue one, is either newspaper cuttings,

273

or bits like the blood and brain bit, all bracketed off, or crossed out; and then entries like buying tomatoes or tea?'

'I suppose it is. It's because I keep trying to write the truth and realising it's not true.'

'Perhaps it is true,' he said suddenly, 'perhaps it is, and you can't bear it, so you cross it out.'

'Perhaps.'

'Why the four notebooks? What would happen if you had one big book without all those divisions and brackets and special writing?'

'I've told you, chaos.'

He turned to look at her. He said sourly: 'You look such a neat little thing and look at what you write.'

Anna said: 'You sounded just like your mother then: that's how she criticises me—in that tone of voice.'

'Don't put me off, Anna. Are you afraid of being chaotic?'

Anna felt her stomach contract in a sort of fear, and said, after a pause: 'I suppose I must be.'

'Then it's dishonest. After all, you take your stand on something, don't you? Yes you do—you despise people like my father, who limit themselves. But you limit yourself too. For the same reason. You're afraid. You're being irresponsible.' He made this final judgement, the pouting, deliberate mouth smiling with satisfaction. Anna realised that this was what he had come to say. This was the point they had been working towards all evening. And he was going on, but in a flash of knowledge she said: 'I often leave my door open—have you been in here to read these notebooks?'

'Yes, I have. I was here yesterday, but I saw you coming up the street so I went out before you could see me. Well I've decided that you're dishonest Anna. You are a happy person but . . .'

'I, happy?' said Anna, derisive.

'Content then. Yes you are. Much more than my mother—or anyone I know. But when you get down to it, it's all a lie. You sit here writing and writing, but no one can see it—that's arrogant, I told you so before. And you aren't even honest enough to let yourself be what you are—everything's divided off and split up. So what's the use of patronising me

274

and saying: You're in a bad phase. If you're not in a bad phase, then it's because you can't be in a phase, you take care to divide yourself up into compartments. If things are a chaos, then that's what they are. I don't think there's a pattern anywhere—you are just making patterns, out of cowardice. I think people aren't good at all, they are cannibals, and when you get down to it no one cares about anyone else. All the best people can be good to one other person or their families. But that's egotism, it isn't being good. We aren't any better than the animals, we just pretend to be. We don't really care about each other at all.' Now he came and sat down opposite her; apparently himself, the obstinate slow-moving boy she knew. Then he gave a sudden bright frightening giggle, and she saw the flash of spite again.

She said: 'Well there's nothing I can say to that, is there?'

He leaned forward and said: 'I'm going to give you another chance Anna.'

'*What?*' she said, startled, almost ready to laugh. But his face was terrifying, and she said, after a pause: 'What do you mean?'

'I'm serious. Now tell me. You used to live by a philosophy—well didn't you?'

'I suppose so.'

'And now you say, the communist myth. So what do you live by now? No don't use words like stoicism, it doesn't mean anything.'

'It seems to me something like this—every so often, perhaps once in a century, there's a sort of—act of faith. A well of faith fills up, and there's an enormous heave forward in one country or another, and that's a forward movement for the whole world. Because it's an act of imagination—of what is possible for the whole world. In our century it was 1917 in Russia. And in China. Then the well runs dry, because, as you say, the cruelty and the ugliness are too strong. Then the well slowly fills again. And then there's another painful lurch forward.'

'A lurch forward?' he said.

'Yes.'

'In spite of everything, a lurch forward?'

'Yes—because every time the dream gets stronger. If people can imagine something, there'll come a time when they'll achieve it.'

'Imagine what?'

'What you said—goodness. Kindness. The end of being animals.'

'And for us now, what is there?'

'Keeping the dream alive. Because there'll always be new people, without—paralysis of the will.' She concluded strongly, with an energetic nod; and thought as she spoke that she sounded like Mother Sugar at the end of a session: One must have faith! Trumpets and fanfares. There must have been a small self-accusatory smile on her face—she could even feel it there, although she believed in what she had said, for Tommy nodded with a sort of malicious triumph. The telephone rang and he said: 'That'll be my mother, checking on how my phase is working itself out.'

Anna answered the telephone, said yes and no, put down the receiver and turned to Tommy.

'No it wasn't your mother, but I'm expecting a visitor.'

'Then I must go.' He got up slowly, with his characteristic lumbering slowness, and arranged on his face the blank inward-looking stare he had entered with. He said: 'Thank you for talking to me.' He was saying: Thank you for confirming what I had expected to find in you.

The moment he had gone Anna telephoned Molly, who had just come in from the theatre. She said: 'Tommy's been here, and he's just left. He frightens me. There's something terribly wrong, but I don't know what, and I don't think I said the right things.'

'What did he say?'

'Well he says everything is rotten.'

'Well it is,' said Molly, loud and cheerful. In the couple of hours since she had last spoken of her son, she had played the part of a jolly landlady—a part she despised in a play she despised—but she was still inside this part. And she had been to the pub with some of the cast and had enjoyed it. She was very far from her earlier mood.

'And Marion has just telephoned me from the phone box

downstairs. She's come up by the last train especially to see me.'

'What on earth for?' said Molly, annoyed.

'I don't know. She's drunk. I'll tell you in the morning. Molly . . .' Anna was filled with panic, remembering how Tommy had gone out. 'Molly, we've got to do something for Tommy, quickly. I'm sure we have.'

'I'll talk to him,' said Molly, practically.

'There's Marion at the door. I must let her in. Good night.'

'Good night. I'll report on the state of Tommy's morale in the morning. I expect we are worrying about nothing. After all, think of how awful we were at that age.' Anna heard her friend's loud, jolly laugh as the receiver clicked down.

Anna pressed the button that released the catch of the front door, and listened to the clumsy sounds of Marion's ascent up the stairs. She could not go to help Marion, who would certainly resent it.

Marion, when she came in, smiled rather as Tommy had: it was a smile prepared before entering, and directed at the whole room. She reached the chair Tommy had sat in, and collapsed heavily into it. She was a heavy woman—tall, with abundant tired flesh. Her face was soft, or rather, blurred-looking, and her brown gaze was both blurred and suspicious. As a girl she had been slender, vivacious, humorous. 'A nut-brown maid,' as Richard said—once with affection, but now with hostility.

Marion was staring about her, alternatively screwing up her eyes and then letting them widen. Her smile had gone. It was clear that she was very drunk, and that Anna should try to get her into bed. Meanwhile Anna sat opposite her, where she could easily be brought into focus—in the same chair she had sat opposite to Tommy.

Marion adjusted her head and her eyes so that she could see Anna, and said with difficulty: 'How lucky—you—are, Anna. I do—think—you—are so lucky to live, to live as you—like. Such a pretty room. And you—you—you are free. Do as you like.'

'Marion, let me put you to bed, we can talk in the morning.'

'You think I'm drunk,' said Marion clearly and with resentment.

'Yes of course you are. It doesn't matter. You should go to sleep.'

Anna was now so tired, and all of a sudden, that fatigue was like heavy hands dragging down her legs and her arms. She sat loose in her chair, fighting waves of tiredness.

'I want a drunk,' said Marion peevishly. 'I want a drunk. I want a drunk.'

Anna roused herself, went to the kitchen next door, filled a glass with some weak tea left in her teapot, added about a teaspoon of whisky, and brought it to Marion.

Marion said 'Thanksh,' took a gulp of the mixture and nodded. She held the glass carefully, lovingly, her fingers clenched around it.

'How is Richard?' she next enquired, carefully, her face tight with the effort of getting the words out. She had prepared this question before she came in. Anna translated it, as it were, into Marion's normal voice, and thought: Good God, Marion's jealous of me, and it never crossed my mind.

She said drily: 'But Marion, surely you're more likely to know than I am?'

She saw the dry tone vanish into the drunken space between herself and Marion; saw Marion's mind working suspiciously on the sense of the words. She said slowly and loudly: 'Marion there's no need to be jealous of me. If Richard has said something then it's not the truth.'

'I'm not jealous of you,' said Marion in a hissing spurt. The word jealous had revived her jealousy; and for a few moments she was a jealous woman, her face contorted as she peered around the room at objects which had played a part in her jealous fantasies, her eyes returning again and again to the bed.

'It's not true,' said Anna.

'Not—that—that it makes much differesh,' said Marion with something like a good-natured laugh. 'Why not you, when there'sh sho many? At least you aren't an insult.'

'But I'm not anything.'

Marion now lifted her chin, and let the tea and whisky mixture go down her throat in three big gulps. 'I needed that,' she said with solemnity, holding out the glass so that Anna could refill it. Anna did not take the glass. She said: 'Marion, I'm glad you've come to see me, but really, you are making a mistake.'

Marion winked, horribly; and said with drunken roguishness: 'Oh but I think I've come because I'm envious. You are what I want to be—you're free, and you have lovers and you do as you like.'

'I'm not free,' said Anna; heard the dryness in her tone and understood she must banish it. She said: 'Marion, I'd like to be married. I don't like living like this.'

'It's easy to say that. But you could get married if you want. Well you'll have to let me sleep here tonight. The last train has gone. And Richard's too mean for me to hire a car. Richard's awfully mean. Yes he is.' (Anna noted that Marion sounded much less drunk, when railing at her husband.) 'Would you believe it, that he could be so mean? He's as rich as hell. Do you know, we are among the one per cent of people as rich as—but he examines my accounts every month. He boasted that we were among the top one per cent, but I bought a model dress and he complained. Of course when he examines my accounts he's finding out how much I spend on liquor, but it's the money as well.'

'Why don't you go to bed?'

'What bed? Who's upstairs?'

'Janet and my lodger. But there's another bed.'

Marion's eyes lit with a delighted suspicion. She said: 'How odd of you to have a lodger. It's a man. How strange of you.'

Again Anna translated, and heard the jokes that Richard and Marion might make about her when Marion was sober. They made jokes about the man lodger. Anna suffered a sudden revulsion, much rarer these days than once, against people like Marion and Richard. She thought: It might be a strain, living as I do, but at least I don't live with people like Marion and Richard, I don't live in that world where a

279

woman can't have a male lodger without spiteful jokes being made.

'What does Janet think, you living here with a man in your flat?'

'Marion, I'm not living here with a man. I have a large flat and I let a room in it. He was the first person who came to see the room and wanted it. There's a tiny room upstairs with no one in it. Please let me put you to bed.'

'But I hate going to bed. Once it was the happiest time of my life. When we were first married. That's why I envy you. No man's ever going to want me again. That's all finished. Sometimes Richard sleeps with me, but he has to make himself. Men are stupid, aren't they, they think we don't know. Anna have you ever slept with a man when you know he's making himself?'

'It was like that when I was married.'

'Yes, but you left him. Good for you. Did you know a man fell in love with me—he wanted to marry me and he said he'd have the children too. Richard pretended to love me again. All he wanted was to keep me as a nursemaid for the children. That's all. I wish I had gone away when I knew that's all he wanted. Did you know, Richard took me for a holiday this summer? It was like that all the time. We went to bed and then he made himself perform. I knew he was thinking all the time about that little tart he's got in his office.' She thrust the glass at Anna, and said peremptorily: 'Fill it.' Anna went next door, made the same mixture of tea and whisky, and came back with it. Marion drank and her voice rolled upwards in a wail of self-pity: 'What would you feel, Anna, if you knew you'd never have a man loving you again? When we went on holiday I thought it would be different. I don't know why I did. On the first night we went to the hotel restaurant and there was an Italian girl at the next table. Richard kept looking at her, I suppose he thought I didn't notice. Then he said I should go up to bed early. He wanted to get the Italian girl. But I wouldn't go to bed early.' She let out a high sobbing screech of satisfaction. ' "Oh no. I said, "You've come on a holiday with me, not to pick up tarts." ' Now her eyes were reddened with vindictive tears, and rough wet red patches appeared on her full cheeks. 'He says to me, "You've got the children, haven't you?" But why should I care about the children if you don't care about me—that's what I say to him. But he doesn't understand that. Why should you care about a man's children if he doesn't love you? Isn't that true, Anna? Well isn't it true? Go on, say something, it's true, isn't it? When he said he wanted to marry me, he said he loved me, he didn't say I'm going to give you three children and then I'm going off to the little tarts leaving you with the children. Well say something Anna. And it's all very well for you, you live with just one child, and you can do exactly as you like. It's easy for you to be attractive for Richard, when he just pops in for a quick one now and again.'

The telephone rang once and then stopped.

'That's one of your men, I suppose,' said Marion. 'Perhaps it's Richard. Well if it is, tell him I'm here, tell him I'm on to him. Tell him so.'

The telephone rang again and kept on ringing.

Anna went to it, thinking: Marion sounds almost sober again. She said: 'Hello.' She heard Molly scream: 'Anna, Tommy's killed himself, he's shot himself.'

'What?'

'Yes. He came in just after you rang. He went upstairs without saying anything. I heard a bang, but I thought he had banged his door shut. Then I heard a groan, much later. So I shouted up to him and he didn't answer, so I thought I'd imagined it. Then I got frightened for some reason and I went out and there was blood trickling down the stairs. I didn't know he had a revolver. He's not dead but he's going to die, I can tell from what the police say. He's going to die,' she screamed out.

'I'll come to the hospital. Which hospital?'

A man's voice now said: 'Now, miss, let me talk to her.' Then on the telephone: 'We are taking your friend and her son to St Mary's Hospital. I think your friend would like to have you with her.'

'I'll come at once.'

Anna turned to Marion. Marion's head had dropped and

her chin was on her upper chest. Anna wrestled her out of the chair, staggered with her to the bed, rolled her on it. Marion lay loose, her mouth open, her face wet with spittle and with tears. Her cheeks flamed with liquor. Anna piled blankets on her, turned out the fires and the lights, and ran into the street as she was. It was long after midnight. No one. No taxi. She ran, half-sobbing, along the street, saw a policeman, and ran towards him. 'I must get to the hospital,' she said, clutching at him. Another policeman appeared from around a corner. One supported her while the other found a taxi, and went with her to the hospital. Tommy was not dead, but he was expected to die before morning.

THE NOTEBOOKS

[The black notebook continued empty under the heading *Source*, on the left-hand side. The right half of the page, under the heading *Money*, was full, however.]

Letter from Mr Reginald Tarbrucke, Amalgamated Vision, to Miss Anna Wulf: Last week I read—by chance, I must confess!—your delightful book, *Frontiers of War*. I was immediately struck by its freshness and sincerity. We are, of course, on the lookout for suitable themes for television plays. I would so much like to discuss this with you. Perhaps you would meet me for a drink at one o'clock on Friday next—do you know the Black Bull in Great Portland Street? Do give me a ring.

Letter from Anna Wulf to Reginald Tarbrucke: Thank you so much for your letter. I think I had better say at once that there are very few plays I see on television which encourage me to write for that medium. I am so sorry.

Letter from Reginald Tarbrucke to Anna Wulf: Thank you so very much for being so frank. I do so agree with you and that is why I wrote to you, the very moment I put down your charming *Frontiers of War*. We desperately need fresh, sincere plays of real integrity. Will you meet me for lunch next Friday at the Red Baron? It's a small unpretentious place, but they do a very good steak.

From Anna Wulf to Reginald Tarbrucke: Thank you so much, but I really did mean what I said. If I believed *Frontiers of War* could be adapted for television in a way which would satisfy me, my attitude would be different. But as it is—Yours sincerely.

From Reginald Tarbrucke to Miss Wulf: What a pity there are not more writers with your delightful integrity! I do promise you that I would not have written to you if we were not desperately searching for real creative talent. Television needs the real thing! Please join me for lunch next Monday at the White Tower. I think we need time for a really long, quiet talk. Very sincerely yours.

Lunch with Reginald Tarbrucke, Amalgamated Vision, at the White Tower.

Bill: £6 15s. 7d.

Dressing for lunch I was thinking of how Molly would enjoy this—playing some role or other. Decided I'd look like a 'lady writer.' I had a skirt, rather too long, and a badly fitting blouse. I put them on and some arty beads. And some long coral ear-rings. Looked the part. But felt enormously uncomfortable—as if I were inside the wrong skin. Irritated. No use thinking of Molly. At the last moment changed into myself. Took a lot of trouble. Mr Tarbrucke (call me Reggie) was surprised: he had expected the lady writer. A soft-faced, good-looking, middle-aged Englishman. Well, Miss Wulf—may I call you Anna—what are you writing now? 'I am living off the royalties from *Frontiers of War*.' Look of slight shock—my tone was one of being only interested in money.

'It must have been very successful?' 'Twenty-five languages,' I said, throwing it away. Humorous grimace—envy. I switch my tone to one of dedicated artist, and say: 'Of course, I don't want to rush the second. The second novel is so important, don't you think?' He is delighted and set at ease. 'Not all of us achieve the first,' he says with a sigh. 'You write of course?' 'How clever of you to guess it!' Again the now automatic humorous grimace, the whimsical gleam. 'I've got a novel half-written in my drawer—but this racket doesn't give one much time for writing.' This theme takes us through scampi and the main course. I wait until he says, inevitably: 'And of course, one fights and fights to get anything halfway decent through the meshes. Of course they haven't a clue, the boys at the top.' (He being half a rung from the top.) 'Not a sausage. Bone-stupid. Sometimes one wonders what one does it for?' Halva and Turkish coffee. He lights a cigar, buys me some cigarettes. We haven't mentioned my charming novel yet. 'Tell me Reggie, do you propose to take the team out to Central Africa to make *Frontiers of War*?' His face, for one second, freezes; then sets into charm. 'Well, I'm glad you asked me that, because of course, that is the problem.' 'The landscape plays quite a part in that novel?' 'Oh, essential, I agree. Marvellous. What a feeling for landscape you have. Really, I could smell the place, quite marvellous.' 'Would you do it inside the studio?' 'Well, that is of course rather the point, and that's why I wanted to talk to you about it. Tell me, Anna, what would you say, if you were asked, what is the central theme of your lovely book? Simply, of course, because television is essentially a simple medium?' 'It is, *simply*, about the colour bar.' 'Oh, I do so agree, a terrible thing, of course I've never experienced it myself, but when I read your book—terrifying! But I wonder if you'll see my point—I do hope you will. It would be impossible to do *Frontiers of War* on the . . .' (whimsical grimace) '. . . magic box, as it is written. It would have to be simplified, leaving its marvellous core intact. So I wondered what you would feel about changing the locale to England—no wait. I don't think you'd object if I can make you see what I see—television is a question of *vision*, isn't it? Can one *see* it? That is always the point and I do feel some of our writers do tend to forget that. Now, let me tell you what I see. It's an air-training base in wartime. In England, I was in the airforce myself—oh, not one of the boys in blue, I was just a pen-pusher. But perhaps that's why your book got me

the way it did. You got the atmosphere so perfectly ...'
'What atmosphere?' 'Oh, my dear, you are so marvellous,
real artists are so really marvellous, half the time you don't
know what you've written ...' I said, suddenly, not meaning
to: 'And perhaps we do, and don't like it.' He frowned,
decided to ignore it, and went on: 'It's the wonderful right-
ness—the desperation of it all—the excitement—I've never
been so alive as I was then ... Well, what I want to suggest
is this. We'll keep the core of your book, because that's so
important, I agree. The airforce base. A young pilot. He falls
in love with a local girl from the village. His parents object—
the class thing, you know, alas it still does exist in this
country. The two lovers must separate. And at the end we
have this marvellous scene on the railway station—he is
going off, and we know he will be killed. No, do think about
it, just for a moment—what do you say?'

'You want me to write an original script?'

'Well yes and no. Your story is basically a simple love
story. Yes it is. The colour thing is really—yes I know it's
desperately important, and I couldn't agree with you more,
how utterly beastly the whole thing is, but your story is really
a simple moving love story. It's all there, trust me, it is—like
another Brief Encounter. I do hope you see that as clearly as
I do—you must remember the telly is just a question of
seeing.' 'Very clearly, but surely one can throw away the
novel Frontiers of War and begin again?' 'Well not entirely,
because the book is so well-known and so marvellous, and I
would like to keep the title, because the Frontier is surely not
geographical? Not in essence? I don't see it like that. It is
frontier of experience.' 'Well, perhaps you'd better write me
a letter setting out your terms for an original television
script?' 'But not altogether original.' (Whimsical twinkle.)
'Don't you think the people who had read the book would be
surprised to see it turn into a sort of Brief Encounter With
Wings?' (Whimsical grimace.) 'But my dear Anna, no,
they're not surprised at anything, how could they be, with the
magic box?' 'Well I've had a lovely lunch.' 'Oh, my dear
Anna, you are so right, of course you are. But obviously with
your intelligence, you must see we couldn't do it in Central

Africa, the boys at the top simply don't let us have that sort of money.' 'No, of course not—but I think I rather suggested that in my letters.' 'It *would* make a lovely film. Tell me, would you like me to mention it to a friend of mine in films?' 'Well, I have been through all that already.' 'Oh, my dear, I do know, I do really. Well all we can do is to keep on plodding I suppose. I know when I go home at night sometimes, and I look at my desk—a dozen books to read for possible stories, and a hundred scripts, and there's my poor novel half-done in a drawer and I haven't had time to look at it for months—I console myself with the thought that I do sometimes get something fresh and authentic through the meshes—please think about my suggestion for *Frontiers of War*, I really do believe it would work.' We are leaving the restaurant. Two waiters bowing. Reginald gets his coat, slips the coin into the man's hand with a small, almost apologetic smile. We are on the pavement. I am very dissatisfied with myself: what am I doing this for? Because I knew exactly what would happen from the first letter from Amalgamated Vision; except they are always one degree worse than one expects, these people. But if I know it, why bother? Just to prove it? My self-disgust begins to turn into another emotion I recognise quite well—a sort of minor hysteria. I know quite well that in a moment I'm going to say something wrong, rude, accusing, or self-accusatory. There is a moment when I know I can either stop myself, or if not, I'll be propelled into speech which I can't stop. We are on the pavement, and he wants to get rid of me. Then we walk towards Tottenham Court Road tube station. I say: 'Reggie, do you know what I'd really like to do with *Frontiers of War*?' 'But my dear, do tell me.' (He frowns involuntarily however.) 'I'd like to make a comedy out of it.' He stops, surprised. Goes on. 'A comedy?' He gives me a quick sideways look, revealing all the dislike for me he in fact feels. Then he says: 'But my dear, it's so marvellously in the grand manner, simple tragedy. I can't even remember a comic scene.' 'Do you remember the excitement you talked about? the pulse of war?' 'My dear, yes, too well.' 'Well I agree with you that that's what the book is really about.' A pause. The good-looking charming face tightens: he looks cautious and wary. My voice is hard, angry, and full of disgust. Self-disgust. 'Now you must tell me exactly what you mean.' We are at the underground entrance. Crowds of people. The man selling newspapers has no face. No nose, rather, his mouth is a rabbit-toothed hole, and his eyes are sunk in scar tissue. 'Well, let's take your story,' I said. 'Young flier, gallant, handsome, reckless. Local girl, pretty daughter of the local poacher. Wartime England. Training base for pilots. Now. Remember that scene we've both seen a thousand times in the films—the aircraft go off over Germany. Shot of pilots' mess—pin-up girls, pretty rather than sexy, doesn't do to suggest our boys have the cruder instincts. A handsome boy reads letter from mother. Sporting trophy on the mantelpiece.' A pause. 'My dear, yes, I do agree with you we do that film rather too often.' 'The aircraft come in to land. Two of them are missing. Groups of men stand around to wait, watching the sky. A muscle tightens in a throat. Shot of pilots' bedroom. Empty bed. One young man comes in. He says nothing. He sits on his bed and looks at the empty bed. A muscle tightens in his throat. Then he goes to the empty bed. There is a teddy bear lying on the bed. He picks up the teddy bear. A muscle tightens in his throat. Shot of aircraft in flames. Cut to young man holding teddy bear, looking at photos of a pretty girl—no, not a girl, better a bull-dog. Cut back to aircraft in flames and the national anthem.' There is a silence. The newsman with the rabbity face and no nose is shouting: 'War in Quemoy. War in Quemoy.' Reggie decides he must be mistaken, so he smiles and says: 'But my dear Anna, you used the word *comedy*.' 'You were acute enough to see what the book was really about—nostalgia for death.' He frowns, and this time the frown sticks. 'Well, I'm ashamed and I'd like to make reparation—let's make a comedy about useless heroism. Let's parody that damned story where twenty-five young men in the flower of their youth, etc., go out to die leaving a wreckage of teddy bears and football trophies and a woman standing at a gate looking stoically at the sky where another wave of aircraft are passing on their way to Germany. A muscle tightens in her throat. How about it?' The newsman is shouting: 'War in Quemoy,' and suddenly I feel as if I'm standing in the middle of a scene from a play that is the parody of something. I begin to laugh. The laugh is hysterical. Reggie is looking at me, frowning and disliking. His mouth, previously mobile with complicity and a desire to be liked, is shrewd and a little bitter. I stop laughing, and suddenly all the propelled laughter, speech, is gone, and I'm quite sane again. He says: 'Well, Anna, I agree with you, but I must keep my job. There is a wonderfully comic idea there—but it's a film, not television. Yes, I can see it.' (He is talking his way back to his normality, because I am normal again.) 'It would be savage of course. I wonder if people would take it?' (His mouth has twisted back into whimsical charm. He glances at me—he can't believe that our moment of pure hate has occurred. I can't either.) 'Well perhaps it *would* work? After all it's ten years since the war ended—but it simply is *not* television. It's a simple medium. And the audience—well I don't have to tell you, it's not the most intelligent audience. We have to remember that.' I buy a newspaper which has the headline: War in Quemoy. I say, conversational: 'This is going to be another of the places we know about only because there's been a war in it.' 'My dear, yes, it is too awful isn't it, the way we are all so ill-informed.' 'But I'm keeping you standing here, and you must be wanting to get back to your office.' 'As it happens I am rather late—good-bye Anna, it was such fun meeting you.' 'Good-bye Reggie, and thank you for the lovely lunch.' At home I collapse into depression, then angry self-disgust. But the only part of that meeting I am not ashamed of is the moment when I was hysterical and stupid. I must not respond to any more of these invitations for TV or films. What for? All I am doing is to say to myself: You are right not to write again. It's all so humiliating and ugly you should just keep out of it. But I know that anyway, so why go on sticking the knife in?

Letter from Mrs Edwina Wright, Representative for the 'Blue Bird' Series of Television One-Hour Plays, U.S.A. Dear Miss Wulf: Watching with hawk-like eyes for plays of durable interest to bring to our screen, it was with great excitement that your novel, *Frontiers of War*, was brought to our attention. I am writing to you in the hope that we may work together on many projects of advantage to us both. I shall be in London for three days on my way to Rome and Paris and hope you will ring me at Black's Hotel so that we may meet for a drink. I am enclosing a brochure we have compiled for the guidance of our authors. Yours sincerely.

The brochure was printed, nine and a half pages long. It began: 'In the course of any year we receive hundreds of plays in our office. Many of these show an authentic feeling for the medium, but fail to meet our requirements through ignorance of the fundamental exigencies of our needs. We present a one-hour play once a week, etc., etc., etc. Clause (a) read: The essence of the Blue Bird series is variety! There are no embargoes on subject matter! We want adventure, romance, travel stories, stories of exotic experience, domestic life, family life, parent-child relationships, fantasy, comedy, tragedy. Blue Bird says *no* to no screenplay that sincerely and authentically grapples with genuine experience, of whatever kind.' Clause (y) read: 'Blue Bird screenplays are viewed weekly by nine million Americans of all ages. Blue Bird brings screenplays of living verity to the ordinary man, woman and child. Blue Bird considers it has a trust and a duty. For this reason Blue Bird writers must remember their responsibility, which they share with Blue Bird: Blue Bird will not consider screenplays dealing with religion, race, politics, or extra-marital sex.

'We are looking forward with eager anticipation to reading *your* screenplay.'

Miss Anna Wulf to Mrs Edwina Wright. Dear Mrs Wright: Thank you for your flattering letter. I see however from your directive brochure to your writers that you do not like plays which touch on race or extra-marital sex. *Frontiers of War* has both. Therefore, I feel there is not much point in our discussing the possibility of adapting this novel for your series. Yours sincerely.

Mrs Edwina Wright to Miss Wulf: A telegram. Thank you so much for prompt and responsible letter stop Please have dinner with me tomorrow night Black's Hotel eight o'clock stop reply pre-paid.

Dinner with Mrs Wright at Black's Hotel. Bill: £11 4s. 6d.

Edwina Wright, forty-five or fifty; a plump, pink-and-white woman, with iron-grey hair, curled and shining; gleaming blue-grey lids; shining pink lips; shining pale-pink nails. A suit of soft blue, very expensive. An expensive woman. Easy chatty friendliness over the Martinis. She has three. I, two. She swallows hers down, she really has to have them. She leads the talk to English literary personalities, finding out which I know personally. I know hardly anyone. Trying to place me. Finally she pigeon-holes me—smiling and saying: 'One of my dearest friends . . .' (mentioning an American writer) '. . . always tells me he hates meeting other writers. I think he's got a very interesting future.' We go into the dining-room. Warm, comfortable, discreet. Seated she looks around, for one second off guard: her crinkling painted lids narrowing, her pink mouth slightly open—she is looking for somebody or something. Then she assumes a regretful, sad look, which however, must be genuine, because she says, meaning it: 'I love England. I love coming to England. I make excuses to be sent here.' I wonder if this hotel is 'England' for her; but she looks too shrewd and intelligent for that. She asks me if I'd like another Martini; I am going to refuse, then see she wants one; I say yes. A tension starts in my stomach; then I see it is her tension, communicating itself to me. I look at the controlled defensive handsome face and I'm sorry for her. I understand her life very well. She orders dinner—she is solicitous, tactful. It is like being taken out by a man. Yet she is not at all masculine; it is that she is used to controlling situations like this. I can feel how this role is not natural to her, what it costs her to play it. While we wait for the melon, she lights a cigarette. She sits, lids lowered, the cigarette dangling, surveying the room again. Her face flashes into relief, which she instantly masks; then she nods and smiles to an American who has come in and is sitting ordering dinner by himself in a corner of the room. He wags a hand back at her, she smiles, the smoke curling up past her eyes. She turns back to me, concentrating on me with an effort. She seems suddenly much older. I like her very much. I see, vividly, how later that night she will be in

her room, wearing something over-feminine. Yes, I see flowered chiffon, something like that ... yes, because of the
strain of having to play this role in her working day. And she
will even look at the chiffon ruffles and make some wisecrack about it to herself. But she is waiting. Then the discreet
knock on the door. She opens it, with a joke. They are both
by then blurred and amiable with alcohol. Another drink.
Then the dry and measured coupling. In New York they will
meet at a party and exchange ironies. She is now critically
eating her melon; finally remarks that food in England has
more taste. She talks of how she intends to leave her job and
go off to live in the country, in New England, and write a
novel. (Her husband is never mentioned.) I realise that
neither of us has any desire to talk about *Frontiers of War*.
She has summed me up; she is neither approving nor disapproving; she took a chance; the dinner is a business loss, but
that's the racket. In a moment she will talk amiably but
perfunctorily about my book. We are drinking a bottle of
good heavy burgundy: steak, mushrooms, celery. Again she
says our food tastes better, but adds that we should learn to
cook it. I'm now as good-natured with alcohol as she is; but
in the pit of my stomach the tension is steadily tightening—
her tension. She keeps glancing over at the American in the
corner. I suddenly realise that unless I'm careful I'll start
talking out of that hysteria which led me, a few weeks ago,
into comic parody for Reginald Tarbrucke. I decide to be
careful; I like her too much. And she frightens me. 'Anna,
I liked your book so much.' 'I'm glad, thank you.' 'Back
home there's a real interest in Africa, in African problems.' I
grin and say: 'But there *is* a race thing in that book.' She
grins, grateful because I have, and says: 'But it is often a
question of degree. Well, in your wonderful novel, you have
the young flier and the Negro girl sleeping together. Well,
now would you say it was important? Would you say their
having sex together was vital to the story?' 'No, I wouldn't.'
She hesitates. Her tired and extraordinarily shrewd eyes
show a gleam of disappointment. She had hoped I would not
compromise; although it is her job to see that I should. For
her, I now see, the sex is in fact the point of the story. Her

manner changes subtly: she is handling a writer who is prepared to sacrifice integrity to get a story on to television. I say: 'But surely, even if they are in love in the purest manner possible, it would be a breach of your code?' 'It's a question of how one handles it.' I see that at this point the whole thing might very well be dropped altogether. Because of my attitude? No; because of her anxiety over the lone American in the corner. Twice I've seen him look at her; I think her anxiety is justified. He is debating whether to come over, or perhaps go off somewhere by himself. Yet he seems to like her well enough. The waiter clears our plates. She is pleased when I say I want coffee, but no sweet: she has been eating business meals twice a day during her trip, and she's relieved we're cutting the thing short by a course. She gives another glance over at her solitary compatriot, who shows no signs of moving yet, and decides to return to work. 'When I was considering how we could use your really wonderful material, it crossed my mind that it would make a marvellous musical—you can get away with a serious message in a musical that you can't in a straight story.' 'A musical set in Central Africa?' 'For one thing, as a musical, it would solve the problem of the scenic background. Your scenic background is so good, but it's not for television.' 'You mean, formalised sets of African scenery?' 'Yes, that would be the idea. And a very simple story. Young English flier in training in Central Africa. The pretty Negro girl he meets at a party. He is lonely. She is kind to him. He meets her folks.' 'But he couldn't conceivably meet a young Negro girl at a party in those parts. Unless it was in a political context—a tiny minority of political people try to break down the colour bar. You didn't have a political musical in mind?' 'Oh, but I didn't realise ... suppose he had an accident in the street and she helped him and took him to her home?' 'She couldn't take him to her home without infringing about a dozen different laws. If she sneaked him in, then it would be very desperate and fearful, and not at all the right atmosphere for a musical.' 'You can be very, very serious in a musical,' she says, rebuking me, but as a matter of form. 'We could use the local songs and dances. The music of Central Africa would

292

be quite new to our viewers.' 'At the time this story is set in, the Africans were listening to jazz from America. They hadn't started developing their own forms.' Now her look at me says: You're simply trying to be difficult. She abandons the musical and says: 'Well, if we bought the property with an idea of doing the story straight, I feel the locale would have to be changed. My suggestion would be an army base in England. An American base. An American G.I. in love with an English girl.' 'A Negro G.I.?' She hesitates. 'Well, that would be difficult. Because after all, this is basically just a very simple love story. I am a very, very great admirer of the British war film. You make such wonderful war films—such restraint. You have such—tact. That kind of feeling, we should aim for that. And the war atmosphere—the Battle of Britain atmosphere, then a simple love story, one of our boys and one of your girls.' 'But if you made him a Negro G.I. you could use all the indigenous folk music from your deep South?' 'Well, yes. But you see it wouldn't be fresh for our viewers.' 'I can see it now,' I say. 'A chorus of American Negro G.I.'s, in an English country village in wartime, with another chorus of fresh young English girls doing indigenous English country folk dances.' I grin at her. She frowns. Then she grins. Then our eyes meet and she lets out a snort of laughter. She laughs again. Then she checks herself and sits frowning. And just as if this subversive laughter had not occurred she takes a deep breath and begins: 'Of course you are an artist, a very fine artist, it is a privilege to meet you and talk to you, and you have a deep and natural reluctance to see anything you have written changed. But you must let me say this, it is a mistake to be over-impatient about television. It is the art form of the future—that is how I see it, and that is why I am so privileged to work with and for it.' She stops: the solitary American is looking around for the waiter—but no, he wants more coffee. She turns her attention to me and continues: 'Art, as a very, very great man once said, is a matter of patience. If you'd like to think over what we've discussed and write to me—or perhaps you'd like to try and write us a screenplay on another theme? Of course we cannot commission work from an artist who has not had

293

previous television experience, but we will be happy to give you all the advice and help we can.' 'Thank you.' 'Are you thinking of visiting the States? I would be so happy if you would give me a call and we could discuss any ideas you might have?' I hesitate. I almost stop myself. Then I know I can't stop myself. I say: 'There is nothing I'd like better than to visit your country, but alas, I wouldn't be let in, I'm a communist.' Her eyes snap into my face, wide and blue and startled. She makes at the same time an involuntary movement—the start of pushing back her chair and going. Her breathing quickens. I see someone who is frightened. Already I am sorry and ashamed. I said that for a variety of reasons, the first being childish: I wanted to shock her. Secondly, equally childish, a feeling that I ought to say it—if someone said afterwards: Of course she is a communist, this woman would feel as if I had been concealing it. Thirdly, I wanted to see what would happen. She sits, opposite me, breathing fast, her eyes uncertain, her pink lips, rather smeared now, parted. She is thinking: Next time I must be careful to make enquiries. She is also seeing herself as a victim—that morning I had read through a batch of cuttings from the States about dozens of people sacked from their jobs, being grilled by Anti-American committees, etc. She says breathlessly: 'Of course things are quite different here in England, I realise that . . .' Her woman-of-the-world mask cracks right across, and she blurts out: 'But my dear, I'd never have guessed in a thousand years that . . .' This means: I like you so how can you be a communist? This suddenly makes me so angry, the provincialism of it, that I feel as I always feel in these circumstances: Better to be a communist, and at almost any cost, better to be in touch than to be so cut off from any reality that one can make a remark as stupid as that. Now we are suddenly both very angry. She looks away from me, recovering herself. And I think of that night I spent talking to the Russian writer two years ago. We used the same language—the communist language. Yet our experience was so different that every phrase we used meant something different to each of us. A feeling of total unreality came over me, and finally, very late at night, or rather, early in the

294

morning, I translated one of the things I had said out of the safe unreal jargon into something that had actually happened—I told him about Jan, who had been tortured in a prison in Moscow. And there was the same moment when his eyes focused on my face in fright, and the involuntary movement away, as if to escape—I was saying something that, if he had said it in his country, would have got him into prison. The fact was, that the phrases of our common philosophy were a means of disguising the truth. The truth was we had nothing in common, except the label, communist. And now with this American woman—we could use the language of democracy all night, but it would describe different experiences. We sat there, she and I, remembering that we liked each other as women. But there was nothing to say: just as after that moment with the Russian writer, there had been nothing more to say. Finally she says: 'Well, my dear, I've never been more surprised. I simply cannot understand it.' It is an accusation this time, and I am angry again. And she even goes on to say: 'Of course I admire your honesty.' Then I think: Well if I was in America now, being hunted by the committees, I wouldn't be sitting at an hotel table saying casually I am a communist. So being angry is dishonest—all the same, it is out of anger that I say drily: 'Perhaps it would be a good idea to check before you invite writers in this country to dinner, because quite a number might cause you embarrassment.' But now her face shows that she has gone a very long distance from me: she is suspicious: I am in the pigeon-hole communist, and therefore I am probably lying. And I remembered that moment with the Russian writer when he had the choice, either to meet me on what I was saying, and to discuss it, or to contract out, which he did by putting on a look of ironical knowledge, and saying: 'Well it's not the first time a friend of our country has turned into an enemy.' In other words: you have succumbed to pressures from the capitalist enemy. Luckily, at this juncture, the American appears, standing by our table. I wonder if the balance has been tipped for him by the fact that she had genuinely, and not from calculation, ceased to be aware of him. I feel sad at this, because I think it is true. 'Well, Jerry,' she says, 'I wondered if we'd run into each other, I heard you were in London.' 'Hi,' he says, 'how are you, good to see you.' Well-dressed, self-possessed, good-natured. 'This is Miss Wulf,' she says, and with difficulty, because what she is feeling is: I am introducing a friend to an enemy, I ought to be warning him in some way. 'Miss Wulf is a very, very well-known writer,' she says; and I see that the words well-known writer have taken some of the edge off her nervousness. I say: 'Perhaps you'll forgive me if I leave you both? I should go home and see to my daughter.' She is obviously relieved. We all leave the dining-room. As I say good-bye and turn away I see her slip her hand into his elbow. I hear her say: 'Jerry, I'm so happy you are here, I thought I was in for a lonely evening.' He says: 'My dear Eddy, when have you ever spent a lonely evening unless you opted one?' I see her smile—dry and grateful to him. As for me, I go home thinking that, in spite of everything, the moment when I broke the comfortable surface of our acquaintanceship was the only honest moment in the evening. Yet I feel ashamed and dissatisfied and depressed, just as I did after the night talking to the Russian.

[The red notebook.]

August 28th, 1954

Spent last evening trying to find out as much as possible about Quemoy. Very little in my bookshelves or in Molly's. We were both frightened, perhaps this will be the beginning of a new war. Then Molly said: 'How often have we done this, sat here worrying, but in the end there isn't a big war.' I could see something else was worrying her. Finally she told me: she had been close friends with the Forest brothers. When they 'disappeared' into—presumably—Czechoslovakia, she went down to H.Q. to make enquiries. They suggested she was not to worry, they were doing important work for the Party. Yesterday it was announced they had been in prison three years, just released. She went to H.Q. again yesterday, asked if they had known the brothers were in jail. It turned out it had been known all along. She said to me: 'I am thinking of leaving the Party.' I said: 'Why not see if things don't get better. After all, they're still cleaning up after Stalin.' She said: 'You said last week you were going to leave. Anyway, that's what I said to Hal—yes, I saw the big chief himself. I said: "All the villains are dead, aren't they? Stalin and Beria, etc. etc.? So why are you still going on as usual?" He said it was a question of standing by the Soviet Union under attack. You know, the usual thing. I said: "How about the Jews in the Soviet Union?" He said it was a capitalist lie. I said: "Oh, Christ, not again." Anyway he gave me a long lecture, ever so friendly and calm, about not panicking. Suddenly I felt as if either I was mad or all of them were. I said to him: "Look, you people have got to understand something pretty soon or you'll have no one left in your Party—you've got to learn to tell the truth and stop all this hole-and-corner conspiracy and telling lies about things." He suggested I was very understandably upset because my friends had been in jug. Suddenly I realised I was getting all apologetic and defensive, when I knew quite well I was in the right and he in the wrong. Isn't it *odd*, Anna? In one minute I'd have started apologising to *him*? I only just stopped myself. I left quickly. I came home and went up to lie down I was so upset.' Michael came in late. I told him what Molly had said. He said to me: 'And so you're going to leave the Party?' It sounded as if he would be sorry if I did, in spite of everything. Then he said, very dry: 'Do you realise, Anna, that when you and Molly talk of leaving the Party, the suggestion always is that leaving it will lead you straight into some morass of moral turpitude. Yet the fact is that literally millions of perfectly sound human beings have left the Party (if they weren't murdered first) and they left it because they were leaving behind murder, cynicism, horror, betrayal.' I said: 'Perhaps that isn't the point at all?' 'Then what is the point?' I said to him: 'A minute ago I got the impression, if I'd said I'm leaving the Party, you'd have been sorry.' He laughed, acknowledging it; then he was silent for some time and then he said, laughing again: 'Perhaps I'm with you, Anna, because it's nice to be with someone full of faith, even though one hasn't got it oneself.' 'Faith!' I said.

297

'Your earnest enthusiasm.' I said: 'I would hardly have described my attitude to the Party in those terms.' 'All the same, you are in it, which is more than could be said for—' He grinned, and I said: 'For you?' He seemed very unhappy, sitting quiet, thinking. Finally he said: 'Well we tried. We did try. It didn't come off, but ... let's go to bed, Anna.'

I dreamed marvellously. I dreamed there was an enormous web of beautiful fabric stretched out. It was incredibly beautiful, covered all over with embroidered pictures. The pictures were illustrations of the myths of mankind but they were not just pictures, they were the myths themselves, so that the soft glittering web was alive. There were many subtle and fantastic colours, but the overall feeling this expanse of fabric gave was of redness, a sort of variegated glowing red. In my dream I handled and felt this material and wept with joy. I looked again and saw that the material was shaped like a map of the Soviet Union. It began to grow: it spread out, lapped outwards like a soft glittering sea. It included now the countries around the Soviet Union, like Poland, Hungary, etc., but at the edges it was transparent and thin. I was still crying with joy. Also with apprehension. And now the soft red glittering mist spread over China and it deepened over China into a hard heavy clot of scarlet. And now I was standing out in space somewhere, keeping my position in space with an occasional down-treading movement of my feet in the air. I stood in a blue mist of space while the globe turned, wearing shades of red for the communist countries, and a patchwork of colours for the rest of the world. Africa was black, but a deep, luminous, exciting black, like a night when the moon is just below the horizon and will soon rise. Now I was very frightened and I had a sick feeling, as if I were being invaded by some feeling I didn't want to admit. I was too sick and dizzy to look down and see the world turning. Then I look and it is like a vision—time has gone and the whole history of man, the long story of mankind, is present in what I see now, and it is like a great soaring hymn of joy and triumph in which pain is a small lively counterpoint. And I look and see that the red areas are being invaded by the bright different colours of the other parts of the world. The colours are melting and flowing into each other, indescribably beautiful so that the world becomes whole, all one beautiful glittering colour, but a colour I have never seen in life. This is a moment of almost unbearable happiness, the happiness seems to swell up, so that everything suddenly bursts, explodes—I was suddenly standing in space, in silence. Beneath me was silence. The slowly turning world was slowly dissolving, disintegrating and flying off into fragments, all through space, so that all around me were weightless fragments drifting about, bouncing into each other and drifting away. The world had gone, and there was chaos. I was alone in chaos. And very clear in my ear a small voice said: Somebody pulled a thread of the fabric and it all dissolved. I woke up, joyful and elated. I wanted to wake Michael to tell him, but I knew, of course, that I couldn't describe the emotion of the dream in words. Almost at once the meaning of the dream began to fade; I said to myself, the meaning is going, catch it, quick; then I thought, but I don't know what the meaning is. But the meaning had gone, leaving me indescribably happy. And I was sitting up in the dark beside Michael, just myself. And I lay down again and put my arms around him and he turned and laid his face on my breasts in his sleep. Then I thought: The truth is I don't care a damn about politics or philosophy or anything else, all I care about is that Michael should turn in the dark and put his face against my breasts. And then I drifted off to sleep. This morning I could remember the dream clearly, and how I had felt. I remembered the words particularly: Somebody pulled a thread of the fabric and it all dissolved. All day the dream has been shrinking and dwindling, so that now it is small and bright and meaningless. But this morning when Michael woke in my arms he opened his eyes and smiled at me. The warm blue of his eyes as he smiled into my face. I thought: so much of my life has been twisted and painful that now when happiness floods right through me like being flooded over with warm glittering blue water, I can't believe it. I say to myself: I am Anna Wulf, this is me, Anna, and I'm happy.

[Here was pasted in some scribbled sheets dated 11th November, 1952.]

Writers' group meeting last night. Five of us—to discuss Stalin on Linguistics. Rex, literary critic, proposes to take this pamphlet sentence by sentence. George 'proletarian writer' from the 'thirties, pipe-smoking and bluff, says: 'Good God, have we got to? Never was a chap for theory.' Clive, communist pamphleteer and journalist, says: 'Yes, we must discuss it seriously.' Dick, the socialist-realist novelist, says: 'We ought to get hold of the main points, at least.' So Rex begins. He speaks of Stalin in the simple respectful tone that has been familiar for years. I am thinking: Yet every one of us in this room, meeting in a pub, or on the street, would use a very different tone, dry and painful. We are silent while Rex makes a short prefatory speech. Then Dick who has just come back from Russia (he is always on some trip to a communist country somewhere) mentions a conversation he had in Moscow with a Soviet writer about one of Stalin's more savage attacks on a philosopher: 'We must remember that their tradition of polemics is much more rough and knockabout than ours.' His tone the simple, bluff, I-am-a-good-fellow tone which I use myself sometimes: 'Well, of course you have to remember their legal traditions are very different from ours,' etc. I am beginning to be uncomfortable whenever I hear this tone; a few days ago, I heard myself use it, and I started to stammer. I usually don't stammer. We all have copies of the pamphlet. I am discouraged because it seems to me nonsense, but I am not philosophically trained (Rex is) and am afraid of making stupid remarks. But it is more than that. I am in a mood that gets more and more familiar: words lose their meaning suddenly. I find myself listening to a sentence, a phrase, a group of words, as if they are in a foreign language—the gap between what they are supposed to mean, and what in fact they say seems unbridgeable. I have been thinking of the novels about the breakdown of language, like *Finnegans Wake*. And the preoccupation with semantics. The fact that Stalin bothers to write a pamphlet on this subject at all is just a sign of a general uneasiness about language. But what right have I to criticise anything when sentences from the most beautiful novel can seem idiotic to me? Nevertheless, this pamphlet seems to me clumsy, and I say: 'Perhaps the translation is bad.' I am astounded that my tone is apologetic. (I know if I were alone with Rex it would not be apologetic.) Instantly I see that I have expressed everyone's feeling that the pamphlet is in fact bad. For years, over pamphlets, articles, novels, pronouncements from Russia we've said: 'Well the translation is probably bad.' And now I am having to fight with myself to say: 'This pamphlet is bad.' I am amazed at the strength of my reluctance to say it. (I wonder how many of us come to such meetings determined to express our uneasiness, our disgust, and find ourselves silenced by this extraordinary prohibition once the meeting starts?) Finally—and my tone has a touch of 'the little girl' in it, a note of charm—I say: 'Look, I'm not equipped to criticise it philosophically, but surely this sentence here is a key sentence, the phrase 'neither superstructure nor base'—surely that is either completely out of the Marxist canon, a new thought completely, or it's an evasion. Or simply arrogance.' (I am relieved that as I go on my tone loses its disarming 'charm' and becomes serious, though over-excited.) Rex blushes, turns the pamphlet over and over and says: 'Yes, I must admit that sentence did strike me as rather ...' There is a silence and then George says bluffly: 'All this theoretical stuff is just over my head.' And now we all look uncomfortable—except for George. A lot of comrades are now using this rough-and-ready attitude, a sort of comfortable philistinism. It has become so much a part of George's personality now, however, that he is quite happy about it. I find myself thinking: Well, it's justified—he does so much good work for the Party, if that's his way of staying in it, then ... Without actually taking a decision that we are not going to discuss the pamphlet, we let it be forgotten; and talk about general matters, communist politics anywhere. Russia, China, France, our own country. All the time I am thinking: Not once does one of us say: something is fundamentally wrong; yet the implication of what we say amounts to that. I can't stop thinking about this phenomenon—that

301

when two of us meet, our discussions are on a totally different level than when there are three people present. Two
people, and it is two persons, from a critical tradition, discussing politics as people not communists would discuss
them. (By people not communists I mean that they wouldn't
be recognised as communists, except for the jargon, by an
outsider listening in.) But more than two, and a different
spirit altogether is present. This is particularly true of what is
said about Stalin. Although I am quite prepared to believe
that he is mad and a murderer (though remembering always
what Michael says—that this is a time when it is impossible
to know the truth about anything), I like to hear people use
that tone of simple, friendly respect for him. Because if that
tone were to be thrown aside, something very important
would go with it, paradoxically enough, a faith in the possibilities of democracy, of decency. A dream would be dead—
for our time, at least.

The talk became desultory, I offered to make tea, everyone
was pleased that the meeting was going to end. I made tea,
and then I remembered a story that was sent to me last
week. By a comrade living somewhere near Leeds. When I
first read it, I thought it was an exercise in irony. Then a
very skilful parody of a certain attitude. Then I realised it
was serious—it was at the moment I searched my memory
and rooted out certain fantasies of my own. But what seemed
to me important was that it could be read as parody, irony or
seriously. It seems to me this fact is another expression of the
fragmentation of everything, the painful disintegration of
something that is linked with what I feel to be true about
language, the thinning of language against the density of our
experience. However, when I'd made the tea, I said I wanted
to read them a story.

[Here were gummed in several sheets of ordinary lined
writing paper torn off a blue writing pad, written over in very
neat tidy handwriting.]

When Comrade Ted knew that he had been chosen to go
on the teachers' delegation to the Soviet Union he felt very

proud. At first he could not believe it. He did not feel worthy of such a great honour. But he wasn't going to miss this chance of going to the first workers' country! At last the great day came when with the other comrades he assembled at the airport. There were three teachers on the delegation who were not Party members, and fine chaps they turned out to be too! Ted found the air trip over Europe delightful—his excitement mounted every minute and when he at last found himself in a very expensively appointed bedroom in the hotel in Moscow he was almost beside himself with excitement! It was nearly midnight when the delegation arrived, so the first thrill of seeing a communist country must wait until the morning! Comrade Ted was seated at the big table—large enough to seat a dozen people at least!—that was provided for him in his bedroom, writing up his notes for the day, for he was determined to keep a record of every precious moment—when there was a knock on the door. He said: 'Please come in,' expecting to see one of the comrades from the delegation, but there were two young chaps wearing cloth caps and workers' boots. One of them said: 'Comrade, please come with us.' They had open simple faces, and I did not ask where they were taking me. (I must confess, to my shame, that I had one bad half-moment, remembering all the stories we had read in the capitalist press—we are all infected by this poison despite ourselves!) I went down in the lift with my two friendly guides. The woman at the reception desk smiled at me and greeted my two new friends. There was a black car waiting. We got into it and sat side by side without speaking. Almost immediately in front of us were the towers of the Kremlin. So it was a short drive. We went through the big gates and the car pulled up outside a discreet side door. My two friends got out of the car, and opened the door for me. They smiled: 'Come with us comrade.' We went up a magnificent marble staircase with works of art on every side and then into a small side corridor that was plain and simple. We stopped outside an ordinary door, a door like any other. One of my guides knocked. A gruff voice said: 'Come in.' Again the two young chaps smiled at me, and nodded. They went off down the passage arm in arm. I went into the room

303

greatly daring, but somehow I knew what I would see. Comrade Stalin sat behind an ordinary desk, that showed much signs of hard use, smoking a pipe, in his shirt-sleeves. 'Come in comrade and sit down,' he said, in a kindly way. I felt at ease, and sat down, looking at the honest kindly face and the twinkling eyes. 'Thank you, comrade,' I said, sitting opposite to him. There was a short silence, while he smiled and examined me. Then he said: 'Comrade, you must forgive me for disturbing you so late at night . . .' 'Oh,' I interrupted eagerly, 'but the whole world knows you are a late worker.' He passed his rough worker's hand across his brow. Now I saw the marks of fatigue and strain—working for us! For the world! I felt proud and humble. 'I have disturbed you so late, comrade, because I have need of your advice. I heard there was a delegation of teachers from your country and I thought I would avail myself of the opportunity.' 'Anything at all I can tell you, Comrade Stalin . . .' 'I often wonder if I am getting the correct advice about our policy in Europe, and in particular, our policy for Great Britain.' I kept silent, but I was enormously proud—yes, this is a truly great man! Like a real communist leader he is prepared to take advice from even rank and file party cadres like myself! 'I would be grateful, comrade, if you would outline for me what our policy ought to be in Great Britain. I realise that your traditions are very different from ours, and I realise that our policy has not been taking these traditions into account.' Now I felt at ease to begin. I told him I often felt that there were many errors and mistakes in the Communist Party of the Soviet Union's policy as it affected Great Britain. I felt this was due to the isolation imposed on the Soviet Union due to the hatred of the capitalist powers for the budding communist country. Comrade Stalin listened and smoked his pipe, nodding the while. When I hesitated, he said, more than once: 'Please continue, comrade, do not be afraid to say exactly what is in your mind.' And so I did. I spoke for about three hours, beginning with a brief analytical account of the historical position of the British C.P. Once he rang a bell, and another young comrade came in with two glasses of Russian tea on a tray, one of which he set before me. Stalin sipped his tea abstemiously, nodding as he listened. I outlined what I considered would be the correct policy for Britain. When I had finished, he said simply: 'Thank you, comrade. I see now I have been very badly advised.' Then he glanced at his watch, and said: 'Comrade, you must forgive me, but I have much work to do before the sun rises.' I rose. He held out his hand. I shook it. 'Good-bye, Comrade Stalin.' 'Good-bye, my good comrade from Britain, and thank you again.' We exchanged a wordless smile. I know my eyes were full—I shall be proud of these tears till I die! As I left Stalin was refilling his pipe, his eyes already on a great pile of papers that awaited his perusal. I went out of the door, after the greatest moment of my life. The two young comrades were waiting for me. We exchanged smiles of profound under-standing. Our eyes were wet. We drove back to the hotel in silence. Only once were words spoken: 'That is a great man,' I said, and they nodded. At the hotel they accompanied me to my bedroom door. They wordlessly pressed my hand. Then I went back to my diary. Now I had something to record indeed! And I was at my work until the sun rose, thinking of the greatest man in the world, less than half a mile away, also awake and working, in custody of the desti-nies of us all!

[And now Anna's writing again:]

When I had finished reading this, no one said anything until George said: 'Good honest basic stuff.' Which could mean anything. Then I said: 'I remember having that fantasy myself, every word of it, except in my case I put right the policy for Europe as well.' Suddenly there was a roar of uncomfortable laughter, and George said: 'I thought it was a parody at first—makes you think, doesn't it.'

Clive said: 'I remember reading something translated from the Russian—early thirties, I think it was. Two young men are in the Red Square, and their tractor has broken down. They don't know what's wrong with it. Suddenly they see a burly figure approaching. He is smoking a pipe. "What's wrong?" he asks. "That's the trouble, comrade, we don't

305

know what's wrong." "So you don't know, eh, that's bad!" The burly man points with the stem of his pipe at some part of the machinery: "Have you thought of *that*?" The young men try—the tractor roars into life. They turn to thank the stranger who is standing watching them with a fatherly twinkle in his eyes. They realise it is Stalin. But he has already turned away, with a salute of his hand, on his solitary walk through the Red Square to the Kremlin.'

We all laughed again, and George said: 'Those were the days, say what you like. Well, I'm off home.'

As we separated, the room was full of hostility: we were disliking each other, and knew it.

[The yellow notebook continued.]

THE SHADOW OF THE THIRD

It was Patricia Brent, editress, who suggested Ella should spend a week in Paris. Because it was Patricia, Ella's instinct was to refuse immediately. 'Mustn't let them get us down,' she had said, the 'them' being men. In short, Patricia was over-eager to welcome Ella into the club of forlorn women; there was kindness in it, but also a private satisfaction. Ella said she thought it was a waste of time to go to Paris. The pretext was that she must interview the editor of a similar French magazine in order to buy the rights of a serial story for Britain. The story, Ella said, might be right for the housewives of Vaugirard; but it was wrong for the housewives of Brixton. 'It's a free holiday,' said Patricia, tart because she knew Ella was rejecting more than a Paris trip. After a few days Ella changed her mind. She had been reminded that it was over a year since Paul had left her and that everything she did, said, or felt, still referred to him. Her life was shaped around a man who would not return to her. She must liberate herself. This was an intellectual decision, unbacked by moral energy. She was listless and flat. It was as if Paul had taken with him, not only all her capacity for joy, but also her will. She said she would go to Paris, like a bad patient agreeing at last to take medicine, but insisting to the doctor that: 'Of course it won't do me any good.'

It was April, Paris, as always, charming; and Ella took a room in the modest hotel on the Left Bank she had last been in, two years before, with Paul. She fitted herself into the room, leaving space for him. It was only when she saw what she was doing that it occurred to her that she should not be in this hotel at all. But it seemed too much effort to leave it and find another. It was still early in the evening. Below her tall windows Paris was animated with greening trees and strolling people. It took Ella nearly an hour to get herself out of the room and into a restaurant to eat. She ate hastily, feeling exposed; and walked home with her eyes kept deliberately preoccupied. Nevertheless two men good-humouredly greeted her, and both times she froze into nervous annoyance, and walked on with hastening steps. She got into her bedroom and locked the door as if against a danger. Then she sat at the window and thought that five years before the dinner alone would have been pleasant because of its solitariness, and because of the possibilities of an encounter; and the walk home from the restaurant alone delightful. And she would certainly have had a cup of coffee or a drink with one or other of the two men. So what had happened to her? It was true that with Paul she had taught herself never to look at a man, even casually, because of his jealousy; she was, with him, like a protected indoors woman from a Latin country. But she had imagined this was an outward conformity to save him from self-inflicted pain. Now she saw that her whole personality had changed.

For some time she sat, listless, at the window, watching the darkening but blossoming city, and told herself she should make herself walk through its streets, and force herself into talking to people; she should let herself be picked up and flirt a little. But she understood she was as incapable of walking down the hotel stairs, leaving her key at the desk and going into the streets, as if she had just served a prison sentence for four years in solitary confinement and then told to behave normally. She went to bed. She was unable to sleep. She put herself to sleep, as always, by thinking of Paul. She had never, since he had left her, been able to achieve a vaginal orgasm; she was able to reach the sharp violence of the exterior orgasm, her hand becoming Paul's hand, mourning as she did so, the loss of her real self. She slept, overstimulated, nervous, exhausted, cheated. And by using Paul thus, brought close to her his 'negative' self, the man full of self-distrust. The real man retreated further and further from her. It was becoming hard for her to remember the warmth of his eyes, the humour of his voice. She would sleep beside a ghost of defeat; and the ghost wore, even when she might wake, briefly, out of habit, to open her arms so that his head might come to her breast, or to lay her head on his shoulder, a small, bitter, self-derisive smile. Yet when she dreamed of him, asleep, he was always to be recognised in the various guises he chose, because his image was one of warmth, a calm masculinity. Paul, whom she had loved, she kept sleeping; awake she retained nothing but shapes of pain.

Next morning she slept too long, as she always did when away from her son. She woke thinking that Michael must have been up, dressed, and breakfasted hours ago with Julia; he would be nearing his lunchtime at school. Then she told herself she had not come to Paris to follow in her mind the stages of her son's day; she reminded herself that Paris lay waiting for her outside, under a light-hearted sun. And it was time for her to dress for her appointment with the editor.

The offices of *Femme et Foyer* were across the river and in the heart of an ancient building that one must enter where once carriages, and before then, troops of privately owned soldiers had pressed under a noble carved archway. *Femme et Foyer* occupied a dozen soberly modern and expensive rooms in decaying piles of masonry that smelt even now of the church, of feudalism. Ella, expected, was shown into Monsieur Brun's office, and was received by Monsieur Brun, a large, well-kept, ox-like young man who greeted her with an excess of good manners which failed to conceal his lack of interest in Ella and in the proposal deal. They were to go out for an apéritif. Robert Brun announced to half a dozen pretty secretaries that since he would be lunching with his fiancée he would not be back until three and received a dozen congratulatory and understanding smiles. Ella and Robert Brun passed through the venerable courtyard, emerged from the ancient gateway, and set out for the café, while Ella enquired politely about his projected marriage. She was informed in fluent and correct English that his fiancée was formidably pretty, intelligent and talented. He was to marry her next month, and they were now engaged in preparing their apartment. Elise (he spoke the name with an already practised propriety, grave and formal) was at that very moment negotiating for a certain carpet they both coveted. She, Ella, would have the privilege of seeing her for herself. Ella hastened to assure him that she would be delighted, and congratulated him again. Meanwhile they had reached the patch of sun-shaded, table-crowded pavement they were to patronise, had sat down, and ordered pernods. This was the moment for business. Ella was at a disadvantage. She knew that if she returned to Patricia Brent with the rights of this serial *Comment J'ai fui un Grand Amour*, that irrepressibly provincial matron would be delighted. For her, the word *French* guaranteed a brand of excellence: discreetly but authentically amorous, high-toned, cultivated. For her, the phrase: by arrangement with the Paris *Femme et Foyer* would exude precisely the same exclusive spiciness as an expensive French scent. Yet Ella knew that no sooner had Patricia actually read it (in translation—she did not read French) she would agree, though reluctantly, that the story wouldn't do at all. Ella could see herself, if she chose, as protecting Patricia against her own weakness. But the fact was Ella had no intention of buying the story, had never had any intention of buying it; and therefore she was wasting this incredibly well-fed, well-washed and correct young man's time. She ought to feel guilty about it; she did not. If she had liked him, she would have been contrite: as it was, she saw him as a species of highly-trained middle-class animal, and was prepared to make use of him: she was unable, so weakened was she as an independent being, to enjoy sitting at a table publicly without a man's protection, and this man would do as well as another. For form's sake, she began explaining to Monsieur Brun how the story would have to be adapted for England. It concerned a young and poor orphan, sorrowing for a beautiful mother who had been brought to an early death-bed by a callous husband. This orphan had been reared in a convent by some good sisters. In spite of her piety, she was seduced at the age of fifteen by the heartless gardener, and, unable to face the innocent nuns, she had run away to Paris where she clung, culpable but utterly innocent at heart, to one man after another, all of whom betrayed her. Finally, at the age of twenty, with an illegitimate child put in the care of yet another set of good sisters, she met the assistant of a baker of whose love she felt herself unworthy. She fled from this, the true love, into several more pairs of uncaring arms, sobbing almost uninterruptedly. But at last the assistant of the baker (but only after a sufficient number of words had been used) caught up with her, forgave her, and promised her undying love, passion and protection. 'Mon amour,' this epic ended, 'Mon amour, I did not know when I ran away from you that I was flying from true love.'

'You see,' said Ella, 'this is so French in flavour that we would have to have it re-written.'

'But, yes? How is that?' The round, prominent, dark brown eyes were resentful. Ella stopped herself on the brink of indiscretion—she had been going to complain of the tone of mingled eroticism and religiosity—thinking that Patricia Brent would stiffen in precisely the same way if someone, perhaps Robert Brun, had said: 'This is so English in flavour.'

Robert Brun said: 'I found the story very sad; it is psychologically very correct.'

Ella remarked: 'The stories written for women's magazines are always psychologically correct. But the point is, on what level are they correct?'

His face, his full eyes, were momentarily immobilised with annoyed incomprehension. Then Ella saw his eyes move away and off in a glance along the pavement: the fiancée was overdue. He remarked: 'I understood from Miss Brent's letter she had decided to buy the story.' Ella said: 'If we were to print it, we should have to re-write it with no convents, no nuns, no religion.' 'But the whole point of that

310

story—surely you must agree?—is the goodness of the poor girl, she is at heart a good girl.' He had understood that the story would not be bought; he did not care one way or the other; and his eyes had now focused themselves, for at the end of the pavement appeared a slight, pretty girl, in type rather like Ella, with a pale little pointed face and fluffy black hair. Ella was thinking: Well I may be his type, but he certainly isn't mine; as the girl approached, and she waited for him to rise and greet his fiancée. But at the last moment he shifted his gaze and the girl passed. Then he returned to his inspection of the end of the pavement. Well, thought Ella; *well*—and sat watching his detailed, analytical, practically sensual appraisal of one woman after another, to the point where the woman in question would glance at him, annoyed or interested; when he would let his eyes move to one side.

Finally there appeared a woman who was ugly, yet attractive; sallow, lumpish in figure, yet made up with skill and very well dressed. This turned out to be the fiancée. They greeted each other with the licensed pleasure of the publicly linked couple. All eyes turned, as they had been intended to, towards the happy pair, and people smiled. Then Ella was introduced. Now the conversation continued in French. It was of the carpet, so much more expensive than either had expected. But it had been bought. Robert Brun grumbled and exclaimed; the future Madame Brun sighed and fluttered her lashes over dark black-rimmed eyes, and murmured with discreet lovingness that for him nothing was too good. Their hands met on a smile. His was complacent; hers pleased, and a trifle anxious. Before the hands had even parted, his eyes had escaped, out of habit, in a quick glance to the end of the pavement where a pretty girl appeared. He frowned as he collected himself. His future wife's smile froze, for a second, as she noted this. Smiling prettily, however, she sat back in her chair, and spoke prettily to Ella of the problems of furnishing in these hard times. Her glances at her fiancé reminded Ella of a prostitute she had seen late one night in the underground in London; just so had this woman caressed and invited a man with small, discreet, pretty glances of her eyes.

Ella contributed facts about furnishing from England, while she thought: now I'm odd-woman-out with an engaged couple. I feel isolated and excluded. I feel exposed again. In a minute they will get up and leave me. And I shall feel even more exposed. *What has happened to me*? And yet I would rather be dead than in this woman's shoes, and that's the truth.

The three remained together for another twenty minutes. The fiancée continued vivacious, feminine, arch, caressing towards her captive. The fiancé remained well-mannered and proprietary. His eyes alone betrayed him. And she, his captive, never for one moment forgot him—her eyes moved with his to note his earnest, minute (though now necessarily curtailed) inspection of the women who passed.

This situation was heartbreakingly clear to Ella; and she felt, surely, to anyone who examined the couple for as long as five minutes? They had been lovers over-long. She had money, and this was necessary to him. She was desperately, fearfully in love with him. He was fond of her, and already chafing at the bonds. The great well-groomed ox was uneasy before the noose had even tightened around his neck. In two years, three years, they would be Monsieur and Madame Brun, in a well-furnished apartment (the money provided by her) with a small child and perhaps a nurse-maid; and she would be caressing and gay and anxious still; and he would be politely good-humoured, but sometimes bad-tempered when the demands of the home prevented his pleasures with his mistress.

And although every phase of this marriage was as clear to Ella as if it were in the past and she was being told of it; although she felt irritable with dislike of the whole situation, yet she dreaded the moment when the couple would rise and leave her. Which they did, with every allowance of their admirable French politeness, he so smoothly indifferently polite, she so anxiously polite, and with an eye on him which said: see how well I behave to your business friends. And Ella was left sitting at the table, at the hour for companionable eating, feeling as if a skin had been peeled off her. Instantly she protected herself by imagining that Paul would come to sit by her, where Robert Brun had sat. She was conscious that two men, now that she was alone, were weighing her up, weighing their chances. In a moment one of them would come over, and she would then *behave like a civilised person*, have a drink or two, enjoy the encounter, and return to her hotel fortified and freed from the ghost of Paul. She was sitting with her back to a low tub of greenery. The sunshade above her enclosed her in a warm yellow glow. She shut her eyes and thought: When I open my eyes perhaps I'll see Paul. (It suddenly seemed inconceivable that he should not be somewhere near, waiting to come and join her.) She thought: What did it mean, my saying I loved Paul—when his going has left me like a snail that has had her shell pecked off by a bird? I should have said that my being with Paul essentially meant I remained myself, remained independent and free. I asked nothing of him, certainly not marriage. And yet now I am in pieces. So it was all a fraud. In fact I was sheltering under him. I was no better than that frightened woman, his wife. I am no better than Elise, future wife of Robert. Muriel Tanner kept Paul by never asking questions, by effacing herself. Elise is buying Robert. But I use the word love and think of myself as free, when the truth is ... a voice, close to her, enquired if the place were free, and Ella opened her eyes to see a small, lively, vivacious Frenchman, in the act of seating himself. She told herself that he looked pleasant, and she would stay where she was; she smiled nervously, said she felt ill and had a headache, and got up and left, conscious that her manner had been that of a frightened schoolgirl.

And now she made a decision. She walked back to the hotel, across Paris, packed, sent a wire to Julia and another to Patricia, and took the coach out to the airport. There was a free seat on an aircraft at nine o'clock, three hours from now. In the airport restaurant she ate at ease—feeling herself; a traveller has the right to be alone. She read a dozen French women's magazines, professionally, marking features and stories that might do for Patricia Brent. She did this work with half her mind; and found herself thinking: Well, the cure for the sort of condition I am in is work. I shall write another novel. But the trouble is, with the last one there was never a point when I said: I shall write a novel. I found I was writing a novel. Well, I must put myself in the same state of mind—a kind of open readiness, a passive waiting. Then perhaps one day I'll find myself writing. But I don't really care about it—I didn't really care about the other. Suppose Paul had said to me, I'll marry you if you promise never to write another word? My God, I would have done it! I would have been prepared to buy Paul, like an Elise buying Robert Brun. But that would have been a double deception, because the act of writing it was irrelevant—it was not an act of creation, but an act of recording something. The story was already written, in invisible ink ... well perhaps somewhere inside me is another story written in invisible ink ... but what's the point? I am unhappy because I have lost some kind of independence, some freedom; but my being 'free' has nothing to do with writing a novel; it has to do with my attitude towards a man, and that has been proved dishonest, because I am in pieces. The truth is that my happiness with Paul was more important to me than anything and where has that landed me? Alone, frightened to be alone, without resources, running from an exciting city because I haven't the moral energy to ring up any one of a dozen people who would be pleased if I did—or at least might turn out to be pleased.

What is terrible is that after every one of the phases of my life is finished, I am left with no more than some banal commonplace that everyone knows: in this case, that women's emotions are all still fitted for a kind of society that no longer exists. My deep emotions, my real ones, are to do with my relationship with a man. One man. But I don't live that kind of life, and I know few women who do. So what I feel is irrelevant and silly ... I am always coming to the conclusion that my real emotions are foolish, I am always having, as it were, to cancel myself out. I ought to be like a man, caring more for my work than for people; I ought to put my work first, and take men as they come, or find an ordinary comfortable man for bread and butter reasons—but I won't do it, I can't be like that ...

314

The loudspeaker was calling the number of the flight; and Ella went with the others across the tarmac and into the aircraft. She sat down and noted a woman sat beside her and that she was relieved it was a woman. Five years ago she would have been sorry. The aircraft taxied forward, turned, and began racing for the take-off. The machine gathered speed, vibrating; seemed to hunch itself up with the effort of getting into the air, then slowed. It stood roaring futilely for a few minutes. Something was wrong. The passengers, crammed so close together in the shaking metal container, looked covertly at each other's brightly-lit faces to see if their own alarm was reflected; understood that their own faces must be preserving masks of unconcern; and lapsed into private fears, glancing at the air hostess, whose look of casualness seemed overdone. Three times the aircraft sped forward, gathered itself for the climb, slowed, and stood roaring. Then it taxied back to the airport building, and the passengers were invited to descend while the mechanics 'adjusted a small fault in the engine.' They all trooped back to the restaurant where officials, outwardly polite, but exuding irritation, announced that a meal would be served. Ella sat by herself in a corner, bored and annoyed. Now it was a silent company, reflecting on their good luck that the engine fault had been discovered in time. They all ate, to fill in time, ordered drinks, and sat looking out of the windows to where mechanics, under bright beams of light, flocked around their aircraft.

Ella found herself in the grip of a sensation which, when she examined it, turned out to be loneliness. It was as if, between her and the groups of people, were a space of cold air, an emotional vacuum. The sensation was of physical cold, of physical isolation. She was thinking of Paul again: so powerfully that it seemed inconceivable that he should not simply walk in through a door and come up to her. She could feel the cold that surrounded her thawing in the powerful belief that he would soon be with her. With an effort she cut this fantasy: she thought in a panic, if I can't stop this, this madness, I'll never become myself again, I'll never recover. She succeeded in banishing the immanence of Paul; felt the

315

chilly spaces open around her again, and inside cold and isolation, leafed through the piles of French magazines and thought of nothing at all. Near her a man was sitting, absorbed in magazines which she saw were medical. He was at first glance an American; short, broad, vigorous; with close-cut glistening hair like brown fur. He was drinking glasses of fruit cordial, one after the other, and seemed unperturbed by the delay. Once their eyes met after both had inspected the aircraft outside, which was swarming with mechanics, and he said with a loud laugh: 'We're going to be stuck here all night.' He returned to his medical publications. It was now after eleven, and they were the only party still waiting in the building. Suddenly a terrific noise of French shouting and exclaiming broke out below: the mechanics were in disagreement, and they were quarrelling. One, apparently in charge, was exhorting the others, or complaining, with much waving of the arms and shrugging of the shoulders. The others at first shouted back, then became sullen. And then the group drifted off back to the main building, leaving the one, alone, under the aircraft. Who, alone, first swore vigorously, and then gave a final heavy angry shrug of the shoulders and followed the others into the building. The American and Ella again exchanged glances. He said, apparently amused: 'I don't care much for that,' while the voice from the loud-speaker invited them to take their seats. Ella and he went together. She remarked: 'Perhaps we should refuse to go?' He said, showing fine, very white teeth and an enthusiastic beam from boyish blue eyes: 'I've got an appointment to-morrow morning.' Apparently the appointment was so important it justified a risk of crashing. The party, most of whom must have overlooked the scene with the mechanics, climbed obediently back into their seats, apparently absorbed into the necessity of putting a good face on things. Even the air hostess, outwardly calm, showed nervousness. In the brightly-lit interior of the aircraft, forty people were in the grip of terror, and concerned with not showing it. All, that is, Ella thought, save for the American, now seated by her, and already at work on his medical books. As for Ella, she had climbed into the aircraft as she would have climbed into a death-chamber; but thinking of the shrug given by the head mechanic: that was her feeling too. As the aeroplane began to vibrate, she thought: I'm going to die, very likely, and I'm pleased.

This discovery was not, after the first moment, a shock. She had known it all the time: I'm so enormously exhausted, so utterly, basically tired, and in every fibre of myself, that to know I haven't got to go through with living is like a reprieve. How extraordinary! And every one of these people, with the possible exception of this exuberant young man, is terrified that the machine is going to crash, and yet we all trooped obediently into it. So perhaps we all feel the same way? Ella glanced curiously at the three people on the other side of the aisle; they were pale with fright, sweat shone on their foreheads. The aircraft again gathered itself for the spring into the air. It roared down the runway, and then, vibrating intensely, lifted itself into the air with an effort, like a tired person. Very low, it climbed over roofs; very low it climbed, painfully gathering height. The American said, on a grin: 'Well, we made that,' and went on reading. The air hostess, who had been standing rigid, smiling brightly, now came to life and went back to prepare more food, and the American said: 'The condemned man will now eat a hearty meal.' Ella shut her eyes. She thought: I'm quite convinced we shall crash. Or that at least there's a good chance of it. And what about Michael? I haven't even thought of him— well Julia will look after him. The thought of Michael was a spur to life for a moment, then she thought: For a mother to die in an aircrash—that's sad, but it's not damaging. Not like a suicide. How odd!—the phrase is, to give a child life; but a child gives life to its parent when the parent decides to live simply because to commit suicide would hurt the child. I wonder how many parents decide to go on living because they have decided not to hurt their children, although they don't care for living themselves? (She was feeling drowsy now.) Well, this way it takes the responsibility off me. Of course I could have refused to get on the plane—but Michael will never know about that scene with the mechanics. It's all over. I feel as if I had been born with a weight of fatigue on

317

me, and I've been carrying it all my life. The only time I wasn't rolling a heavy weight up hill was when I was with Paul. Well, enough of Paul and enough of love and enough of me—how boring these emotions are that we're caught in and can't get free of, no matter how much we want to ... she could feel the machine vibrating roughly. It will fly into pieces in the air, she thought, and I will go spinning off down like a leaf into the dark, into the sea, I'll go spinning weightlessly down into the black cold obliterating sea. Ella slept and woke to find the plane stationary and the American shaking her. They had landed. It was already one in the morning; and by the time the coach load of people were deposited at the terminus it was getting on for three. Ella was numb, cold, heavy with tiredness. The American was still beside her, still cheerful, efficient, his broad pink face gleaming with health. He invited her to share his taxi; there weren't enough to go round.

'I thought we'd had it,' Ella said, noting that her voice sounded as cheerfully unconcerned as his.

'Yeah. It certainly looked like it.' He laughed, all his teeth showing. 'When I saw that guy shrug his shoulders back there—I thought, boy! that's it. Where do you live?' Ella told him, and added: 'Have you got somewhere?' 'I'll find myself a hotel.' 'At this time of night it won't be easy. I'd ask you to stay with me, but I've got two rooms, and my son's in one of them.' 'That's very sweet of you, no, I'm not worried.' And he wasn't. It would soon be dawn; he had no place to sleep; and he was as exuberant and fresh as he had been early in the evening. He dropped her, saying that he would be very happy if she would dine with him. Ella hesitated, then agreed. They would meet, therefore, the following evening, or rather, that evening. Ella went upstairs, thinking that she and the American would have nothing to say to each other and that the thought of the coming evening already bored her. She found her son sleeping in a room that was like the cave of a young animal; it smelled of healthy sleep. She adjusted the covers over him, and sat for a while to watch the pink young face, already visible in the creeping grey light from the window, to see the soft gleam from his tufted brown hair. She thought: He's like the American in type—both are square and large and loaded with strong pink flesh. Yet the American repels me physically; yet I don't dislike him, the way I disliked that fine young ox, Robert Brun. Why not? Ella went to bed, and for the first time in many nights, did not summon the memory of Paul. She was thinking that forty people who had given themselves up for dead were lying in bed, alive, scattered all over the city.

Her son woke her two hours later, radiant with surprise at her being there. Since she was still officially on holiday, she did not go to the office, but informed Patricia on the telephone that the serial was unbought, and that she was unredeemed by Paris. Julia was rehearsing for a new play. Ella spent the day alone, cleaning, cooking, re-arranging the flat; and playing with the boy when he came home from school. It was not until late that the American, whose name now turned out to be Cy Maitland, telephoned to say he was in her hands: what would she like to do? The theatre? The opera? Ballet? Ella said it was too late for any of these, and suggested dinner. He was at once relieved. 'To tell you the truth, shows aren't in my line, I don't go to shows much. Now tell me where you'd like to have dinner?' 'Do you want to go somewhere special? Or a place where you can get steak, something like that?' Again he was relieved. 'That'd suit me fine—I've got pretty simple tastes in the food line.' Ella named a good solid restaurant and put aside the dress she had chosen for the evening: it was the kind of dress she had never worn with Paul, out of all kinds of inhibitions; and which she had been wearing since, defiantly. She now put on a skirt and a shirt, and made herself up to look healthy rather than interesting. Michael was sitting up in bed surrounded by comics. 'Why are you going out when you only just got home?' He sounded deliberately aggrieved. 'Because I feel like it,' she said, grinning in answer to his tone. He gave a conscious smile, then frowned, and said in an injured voice: 'It isn't fair.' 'But you'll be asleep in an hour—I hope.' 'Is Julia going to read to me?' 'But I've already read to you for hours. Besides, it's a school-day tomorrow, and you've got to go to sleep.' 'But when you've gone I expect I'll talk her into

319

it.' 'You'd better not tell me about it then, because I'll be cross!' He sauced her with his eyes; sitting up broad, solid, pink-cheeked; very sure of himself and his world in this house. 'Why haven't you put on the dress you said you were going to wear?' 'I've decided to wear this instead.' 'Women,' said the nine-year-old, in a lordly way. 'Women and their dresses.' 'Well, good night,' she said, holding her lips for a moment against the smooth warm cheek; sniffing with pleasure at the fresh soap smell of his hair. She went downstairs, and found Julia in her bath. She shouted: 'I'm off!' and Julia shouted back: 'You'd better get home early, you didn't get any sleep last night.'

In the restaurant Cy Maitland was waiting for her. He looked fresh and vital. His clear blue eyes were undimmed by sleeplessness; and Ella said, sliding into the seat beside him and feeling suddenly fatigued: 'Aren't you sleepy at all?' He said, at once triumphant: 'I never sleep more than three or four hours a night.' 'Why not?' 'Because I'll never get where I want if I waste time sleeping.' 'You tell me about you,' said Ella, 'and then I'll tell you about me.' 'Fine,' he said. 'Fine. To tell you the truth, you are an enigma to me, so you'll have to do a lot of talking.' But now the waiters were ostensibly at their service, and Cy Maitland ordered 'the biggest steak they had in the place' and coca-cola, no potatoes because he had to lose a stone in weight, and tomato sauce. 'Don't you ever drink alcohol?' 'Never, only fruit juice.' 'Well, I'm afraid you are going to have to order me wine.' 'It's a pleasure,' he said; and instructed the wine waiter to bring a bottle of 'the best he had.' The waiters having departed, Cy Maitland said, relishing it: 'In Paris the garcongs go out of their way to let you know you're a hick; but here I see they just let you know it, without trying.' 'And are you a hick?' 'Sure, sure,' he said, his batteries of fine teeth gleaming. 'Well now it's time for the story of your life.' It took them to the end of the meal—over, as far as Cy was concerned, in ten minutes. But he waited agreeably enough for her, answering her questions. He had been born a poor boy. But he had also been born with brains and had used them. Scholarships and grants had taken him where he wanted to be—a brain surgeon, on his way up, married well with five children, a position and a great future, even if he said it himself. 'And what does a poor boy mean in America?' 'My pop was selling ladies' hose all his life and he still is. I'm not saying anyone ever went hungry, but there aren't any brain surgeons anywhere in our family, you can bet your life.' His boasting was so simple, so natural to him, that it was not boasting. And his vitality was beginning to infect Ella. She had forgotten she was tired. When he suggested it was now time for her to tell him about herself, she postponed what she now understood would be an ordeal. For one thing, it occurred to her that her life, as far as she was concerned, could not be described by simple succession of statements: my parents were so and so; I've lived in such and such places; I do such and such work. And for another, she had understood that she was attracted to him, and this discovery had upset her. When he laid his large white hand on her arm, she felt her breasts lift and sting. Her thighs were wet. But she had nothing in common with him. She could not remember ever, not once in her life, feeling a physical response for a man who was not in some way kin to her. She had always responded to a look, a smile, the tone of a voice, a laugh. As far as she was concerned, this man was a healthy savage; and the discovery that she wanted to be in bed with him split her. She felt irritation and annoyance; she remembered feeling precisely like this when her husband attempted to rouse her by physical manipulation against her emotions. The end of that was frigidity. She thought: I might easily be a frigid woman. Then she was struck by the humour of it: she was sitting here, soft with desire for this man; worrying about a hypothetical frigidity. She laughed, and he enquired: 'What's funny?' She replied at random, and he said good-humouredly: 'O.K., you think I'm a hick too. Well that's O.K. with me. Now I have a suggestion. I've got about twenty telephone calls to make, and I want to make them from my hotel. Come back with me, I'll give you a drink, and then when I've finished the telephone calls, you can tell me about you.' Ella agreed; then wondered if he interpreted this as a willingness on her part to go to bed with him? If so, he showed no signs of it. It struck her that with the men she met in her world, she could interpret what they felt or were thinking from a glance, a gesture, or an atmosphere; so that words told her nothing about them she did not know already. But with this man, she knew nothing at all. He was married; but she did not know, as she would have done for instance with Robert Brun, what his attitude would be to infidelity. Since she knew nothing about him, it followed he knew nothing about her: he did not know, for instance, that her nipples were burning. She agreed, therefore, and casually, to go with him to his hotel.

He had a bed-sitting-room and a bath in an expensive hotel. The rooms were in the heart of the building, air-conditioned, windowless, claustrophobic, neatly and anonymously furnished. Ella felt caged; but he seemed quite at home. He supplied her with a whisky, then drew the telephone to him and made, as he had said he would, about twenty telephone calls, a process that took half an hour. Ella listened, and noted that tomorrow he had at least ten appointments, including four visits to well-known London hospitals. When he had finished the calls, he began striding exuberantly up and down the small room. 'Boy,' he exclaimed, 'boy! But I feel great.' 'If I weren't here, what would you be doing?' 'I'd be working.' There was a great heap of medical journals on his night-table, and she said: 'Reading?' 'Yes. There's a lot to read, if you're going to keep up.' 'Do you ever read, except for your work?' 'Nope.' He laughed, and said: 'My wife's the one for culture. I haven't time.' 'Tell me about her.' He instantly produced a photograph. She was a pretty baby-faced blonde surrounded by five small children. 'Boy! Isn't she pretty? She's the prettiest girl in the whole town!' 'Is that why you married her?' 'Why, sure . . .' He caught her tone, laughed at himself with her, and said, shaking his head as if in wonder at himself: 'Sure! I said to myself, I'm going to marry the prettiest and classiest girl in this town and I did. That's just what I did.' 'And you're happy?' 'She's a great girl,' he said at once, enthusiastic. 'She's fine, and I've got five fine boys. I wish I had a girl, but

322

my boys are fine. And I just wish I had more time to be with them, but when I am, then I feel fine.'

Ella was thinking: If I get up now and say I must go, he'd agree, without rancour, with good-nature. Perhaps I'll see him again. Perhaps not. Neither of us will care. But I have to do the directing now, because he doesn't know what to do with me. I ought to go—but why? Only yesterday I decided it was ridiculous, women like me, having emotions that don't fit our lives. A man now, in this situation, *the sort of man I would be if I'd been born a man,* would go to bed and think no more of it. He was saying: 'And now, Ella, I've been talking about myself, and you're a darned fine listener, I must say that, but do you know, I don't know the first thing about you, not the first thing.'

Now, thought Ella. Now.

But she temporised: 'Did you know it was after twelve?'

'No? Is it? Too bad. I never go to bed before three or four and I'm up by seven, every day of my life.'

Now, thought Ella. It's ridiculous, she thought, that it should be so difficult. To say what she now said was going against every one of her deepest instincts, and she was surprised that it came out apparently casual, and only slightly breathless: 'Would you like to go to bed with me?'

He looked at her, grinning. He was not surprised. He was—interested. Yes, thought Ella, he's interested. Well good for him; she liked him for it. Suddenly he put back his broad healthy head and whooped: 'Boy, oh boy, would I? Yes, sir, Ella, if you hadn't said that I wouldn't have known what to say.'

'I know,' she said, smiling demurely. (She could feel this demure smile, and marvelled at it.) She said, demurely; 'Well, now, sir, I think you should set me at my ease, or something.'

He grinned. He was standing across the room from her; and she saw him as all flesh, a body of warm, abundant, exuberant flesh. Very well then, that's what it would be. (At this point, Ella detached herself from Ella, and stood to one side, watching and marvelling.)

323

She got up, smiling, and deliberately pulled off her dress. He, smiling, took off his jacket, and stripped off his shirt.

In bed, it was a delightful shock of warm tense flesh. (Ella was standing to one side, thinking ironically: Well, well!) He penetrated her almost at once, and came after a few seconds. She was about to console or be tactful, when he rolled on his back, flung up his arms, and exclaimed: 'Boy. Oh boy!'

(At this point Ella became herself, one person, both of them thinking as one.)

She lay beside him, controlling physical disappointment, smiling.

'Oh boy!' he said, contented. 'That's what I like. No problems with you.'

She thought this one out slowly, her arms around him. Then he began talking of his wife, apparently at random. 'Do you know what? We go to the club, dancing, two, three nights a week. You know, that's the best club in the town. All the boys look at me and think, lucky bastard! She's the prettiest girl there, even after five kids. They are thinking we have a whale of a time. Oh boy, and sometimes I think, suppose I told them—we have five kids. And we've had it five times since we married. Well, I'm exaggerating, but that's about it. She's not interested, though she looks as if she is.'

'What's the trouble?' asked Ella, demure.

'Search me. Before we got married, when we were dating, she was hot enough then. Oh boy, when I think!'

'How long were you—dating?'

'Three years. Then we got engaged. Four years.'

'And you never made love?'

'Made love—oh, I see. No, she wouldn't let me, and I wouldn't have wanted her to. But everything but. And she was hot then, boy, when I think! And then on the honeymoon she froze up. And now I never touch her. Well if we're tight after a party sometimes.' He let out his youthful energetic laugh, throwing his large brown legs up and letting them fall. 'And we go dancing, she's all dressed to kill, and all the boys looking at her and envying me, and I think: if they just knew!'

'Don't you mind?'

'Hell, of course I mind. But I'm not going to force myself on anyone. That's what I like about you—let's go to bed, you say, and that's fine and easy. I like you.'

She lay beside him, smiling. His large healthy body was pulsing with well-being. He said: 'Wait a while, I'll make it again. Out of practice, I guess.'

'Do you have other women?'

'Sometimes. When I get the chance. I don't chase any. Haven't the time.'

'Too busy getting where you want to go?'

'That's right.'

He put his hand down and felt himself.

'You wouldn't rather I did that?'

'What? You don't mind?'

'Mind?' she said, smiling, lying on her elbow beside him.

'Hell, my wife won't touch me. Women don't like it.' He let out another whoop of laughter. 'You don't mind then?'

After a moment, his face changed into wondering sensuality. 'Hell,' he said. 'Hell. Oh boy!'

She made him big, taking her time; and then said: 'And now, don't be in such a hurry.'

He frowned in thought; Ella could see him thinking this out; well, he wasn't stupid—but she was wondering about his wife, about the other women he had had. He came into her; and Ella was thinking: I've never done this before—I'm *giving pleasure*. Extraordinary; I've never used the phrase before, or even thought of it. With Paul, I went into the dark and ceased to think. The essence of this is, I'm conscious, skilled, discreet—I'm giving pleasure. It has nothing to do with what I had with Paul. But I'm in bed with this man and this is intimacy. His flesh moved in hers, too fast, unsubtle. Again she did not come, and he was roaring with delight, kissing her and shouting: 'Oh boy, oh boy, oh boy!'

Ella was thinking: But with Paul, I would have come in that time—so what's wrong?—it's not enough to say, I don't love this man? She understood suddenly that she would never come with this man. She thought: for women like me, integrity isn't chastity, it isn't fidelity, it isn't any of the old words. Integrity is the orgasm. That is something I haven't

325

any control over. I could never have an orgasm with this man, I can give pleasure and that's all. But why not? Am I saying that I can never come except with a man I love? Because what sort of a desert am I condemning myself to if that's true?

He was enormously pleased with her, generously appreciative, glistening with well-being. And Ella was delighted with herself, that she could make him so happy.

When she had dressed to go home, and was telephoning for a taxi, he said: 'I wonder what it would be like, being married to someone like you—*hell*!'

'You'd enjoy it?' asked Ella, demure.

'It'd be—man! a woman you can talk to, and have such fun in the sack too—man, I can't even imagine it!'

'Don't you talk to your wife?'

'She's a fine girl,' he said soberly. 'I think the world of her and of the kids.'

'Is she happy?'

This question so surprised him that he leaned up on his elbow to consider it and her—he was frowning with seriousness. Ella found herself liking him enormously; she sat dressed, on the side of the bed, liking him. He said, after thinking it out: 'She's got the best house in the town. She's got everything she ever asks for, for the house. She's got five boys—I know she wants a girl, but perhaps next time . . . She has a fine time with me—we go out dancing once or twice a week, and she's always the smartest girl wherever we go. And she's got me—and I'm telling you Ella, I don't mean to boast, I can see from your smile when I say it—but she's got a man who's doing pretty well.'

Now he lifted down the photograph of his wife from where it stood by the bed and said: 'Does she look like an unhappy woman?' Ella looked at the pretty little face and said: 'No, she doesn't.' She added: 'I could no more understand a woman like your wife than fly.'

'No, I don't think you would, at that.'

The taxi was waiting; and Ella kissed him and left, after he had said: 'I'll ring you tomorrow. Boy, but I want to see you again.'

326

Ella spent the following evening with him. Not out of any promise of pleasure, but out of liking. And besides, she felt that if she refused to see him, he might be hurt.

They had dinner again, and in the same restaurant. ('This is our restaurant, Ella,' he said sentimentally; as he might have said: 'This is our tune, Ella.')

He talked about his career.

'And when you've passed all your examinations and attended all the conferences, what then?'

'I'm going to try for Senator.'

'Why not President?'

He laughed with her, at himself, good-natured as always. 'No, not President. But Senator—yes. I tell you, Ella, you watch for my name. You'll find it, fifteen years' time, head of my profession. I've done everything I said I would do up till now, haven't I? So I know what I'll do in the future. Senator Cy Maitland, Wyoming. Want to bet?'

'I never make bets I know I'll lose.'

He was leaving for the States again next day. He had interviewed a dozen top doctors in his field, seen a dozen hospitals, attended four conferences. He was finished with England.

'I'd like to go to Russia,' he said. 'But I can't, not with things as they are now.'

'You mean McCarthy?'

'You've heard of him then?'

'Well, yes, we've heard of him.'

'Those Russians, they're pretty well up in my field, I read them up, I wouldn't mind a trip, but not with things as they are.'

'When you're Senator, what'll your attitude be to McCarthy?'

'My attitude? You're kidding me again?'

'Not at all.'

'My attitude—well, he's right, we can't have the Reds taking over.'

Ella hesitated, then said, demure: 'The woman I share a house with is a communist.'

She felt him stiffen; then he thought; then he loosened

327

again. He said: 'I know things are different here with you. I don't get it, I don't mind telling you that.'

'Well, it doesn't matter.'

'No. You coming back to the hotel with me?'

'If you like.'

'If I like!'

Again, she gave pleasure. She liked him, and that was all.

They talked about his work. He specialised in leucotomies: 'Boy, I've cut literally hundreds of brains in half!'

'It doesn't bother you, what you're doing?'

'Why should it?'

'But you know when you've finished that operation, it's final, the people are never the same again?'

'But that's the idea, most of them don't want to be the same again.' Then, with the fairness which characterised him, he added: 'But I'll admit it, sometimes when I think, I've done hundreds, and it is pretty final.'

'The Russians wouldn't approve of you at all,' said Ella.

'No. That's why I wouldn't mind a trip, to find out what they do instead. Tell me, how come you know about leucotomies?'

'I once had an affair with a psychiatrist. He was a neurologist too. But not a brain surgeon—he told me he never recommended leucotomies—except very rarely.'

He suddenly said: 'Ever since I told you I was a specialist in that operation you haven't liked me as much.'

She said, after a pause: 'No. But I can't help it.'

Then he laughed, and said: 'Well, I can't help it either.' Then he said: 'You say, I once had an affair, just like that?'

Ella had been thinking that when she used the phrase, of Paul: I once had an affair, it was the exact equivalent of his 'a pretty flighty piece'—or whatever the words were he had used that meant the same. She found herself thinking, involuntarily: Good! he said I was like that! Well, I am, and I'm glad of it.

Cy Maitland was saying: 'Did you love him?'

The word love had not been used before between them; he had not used it in connection with his wife.

She said: 'Very much.'

328

'You don't want to get married?'

She said, demurely: 'Every woman wants to get married.'

He gave a snort of laughter; and then turned to look at her, shrewd. 'I don't get you, Ella, you know that? I don't understand you at all. But I understand you are a pretty independent sort of woman.'

'Well, yes, I suppose I am.'

Now he put his arms around her and said: 'Ella, you've taught me things.'

'I'm glad. I hope they were pleasant.'

'Well, yes, they were too.'

'Good.'

'You kidding me?'

'Just a little.'

'That's all right, I don't mind. You know Ella, I mentioned your name to someone today and they said you had written a book?'

'Everyone has written a book.'

'If I told my wife I'd met a real writer, she'd never get over it, she's mad about culture and that kind of thing.'

'But perhaps you'd better not tell her.'

'What if I read your book?'

'But you don't read books.'

'I can read,' he said, good-humoured. 'What's it about?'

'Well . . . let me see. It's full of insight and integrity and one thing and another.'

'You don't take it seriously?'

'Of course I take it seriously.'

'O.K. then. O.K. You're not going?'

'I have to—my son'll wake up in about four hours from now, and unlike you, I need to sleep.'

'O.K. I won't forget you, Ella. I wonder what it would be like, married to you.'

'I've got a feeling you wouldn't like it very much.'

She was dressing; he lay at ease in bed, watching her, shrewd and thoughtful.

'Then I wouldn't like it,' he said and laughed, stretching his arms. 'I probably wouldn't at that.'

'No.'

They parted, with affection.

She went home in a taxi, and crept up the stairs so as not to disturb Julia. But there was a light under Julia's door, and she called out: 'Ella?'

'Yes. Was Michael all right?'

'Not a cheep out of him. How was it?'

'Interesting,' said Ella, with deliberation.

'Interesting?'

Ella went into the bedroom. Julia lay propped on pillows, smoking and reading. She examined Ella, thoughtfully.

Ella said: 'He was a very nice man.'

'That's good.'

'And I'm going to be extremely depressed in the morning. In fact I can feel it coming on already.'

'Because he's going back to the States?'

'No.'

'You look terrible. What's the matter, wasn't he any good in bed?'

'Not much.'

'Oh well,' said Julia, tolerant. 'Have a cigarette?'

'No. I'm going to sleep before it hits me.'

'It's hit you already. Why do you go to bed with a man who doesn't attract you?'

'I didn't say he didn't attract me. The point is, there's no use my going to bed with anyone but Paul.'

'You'll get over it.'

'Yes, of course. But it takes a long time.'

'You must persevere,' said Julia.

'I intend to,' said Ella. She said good night and went up to her rooms.

[The blue notebook continued.]

15th September, 1954

Last night Michael said (I had not seen him for a week): 'Well, Anna, and so our great love affair is coming to an end?' Characteristic of him that it is a question mark: he is bringing it to an end, but talks as if I am. I said, smiling but

330

ironical in spite of myself: 'But at least it has been a great love affair?' He, then: 'Ah, Anna, you make up stories about life and tell them to yourself, and you don't know what is true and what isn't.' 'And so we haven't had a great love affair?' This was breathless and pleading; though I had not meant it. I felt a terrible dismay and coldness at his words, as if he were denying my existence. He said, whimsically: 'If you say we have, then we have. And if you say not, then not.' 'So what you feel doesn't count?' 'Me? But Anna, why should I count?' (This was bitter, mocking, but affectionate.) Afterwards I fought with a feeling that always takes hold of me after one of these exchanges: unreality, as if the substance of my self were thinning and dissolving. And then I thought how ironical it was that in order to recover myself I had to use precisely that Anna which Michael dislikes most; the critical and thinking Anna. Very well then; he says I make up stories about our life together. I shall write down, as truthfully as I can, every stage of a day. Tomorrow. When tomorrow ends I shall sit down and write.

17th September, 1954

I could not write last night because I was too unhappy. And now of course I am wondering if the fact that I chose to be very conscious of everything that happened yesterday changed the shape of the day. That just because I was conscious I made it a special day? However, I shall write it and see how it looks. I woke early, about five, tensed, because I thought I heard Janet move in the room through the wall. But she must have moved and gone to sleep again. A grey stream of water on the windowpane. The light grey. The shapes of furniture enormous in the vague light. Michael and I were lying facing the window, I with my arms around him under his pyjama jacket, my knees tucked into the angle of his knees. A fierce healing warmth from him to me. I thought: Very soon now he won't come back. Perhaps I'll know it is the last time, perhaps not. Perhaps this is the last time? But it seemed impossible to associate the two feelings: Michael warm in my arms, asleep; and knowing that soon he would not be there. I moved my hand up and the hair on his breast was slippery yet rough against my palm. It gave me intense delight. He started up, feeling me awake, and said sharply: 'Anna, what is it?' His voice came out of a dream, it was frightened and angry. He turned on his back, and was asleep again. I looked at his face to see the shadow of the dream on it; his face was clenched up. Once he said, waking abrupt and frightened out of a dream: 'My dear Anna, if you insist on sleeping with a man who is the history of Europe over the last twenty years, you mustn't complain if he has uneasy dreams.' This was resentful: the resentment was because I wasn't part of that history. Yet I know that one of the reasons he is with me is that I wasn't part of it, and haven't had something destroyed in me. This morning I looked at the tight sleeping face and again tried to imagine it, so that it was part of my own experience, what it would mean: 'Seven of my family, including my mother and father, were murdered in the gas chambers. Most of my close friends are dead: communists murdered by communists. The survivors are mostly refugees in strange countries. I shall live for the rest of my life in a country which will never really be my home.' But as usual, I failed to imagine it. The light was thick and heavy because of the rain outside. His face unclenched, relaxed. It was now broad, calm, assured. Calm sealed lids, and above them the lightly-marked, glossy brows. I could see him as a child, fearless, cocky, with a clear candid, alert smile. And I could see him old: he will be an irascible, intelligent, energetic old man, locked in a bitter intelligent loneliness. I was filled with an emotion one has, women have, about children: a feeling of fierce triumph: that against all odds, against the weight of death, this human being exists, here, a miracle of breathing flesh. I shored this feeling up, strengthened it, against the other one, that he would soon be leaving me. He must have felt it in his sleep, because he stirred and said: 'Go to sleep, Anna.' He smiled, his eyes shut. The smile was strong and warm; out of another world than the one where he says: But Anna, why should I count? I felt 'nonsense,' of course he won't leave me; he can't smile at me, like that, and mean to leave me. I lay down beside him, on my back. I was careful not to sleep, because very soon Janet would wake. The light in the room was like thin greyish water, moving, because of the streaming wet on the panes. The panes shook slightly. On windy nights they batter and shake, but I don't wake. Yet I wake if Janet turns over in bed.

It must be about six o'clock. My knees are tense. I realise that what I used to refer to, to Mother Sugar, as 'the housewife's disease' has taken hold of me. The tension in me, so that peace has already gone away from me, is because the current has been switched on: I must-dress-Janet-get-her-breakfast-send-her-off-to-school-get-Michael's-breakfast-don't-forget-I'm-out-of-tea-etc.-etc. With this useless but apparently unavoidable tension resentment is also switched on. Resentment against what? An unfairness. That I should have to spend so much of my time worrying over details. The resentment focuses itself on Michael; although I know with my intelligence it has nothing to do with Michael. And yet I do resent him, because he will spend his day, served by secretaries, nurses, women in all kinds of capacities, who will take this weight off him. I try to relax myself, to switch off the current. But my limbs have started to ache, and I must turn over. There is another movement from beyond the wall—Janet is waking. Simultaneously, Michael stirs and I feel him growing big against my buttocks. The resentment takes the form: Of course he chooses now, when I am unrelaxed and listening for Janet. But the anger is not related to him. Long ago, in the course of the sessions with Mother Sugar, I learned that the resentment, the anger, is impersonal. It is the disease of women in our time. I can see it in women's faces, their voices, every day, or in the letters that come to the office. The woman's emotion: resentment against injustice, an impersonal poison. The unlucky ones, who do not know it is impersonal, turn it against their men. The lucky ones like me—fight it. It is a tiring fight. Michael takes me from behind, half asleep, fierce and close. He is taking me impersonally, and so I do not respond as I do when he is loving Anna. And besides with one half of my mind I am thinking how, if I hear Janet's soft feet outside, I must be up

333

and across the room to stop her coming in. She never comes in until seven; that is the rule; I do not expect her to come in; yet I have to be alert. While Michael grips me and fills me the noises next door continue, and I know he hears them too, and that part of the pleasure, for him, is to take me in hazard; that Janet, the little girl, the eight-year-old, represents for him partly women—other women, whom he betrays to sleep with me; and partly, child; the essence of child, against whom he is asserting his rights to live. He never speaks of his own children without a small, half-affectionate, half-aggressive laugh—his heirs, and his assassins. My child, a few feet away through the wall, he will not allow to cheat him of his freedom. When we are finished, he says: 'And now, Anna, I suppose you are going to desert me for Janet?' And he sounds like a child who feels himself slighted for a younger brother or sister. I laugh and kiss him; although the resentment is suddenly so strong I clench my teeth against it. I control it, as always, by thinking: If I were a man I'd be the same. The control and discipline of being a mother came so hard to me, that I can't delude myself that if I'd been a man, and not forced into self-control, I'd have been any different. And yet for the few moments it takes for me to put on the wrap to go into Janet, the resentment is like a raging poison. Before I go in to Janet I wash myself quickly between the legs so that the smell of sex may not disturb her, even though she doesn't yet know what it is. I like the smell, and hate to wash it off so quickly; and the fact that I must adds to my bad temper. (I remember thinking that the fact I was deliberately watching all my reactions was exacerbating them; normally they would not be so strong.) Yet when I close Janet's door behind me, and see her sitting up in bed, her black hair wild, in elf-locks, her small pale face (mine) smiling, the resentment vanishes under the habit of discipline, and almost at once becomes affection. It is six-thirty and the little room is very cold. Janet's window is also streaming with grey wet. I light the gas fire, while she sits up in bed, surrounded by bright patches of colour from her comics, watching me to see if I do everything as usual, and reading at the same time. I shrink, in affection, to Janet's size, and

334

become Janet. The enormous yellow fire like a great eye; the window, enormous, through which anything can enter; a grey and ominous light which waits for the sun, a devil or an angel, which will shake away the rain. Then I make myself be Anna: I see Janet, a small child in a big bed. A train passes, and the walls shake slightly. I go over to kiss her, and smell the good smell of warm flesh, and hair, and the stuff of her pyjamas, heated by sleep. While her room warms I go into the kitchen and prepare her breakfast—cereal, fried eggs and tea, on a tray. I take the tray back into her room, and she eats her breakfast sitting up in bed, and I drink tea and smoke. The house is dead still—Molly will be asleep for another two or three hours. Tommy came in late with a girl; they'll be asleep too. Through the wall, a baby is crying. It gives me a feeling of continuity, of rest, the baby crying, as Janet once cried. It is the contented half-sleepy cry of a baby who has been fed and will be asleep in a moment. Janet says: 'Why don't we have another baby?' She says this often. And I say: 'Because I haven't got a husband and you must have a husband to get a baby.' She asks this question partly because she would like me to have a baby; and partly to be reassured about the role of Michael. Then she asks: 'Is Michael here?' 'Yes he is, and he is asleep,' I say firmly. My firmness reassures her; and she goes on with her breakfast. Now the room is warm, and she gets out of bed in her white sleeping suit, looking fragile and vulnerable. She puts her arms around my neck and swings on it, back and forth, singing: Rockabye baby. I swing her and sing—babying her, she has become the baby next door, the baby I won't have. Then, abruptly, she lets me go, so that I feel myself spring up like a tree that has been bent over by a weight. She dresses herself, crooning, still half-drowsy, still peaceful. I think that she will retain the peace for years, until the pressure comes on her, and she must start thinking. In half an hour I must remember to cook the potatoes and then I must write a list for the grocer and then I must remember to change the collar on my dress and then . . . I want very much to protect her from the pressure, to postpone it; then I tell myself I must protect her from nothing, this need is really Anna wanting to protect Anna. She dresses slowly, chattering a little, humming; she has the lazy bumbling movements of a bee in the sun. She wears a short red pleated skirt and a dark blue jersey and long dark blue socks. A pretty little girl. Janet. Anna. The baby is asleep next door; there is the silence of content from the baby. Everyone asleep save me and Janet. It is a feeling of intimacy and exclusiveness—a feeling that began when she was born, when she and I were awake together at times when the city slept around us. It is a warm, lazy, intimate gaiety. She seems to me so fragile that I want to put out my hand to save her from a wrong step, or a careless movement; and at the same time so strong that she is immortal. I feel what I felt with sleeping Michael, a need to laugh out in triumph, because of this marvellous, precarious, immortal human being, in spite of the weight of death.

Now it is nearly eight o'clock and another pressure starts; this is Michael's day for going to the hospital in South London, so he must wake at eight to be in time. He prefers Janet to have left for school before he wakes. And I prefer it, because it divides me. The two personalities—Janet's mother, Michael's mistress, are happier separated. It is a strain having to be both at once. It is no longer raining. I wipe the fog of condensed breath and night-sweat from the windowpane, and see it is a cool, damp, but clear day. Janet's school is close, a short walk. I say: 'You must take your raincoat.' Instantly her voice raises into protest: 'Oh no, mummy, I hate my raincoat, I want my duffle coat.' I say, calm and firm: 'No. Your raincoat. It's been raining all night.' 'How do you know when you were asleep?' This triumphant retort puts her into a good humour. She will now take the raincoat and put on her gum-boots without any further fuss. 'Are you going to fetch me from school this afternoon?' 'Yes, I think so, but if I'm not there, then come back, and Molly will be here.' 'Or Tommy.' 'No, not Tommy.' 'Why not?' 'Tommy's grown-up now, and he's got a girl-friend.' I say this on purpose because she has shown signs of jealousy of Tommy's girl. She says, calmly: 'Tommy will always like me best.' And adds: 'If you're not there to pick me up, I'll go and play at Barbara's house.' 'Well, if you do

I'll come and fetch you at six.' She rushes off down the stairs, making a terrific din. It sounds like an avalanche sliding down the centre of the house. I am afraid Molly might wake. I stand at the head of the stairs, listening, until, ten minutes later, the front door slams; and I make myself shut out all thoughts of Janet until the proper time. I go back into the bedroom. Michael is a dark hump under the bedclothes. I draw the curtains right back, and sit on the bed and kiss Michael awake. He grips me and says: 'Come back to bed.' I say: 'It's eight o'clock. After.' He puts his hands on my breasts. My nipples begin to burn, and I control my response to him and say: 'It's eight o'clock.' 'Oh, Anna, but you're always so efficient and practical in the morning.' 'It's just as well I am,' I say, lightly, but I can hear the annoyance in my voice. 'Where is Janet?' 'Gone to school.' He lets his hands fall from my breasts, and now I feel disappointment— perversely—because we won't make love. Also relief; because if we did he would be late, and short-tempered with me. And of course, the resentment: my affliction, my burden, and my cross. The resentment is because he said: 'You are always so efficient and practical,' when it is precisely my efficiency and practicality that gains him an extra two hours in bed.

He gets up and washes and shaves and I make his breakfast. We always eat it on a low table by the bed, whose covers have been hastily pulled up. Now we have coffee and fruit and toast; and he is already the professional man, smooth-suited, clear-eyed, calm. He is watching me. I know this is because he plans to tell me something. Is today the day he will break it off? I remember this is the first morning together for a week. I don't want to think about this because it is unlikely that Michael, feeling confined and unhappy in his home, as he does, has been with his wife for the last six days. Where then? My feeling is not so much of jealousy, as of a dull heavy pain, the pain of loss. But I smile, pass him the toast, offer him the newspapers. He takes the papers, glances at them, and remarks: 'If you can put up with me two nights running—I have to be at the hospital down the road this evening to give a lecture.' I smile; for a moment we exchange irony, because of the years we have spent night

337

after night together. Then he slides off into sentimentality, but parodying it at the same time: 'Ah, Anna, but look how it has worn thin for you.' I merely smile again, because there's no point in saying anything, and then he says, this time gaily, in the parody of a rake's manner: 'You get more and more practical with every day that dawns. Every man with sense knows that when a woman gets all efficient on him, the time has come to part.' Suddenly it's too painful for me to play this game, and I say: 'Well, anyway, I'll love you to come this evening. Do you want to eat here?' He says: 'It's not likely I should refuse to eat with you when you're such a cook, now is it?' 'I shall look forward to it,' I say.

He says: 'If you can get dressed quickly, I can give you a lift to your office.' I hesitate, because I am thinking: If I have to cook this evening, then I must buy food before I go to work. He says quickly, because of the hesitation: 'But if you'd rather not, then I'll be off.' He kisses me; and the kiss is a continuation of all the love we've had together. He says, cancelling the moment of intimacy, for his words continue the other theme: 'If we have nothing else in common, we have sex.' Whenever he says this, and it is only recently he has been saying it, I feel the pit of my stomach go cold; it is the total rejection of me, or so I feel it; and there is a great distance between us. Across the distance I say ironically: 'Is that all we have together?' and he says: '*All*? But my dear Anna, my dear Anna—but I must go, I'll be late.' And he goes, with the bitter rueful smile of a rejected man.

And now I must hurry. I wash again and dress. I choose a black and white wool dress with a small white collar, because Michael likes it, and there mightn't be time to change before this evening. Then I run down to the grocer and the butcher. It is a great pleasure, buying food I will cook for Michael; a sensuous pleasure, like the act of cooking itself. I imagine the meat in its coat of crumbs and egg; the mushrooms, simmering in sour cream and onions, the clear, strong, amber-coloured soup. Imagining it I create the meal, the movements I will use, checking ingredients, heat, textures. I take the provisions up and put them on the table; then I remember the veal must be beaten and I must do it now, because later

338

it will wake Janet. So I beat the veal flat and fold the tissues of meat in paper and leave them. It is now nine o'clock. I'm short of money so I must go by bus, not taxi. I have fifteen minutes in hand. I hastily sweep the room and make the bed, changing the undersheet which is stained from last night. As I push the stained sheet into the linen-basket I notice a stain of blood. But surely it's not time yet for my period? I hastily check dates, and realise yes, it's today. Suddenly I feel tired and irritable, because these feelings accompany my periods. (I wondered if it would be better not to choose today to write down everything I felt; then decided to go ahead. It was not planned; I had forgotten about the period. I decided that the instinctive feeling of shame and modesty was dishonest: no emotion for a writer.) I stuff my vagina with the tampon of cotton wool, and am already on my way downstairs, when I remember I've forgotten to take a supply of tampons with me. I am late. I roll tampons into my handbag, concealing them under a handkerchief, feeling more and more irritable. At the same time I am telling myself that if I had not noticed my period had started, I would not be feeling nearly so irritable. But all the same, I must control myself now, before leaving for work, or I'll find myself cracking into bad temper in the office. I might as well take a taxi after all—that way I'll have ten minutes in hand. I sit down and try to relax in the big chair. But I am too tense. I look for ways to relax tension. There are half a dozen pots of creeper on the window sill, a greenish-grey wandering plant I don't know the name of. I take the six earthenware pots to the kitchen and submerge them, one after another, in a basin of water, watching the bubbles rise as the water sinks down and drives up the air. The leaves sparkle with water. The dark earth smells of damp growth. I feel better. I put the pots of growth back on the window sill where they can catch the sun, if there is any. Then I snatch up my coat and run downstairs, passing Molly, sleepy in her housecoat. 'What are you in such a hurry for?' she asks; and I shout back: 'I'm late,' hearing the contrast between her loud, lazy, unhurried voice, and mine, tense. There isn't a taxi before I reach the bus-stop, and a bus comes along so I get on, just as the rain comes down. My stockings are slightly splashed; I must remember to change them tonight; Michael notices this sort of detail. Now, sitting on the bus, I feel the dull drag at my lower belly. Not bad at all. Good, if this first pang is slight, then it will all be over in a couple of days. Why am I so ungrateful when I suffer so little compared to other women?— Molly, for instance, groaning and complaining in enjoyable suffering for five or six days. I find my mind is on the practical treadmill again, the things I have to do today, this time in connection with the office. Simultaneously I am worrying about this business of being conscious of everything so as to write it down, particularly in connection with my having a period. Because, whereas to me, the fact I am having a period is no more than an entrance into an emotional state, recurring regularly, that is of no particular importance; I know that as soon as I write the word 'blood,' it will be giving a wrong emphasis, and even to me when I come to read what I've written. And so I begin to doubt the value of a day's recording before I've started to record it. I am thinking, I realise, about a major problem of literary style, of tact. For instance, when James Joyce described his man in the act of defecating, it was a shock, shocking. Though it was his intention to rob words of their power to shock. And I read recently in some review, a man said he would be revolted by the description of a woman defecating. I resented this; because, of course, what he meant was, he would not like to have that romantic image, a woman, made less romantic. But he was right, for all that. I realise it's not basically a literary problem at all. For instance, when Molly said to me, with her loud jolly laugh: I've got the curse; I have instantly to suppress distaste, even though we are both women; and I begin to be conscious of the possibility of bad smells. Thinking of my reaction to Molly, I forget about my problems of being truthful in writing (which is being truthful about oneself), and I begin to worry: Am I smelling? It is the only smell I know of that I dislike. I don't mind my own immediate lavatory smells; I like the smell of sex, of sweat, of skin, or hair. But the faintly dubious, essentially stale smell of menstrual blood I hate. And resent. It is a smell that I

340

feel as strange even to me, an imposition from outside. Not from me. Yet for two days I have to deal with this thing from outside—a bad smell, emanating from me. I realise that all these thoughts would not have been in my head at all had I not set myself to be conscious. A period is something I deal with, without thinking about it particularly, or rather I think of it with a part of my mind that deals with routine problems. It is the same part of my mind that deals with the problem of routine cleanliness. But the idea that I will have to write it down is changing the balance, destroying the truth; so I shut the thoughts of my period out of my mind; making, however, a mental note that as soon as I get to the office I must go to the washroom to make sure there is no smell. I ought really to be thinking over the coming encounter with Comrade Butte. I call him comrade ironically; as he calls me, ironically, Comrade Anna. Last week I said to him, furious about something: 'Comrade Butte, do you realise that if by some chance we had both been Russian communists, you would have had me shot years ago?' 'Yes, Comrade Anna, that seems to me more than likely.' (This particular joke is characteristic of the Party in this period.) Meanwhile, Jack sat and smiled at us both behind his round spectacles. He enjoys my fights with Comrade Butte. After John Butte had left, Jack said: 'There's one thing you don't take into account, and that you might very well have been the one to order the shooting of John Butte.' This remark came close to my private nightmare, and to exorcise it I joked: 'My dear Jack, the essence of my position is that I am essentially the one to be shot—this is, traditionally, my role.' 'Don't be too sure, if you'd known John Butte in the 'thirties you wouldn't be so ready to cast him in the role of a bureaucratic executioner.' 'And anyway, that isn't the point.' 'Which is?' 'Stalin's been dead nearly a year, and nothing has changed.' 'A great deal has changed.' 'They're letting people out of prison; nothing is being done to change the attitudes that put them there.' 'They're considering changing the law.' 'The legal system's being changed this way and that way'll do nothing to change the spirit I'm talking about.' After a moment he nodded. 'Quite possibly, but we don't know.' He was examining me, mildly. I've often wondered if this mildness, this detachment, which makes it possible for us to have these conversations, is a sign of a broken personality; the sell-out most people make at some time or another; or whether it is a self-effacing strength. I don't know. I do know that Jack is the only person in the Party with whom I can have this kind of discussion. Some weeks ago I told him I was thinking of leaving the Party, and he replied in jest: 'I've been in the Party thirty years, and sometimes I think I and John Butte will be the only people, of the thousands I've known, who will remain in it.' 'Is that a criticism of the Party or of the thousands who have left?' 'Of the thousands who have left, naturally,' he said, laughing. Yesterday he said: 'Well, Anna, if you are going to leave the Party, please give me the usual month's notice, because you're very useful and I shall need time to replace you.'

Today I am to report on two books I have read, for John Butte. It will be a fight. Jack employed me, as a weapon in the battle he carries on with the spirit of the Party—the spirit which he is only too ready to describe as dead and dry. Jack is supposed to run this publishing house. In fact he is a kind of administrator; over him, set over him by 'the Party,' is John Butte; and the final decisions about what will and will not be published are taken in the Party H.Q. Jack is a 'good communist.' That is, he has genuinely and honestly driven out of himself the false pride that might make him resent his lack of independence. He does not resent, in principle, the fact that it is a sub-committee, under John Butte, in H.Q., that takes decisions he must carry out. On the contrary, he is all for this sort of centralism. But he thinks the policy of H.Q. is wrong; and, more than that, it's not a question of a person, or a group that he disapproves of; he quite simply states that the Party 'in this epoch' is in an intellectual dead-water and there is nothing for it but to wait for things to change. Meanwhile he is prepared to have his name associated with intellectual attitudes he despises. The difference between him and me is that he sees the Party in terms of decades, and even centuries (I pull his leg saying: Like the Catholic Church); whereas I think the intellectual collapse is probably final. We discuss this interminably, over lunches, in gaps of work at the office. Sometimes John Butte is there, listens, even joins in. And this fascinates and angers me: because the kind of talk we use in this type of argument is a thousand miles away from the public 'line' of the Party. More, this kind of talk would be treason in a communist country. Yet when I leave the Party, this is what I am going to miss—the company of people who have spent their lives in a certain kind of atmosphere, where it is taken for granted that their lives must be related to a central philosophy. This is why so many people who would like to leave, or think they should leave, the Party, do not. There is no group of people or type of intellectual I have met outside the Party who aren't ill-informed, frivolous, parochial, compared with certain types of intellectual inside the Party. And the tragedy is that this intellectual responsibility, this high seriousness, is in a vacuum: it relates, not to Britain; not to communist countries as they are now; but to a spirit which existed in international communism years ago, before it was killed by the desperate, crazed spirit of struggle for survival to which we now give the name Stalinism.

When I get off the bus I realise that thinking about the coming fight has over-excited me: the essence of a successful battle with Comrade Butte is that one has to remain calm. I am not calm; and besides my lower stomach is painful. And I am half an hour late. I am always careful to be on time, to work the usual hours, because I am unpaid, and I don't want special privileges because of that. (Michael jokes: You're in the great British tradition of upper-class service to the community, my dear Anna; you work for the Communist Party, unpaid, the way your grandmother would have worked for the starving poor. It's the kind of joke I make myself; but when Michael makes it it hurts me.) I go at once to the washroom, quickly because I am late, and I examine myself and change the tampon and pour jug after jug of warm water between my thighs to defeat the sour musty smell. Then I scent my thighs and forearms, and remind myself to come down in an hour or two; and I go upstairs to Jack's office, by-passing my own. Jack is there with John Butte. Jack says:

343

'You smell lovely, Anna,' and at once I feel at ease and able to manage everything. I look at the creaking, grey John Butte, an elderly man with all his juices gone dry, and remember that Jack has told me that in his youth, in the early 'thirties, he was gay, brilliant, witty. He was a brilliant public speaker; he was in opposition to the then Party officialdom; he was essentially critical and irreverent. And after Jack had told me all this, rather wryly enjoying my disbelief, he handed me a book John Butte wrote twenty years ago, a novel about the French Revolution. It was a sparkling, vivid, courageous book. And now I look at him again and think, involuntarily: The real crime of the British Communist Party is the number of marvellous people it has either broken, or turned into dry-as-dust hair-splitting office men, living in a closed group with other communists, and cut off from everything that goes on in their own country. Then the words I use surprise and displease me: the word 'crime' is from the communist arsenal, and is meaningless. There's some kind of social process involved which makes words like 'crime' stupid. And as I think this, I feel the birth of a new sort of thought; and I go on to think, clumsily: The Communist Party, like any other institution, continues to exist by a process of absorbing its critics into itself. It either absorbs them or destroys them. I think: I've always seen society, societies, organised like this: a ruling section or government with other sections in opposition; the stronger section either ultimately being changed by the opposing section or being supplanted by it. But it's not like that at all: suddenly I see it differently. No, there's a group of hardened, fossilised men opposed by fresh young revolutionaries as John Butte once was, forming between them a whole, a balance. And then a group of fossilised hardened men like John Butte, opposed by a group of fresh and lively-minded and critical people. But the core of deadness, of dry thought, could not exist without lively shoots of fresh life, to be turned so fast, in their turn, into dead sapless wood. In other words, I, 'Comrade Anna'— and the ironical tone of Comrade Butte's voice now frightens me when I remember it—keep Comrade Butte in existence, feed him, and in due course will become him. And as I think this, that there is no right, no wrong, simply a process, a wheel turning, I become frightened, because everything in me cries out against such a view of life, and I am back inside a nightmare which it seems I've been locked in for years, whenever I'm off guard. The nightmare takes various forms, comes in sleep, or in wakefulness, and can be pictured most simply like this: There is a blindfolded man standing with his back to a brick wall. He has been tortured nearly to death. Opposite him are six men with their rifles raised ready to shoot, commanded by a seventh, who has his hand raised. When he drops his hand, the shots will ring out, and the prisoner will fall dead. But suddenly there is something unexpected—yet not altogether unexpected, for the seventh has been listening all this while in case it happens. There is an outburst of shouting and fighting in the street outside. The six men look in query at their officer, the seventh. The officer stands waiting to see how the fighting outside will resolve itself. There is a shout: 'We have won!' At which the officer crosses the space to the wall, unties the bound man, and stands in his place. The man, hitherto bound, now binds the other. There is a moment, and this is the moment of horror in the nightmare, when they smile at each other: it is a brief, bitter, accepting smile. They are brothers in that smile. The smile holds a terrible truth that I want to evade. Because it cancels all creative emotion. The officer, the seventh, now stands blindfolded and waiting with his back to the wall. The former prisoner walks to the firing squad who are still standing with their weapons ready. He lifts his hand, then drops it. The shots ring out, and the body by the wall falls twitching. The six soldiers are shaken and sick; now they will go and drink to drown the memory of their murder. But the man who was bound, is now free, smiles as they stumble away, cursing and hating him, just as they would have cursed and hated the other, now dead. And in this man's smile at the six innocent soldiers there is a terrible understanding irony. This is the nightmare. Meanwhile Comrade Butte sits waiting. As always he smiles his small, critical defensive smile, like a grimace. 'Well, Comrade Anna, and are we going to be allowed to publish these two masterpieces?' Jack grimaces

345

involuntarily; and I realise that he has just understood, like myself, that these two books are going to be published: the decision has already been made. Jack has read them both, and remarked with his characteristic mildness that: 'they aren't much but I suppose they could be worse.' I say: 'If you are really interested in what I think, then you should publish one of them. Mind you, I don't think either is much good.' 'But naturally I don't expect them to reach the heights of critical acclaim your masterpiece did.' This does not mean he did not like *Frontiers of War;* he told Jack he liked it, he has never mentioned it to me. He is suggesting that it did so well because of what he would describe as 'the capitalist publishing racket.' And of course I agree with him; except that the word capitalist can be supplanted by others, like communist, or woman's magazine, for instance. His tone is merely part of the game we play, the playing out of our roles. I am a 'successful bourgeois writer'; he the custodian of the purity of working-class values. (Comrade Butte comes from an upper-middle-class English family, but this is of course irrelevant.) I suggest: 'Perhaps we might discuss them separately?' I put two packets of manuscript on the desk and push one towards him. He nods. It is called: 'For Peace and Happiness,' and is written by a young worker. At least, that is how he is described by Comrade Butte. In fact, he is nearly forty, has been a Communist Party official these twenty years, was once a bricklayer. The writing is bad, the story lifeless, but what is frightening about this book is that it is totally inside the current myth. If that useful imaginary man from Mars (or for that matter, a man from Russia) should read this book he would get the impression that (a) the cities of Britain were locked in deep poverty, unemployment, brutality, a Dickensian squalor; and that (b) the workers of Britain were all communist or at least recognised the Communist Party as their natural leader. This novel touches reality at no point at all. (Jack described it as: 'communist cloud-cuckoo spit.') It is, however, a very accurate re-creation of the self-deceptive myths of the Communist Party at this particular time; and I have read it in about fifty different shapes or guises during the last year. I say: 'You know quite

346

well this is a very bad book.' A look of dry stubbornness comes over Comrade Butte's long, bony face. I remember that novel he wrote himself, twenty years ago, which was so fresh and good and marvel that this can be the same man. He now remarks: 'It's no masterpiece, I didn't say it was, but it's a good book, I think.' This is the overture, so to speak, to what is expected to follow. I will challenge him, and he will argue. The end will be the same, because the decision has already been taken. The book will be published. People in the Party with any discrimination will be even more ashamed because of the steadily debasing values of the Party; the *Daily Worker* will praise it: 'In spite of its faults, an honest novel of Party life'; the 'bourgeois' critics who notice it will be contemptuous. Everything will be as usual, in fact. But suddenly I lose interest. I say: 'Very well, you'll publish it. There's no more to be said.' There is a startled silence; and Comrade Jack and Butte even exchange glances. Comrade Butte lowers his eyes. He is annoyed. I realise that my role or function is to argue, to play the part of critic, so that Comrade Butte may have the illusion that he has fought his way through informed opposition. I am, in fact, his youthful self, sitting opposite him, which he has to defeat. I am ashamed I have never understood this very obvious fact before; and even think—perhaps those other books wouldn't have been published if I had refused to play this role of captive critic? Jack says, mildly, after a time: 'But Anna, this won't do. You're expected to make a criticism for the edification of Comrade Butte here.' I say: 'You know it's bad. Comrade Butte knows it's bad ...' Comrade Butte lifted his faded, crease-surrounded eyes to stare at me, '. . . and I know it's bad. And we all know it will be published.' John Butte says: 'Can you please tell me, Comrade Anna, in six words, or perhaps eight, if you can spare so much of your valuable time, why this is a bad book?' 'As far as I can see the author has lifted his memories from the 'thirties intact and made them true of Britain 1954, and apart from that he appears to be under the impression that the great British working-class owe some kind of allegiance to the Communist Party.' His eyes flash with anger. He suddenly lifts a fist and

347

crashes it on Jack's desk. 'Publish and be damned!' he shouts. 'Publish and be damned! That's what I say.' This is so bizarre, that I laugh. Then I see how much to be expected it was. At the laugh, and at Jack's smile, John Butte seems to shrivel with anger; he goes behind barricade after barricade of himself into an inner fortress, staring out of it with steady angry eyes. 'I seem to amuse you, Anna. Would you be kind enough to explain why?' I laugh and look at Jack, who nods at me: yes, explain. I look back at John Butte, think, and say: 'What you've said sums up everything that is wrong with the Party. It's a crystallisation of the intellectual rottenness of the Party that the cry of nineteenth-century humanism, courage against odds, truth against lies, should be used now to defend the publication of a lousy lying book by a communist firm which will risk nothing at all by publishing it, not even a reputation for integrity.' I am terribly angry. Then I remember that I work for this firm, and am in no position to criticise; and that Jack runs it, and will in fact have to publish this book. I am afraid I have hurt Jack, and look at him: he looks back, quietly, and then he nods, just once, and smiles. John Butte sees the nod and the smile. Jack turns to meet John's anger. Butte is literally shrivelled with his anger. But it is a righteous anger, he is defending the good and the right and the true. Later, these two will discuss what has happened; Jack will agree with me; the book will be published. 'And about the other book?' Butte asks. But I am bored and impatient. I am thinking, after all, this is the level on which the Party should be judged, the level on which it actually makes decisions, does things; not on the level of the conversations I have with Jack which do not affect the Party at all. Suddenly I decide I must leave the Party. It interests me that it should be this moment instead of another. 'And so,' I say pleasantly, 'both books will be published, and this has been a very interesting discussion.' 'Yes, thank you, Comrade Anna, it has indeed,' says John Butte. Jack is watching me; I think that he knows I have made my decision. But these men now have other things to discuss which do not concern me, so I say good-bye to John Butte and go into my room next door. It is shared by Jack's secretary,

Rose. We dislike each other, and we greet each other coolly. I settle down to the piles of magazines and papers on my desk.

I read magazines and periodicals published in English in the communist countries: Russia, China, East Germany, etc. etc., and if there is a story or an article or a novel 'suitable for British conditions,' I draw Jack's, and therefore John Butte's, attention to it. Very little is 'suitable for British conditions'; an occasional article or a short story. Yet I read all this material avidly, as Jack does, and for the same reasons: we read between and behind lines, to spot trends and tendencies.

But—as I became aware recently—there is more to it than that. The reason for my fascinated absorption is something else. Most of this writing is flat, tame, optimistic, and on a curiously jolly note, even when dealing with war and suffering. It all comes out of the myth. But this bad, dead, banal writing is the other side of my coin. I am ashamed of the psychological impulse that created *Frontiers of War*. I have decided never to write again, if that is the emotion which must feed my writing.

During the last year, reading these stories, these novels, in which there might be an occasional paragraph, a sentence, a phrase, of truth, I've been forced to acknowledge that the flashes of genuine art are all out of deep, suddenly stark, undisguisable private emotion. Even in translation there is no mistaking these lightning flashes of genuine personal feeling. And I read this dead stuff praying that just once there may be a short story, a novel, even an article, written wholly from genuine personal feeling.

And so this is the paradox: I, Anna, reject my own 'unhealthy' art; but reject 'healthy' art when I see it.

The point is that this writing is essentially impersonal. Its banality is that of impersonality. It is as if there were a new Twentieth Century Anon at work.

Since I have been in the Party, my 'Party work' has consisted mostly of giving lectures on art to small groups. I say something like this: 'Art during the Middle Ages was communal, unindividual; it came out of a group consciousness. It was without the driving painful individuality of the art of the bourgeois era. And one day, we will leave behind the driving egotism of individual art. We will return to an art which will express not man's self-divisions and separateness from his fellows but his responsibility for his fellows and his brotherhood. Art from the West . . .' to use the useful catchphrase '—becomes more and more a shriek of torment from souls recording pain. Pain is becoming our deepest reality . . .' I've been saying something like this. About three months ago, in the middle of this lecture, I began to stammer and couldn't finish. I have not given any more lectures. I know what that stammer means.

It occurred to me that the reason I came to work for Jack, without knowing, was that I wanted to have my deep private preoccupations about art, about literature (and therefore about life), about my refusal to write again, put into a sharp focus, where I must look at it, day after day.

I have been discussing this with Jack. He listens and understands. (He always understands.) And he says: 'Anna, communism isn't four decades old yet. So far, most of the art it has produced is bad. But what makes you think these aren't the first steps of a child learning to walk? And in a century's time . . .' 'Or in five centuries,' I say, teasing him— 'In a century's time the new art may be born. Why not?' And I say: 'I don't know what to think. But I'm beginning to be afraid that I've been talking nonsense. Do you realise that all the arguments we ever have are about the same thing—the individual conscience, the individual sensibility?' And he teases me saying: 'And is the individual conscience going to produce your joyful communal unselfish art?' 'Why not? Perhaps the individual conscience is also a child learning how to walk?' And he nods; and the nod means: Yes, this is all very interesting, but let's get on with our work.

Reading all this mass of dead literature is only a small part of my work. Because without anyone intending it or expecting it, my work has become something quite different. It is 'welfare work'—a joke Jack makes, I make; and also Michael: 'How is your welfare work going, Anna? Saved any more souls recently?'

350

Before I start on the 'welfare work,' I go down to the washroom, and make up my face, and wash myself between my legs, and wonder if the decision I have just come to, to leave the Party, is because I've been thinking more clearly than usual, out of the decision to record everything about today? In which case, who is that Anna who will read what I will write? Who is this other I whose judgement I fear; or whose gaze, at least, is different from mine when I am not thinking, recording, and being conscious. And perhaps tomorrow, when that other Anna's eye is on me, I will decide not to leave the Party? For one thing, I am going to miss Jack—with whom else could I discuss, and without reservations, all these problems? With Michael, of course—but he is leaving me. And besides, it is always in bitterness. But what is interesting is this: Michael is the ex-communist, the traitor, the lost soul; Jack the communist bureaucrat. In a sense it is Jack who murdered Michael's comrades (but then so did I, because I am in the Party). It is Jack who labels Michael a traitor. And it is Michael who labels Jack a murderer. And yet these two men (if they met they would not exchange one word out of mistrust) are the two men who I can talk to, and who understand everything I feel. They are part of the same experience. I stand in the washroom, putting scent on to my arms, so as to defeat the smell from the stale leak of blood; and suddenly I realise that what I am thinking about Michael and Jack is the nightmare about the firing party and the prisoners who exchange places. I feel dizzy and confused, and I go upstairs to my office and push away the great piles of magazines: *Voks, Soviet Literature, Peoples for Freedom Awake! China Reborn,* etc., etc. (the mirror into which I have been looking for over a year), and I think that I can't read this again. I simply can't read it. I've gone dead on it, or it on me. I'll see what 'welfare work' there is today. And as I reach this point Jack comes in, because John Butte has now gone back to H.Q., and he says: 'Anna will you share my tea and sandwiches with me?' Jack lives on the official Party wage, which is eight pounds a week; and his wife earns about the same as a teacher. So he must economise; and one of the economies is, not going out to lunch. I say thank you, and I go into his office and we talk. Not about the two novels, because there is nothing further to be said: they will be published, and we both in our different ways feel ashamed. Jack has a friend who has just come back from the Soviet Union with private information about the anti-Semitism there. And rumours about murders, tortures, and every kind of bullying. And Jack and I sit and check every piece of information: Is that true? Does that sound true? If that is true then that means that ... And I think, for the hundredth time, how strange it is that this man is part of the communist bureaucracy, and yet he knows no more than I, or any rank and file communist, what to believe. We finally decide, not for the first time, that Stalin must have been clinically mad. We sit drinking tea and eating sandwiches and speculate about whether, if we had lived in the Soviet Union during his last years, we would have decided it was part of our duty to assassinate him. Jack says no; Stalin is so much a part of his experience, his deepest experience, that even if he knew him to be criminally insane, when the moment came to pull the trigger he couldn't do it: he would turn the revolver on himself instead. And I say I couldn't either, because 'political murder is against my principles.' And so on and so on; and I think how terrible this talk is, and how dishonest, sitting in safe, comfortable, prosperous London, with our lives and freedom in no danger at all. And something happens I get more and more afraid of—words lose their meaning. I can hear Jack and I talking—it seems the words come out from inside me, from some anonymous place—but they don't mean anything. I keep *seeing*, before my eyes, pictures of what we are talking about—scenes of death, torture, cross-examination and so on; and the words we are using have nothing to do with what I am seeing. They sound like an idiotic gabbling, like mad talk. Suddenly Jack says: 'Are you going to leave the Party, Anna?' I say: 'Yes.' Jack nods. It is a friendly unjudging nod. And very lonely. There is at once a gulf between us—not of trust, because we trust each other, but of future experience. He will stay, because he has been in it so long, because it has been his life, because all his friends are in and will stay in. And soon, when we meet, we will be strangers. And I think what a good man he is, and the men like him; and how they have been betrayed by history—and when I use that melodramatic phrase, it is not melodramatic, it is accurate. And if I said it to him now, he would give his simple friendly nod. And we would look at each other in ironical understanding—there but for the grace of God, etc. (like the two men exchanging places in front of the firing squad).

I examine him—he sits on his desk, with a half-eaten dry and tasteless sandwich in his hand, looking, despite everything, like a Don—which is what he might have chosen to be. Rather boyish, bespectacled, pale, intellectual. And decent. Yes, that is the word, decent. And yet behind him, part of him, like myself, the miserable history of blood, murder, misery, betrayal, lies. He says: 'Anna, are you crying?' 'I might very easily,' I say. He nods, and says: 'You must do what you feel you have to do.' Then I laugh, because he has spoken out of his British upbringing, the decent nonconformist conscience. And he knows why I am laughing, and he nods and says: 'We are all the product of our experience. I had the ill-luck to be born as a conscious human being into the early 'thirties.' Suddenly I am unbearably unhappy, and I say: 'Jack, I'm going back to work,' and I go back to my office, and put my head down on my arms, and thank God that the stupid secretary has gone out to lunch. I think: Michael is leaving me, that's finished; and although he left the Party years ago, he's part of the whole thing. And I'm leaving the Party. It's a stage of my life finished. And what next? I'm going out, willing it, into something new, and I've got to. I'm shedding a skin, or being born again. The secretary, Rose, comes in, catches me with my head on my arms, asks me if I'm ill. I say I am short of sleep and was having a nap. And I start on the 'welfare work.' I'm going to miss it when I leave: I find myself thinking: I'm going to miss the illusion of doing something useful, and wonder if I really believe it is an illusion.

About eighteen months ago, in one of the Party magazines, there was a small paragraph to the effect that Boles and Hartley, this firm, had decided to publish novels as well

353

as the sociology, history, etc., that is its main business. And all at once the office was flooded with manuscripts. We used to make jokes that every member of the Party must be a part-time novelist, but then it stopped being a joke. Because with every manuscript—some of them obviously hoarded in drawers for years, came a letter; and these letters have become my business. Most of the novels are pretty bad, either written by the banal Anon, or ordinarily incompetent. But the letters come out of a different climate altogether. I've been saying to Jack what a pity we couldn't print a selection of fifty or so of these letters, as a book. To which he replies: 'But my dear Anna, that would be an anti-party act, what *are* you suggesting!'

A typical letter: 'Dear Comrade Preston: I don't know what you think of what I'm sending you. I wrote it about four years ago. I sent it to a selection of the usual "reputable" publishers—enuff said! When I saw Boles and Hartley had decided to encourage creative writing as well as the usual philosophical tracts I felt emboldened to try my luck again. Perhaps this decision is the long-awaited sign of a new attitude towards real creativity in the Party? Howsoever that may be, I await your decision with anticipation—needless to say! With comradely greetings. P.S. It is very hard for me to find time to write. I am secretary of the local Party Branch (dwindled in the last ten years from fifty-six members to fifteen—and most of the fifteen are sleeping members). I am active in my trade union. I am also secretary of the local musical society—sorry, but I'm afraid I think such evidences of local culture are not to be despised, though I know what H.Q. would say to *that!* I have a wife and three children. So in order to write this novel (if it deserves the name!) I got up every morning at four, and wrote for three hours before the children and my better half woke up. And then off to the office and heigh-ho for another day's grind for the bosses, in this case the Beckly Cement Co. Ltd. Never heard of them? Well believe you me, if I could write a novel about them and their activities I'd be in dock for libel. Enuff said?'

And another: 'Dear Comrade. With great fear and trembling I send you my stories. From you I expect a *fair* and

354

just judgement—they have been sent back far too many times by our so-called cultural magazines. I'm glad to see that the Party has at last seen fit to encourage talent in its midst, instead of making speeches about Culture at every conference and never doing anything practical about it. All these tomes about dialectical materialism and the history of the peasants' revolts are all very well, but how about the living article? I have had a good deal experience of writing. I started in the War (Second World) when I wrote for our Battalion Rag. I've been writing ever since when I've had the time. But there is the rub. With a wife and two children (and my wife fully agrees with the pundits of King Street that a comrade is better occupied distributing leaflets than *wasting time scribbling*) it means a running fight not only with her but with the local Party officials all of whom take a dim view when I say I want to take off time for writing. With comradely greetings.'

'Dear Comrade. How to start this letter is my greatest difficulty, and yet if I am reluctant and fear the effort I shall never know if you will find it in your heart to kindly help me, or put my letter into the waste-paper basket. I am writing as a mother first. I, like thousands of other women, had my home broken up during the latter stages of the war and had to fend for both my children, though that was just the time when I had finished a chronicle (not a novel) of my girlhood which was spoken very highly of by the reader of one of our best publishing firms (capitalist, I fear, and one must assume some prejudice of course—I made no secret of my political faith!). But with two children on my hands I had to give up all hope of expressing myself through the word. I was fortunate enough to get a post as housekeeper to a widower with three children, and so five years merrily passed, then he re-married (not very wisely, but that is another story) and I was no longer necessary to his household and I and my children had to leave. Then I got a job as dentist's receptionist, and on £10 a week had to feed my children and myself and keep an outward semblance of respectability. Now my two boys are both working and my time is suddenly my own. I am forty-five years old but rebel against the idea that my life is over. Friends and/or comrades tell me my duty is to spend what spare time I have in the Party—to which I have remained faithful in my thoughts despite lack of time to be of practical use. But—dare I confess this?—my thoughts about the Party are confused and often negative. I cannot reconcile my early faith in the glorious future of mankind with what we read (though of course in the capitalist press—though it appears to be a case of no smoke without a fire?) and I believe I would better serve my true self by writing. Meanwhile time has passed in domestic chores and the business of earning a living and I am out of touch with the finer things of life. Please recommend to me what I should read, how I should develop myself, and how I can make up for lost time. With fraternal greetings. P.S. Both my sons went to grammar school, and both far beyond me, I fear, in their knowledge. This has given me a feeling of inferiority which it is hard to combat. I would appreciate more than I can express, your kindly advice and help.'

For a year I have been answering these letters, meeting the writers, giving practical advice. For instance, I asked the people who have to fight their local Party officials for time to write to come up to London. Then Jack and I take them out to lunch or tea and tell them (Jack is essential for this, because he is high up in the Party) to fight these officials, to insist that they are in the right to want time to themselves. Last week I helped a woman to the Legal Aid Bureau so that she might get advice about divorcing her husband.

While I deal with these letters, or with their writers, Rose Latimer works opposite, stiff with hostility. She is a typical Party member of this time; lower-middle-class by origin, the word 'worker' literally fills her eyes with tears. When she makes speeches, and uses the phrases: The British Worker, or The Working Class, her voice goes soft with reverence. When she goes off into the provinces to organise meetings or make speeches, she returns exalted: 'Wonderful people,' she says, 'wonderful marvellous people. They are *real*.' A week ago I got a letter from the wife of a trade union official she, Rose, had spent the weekend with a year ago, returning with the usual hymn of marvellous real people. This wife complained she was at the end of her tether: her husband spent all his time either with his brother trade union officials or in the pub; and that she never got any help from him with her four children. The usual illuminating postscript added that they had had 'no love-life' for eight years. I handed this letter, without comment, to Rose, and she read it and said quickly, defensive and angry: 'I didn't see anything of that when *I* was there. He's the salt of the earth. They are the salt of the earth, these people.' And then, handing the letter back with a bright false smile: 'I suppose you are going to encourage her to feel sorry for herself.'

I realise what a relief it will be to be rid of the company of Rose. I don't often dislike people (or at least not longer than for a few moments) but I dislike her actively and all the time. And I dislike her physical presence. She has a long thin straggly neck and there are blackheads on it and traces of grime. And above this unpleasant neck, a narrow glossy pert head, like a bird's. Her husband, also a Party official, a pleasant, not very intelligent man, is hen-pecked by her; and she has two children, whom she brings up in the most conventional middle-class way, fearful about their manners and their futures. She was once a very pretty girl—I was told that in the 'thirties she was 'one of the glamour girls' of the Party. Of course she frightens me: I am frightened by her the way I am frightened by John Butte—what is to stop me becoming like her?

Looking at Rose, hypnotised by that dirty neck of hers, I remember I have special reasons today for worrying about my own cleanliness, and I make another visit to the washroom. When I get back to my desk the afternoon post has arrived, and there are two more manuscripts and with them, two more letters. One of the letters is from an old-age pensioner, a man of seventy-five, living alone and pinning his hopes on the belief that the publication of this book (it looks pretty bad) will 'soften my old age for me.' I decide to go and visit him before remembering that I am quitting this job. Is someone going to do this work if I don't? Probably not. Well, does it make all that difference? In this year of 'welfare

357

work' I can't imagine that the letters I've written, the visits I've paid, the advice I've given, even the practical help has made all that difference. Perhaps a little less frustration, a little less unhappiness—but this is a dangerous way of thinking, one too natural to me, and I'm afraid of it.

I go in to Jack, who is sitting alone, shirt-sleeved, his feet on the desk, smoking a pipe. His pale, intelligent face is concentrated and frowning, and he seems more than ever like a university lecturer at ease. He is thinking, I know, about his private work. His speciality is the history of the Communist Party in the Soviet Union. He has written something like half a million words on the subject. But impossible to print it now, because he has written truthfully of the roles of people like Trotsky and similar people. He accumulates manuscript, notes, records of conversations. I tease Jack, saying: 'In two centuries' time the truth can be told.' He smiles calmly and says: 'Or in two decades or five.' It does not trouble him at all that this detailed work will receive no practical recognition for years, perhaps not even in his lifetime. He once said: 'I wouldn't be at all surprised if someone fortunate enough to be outside the Party publishes all this first. But on the other hand, someone outside the Party won't have the access I have to certain people and documents. So it cuts both ways.'

I say: 'Jack, when I leave, will there be anyone to do something about all these people in trouble?' He says: 'Well, I can't afford to pay someone to do it. It's not many comrades who can afford to live off royalties, like you.' Then he softens and says: 'I'll see what I can do about the worst cases.' 'There's an old-age pensioner,' I say; and I sit down and we discuss what might be done. Then he says: 'I take it you're not going to give me a month's notice? I always thought you'd do this—decide to leave and then just walk out.' 'Well, if I didn't, I probably wouldn't be able to leave at all.' He nods. 'Are you going to take another job?' 'I don't know, I want to think.' 'Sort of go into retreat for a while?' 'The point is, it seems to me that my mind is a mass of totally contradictory attitudes about everything.' 'Everyone's mind is a mass of contradictory attitudes. Why should it matter?' 'It should matter to *us*, surely?' (Meaning, it should matter to communists.) 'But Anna, has it occurred to you that throughout history . . .' 'Oh Jack, don't let's talk about history, about the five centuries, it's such an evasion.' 'No, it is not an evasion. Because throughout history, there have perhaps been five, ten, fifty people, whose consciousness truly matched their times. And if our consciousness of reality doesn't fit our time, what's so terrible about that? Our children . . .' 'Or our great-great-great grandchildren,' I say, sounding irritable. 'All right—our great-great-great-great grandchildren will look back and it will be perfectly clear to them that the way we saw the world, the way we see the world now, was incorrect. But then their view will be, of their time. It doesn't matter.'

'But Jack, that's such nonsense . . .' I hear my voice shrill and stop myself. I realise my period has caught up with me; there's a moment in every month when it does, and then I get irritated, because it makes me feel helpless and out of control. Also I'm irritated because this man has spent years in university studying philosophy; and I can't say to him: I know you're wrong because I feel you are. (And besides there's something dangerously attractive in what he's saying, and I know part of the irritation comes from fighting this attraction.) Jack ignores my shrillness; and he says mildly: 'All the same, I wish you'd think about it Anna—there's something very arrogant about insisting on the right to be right.' (The word arrogant hits me; because I've convicted myself so often of being arrogant.) I say, feebly enough: 'But I think and think and think.' 'No, let me try again: In the last decade or two the scientific achievements have been revolutionary. And in every sort of field. There's probably not one scientist in the world who can comprehend the implications of all the scientific achievements, or even part of them. There's perhaps a scientist in Massachusetts who understands one thing, and another in Cambridge understanding another, and another in the Soviet Union for a third—and so on. But I doubt even that. I doubt if there's anyone alive who can really imaginatively comprehend all the implications of let's say the use of atomic energy for industry . . .' I am feeling that he's terribly off the point; and I stick stubbornly

359

to mine: 'All you are saying is, we must submit to being split.' 'Split,' he said. 'Yes.' 'I'm certainly saying you're not a scientist, you haven't the scientific imagination.' I say: 'You're a humanist, that's been your education, and suddenly you throw up your hands and say you can't judge anything because you haven't been trained in physics and mathematics?' He looks uncomfortable; and he so seldom does, it makes me feel uncomfortable. I continue however with my point: 'Alienation. Being split. It's the moral side, so to speak, of the communist message. And suddenly you shrug your shoulders and say because the mechanical basis of our lives is getting complicated, we must be content to not even try to understand things as a whole?' And now I see his face has put on a stubborn closed look that reminds me of John Butte's: and he looks angry. He says: 'Not being split, it's not a question of imaginatively understanding everything that goes on. Or trying to. It means doing one's work as well as possible, and being a good person.' I feel he's a traitor to what he's supposed to be standing for. I say: 'That's treachery.' 'To what?' 'To humanism.' He thinks and says: 'The idea of humanism will change like everything else.' I say: 'Then it will become something else. But humanism stands for the whole person, the whole individual, striving to become as conscious and responsible as possible about everything in the universe. But now you sit there, quite calmly, and as a humanist you say that due to the complexity of scientific achievement the human being must never expect to be whole, he must always be fragmented.' He sits thinking. And all at once I think there is an undeveloped and incomplete look about him; and I wonder if this reaction is because I've decided to leave the Party and I'm already projecting emotions on to him; or if he is in fact not what I've been seeing him all this time. But I can't help remarking to myself that his face is that of an elderly boy; and I remember he is married to a woman who looks old enough to be his mother, and that it is very clear this is a marriage of affection.

I insist: 'When you said, not being split is just going to be a question of doing one's work well, etc., well you could say that of Rose next door.' 'Well, yes, I could, and do.' I can't believe he really means it, and I even look for the gleam of humour that surely must accompany this. Then I see he does mean it; and again I wonder why it is only now, after I've said I'm leaving the Party, that these discordancies begin between us.

Suddenly he takes the pipe out of his mouth and says: 'Anna, I think your soul is in danger.'

'That's more than likely. And is that so terrible?'

'You are in a very dangerous position. You are earning enough money not to have to work, due to the arbitrary rewards of our publishing system . . .'

'I've never pretended it was due to any special merit of mine.' (I note that my voice is shrill again, and add a smile.) 'No, you haven't. But it's possible that that nice little book of yours will go on bringing you enough money not to work for some time. And your daughter is at school and doesn't give you so much trouble. And so there's nothing to stop you sitting in a room somewhere doing nothing at all very much except brood about everything.' I laugh. (Sounding irritated.) 'Why are you laughing?' 'I used to have a school-teacher, that was during my stormy adolescence, she used to say: "Don't brood, Anna. Stop brooding and go out and do something." ' 'Perhaps she was right.' 'The thing is, I don't believe she was. And I don't believe you are.' 'Well, Anna, there's no more to be said.' 'And I don't believe for a moment *you* believe you are right.' At this he flushes slightly and he gives me a quick hostile glance. I can feel the hostile look on my face. It astounds me that there's this antagonism between us suddenly; particularly as the moment has come to part. Because at the moment of antagonism, it's not so painful to part as I expected. Both our eyes are wet, we kiss each other on the cheek, hold each other close; but there's no doubt the last argument has changed our feeling for each other. I go into my own office quickly, take my coat and my bag and go downstairs, thankful that Rose is not around, so that there's no need for explanations.

It is raining again, a small tedious drizzle. The buildings are big and dark and wet, hazed by reflected light; and the buses are scarlet and alive. I am too late to be at the school in time for Janet, even if I take a taxi. So I climb onto a bus, and sit surrounded by damp and stuffy-smelling people. I want more than anything to have a bath, quickly. My thighs are rubbing stickily together, and my armpits are wet. On the bus I collapse into emptiness; but I decide not to think about it; I have to be fresh for Janet. And it is in this way that I leave behind the Anna who goes to the office, argues interminably with Jack, reads the sad frustrated letters, dislikes Rose. When I get home the house is empty so I ring up Janet's friend's mother. Janet will be home at seven; she's finishing a game. Then I run the bath, and fill the bathroom with steam, and bathe, with pleasure, slowly. Afterwards I look at the black and white dress, and see that the collar is slightly grimy, so I can't wear it. It irritates me that I wasted that dress on the office. I dress again; this time wearing my striped gay trousers and my black velvet jacket; but I can hear Michael say: Why are you looking so boyish tonight, Anna?—so I'm careful to brush my hair so that it doesn't look boyish at all. I have all the fires on by now. I start two meals going: one for Janet. One for Michael and me. Janet at the moment has a craze for creamed spinach baked with eggs. And for baked apples. I have forgotten to buy brown sugar. I rush downstairs to the grocer's, just as the doors are closing. They let me in, good-humouredly; and I find myself playing the game they enjoy: the three serving men in their white coats joke and humour me and call me love and duck. I am dear little Anna, a dear little girl. I rush upstairs again and now Molly has come in and Tommy is with her. They are arguing loudly so I pretend not to hear and go upstairs. Janet is there. She is animated, but cut off from me; she has been in the child's world at school, and then with her little friend in a child's world, and she doesn't want to come out of it. She says: 'Can I have supper in bed?' and I say, for form's sake: 'Oh, but you're lazy!' and she says: 'Yes, but I don't care.' She goes, without being told, to the bathroom and runs her bath. I hear her and Molly laughing and talking together down three flights of stairs. Molly, without an effort, becomes a child when with children. She is telling a nonsensical tale about some animals who took over a theatre and ran it, and

362

no one noticed they weren't people. This story absorbs me so that I go to the landing to listen; on the landing below is Tommy, also listening, but with a bad-tempered critical look on his face—his mother never irritates him more than when with Janet, or another child. Janet is laughing and sploshing the water all around the bath, and I can hear the sound of water landing on the floor. In my turn, I am irritated, because now I shall have to wipe all this water up. Janet comes up, in her white dressing-gown and white pyjamas, already sleepy. I go down and wipe up the seas of water in the bathroom. When I return, Janet is in bed, her comics all around her. I bring in the tray with the baked dish of spinach and eggs and the baked apple with the clot of crumbly cream. Janet says, tell me a story. 'There was once a little girl called Janet,' I begin, and she smiles with pleasure. I tell how this little girl went to school on a rainy day, did lessons, played with the other children, quarrelled with her friend . . . 'No, mummy, I didn't, that was yesterday. I *love* Marie for ever and ever.' So I change the story so that Janet loves Marie for ever and ever. Janet eats dreamily, conveying her spoon back and forth to her mouth, listening while I create her day, give it form. I watch her, seeing Anna watch Janet. Next door the baby is crying. Again the feeling of continuity, of gay intimacy, starts, and I finish the story: 'And then Janet had a lovely supper of spinach and eggs and apples with cream and the baby next door cried a little, and then it stopped crying and went to sleep, and Janet cleaned her teeth and went to sleep.' I take the tray and Janet says: 'Do I have to clean my teeth?' 'Of course, it's in the story.' She slides her feet over the edge of the bed, into her slippers, goes like a sleep-walker to the basin, cleans her teeth, comes back. I turn off her fire and draw the curtains. Janet has an adult way of lying in bed before sleeping: on her back, her hands behind the back of her neck, staring at the softly moving curtains. It is raining again, hard. I hear the door at the bottom of the house shut: Molly has gone to her theatre. Janet hears it and says: 'When I grow up I'm going to be an actress.' Yesterday she said, a teacher. She says sleepily: 'Sing to me.' She shuts her eyes, and mumbles: 'Tonight I'm

363

a baby. I'm a baby.' So I sing over and over again, while Janet listens for what known change I will use, for I have all kinds of variations in the words: 'Rockabye baby, in your warm bed, there are lovely new dreams coming into your head, you will dream, dream, all through the dark night and wake warm and safe with the morning light.' Often if Janet finds the words I've chosen don't fit her mood, she stops me and demands another variation; but tonight I've guessed right, and I sing it again and again and again, until I see she's asleep. She looks defenceless and tiny when she's asleep, and I have to check in myself a powerful impulse to protect her, to shut her away from possible harm. This evening it is more powerful than usual; but I know it is because I have my period and need to cling to somebody myself. I go out, shutting the door softly.

And now the cooking for Michael. I unroll the veal that I remembered to batter out flat this morning; and I roll the pieces in the yellow egg, and the crumbs. I baked crumbs yesterday, and they still smell fresh and dry, in spite of the dampness in the air. I slice mushrooms into cream. I have a pan full of bone-jelly in the ice-box, which I melt and season. And the extra apples I cooked when doing Janet's I scoop out of the still warm crackling skin, and sieve the pulp and mix it with thin vanilla'd cream, and beat it until it goes thick; and I pile the mixture back into the apple skins and set them to brown in the oven. All the kitchen is full of good cooking smells; and all at once I am happy, so happy I can feel the warmth of it through my whole body. Then there is a cold feeling in my stomach, and I think: Being happy is a lie, it's a habit of happiness from moments like these during the last four years. And the happiness vanishes, and I am desperately tired. With the tiredness comes guilt. I know all the forms and variations of this guilt so well that they even bore me. But I have to fight them nevertheless. Perhaps I don't spend enough time with Janet—oh, nonsense, she wouldn't be so happy and easy if I wasn't doing it right. I am too egotistical, Jack is right, I should simply be concerned with some sort of work, and not bothered about my conscience— nonsense, I don't believe that. I shouldn't dislike Rose so much—well only a saint wouldn't, she's a terrible woman. I am living on unearned money, because it's only luck that book was a best-seller, and other people with more talent have to sweat and suffer—nonsense, it's not my fault. The fight with my various forms of dissatisfaction tires me; but I know this is not a personal fight. When I talk about this with other women, they tell me they have to fight all kinds of guilt they recognise as irrational, usually to do with working, or wanting time for themselves; and the guilt is a habit of the nerves from the past, just as my happiness a few moments ago was a habit of the nerves from a situation that is finished. I set a bottle of wine to warm, and go into my room, getting pleasure from the low white ceiling, the pale shadowed walls, the glow of red from the fire. I sit in the big chair, and now I'm so depressed I have to fight against tears. I think, I'm bolstering myself up: the cooking for Michael and the waiting for him—what does it mean? He already has another woman, whom he cares for more than he does for me. I know it. He'll come tonight out of habit or kindness. And then I again fight this depression by putting myself back into a mood of confidence and trust (like entering another room inside myself) and I say: He'll come quite soon, and we will eat together, and drink the wine, and he will tell me stories about the work he's done today, and then we'll have a cigarette, and he will take me in his arms. I'll tell him I have my period and as usual he'll laugh at me and say: My dear Anna, don't put your guilt feelings on to me. When I have my period I rest on the knowledge that Michael will love me, at night; it takes away the resentment against the wound inside my body which I didn't choose to have. And then we will sleep together, all night.

I realise it is getting late. Molly comes back from her theatre. She says: 'Is Michael coming?' and I say: 'Yes,' but I see from her face that she doesn't think he will. She asks me how the day has been, and I say I've decided to leave the Party. She nods, and says that she's noticed that whereas she used to be on half a dozen different committees and was always busy on Party work, she's now on one committee and can't bring herself to do Party work. 'So it comes to the same

365

thing, I suppose,' she says. But what's worrying her this evening is Tommy. She doesn't like his new girl-friend. (I didn't either.) She says: 'It's just occurred to me, his girl-friends are all of the same type—the type that are bound *not* to like me. Whenever they are here, they simply radiate disapproval of me all the time; and instead of seeing we don't meet, Tommy simply pushes us together. In other words, he is using his girl-friends as a kind of alter ego, to say about me what he thinks but doesn't say aloud. Does that strike you as too far-fetched?' Well it doesn't, because I think she's right, but I say it is. I am being tactful over Tommy, the way she is tactful about Michael's leaving me—we shield each other. Then she says again about being sorry that Tommy was a conscientious objector, because his two years in the coal mines have made him a sort of hero in a certain small circle, and 'I can't stand that awful self-satisfied exalted air of his.' It irritates me too, but I say that he's young and will grow out of it. 'And I said an awful thing tonight: I said, thousands of men work down the coal-mines all their lives, and think nothing of it, for God's sake don't make such a thing out of it. And of course that was unfair, because it *is* a big thing, a boy of his background working down the coal mines. And he did stick it out . . . all the same!' She lights a cigarette, and I watch her hands lying on her knees; they look limp and discouraged. Then she says: 'What frightens me is, I never seem to be able to see anything *pure* in what people do—do you know what I mean? Even when they do something good, I find myself getting all cynical and psychological about it—that *is* awful, Anna, isn't it?' I know only too well what she means, and say so, and we sit in a depressed silence until she says: 'I think Tommy is going to marry this one, I just have a hunch.' 'Well, he's bound to marry one of them.' 'And I know that this sounds just like a mother resenting her son getting married—well, there's that in it. But I swear I'd think she was awful anyway. She's so bloody middle-class. And she's ever such a socialist. You know, when I met her first I thought: Good God, who is this awful little Tory Tommy's inflicted on me? Then it turns out she's a socialist, you know, one of those academic socialists from

Oxford. Studying sociology. You know, one gets into the mood where one keeps seeing the ghost of Keir Hardie. Well, that lot'd be surprised if they could see what they've spawned. Tommy's new girl'd be a real eye-opener to them. You know, you can positively see the insurance policies and the savings accounts taking shape in the air all round them while they talk about making the Labour Party fulfil its pledges. Yesterday she even told Tommy that he ought to be planning for his old age. Can you beat it?' We laugh together, but it's no good. She goes downstairs, saying good night. She says it gently (as I said good night to Janet) and I know it is because she is unhappy for me because Michael won't come. It is nearly eleven now; and I know he won't come. The telephone rings and it is Michael. 'Anna, forgive me, but I can't come tonight after all.' I say it is quite all right. He says: 'I'll ring you tomorrow—or in a couple of days. Good night Anna.' He adds, fumbling with the words: 'I'm sorry if you cooked especially for me.' The *if* suddenly makes me furious. Then it strikes me as odd that I should be angry over such a little thing, and I even laugh. He hears the laugh, and says: 'Ah, yes, Anna, yes . . .' Meaning that I am heartless and don't care for him. But I suddenly can't stand this, and say: 'Good night, Michael,' and ring off.

I take all the food off the stove, carefully saving what can be used, and throwing the rest away—nearly everything. I sit and think: Well, if he rings me tomorrow . . . But I know he won't. I realise, at last, that this is the end. I go to see if Janet is asleep—I know she is, but I have to look. Then I know that an awful black whirling chaos is just outside me, waiting to move into me. I must go to sleep quickly, before I become that chaos. I am trembling with misery and with tiredness. I fill a tumbler full of wine and drink it, quickly. Then I get into bed. My head is swimming with the wine. Tomorrow, I think—tomorrow—I'll be responsible, face my future, and refuse to be miserable. Then I sleep, but before I am even asleep I can hear myself crying, the sleep-crying, this time all pain, no enjoyment in it at all.

[The whole of the above was scored through—cancelled

367

out and scribbled underneath: No, it didn't come off. A failure as usual. Underneath was written, in different handwriting, more neat and orderly than the long entry, which was flowing and untidy:]

15th September, 1954

A normal day. During the course of a discussion with John Butte and Jack decided to leave the Party. I must now be careful not to start hating the Party in the way we do hate stages of our life we have outgrown. Noted signs of it already: moments of disliking Jack which were quite irrational. Janet as usual, no problems. Molly worried, I think with reason, over Tommy. She has a hunch he will marry his new girl. Well, her hunches usually come off. I realised that Michael had finally decided to break it off. I must pull myself together.

■ **FREE WOMEN: 3** ■

■ FREE WOMEN: 3 ■

Tommy adjusts himself to being blind
while the older people try to help him

TOMMY hovered for a week between life and death.
The end of that week was marked by Molly's use of
these words; her voice very far from its usual note of ringing
confidence: 'Isn't it odd, Anna? He's been hovering between
life and death. Now he's going to live. It seems impossible he
shouldn't. But if he had died, then I suppose we'd have felt
that was inevitable too?' For a week the two women had sat
by Tommy's bed in the hospital; waited in side-rooms while
doctors conferred, judged, operated; returned to Anna's flat
to care for Janet; received letters and visits of sympathy; and
called on their reserves of energy to deal with Richard, who
was openly condemning them both. During this week, while
time stopped, and feeling stopped (they asked themselves and
each other why they felt nothing but numbing suspense,
although of course tradition authorised this reaction), they
talked, though briefly and in shorthand, so to speak, since the
points in question were so familiar to them both, of Molly's
care of Tommy, Anna's relationship with him, to pinpoint the
event or the moment when they had definitely failed him.
Because Molly had gone away for a year? No, she still felt
that was the right thing to have done. Because of the formlessness of their own lives? But how could they have been
anything different? Because of something said or not said
during Tommy's last visit to Anna? Possibly, but they felt
not; and how was one to know? They did not refer the
catastrophe to Richard's account; but when he accused them,
replied: 'Look, Richard, there's no point in abusing each
other. The thing is, what to do next for him?'

Tommy's optic nerve was damaged; he would be blind. The brain was undamaged, or at least, would recover.

Now that he was pronounced out of danger, time established itself again, and Molly collapsed into hours of low and helpless weeping. Anna was very busy with her and with Janet, who had to be shielded from the knowledge that Tommy had tried to kill himself. She had used the phrase: '—had an accident,' but it was a stupid one, because now she could see in the child's eyes the knowledge that the possibilities of an accident terrible enough to lay one flat on one's back, permanently blinded, in hospital, lurked in the objects and habits of an every day. So Anna amended the phrase and said Tommy had accidentally wounded himself cleaning a revolver. Janet then remarked that there was no revolver in their flat; and Anna said no, and there never would be, etc.; and the child came out of her anxiety.

Meanwhile Tommy, having been a silent shrouded figure in a darkened room, ministered to by the living and helpless in their hands, moved, came to life, and spoke. And that group of people, Molly, Anna, Richard, Marion, who had stood waiting, had sat waiting, had kept vigil through a timeless week, understood how far they had allowed him, in their minds, to slip beyond them into death. When he spoke it was a shock. For that quality in him, the accusing dogged obstinacy that had led him to try to put a bullet in his brain, had been obliterated in their thoughts of him as the victim lying shrouded under white sheets and bandages. The first words he said—and they were all there to hear them—were: 'You're there, aren't you? Well, I can't see you.' The way this was said kept them silent. He continued: 'I *am* blind, aren't I?' And again, the way this was spoken made it impossible to soften the boy's coming back to life as it was their first impulse to do. After a moment, Molly told him the truth. The four stood around the bed, looking down at the head blind under moulding white tissues, and they were all of them sick with horror and with pity, imagining the lonely and brave struggle that must be going on. And yet Tommy said nothing. He lay still. His hands, the clumsy thick hands he had from his father, were lying by his sides. He lifted them, fumbled them together, and folded them on his chest, in an attitude of endurance. But in his way of making the gesture was something that caused Molly and Anna to exchange a look in which there was more than pity. It was a kind of terror—the look was like a nod. Richard saw the two women communicate this feeling, and literally ground his teeth with rage. It was no place to say what he felt; but outside he said it. They were walking together away from the hospital, Marion a little behind—the shock of what had happened to Tommy had stopped her drinking for the time, but she still seemed to move in a slowed world of her own. Richard spoke fiercely to Molly, turning hot and angry eyes on Anna, so as to include her: 'That was a pretty bloody thing you did, wasn't it?' 'What?' said Molly, from inside Anna's supporting arm. Now they were out of the hospital, she was shaking with sobs. 'Telling him just like that, he's blind for life. What a think to do.' 'He knew it,' said Anna, seeing that Molly was too shaken to talk, and knowing also that this was not what he was accusing them of. 'He knew it, he knew it,' Richard hissed at them. 'He had just come out of being unconscious and you tell him, he's blind for life.' Anna said, answering his words but not his feeling: 'He had to know.' Molly said to Anna, ignoring Richard, continuing the dialogue with Anna which had been begun in that silent confirming horrified glance over the hospital bed: 'Anna, I believe he had been conscious for some time. He was waiting for us all to be there—it's as if he were pleased about it. Isn't it *awful*, Anna?' Now she broke into hysterical weeping, and Anna said to Richard: 'Don't take it out on Molly now.' Richard let out a disgusted inarticulate exclamation, wheeled back to Marion, who was vaguely following the three of them, impatiently took her arm, and went off with her across the vivid green hospital lawn that was systematically dotted with bright flower-beds. He drove off with Marion, not looking back, leaving them to find a taxi for themselves.

There never was a moment at which Tommy broke down. He gave no evidence of a collapse into unhappiness or self-pity. From the first moment, from his first words, he was patient, calm, co-operated pleasantly with the nurses and doctors, and discussed with Anna and Molly, and even with Richard, plans for his future. He was, as the nurses kept repeating—not without a touch of that uneasiness which Anna and Molly felt so strongly—'A model patient.' They had never known anyone, they said, and kept saying, let alone a poor young lad of twenty, faced with such an awful fate, take it so bravely.

It was suggested that Tommy should spend some time in a training hospital for the newly blind, but he insisted on returning home. And he had made such good use of his weeks in hospital that he was already handling his food, could wash and care for himself, could move slowly around his room. Anna and Molly would sit and watch him: normal again, apparently the same as he was before, save for the black shield over sightless eyes, moving with dogged patience from bed to chair, from chair to wall, his lips pursed in concentration, the effort of his will behind every small movement. 'No thank you nurse, I can manage.' 'No, mother, please don't help me.' 'No, Anna, I don't need help.' And he didn't.

It was decided that Molly's living-room on the first floor must be turned over to Tommy—there would be fewer stairs for him to manage. This adaptation he was prepared to accept, but he insisted that her life and his should continue as before. 'There's no need to make any changes, mother, I don't want anything to be different.' His voice had gone back to what they knew: the hysteria, the immanent giggle, the shrillness that had been in it on that evening he had visited Anna, had gone entirely. His voice, like his movements, was slow, full and controlled, every word authorised by a methodical brain. But when he said: 'There's no need to make changes,' the two women looked at each other, which it was safe to do now that he couldn't see them (although they could not rid themselves of the suspicion that he knew it all the same) and they both felt the same dulled panic. For he used the words as if there had been no change, as if the fact that he was now blind was almost incidental, and that if his mother was unhappy about it it was because she chose to be, or was being fussy or nagging, like a woman becoming

374

irritated by untidiness or a bad habit. He humoured them like a man humouring difficult women. The two watched him, looked, appalled, at each other, looked away again, watched helplessly while the boy made his tedious but apparently unpainful adjustment to the dark world which was now his.

The white cushioned window sills on which Molly and Anna had so often sat to talk, with the boxes of flowers behind them, the rain or the pale sunshine on the panes, were all that remained the same in this room. It now contained a narrow tidy bed; a table with a straight chair; some conveniently placed shelves. Tommy was learning Braille. And he was teaching himself to write again with an exercise book and a child's ruler. His writing was quite unlike what it had been: it was large, square and clear, like a child's. When Molly knocked to come in, he would raise his black-shaded face over the Braille or his writing and say 'Come in,' with the temporarily though courteously granted attention of a man behind a desk in an office.

So Molly, who had refused a part in a play so as to be able to nurse Tommy, went back to her work and acted again. Anna ceased dropping over in the evenings when Molly was out at the theatre, for Tommy said: 'Anna, you are very kind to come and take pity on me, but I'm not at all bored. I like being alone.' As he would have said it had he been an ordinary man who chose to prefer solitude. And Anna, who had been trying to get back to her intimacy with Tommy before the accident, and failing (she felt as if the boy were a stranger she had never known), took him at his word. She literally could not think of anything to say to him. And besides, alone in a room with him, she kept succumbing to waves of pure panic, which she did not understand.

And now Molly rang Anna, no longer from her home, since the telephone was immediately outside Tommy's room, but from telephone boxes or from the theatre. 'How is Tommy?' Anna would ask. And Molly's voice, loud and in command again, but with a permanent note of challenging query, of pain defied, would reply: 'Anna, it's all so odd I don't know what to say or do. He just stays in that room, working away, always quiet; and when I can't stand it another moment I go in, and he looks up and says: "Well mother, and what can I do for you?" ' 'Yes, I know.' 'So naturally I say something silly, like—I thought you might like a cup of tea. Usually he says no, very politely of course, so I go out again. And now he's learning to make his own tea and coffee. Even to cook.' 'He's handling kettles and things?' 'Yes. I'm petrified. I have to go out of the kitchen, because he knows what I am feeling, and he says, Mother, there's no need to be frightened, I'm not going to burn myself.' 'Well Molly I don't know what to say.' (Here there was a silence, because of what they were both afraid to say.) Then Molly went on: 'And people come up, oh ever so sweet and kind, *you know*?' 'Yes, indeed I do.' 'Your poor son, your unfortunate Tommy ... I always knew everything was a jungle, but never as clearly as I do now.' Anna understood this because mutual friends and acquaintances used her as a target for the remarks, on the surface kindly, but concealing malice, which they would have liked to direct at Molly. 'Of course it was a pity that Molly went off and left the boy for that year.' 'I don't think that had anything to do with it. Besides, she did it after careful thought.' Or: 'Of course, there was that broken marriage. It must have affected Tommy more than anyone guessed.' 'Oh quite so,' Anna would say, smiling. 'And there's my broken marriage. I do so trust that Janet won't end up the same way.' And all the time, while Anna defended Molly, and herself, there was something else, the cause of the panic they both felt, the something they were afraid to say.

It was expressed by the single fact that whereas not six months before she, Anna, rang Molly's home to chat with Molly, sending messages to Tommy; visited Molly, and perhaps dropped into Tommy's room for a chat; went to Molly's parties at which Tommy was a guest, among others; was a participant in Molly's life, her adventures with men, her need, and her failure to marry—now all this, the years' long, slow growth of intimacy was checked and broken. Anna never telephoned Molly except for the most practical reasons, because even if the telephone had not been outside Tommy's door, he was able to intuit what was said by people apparently through a new sixth sense. For instance, once Richard, who was still aggressively accusing, telephoned Molly saying: 'Answer yes or no, that's all that's necessary: I want to send Tommy off on a holiday with a trained blind-nurse. Will he go?' And before Molly could even reply, Tommy raised his voice from the room inside with: 'Tell my father that I'm quite all right. Thank him and say I'll telephone him tomorrow.'

No longer did Anna visit Molly casually and lightly for an evening, or drop in when going past. She rang the door-bell after a preparatory telephone call, heard it vibrate upstairs, and was convinced that Tommy already knew who it was. The door opened on Molly's shrewd, painful, still forcibly gay smile. They went up to the kitchen, speaking of neutral matters, conscious of the boy through the wall. The tea or the coffee would be made; and a cup offered to Tommy. He always refused. The two women went up to the room that had been Molly's bedroom, and was now a sort of bed-sitting-room. There they sat, thinking in spite of themselves of the mutilated boy just below them, who was now the centre of the house, dominating it, conscious of everything that went on in it, a blind but all-conscious presence. Molly would chatter a little, offer theatre gossip, from habit. Then she fell silent, her mouth twisted in anxiety, her eyes reddened with checked tears. She had now the tendency to burst suddenly and without warning into tears—on a word, in the middle of a sentence, helpless and hysterical tears which she instantly checked. Her life had changed completely. She now went to the theatre to work, shopped for what was necessary, then came home and sat alone in the kitchen or in her bed-sitting-room.

'Aren't you seeing anybody?' Anna asked.

'Tommy asked me that. Last week he said: "I don't want you to stop your social life, just for me, mother. Why don't you bring your friends home?" Well so I took him at his word. And so I brought home that producer, you know, the one that wanted to marry me. Dick. You remember? Well he's been very sweet over Tommy—I mean really sweet and kind, not spiteful. And I was sitting here with him, and we were drinking some Scotch. And for the first time I thought,

377

well I wouldn't mind—he *is* kind, and I'd settle tonight for just a kind masculine shoulder. And I was on the point of flashing the green light, and then I realised—it wouldn't be possible for me to give him so much as a sisterly kiss without Tommy knowing it. Though of course Tommy would never hold it against me, would he? In the morning he would very likely have said, Did you have a pleasant evening, mother? I'm so glad.'

Anna stopped an impulse to say: You're exaggerating. Because Molly was not exaggerating, and she could not offer this sort of dishonesty to Molly. 'So you know, Anna, when I look at Tommy, with that ghastly black thing over his eyes—*you know*, all neat and tidy, and his mouth—you know that mouth of his, set, dogmatic ... I get suddenly so irritated ...' 'Yes, I can understand.' 'But isn't it awful? I get physically irritated. Those slow careful movements, you know.' 'Yes.' 'Because the point is, it's like he was before, only—confirmed, if you know what I mean.' 'Yes.' 'Like some kind of zombie.' 'Yes.' 'I could scream with irritation. And the thing is, I have to leave the room because I know quite well *he* knows I'm feeling like that and ...' She stopped herself. Then she made herself go on, defiantly: 'He enjoys it.' She gave a high yelp of laughter, and said: 'He's happy, Anna.' 'Yes.' Now it was out at last, they both felt easier. 'He's happy for the first time in his life. That's what's so terrible ... you can see it in how he moves and talks—he's all in one piece for the first time in his life.' Molly gasped in horror at her own words, hearing what she had said: *all in one piece*, and matching them against the truth of that mutilation. Now she put her face in her hands and wept, differently, through her whole body. When she had finished crying, she looked up and said, trying to smile: 'I oughtn't to cry. He'll hear me.' There was gallantry in that smile even now.

Anna noticed, for the first time, that her friend's cap of rough gold hair had streaks of grey; and that around her direct but sad eyes were dark hollows, where the bones showed, thin and sharp. 'I think you should dye your hair,' said Anna. 'What's the point?' said Molly, angry. Then she made herself laugh, and said: 'I can hear him now: I'd come up the stairs with ever-such a posh hair-do, and I'd be so pleased with myself, and Tommy'd smell the dye or something, just sense the vibrations, and he'd say: Mother, have you had your hair dyed? Well, I'm glad you're not letting yourself go.' 'Well I'll be glad if you don't, even if he wouldn't be.' 'I expect I'll be sensible again when I've got used to it all . . . I was thinking yesterday about that—the words, getting used to it, I mean. That's what life is, getting used to things that are really intolerable . . .' Her eyes reddened and filled, and again she determinedly blinked them clear.

A few days later Molly telephoned from a telephone box to say: 'Anna, something very odd's happening. Marion's started dropping in all hours of the day to see Tommy.'

'How is she?'

'She's hardly drunk anything since Tommy's accident.'

'Who told you?'

'She told Tommy and Tommy told me.'

'Oh. What did he say?'

Molly imitated her son's slow pedantic voice: ' "Marion's really doing quite well, on the whole. She's coming on quite nicely." '

'He didn't?'

'Oh yes he did.'

'Well at least Richard must be pleased.'

'He's furious. He writes me long furious letters—and when I open one of them, even if I've ten other letters by the same post, Tommy says: And what does my father have to say?—Marion comes nearly every day and spends hours with him. He's like an elderly professor welcoming his favourite pupil.'

'Well . . .' said Anna helplessly. 'Well.'

'Yes, I know.'

Anna was summoned to Richard's office a few days later. He telephoned, brusque with hostility, to say: 'I'd like to see you. I *could* come to your place if you want.' 'But obviously you don't want.' 'I daresay I could spare an hour or two tomorrow afternoon.' 'Oh no, I'm sure you really haven't the time. I'll come to you. Shall we make an appointment?' 'Would three o'clock tomorrow suit you?' 'Three it is,' said

Anna, conscious she was pleased Richard was not coming to her flat. During the last months she had been haunted by the memory of Tommy standing over her notebooks, turning page after page, on the evening he had tried to kill himself. She had made few entries recently; and then with effort. She felt as if the boy, his hot dark eyes accusing, stood at her elbow. She felt that her room was no longer her own. And having Richard in it would have made things worse.

At precisely three o'clock she was presenting herself to Richard's secretary, telling herself that of course he would make a point of keeping her waiting. About ten minutes she judged would be the amount of time necessary to feed his vanity. Fifteen minutes later she was informed she might enter.

As Tommy had said, Richard behind his desk was impressive in a way she would never have expected possible. The head offices of this empire occupied four floors of an ancient and ugly building in the City. These offices were of course not where the actual business was done; but rather a showcase for the personalities of Richard and his associates. The décor was tactful and international. One would not have been surprised to see it anywhere in the world. From the moment one entered the great front door, the lift, corridors, waiting rooms, were a long but discreet preparation for the moment one finally entered Richard's office. The floor was six inches deep in thick dark pile. The walls were of dark glass between white panels. It was lit unemphatically; and apparently from behind the various wall plants that trailed well-tended greenery from level to level. Richard, his sullen and obstinate body cancelled by anonymous suiting, sat behind a desk that looked like a tomb in greenish marble.

Anna had been examining the secretary while she was waiting; and had noted that she was in type similar to Marion: another nut-brown maid, tending to glossy and lively untidiness. She took care to watch how Richard and this girl behaved together in the few seconds it took to usher in herself, caught a glance between them, and understood they were having an affair. Richard saw that Anna had come to

380

conclusions, and said: 'I don't want any of your lectures, Anna. I want to talk seriously.'

'But that's what I'm here for, isn't it?'

He was suppressing annoyance. Anna refused the seat opposite his desk which he offered her, and sat on a window ledge some distance from him. Before he could speak, a green light went up on the panel of his office telephone, and he excused himself to speak into it. 'Excuse me a moment,' he said again; and an inner door opened and a young man came in with a file, which he laid in the most unobtrusively charming manner possible on the marbled stone before Richard, almost bowing, before tiptoeing out again.

Richard hastily laid open the file, made a pencil note, was about to press another button, when he saw Anna's face and said: 'Anything especially funny?'

'Not especially. I remember someone saying that the importance of any public man can be gauged by the number of mellifluous young men he has about him.'

'Molly, I suppose.'

'Well yes, actually. How many do you have, as a matter of interest?'

'A couple of dozen, I suppose.'

'The Prime Minister couldn't say as much.'

'I dare say not. Anna, do you have to?'

'I was just making conversation.'

'In that case I'll save you the trouble. It's about Marion. Did you know she was spending all her time with Tommy?'

'Molly told me. She also told me she had stopped drinking.'

'She comes into town every morning. She buys all the newspapers, and spends the time reading them to Tommy. She gets back home at seven or eight. All she can talk about is Tommy and politics.'

'She's stopped drinking,' Anna said again.

'And what about her children? She sees them at breakfast, and if they're lucky for an hour in the evening. I don't suppose she even remembers they exist, half the time.'

'I think you should employ someone for the time being.'

'Look, Anna, I asked you here to discuss it seriously.'

'I am serious. I suggest you employ some nice sort of woman to be with the boys until—things sort themselves out.'

'My God, what's that going to cost . . .' But here Richard stopped himself, frowning, embarrassed.

'You mean you don't want a strange woman around the house, even temporarily? It can't possibly be the money. Marion says you earn thirty thousand a year even before you start on the perks and the expenses.'

'What Marion says about money is usually nonsense. All right then, I don't want a strange woman around the house. The whole thing's impossible! Marion's never given a thought to politics. Suddenly she cuts bits out of the newspapers and spouts out of the *New Statesman*.'

Anna laughed. 'Richard, what's really the matter? Well, what is it? Marion was drinking herself silly. She's stopped. Surely that's worth almost anything? I should imagine she's a better mother than she was.'

'Well that's certainly saying a lot!'

Richard's lips actually trembled; and his whole face swelled and reddened. Seeing Anna's face, which openly diagnosed self-pity, he restored himself by again pressing the buzzer, and when the discreetly attentive young man entered— another one—handed over the file and said: 'Telephone Sir Jason and ask him to lunch with me on Wednesday or Thursday at the club.'

'Who is Sir Jason?'

'You know quite well you don't care.'

'I'm interested.'

'He's a very charming man.'

'Good.'

'He's also an opera fan—knows everything about music.'

'Delightful.'

'And we are about to buy a controlling interest in his company.'

'Well that's all very satisfactory, isn't it? I do wish you'd come to the point, Richard. What's really on your mind?'

'If I paid a woman to come in and take Marion's place

with the children it would turn my whole life upside-down. Apart from the cost,' he could not prevent himself adding.

'It occurs to me that you're so extraordinary about money because of your bohemian phase in the 'thirties? I've never before met a man who was born rich who had your attitude to money. I suppose when your family cut you off with that shilling it was a real shock to you? You go on like a suburban factory manager who's done better than he expected.'

'Yes, you're right. It was a shock. It was the first time in my life I realised what money was worth. I've never forgotten it. And I agree—I've got the attitude to money of someone who's had to make it. Marion has never understood that—and you and Molly keep telling me she's so intelligent!'

This last was on such a note of aggrieved righteousness that Anna laughed again, genuinely. 'Richard, you are funny. Well you really are. All right, let's not argue. You suffered a deep trauma when your family took your flirtation with communism seriously; as a result of which you can never enjoy money. And you've always been ever so unlucky with your women. Molly and Marion are both rather stupid, and their characters are disastrous.'

Richard now faced Anna with his characteristic stubbornness: 'That's how I see it, yes.'

'Good. And now?'

But now Richard let his eyes move away from hers; and sat frowning at a stream of delicate green leaves mirrored in dark glass. It occurred to Anna that he wanted to see her—not for the usual reason, to attack Molly through her, but to announce a new plan.

'What do you have in mind, Richard? Are you going to pension off Marion? Is that it? Are you planning that Marion and Molly should live out their old age together somewhere while you . . .' Anna saw that this flight of fancy was in fact stumbling on the truth. 'Oh Richard,' she said. 'You can't abandon Marion now. Particularly when she's just begun to cope with her drinking.'

Richard said hotly: 'She doesn't care for me. She has no time for me. I might just as well not be there at all.' Wounded vanity rang in his voice. And Anna was amazed.

383

For he was genuinely wounded. Marion's escape from her position as prisoner, or fellow-victim, had left him alone and hurt.

'For God's sake Richard! You've ignored her for years. You've simply used her as . . .'

Again his lips were hotly trembling and his full dark eyes swelling with tears.

'Good Lord!' said Anna, simply. She was thinking: Molly and I are very stupid, after all. It amounts to this, that's his way of loving someone, and he doesn't understand anything else. And it's probably what Marion understands too.

She said: 'What's your plan then? I got the impression you're involved with that girl out there. Is that it?'

'Yes, that is it. She loves me, at least.'

'Richard,' said Anna helplessly.

'Well it's true. I might as well not exist as far as Marion is concerned.'

'But if you divorce Marion now it might crack her up altogether.' 'I doubt if she'd even notice it. Anyway, I didn't mean to do anything suddenly. That's why I wanted to see you. I want to suggest that Marion and Tommy should go off on some holiday together. After all, they spend all their time together as it is. I'd send them anywhere they want to go. For as long as they like. Anything they like. And while they were away, I'd introduce Jean to the children—gradually. They know her of course, and they like her, but I'd ease them into the idea of my marrying her in due course.'

Anna sat silent until he insisted: 'Well, what do you say?'

'You mean, what would Molly say?'

'I'm asking you, Anna. I can see it might be a shock for Molly.'

'It wouldn't be a shock to Molly at all. Nothing you did would. You know that. So what is it you really want to know?'

Refusing to help him, not only out of dislike for him, but out of dislike for herself—sitting there judging, critical and cool while he looked so unhappy—Anna continued to sit hunched up on the window sill, smoking.

'Well Anna?'

'If you asked Molly, I think she'd be relieved if Marion and Tommy went away for a while.'

'Of course she would. She'd be rid of the burden!'

'Look, Richard, you can abuse Molly to other people, but not to me.'

'Then what's the problem, if Molly wouldn't mind?'

'Well, obviously, Tommy.'

'Why? Marion tells me that it's evident he doesn't even like having Molly in the room—he's only happy with her. With Marion, I mean.'

Anna hesitated, then said: 'Tommy's set everything up so that he has his mother in the house, not next to him, but close. As his prisoner. And he's not likely to give that up. He might consider, as a great favour, going away for a holiday with Marion, provided Molly tagged along well under control . . .'

Richard exploded into fury: 'God, I might have known. You're a filthy-minded, loathsome, cold-brained pair of . . .' He spluttered into inarticulate silence, breathing heavily. Yet he was watching her curiously, he was waiting to hear what she would say.

'You asked me here so that I should say what I've said, in order that you could call me names. Or call Molly names. And now I've obliged you by saying it and I'm going home.' Anna slid off the high window ledge on to her feet and stood ready to go. She was full of self-dislike, thinking: Of course Richard asked me here for the usual reasons—so that I would eventually abuse him. But I must have known that. So I'm here because I need to abuse him and what he stands for. I'm part of the whole stupid game and I should be ashamed of myself. But although she was thinking this, and it was genuine, Richard was standing opposite her in the pose of someone waiting to be whipped and she went on: 'There are people who need victims, dear Richard. Surely you understand that? After all, he is your son.' She went towards the door she came in at. But the door was blank without a handle. In this office it would open only at the touch of a button either outside or from Richard's desk.

'What am I going to do, Anna?'

385

'I don't think you'll be able to do anything.'

'I'm not going to be outwitted by Marion!' Again Anna was startled into laughter. 'Richard, do stop it! Marion's had enough, that's all. Even the softest-willed people have escape routes. Marion's turned towards Tommy because he needs her. That's all. I'm sure she's never planned anything—to use the word outwit of Marion is so . . .'

'All the same, she knows quite well, she's glorying in it. Do you know what she said to me a month ago? She said: You can sleep alone Richard and . . .' But he stopped on the verge of finishing what she had said.

'But Richard, you were complaining of having to share a bed with her at all!'

'I might just as well not be married at all. Marion's got her own room now. And she's never at home. Why should I be cheated out of a normal life?'

'But Richard . . .' Futility stopped her. But he was still waiting, wanting to hear what she would say. She said: 'But you've got Jean, Richard. Surely you must see some connection somewhere. You've got your secretary.'

'She's not going to hang around forever. She wants to get married.'

'But Richard, the supply of secretaries is unlimited. Oh don't look so wounded. You've had affairs with at least a dozen of your secretaries, haven't you?'

'I want to marry Jean.'

'Well I don't think it's going to be easy. Tommy won't let it be, even if Marion divorces you.'

'She said she wouldn't divorce me.'

'Give her time then.'

'Time. I'm not getting any younger. I'll be fifty next year. I can't afford to waste time. Jean's twenty-three. Why should she hang around wasting her chances while Marion . . .'

'You should be talking to Tommy. Surely you can see that he's the key to everything?'

'A lot of sympathy I'll get from him. He's always been on Marion's side.'

'Perhaps you should try to get him on to yours?'

'There's no chance of that.'

'No, I don't think there is. I think you'll have to dance to Tommy's tune. Just as Molly is, and Marion too.'

'Just what I expected from you—the boy's a cripple and you talk of him as if he's a sort of criminal.'

'Yes I know it was what you expected. I can't forgive myself for supplying it. Please let me go home Richard. Open the door.' She stood by it, waiting for him to let it open.

'And you're even laughing, at this awful pitiful mess.'

'I'm laughing, as you know quite well, at the sight of one of the financial powers of this our great country dancing with rage like a child of three in the middle of his ever-so-expensive carpet. Please let me out Richard.'

Richard with an effort took himself to his desk, pushed a button, and the door swung open.

'If I were you, I'd wait a few months and offer Tommy a job here. A nice important one.'

'You mean he'd be kind enough to accept it now? You're crazy. He's on a left-wing political kick, he and Marion, getting all hot under the collar about the wrongs of those poor bloody blacks at this very moment.'

'Well, well. Why not? It's very fashionable. Didn't you know? You just lack a sense of timing, Richard. You always did, you know. That's not left wing. That's *à la mode*.'

'You would have been pleased, I should have thought.'

'Oh but I am. Remember what I said—if you handle things right, Tommy'll be pleased to accept a job here. Probably take yours over.'

'Well I'd be happy. You've always been wrong about me Anna. I don't really enjoy this racket. I want to retire, just as soon as I can, and go and live a quiet sort of life with Jean and perhaps have some more children. That's what I'm planning to do. I wasn't cut out for the financial racket.'

'Except that you've quadrupled the holdings and profits of your empire since you took over, so Marion says. Good-bye Richard.'

'Anna.'

'Well what is it?'

He hastily moved around to stand between her and the half-open door. He now bumped it shut, with an impatient jerk of his buttocks. The contrast between this movement and the smooth invisibly managed machinery of the rich office, or display room, affected Anna like a reminder of her own discordant self as she stood there waiting to leave. She saw herself: small, pale, pretty, maintaining an intelligent and critical smile. She could feel herself, under this shape of order, as a chaos of discomfort and anxiety. That ugly little jerk of Richard's well-clothed buttocks matched her own just-concealed turmoil; and therefore it was hypocrisy to feel distaste. Telling herself this, she felt, instead, exhaustion, and said: 'Richard, I don't see any use in this. Every time we meet it's the same thing.'

Richard had sensed her momentary lapse into discouragement. He stood just in front of her, breathing heavily, his dark eyes narrowed. Then he slowly, sarcastically smiled. What's he trying to remind me of? Anna wondered. Surely it couldn't be—yes, it was. He was reminding her of that evening when she might, just possibly, have gone to bed with him. And instead of feeling angry, or contemptuous, she knew she was looking self-conscious. She said: 'Richard, please open the door.' He stood, maintaining his sarcastic pressure on her, enjoying it; then she went past him to the door and tried to push it open. She could see herself, awkward and flustered, uselessly pushing at the door. Then it opened: Richard had gone back to his desk and touched the appropriate button. Anna walked straight out, past the luxuriant secretary, Marion's probable successor, and descended through the cushioned gleaming carpeted foliaged centre of the building to the ugly street, which she greeted with relief.

She went to the nearest underground, not thinking, knowing she was in a state of near-collapse. The rush hour had begun. She was being jostled in a herd of people. Suddenly she was panicking, so badly that she withdrew from the people pressing towards the ticket booth, and stood, her palms and armpits wet, leaning against a wall. This had happened to her twice recently at rush hour. Something is happening to me, she thought, struggling for control. I'm only just managing to skate on the surface of something—but what? She remained by the wall, unable to move forward

388

into the crowd again. The city at rush hour—it was impossible for her to get from here, the five or six miles to her flat, in a hurry, save by the underground. No one could. They were all of them, all these people, caught by the terrible pressure of the city. All except Richard and people like him. If she went upstairs again and asked him to send her home by car, of course he would. He'd be delighted. And of course she would not. There was nothing for it except to make herself go forward. Anna forced herself forward, fitted herself into the press of people, waited her turn for a ticket, went down the escalator in an ooze of people. On the platform four trains came in before she was able to squeeze herself into a compartment. Now the worst was over. She had only to stand, held upright by the pressure of people, in the brightly lit, crammed, smelling place, and in ten or twelve minutes she would be at her home station. She was afraid she might faint.

She was thinking: If someone cracks up, what does that mean? At what point does a person about to fall to pieces say: I'm cracking up? And if I were to crack up, what form would it take? She shut her eyes, seeing the glare of the light on her lids, feeling the pressure of bodies, smelling sweat and dirt; and was conscious of Anna, reduced to a tight knot of determination somewhere in her stomach. Anna, Anna, I am Anna, she kept repeating; and anyway, I can't be ill or give way, because of Janet; I could vanish from the world tomorrow, and it wouldn't matter to anyone except to Janet. What then am I, Anna?—something that is necessary to Janet. But that's terrible, she thought, her fear becoming worse. That's bad for Janet. So try again: Who am I, Anna? Now she did not think of Janet, but shut her out. Instead she saw her room, long, white, subdued, with the coloured notebooks on the trestle table. She saw herself, Anna, seated on the music-stool, writing, writing; making an entry in one book, then ruling it off, or crossing it out; she saw the pages patterned with different kinds of writing; divided, bracketed, broken—she felt a swaying nausea; and then saw Tommy, not herself, standing with his lips pursed in concentration, turning the pages of her orderly notebooks.

She opened her eyes, giddy and afraid, and saw the sway of the glistening ceiling, a confusion of advertisements, and faces blank and staring with the effort of keeping a balance on the train. A face, six inches away: the flesh was yellowish grey and large-pored, the mouth crumpled-looking and damp. The eyes were fixed on hers. The face smiled, half frightened, half inviting. She thought: While I stood here with my eyes shut he was looking into my face and imagining it under him. She felt sick; turned her neck; and stared away from him. His uneven breath staled her cheek. There were still two stations to go. Anna edged herself away, inch by inch, feeling in the shake and sway of the train how the man pressed after her, his face sickly with excitement. He was ugly. Lord, but they are ugly, we are so ugly, thought Anna, her flesh, menaced by his nearness, crawling with repulsion. At the station she squeezed out of the train as others squeezed in; and the man stepped down after her, pressed behind her on to the escalator and stood behind her at the ticket barrier. She handed in her ticket and hastened on, turning to frown at him as he said just behind her: 'Like a walk? Like a walk?' He was grinning in triumph; in his fantasy he had humiliated and triumphed over her while she stood, eyes shut, on the train. She said: 'Go away,' and walked on and out of the underground into the street. He was still following her. Anna was frightened; and then she was amazed at herself—and frightened because she was afraid. What's happened to me? This happens every day, this is living in the city, it doesn't affect me—but it *was* affecting her; just as Richard's aggressive need to humiliate her had affected her, half an hour before, in his office. The knowledge that the man still followed her, grinning unpleasantly, made her want to break into a run of panic. She thought: If I could see something or touch something that wasn't ugly . . . there was a fruit barrow just ahead, offering tidy coloured loads of plums, peaches, apricots. Anna bought fruit: smelling at the tart clean smell, touching the smooth or faintly hairy skins. She was better. The panic had gone. The man who had been following her stood near, waiting and grinning; but now she was immune from him. She walked past him, immune.

She was late, but was not worried—Ivor would be there. During the time Tommy was in hospital, and Anna so often with Molly, Ivor had moved into their lives. From being the almost unknown young man who lived in the upper room, saying good night and good morning, coming and going with discretion, he had become Janet's friend. He had taken her to the pictures when Anna was at the hospital, he helped her with her homework, and he repeated to Anna that she should not worry, he was only too happy to look after Janet. And he was. And yet this new situation made Anna uneasy. Not on his account, or on Janet's, for with the child he showed the most simple, the most charming perception.

She was thinking now, as she climbed the ugly stairs to the door of her own flat: Janet needs a man in her life, she misses a father. Ivor's very kind to her. And yet because he's not a man—what do I mean when I say he's not a man? Richard's a man; Michael's a man. And yet Ivor isn't? I know that with 'a real man' there would be a whole area of tension, of wry understanding that there can't be with Ivor; there would be a whole dimension there isn't now; and yet he's charming with her, and so what do I mean by 'A real man'? For Janet adored Ivor. And she adored—or said that she did—his friend Ronnie.

Some weeks ago Ivor had asked if he could have a friend to share his room, who was short of money and out of a job. Anna had gone through the conventional motions of offering to put another bed in the room, and so on. Both sides had played their parts, but Ronnie, an actor out of work, had moved into Ivor's room and to his bed, and as it made no difference to Anna, she said nothing. Apparently Ronnie had every intention of staying for as long as she said nothing. Anna knew that Ronnie was the price she was expected to pay for Ivor's new friendship with Janet.

Ronnie was a dark graceful young man with carefully-waved glossy hair, and a white flashing smile, carefully prepared. Anna disliked him, but, realising she disliked the type rather than the person, controlled the feeling. He also was pleasant with Janet, but not (as Ivor was) from the heart; but out of policy. Probably his relation with Ivor was policy too. All this did not concern Anna, and it did not impinge on Janet, for she trusted Ivor that the child would never be shocked. And yet she was uneasy. Suppose I were living with a man—a 'real man'—or was married. There would certainly be tension for Janet. Janet would resent him, would have to accept him, have to come to terms. And the resentment would be precisely because of the quality of sex, of being a man. Or even if there was a man living here I didn't sleep with, or didn't want to sleep with, even then the business of his being 'a real man' would spark off tensions, set a balance. Well then? Why then should I feel that in fact I ought to have a real man and even for Janet's sake, let alone mine, instead of that charming friendly perceptive young man Ivor? Am I then saying, or assuming (is everyone assuming?); that children need the tension to grow up? But why? And yet I obviously do feel it, or I wouldn't be uneasy when I see Ivor with Janet because he's like a big friendly dog, or a sort of harmless elder brother—I use the word harmless. Contempt. I feel contempt. It's contemptible of me that I should. A real man—Richard? Michael? Both of them are very stupid with their children. And yet there is no doubt I feel that their quality, their liking women rather than men, would be better for Janet than what Ivor has.

Anna reached the cleanliness of her own flat from the dark and dusty stairs, and heard Ivor's voice over her head. He was reading to Janet. She passed the door of her big room, climbed the white staircase, and found Janet sitting cross-legged on her bed, a black-haired urchin of a girl, and Ivor, dark, shaggy and friendly, sitting on the floor, one hand raised, reading with emphasis a story about some girls' school. Janet shook her head at her mother, in a warning not to interrupt. Ivor, using his raised hand as a sort of baton, winked and raised his voice as he read: 'And so Betty put her name down for the hockey team. Would she be chosen? Would she be lucky?' He said to Anna in his normal voice: 'We'll call you when we're finished,' and went on: 'Everything depended on Miss Jackson. Betty wondered if she had been sincere when she wished her luck last Wednesday after the match? Had she really meant it?' Anna paused outside the door listening: there was a new quality in Ivor's voice: mockery. The mockery was aimed at the world of the girls' school, at the feminine world, not at the absurdity of the story; and had started from the moment Ivor had become aware of Anna's presence. Yes, but there was nothing new in that; that she was familiar with. Because the mockery, the defence of the homosexual, was nothing more than the polite over-gallantry of a 'real' man, the 'normal' man who intends to set bounds to his relationship with a woman, consciously or not. Usually unconsciously. It was the same cold evasive emotion, taken a step further; there was a difference in degree but not in kind. Anna glanced round the edge of the door at Janet, and saw the child's face showed a delighted but half-uneasy grin. She sensed the mockery being directed at her, a female. Anna directed the silent, compassionate thought towards her daughter: Well my poor girl, you'd better get used to it early, because you're going to have to live in a world full of it. And now that she, Anna, was well removed from the scene, Ivor's voice had lost its element of parody and gone back to normal.

The door into the room shared by Ivor and Ronnie was standing open. Ronnie was singing, also on a note of parody. It was a song being sung everywhere in tones of yearning, howling desire. 'Give me what I want tonight baby, I don't want you and me to fight baby, kiss me, squeeze me, etc.' Ronnie, too, was mocking 'normal' love; and on a jeering, common, gutter level. Anna thought: Why do I assume that all this won't touch Janet? Why do I take it for granted that children can't be corrupted? What it amounts to is, I'm certain that my influence, the healthy female influence, is strong enough to outweigh theirs. But why should I? She turned to go downstairs. Ronnie's voice stopped, and his head appeared around the angle of the door. It was a charming coiffured head, the head of a boyish young girl. He smiled, spitefully. He was saying, as clearly as he could, that he thought Anna had been spying on him: one of the disturbing things about Ronnie was that he always assumed that the things people said or did referred to him; and so one was always conscious of him. Anna nodded at him. She was thinking: In my home I can't move freely because of these two. I'm on the defensive all the time, in my own flat. Ronnie now chose to conceal his malice, and came out, standing negligently, his weight on one hip. 'Why Anna, I didn't know you, too, were partaking of the joys of children's hour?' 'I dropped up to see,' said Anna shortly. He was now the image of winning charm. 'Such a delightful child, your Janet.' He had remembered that he was living here for nothing, and dependent on Anna's good humour. He was now the very image of—well, yes, Anna thought—a well-brought-up young girl, almost lispingly correct. Very *jeune fille,* you are, Anna addressed him silently, giving him a smile which she intended to convey: You're not taking me in, and don't you think it. She went downstairs: a glance upwards, however, showed him still there, not looking at her, but staring at the wall of the stairs. His pretty, oh-so-neat little face was now haggard. With fear. Oh Christ, Anna thought; I can see what's going to happen already—I want him out, but I'm not going to have the heart to do it, because I'm going to be sorry for him, if I'm not careful.

She went into her kitchen, and ran a glass of water, slowly; running the water to watch it splash and sparkle, to hear its cool noise. She was using the water as she had used the fruit earlier—to calm herself, to assure herself of the possibility of normality. Yet all the time she was thinking: I'm right off balance. I feel as if the atmosphere of this flat were being poisoned, as if a spirit of perverse and ugly spite were everywhere. Yet it's nonsense. The truth is, everything I'm thinking at the moment is wrong. I can *feel* it is . . . and yet I'm saving myself by this sort of thinking. Saving myself from what? She felt ill again, and frightened, as she had on the tube. She thought: I've got to stop it, I simply must— though she could not have said what she had to stop. I'll go next door, she decided, and sit down, and—she did not finish the thought, but she had a mental image of a dry well, slowly filling up with water. Yes; that's what's wrong with me—I'm dry. I'm empty. I've got to touch some source somewhere or . . . she opened the door of her big room and there, black against the light from the windows, was a large female shape

394

which had something menacing about it. Anna said sharply: 'Who are you?' and turned on the light switch; so that the figure sprang into shape and personality against the defining light. 'Good Lord, Marion, is that you?' Anna sounded cross. She was confused because of her mistake, and looked closely at Marion because during all the years she had known her, she had seemed a pathetic figure, but never a menacing one. And as she did so she could *see* herself go through a process which, it seemed to her, she was now having to make use of a hundred times a day: she straightened herself, toughened herself, became wary; and because she was so tired, because 'the well was dry,' she set her brain on the alert, a small critical, dry machine. She could even feel that intelligence there, at work, defensive and efficient—a machine. And she thought: this intelligence, it's the only barrier between me and—but this time she did finish it, she knew how to end the sentence. Between me and cracking up. Yes.

Marion said: 'I'm sorry if I gave you a fright, but I came upstairs, and heard your young man reading to Janet and I didn't want to disturb them. And then I thought, how nice to sit in the dark.' Anna heard the words 'Your young man' which had a lisping coyness about them; as from a society matron, flattering a young woman?—she thought that within five minutes of meeting Marion there was always this jarring moment; and then reminded herself of the world Marion had been brought up in. She said: 'I'm sorry I sounded cross. I'm tired. I got caught in the rush hour.' She was drawing curtains, and restoring to her room the quiet severity she needed from it. 'But Anna, you're so spoiled, us poor ordinary people have to face these things every day.' Anna glanced, startled, at Marion, who had never, in the whole of her life, had to face anything as ordinary as rush hours. She saw Marion's face: innocent, bright-eyed, full of enthusiasm. She said: 'I need a drink, do you want one?'—remembered, then was glad she had forgotten, and offered Marion a drink with genuine casualness; for now she said: 'Oh yes, I'd love just a little one. Tommy says it's much braver to decide to drink just normally, instead of giving it up altogether. Do you think he's right? I do. I do think he's so clever and so strong.'

'Yes, but it must be very much more difficult.' Anna poured whisky into glasses, her back turned to Marion, trying to think: Is she here because she knows I've just seen Richard? And if another reason, what? She said, 'I've just come from seeing Richard,' and Marion said, taking her glass which she set beside her with an apparently genuine lack of interest: 'Have you? Well you always were such chums.' Anna refused to wince at the word chums; noted with alarm her own steadily rising irritation, strengthened the bright beam of her cold intelligence, and heard from upstairs Ivor's bellowing out: 'Shoot! shouted fifty eager voices and Betty, running for her life across the field, hit the ball straight into the goal. She had done it! The air rang with young cheering voices, and Betty saw the faces of her pals through a mist of happy tears.'

'I did so adore those marvellous school stories when I was a child,' said Marion, lisping girlishly.

'I loathed them.'

'But you always were such an intellectual little thing.'

Anna now sat down with her whisky and examined Marion. She was wearing an expensive brown suit, obviously new. Her dark, slightly greying hair was newly waved. Her hazel eyes were bright, her cheeks pink. She was the image of an abundant, happy, lively matron.

'And that's why I've come to see you,' Marion was saying. 'It was Tommy's idea. We need your help Anna. Tommy's had the most marvellous idea, I do think he's such a fine clever boy, and we both thought we should ask you.'

Here Marion took a sip of her whisky, made a small *moue* of pretty distaste, and put down the glass, chattering on: 'Thanks to Tommy I've just realised how awfully ignorant I am. It began with my reading the newspapers to him. I never read anything before. And of course he's so well-informed, and he explained things to me, and I really do feel quite a different person, and so ashamed that I never cared for anything but myself before.'

'Richard mentioned that you had become interested in politics.'

'Oh yes, and he's so cross. And of course mother and my

396

sisters are *furious*.' A naughty girl, she sat smiling, with naughty little compressions of the lips, and flickering guilty little glances from the corners of her eyes.

'I can imagine.' Marion's mother being the widow of a general, and her sisters all ladies or honourables, Anna could see what a pleasure it must be to annoy them.

'But of course they have no idea, none at all, any more than I had until Tommy took me in hand. I feel as if my life began from that moment. I feel a new person.'

'You look a new person.'

'I know I do. Anna, have you seen Richard today?'

'Yes—I told you—in his office.'

'Did he say anything about a divorce? I'm asking because if he said something to you, then I suppose I must take it seriously. He's always been threatening and bullying—he's a terrible bully. So I didn't take it seriously. But if he's really talking about it, then I suppose Tommy and I must take it seriously.'

'I think he wants to marry his secretary. Or so he said.'

'Have you seen her?' Marion positively giggled and looked roguish.

'Yes.'

'Did you notice anything?'

'That she looks like you did at her age?'

'Yes.' Marion giggled again. 'Isn't it funny?'

'If you think so.'

'Yes, I do.' Marion suddenly sighed and her face changed. Before Anna's eyes she changed from a little girl into a sombre woman. She sat staring: serious, ironical. 'Don't you see, I've *got* to think it's funny?' 'Yes, I do.' 'It happened all at once, at breakfast one morning. Richard's always been horrid at breakfast. He's always bad tempered and he nags at me. But the funny thing is, why did I let him? And he was going on and on, nagging away about me seeing Tommy so much. And suddenly, it was like a sort of revelation. It really was, Anna. He was sort of *bouncing* up and down the breakfast room. And his face was red. And he was so bad tempered. And I was listening to his voice. He's got an ugly voice, hasn't he? It's a bully's voice, isn't it?'

397

'Yes, it is.'

'And I thought—Anna I wish I could explain it. It was really a revelation. I thought: I've been married to him for years and years, and all that time I've been—wrapped up in him. Well women are, aren't they? I've thought of nothing else. I've cried myself to sleep night after night for years. And I've made scenes, and been a fool and been unhappy and ... The point is, what for? I'm serious Anna.' Anna smiled, and Marion went on: 'Because the point is, he's not anything, is he? He's not even very good-looking. He's not even very intelligent—I don't care if he is ever so important and a captain of industry. Do you see what I mean?' 'Well, and then?' 'I thought, My God, for that creature I've ruined my life. I remember the moment exactly. I was sitting at the breakfast-table, wearing a sort of negligee thing I'd bought because he likes me in that sort of thing—you know, frills and flowers, or well, he *used* to like me in them. I've always *hated* them. And I thought, for years and years I've even been wearing clothes I hated, just to please this *creature.*'

Anna laughed. Marion was laughing, her handsome face alive with self-critical irony, and her eyes sad and truthful. 'It's humiliating, isn't it Anna?'

'Yes, it is.'

'But I bet you've never made a fool of yourself about any stupid man. You've got too much sense.'

'That's what you think,' said Anna drily. But she saw this was a mistake; it was necessary for Marion to see her, Anna, as self-sufficient, and non-vulnerable.

Marion, not hearing what Anna had said, insisted: 'No, you've got too much sense, and that's why I admire you.' Marion now held her glass between tense fingers. She took a gulp of whisky; another, another, another—Anna forced herself not to look. She heard Marion's voice: 'And then there's that girl Jean. When I saw her it was another revelation. He's in love with her, so he says. But who's he in love with, that's the point. He's just in love with a type, something that strikes his box.' The crudity of the words *strikes his box,* surprising from Marion, made Anna look back at her. Marion sat tense, her large body rigid and upright in the chair, lips tight,

398

fingers claw-like around the empty glass into which she gazed, avidly.

'And so what's this love? He never loved me. He loves large brown-haired girls with large bosoms. I used to have a lovely bosom when I was young.'

'Nut-brown maid,' said Anna, watching the avid hand curl around the empty glass.

'Yes. And so it's got nothing to do with me. That's what I've decided. He probably doesn't even know what I'm like. And so why do we talk about love?'

Marion laughed, with difficulty. She put back her head and sat with her eyes shut: shut so tight that the brown lashes quivered on cheeks that were now haggard. Then her eyes opened, and blinked and searched; they were searching for the bottle of whisky which stood on the trestle table against the wall. If she asks me for another drink I shall have to give it to her, Anna thought. It was as if she, Anna, were involved with her whole self in Marion's silent struggle. Marion shut her eyes, gasped, opened them, looked at the bottle, twitched the empty glass between her fingers, shut her eyes again.

All the same, Anna thought, better for Marion to be a lush and a whole person; better a drunkard, and bitter and truthful than sober, if the price of being sober is that she must be an awful dripping coy little girl—the tension had become so painful she found herself breaking it with: 'What did Tommy want me to do?' Marion sat up, put down the glass, and in one moment changed from a sad, honest defeated woman into a little girl.

'Oh he's so marvellous, he's so marvellous about everything Anna. I told him Richard said he wanted a divorce and he was so marvellous.'

'What did he say?'

'He says I must do what's right, what I really believe to be right, and I mustn't humour Richard in an infatuation just because I think it would be high-minded or I want to be noble. Because my first reaction was, let him have a divorce, what's it matter to me? I've got enough money of my own, that's no problem. But Tommy said no, I must think what's best for Richard in the long run. And so I should make him

399

face up to his responsibilities.' 'I see.' 'Yes. He's so clear-headed. And when you think, he's just twenty-one. Though I suppose the terrible thing that happened to him accounts for it—I mean, it's terrible, but you can't even think it's a tragedy when you see him so brave and never giving way, and being such a marvellous person.' 'No, I suppose not.' 'And so Tommy says I shouldn't take any notice of Richard, just ignore him. Because I'm quite serious when I say I'm going to spend my life on bigger things. Tommy is showing me the way. I'm going to live for others and not myself.' 'Good.' 'And that's why I dropped in to see you. You must help Tommy and me.'

'Of course, what shall I do?'

'Do you remember that black leader, the African man you used to know? Mathews, or something like that?'

This was not at all what Anna had expected. 'You don't mean Tom Mathlong?'

Marion had actually taken out a notebook and was sitting with a poised pencil. 'Yes. Please give me his address.'

'But he's in prison,' said Anna. She sounded helpless. Hearing her own feebly objecting voice, she realised she felt not only helpless but frightened. It was the panic that assaulted her when with Tommy.

'Yes of course he's in prison, but what's its name?'

'But Marion, what are you planning to do?'

'I told you, I'm not going to live for myself any longer. I want to write to the poor thing, and see what I can do for him.'

'But Marion . . .' Anna looked at Marion, trying to make contact with the woman she had been talking to only a few minutes before. She was met by a gaze from brown eyes glazed with a guilty but happy hysteria. Anna went on, firmly: 'It's not a nice organised prison like Brixton or somewhere like that. It's probably a shack in the bush, hundreds of miles from anywhere, about fifty political prisoners, and very likely they don't even get letters. What did you think?—that they had visiting days and rights and things like that?'

Marion pouted and said: 'I think that's an awfully negative attitude to take about the poor things.'

Anna thought: negative attitude is Tommy's—echoes from the Communist Party; but poor things is all Marion's—probably her mother and sisters give old clothes to charities.

'I mean,' said Marion happily, 'it's a continent in chains, well, isn't it?' (*Tribune,* thought Anna; or possibly the *Daily Worker.*) 'And measures ought to be taken immediately to restore the Africans' faith in justice if it is not already too late.' (The *New Statesman,* thought Anna.) 'Well at least the situation ought to be thoroughly gone into in the interests of everybody.' (*The Manchester Guardian,* at a time of acute crisis.) 'But Anna, I don't understand your attitude. Surely you'll admit there's evidence that something's gone wrong?' (*The Times,* editorialising a week after the news that the white administration has shot twenty Africans and imprisoned fifty more without trial.)

'Marion, what's got into you?'

Marion sat anxiously leaning forward, her tongue exploring her smiling lips, blinking earnestly.

'Look, if you want to get involved in African politics, there are organisations you can join, Tommy must know that.'

'But the poor things, Anna,' Marion said, very reproachful.

Anna thought: Tommy's political development before his accident was so far in advance of the 'poor things' that either his mind has been seriously affected or . . . Anna sat silent, considering for the first time whether Tommy's mind had been affected.

'Tommy told you to come and ask me for the prison address of Mr Mathlong so that you and he could send the poor prisoners food parcels and consoling letters? He knows quite well they'd never reach the prison at all—apart from anything else.'

Marion's bright brown eyes, fixed on Anna, did not see her. Her girlish smile was directed towards some charming but wilful friend.

'Tommy said, your advice would be so useful. And we all three could work together for the common cause.'

Anna, beginning to understand, was angry. She said aloud,

drily: 'Tommy hasn't used the word "cause" except ironically for years. If he's using it now then . . .'

'But Anna, that sounds so cynical, it doesn't sound like you at all.'

'But you forget that all of us, including Tommy, have been plunged in the atmosphere of good causes for years, and I assure you that if we had always used the word with your reverence we would never have got anything done at all.'

Marion stood up. She looked extremely guilty, sly, and delighted with herself. Anna now understood that Marion and Tommy had discussed her, and had decided to save her soul. For what? She was quite extraordinarily angry. The anger was out of all proportion to what had actually happened; she knew it; and was all the more frightened.

Marion saw the anger, was both pleased and confused, and now said: 'I'm so sorry I've disturbed you for nothing.'

'Oh but it wasn't for nothing. Write a letter to Mr Mathlong, c/o Prison Administration, Northern Province. He won't get it of course, but it's the gesture that counts in these matters, isn't it?'

'Oh thank you, Anna, you're so helpful, we knew you would be. And now I must go.'

Marion left, creeping downstairs, in a way that parodied a guilty but defiant little girl's. Anna watched her and saw herself standing there, on the landing—cool, rigid, critical. Marion having gone out of sight, Anna went to the telephone and rang Tommy.

His voice came slow and formal over the half mile or so of streets. 'Double o five six seven?'

'This is Anna. Marion has just left. Tell me, was it really your idea to adopt African political prisoners as pen-pals? Because if so, I can't help feeling you are just a bit out of touch.'

A slight pause. 'I'm glad you rang me, Anna. I think it would be a good thing.'

'For the poor prisoners?'

'To be quite frank, I think it would be good for Marion. Don't you? I think she needs some interest outside herself.'

Anna said: 'A sort of therapy, you mean?'

'Yes. Don't you agree with me?'

'But Tommy, the point is, *I* don't think I need therapy—at least, not this particular kind.'

Tommy said carefully, after a pause: 'Thanks for ringing me up and giving me your views, Anna. I'm very grateful.'

Anna laughed, angrily. She expected him to laugh with her; but in spite of everything she had been thinking of the old Tommy, who would have laughed. She put down the receiver and stood trembling—she had to sit down.

Sitting, she thought: This boy, Tommy—I've known him since he was a child. He's had this terrible damage done to him—and yet now I see him as a sort of zombie, a menace, something to be frightened of. And we all feel it. No, he's not mad, that's not it, but he's turned into something else, something new . . . but I can't think about it now—later. I've got to give Janet her supper.

It was after nine, and Janet's supper overdue. Anna put food on a tray and took it upstairs, arranging her mind so that Marion and Tommy and what they represented were out of sight. For the time being.

Janet took the tray on her knees and said: 'Mother?'

'Yes.'

'Do you like Ivor?'

'Yes.'

'I like him very much. He's kind.'

'Yes he is.'

'Do you like Ronnie?'

'Yes,' said Anna, after a hesitation.

'But you don't really like him.'

'What makes you say that?' asked Anna, startled.

'I don't know,' said the child. 'I just thought you didn't like him. Because he makes Ivor behave in a silly way.' She said no more, but ate her supper in an abstracted thoughtfulness. She looked several times, very shrewd, at her mother, who sat, allowing herself to be shrewdly inspected, preserving a surface of calm competence.

When she had gone to sleep Anna descended to the kitchen and smoked over cups of tea. She was worrying now over Janet: Janet's upset by it all, but she doesn't know why she

403

is. But it's not Ivor—it's the atmosphere created by Ronnie. I could tell Ivor that Ronnie must go. He'll certainly offer to pay rent for Ronnie, but that isn't the point. I feel exactly as I did over Jemmie . . .

Jemmie was a student from Ceylon who had had the empty room upstairs for a couple of months. Anna disliked him, but couldn't bring herself to give him notice because he was coloured. The problem was solved in the end because he went back to Ceylon. And now Anna could not ask a couple of young men who were disturbing her peace of mind to leave, because they were homosexuals, and they, like a coloured student, would find it hard to get a room.

Yet why should Anna feel responsible? . . . It isn't as if one doesn't have enough trouble with 'normal' men, she said to herself, trying to dissipate her uneasiness with humour. But the humour failed. She tried again: It's my home, my home, my home—this time attempting to fill herself with strong proprietary emotions. This failed too: she sat thinking: Yet why do I have a home at all? Because I wrote a book I am ashamed of, and it made a lot of money. Luck, luck, that's all. And I hate all that—*my* home, *my* possessions, *my* rights. And yet come to the point where I'm uncomfortable, I fall back on it just like everyone else. Mine. Property. Possessions. I'm going to protect Janet because of *my* property. What's the use of protecting her? She will grow up in England, a country full of men who are little boys and homosexuals and the half-homosexuals . . . but this tired thought vanished in a strong wave of genuine emotion—By God, there are a few real men left, and I'm going to see she gets one of them. I'm going to see she grows up to recognise a real man when she meets one. Ronnie's going to have to leave.

With which she went to the bathroom, to get ready for bed. The lights were on. She stopped at the door. Ronnie stood anxiously peering into the mirror over the shelf where she kept her cosmetics. He was patting lotion on to his cheeks with her cottonwool, and trying to smooth out the lines on his forehead.

Anna said: 'Like my lotion better than yours?'

404

He turned, without surprise. She saw that he had intended her to find him there.

'My dear,' he said, graceful and coquettish, 'I was trying your lotion out. Does it do anything for you?'

'Not much,' said Anna. She leaned at the door, watching, waiting to be enlightened.

He was wearing an expensive silk dressing-gown in a soft hazy purple, with a reddish cravat tucked into it. He wore expensive red leather Moorish slippers, thonged with gold. He looked as if he should be in some harem, and not in this flat in the wastes of London's student-land. Now he stood with his head on one side, patting the waves of black, faintly greying hair with a manicured hand. 'I did try a rinse,' he remarked, 'but the grey shows through.'

'Distinguished, really,' said Anna. She had now understood: terrified that she might throw him out, he was appealing to her as one girl to another. She tried to tell herself she was amused. The truth was she was disgusted, and ashamed that she was.

'But my dear Anna,' he lisped winningly, 'looking distinguished is all very well, if one is—if I can put it that way—on the employing side.'

'But Ronnie,' Anna said, succumbing despite her disgust, and playing the role she was expected to play, 'you look very charming, in spite of the odd grey hair. I'm sure dozens of people must find you devastating.'

'Not as many as before,' he said. 'Alas, I must confess it. Of course I do pretty well, in spite of ups and downs, but I do have to take pretty good care of myself.'

'Perhaps you should find a permanent rich protector very soon.'

'Oh my dear,' he exclaimed, with a little writhing movement of the hips that was quite unconscious, 'you can't imagine that I haven't tried?'

'I didn't realise that the market was so badly oversupplied,' said Anna, speaking out of her disgust, and already ashamed of doing so before the words were out. Good Lord! she thought, to be born a Ronnie! to be born like that—I complain about the difficulties of being my kind of woman, but good Lord!—I might have been born a Ronnie.

He gave her a quick frank look full of hatred. He hesitated, an impulse was too strong for him, and he said: 'I think after all that I do prefer your lotion to mine.' He had his hand on the bottle, claiming it. He smiled at her sideways, challenging her, hating her openly.

She, smiling, put her hand out and took the bottle. "Well you'd better buy some of your own, hadn't you?'

And now his smile was quick, impertinent, and acknowledged that she had defeated him, that he hated her for it, that he proposed to try again soon. Then the smile faded and was succeeded by the cold haggard fear she had seen earlier. He was telling himself that his spiteful impulses were dangerous, and that he should be placating her, not challenging her.

He excused himself quickly, in a charming placating murmur, said good night, and tripped upstairs to Ivor.

Anna took her bath and went upstairs to see if Janet was settled for the night. The door into the young men's room stood open. Anna was surprised, knowing that they knew she came upstairs at this time every night to see Janet. Then she realised it was open on purpose. She heard: 'Fat buttocky cows . . .' That was Ivor's voice, and he added an obscene noise. Then Ronnie's voice: 'Sagging sweaty breasts . . .' And he made the sound of vomiting.

Anna, furious, was on the point of going forward to quarrel with them. She found herself, instead, shaken, trembling, and frightened. She crept downstairs, hoping they had not known she was there. But now they shut their door with a bang, and she heard shouts of laughter—from Ivor; and shrill graceful peals from Ronnie. She got into bed, appalled. At herself. For she saw that the obscene little play that had been prepared for her was nothing more than the night-face of Ronnie's girlishness, Ivor's big-dog friendliness, and that she might have deduced it all for herself without waiting to have it demonstrated. She was frightened because she was affected. She sat up in bed in the big dark room, smoking, and felt herself as vulnerable and helpless. She said again: If I cracked up then . . . The man on the train had shaken her;

406

the two young men upstairs had reduced her to trembling. A week ago, coming home late from the theatre, a man had exposed himself on a dark street corner. Instead of ignoring it, she had found herself shrinking inwardly, as if it had been a personal attack on Anna—she had felt as if she, Anna, had been menaced by it. Yet, looking back only a short time, she saw Anna who walked through the hazards and ugliness of the big city unafraid and immune. Now it seemed as if the ugliness had come close and stood so near to her she might collapse, screaming.

And when had this new frightened vulnerable Anna been born? She knew: it was when Michael had abandoned her.

Anna, frightened and sick, nevertheless grinned at herself, smiled at the knowledge that she, the independent woman, was independent and immune to the ugliness of perverse sex, violent sex, just so long as she was loved by a man. She sat in the dark grinning, or rather, forcing herself to grin, and thinking that there was no one in the world she could share this amusement with but Molly. Only Molly was in such trouble this was no moment to talk to her. Yes—she must ring up Molly tomorrow and talk to her about Tommy.

And now Tommy came back into the front of Anna's mind, with her worry over Ivor and Ronnie; and it was all too much. She crept in and under the clothes, clinging on to them.

The fact is, said Anna, trying to be calm about it, to herself: that I'm not fit to cope with anything. I stay above all this—chaos, because of this increasingly cold, critical, balancing little brain of mine. (Anna again saw her brain, like a cold little machine, ticking away in her head.)

She lay, frightened, and again the words came into her head: the spring has gone dry. And with the words, came the image: she saw the dry well, a cracked opening into the earth that was all dust.

Laying about her for something to hold on to, she clutched to the memory of Mother Sugar. Yes. I have to dream of water, she told herself. For what was the use of that long 'experience' with Mother Sugar if now, in time of drought,

407

she could not reach out for help. I must dream of water, I must dream of how to get back to the spring.

Anna slept and dreamed. She was standing on the edge of a wide yellow desert at midday. The sun was darkened by the dust hanging in the air. The sun was a baleful orange colour over the yellow dusty expanse. Anna knew she had to cross the desert. Over it, on the far side, were mountains—purple and orange and grey. The colours of the dream were extraordinarily beautiful and vivid. But she was enclosed by them, enclosed by these vivid dry colours. There was no water anywhere. Anna started off to walk across the desert, so that she might reach the mountains.

That was the dream she woke with in the morning; and she knew what it meant. The dream marked a change in Anna, in her knowledge of herself. In the desert she was alone, and there was no water, and she was a long way from the springs. She woke knowing that if she was to cross the desert she must shed burdens. She had gone to sleep confused about what to do about Ronnie and Ivor, but woke knowing what she would do. She stopped Ivor on his way out to work (Ronnie was still in bed, sleeping the just sleep of a petted mistress) and said: 'Ivor, I want you to go.' This morning he was pale, apprehensive, and appealing. He could not have said more clearly, without using the words to say it: I'm sorry, I'm in love with him and I can't help myself.

Anna said: 'Ivor, you must see that it can't go on.'

He said: 'I've been meaning to say this for some time— you've been so good, I really would like to pay you for Ronnie's being here.'

'No.'

'Whatever rent you say,' he said, and even now, while he was certainly ashamed of his last-night's personality, and above all frightened because his idyll might be shattered, he could not prevent the jeering mocking note coming back into his voice.

'Since Ronnie's been here weeks now, and I've never mentioned rent, it obviously isn't money,' said Anna, disliking the cold critical person who stood there, using this voice.

He hesitated again; his face the most remarkable mixture

of guilt, impertinence and fear. 'Look Anna, I'm terribly late for work. I'll drop down this evening and we'll talk it over.' He was already halfway down the stairs, he was bounding down them in desperation to get away from her, and his own impulse to jeer and provoke her.

Anna went back into her kitchen. Janet was eating her breakfast.

She asked: 'What were you talking to Ivor about?'

'I was suggesting he should go, or at least, that Ronnie should go.' She added quickly, for Janet was on the point of protesting: 'That room is for one person, not for two. And they're friends, they'd probably prefer to live together.'

To Anna's surprise Janet decided not to protest. She was quiet and thoughtful through the meal, as she had been at supper the night before. At the end of it she remarked: 'Why can't I go to school?'

'But you are at school.' 'No, I mean a real school. A boarding-school.' 'Boarding-schools aren't at all like that story Ivor was reading to you last night.' Janet seemed as if she might go on, but let the subject slip. She went off to her school as usual.

Ronnie descended the stairs a short time later, much earlier than he usually did. He was carefully dressed, and very pale under the faint rouge on his cheeks. For the first time he offered to shop for Anna. 'I'm awfully good at little jobs around the house.' When Anna refused, he sat in the kitchen chatting delightfully, and all the time his eyes pleaded with her.

But Anna was determined, and when Ivor came to her room that evening for the interview, she remained determined. So Ivor suggested Ronnie should leave and he should stay.

'After all, Anna, I've been here months and months, and we've never got in each other's hair before. I agree with you, Ronnie was asking a bit much. But he's moving out, I promise you.' Anna hesitated, and he pressed her: 'And there's Janet. I'd miss her. And I don't think I'm saying too much if I think she'd miss me. We saw an awful lot of each

409

other while you were so busy holding your poor friend's hand during that awful business with her son.'

Anna gave in. Ronnie left. He made an exhibition of leaving. It was made clear to Anna that she was a bitch for turning him out. (And she felt a bitch.) And it was made clear to Ivor that he had lost his mistress, whose minimum price was a roof over his head. Ivor resented Anna for his loss, and showed it. He sulked.

But Ivor's sulking meant that things returned to what they had been before Tommy's accident. They hardly saw him. He had become again the young man who said good evening and good morning when they met on the stairs. He was out most nights. Then Anna heard that Ronnie had failed to hold his new protector, had installed himself in a small room in a nearby street, and that Ivor was keeping him.

THE NOTEBOOKS

[The black notebook now fulfilled its original plan, for both sides had been written on. Under the left side heading, *The Source*, was written:]

11th November, 1955

Today on the pavement a fat domestic London pigeon waddling among the boots and shoes of people hurrying for a bus. A man takes a kick at it, the pigeon lurches into the air, falls forward against a lamppost, lies with its neck stretched out, its beak open. The man stands, bewildered: he had expected the pigeon to fly off. He casts a furtive look around, so as to escape. It is too late, a red-faced virago is already approaching him. 'You brute! Kicking a pigeon!' The man's face is by now also red. He grins from embarrassment and a comical amazement. 'They always fly away,' he observes, appealing for justice. The woman shouts: 'You've killed it—kicking a poor little pigeon!' But the pigeon is not dead, it is stretching out its neck by the lamppost, trying to lift its head, and its wings strive and collapse, again and again. By now there is a small crowd including two boys of about fifteen. They have the sharp watchful faces of the freebooters of the streets, and stand watching, unmoved, chewing gum. Someone says: 'Call the R.S.P.C.A.' The woman shouts: 'There'd be no need for that if this bully hadn't kicked the poor thing.' The man hangs about, sheepish, a criminal hated by the crowd. The only people not emotionally involved are the two boys. One remarks to the air: 'Prison's the place for criminals like 'im.' 'Yes, yes,' shouts the woman. She is so busy hating the kicker she doesn't look at the pigeon. 'Prison,' says the second boy, 'flogging, I'd say.' The woman now sharply examines the boys, and realises they are making fun of her. 'Yes, and you too!' she gasps at them, her voice almost squeezed out of her by her anger. 'Laughing while a poor little bird suffers.' By now the two boys are in fact grinning, though not in the same shame-faced incredulous way as the villain of the occasion. 'Laughing,' she says. 'Laughing. You *should* be flogged. Yes. It's true.' Meanwhile an efficient frowning man bends over the pigeon, and examines it. He straightens himself and pronounces: 'It's going to die.' He is right: the bird's eyes are filming, and blood wells from its open beak. And now the woman, forgetting her three objects of hatred, leans forward to look at the bird. Her mouth is slightly open, she has a look of unpleasant curiosity as the bird gasps, writhes its head, then goes limp.

'It's dead,' says the efficient man.

The villain, recovering himself, says apologetically, but clearly determined to have no nonsense: 'I'm sorry, but it was an accident. I've never seen a pigeon before that didn't move out of the way.'

We all look with disapproval at this hardened kicker of pigeons.

'An accident!' says the woman. 'An accident!'

But now the crowd is dissolving. The efficient man picks up the dead bird, but that's a mistake, for now he doesn't

411

know what to do with it. The kicker moves off, but the woman goes after him, saying: 'What's your name and address? I'm going to have you prosecuted.' The man says, annoyed: 'Oh, don't make such a mountain out of a molehill.' She says: 'I suppose you call murdering a poor little bird a molehill.' 'Well, it isn't a mountain, murder isn't a mountain,' observes one of the fifteen-year-olds, who stands grinning with his hands in his jacket pockets. His friend takes it up, sagaciously: 'You're right. Molehills is murder, but mountains isn't.' 'That's right,' says the first, 'when's a pigeon a mountain? When it's a molehill.' The woman turns on them, and the villain thankfully makes his escape, looking incredibly guilty, despite himself. The woman is trying to find the right words of abuse for the two boys, but now the efficient man stands holding the corpse, and looking helpless, and one of the boys asks derisively: 'You going to make pigeon pie, mister?' 'You cheek me and I'll call the police,' the efficient one says promptly. The woman is delighted, and says: 'That's right, that's right, they should have been called long ago.' One of the boys lets out a long, incredulous, jeering, admiring whistle. 'That's the ticket,' he says, 'call the coppers. They'll put you down for stealing a public pigeon, mister!' The two go off, rolling with laughter, but fast as they can without losing face, because the police have been mentioned.

The angry woman, the efficient man, the corpse, and a few bystanders remain. The man looks around, sees a rubbish receptacle on the lamppost, and moves forward to drop the dead bird into it. But the woman intercepts him, grasps the pigeon. 'Give it to me,' she says, her voice suffused with tenderness. 'I'll bury the poor little bird in my window-box.' The efficient man thankfully hurries off. She is left, looking down with disgust at the thick blood dropping from the beak of the pigeon.

12th November

Last night I dreamed of the pigeon. It reminded me of

412

something, I didn't know what. In my dream I was fighting to remember. Yet when I woke up I knew what it was—an incident from the Mashopi Hotel week-ends. I haven't thought of it for years, yet now it is clear and detailed. I am again exasperated because my brain contains so much that is locked up and unreachable, unless, by a stroke of luck, there is an incident like yesterday's. It must have been one of the intermediate week-ends, not the climacteric last week-end, for we were still on good terms with the Boothbys. I remember Mrs Boothby coming into the dining-room with a .22 rifle at breakfast and saying to our group: 'Can any of you shoot?' Paul said, taking the rifle: 'My expensive education has not failed to include the niceties of grouse and pheasant murder.' 'Oh, nothing so fancy like that,' said Mrs Boothby. 'There are grouse and pheasant about, but not too many. Mr Boothby mentioned he fancied a pigeon pie. He used to take out a gun now and then, but he's lost the figure for it, so I thought if you could oblige . . . ?'

Paul was handling the weapon quizzically. He finally said: 'Well, I'd never thought of shooting birds with a rifle, but if Mr Boothby can do it, so can I.'

'It's not hard,' said Mrs Boothby, as usual letting herself be taken in by the polite surface of Paul's manner. 'There's a small vlei down there between the kopjes that's full of pigeons. You let them settle and just pick them off.'

'It's not sporting,' said Jimmy, owlish.

'My God, it's not sporting!' cried Paul, playing up, clutching at his brow with one hand and holding the rifle away from him with the other.

Mrs Boothby was not sure whether to take him seriously, but she explained: 'It's fair enough. Don't shoot unless you're sure of killing, and then where's the harm?'

'She's right,' said Jimmy to Paul.

'You're right,' said Paul to Mrs Boothby. 'Dead right. We'll do it. How many pigeons for Host Boothby's pigeon pie?'

'There's not much use with less than six, but if you can get enough I can make pigeon pie for you as well. It'd make a change.'

'True,' said Paul. 'It *would* make a change. Rely on us.'

She thanked him, gravely, and left us with the rifle.

Breakfast was over, it was about ten in the morning, and we were glad to have something to fill our time until lunch. A short way past the hotel a track turned off the main road at right-angles and wandered ruttily over the veld, following the line of an earlier African footpath. This track led to the Roman Catholic Mission about seven miles off in the wilderness. Sometimes the Mission car came in for supplies; sometimes farm labourers went by in groups to or from the Mission, which ran a large farm, but for the most part the track was empty. All that country was high-lying sandveld, undulating, broken sharply here and there by kopjes. When it rained the soil seemed to offer resistance, not welcome. The water danced and drummed in a fury of white drops to a height of two or three feet over the hard soil, but an hour after the storm, it was already dry again and the gullies and vleis were running high and noisy. It had rained the previous night so hard that the iron roof of the sleeping block had shaken and pounded over our heads, but now the sun was high, the sky unclouded, and we walked beside the tarmac over a fine crust of white sand which broke drily under our shoes to show the dark wet underneath.

There were five of us that morning, I don't remember where the others were. Perhaps it was a week-end when only five of us had come down to the hotel. Paul carried the rifle, looking every inch a sportsman and smiling at himself in this role. Jimmy was beside him, clumsy, fattish, pale, his intelligent eyes returning always to Paul, humble with desire, ironical with pain at his situation. I, Willi and Maryrose came along behind. Willi carried a book. Maryrose and I wore holiday clothes—coloured dungarees and shirts. Maryrose wore blue dungarees and a rose-coloured shirt. I wore rose dungarees and a white shirt.

As soon as we turned off the main road on to the sand track we had to walk slowly and carefully, because this morning after the heavy rain there was a festival of insects. Everything seemed to riot and crawl. Over the low grasses a million white butterflies with greenish-white wings hovered and lurched. They were all white, but of different sizes. That morning a single species had hatched or sprung or crawled from their chrysalises, and were celebrating their freedom. And on the grass itself and all over the road were a certain species of brightly-coloured grasshopper, in couples. There were millions of them too.

'And one grasshopper jumped on the other grasshopper's back,' observed Paul's light but grave voice, just ahead. He stopped. Jimmy, beside him, obediently stopped too. We came to a standstill behind them both. 'Strange,' said Paul, 'but I've never understood the inner or concrete meaning of that song before.' It was grotesque, and we were all not so much embarrassed as awed. We stood laughing, but our laughter was too loud. In every direction, all around us, were the insects, coupling. One insect, its legs firmly planted on the sand, stood still; while another, apparently identical, was clamped firmly on top of it, so that the one underneath could not move. Or an insect would be trying to climb on top of another, while the one underneath remained still, apparently trying to aid the climber whose earnest or frantic heaves threatened to jerk both over sideways. Or a couple, badly-matched, would topple over, and the one that had been underneath would right itself and stand waiting while the other fought to resume its position, or another insect, apparenly identical, ousted it. But the happy or well-mated insects stood all around us, one above the other, with their bright round idiotic black eyes staring. Jimmy went off into fits of laughter, and Paul thumped him on the back. 'These extremely vulgar insects do not merit our attention,' observed Paul. He was right. One of these insects, or half a dozen, or a hundred would have seemed attractive, with their bright paint-box colours, half-submerged in thin emerald grasses. But in thousands, crude green and crude red, with the black blank eyes staring—they were absurd, obscene, and above all, the very emblem of stupidity. 'Much better watch the butterflies,' said Maryrose, doing so. They were extraordinarily beautiful. As far as we could see, the blue air was graced with white wings. And looking down into a distant vlei, the butterflies were a white glittering haze over green grass.

'But my dear Maryrose,' said Paul, 'you are doubtless imagining in that pretty way of yours that these butterflies are celebrating the joy of life, or simply amusing themselves, but such is not the case. They are merely pursuing vile sex, just like those ever-so-vulgar grasshoppers.'

'How do you know?' inquired Maryrose, in her small voice, very earnest; and Paul laughed his full-throated laugh which he knew was so attractive, and fell back and came beside her, leaving Jimmy alone in front. Willi, who had been squiring Maryrose, gave way to Paul and came to me, but I had already moved forward to Jimmy, who was forlorn.

'It really *is* grotesque,' said Paul, sounding genuinely put-out. We looked where he was looking. Among the army of grasshoppers were two obtrusive couples. One was an enormous powerful-looking insect, like a piston with its great spring-like legs, and on its back a tiny ineffectual mate, unable to climb high enough up. And next to it, the position reversed: a tiny bright pathetic grasshopper was straddled by, dwarfed, almost crushed by an enormous powerful driving insect. 'I shall try a small scientific experiment,' announced Paul. He stepped carefully among the insects to the grasses at the side of the road, laid down his rifle, and pulled a stem of grass. He went down on one knee in the sand, brushing insects aside with an efficient and indifferent hand. Neatly he levered the heavy-bodied insect off the small one. But it instantly sprang back to where it was, with a most surprisingly determined single leap. 'We need two for this operation,' announced Paul. Jimmy was at once tugging at a grass-stem, and took his place beside him, although his face was wrenched with loathing at having to bend down so close to the swarm. The two young men were now kneeling on the sandy road, operating their grass-stems. I and Willi and Maryrose stood and watched. Willi was frowning. 'How frivolous,' I remarked, ironical. Although, as usual, we were not on particularly good terms that morning, Willi allowed himself to smile at me and said with real amusement: 'All the same, it is interesting.' And we smiled at each other, with affection and with pain because these moments were so seldom. And across the kneeling boys Maryrose watched us,

416

with envy and pain. She was seeing a happy couple and feeling shut out. I could not bear it, and I went to Maryrose, abandoning Willi. Maryrose and I bent over the backs of Paul and Jimmy and watched.

'Now,' said Paul. Again he lifted his monster off the small insect. But Jimmy was clumsy and failed, and before he could try again Paul's big insect was back in position. 'Oh, you idiot,' said Paul, irritated. It was an irritation he usually suppressed, because he knew Jimmy adored him. Jimmy dropped the grass-stem and laughed painfully, tried to cover up his hurt—but by now Paul had grasped the two stems, had levered the two covering insects, large and small, off the two others, large and small, and now they were two well-matched couples, two big insects together and two small ones.

'There,' said Paul. 'That's the scientific approach. How neat. How easy. How satisfactory.'

There we all stood, the five of us, surveying the triumph of common-sense. And we all began to laugh again, helplessly, even Willi; because of the utter absurdity of it. Meanwhile all around us thousands and thousands of painted grasshoppers were getting on with the work of propagating their kind without any assistance from us. And even our small triumph was soon over, because the large insect that had been on top of the other large insect, fell off, and immediately the one which had been underneath mounted him or her.

'Obscene,' said Paul gravely.

'There is no evidence,' said Jimmy, trying to match his friend's light grave tone, but failing, since his voice was always breathless, or shrill, or too facetious: 'There is no evidence that in what we refer to as nature things are any better-ordered than they are with us. What evidence have we that all these—miniature troglodites are nicely sorted out male above female? Or even—' he added daringly, on his fatally wrong note '—male with female at all? For all we know, this is a riot of debauchery, males with males, females with females . . .' He petered out in a gasp of laughter. And looking at his heated, embarrassed, intelligent face, we all knew that he was wondering why it was that nothing he ever

said, or could say, sounded easy, as when Paul said it. For if
Paul had made that speech, as he might very well have done,
we would all have been laughing. Instead of which we were
uncomfortable, and were conscious that we were hemmed in
by these ugly scrambling insects.

Suddenly Paul sprang over and trod deliberately, first on
the monster couple, whose mating he had organised, and then
on the small couple.

'Paul,' said Maryrose, shaken, looking at the crushed mess
of coloured wings, eyes, white smear.

'A typical response of a sentimentalist,' said Paul, deliberately parodying Willi—who smiled, acknowledging that he
knew he was being mocked. But now Paul said seriously:
'Dear Maryrose, by tonight, or to stretch a point, by tomorrow night, nearly all these things will be dead—just like your
butterflies.'

'Oh no,' said Maryrose, looking at the dancing clouds of
butterflies with anguish, but ignoring the grasshoppers. 'But
why?'

'Because there are too many of them. What would happen
if they all lived? It would be an invasion. The Mashopi
Hotel would vanish under a crawling mass of grasshoppers, it
would be crushed to the earth, while inconceivably ominous
swarms of butterflies danced a victory dance over the deaths
of Mr and Mrs Boothby and their marriageable daughter.'

Maryrose, offended and pale, looked away from Paul. We
all knew she was thinking about her dead brother. At such
moments she wore a look of total isolation, so that we all
longed to put our arms around her.

Yet Paul continued, and now he began by parodying
Stalin: 'It is self-evident, it goes without saying—and in fact
there is no need at all to say it, so why should I go to the
trouble?—However, whether there is any need to say a thing
or not is clearly besides the point. As is well-known, I say,
nature is prodigal. Before many hours are out, these insects
will have killed each other by fighting, biting, deliberate
homicide, suicide, or by clumsy copulation. Or they will have
been eaten by birds which even at this moment are waiting
for us to remove ourselves so that they can begin their feast.

When we return to this delightful pleasure resort next week-end, or, if our political duties forbid, the week-end after, we shall take our well-regulated walks along this road and see perhaps one or two of these delightful red and green insects at their sport in the grass, and think, how pretty they are! And little will we reck of the million corpses that even then will be sinking into their last resting place all about us. I do not even mention the butterflies who, being incomparably more beautiful, though probably not more useful, we will actively, even assiduously miss—if we are not more occupied with our more usual decadent diversions.'

We were wondering why he was deliberately twisting the knife in the wound of Maryrose's brother's death. She was smiling painfully. And Jimmy, tormented continuously by fear that he would crash and be killed, had the same small wry smile as Maryrose.

'The point I am trying to make comrades . . .'

'We know what point you are trying to make,' said Willi, roughly and angrily. Perhaps it was for moments like these that he was the 'father-figure' of the group, as Paul said he was. 'Enough,' said Willi. 'Let's go and get the pigeons.'

'It goes without saying, it is self-evident,' said Paul, return-ing to Stalin's favourite opening phrases just so as to hold his own against Willi, 'that mine host Boothby's pigeon pie will never get made, if we go on in this irresponsible fashion.'

We proceeded along the track, among the grasshoppers. About half a mile further on there was a small kopje, or tumbling heap of granite boulders; and beyond it, as if a line had been drawn, the grasshoppers ceased. They were simply not there, they did not exist, they were an extinct species. The butterflies, however, continued everywhere, like white petals dancing.

I think it must have been October or November. Not because of the insects, I'm too ignorant to date the time of the year from them, but because of the quality of the heat that day. It was a sucking, splendid, menacing heat. Late in a rainy season there would have been a champagne tang in the air, a warning of winter. But that day I remember the heat was striking our cheeks, our arms, our legs even, through our

419

clothing. Yes, of course it must have been early in the season, the grass was short, tufts of clear sharp green in white sand. So that week-end was four or five months before the final one, which was just before Paul was killed. And the track we strolled along that morning was where Paul and I ran hand in hand that night months later through a fine seeping mist to fall together in the damp grass. Where? Perhaps near where we sat to shoot pigeons for the pie.

We left the small kopje behind, and now a big one rose ahead. The hollow between the two was the place Mrs Boothby had said was visited by pigeons. We struck off the track to the foot of the big kopje, in silence. I remember us walking, silent, with the sun stinging our backs. I can *see* us, five small brightly coloured young people, walking in the grassy vlei through reeling white butterflies under a splendid blue sky.

At the foot of the kopje stood a clump of large trees under which we arranged ourselves. Another clump stood about twenty yards away. A pigeon cooed somewhere from the leaves in this second clump. It stopped at the disturbance we made, decided we were harmless and cooed on. It was a soft, somnolent drugging sound, hypnotic, like the sound of cica-dae, which—now that we were listening—we realised were shrilling everywhere about us. The noise of cicadae is like having malaria and being full of quinine, an insane incessant shrilling noise that seems to come out of the ear-drums. Soon one doesn't hear it, as one ceases to hear the fevered shrilling of quinine in the blood.

'Only one pigeon,' said Paul. 'Mrs Boothby has misled us.'

He rested his rifle barrel on a rock, sighted the bird, tried without the support of the rock, and just when we thought he would shoot, laid the rifle aside.

We prepared for a lazy interval. The shade was thick, the grass soft and springy and the sun climbing towards midday position. The kopje behind us towered up into the sky, dominating, but not oppressive. The kopjes in this part of the country are deceptive. Often quite high, they scatter and diminish on approach, because they consist of groups or piles of rounded granite boulders; so that standing at the base of a kopje one might very well see clear through a crevice or small ravine to the vlei on the other side, with great, toppling glistening boulders soaring up like a giant's pile of pebbles. This kopje, as we knew, because we had explored it, was full of the earthworks and barricades built by the Mashona seventy, eighty years before as a defence against the raiding Matabele. It was also full of magnificent Bushman paintings. At least, they had been magnificent until they had been defaced by guests from the hotel who had amused themselves throwing stones at them.

'Imagine,' said Paul. 'Here we are, a group of Mashona, besieged. The Matabele approach, in all their horrid finery. We are outnumbered. Besides, we are not, so I am told, a warlike folk, only simple people dedicated to the arts of peace, and the Matabele always win. We know, we men, that we will die a painful death in a few moments. You lucky women, however, Anna and Maryrose, will merely be dragged off by new masters in the superior tribe of the altogether more warlike and virile Matabele.'

'They would kill themselves first,' said Jimmy. 'Wouldn't you, Anna? Wouldn't you, Maryrose?'

'Of course,' said Maryrose, good-humoured.

'Of course,' I said.

The pigeon cooed on. It was visible, a small, shapely bird, dark against the sky. Paul took up the rifle, aimed and shot. The bird fell, turning over and over with loose wings, and hit earth with a thud we could hear from where we sat. 'We need a dog,' said Paul. He expected Jimmy to leap up and fetch it. Although we could see Jimmy struggling with himself, he in fact got up, walked across to the sister clump of trees, retrieved the now graceless corpse, flung it at Paul's feet, and sat down again. The small walk in the sun had flushed him, and caused great patches to appear on his shirt. He pulled it off. His torso, naked, was pale, fattish, almost childish. 'That's better,' he said, defiantly, knowing we were looking at him, and probably critically.

The trees were now silent. 'One pigeon,' said Paul. 'A toothsome mouthful for our host.'

From trees far away came the sound of pigeons cooing, a

murmuring gentle sound. 'Patience,' said Paul. He rested his rifle again and smoked.

Meanwhile, Willi was reading. Maryrose lay on her back, her soft gold head on a tuft of grass, her eyes closed. Jimmy had found a new amusement. Between isolated tufts of grass was a clear trickle of sand where water had coursed, probably last night in the storm. It was a miniature river-bed, about two feet wide, already bone dry from the morning's sun. And on the white sand were a dozen round shallow depressions, but irregularly spaced and of different sizes. Jimmy had a fine strong grass-stem, and, lying on his stomach, was wriggling the stem around the bottom of one of the larger depressions. The fine sand fell continuously in avalanches, and in a moment the exquisitely regular pit was ruined.

'You clumsy idiot,' said Paul. He sounded, as always in these moments with Jimmy, pained and irritated. He really could not understand how anybody could be so awkward. He grabbed the stem from Jimmy, poked it delicately at the bottom of another sand-pit, and in a second had fished out the insect which made it—a tiny ant-eater, but a big specimen of its kind, about the size of a large match-head. This insect, toppling off Paul's grass-stem on to a fresh patch of white sand, instantly jerked itself into frantic motion, and in a moment had vanished beneath the sand which heaved and sifted over it.

'There,' said Paul roughly to Jimmy, handing back his stem. Paul looked embarrassed at his own crossness; Jimmy, silent and rather pale, said nothing. He took the stem and watched the heaving of the minute patch of sand.

Meanwhile we had been too absorbed to notice that two new pigeons had arrived in the trees opposite. They now began to coo, apparently without any intention of co-ordination, for the two streams of soft sound continued, sometimes together, sometimes not.

'They are very pretty,' said Maryrose, protesting, her eyes still shut.

'Nevertheless, like your butterflies, they are doomed.' And Paul raised his rifle and shot. A bird fell off a branch, this time like a stone. The other bird, startled, looked around, its sharp head turning this way and that, an eye cocked up sky-wards for a possible hawk that had swooped and taken off its comrade, then cocked earth-wards where it apparently failed to identify the bloody object lying in the grass. For after a moment of intense waiting silence, during which the bolt of the rifle snapped, it began again to coo. And immediately Paul raised his gun and shot and it, too, fell straight to the ground. And now none of us looked at Jimmy, who had not glanced up from his observation of his insect. There was already a shallow, beautifully regular pit in the sand, at the bottom of which the invisible insect worked in tiny heaves. Apparently Jimmy had not noticed the shooting of the two pigeons. And Paul did not look at him. He merely waited, whistling very softly, frowning. And in a moment, without looking at us or at Paul, Jimmy began to flush, and then he clambered up, walked across to the trees, and came back with the two corpses.

'We don't need a dog after all,' remarked Paul. It was said before Jimmy was half-way back across the grass, yet he heard it. I should imagine that Paul had not intended him to hear, yet did not particularly care that he had. Jimmy sat down again, and we could see the very white thick flesh of his shoulders had begun to flush scarlet from the two short journeys in the sun across the bright grass. Jimmy went back to watching his insect.

There was again an intense silence. No doves could be heard cooing anywhere. Three bleeding bodies lay tumbled in the sun by a small jutting rock. The grey rough granite was patched and jewelled with lichens, rust and green and purple; and on the grass lay thick glistening drops of scarlet.

There was a smell of blood.

'Those birds will go bad,' remarked Willi, who had read steadily during all this.

'They are better slightly high,' said Paul.

I could see Paul's eyes hover towards Jimmy, and see Jimmy struggling with himself again, so I quickly got up and threw the limp wing-dragging corpses into the shade.

423

By now there was a prickling tension between us all, and Paul said: 'I want a drink.'

'It's an hour before the pub opens,' said Maryrose.

'Well, I can only hope that the requisite number of victims will soon offer themselves, because at the stroke of opening time I shall be off. I shall leave the slaughter to someone else.'

'None of us can shoot as well as you,' said Maryrose.

'As you know perfectly well,' said Jimmy, suddenly spiteful.

He was observing the rivulet of sand. It was now hard to tell which ant-pit was the new one. Jimmy was staring at a largish pit, at the bottom of which was a minute hump—the body of the waiting monster; and a tiny black fragment of twig—the jaws of the monster. 'All we need now is some ants,' said Jimmy. 'And some pigeons,' said Paul. And, replying to Jimmy's criticism, he added: 'Can I help my natural talents? The Lord gives. The Lord takes. In my case, He has given.'

'Unfairly,' I said. Paul gave me his charming wry appreciative smile. I smiled back. Without raising his eyes from his book, Willi cleared his throat. It was a comic sound, like bad theatre, and both I and Paul burst out into one of the wild helpless fits of laughing that often took members of the group, singly, in couples, or collectively. We laughed and laughed, and Willi sat reading. But I remember now the hunched enduring set of his shoulders, and the tight painful set of his lips. I did not choose to notice it at the time.

Suddenly there was a wild shrill silken cleaving of wings and a pigeon settled fast on a branch almost above our heads. It lifted its wings to leave again at the sight of us, folded them, turned round on its branch several times, with its head cocked sideways looking down at us. Its black bright open eyes were like the round eyes of the mating insects on the track. We could see the delicate pink of its claws gripping the twig, and the sheen of sun on its wings. Paul lifted the rifle—it was almost perpendicular—shot, and the bird fell among us. Blood spattered over Jimmy's forearm. He went pale again, wiped it off, but said nothing.

'This is getting disgusting,' said Willi.

'It has been from the start,' said Paul composedly.

He leaned over, picked the bird off the grass and examined it. It was still alive. It hung limp, but its black eyes watched us steadily. A film rolled up over them, then with a small perceptible shake of determination it pushed death away and struggled for a moment in Paul's hands. 'What shall I do?' Paul said, suddenly shrill; then, instantly recovering himself with a joke: 'Do you expect me to kill the thing in cold blood?'

'Yes,' said Jimmy, facing Paul and challenging him. The clumsy blood was in his cheeks again, mottling and blotching them, but he stared Paul out.

'Very well,' said Paul, contemptuous, tight-lipped. He held the pigeon tenderly, having no idea how to kill it. And Jimmy waited for Paul to prove himself. Meanwhile the bird sank in a glossy welter of feathers between Paul's hands, its head sinking on its neck, trembling upright again, sinking sideways, as the pretty eyes filmed over and it struggled again and again to defeat death.

Then, saving Paul the ordeal, it was suddenly dead, and Paul flung it on to the heap of corpses.

'You are always so damned lucky about everything,' said Jimmy, in a trembling, angry voice. His full carved mouth, the lips he referred to with pride as 'decadent,' visibly shook.

'Yes, I know,' said Paul. 'I know it. The Gods favour me. Because I'll admit to you, dear Jimmy, that I could not have brought myself to wring this pigeon's neck.'

Jimmy turned away, suffering, to his observation of the ant-eaters' pits. While his attention had been with Paul, a very tiny ant, as light as a bit of fluff, had fallen over the edge of a pit and was at this moment bent double in the jaws of the monster. This drama of death was on such a small scale that the pit, the ant-eater and the ant could have been accommodated comfortably on a small finger-nail—Mary-rose's pink little finger-nail for instance.

The tiny ant vanished under a film of white sand, and in a moment the jaws appeared, clean and ready for further use.

Paul ejected the case from his rifle and inserted a bullet

with a sharp snap of the bolt. 'We have two more to get before we satisfy Ma Boothby's minimum needs,' he remarked. But the trees were empty, standing full and silent in the hot sun, all their green boughs light and graceful, very slightly moving. The butterflies were now noticeably fewer; a few dozen only danced on in the sizzling heat. The heat-waves rose like oil off the grass, the sand patches, and were strong and thick over the rocks that protruded from the grass.

'Nothing,' said Paul. 'Nothing happens. What tedium.'

Time passed. We smoked. We waited. Maryrose lay flat, eyes closed, delectable as honey. Willi read, doggedly improving himself. He was reading *Stalin on the Colonial Question.*

'Here's another ant,' said Jimmy, excited. A larger ant, almost the size of the ant-eater, was hurrying in irregular dashes this way and that between grass-stems. It moved in the irregular apparently spasmodic way that a hunting dog does when scenting. It fell straight over the edge of the pit, and now we were in time to see the brown shining jaws reach up and snap the ant across the middle, almost breaking it in two. A struggle. White drifts of sand down the sides of the pit. Under the sand they fought. Then stillness.

'There is something about this country,' said Paul, 'that will have marked me for life. When you think of the sheltered upbringing nice boys like Jimmy and I have had—our nice homes and public school and Oxford, can we be other than grateful for this education into the realities of nature red in beak and claw?'

'I'm not grateful,' said Jimmy. 'I hate this country.'

'I adore it. I owe it everything. Never again will I be able to mouth the liberal and high-minded platitudes of my democratic education. I know better now.'

Jimmy said: 'I may know better, but I shall continue to mouth high-minded platitudes. The very moment I get back to England. It can't be too soon for me. Our education has prepared us above all for the long littleness of life. What else has it prepared us for? Speaking for myself, I can't wait for the long littleness to begin. When I get back—if I ever do get back that is, I shall . . .'

'Hallo,' exclaimed Paul, 'here comes another bird. No it

doesn't.' A pigeon cleaved towards us, saw us, and swerved off and away in mid-air, nearly settled on the other clump of trees, changed its mind and sped into the distance. A group of farm labourers were passing on the track a couple of hundred yards off. We watched them, in silence. They had been talking and laughing until they saw us, but now they, too, were silent, and went past with averted faces, as if in this way they might avert any possible evil that might come from us, the white people.

Paul said softly: 'My God, my God, my God.' Then his tone changed, and he said jauntily: 'Looking at it objectively, with as little reference as we can manage to Comrade Willi and his ilk—Comrade Willi, I'm inviting you to consider something objectively.' Willi laid down his book, prepared to show irony. 'This country is larger than Spain. It contains one and a half million blacks, if one may mention them at all, and one hundred thousand whites. That, in itself, is a thought which demands two minutes silence. And what do we see? One might imagine—one would have every excuse for imagining, despite what you say, Comrade Willi, that this insignificant handful of sand on the beaches of time—not bad, that image?—unoriginal, but always apt—this million-and-a-little-over-a-half people exist in this pretty piece of God's earth solely in order to make each other miserable. . . .' Here Willie picked up his book again and applied his attention to it. 'Comrade Willi, let your eyes follow the print but let the ears of your soul listen. For the *facts* are—the *facts*—that there's enough food here for everyone!—enough materials for houses for everyone!—enough talent though admittedly so well hidden under bushels at the moment that nothing but the most generous eye could perceive it—enough talent, I say, to create light where now darkness exists.'

'From which you deduce?' said Willi.

'I deduce nothing. I am being struck by a new . . . it's a blinding light, nothing less . . .'

'But what you say is the truth about the whole world, not just this country,' said Maryrose.

'Magnificent Maryrose! Yes. My eyes are being opened to—Comrade Willi, would you not say that there is some principle at work not yet admitted to your philosophy? Some principle of destruction?'

Willi said, in exactly the tone we had all expected: 'There is no need to look any further than the philosophy of the class struggle,' and as if he'd pressed a button, Jimmy, Paul and I burst out into one of the fits of irrepressible laughter that Willi never joined.

'I'm delighted to see,' he remarked, grim-mouthed, 'that good socialists—at least two of you call yourselves socialists, should find that so very humorous.'

'I don't find it humorous,' said Maryrose.

'You never find anything humorous,' said Paul. 'Do you know that you never laugh, Maryrose? Never? Whereas I, whose view of life can only be described as morbid, and increasingly morbid with every passing minute, laugh continuously? How would you account for that?'

'I have no view of life,' said Maryrose, lying flat, looking like a neat soft little doll in her bright bibbed trousers and shirt. 'Anyway,' she added, 'you weren't laughing. I listen to you a lot—' (she said this as if she were not one of us, but an outsider) '—and I've noticed that you laugh most when you're saying something terrible. Well I don't call that laughing.'

'When you were with your brother, did you laugh, Maryrose? And when you were with your lucky swain in the Cape?'

'Yes.'

'Why?'

'Because we were happy,' said Maryrose simply.

'Good God,' said Paul in awe. 'I couldn't say that. Jimmy, have you ever laughed because you were happy?'

'I've never been happy,' said Jimmy.

'You, Anna?'

'Nor me.'

'Willi?'

'Certainly,' said Willi, stubborn, defending socialism, the happy philosophy.

'Maryrose,' said Paul, 'you were telling the truth. I don't

believe Willi but I believe you. You are very enviable Maryrose, in spite of everything. Do you know that?'

'Yes,' said Maryrose. 'Yes, I think I'm luckier than any of you. I don't see anything wrong with being happy. What's wrong with it?'

Silence. We looked at each other. Then Paul solemnly bowed towards Maryrose: 'As usual,' he said humbly, 'we have nothing to say in reply.'

Maryrose closed her eyes again. A pigeon alighted fast on a tree in the opposite clump. Paul shot and missed. 'A failure,' he exclaimed, mock tragic. The bird stayed where it was, surprised, looking about it, watching a leaf dislodged by Paul's bullet float down to the earth. Paul ejected his empty case, refilled at leisure, aimed, shot. The bird fell. Jimmy obstinately did not move. He did not move. And Paul, before the battle of wills could end in defeat for himself, gained victory by rising and remarking: 'I shall be my own retriever.' And he strolled off to fetch the pigeon; and we all saw that Jimmy had to fight with himself to prevent his limbs from jumping him up and over the grass after Paul, who came back with the dead bird yawning, flinging it with the other dead birds.

'There's such a smell of blood I shall be sick,' said Maryrose.

'Patience,' said Paul. 'Our quota is nearly reached.'

'Six will be enough,' said Jimmy. 'Because none of us will eat this pie. Mr Boothby can have the lot.'

'I shall certainly eat of it,' said Paul. 'And so will you. Do you really imagine that when that toothsome pie, filled with gravy and brown savoury meat, is set before you, that you will remember the tender songs of these birds so brutally cut short by the crack of doom?'

'Yes,' said Maryrose.

'Yes,' I said.

'Willi?' asked Paul, making an issue of it.

'Probably not,' said Willi, reading.

'Women are tender,' said Paul. 'They will watch us eat, toying the while with Mrs Boothby's good roast beef, making delicate little mouths of distaste, loving us all the more for our brutality.'

'Like the Mashona women and the Matabele,' said Jimmy.

'I like to think of those days,' said Paul, settling down with his rifle at the ready, watching the trees. 'So simple. Simple people killing each other for good reasons, land, women, food. Not like us. Not like us at all. As for us—do you know what is going to happen? I will tell you. As a result of the work of fine comrades like Willi, ever-ready to devote themselves to others, or people like me, concerned only with profits, I predict that in fifty years all this fine empty country we see stretching before us filled only with butterflies and grasshoppers will be covered by semi-detached houses filled by well-clothed black workers.'

'And what is the matter with that?' enquired Willi.

'It is progress,' said Paul.

'Yes it is,' said Willi.

'Why should they be semi-detached houses?' enquired Jimmy, very seriously. He had moments of being serious about the socialist future. 'Under a socialist government there'll be beautiful houses in their own gardens or big flats.'

'My dear Jimmy!' said Paul. 'What a pity you are so bored by economics. Socialist or capitalist—in either case, all this fine ground, suitable for development, will be developed at a rate possible for seriously undercapitalised countries—are you listening, Comrade Willi?'

'I am listening.'

'And because a government faced with the necessity of housing a lot of un-housed people fast, whether socialist or capitalist, will choose the cheapest available houses, the best being the enemy of the better, this fair scene will be one of factories smoking into the fair blue sky, and masses of cheap identical housing. Am I right, Comrade Willi?'

'You are right.'

'Well then?'

'It's not the point.'

'It's my point. That is why I dwell on the simple savagery of the Matabele and the Mashona. The other is simply too hideous to contemplate. It is the reality for our time, socialist or capitalist—well, Comrade Willi?'

Willi hesitated, then said: 'There will be certain outward similarities but . . .' He was interrupted by Paul and myself, then Jimmy, in a fit of laughter.

Maryrose said to Willi: 'They're not laughing at what you say, but because you always say what they expect.'

'I am aware of that,' said Willi.

'No,' said Paul, 'you are wrong Maryrose. I'm also laughing at what he's saying. Because I'm horribly afraid it's not true. God forbid, I should be dogmatic about it, but I'm afraid that—as for myself, from time to time I shall fly out from England to inspect my overseas investments and peradventure I shall fly over this area, and I shall look down on smoking factories and housing estates and I shall remember these pleasant, peaceful pastoral days and . . .' A pigeon landed on the trees opposite. Another and another. Paul shot. A bird fell. He shot, the second fell. The third burst out of a bunch of leaves skywards as if it had been shot from a catapult. Jimmy got up, walked over, brought back two bloodied birds, flung them down with the others and said: 'Seven. For God's sake, isn't it enough?'

'Yes,' said Paul, laying aside his rifle. 'And now let's make tracks fast for the pub. We shall just have time to wash the blood off before it opens.'

'Look,' said Jimmy. A small beetle about twice the size of the largest ant-eater was approaching through the towering grass-stems.

'No good,' said Paul, 'that is not a natural victim.'

'Maybe not,' said Jimmy. He twitched the beetle into the largest pit. There was a convulsion. The glossy brown jaws snapped on the beetle, the beetle jumped up, dragging the ant-eater half-way up the sides of the pit. The pit collapsed in a wave of white sand, and for a couple of inches all around the suffocating silent battle the sand heaved and eddied.

'If we had ears that could hear,' said Paul, 'the air would be full of screams, groans, grunts and gasps. But as it is, there reigns over the sunbathed veld the silence of peace.'

A cleaving of wings. A bird alighted.

'No don't,' said Maryrose in pain, opening her eyes and raising herself on her elbow. But it was too late. Paul had shot, the bird fell. Before it had even hit the ground another bird had touched down, swinging lightly on a twig at the very end of a branch. Paul shot, the bird fell; this time with a cry and a fluttering of helpless wings. Paul got up, raced across the grass, picked up the dead bird and the wounded one. We saw him give the wounded struggling bird a quick determined tight-mouthed look, and wring its neck.

He came back, flung down the two corpses and said: 'Nine. And that's all.' He looked white and sick, and yet in spite of it, managed to give Jimmy a triumphant amused smile.

'Let's go,' said Willi, shutting his book.

'Wait,' said Jimmy. The sand was now unmoving. He dug into it with a fine stem and dragged out, first the body of the tiny beetle, and then the body of the ant-eater. Now we saw the jaws of the ant-eater were embedded in the body of the beetle. The corpse of the ant-eater was headless.

'The moral is,' said Paul, 'that none but natural enemies should engage.'

'But who should decide which are natural enemies and which are not?' said Jimmy.

'Not you,' said Paul. 'Look how you've upset the balance of nature. There is one ant-eater the less. And probably hundreds of ants that should have filled its maw will now live. And there is a dead beetle, slaughtered to no purpose.'

Jimmy stepped carefully over the shining round-pitted river of sand, so as not to disturb the remaining insects lying in wait at the bottom of their sand-traps. He dragged on his shirt over his sweaty reddened flesh. Maryrose got up in the way she had—obedient, patient, long-suffering, as if she had no will of her own. We all stood on the edge of the patch of shade, reluctant to plunge into the now white-hot midday, made dizzy and giddy by the few remaining butterflies who reeled drunk in the heat. And as we stood there, the clump of trees we had lain under sang into life. The cicadae which inhabited this grove, patiently silent these two hours waiting for us to go, burst one after another into shrill sound. And in the sister clump of trees, unnoticed by us, had arrived two pigeons who sat there cooing. Paul contemplated them, his rifle swinging. 'No,' said Maryrose. 'Please don't.'

'Why not?'

'Please Paul.'

The heap of nine dead pigeons, tied together by their pink feet, dangled from Paul's free hand, dripping blood.

'It is a terrible sacrifice,' said Paul gravely, 'but for you, Maryrose, I will refrain.'

She smiled at him, not in gratitude, but in the cool reproachful way she always used for him. And he smiled back, his delightful, brown, blue-eyed face all open for her inspection. They walked off together in front, the dead birds trailing their wings over jade-coloured clumps of grass.

The three of us followed.

'What a pity,' remarked Jimmy, 'that Maryrose disapproves so much of Paul. Because there is no doubt they are what is known as a perfectly-matched couple.' He had tried the light ironic tone, and almost succeeded. Almost, not quite; his jealousy of Paul grated in his voice.

We looked: they were, those two, a perfect couple, both so light and graceful, the sun burnishing their bright hair, shining on their brown skins. And yet Maryrose strolled on without looking at Paul who gave her his whimsically appealing blue glances all in vain.

It was too hot to talk on the way back. Passing the small kopje on whose granite chunks the sun was beating, waves of dizzying heat struck at us so that we hurried past it. Everything was empty and silent, only the cicadae and a distant pigeon sang. And past the kopje we slowed and looked for the grasshoppers, and saw that the bright clamped couples had almost disappeared. A few remained, one above another, like painted clothes-pegs with painted round black eyes. A few. And the butterflies were almost gone. One or two floated by, tired, over the sun-beaten grass.

Our heads ached with heat. We were slightly sick with the smell of blood.

At the hotel we separated with hardly a word.

[The right side of the black notebook, under the heading *Money,* continued.]

Some months ago I got a letter from the *Pomegranate Review,* New Zealand, asking for a story. Write back, saying I did not write stories. They replied asking for 'portions of your journals, if you keep them.' Replied saying I did not believe in publishing journals written for oneself. Amused myself composing imaginary journal, of the right tone for a literary review in a colony or the Dominions: circles isolated from the centres of culture will tolerate a far more solemn tone than the editors and their customers in let's say London or Paris. (Though sometimes I wonder.) This journal is kept by a young American living on an allowance from his father who works in insurance. He has had three short stories published and has completed a third of a novel. He drinks rather too much, but not as much as he likes people to think; takes marihuana, but only when friends from the States visit him. He is full of contempt for that crude phenomenon, the United States of America.

April 16th. *On the steps of the Louvre.* Remembered Dora. That girl was in real trouble. I wonder if she has solved her problems. Must write to my father. The tone of his last letter hurt me. Must we be always isolated from each other? I am an artist—Mon Dieu!

April 17th. *The Gare de Lyon.* Thought of Lise. My God, and that was two years ago! What have I done with my life? Paris has stolen it . . . must re-read Proust.

April 18th. *London. The Horseguards' Parade.* A writer is the conscience of the world. Thought of Marie. It is a writer's duty to betray his wife, his country and his friend if it serves his art. Also his mistress.

April 18th. *Outside Buckingham Palace.* George Eliot is the rich man's Gissing. Must write to my father. Only ninety dollars left. Will we ever speak the same language?

May 9th. *Rome. The Vatican.* Thought of Fanny. My God, those thighs of hers, like the white necks of swans. Did she have problems! A writer is, must be, the Machiavelli of the soul's kitchen. Must re-read Thom (Wolfe).

434

May 11th. *The Campagna.* Remembered Jerry—they killed him. Salauds! The best die young. I have not long to live. At thirty I shall kill myself. Thought of Betty. The black shadows of the lime trees on her face. Looked like a skull. I kissed the sockets of her eyes so as to feel the white bone on my lips. If I don't hear from my father before next week shall offer this journal for publication. On his head be it. Must re-read Tolstoy. He said nothing that wasn't obvious, but perhaps now that reality is draining the poetry from my days I can admit him to my Pantheon.

June 21st. *Les Halles.* Spoke to Marie. Very busy but she offered me one of her nights for free. Mon Dieu, the tears stand in my eyes as I remember it! When I kill myself I shall remember that a woman of the streets offered me one of her nights, for love. No greater compliment has been paid me. It is not the journalist but the critic who is the prostitute of the intellect. Re-reading Fanny Hill. Am thinking of writing an article called 'Sex Is the Opium of the People.'

June 22nd. *Café de Flore.* Time is the River on which the leaves of our thoughts are carried into oblivion. My father says I must come home. Will he never understand me? Am writing a porno for Jules called *Loins.* Five hundred dollars, so my father can go hang. Art is the Mirror of our betrayed ideals.

July 30th. *London. Public Convenience, Leicester Square.* Ah, the lost cities of our urban nightmare! Thought of Alice. The lust I feel in Paris is of a different quality from the lust I feel in London. In Paris sex is scented with *je ne sais quoi.* In London it is just sex. Must go back to Paris. Shall I read Bossuet? Am reading my book *Loins* for the third time. Pretty good. Have put, not my best self, but my second-best self into it. Pornography is the true journalism of the fifties. Jules said he would only pay me three hundred dollars for it. Salaud! Wired my father, told him I had finished a book which had been accepted. He sent me a thousand dollars. *Loins* is a real spit in the eye for Madison Avenue. Leautard is the poor man's Stendhal. Must read Stendhal.

• •

435

Came to know the young American writer James Schafter. Showed him this journal. He was delighted. We concocted another thousand or so words, and he sent it to an American little review as the work of a friend too shy to send it himself. It was printed. He took me out to lunch to celebrate. Told me the following: the critic, Hans P., a very pompous man, had written an article about James' work, saying it was corrupt. The critic was due in London. James, who had previously snubbed Hans P., because he dislikes him, sent a sycophantic telegram to the airport and a bunch of flowers to the hotel. He was waiting in the foyer when Hans P. arrived from the airport, with a bottle of Scotch and yet another bunch of flowers. Then he offered himself as a guide around London. Hans P., flattered but uneasy. James kept this up for the two weeks of Hans P.'s visit, hanging on Hans' every word. When Hans P. left he said from a steep moral height: 'Of course you must understand that I never allow personal feelings to interfere with my critical conscience.' To which James replied: 'writhing with moral turpitude,' as he describes it—'Yeah, but yeah, I see *that*, but man, it's communication that *counts*—yeah.' Two weeks later Hans P. wrote an article about James' work in which he says that the element of corruption in James' work is more the honest cynicism of a young man due to the state of society than an enduring element of James' view of life. James rolled on the floor laughing all afternoon.

James reverses the usual mask of the young writer. All, or nearly all, naïve enough to begin with, half-consciously, half-unconsciously begin to use naivety as a protection. But James plays at being corrupt. Faced, for instance, with a film-director who plays the usual game of pretending to make a movie of a story of James', 'just as it is, though of course we must make some alterations'—James will spend an afternoon, straight-faced, stammering with earnestness, offering to make wilder and wilder alterations for the sake of the box office, while the director gets more and more uneasy. But, as James says, no suggestion of change one can make to them can be more incredible than they would be prepared to make themselves, and so they never know whether he is laughing at

436

them or not. He leaves them, 'inarticulate with grateful emotion.' 'Unaccountably,' they are offended, and don't get in touch with him again. Or at a party where there is a critic or a mandarin who has any flavour of pomposity, James will sit at his or her feet, positively begging for favours, and pouring out flattery. Afterwards, he laughs. I told him all this was very dangerous; he replied it was no more dangerous than being 'the honest young artist with built-in integrity.' 'Integrity,' he says, with an owlish look, scratching at his crotch, 'is a red rag to the bull of Mammon, or, to put it another way, integrity is the poor man's codpiece.' I said this was all very well—he replied: 'Well, Anna, and how do you describe all this pastiching about? What's the difference between you and me?'

I agreed he was right; but then, inspired with our success over the young American's journal, we decided to invent another as written by a lady author of early middle-age, who had spent some years in an African colony, and was afflicted with sensibility. This is aimed at Rupert, editor of *Zenith*, who has asked me for 'something of yours—at last!'

James had met Rupert and hated him. Rupert is wet, limp, hysterical, homosexual, intelligent.

Easter week. The doors of the Russian Orthodox Church in Kensington stand flush with the mid-twentieth century street. Inside flickering shadows, incense, the kneeling bowed figures of immemorial piety. The bare vast floor. A few priests absorbed in the ritual of their service. The few worshippers kneeling on the hard wood, bending forward to touch their foreheads to the floor. Few, yes. But *real*. This was reality. I was aware of reality. After all, it is in the majority of mankind who have their beings inside a religion, the minority who are pagan. Pagan? Ah, that is a joyous word for the aridity of Godless modern man! I stood while the others kneeled. I, stubborn little me, I could feel my knees buckle under, I, who was the only one obstinately standing. The priests grave, harmonious, *masculine*. A handful of delightful pale young boys charmingly grave with piety. The thundering rich *virile* waves of the Russian singing. My knees, faint ... I found myself kneeling. Where was

437

my little individuality which usually asserts itself? I did not care. I was aware of deeper things. I found the grave figures of the priests wavering and blurring through the tears in my eyes. It was *too* much. I stumbled up and fled that soil, not mine; that solemnity, not mine ... should I perhaps no longer describe myself as an atheist but an agnostic? There is something so barren about the word atheist when I think (for instance) of the majestic fervour of those priests. Agnostic has more of a *tone?* I was late for the cocktail party. No matter, the countess did not notice. How sad, I felt, as I always do, to be the Countess Pirelli ... a come down, surely, after having been the mistress of four famous men? But I suppose we each of us need our little mask against the cruel world. The rooms crowded as always with the cream of literary London. Spied my dear Harry at once. I am so fond of these tall, pale-browed equine Englishmen—so *noble.* We talked, under the meaningless din of the cocktail party. He suggested I should do a play based on *Frontiers of War.* A play which should take no sides but emphasise the essential tragedy of the colonial situation, the tragedy of the whites. It is true, of course ... what is poverty, what are hunger, malnutrition, homelessness, the *pedestrian* degradations (his word—how sensitive, how full of *true* sensibility are a certain type of Englishman, far more intuitive than any woman!) compared to the reality, the human reality of the white dilemma? Listening to him talk, I understood my own book better. And I thought of how, only a mile away, the kneeling figures on the cold stone of the Russian church bowed their foreheads in reverence to a deeper truth. My truth? Alas no! Nevertheless I have decided I shall henceforth describe myself as an agnostic and not an atheist, and I shall lunch with my dear Harry tomorrow and discuss my play. As we parted, he—so delicately—squeezed my hand, a chill, essentially poetic pressure. I went home, nearer to reality I think than ever in my life. And, in silence, to my fresh narrow bed. So essential, I feel, to have clean linen on one's bed every day. Ah, what a sensuous (not sensual) pleasure to creep, fresh-bathed, between the cool *clean* linen, and to lie awaiting sleep. Ah, lucky little me ...

438

Easter Sunday

I lunched with Harry. How charming his house is! He had already made a sketch of how he thought the play should go. His close friend is Sir Fred, who he thinks would play the lead and then, of course, there would be none of the usual trouble of finding a backer. He suggested a slight change in the story. A young white farmer should notice a young African girl of rare beauty and intelligence. He tries to influence her to educate herself, to raise herself, for her family are nothing but crude Reserve Natives. But she misunderstands his motives and falls in love. Then, when he (oh, so gently) explains his real interest in her, she turns virago and calls him ugly names. Taunts him. He, patient, bears it. But she goes to the police and tells them he has tried to rape her. He suffers the social obloquy in silence. He goes to prison accusing her only with his eyes, while she turns away in shame. It could be real, strong drama! It symbolises, as Harry says, the superior spiritual status of the white man trapped by history, dragged down into the animal mud of Africa. So true, so penetrating, so *new*. True courage consists of swimming *against* the tide. When I left Harry I walked home and reality touched me with her white wings. I walked in little slow steps, so as not to waste this *beautiful* experience. And so to bed, bathed and *clean*, to read the *Imitation of Christ*, which Harry had lent me.

I thought all this was a bit thick, but James said no, he'd swallow it. James turned out to be right; but unfortunately my rare sensibility overcame me at the last moment and I decided to keep my privacy. Rupert sent me a note saying that he so understood, some experiences were too personal for print.

[At this point in the black notebook was pinned to the page a carbon copy of a short story written by James Schaffer after being asked to review a dozen novels for a certain literary magazine. He sent in this piece to the editor, suggesting it should be printed in place of the review. The editor wrote back with enthusiasm for the story, asking to be allowed to publish it in the magazine—'but where is your review, Mr Schaffer? We expected it for this issue.' It was at this point that James and Anna decided they were defeated; that something had happened in the world which made parody impossible. James wrote a serious review about the dozen novels, taking them one by one; using his thousand words. Anna and he wrote no more bits of pastiche.[

Blood on the Banana Leaves

Frrrrrr, frrr, frrr, say the banana trees ghosting the age-tired moon of Africa, sifting the wind. Ghosts. Ghosts of time and of my pain. Black wings of night-jars, white wings of night-moths, cut, sift, the moon. Frrrr, frrr, say the banana trees, and the moon slips pale with pain on the wind-tilting leaves. John, John, sings my girl, brown, cross-legged in the dark of the eaves of the hut, the moon mysterious on her eye-balls. Eyes that I have kissed in the night, victim-eyes of impersonal tragedy, to be impersonal no longer. Oh, Africa! for soon the banana leaves will be senile with dark red, the red dust will be redder yet, redder than the new-lipsticked lips of my dark love, store-betrayed to the commerce-lust of the white trader.

'Be still and sleep now Noni, the moon is four-horned with menace and I am making my fate and yours, the fate of our people.'

'John, John,' says my girl, and her voice is sighing with longing like the sigh of the incandescent leaves, wooing the moon.

'Sleep now my Noni.'

'But my heart is ebony with uneasiness and the guiltiness of my fate.'

'Sleep, sleep, I do not hate you my Noni, I have often been seeing the white man pointing his eyes like arrows at the swing and the sway of your hips my Noni. I have seen it. I have seen it as I see the banana leaves answering the moon and the white-spears of the rain murdering the cannibal-raped soil of our land. Sleep.'

'But John, my John, I am sickening with the knowing of my betraying you, my man, my lover, and yet was I being taken by force, not in having of my true self, by the white man from the store.'

Frrrrr, frrr, say the banana leaves and the night-jars cry black murder to the sick-grey moon.

'But John, my John, it was only one little lipstick, one little red lipstick that I bought, for the making of my thirsty lips more beautiful for you, my love, and when I was buying of it I saw his cold blue eyes hot on my maiden thighs, and I ran, I was running my love, back from the store to you, to my love, my lips red for you, for you my John my man.'

'Sleep now, Noni. Sit no longer cross-legged in the grinning moon-shadows. Sit no longer, crying from your pain which is my pain and the pain of our people crying for my pity, which you are having now and for always my Noni my girl.'

'But your love, my John, where is your love for me?'

Ah, dark coils of the red snake of hate, sliding at the roots of the banana tree, swelling in the latticed windows of my soul.

'My love, Noni, is yours and for our people and for the red hooded snake of hate.'

'Aie, Aie, Aie,' screams my love, my love Noni, speared to her mysterious giving womb by the lust of the white man, by his lust for having, by his trader's lust.

And 'Aie, Aie, Aie,' wail the old women in their huts hearing my purposefulness in the wind and in the sign of the raped banana leaves. *Voices of the wind, call my pain to the free world, the snake in the echoing dust, bite the heel of the heartless world for me!*

'Aie, Aie, my John, and what of the child I am having, it is being heavy on my heart, the child I am giving to you, my love, my man, and not to the hated white man from the store who tripped my frantic fleeing heels as I sped from him, and was being flung into the sightless dust at the hour of setting sun, the hour when all the world is being betrayed by the ageless night?'

'Sleep, sleep, my girl, my Noni, the child is for the world, heavy with fate, and crossed with the mystery of mingling bloods, it is a child of vengeful shadows, the child of the gathering snake of my hate.'

441

'Aie, Aie,' screams my Noni, writhing deep and mystical in the shadows of the eaves of the hut.

'Aie, Aie,' scream the old women, hearing my purposefulness, the old women, auditors of life's stream, their wombs dry for living, hearing the silent screams of living from their huts.

'Sleep now, my Noni. I will return after many years. But now I have a man's purpose. Do not stop me.'

Dark blue and green the ghosts in the moonlight, the ghosts sub-divided by my hate. And dark red the snake in the purple dust under the banana tree. Within a myriad answers, the answer. Behind a million purposes, the purpose. Frrrrr, frrr, say the banana leaves, and my love sings: John and where will you go from me, who wait for you always with my womb filled with longing.

I go to the city now to the gun-metal-writhing-grey streets of the white man and I find my brothers and into their hands I will place the red snake of my hate and together we will seek out the white man's lust and kill it, so that no longer will the banana trees bear alien fruit, and the soil of our raped country cry, and the dust of souls weep for rain.

'Aie, Aie,' scream the old women.

In the moon-menaced night a scream, the scream of anonymous murder.

My Noni creeps, double, into the hut and the purple-green shadows of the moon are empty and empty my heart save for its snake-purpose.

Ebony lighting hates the leaves. Jacaranda thunder kills the trees. Sweet globes of paw paws receive indigo vengeance. Frrr, frr, say the banana leaves, ghosting the time-tired moon. I am going, I am saying to the banana leaves. Multitudes of perverted shudders rip the criss-crossing dreams of the thwarted forest.

I go on fated feet and the dust-echoes are swamp-dark in the loom of time. I go past the banana tree and red snakes of loving hatred are singing after me: Go, man, go, for vengeance to the city. *And the moon on the banana leaves is crimson, singing frrrr, frr, scream, cry and croon, oh red is*

442

my pain, crimson my twining pain, oh red and crimson are
dripping the moon-echoing leaves of my hate.

[Here was pinned to the page a review of *Frontiers of War* cut from *Soviet Writing,* and dated August, 1952.]

Terrible indeed is the exploitation in British colonies revealed in this courageous first novel, written and published under the very eye of the oppressor to reveal to the world the real truth behind British Imperialism! Yet admiration for the courage of the young writer, daring all for her social conscience, must not blind us to the incorrect emphasis she gives to the class struggle in Africa. This is the story of a young airman, a true patriot, so soon to die for his country in the Great Anti-Fascist War who falls in with a group of so-called socialists, decadent white settlers who play at politics. Sickened by his experience with this gang of rich cosmopolitan socialites, he turns to the people, to a simple black girl who teaches him the realities of true working-class life. Yet this is precisely the weak point of this well-intentioned but misguided novel. For what contact can a young upper-class Englishman have with the daughter of a cook? What a writer must search for in her calvary towards true artistic verity is the typical. Such a situation is not, cannot be, typical. Suppose the young writer, daring the Himalayas of truth itself, had made her hero a young white working man and her heroine an African organised worker from a factory? In such a situation she might have found a solution, political, social, spiritual, that could have shed light on the future struggle for Freedom in Africa. Where are the working masses in this book? Where the class conscious fighters? They do not appear. But let not this talented young writer lose heart! The artistic heights are for the great in spirit! Forward! for the sake of the world!

[Review of *Frontiers of War, Soviet Gazette,* dated August, 1954.]

Majestic and untamed is Africa! What a burst of splendour

443

is revealed before us in the pages of this novel which has just reached us from Great Britain depicting a wartime incident in the very heart of the plains and jungles of the African land.

It goes without saying that typical characters in art differ from scientific concepts of types in content, and accordingly, in form. Hence, when this author quotes at the beginning of her book a saying which, redolent as it is of Western sociological mumbo-jumbo, nevertheless contains a profound verity: 'It is said, it was because Adam ate the apple that he was lost, or fell. I say it was because of his claiming something for his own, and because of his I, Mine, Me, and the like'—we look at her work with an eager expectation which is not justified. Yet let us welcome what she has given, looking forward with hope to what she might, indeed will, give us, when she comes to understand that a true artistic work must have a revolutionary life—asserting content, ideological profundity, humaneness, as well as artistic quality. The feeling grows, as page follows page: How noble, how truly profound must be the human types evolved by this still undeveloped continent; the feeling remains with you and repeatedly evokes a response in your heart. For the young English flier, and the trusting black girl, never-to-be-forgotten as they are, thanks to the author's entrancing power, are not yet typical of the deep moral potentialities of the future. Our readers say to you, dear author, with one voice: 'Work on! Remember that art must ever be bathed in the clear light of truth! Remember that the process of creating new concrete forms of realism in the literature of Africa and in general those of underdeveloped countries with a strong national-liberation movement is a very difficult and intricate process!

(Review of *Frontiers of War* in *Soviet Journal for Literature for Colonial Freedom,* dated Dec. 1956.)

The struggle against Imperialist Oppression in Africa has its Homers and its Jack Londons. It also has its petty psy-

444

chologisers, not without a certain minor merit. With the black masses on the march, with every day a new heroic stand by the nationalist movements, what can we say of this novel which chronicles the story of a love affair between a young Oxford-educated Britisher and a black girl? She is the only representative of the people in this book, and yet her character remains shadowy, undeveloped, unsatisfying. No, this author must learn from our literature, the literature of health and progress, that no one is benefited by despair. This is a negative novel. We detect Freudian influences. There is an element of mysticism. As for the group of 'socialists' portrayed here, the author has essayed satire and failed. There is something unhealthy, even ambiguous in her writing. Let her learn from Mark Twain, whose wholesome humour is so dear to progressive readers, how to make mankind laugh at what is already dead, backward, outmoded by history.

[The red notebook continued:]

13th November, 1955

Ever since Stalin's death in 1953 there has been a state of affairs in the C.P. that the old hands say would have been impossible at any time before. Groups of people, ex-communists and communists together, have been meeting to discuss what is going on in the Party, in Russia and in Britain. The first meeting I was asked to attend (and I've been out of the Party for over a year now) consisted of nine members and five ex-members. And none of us, the ex-members, had the usual 'You are traitors' inflicted on us. We met as socialists, with full trust. The discussions have slowly developed and there is now a sort of vague plan—to remove the 'dead bureaucracy' at the centre of the Party, so that the C.P. should be completely changed, a genuinely British Party, without the deadly loyalty to Moscow and the obligation to tell lies, etc., a genuinely democratic Party. I again find myself among people filled with excitement and purpose—

among them people who left the Party years ago. The plan can be summarised thus: (a) The Party, shorn of its 'old hands' who are incapable of thinking straight after so many years 'of lying and double-cross, should make a statement repudiating its past. This, first. (b) to break all ties with foreign communist parties, in the expectation that other communist parties will also be rejuvenating themselves and breaking with the past. (c) to call together the thousands and thousands of people who have been communist and who have left the Party in disgust, inviting them to join the revitalised party. (d) To . . .

[At this point the red notebook was stuffed full of newspaper cuttings to do with the Twentieth Congress of the Russian Communist Party, letters from all kinds of people about politics, agendas for political meetings, etc. This mass of paper had been fastened together by rubber bands and clipped to the page. Then Anna's handwriting began again:]

11th August, 1956

Not for the first time in my life I realise I have spent weeks and months in frenzied political activity and have achieved absolutely nothing. More, that I might have foreseen it would achieve nothing. The Twentieth Congress has doubled and trebled the numbers of people, both in and out of the Party, who want a 'new' communist party. Last night I was at a meeting which went on till nearly morning. Towards the end a man who had not spoken before, a socialist from Austria, made a short humorous speech, something like this: 'My dear Comrades. I have been listening to you, amazed at the wells of faith in human beings! What you are saying amounts to this: that you know the leadership of the British C.P. consists of men and women totally corrupted by years of work in the Stalinist atmosphere. You know they will do anything to maintain their position. You know, because you have given a hundred examples of it here this evening, that they suppress resolutions, rig ballots, pack meetings, lie and twist. There is no way of getting them out of office by

446

democratic means partly because they are unscrupulous, and partly because half of the Party members are too innocent to believe their leaders are capable of such trickery. But every time you reach this point in your deliberations you stop, and instead of drawing the obvious conclusions from what you have said, you go off into some day-dream and talk as if all you have to do is to appeal to the leading comrades to resign all at once because it would be in the best interests of the Party if they did. It is as if you proposed to appeal to a professional burglar to retire because his efficiency was giving his profession a bad name.'

We all laughed, but continued with the discussion. The humorous note he used absolved him, as it were, from the necessity of a serious answer.

Afterwards I thought about it. Long ago I decided that at a political meeting the truth usually comes out in just such a speech or a remark ignored at the time because its *tone* is not that of the meeting. Humorous, or satirical, or even angry or bitter—yet it's the truth, and all the long speeches and contributions are nonsense.

I've just read what I wrote on the 13th November last year. I am amazed at our naivety. Yet I was really inspired by a belief in the possibility of a new honest C.P. I really did believe it was possible.

20th September, 1956

Have been to no more meetings. The idea in the air, so I'm told, is to start a new 'really British C.P.' as an example and an alternative to the existing C.P. People are contemplating, apparently without misgivings, the existence of two rival C.P.'s. Yet it's obvious what would happen. The energies of both would be occupied by throwing insults at each other and denying each other's right to be communist at all. A recipe for farce. But it's no more stupid than the idea of 'throwing out' the old guard by democratic means and reforming the Party 'from within.' Stupid. Yet I was wrapped up in it for months, like hundreds of other normally intelligent people who have been involved in politics for years. Sometimes I

447

think the one form of experience people are incapable of learning from is the political experience.

People are reeling off from the C.P. in dozens, broken-hearted. The irony is that they are broken-hearted and cynical to the degree that they were loyal and innocent before. People like myself who had few illusions (we all had some illusions—mine was that anti-Semitism was 'impossible') remain calm and ready to start again, accepting the fact that the British C.P. will probably slowly degenerate into a tiny little sect. The new phrase in the air is 're-think the socialist position.'

Today Molly rang me. Tommy is involved with the new group of young socialists. Molly said she had sat in a corner listening while they talked. She felt as if 'she had gone back a hundred years to her own youth' when she was first in the C.P. 'Anna, it was extraordinary! It was really so *odd*. Here they are, with no time for the C.P., and quite right too, and no time for the Labour Party, and I wouldn't be surprised if they weren't right about that, there are a few hundred of them, scattered up and down Britain, yet they all talk as if Britain will be socialist in about ten years at the latest, and through their efforts of course. You know, as if they will be running the new beautiful socialist Britain that will be born on Tuesday week. I felt as if they were mad, or as if I were mad . . . but the point is, Anna, it's just like us, isn't it? Well? And even using that awful jargon we've been making fun of for years and years, just as if they'd just thought it all up for themselves.' I said: 'But surely, Molly, you're pleased he's become a socialist and not some sort of career-type?' 'But, of course. Naturally. The point is, oughtn't they to be more intelligent than we were, Anna?'

[The yellow notebook continued:]

The Shadow of the Third

From this point of the novel 'the third,' previously Paul's wife; then Ella's younger *alter ego* formed from fantasies

448

about Paul's wife; then the memory of Paul; becomes Ella herself. As Ella cracks and disintegrates, she holds fast to the idea of Ella whole, healthy, and happy. The link between the various 'thirds' must be made very clear: the link is normality, but more than that—conventionality, attitudes or emotions proper to the 'respectable' life which in fact Ella refuses to have anything to do with.

Ella moves into a new flat. Julia resentful. An area of their relationship obscured before is now exposed by Julia's attitude. Julia had dominated Ella. Ella had been prepared to be dominated, or at least been prepared to look as if she was. Julia's nature was essentially generous—kind, warm, giving. Yet now she even goes to the length of complaining to mutual friends that Ella had taken advantage of her, had made use of her. Ella, alone with her son in the big ugly dirty flat which she now has to clean and paint, thinks that in a sense what Julia complains of was true. She had been rather like a willing captive, with the captive's hidden core of independence. Leaving Julia's house was like a daughter leaving a mother. Or, she thinks wryly, remembering Paul's unfriendly jokes that she was 'married to Julia'—like the break-up of a marriage.

•   •

Ella is for a while more alone than she has ever been. She thinks a great deal about her ruptured friendship with Julia. For she is closer to Julia than anyone, if being 'close' means mutual confidence and shared experience. Yet at the moment this friendship is all hatred and resentment. And she cannot stop herself thinking about Paul who left her months ago. Over a year now.

•   •

Ella understands that, living with Julia, she has been protected from a certain kind of attention. She is now definitely 'a woman living alone'; and that, although she has not realised it before, is very different from 'two women sharing a house.'

For instance. Three weeks after she has moved into the

449

new flat, Dr West telephones her. He informs her that his wife is on holiday and asks her to dinner. Ella goes, unable to believe, in spite of the too-carefully dropped information about his wife's being away, that this is not to be a dinner about some aspect of office-work. During the dinner Ella slowly understands that Dr West is offering her an affair. She remembers the unkind remarks that he so carefully passed on to her at the time that Paul left her, and thinks that he has probably pigeon-holed her in his mind for an occasion like this. She also understands, that if she, Ella, turns him down this evening he will work through a short list of three or four women, for he remarks spitefully: 'There are others, you know. You aren't condemning me to solitude.'

Ella watches developments in the office, and sees, that towards the end of a week, Patricia Brent has a new manner with Dr West. The tough, efficient, professional woman's manner has become soft, almost girlish. Patricia has been the last on Dr West's short list, for he has tried and failed with two of the secretaries. Ella watches: maliciously pleased that Dr West has ended up with what, for him, was the worst choice; angry on behalf of her sex that Patricia Brent is positively grateful and flattered; terror that accepting the favours of a Dr West might be the end of her own road; angry amusement that Dr West, turned down by herself, made a point of indicating: You wouldn't have me, but you see, I don't care!

And all these emotions are uncomfortably strong, rooted in a resentment that has nothing to do with Dr West. Ella dislikes feeling them, and is ashamed. She asks herself why she is not sorry for Dr West, a middle-aged, not very attractive man, married to an essentially competent and probably dull wife. Why shouldn't he try to attract some romance to himself? But it is no use. She resents and despises him.

Meeting Julia at a friend's house, their relations are chilly. Ella, 'by chance,' starts telling her about Dr West. In a few moments the two women are friendly again, as if there had never been a coldness. But they are now friends on the basis of an aspect of their relationship which had always been subordinate before—criticism for men.

450

Julia caps Ella's story about Dr West with this one: an actor at the theatre Julia was playing in brought her home one night and came up for coffee and sat complaining about his marriage. Julia: 'I was all kind and full of good advice as usual, but I was so bored at hearing it all again I wanted to scream.' Julia, at four in the morning, suggested she was tired and he should go home. 'But my dear, you'd think I'd mortally insulted him. I could see that if he didn't make me that night his ego would be all deflated, and so I went to bed.' The man was impotent, Julia good-humoured. 'In the morning, he said could he come over again that night. He said, it was the least I could do, to give him a chance to redeem himself. He's got a sense of humour at least.' And so this man spent a second night with Julia. With no better results. 'Naturally he left at four, so that the little woman could believe he had been working late. Just as he left he turned on me and said: "You're a castrating woman, I thought you were from the moment I saw you."'

'Jesus,' said Ella.

'Yes,' said Julia fiercely. 'And the funny thing is, he's a nice man. I mean, I would never have expected that sort of remark from him.'

'You shouldn't have gone to bed.'

'But you know how it is—it's always that moment, when a man looks all wounded in his masculinity, one can't bear it, one needs to bolster him up.'

'Yes, but they just kick us afterwards as hard as they can, so why do we do it?'

'Yes, but I never seem to learn.'

A few weeks later, Ella sees Julia, tells her: 'Four men, and I haven't even flirted with them before, have telephoned to say their wives are away, and every time they have a delightful coy note in their voices. It really is extraordinary—one knows a man, to work with, for years, then it's enough that their wives should go away for them to change their voices and they seem to think you're going to fall over yourself to get into bed. What on earth do you suppose goes through their minds?'

'Much better not think about *that*.'

Ella says to Julia, out of an impulse to placate, to charm (and she recognises it as she speaks as the same need she has to charm or placate a man: 'Well at least when I was living in your house, this didn't happen. Which is odd in itself, isn't it?'

Julia shows a flash of triumph, as if she would like to say: Well, I was good for something, then ...

There is now a moment of discomfort: Ella lets slide, out of cowardice, the chance of saying that Julia has behaved badly about her leaving; the chance of 'getting it all out into the open.' And in the silence of this discomfort, there is the thought, which follows naturally from the 'it is odd in itself, isn't it?'—is it possible they thought us Lesbians?

Ella had considered this before, with amusement. But she is thinking: No. If they had thought us Lesbian it would have attracted them, they would have been around in swarms. Every man I've ever known has spoken with relish—either openly or unconsciously, about Lesbians. It's an aspect of their incredible vanity: seeing themselves as redeemers of these lost females.

Ella listens to the bitter words she is using in her mind and is shaken by them. At home she tries to analyse the bitterness which possesses her. She literally feels poisoned by it.

She thinks that nothing has occurred which has not been happening all her life. Married men, temporarily wifeless, trying to have an affair with her—etc., etc., ten years ago she would not have even noticed or remarked on it. All this was taken by her as part of the hazards and chances of being a 'free woman.' But ten years ago, she realised, she had been feeling something that she had not then recognised. An emotion of satisfaction, of victory over the wives; because she, Ella, the free woman, was so much more exciting than the dull tied women. Looking back and acknowledging this emotion she is ashamed.

She thinks, too, that the quality of her tone with Julia is that of a bitter spinster. Men. The enemy. They. She decides not to confide in Julia again, or at least to banish the tone of dry bitterness.

Soon afterwards, the following incident. One of the subeditors at the office is working with Ella on a series of articles giving advice about emotional problems—the problems which arise most often in the letters which come in. Ella and this man spend several evenings together at the office. There are to be six articles, and each has two titles, an official one and one for jocular use by Ella and her colleague. For instance, Do you sometimes feel Bored with Your Home? is for Ella and Jack: Help! I'm going round the bend. And: The Husband who neglects his Family, becomes My Husband sleeps around. And so on. Both Ella and Jack laugh a great deal, and make fun of the over-simple style of the articles, yet they write them carefully, taking trouble with them. They both know their joking is because of the unhappiness and frustration of the letters which pour into the office, and which they do not believe their articles will do anything to alleviate.

On the last evening of their collaboration Jack drives Ella home. He is married, has three children, is aged about thirty. Ella likes him very much. She offers him a drink, he goes upstairs with her. She knows the moment will soon approach when he will invite her to make love. She is thinking: But I'm not attracted to him. But I might be, if only I could shake off the shadow of Paul. How do I know I won't be attracted to him once I'm in bed? After all, I was not immediately attracted to Paul. This last thought surprises her. She sits listening, while the young man talks and entertains her, and is thinking: Paul always used to say, joking, but really serious, that I had not been in love with him at first. Now I say it myself. But I don't think it's true. I probably only say it because he said it . . . but no wonder I can never work up any interest in a man if I'm thinking all the time of Paul.

Ella goes to bed with Jack. She classifies him as the efficient type of lover. 'The man who is not sensual, has learned love-making out of a book, probably called *How to Satisfy Your Wife*.' He gets his pleasure from having got a woman into bed, not from sex itself.

These two are cheerful, friendly, continuing the good sense of their work together in the office. Yet Ella is fighting down a need to cry. She is familiar with this sudden depression and combats it thus: It's not my depression at all; it is guilt, but not my guilt; it is the guilt from the past, it has to do with the double standard which I repudiate.

Jack, announcing the fact that he must return home, begins talking about his wife. 'She is a good girl,' he remarks, and Ella freezes at the condescension in his voice. 'I make damned sure she never suspects me when I go off the rails. Of course, she gets pretty fed up, stuck with the kids, they're a bit of a handful, but she copes.' He is putting on his tie, pulling on his shoes as he sits on Ella's bed. He is full of well-being; his face is the unmarked, open face of a boy. 'I'm pretty lucky in my old woman,' he goes on; but now there is resentment in it, against his wife; and Ella knows that this occasion, his sleeping with her, is going to be used subtly as a means to denigrate his wife. And he is jaunty with satisfaction, not because of the pleasures of love, about which he knows very little, but because he has proved something to himself. He says good-bye to Ella, remarking: 'Well, back to the grindstone. My wife's the best in the world, but she's not exactly an exhilarating conversationalist.' Ella checks herself, does not say that a woman with three small children, stuck in a house in the suburbs with a television set, has nothing much exhilarating to talk about. The depths of her resentment amaze her. She knows that his wife, the woman who is waiting for him miles away somewhere across London, will know, the moment he enters the bedroom, that he has been sleeping with another woman, from his self-satisfied jauntiness.

Ella decides (a) that she will be chaste until she falls in love and (b) that she will not discuss this incident with Julia.

Next day she telephones Julia, they meet for lunch and she tells Julia. She is reflecting, as she does so, that while she has always steadily refused to confide in Patricia Brent, or at least refused to be an accomplice in her sardonic criticism of men (Ella thinks that the sardonic, almost good-natured quality of Patricia's criticism of men is what her own present bitterness will mellow into and she is determined that it won't) yet she is prepared to confide in Julia whose bitterness is turning rapidly into a corroding contempt. She again decides not to indulge in these conversations with Julia, thinking that two women, friends on a basis of criticism of men, are Lesbian, psychologically if not physically.

This time she keeps her promise to herself not to talk to Julia. She is isolated and lonely.

Now something new happens. She begins to suffer torments of sexual desire. Ella is frightened because she cannot remember feeling sexual desire, as a thing in itself, without reference to a specific man before, or at least not since her adolescence, and then it was always in relation to a fantasy about a man. Now she cannot sleep, she masturbates, to accompaniment of fantasies of hatred about men. Paul has vanished completely: she has lost the warm strong man of her experience, and can only remember a cynical betrayer. She suffers sex desire in a vacuum. She is acutely humiliated, thinking that this means she is dependent on men for 'having sex,' for 'being serviced,' for 'being satisfied.' She uses this kind of savage phrase to humiliate herself.

Then she realises she is falling into a lie about herself, and about women, and that she must hold on to this knowledge: that when she was with Paul she felt no sex hungers that were not prompted by him; that if he was apart from her for a few days, she was dormant until he returned; that her present raging sexual hunger was not for sex, but was fed by all the emotional hungers of her life. That when she loved a man again, she would return to normal: a woman, that is, whose sexuality would ebb and flow in response to his. A woman's sexuality is, so to speak, contained by a man, if he is a real man; she is, in a sense, put to sleep by him, she does not think about sex.

Ella holds on fast to this knowledge, and thinks: every time in life I go through a dry time, a period of deadness, I always do this: hold on to a set of words, the phrases of a kind of knowledge, even while they are dead and meaningless, but knowing that life will come back and make them live too. But how strange that one should hold on to a set of sentences, and have faith in them.

Meantime, men approached her and she refused them,

455

because she knew she could not love them. The words she used to herself were: I won't sleep with a man until I know I could love him.

Yet, some weeks later, the following incident: Ella meets a man at a party. She is again conscientiously going to parties, hating the process of 'being on the market again.' The man is a script-writer, Canadian. He does not attract her particularly physically. Yet he is intelligent, with the cool wise-cracking transatlantic humour she enjoys. His wife, at the party, is a beautiful girl, as it were professionally beautiful. Next morning, this man arrives at Ella's flat, unannounced. He has brought gin, tonic, flowers; he makes a game of the situation 'man coming to seduce girl met at a party the night before, bringing flowers and gin.' Ella is amused. They drink and laugh and make jokes. Out of the laughter, they go to bed. Ella gives pleasure. She feels nothing, and is even prepared to swear that he feels nothing either. For at the moment of penetration the knowledge goes through her that this is something that he set himself to do and that's all. She thinks: Well, I'm doing this without feeling so why am I criticising him? It's not fair. Then she thinks, rebellious: But that's the point. The man's desire creates a woman's desire, or should, so I'm right to be critical.

Afterwards they continue to drink and to make jokes. Then he remarks, at random, not from anything that has gone before: 'I have a beautiful wife whom I adore. I have work I like to do. And now I have a girl.' Ella understands that she is the girl, and that this enterprise, sleeping with her, is a sort of project or plan for a happy life. She realises that he expects the relationship to continue, he takes it for granted that it will. She indicates that as far as she is concerned the exchange is over; as she speaks there is a flash of ugly vanity on his face, though she has said it gently, positively compliantly, as if her refusal were due to circumstances beyond her control.

He studies her, hard-faced. 'What's wrong, baby, haven't I satisfied you?' He says this wearily, at a loss. Ella hastens to assure him that he has; although he has not. But she under-

456

stands this is not his fault, she has not had a real orgasm since Paul left her.

She says, dry in spite of herself: 'Well, I don't think there's much conviction in it for either of us.'

Again the hard, weary, clinical look. 'I have a beautiful wife,' he announces. 'But she doesn't satisfy me sexually. I need more.'

This silences Ella. She feels as if she's in some perverse emotional no-man's-land that has nothing to do with her, although she has temporarily strayed into it. Yet she realises that he really does not understand what is the matter with what he offers her. He has a large penis; he is 'good in bed.' And that's it. Ella stands, silent, thinking that the weariness of sensuality he has in bed is the other side of his cold world-weariness out of it. He stands looking her over. *Now*, thinks Ella, now he's going to lash out, he's going to let me have it. She sets herself to take it.

'I've learned,' he drawls, sharp with wounded vanity, 'that it's not necessary to have a beautiful woman in the sack. It's enough to concentrate on one part of her—anything. There's always something beautiful in even an ugly woman. An ear for instance. Or a hand.'

Ella suddenly laughs and tries to catch his eye thinking that surely he will laugh. Because for the couple of hours before they had got into bed, their relationship had been good-humoured and humorous. What he has just said is positively the parody of a worldly-wise philanderer's remark. Surely he will smile at it? But no, it had been intended to hurt, and he would not withdraw it, even by a smile.

'Lucky I have nice hands, if nothing else,' says Ella at last, very dry.

He comes to her, picks up her hands, kisses them, wearily, rake-like: 'Beautiful, doll, beautiful.'

He leaves and she thinks for the hundredth time that in their emotional life all these intelligent men use a level so much lower than anything they use for work, that they might be different creatures.

That evening Ella goes to Julia's house, and finds Julia in

457

what she classified as 'Patricia's mood'—that is, sardonic rather than bitter.

Julia tells Ella, humorous, that the man, the actor who had called her a 'castrating woman,' had turned up a few days before with flowers, just as if nothing had happened. 'He was really quite surprised that I wouldn't play. He was ever so jolly and companionable. And I sat there, looking at him, and remembering how I had cried my eyes out after he had left—you remember, there were two nights, and I had been ever so sweet and kind putting him at his ease, and then he said I was . . . and even then I couldn't hurt his damned feelings. And I sat there and I thought: Do you suppose he's forgotten what he said or why he said it? Or aren't we supposed to care what they say? We're just supposed to be tough enough to take anything? Sometimes I think we're all in a sort of sexual mad house.'

Ella says drily: 'My dear Julia, we've chosen to be free women, and this is the price we pay, that's all.'

'Free,' says Julia. 'Free! What's the use of us being free if they aren't? I swear to God, that every one of them, even the best of them, have the old idea of good women and bad women.'

'And what about us? Free, we say, yet the truth is they get erections when they're with a woman they don't give a damn about, but we don't have an orgasm unless we love him. What's free about that?'

Julia says: 'Then you're luckier than I have been. I was thinking yesterday: of the ten men I've been in bed with during the last five years, eight have been impotent or come too quickly. I was blaming myself—of course, we always do, isn't it odd, the way we positively fall over ourselves to blame ourselves for everything? But even that damned actor, the one who said I was castrating, was kind enough to remark, oh, only in passing of course, that he had only found one woman in his life he could make it with. Oh, don't run away with the idea that he mentioned it to make me feel better, not at all.'

'My dear Julia, you didn't sit down to count them?'

'Not until I started thinking about it, no.'

458

Ella finds herself in a new mood or phase. She becomes completely sexless. She puts it down to the incident with the Canadian script-writer, but does not care particularly. She is now cool, detached, self-sufficient. Not only can she not remember what it was like, being afflicted with sexual desire, but she cannot believe she will ever feel desire again. She knows, however, that this condition, being self-sufficient and sexless, is only the other side of being possessed by sex.

She rings up Julia to announce that she has given up sex, given up men, because 'she can't be bothered.' Julia's good-humoured scepticism positively crackles in Ella's ear, and she says: 'But I mean it.' 'Good for you,' says Julia.

Ella decides to write again, searches herself for the book which is already written inside her, and waiting to be written down. She spends a great deal of time alone, waiting to discern the outlines of this book inside her.

• •

I see Ella, walking slowly about a big empty room, thinking, waiting. I, Anna, see Ella. Who is, of course, Anna. But that is the point, for she is not. The moment I, Anna, write: Ella rings up Julia to announce, etc., then Ella floats away from me and becomes someone else. I don't understand what happens at the moment Ella separates herself from me and becomes Ella. No one does. It's enough to call her Ella, instead of Anna. Why did I choose the name Ella? Once I met a girl at a party called Ella. She reviewed books for some newspaper and read manuscripts for a publisher. She was small, thin, dark—the same physical type as myself. She wore her hair tied back with a black bow. I was struck by her eyes, extraordinarily watchful and defensive. They were windows in a fortress. People were drinking heavily. The host came over to fill our glasses. She put out her hand—a thin, white delicate hand, at just that moment when he had put an inch of liquor in her glass, to cover it. She gave a cool nod: 'That's enough.' Then a cool shake, as he pressed to fill the glass. He went off; she saw I had been looking. She picked up the glass with just an inch of red wine in it, and said: 'That's the *exact* amount I need for the right degree of intoxication.'

459

I laughed. But no, she was serious. She drank the inch of red wine, and then remarked: 'Yes, that's right.' Assessing how the alcohol was affecting her—she gave another small, cool nod. 'Yes, that was just right.'

Well, I would never do that. That's not Anna at all.

I see Ella, isolated, walking about her big room, tying back her straight black hair with a wide black ribbon. Or sitting hour after hour in a chair, her white delicate hands loose in her lap. She sits frowning at them, thinking.

• •

Ella finds this story inside herself: A woman, loved by a man who criticises her throughout their long relationship for being unfaithful to him and for longing for the social life which his jealousy bars her from and for being 'a career woman.' This woman who, throughout the five years of their affair, in fact never looks at another man, never goes out, and neglects her career becomes everything he has criticised her for being at that moment when he drops her. She becomes promiscuous, lives only for parties, and is ruthless about her career, sacrificing her men and her friends for it. The point of the story is that this new personality has been created by him; and that everything she does—sexual acts, acts of betrayal for the sake of her career, etc., are with the revengeful thought: There, that's what you wanted, that's what you wanted me to be. And, meeting this man again after an interval, when her new personality is firmly established, he falls in love with her again. This is what he always wanted her to be; and the reason why he left her was in fact because she was quiet, compliant and faithful. But now, when he falls in love with her again, she rejects him and in bitter contempt: what she is now is not what she 'really' is. He has rejected her 'real' self. He has betrayed a real love and now loves a counterfeit. When she rejects him, she is preserving her real self, whom he has betrayed and rejected.

Ella does not write this story. She is afraid that writing it might make it come true.

She looks inside herself again and finds:

A man and a woman. She, after years of freedom, is

460

over-ready for a serious love. He is playing at the role of a serious lover because of some need for asylum or refuge. (Ella gets the idea of this character from the Canadian script-writer—from his cool and mask-like attitude as a lover: he was watching himself in a role, the role of a married man with a mistress. It is this aspect of the Canadian that Ella uses—a man watching himself play a role.) The woman, over-hungry, over-intense, freezes the man even more than he is; although he only half-knows he is frozen. The woman, having been unpossessive, unjealous, undemanding, turns into a jailor. It is as if she is possessed by a personality not hers. And she watches her own deterioration into this possessive termagant with surprise, as if this other self has nothing to do with her. And she is convinced it has not. For when the man accuses her of being a jealous spy, she replied and with sincerity: 'I'm not jealous, I've never been jealous.' Ella looked at this story with amazement; because there was nothing in her own experience that could suggest it. Where, then, had it come from? Ella thinks of Paul's wife—but no; she had been too humble and accepting to suggest such a character. Or perhaps her own husband, self-abasing, jealous, abject, making feminine hysterical scenes because of his incapacity as a man? Presumably, thinks Ella, this figure, her husband, with whom she was linked so briefly and apparently without any real involvement, is the masculine equivalent of the virago in her story? Which, however, she decides not to write. It is written, within her, but she does not recognise it as hers. Perhaps I read it somewhere?—she wonders; or someone told it to me and I've forgotten hearing about it?

About this time Ella pays a visit to her father. It is some time since she has seen him. Nothing has changed in his life. He is still quiet, absorbed in his garden, his books, a military man turned some sort of mystic. Or had always been a mystic? Ella, and for the first time, wonders: What must it have been like, married to such a man? She seldom thinks of her mother, so long dead, but now tries to revive memories of her. She sees a practical, cheerful bustling woman. One evening, sitting across the fireplace from her father, in a white-ceilinged black-beamed room full of books, she watches him read and sip whisky and at last brings herself to talk of her mother.

Her father's face takes on the most comical look of alarm; clearly he, too, has not thought of the dead woman for years. Ella persists. He says at last, abruptly: 'Your mother was altogether too good for me.' He laughs, uncomfortably; and his remote blue eyes suddenly have the startled rolling look of a surprised animal. The laugh offends Ella; but she recognises why: she is annoyed on behalf of the wife, her mother. She thinks: What's wrong with Julia and me is quite simple: we're being mistress figures long past the age for it. She says aloud: 'Why too good?' although her father has picked up his book again as a shield. He says, over the top of the book, an elderly burned-leather man, suddenly agitated with emotions thirty years old: 'Your mother was a good woman. She was a good wife. But she had no idea, absolutely no idea at all, all that sort of thing was left completely out of her.' 'You mean sex?' asks Ella, forcing herself to speak in spite of her distaste for associating these ideas with her parents. He laughs, offended; his eyes rolling again: 'Of course all you people don't mind talking about that sort of thing. I never talk about it. Yes, sex, if that's what you call it. Was left clean out of her make-up, that sort of thing.' The book, a memoir of some British General, is raised against Ella. Ella insists: 'Well, what did you do about it?' The edges of the book seem to tremble. A pause. She has meant: Didn't you teach her? But her father's voice says from behind the book—the clipped yet hesitant voice, clipped from training, hesitant because of the vagueness of his private world: 'When I couldn't stick it, I went out and bought myself a woman. What did you expect?' The *what did you expect* is addressed, not to Ella, but to her mother. 'And jealous! She didn't give a damn about me, but she was jealous as a sick cat.'

Ella says: 'I meant, perhaps she was shy. Perhaps you should have taught her?' For she is remembering Paul's saying: There is no such thing as a frigid woman, there are only incompetent men.

The book slowly lowers to her father's lean and stick-like thighs. The yellowish, dry, lean face has flushed, and the blue

462

eyes were protuberant, like an insect's: 'Look here. Marriage as far as I'm concerned—well! Well, you're sitting there, so I suppose that's a justification of it.'

Ella says: 'I suppose I ought to say I'm sorry—but I want to know about her. She was my mother after all.'

'I don't think of her. Not for years. I think of her sometimes when you do me the honour of a visit.'

'Is that why I feel you don't like seeing me much?' says Ella, but smiling and forcing him to look at her.

'I never said that, did I? I don't feel it. But all these family ties—family stuff, marriage, that sort of thing, it seems pretty unreal to me. You're my daughter, so I believe. Must be, knowing your mother. I don't feel it. Blood ties—do you feel it? I don't.'

'Yes,' says Ella. 'When I'm here with you, I feel some sort of a bond. I don't know what.'

'No, I don't either.' The old man has recovered himself, and is again in a remote place, safe from the hurt of personal emotions. 'We're human beings—whatever that may mean. I don't know. I'm pleased to see you, when you do me the honour. Don't think you're not welcome. But I'm getting old. You don't know what that means yet. All that stuff, family, children, that sort of thing, seems unreal. It's not what matters. To me at least.'

'What does matter then?'

'God, I suppose. Whatever that may mean. Oh, of course, I know it means nothing to you. Why should it? Used to get a glimpse sometimes. In the desert—the army, you know. Or in danger. Sometimes now, at night. I think being alone—it's important. People, human beings, that kind of thing, it's just a mess. People should leave each other alone.' He takes a sip of whisky, stares at her, with a look of being astonished at what he sees. 'You're my daughter. So I believe. I know nothing about you. Help you any way I can of course. You'll get what money I have when I go—but you know that. Not that it's much. But I don't want to know about your life— shouldn't approve of it anyway, I suppose.'

'No, I don't think you would.'

'That husband of yours, a stick, couldn't understand it.'

463

'It was a long time ago. Suppose I told you that I'd loved a married man for five years and that was the most important thing in my life?'

'Your business. Not mine. And men since, I suppose. You're not like your mother, that's something. More like a woman I had after she died.'

'Why didn't you marry her?'

'She was married. Stuck to her husband. Well, she was right, I suppose. In that line it was the best thing in my life, but that line—it never was the most important to me.'

'You don't ever wonder about me? What I'm doing? You don't think about your grandson?'

And now he was clearly in full retreat, he didn't like this pressure at all.

'No. Oh, he's a jolly little chap. Always pleased to see him. But he'll turn into a cannibal like everyone else.'

'A cannibal?'

'Yes, cannibals. People are just cannibals unless they leave each other alone. As for you—what do I know about you? You're a modern woman, don't know anything about them.'

'A modern woman,' says Ella drily, smiling.

'Yes. Your book, I suppose. I suppose you're after something of your own the way we all are. And good luck to you. We can't help each other. People don't help each other, they are better apart.'

With which he lifts his book, having given her a final warning that the conversation is over by means of a short abrupt stare.

Ella, alone in her room, looks into her private pool, waiting for the shadows to form, for the story to shape itself. She sees a young professional officer, shy, proud and inarticulate. She sees a shy and cheerful young wife. And now a memory, not an image, rises to the surface: she sees this scene: late at night, in her bedroom, she is pretending to be asleep. Her father and mother are standing in the middle of the room. He puts his arms about her, she is bashful and coy like a girl. He kisses her, then she runs fast out of the bedroom in tears. He stands alone, angry, pulling at his moustache.

He remains alone, withdrawing from his wife into books and the dry, spare dreams of a man who might have been a poet or a mystic. And in fact, when he dies, journals, poems, fragments of prose are found in locked drawers.

Ella is surprised by this conclusion. She had never thought of her father as a man who might write poetry, or write at all. She visits her father again, as soon as she can.

Late at night, in the silent room where the fire burns slowly in the wall, she asks: 'Father, have you ever written poetry?' The book descends to his lean thighs with a bump and he stares at her. 'How the hell did you know?'

'I don't know. I just thought perhaps you did.'

'I've never told a soul.'

'Can I see them?'

He sits a while, pulling at his fierce old moustache that is now white. Then he gets up and unlocks a drawer. He hands her a sheaf of poems. They are all poems about solitude, loss, fortitude, the adventures of isolation. They are usually about soldiers. T. E. Lawrence: 'A lean and austere man among lean men.' Rommel: 'And at evening lovers pause outside the town, where an acre or so of crosses lean in the sand.' Cromwell: 'Faiths, mountains, monuments and rocks . . .' T. E. Lawrence again: '. . . yet travels wild escarpments of the soul.' And T. E. Lawrence again who renounced: 'The clarity, the action and the clean rewards, and owned himself beat, like all who come to words.'

Ella hands them back. The wild old man takes the poems and locks them up again.

'You've never thought of having them published.'

'Certainly not. What for?'

'I just wondered.'

'Of course you're different. You write to get published. Well, I suppose people do.'

'You never said, did you like my novel? Did you read it?'

'Like it? It was written well, that sort of thing. But that poor stick, what did he want to kill himself for?'

'People do.'

'What? Everyone wants to at some time or another. But why write about it?'

'You may be right.'

'I'm not saying I'm right. That's what I feel. It's the difference between my lot and yours.'

'What, killing ourselves?'

'No. You ask such a lot. Happiness. That sort of thing. Happiness! I don't remember thinking about it. Your lot—you seem to think something's owed to you. It's because of the communists.'

'What?' says Ella, startled and amused.

'Yes, your lot, you're all reds.'

'But I'm not a communist. You're mixing me up with my friend Julia. And even she's stopped being one.'

'It's all the same thing. They've got at you. You all think you can do anything.'

'Well, I think that's true—somewhere at the back of the minds of "our lot" is the belief that anything is possible. You seemed to be content with so little.'

'Content? Content! What sort of word is that.'

'I mean that for better or worse, we are prepared to experiment with ourselves, to try and be different kinds of people. But you simply submitted to something.'

The old man sits, fierce and resentful. 'That young sap in your book, he thought of nothing but killing himself.'

'Perhaps because something *was* owed to him, it's owed to everyone, and he didn't get it.'

'Perhaps, you say? Perhaps? You wrote it, so you ought to know.'

'Perhaps next time I'll try to write about that—people who deliberately try to be something else, try to break their own form as it were.'

'You talk as if—a person is a person. A man is what he is. He can't be anything else. You can't change that.'

'Well then, I think that's the real difference between us. Because I believe you can change it.'

'Then I don't follow you. And I don't want to. Bad enough to cope with what one is, instead of complicating things even more.'

This conversation with her father starts a new train of thought for Ella.

466

Now, looking for the outlines of a story and finding, again and again, nothing but patterns of defeat, death, irony, she deliberately refuses them. She tries to force patterns of happiness or simple life. But she fails.

Then she finds herself thinking: I've got to accept the patterns of self-knowledge which mean unhappiness or at least a dryness. But I can twist it into victory. A man and a woman—yes. Both at the end of their tether. Both cracking up because of a deliberate attempt to transcend their own limits. And out of the chaos, a new kind of strength.

Ella looks inwards, as into a pool, to find this story imaged; but it remains a series of dry sentences in her mind. She waits, she waits patiently, for the images to form, to take on life.

[For something like eighteen months the blue notebook consisted of short entries different in style not only from previous entries in the blue notebook but from anything else in the notebooks. This section began:]

17th October, 1954: Anna Freeman, born 10th November, 1922, a daughter of Colonel Frank Freeman and May Fortescue; lived 23 Baker Street; educated Girls' High School, Hampstead; spent six years Central Africa—1939 to 1945; married Max Wulf 1945; one daughter, born 1946; divorced Max Wulf 1947; joined Communist Party 1950, left it 1954.

[Each day had its entry, consisting of short factual statements: 'Got up early. Read so-and-so. Saw so-and-so. Janet is sick. Janet is well. Molly is offered a part she likes/doesn't like, etc.' After a date in March 1956, a line in heavy black was drawn across the page, marking the end of the neat small entries. And the last eighteen months had been ruled out, every page, with a thick black cross. And now Anna continued in a different writing, not the clear small script of the daily entries, but fluent, rapid, in parts almost unintelligible with the speed it had been written:]

So all that is a failure too. The blue notebook, which I had expected to be the most truthful of the notebooks, is worse than any of them. I expected a terse record of facts to present some sort of a pattern when I read it over, but this sort of record is as false as the account of what happened on 15th September, 1954, which I read now embarrassed because of its emotionalism and because of its assumption that if I wrote 'at nine-thirty I went to the lavatory to shit and at two to pee and at four I sweated,' this would be more real than if I simply wrote what I thought. And yet I still don't understand why. Because although in life things like going to the lavatory or changing a tampon when one has one's period are dealt with on an almost unconscious level, I can recall every detail of a day two years ago because I remember that Molly had blood on her skirt and I had to warn her to go upstairs and change before her son came in.

And of course this is not a literary problem at all; it is the same as the 'experience' with Mother Sugar. I remember saying to her that for the larger part of our time together her task was to make me conscious of, to become preoccupied by, physical facts which we spend our childhood learning to ignore so as to live at all. And then she made the obvious reply: that the 'learning' in childhood was of the wrong kind, or otherwise I would not need to be sitting opposite her in a chair asking for her help three times a week. To which I replied, knowing I would get no answer to it, or at least, not on the level I wanted, since I knew that what I was saying was the 'intellectualising' to which she attributed my emotional troubles: 'It seems to me that being psycho-analysed is essentially a process where one is forced back into infantilism and then rescued from it by crystallising what one learns into a sort of intellectual primitivism—one is forced back into myth, and folk lore and everything that belongs to the savage or undeveloped stages of society. For if I say to you: I recognise in that dream, such and such a myth; or in that emotion about my father, that folk-tale; or the atmosphere of that memory is the same as an English ballad—then you smile, you are satisfied. As far as you are concerned, I've gone beyond the childish, I've transmuted it and saved it, by embodying it in myth. But in fact all I do, or you do, is to fish among the childish memories of an individual, and merge them with the art or ideas that belong to the childhood of a people. At which, of course, she smiled. And I said: 'I'm now using your own weapons against you. I'm talking not of what you say, but how you react. Because the moments when you're really pleased and excited; the moments when your face comes alive are those when I say the dream I had last night was of the same stuff of Hans Andersin's story about the Little Mermaid. But when I try to use an experience, a memory, a dream, in modern terms, try to speak of it critically or drily or with complexity, you almost seem bored or impatient. So I deduce from this that what really pleases you, what really moves you, is the world of the primitive. Do you realise that I've never once, not once, spoken of an experience I've had, or a dream, in the way one would speak of it to a friend, or the way you would speak of it, outside this room, to a friend, without earning a frown from you—and I swear the frown or the impatience is something you aren't conscious of. Or are you going to say that the frown is deliberate, because you think I'm not really ready to move forward out of the world of myth?'

'And so?' she said, smiling.

I said: 'That's better—you'd smile like that if I were talking to you in a drawing-room—yes, I know you're going to say that this isn't a drawing-room, and I'm here because I'm in trouble.'

'And so?'—smiling.

'I'm going to make the obvious point that perhaps the word neurotic means the condition of being highly conscious and developed. The essence of neurosis is conflict. But the essence of living now, fully, not blocking off to what goes on, is conflict. In fact I've reached the stage where I look at people and say—he or she, they are whole at all because they've chosen to block off at this stage or that. People stay sane by blocking off, by limiting themselves.'

'Would you say you were better or worse for your experience with me?'

'But now you're back in the consulting room. Of course

I'm better. But that's a clinical term. I'm afraid of being better at the cost of living inside myth and dreams. Psychoanalysis stands or falls on whether it makes better human beings, morally better, not clinically more healthy. What you are really asking me now is: Am I able to live more easily now than I did? Am I less in conflict, less in doubt, less neurotic in short? Well, you know that I am.'

I remember how she sat opposite me, the alert, vigorous old woman, with her efficient blouse and skirt, her white hair dragged back into a hasty knot, frowning at me. I was pleased because of the frown—we were outside, for a moment, the analyst-patient relationship.

'Look,' I said. 'If I were sitting here, describing a dream I'd had last night, the wolf-dream, let's say, more highly developed, there'd be a certain look on your face. And I know what the look means because I feel it myself—recognition. The pleasure of recognition, of a bit of rescue-work, so to speak, rescuing the formless into form. Another bit of chaos rescued and "named." Do you know how you smile when I "name" something? It's as if you'd just saved someone from drowning. And I know the feeling. It's joy. But there's something terrible in it—because I've never known joy, awake, as I do, asleep, during a certain kind of dream—when the wolves come down out of the forest, or when the castle gates open, or when I'm standing before the ruined white temple on the white sands with the blue sea and sky behind it, or when I'm flying like Icarus—during these dreams, no matter what frightening material they incorporate, I could cry with happiness. And I know why—it's because all the pain, and the killing and the violence is safely held in the story and it can't hurt me.'

She was silent, looking at me intently.

I said: 'Are you saying perhaps that I'm not ready to go on further? Well, I think that if I'm capable of being impatient, of wanting it, I must be ready for the next stage?'

'And what is the next stage?'

'The next stage is, surely, that I leave the safety of myth and Anna Wulf walks forward alone.'

'Alone?' she said, and added drily, 'You're a communist, or

so you say, but you want to go alone. Isn't that what you'd call a contradiction?'

And so we laughed, and it might have ended there, but I went on: 'You talk about individuation. So far what it has meant to me is this: that the individual recognises one part after another of his earlier life as an aspect of the general human experience. When he can say: What I did then, what I felt then, is only the reflection of that great archetypal dream, or epic story, or stage in history, then he is free, because he has separated himself from the experience, or fitted it like a piece of mosaic into a very old pattern, and by the act of setting it into place, is free of the individual pain of it.'

'Pain?' she queried softly.

'Well, my dear, people don't come to you because they are suffering from an excess of happiness.'

'No, they usually come, like you, because they say they can't feel.'

'But now I can feel. I'm open to everything. But no sooner do you accomplish that, than you say quickly—put it away, put the pain away where it can't hurt, turn it into a story or into history. But I don't want to put it away. Yes, I know what you want me to say—that because I've rescued so much private pain-material—because I'm damned if I'll call it anything else, and "worked through it" and accepted it and made it general, because of that I'm free and strong. Well all right, I'll accept it and say it. And what now? I'm tired of the wolves and the castles and the forests and the priests. I can cope with them in any form they choose to present themselves. But I've told you, I want to walk off, by myself, Anna Freeman.'

'By yourself?' she said again.

'Because I'm convinced that there are whole areas of me made by the kind of experience women haven't had before . . .'

The small smile was already beginning on her face—it was the 'conducting smile' of our sessions together, we were back as analyst and patient.

I said: 'No, don't smile yet. I believe I'm living the kind of life women never lived before.'

'Never?' she said, and behind her voice I could hear the sounds she always evoked at such moments—seas lapping on old beaches, voices of people centuries dead. She had the capacity to evoke a feeling of vast areas of time by a smile or a tone of voice that could delight me, rest me, fill me with joy—but I didn't want it just then.

'Never,' I said.

'The details change, but the form is the same,' she said.

'No,' I insisted.

'In what way are you different? Are you saying there haven't been artist-women before? There haven't been women who were independent? There haven't been women who insisted on sexual freedom! I tell you, there are a great line of women stretching out behind you into the past, and you have to seek them out and find them in yourself and be conscious of them.'

'They didn't look at themselves as I do. They didn't feel as I do. How could they? I don't want to be told when I wake up, terrified by a dream of total annihilation, because of the H-bomb exploding, that people felt that way about the cross-bow. It isn't true. There is something new in the world. And I don't want to hear, when I've had encounter with some Mogul in the film industry, who wields the kind of power over men's minds that no emperor ever did, and I come back feeling trampled on all over, that Lesbia felt like that after an encounter with her wine-merchant. And I don't want to be told when I suddenly have a vision (though God knows it's hard enough to come by) of a life that isn't full of hatred and fear and envy and competition every minute of the night and the day that this is simply the old dream of the golden age brought up to date . . .'

'Isn't it?' she said, smiling.

'No, because the dream of the golden age is a million times more powerful because it's possible, just as total destruction is possible. Probably *because* both are possible.'

'What do you want me to say then?'

'I want to be able to separate in myself what is old and

cyclic, the recurring history, the myth, from what is new, what I feel or think that might be new . . .' I saw the look on her face, and said: 'You are saying that nothing I feel or think is new?'

'I have never said . . .' she began, and then switched to the royal *we* . . . 'we have never said or suggested that further development of the human race isn't possible. You aren't accusing me of that, are you? Because it's the opposite of what we say.'

'I'm accusing you of behaving as if you didn't believe it. Look, if I'd said to you when I came in this afternoon: Yesterday I met a man at a party and I recognised in him the wolf, or the knight, or the monk, you'd nod and you'd smile. And we'd both feel the joy of recognition. But if I'd said: Yesterday I met a man at a party and suddenly he said something, and I thought: *Yes,* there's a hint of something— there's a crack in that man's personality like a gap in a dam, and through that gap the future might pour in a different shape—terrible perhaps, or marvellous, but something new—if I said that, you'd frown.'

'Did you meet such a man?' she demanded, practically.

'*No.* I didn't. But sometimes I meet people, and it seems to me the fact they are cracked across, they're split, means they are keeping themselves open for something.'

She said, after a long, thoughtful silence: 'Anna, you shouldn't be saying this to me at all.'

I was surprised. I said: 'You're not deliberately inviting me to be dishonest with you?'

'No. I'm saying that you should be writing again.'

I was angry, of course, and of course she knew I was going to be.

'You're suggesting I should write of our experience? How? If I set down every word of the exchange between us during an hour, it would be unintelligible unless I wrote the story of my life to explain it.'

'And so?'

'It would be a record of how I saw myself at a certain point. Because the record of an hour in the first week, let's

473

say, of my seeing you, and an hour now, would be so different that . . .'

'And so?'

'And besides, there are literary problems, problems of taste you never seem to think of. What you and I have done together is essentially to break down shame. In the first week of knowing you I wouldn't have been able to say: I remember the feeling of violent repulsion and shame and curiosity I felt when I saw my father naked. It took me months to break down barriers in myself so I could say something like that. But now I can say something like: . . . because I wanted my father to die and—but the person reading it, without the subjective experience, the breaking down, would be shocked, as by the sight of blood or a word that has associations of shame, and the shock would swallow everything else.'

She said drily: 'My dear Anna, you are using our experience together to re-enforce your rationalisations for not writing.'

'Oh, my God no, that is not all I'm saying.'

'Or are you saying that some books are for a minority of people?'

'My dear Mrs Marks, you know quite well it would be against my principles to admit any such idea, even if I had it.'

'Very well then, *if* you had it, tell me why some books are for the minority.'

I thought, and then said: 'It's a question of form.'

'Form? What about the content of yours? I understood that you people insisted on separating form and content?'

'My people may separate them, I don't. At least, not till this moment. But now I'll say it's a question of form. People don't mind immoral messages. They don't mind art which says that murder is good, cruelty is good, sex for sex's sake is good. They like it, provided the message is wrapped up a little. And they like messages saying that murder is bad, cruelty is bad, and love is love is love is love. What they can't stand is to be told it all doesn't matter, they can't stand formlessness.'

474

'So it is formless works of art, if such a thing were possible, that are for the minority?'

'But I don't hold the belief that some books are for the minority. You know I don't. I don't hold the aristocratic view of art.'

'My dear Anna, your attitude to art is so aristocratic that you write, when you do, for yourself only.'

'And so do all the others,' I heard myself muttering.

'What others?'

'The others, all over the world, who are writing away in secret books, because they are afraid of what they are thinking.'

'So you are afraid of what you are thinking?' And she reached out for her appointment book, marking the end of our hour.

[At this point, another thick black line across the page.]

When I came to this new flat and arranged my big room the first thing I did was to buy the trestle table and lay my notebooks on it. And yet in the other flat in Molly's house, the notebooks were stuffed into a suitcase under the bed. I didn't buy them on a plan. I don't think I ever, until I came here, actually said to myself: I keep four notebooks, a black notebook, which is to do with Anna Wulf the writer; a red notebook, concerned with politics; a yellow notebook, in which I make stories out of my experience; and a blue notebook which tries to be a diary. In Molly's house the notebooks were something I never thought about; and certainly not as work, or a responsibility.

The things that are important in life creep up on one unawares, one doesn't expect them, one hasn't given them shape in one's mind. One recognises them, when they've appeared, that's all.

When I came to this flat it was to give room, not only to a man (Michael or his successor) but to the notebooks. And in fact I now see moving to this flat as giving room to the notebooks. For I hadn't been here a week before I had bought the trestle table and laid out the books on it. And

475

then I read them. I hadn't read them through since I first began to keep them. I was disturbed by reading them. First, because I had not realised before how the experience of being rejected by Michael had affected me; how it had changed, or apparently had changed, my whole personality. But above all, because I didn't recognise myself. Matching what I had written with what I remembered it all seemed false. And this—the untruthfulness of what I had written was because of something I had not thought of before—my sterility. The deepening note of criticism, of defensiveness, of dislike.

It was then I decided to use the blue notebook, this one, as nothing but a record of facts. Every evening I sat on the music-stool and wrote down my day, and it was as if I, Anna, were nailing Anna to the page. Every day I shaped Anna, said: Today I got up at seven, cooked breakfast for Janet, sent her to school, etc. etc., and felt as if I had saved that day from chaos. Yet now I read those entries and feel nothing. I am increasingly afflicted by vertigo where words mean nothing. Words mean nothing. They have become, *when I think*, not the form into which experience is shaped, but a series of meaningless sounds, like nursery talk, and away to one side of experience. Or like the sound track of a film that has slipped its connection with the film. *When I am thinking* I have only to write a phrase like 'I walked down the street,' or take a phrase from a newspaper 'economic measures which lead to the full use of . . .' and immediately the words dissolve, and my mind starts spawning images which have nothing to do with the words, so that every word I see or hear seems like a small raft bobbing about on an enormous sea of images. So I can't write any longer. Or only when I write fast, without looking back at what I have written. For if I look back, then the words swim and have no sense and I am conscious only of me, Anna, as a pulse in a great darkness, and the words that I, Anna, write down are nothing, or like the secretions of a caterpillar that are forced out in ribbons to harden in the air.

It occurs to me that what is happening is a breakdown of me, Anna, and this is how I am becoming aware of it. For words are form, and if I am at a pitch where shape, form, expression are nothing, then I am nothing, for it has become clear to me, reading the notebooks, that I remain Anna because of a certain kind of intelligence. This intelligence is dissolving and I am very frightened.

Last night I had a recurrence of that dream which, as I told Mother Sugar, was the most frightening of all the different types of cycles of dreams. When she asked me to 'give a name to it' (to give it form), I said it was the nightmare about destruction. Later, when I dreamed it again, and she said: Give it a name, I was able to go further: I said it was the nightmare about the principle of spite, or malice—joy in spite.

The first time I dreamed it, the principle, or figure, took form in a certain vase I had then, a peasant wooden vase from Russia, that someone had brought back. It was bulbous, rather jolly and naïve in shape, and covered with crude red and black and gilt patterns. This vase, in my dream, had a personality, and the personality was the nightmare, for it represented something anarchistic and uncontrollable, something destructive. This figure, or object, for it was not human, more like a species of elf or pixie, danced and jumped with a jerky cocky liveliness and it menaced not only me, but everything that was alive, but impersonally, and without reason. This was when I 'named' the dream as about destruction. The next time I dreamed, months later, but instantly recognised it as the same dream, the principle or element took shape in an old man, almost dwarf-like, infinitely more terrifying than the vase-object, because he was part human. This old man smiled and giggled and sniggered, was ugly, vital and powerful, and again, what he represented was pure spite, malice, joy in malice, joy in a destructive impulse. This was when I 'named' the dream as about joy in spite. And I dreamed the dream again, always when particularly tired, or under stress, or in conflict, when I could feel that the walls of myself were thin or in danger. The element took a variety of shapes, usually that of a very old man or woman (yet there was a suggestion of a double sex, or even sexlessness) and the figure was always very lively, in spite of having

477

a wooden leg, or a crutch, or a hump, or being deformed in some way. And the creature was always powerful, with an inner vitality which I knew was caused by a purposeless, undirected, causeless spite. It mocked and jibed and hurt, wished murder, wished death. And yet it was always vibrant with joy. Telling Mother Sugar of this dream, re-created for perhaps the sixth or seventh time, she asked as usual: 'And how do you name it?' and I replied as usual with the words spite, malice, pleasure in hurt; and she enquired: 'Only negative qualities, nothing good about it?' 'Nothing,' I said, surprised. 'And there is nothing creative at all there?' 'Not for me.'

She then smiled in the way I knew meant that I should think more about it, and I asked: 'If this figure is an elemental and creative force, for good as well as for evil, then why should I fear it so terribly?' 'Perhaps as you dream deeper you'll feel the vitality as good as well as bad.'

'It's so dangerous to me that as soon as I feel the atmosphere of that figure, even before the figure has appeared, and I know the dream is beginning, I struggle and scream to wake up.'

'It is dangerous to you as long as you fear it—' This with the homely, emphatic, mother-nod, which always, in spite of everything, and no matter how deep I was embroiled in some hurt or problem, made me want to laugh. And I did laugh, often, helpless in my chair, while she sat smiling, for she had spoken as people do of animals or snakes: they won't hurt you if you don't fear them.

And I thought, as I often did, that she was having it both ways: for if this figure, or element, was so familiar to her in the dreams or fantasies of her patients that she instantly recognised it, then why was it my responsibility that the thing was totally evil? Only the word evil is too human a word for a principle felt to be, in spite of what part-human shapes it chose to assume, as essentially inhuman.

In other words, it was up to me to force this thing to be good as well as bad? That was what she was saying?

Last night I dreamed the dream again, and this time it was more terrifying than anything I've experienced, because I felt

478

the terror, the helplessness, in face of the uncontrolled force for destruction, when there was no object or thing or even a dwarf to hold it. I was in a dream with another person, who I did not immediately recognise; and then I understood that this terrible malicious force was in that person who was a friend. And so I forced myself awake out of the dream, screaming, and when I awoke I put a name to the person in my dream, knowing that for the first time the principle was embodied in a human being. And when I knew who the person was, I was even more frightened. For it was safer to have that terrible frightening force held in a shape associated with the mythical or the magical, than loose, or as it were at large, in a person, and in a person who had the power to move me.

Once really awake, and looking back at the dream from the condition of being awake, I was frightened because if the element is now outside of myth, and inside another human being, then it can only mean it is loose in me also, or can only too easily be evoked.

I should now write down the experience to which the dream related.

[At this point Anna had drawn a heavy black line across the page. After it she had written:]

I drew that line because I didn't want to write it. As if writing about it sucks me even further into danger. Yet I have to hold fast to this—that Anna, the thinking Anna, can look at what Anna feels and 'name' it.

What is happening is something new in my life. I think many people have a sense of shape, of unfolding, in their lives. This sense makes it possible for them to say: Yes, this new person is important to me: he, or she, is the beginning of something I must live through. Or: This emotion, which I have not felt before, is not the alien I believed it to be. It will now be part of me and I must deal with it.

It is easy now, looking back over my life, to say: That Anna, in that time, was such and such a person. And then, five years later, she was such and such. A year, two years, five years of a certain kind of being can be rolled up and tucked away, or 'named'—yes, during that time I was like that. Well now I am in the middle of such a period, and when it is over I shall glance back at it casually and say: Yes, that's what I was. I was a woman terribly vulnerable, critical, using femaleness as a sort of standard or yardstick to measure and discard men. Yes—something like that. I was an Anna who invited defeat from men without even being conscious of it. (But I am conscious of it. And being conscious of it means I shall leave it all behind me and become—but what?) I was stuck fast in an emotion common to women of our time, that can turn them bitter, or Lesbian, or solitary. Yes, that Anna, during that time was ...

[Another black line across the page:]

About three weeks ago I went to a political meeting. This one was informal, at Molly's house. Comrade Harry, one of the top academics in the C.P., recently went to Russia, to find out, as a Jew, what had happened to the Jews in the 'black years' before Stalin died. He fought the communist brass to go at all; they tried to stop him. He used threats, saying if they would not let him go, would not help him, he would publicise the fact. He went; came back with terrible information; they did not want any of it made known. His argument the usual one from the 'intellectuals' of this time: just for once the communist party should admit and explain what everyone knew to be true. Their argument, the old argument of the communist bureaucracy—solidarity with the Soviet Union at all cost, which means admitting as little as possible. They agreed to publish a limited report, leaving out the worst of the horrors. He has been conducting a series of meetings for communists and ex-communists in which he has been speaking about what he discovered. Now the brass are furious, and are threatening him with expulsion; threatening members who go to his meetings with expulsion. He is going to resign.

There were forty-odd people in Molly's living-room. All 'intellectuals.' What Harry told us was very bad, but not

480

much worse than we knew from the newspapers. I noticed a man sitting next to me listening quietly. His quietness impressed me in an emotional gathering. We smiled at each other at one point with the painful irony that is the mark of our kind now. The formal meeting ended, and about ten people remained. I recognised the atmosphere of the 'closed meeting'—more was to follow, the non-communists were expected to leave. But after a hesitation Harry and the others said we could stay. Harry then spoke again. What we had heard before was terrible; what we heard now worse even than what the most virulent anti-communist papers were printing. They were in no position to get the real facts and Harry had been. He spoke of the tortures, the beatings-up, the most cynical kinds of murder. About Jews being locked in cages designed in the Middle Ages for torture, of being tortured with instruments taken from museums. And so on.

What he was saying now was on a different level of horror from what he had said before, to the meeting of forty people. When he had finished, we asked questions; each answer brought out something new and terrible. What we were seeing was something we knew very well from our own experience: a communist, determined to be honest, yet fighting every inch of the way even now not to have to admit the truth about the Soviet Union. When he had finished speaking, the quiet man, whose name turned out to be Nelson (an American), got up and broke into passionate oratory. The word comes easily because he spoke well, and obviously out of a great deal of political experience. A strong voice, and practised. But now he was accusatory. He said that the reason why the communist parties of the West had collapsed, or would collapse, was because they were incapable of telling the truth about anything; and because of their long habit of telling lies to the world, could no longer distinguish the truth even to themselves. Yet tonight, he said, after the Twentieth Congress and everything we had learned about the conditions of communism, we saw a leading comrade and one we all know to have fought for the truth inside the Party against people more cynical than he, deliberately dividing the truth into two—one, a mild truth, for the public

481

meeting of forty, and another, a harsher truth, for a closed group. Harry was embarrassed and upset. We did not know then of the threats being used against him by the top brass to stop him speaking at all. He said, however, that the truth was so terrible that as few people as possible should know about it—used the same arguments, in short, that he was fighting the bureaucrats for using.

And now suddenly Nelson got up again and launched into an even more violent, self-accusing denunciation. It was hysterical. And everyone was becoming hysterical—I could feel the hysteria rising in myself. I recognised an atmosphere I recognised from 'the dream about destruction.' It was the feeling or atmosphere that was a prelude to the entrance of the figure of destruction. I got up, and thanked Harry—after all, it was two years since I had been a Party member, with no right in the closed meeting. I went downstairs—Molly was crying in the kitchen. She said: 'It's all very well for you, you aren't Jewish.'

In the street I found Nelson had come down behind me. He said he would take me home. He was quiet again; and I forgot the self-beating note of his speech. He is a man of about forty, Jewish, American, pleasant-looking, a bit of a paterfamilias. I knew I was attracted to him and . . .

[Another heavy black line. Then:]

The reason why I don't want to write this is because I have to fight to write about sex. Extraordinary how strong this prohibition is.

I am making this too complicated—too much about the meeting. Yet Nelson and I would not have so easily been in communion without having shared all that experience, even though it had been in different countries. On that first evening he stayed late. He was courting me. He was talking about me, the sort of life I led. And women always respond at once to men who understand we are on some kind of frontier. I suppose I could say that they 'name' us. We feel safe with them. He went up to see Janet, sleeping. His interest in her was genuine. Three children of his own. Married for seventeen years. His marriage a direct consequence of his having fought in Spain. The tone of the evening was serious, responsible, grown-up. After he left I used the word—grown-up. And I matched him against the men I've been encountering recently (why?) the men-babies. My spirits so high I cautioned myself. I was marvelling, again, how easy it is, living deprived, to forget love, joy, delight. For nearly two years now, the disappointing encounters, one emotional snub after another. I had drawn in my emotional skirts, became guarded in my responses. Now, after one evening with Nelson I had forgotten all that. He came to see me next day. Janet just on her way out to play with friends. Nelson and she instantly friendly. He was speaking as more than a potential lover. He was leaving his wife, he said, needed a real relationship with a woman. He would come that evening 'after Janet was asleep.' I loved him for the sense of the 'after Janet was asleep' and the understanding of the sort of life I have. When he came that evening he was very late, and in a different mood—garrulous, talking compulsively, his eyes darting everywhere, never meeting mine. I felt my spirits sink; it was from my own sudden nervousness and apprehension that I understood, before my mind understood it, that this was going to be another disappointment. He talked of Spain, of the war. He was condemning himself, as he had at the meeting, breast-beating, hysterical, for taking part in the Communist Party betrayals. He said that innocent people had been shot, through him, though he had not believed at the time they were innocent. (Yet as he spoke of this, the feeling kept going through me: he's not really sorry, not really; his hysteria and the noise are a defence against feeling, because it's too terrible, the guilt he would have to feel.) He was also, at moments, very funny, with the American self-punishing humour. At midnight he left, or rather slunk off, still talking at the top of his voice, looking guilty. He talked himself out, so to speak. I began thinking about his wife. But I wouldn't admit what my instincts told me quite clearly was wrong. Next morning, unannounced, he came back. I couldn't recognise him as the loud hysterical man—he was sober and responsible and humorous. He took me into bed and then I knew what was wrong. I asked him if it was always like this. He was disconcerted (and this told me more about his sex relationships than anything) that I frankly spoke about it while he tried to pretend he didn't understand me. Then he said he had a mortal terror of sex, could never stay inside a woman for longer than a few seconds, and had never been different. And I saw, from the nervous, instinctively repulsive haste with which he moved away from me, the haste with which he dressed, how deep was his fear. He said he had started psycho-analysis, expected to be 'cured' soon. (I could not help wanting to laugh at the word 'cured' which is how people talk, going into psycho-analysis, the clinical talk, as if one were submitting finally to a desperate operation that would change one into something else.) Afterwards, our relation had changed—a friendliness, a trust. Because of the trust, we would go on seeing each other.

We did. That was months ago. What frightens me now is—why did I go on with it? It wasn't the self-flattery: I can cure this man. Not at all. I know better, I've known too many of the sexual cripples. It wasn't really compassion. Though that was part of it. I am always amazed, in myself and in other women, at the strength of our need to bolster men up. This is ironical, living as we do in a time of men's criticising us for being 'castrating,' etc.—all the other words and phrases of the same kind. (Nelson says his wife is 'castrating'—this makes me angry, thinking of the misery she must have lived through.) For the truth is, women have this deep instinctive need to build a man up as a man. Molly for instance. I suppose this is because real men become fewer and fewer, and we are frightened, trying to create men.

No, what terrifies me is my willingness. It is what Mother Sugar would call 'the negative side' of the women's need to placate, to submit. Now I am not Anna, I have no will, I can't move out of a situation once it has started, I just go along with it.

Within a week of my having gone to bed with Nelson the first time I was in a situation I had no control over. The man Nelson, the responsible quiet man, had vanished. I could no longer even remember him. Even the words, the language of

484

emotional responsibility had gone. He was driven by a shrill compulsive hysteria, in which I was also caught up. We went to bed for the second time: to the accompaniment of a highly verbal, bitterly humorous self-denunciation which switched at once into hysterical abuse of all women. Then he vanished from my life for nearly two weeks. I was more nervous, more depressed than I can remember being. I was sexless, too. I had no sex—nothing. A long way off I could see Anna, who belonged to a world of normality and warmth. I could see her but I could not remember what it was like to be alive, as she was. He rang me twice, making excuses, insultingly obvious, because there was no need for them—they were excuses made to 'a woman,' to 'women,' to 'the enemy,' not to Anna; in his good moments he'd be incapable of such insensitivity. I had, in my mind, written him off as a lover, but intended to keep him as a friend. There's a kinship between us, the relationship of a certain kind of self-knowledge, of despair. Well, and then one evening he came over, unannounced, and in his other, his 'good' personality. And listening to him then I could not remember what he was like when hysterical and driven. I sat there and looked at him, in the same way as I look at the sane and happy Anna—he's out of reach, she's out of reach, moving beyond a glass wall. Oh, yes, I understand that glass wall certain kinds of Americans live behind, I understand it too well—don't touch me, for God's sake don't touch me, don't touch me because I'm afraid of feeling.

That evening he asked me to an evening party at his house. I said I'd go. After he left I knew I shouldn't go because I felt uneasy about it. Yet on the face of it, why not? He'd never be my lover, and so we were friends, so why not go and meet his friends, his wife?

As soon as I entered their flat I realised how much I had not been using my imagination, how stupid I had chosen to be. Sometimes I dislike women, I dislike us all, because of our capacity for not-thinking when it suits us; we choose not to think when we are reaching out for happiness. Well, entering the flat, I knew I had chosen not to think, and I was ashamed and humiliated.

A large rented flat, full of tasteless, anonymous furniture. And I knew that when they moved into a house and filled it with their own chosen things, they would still be anonymous—that was the quality, anonymity. The safety of anonymity. Yes, and I understand that too, too well. They mentioned the rent of this flat and I was filled with disbelief. Thirty pounds a week, it's a fortune, it's crazy. There were about twelve people, all Americans to do with television or the films—'show business' people; and of course they joked about it. 'We're show biz, and why not? Nothing wrong with *that*, is there?' They all knew each other, their 'knowing each other' was on the basis of being show business, on the arbitrary contacts of their work; yet they were friendly, it was an attractive, accepting, casual friendliness. I liked it, it reminded me of the casual, informal friendliness of the white people of Africa. 'Hallo. Hallo! How are you? My house is yours, though I've only met you once.' Yet I liked it. By English standards they were all rich. In England people as rich as they are don't talk about it. An atmosphere of money all the time, anxious money, with these American people. Yet, with all the money, everything so expensive (which they apparently take for granted), a middle-class atmosphere that is hard to define. I sat there, trying to define it. It's a kind of deliberate ordinariness, a scaling-down of the individual; it's as if they all have, built in, a need to fit themselves to what is expected. And yet one likes them so much, they are such good people, one watches them full of pain because they choose to scale themselves down, to set limits. The limits are money-limits. (Yet why?—half of them were left-wingers, had been black-listed, were in England because they couldn't earn in America. Yet money, money, money all the time.) Yes, I could feel the money-anxiety, it was in the air, like a question. Yet the rent of Nelson's big ugly flat would keep an English middle-class family in comfort.

I was secretly fascinated by Nelson's wife—half the ordinary curiosity—what is this new person like? But the other half I was ashamed of—what does she lack that I have? Nothing—that I could see.

She is attractive. A tall, very thin, almost bony, Jewish

486

woman; very attractive, with striking bold features, everything emphasised, big mobile mouth, big, rather beautiful curved nose, large prominent striking black eyes. And colourful dashing clothes. A loud shrill voice (which I hated, I hate loud voices), and an emphatic laugh. A great style and assurance about her, which of course I envied, I always do. And then, looking at her, I knew it was a superficial self-assurance. For she never took her eyes off Nelson. Never, not for one moment. (Whereas he wouldn't look at her, he was afraid to.) That quality I begin to recognise in American women—the surface competence, the assurance. And underneath the anxiety. They have a nervous, frightened look to their shoulders. They are frightened. They look as if they were out in a space somewhere by themselves, pretending that they are not alone. They have the look of people alone, people isolated. But pretending not to be alone. They frighten me.

Well, from the moment Nelson came in, she never took her eyes off him. He came in with a wisecrack, the self-punishing, self-defining humour that scares me, because it accepts so much: 'The man is two hours late, and for why?—because he was getting loaded, to face the social happy evening ahead of him.' (And all his friends laughed—though they were the social happy evening.) And she replied, in the same style, gay and tense and accusing: 'But the woman knew he'd be two hours late, because of the happy social evening, so the dinner's fixed to be ready at ten, please don't give yourself one minute's concern over it!' And so they all laughed, and her eyes, apparently so black and bold, so full of apparent self-assurance, were fixed on him, anxious and afraid. 'Scotch? Nelson?' she asked, after serving the others; and her voice was suddenly a shrill plea. 'Double,' he said; aggressive and challenging; and they looked at each other a moment, it was a sudden exposed moment; and the others joked and laughed to cover it. That was another thing that I began to understand—they covered up for each other, all the time. It gave me the most uneasy feeling, watching the easy friendliness, knowing that they were on guard for dangerous moments like this one, so that they could cover up. I was the only English person present, and they were nice about it, for they are nice people, with an instinct for generosity: they made a lot of self-mocking jokes about the stock American attitudes towards the English; and they were very funny, and I laughed a great deal, and felt bad, because I didn't know how to be easily self-mocking in return. We drank a lot; it was a gathering where people set themselves, from the moment of entering, to get just so much drink inside them as soon as possible. Well, I'm not used to it, and so I was drunker than anyone, and very quickly, though they drank very much more than I did. I noticed a tiny blonde woman, in a tight Chinese green-brocade dress. Really beautiful she was, with a tiny neat exquisiteness. She was, or is, the fourth wife of a big ugly dark man, a film tycoon of some kind. She had four doubles in an hour, yet she was cool, controlled, charming; watching her husband's drinking anxiously, babying him out of getting really drunk. 'My baby doesn't really need that new drink,'—cooing at him, baby talk. And he: 'Oh, yes, your baby needs that drink and he's going to have it.' And she stroked and patted him: 'My little baby's not going to drink, no he isn't, because his momma says so.' And good Lord, he didn't. She caressed and babied him, and I thought it was insulting; until I saw this was the basis of this marriage—the beautiful green Chinese dress and the long beautiful earrings, in return for mothering him, babying him. I was embarrassed. No one else was embarrassed. I realised, as I sat there, much too tight, watching them; out of it because I can't talk the cool wise-cracking talk, that I was above all embarrassed; and afraid that next time there was a dangerous corner they wouldn't cover up in time, there'd be some awful explosion. Well, about midnight there was; but I understood there was no need to be scared, because they were all far ahead of me in some area of sophistication well beyond anything I was used to; and it was their self-aware, self-parodying humour that insulated them against real hurt. Protected them, that is, until the moment when the violence exploded into another divorce, or drunken breakdown.

I kept watching Nelson's wife, so bold and attractive and vital, her eyes fixed on Nelson every moment of the evening. Her eyes had a kind of wide, blank, disorganised look about them. I knew the look, but couldn't place it, then at last remembered: Mrs Boothby's eyes were like that when she was cracking up, at the end of the story; they were frantic and disorganised, yet staring wide with the effort not to show the state she was in. And Nelson's wife was locked, I could see, in some permanent, controlled hysteria. Then I understood that they all were; they were all people on the extreme edge of themselves, controlling it, holding it, while hysteria flickered in the good-humoured barbed talk, in the shrewd, on-guard eyes.

Yet they were all used to it, they had been living inside it for years; it was not strange to them, only to me. And yet, sitting there in a corner, not drinking any more, because I had got tight too quickly, and was in the over-aware, over-sensitive state of having drunk too much too quickly and waiting for it all to subside—I understood that this was not so new to me as I imagined; this was nothing more than I had seen in a hundred English marriages, English homes; it was the same thing taken a stage further, taken into awareness and self-consciousness. They were, I understood, above all self-conscious people, aware of themselves all the time; and it was from the awareness, a self-disgusted awareness, that the humour came. The humour was not at all the verbal play, harmless and intellectualised, that the English use; but a sort of disinfection, a making-harmless, a 'naming' to save themselves from pain. It was like peasants touching amulets to avert the evil eye.

It was quite late, as I've said, about midnight, that I heard Nelson's wife's voice, loud and shrill, saying: 'O.K., O.K., I know what's coming next. You're not going to write that script. So why waste your time on Nelson, Bill?' (Bill was the big aggressive husband of the tiny tactful mothering blonde.) She went on, to Bill, who looked determinedly good-humoured: 'He's going to talk and talk again for months, but he'll turn you down at the end of it, and waste his time on another masterpiece that never gets itself on the stage . . .' Then she laughed, a laugh full of apology, but wild and hysterical. Then Nelson, grabbing the stage, so to speak, before Bill could shield him, which he was ready to do:

489

'That's right, that's my wife, her husband wastes time writing masterpieces—well, did I have a play on Broadway, or didn't I?' He shrieked this last at her, shrieking like a woman, his face black with hate of her, and a naked, panicking fear. And they all began laughing, the roomful of people began to laugh and joke, to cover the dangerous moment, and Bill said: 'How do y'know I won't turn Nelson down, it might come to that, it might be my turn to write the masterpiece, I can feel it coming on.' (With a look at his pretty blonde wife which said: Don't worry honey, you know I'm just covering up, don't you?) But it was no good their covering up, the group self-protection was not strong enough for the moment of violence. Nelson and his wife were alone, forgetting all of us, standing at the other side of the room, locked in hatred for each other, and a desperate yearning plea to each other; they were not conscious of us any longer; yet in spite of everything, they were using the deadly, hysterical, self-punishing humour. The wisecrack:

NELSON: Yeah. Hear that baby? Bill's going to write the *Death of a Salesman* for our time, he's going to beat me to it, and whose fault will that be—my ever-loving wife's fault, who else?

SHE (*shrill and laughing, her eyes frantic with anxiety, moving in her face uncontrolled, like small black molluscs, writhing under a knife*): Oh, it's my fault, of course, who else's could it be? That's what I'm for, isn't it?

NELSON: Yes, of course that's what you are for. You cover up for me, I know it. *And I love you for it.* But did I or did I not have that play on Broadway? And all those fine notices? Or did I just imagine it?

SHE: Twelve years ago. Oh, you were a fine American citizen then, no black-lists in sight. *And what have you been doing since?*

HE: *O.K., so they've beaten me.* Do you imagine I don't know it? Do you have to rub it in? I tell you, they don't need firing squads and prison to beat people. It's much easier than that ... well, about *me*. Yeah, about *me* ...

SHE: You're black-listed, you're a hero, that's your alibi for the rest of your life ...

HE: No, dove; no baby, you're my alibi for the rest of my life—who wakes me every morning of my life at four a.m., screaming and wailing that you and your children'll end up on the Bowery if I don't write some more crap for our good friend Bill here?

SHE (*laughing, her face distorted with laughter*): O.K., so I wake up at four every morning. O.K., so I'm scared. Want me to move to the spare room?

HE: Yeah, I want you to move to the spare room. I could use that three hours every morning for working in. If I could remember how to work. (*Suddenly laughing.*) Except that I'd be in the spare room with you saying I was scared I might end up on the Bowery. How's that for a project? You and I on the Bowery together, together until death-do-us-part, love until death.

SHE: You could make a comedy of it, I'd laugh my head off.

HE: Yeah, my ever-loving wife'd laugh her head off if I ended on the Bowery. (*Laughing.*) But the joke is, if you were there, stranded drunk in a doorway, I'd come after you for assurance, yeah, it's the truth. If you were there I'd come after you. I need security, yes, that's what I need from you, my analyst says so, and who am I to contradict?

SHE: Yeah, that's right, that's what you need from me. And it's what you get. You need Mom, God help me.

(*They are both laughing, leaning towards each other, screaming with laughter, helpless with it.*)

HE: Yeah, you're my mom. *He* says so. He's always right. Well it's O.K. to hate your mom, it's in the book. I'm right on the line. I'm not going to feel guilty about *that*.

SHE: Oh no, why should you feel guilty, why should you ever feel guilty at all?

HE (*shouting, his dark handsome face distorted*): Because you make me guilty, I'm always in the wrong with you, I have to be, mom's always right.

SHE (*suddenly not laughing, but desperate with anxiety*): Oh, Nelson, don't get at me all the time, don't do it, I can't stand it.

HE (*soft and menacing*): So you can't stand it? Well, you've got to stand it. For why? Because I need you to stand it,

that's why. Hey, perhaps *you* should go to the analyst. Why
should I do all the hard work? Yeah, that's it; you can go
to the analyst, I'm not sick, *you're* sick. You're *sick*!

(*But she has given in, turned away from him, limp and
desperate. He jumps towards her victorious but appalled*):
And now what's wrong with you! Can't take it, huh? Why
not? How d'you know it's not you that's sick: why should
it always be me that's in the wrong? Oh, don't look like
that! Trying to make me feel bad, as usual, huh? Well,
you're succeeding. O.K., so I'm in the wrong. But please
don't worry—not for a moment. It's always me that is in
the wrong. I said so, didn't I? I've confessed, haven't I?
You're a woman, so you're in the right. O.K., O.K., I'm
not complaining. I'm just stating a fact—I'm a man, so I'm
in the wrong. O.K.?

But now, suddenly, the tiny blonde woman (who has drunk
at least three-quarters of a bottle of Scotch and is as cool
and controlled as a soft little kitten with sweet, just-open
misty blue eyes) gets up and says: 'Bill, Bill, I want to dance.
I want to dance, baby.' And Bill jumps up towards the record
player, and the room is full of late Armstrong, the cynical
trumpet and the cynical good-humoured voice of the older
Armstrong. And Bill has gathered his beautiful little wife in
his arms, and they are dancing. But it is a parody, a parody
of good-humoured sexy dancing. Now everyone is dancing,
and Nelson and his wife are away on the edge of the group,
ignored. No one is listening to them, people can't stand it any
more. And then Nelson says, loud, jerking his thumb at me:
'I'm going to dance with Anna. I can't dance, I can't do
anything, you don't have to tell me that, but I'm going to
dance with Anna.' I stand up, because everyone is looking at
me, saying with their eyes: Go on, you've got to dance,
you've got to.

Nelson comes over, and says loudly in parody: 'I'm going
to dance with Anna. Dance with *m—e—e*—! Da—a—a—
ance with me, Anna.'

His eyes are desperate with self-dislike, misery, pain. And
then, in parody: 'Com'n, let's fuck, baby, I like your style.'

I laugh. (I hear my laugh, shrill and pleading.) They all

laugh, in relief, because I'm playing my role; and the dangerous moment is passed. And Nelson's wife laughs loudest. She gives me, however, an acute, fearful inspection; and I know that I've already become part of the marital battle; and that the whole point of me, Anna, was probably to add fuel to the battle. They've probably fought over me, interminably, in the terrible hours between four and seven in the morning, when they wake in anxiety (but anxiety about what?) and fight to the death. I can even hear the dialogue: I dance with Nelson, while his wife watches, smiling in painful anxiety, and listen to the dialogue:

SHE: Yes, I suppose you think I don't know about you and Anna Wulf.

HE: That's right, you don't know and you'll never know, will you?

SHE: So you think I don't know, well I do know, I've just got to look at you!

HE: Look at me, baby! Look at me, doll! Look at me, honey, look, look, look! What do you see? Lothario? Don Juan? Yes, that's me. That's right. I've been screwing Anna Wulf, she's just my style, my analyst says she is, and who am I to argue with my analyst?

After the wild, painful, laughing dance, everyone dancing in parody, and *urging* all the other members of the group to keep up the parody, for their dear lives' sake, we all say good night and go home.

Nelson's wife kisses me at parting. We all kiss each other, one big happy family, though I know, and they know, that any member of this group could fall out of it tomorrow, from failure, or drunkenness or unconformity, and never be seen again. Nelson's wife's kiss on my cheeks—first left, then right, is half warm and genuine, as if to say: I'm sorry, we can't help it, it's nothing to do with you; and half exploratory, as if to say: I want to know what you've got for Nelson that I haven't.

And we even exchange glances, ironic and bitter, saying: Well, it's got nothing to do with either of us, not really!

The kiss makes me uncomfortable, nevertheless, and I feel an impostor. Because I was realising something I should have

493

known by using my intelligence, without ever having gone to their flat at all: that the ties between Nelson and his wife are bitterly close, and never to be broken in their lives. They are tied by the closest of all bonds, neurotic pain-giving; the experience of pain dealt and received; pain as an aspect of love; apprehended as a knowledge of what the world is, what growth is.

Nelson is about to leave his wife; he will never leave her. She will wail at being rejected and abandoned; she does not know she will never be rejected.

The evening after the party I was at home sitting in a chair, exhausted. An image kept coming into my mind: it was like a shot from a film, then it was as if I was seeing a sequence from a film. A man and a woman, on a roof-top above a busy city, but the noise and the movement of the city are far beneath them. They wander aimlessly on the roof-top, sometimes embracing, but almost experimentally, as if they are thinking: How does this taste?—then they separate again and aimlessly move about the roof. Then the man goes to the woman and says: I love you. And she says, in terror: What do you mean? He says: I love you. So she embraces him, and he moves away, with nervous haste, and she says: Why did you say you loved me? And he says: I wanted to hear how it would sound. And she says: But I love you, I love you, I love you—and he goes off to the very edge of the roof and stands there, ready to jump—he will jump if she says even once again: I love you.

When I slept I dreamed this film sequence—in colour. Now it was not on a roof-top, but in a thin tinted mist or fog, an exquisitely-coloured fog swirled and a man and a woman wandered in it. She was trying to find him, but when she bumped into him, or found him, he nervously moved away from her; looking back at her, then away, and away again.

The morning after the party Nelson telephoned and announced that he wanted to marry me. I recognised the dream. I asked him why he had said that. He shouted: 'Because I wanted to.' I said he was closely bound to his wife. Then the dream, or film sequence stopped, and his voice changed and he said, humorous: 'My God, if that's true, I'm in trouble.' We talked a bit longer, then he said he had told his wife he had slept with me. I was very angry, I said he was using me in his fight with his wife. He started screaming and reviling me as he had screamed at her the night before at the party.

I put down the receiver and he was over in a few minutes. He was now defending himself about his marriage, not to me, but to some invisible observer. I don't think he was very conscious of my being there. I realised who it was when he said his analyst was on holiday for a month.

He went off, shouting and screaming at me—at women. An hour later he telephoned me to say he was sorry, he was 'nuts' and that was all there was to it. Then he said: 'I haven't hurt you, Anna, have I?' This stunned me—I felt the atmosphere of the terrible dream again. But he went on: 'Believe me, I wanted nothing more than to have the real thing with you—' and then, switching into the painful bitterness—'If the love they say is possible is more real than what we seem to get.' And then again, insistent and strident: 'But what I want you to say is that I haven't hurt you, you've got to say it.' I felt as if a friend had slapped me across the face, or spat at me, or, grinning with pleasure, had taken a knife out and was turning it in my flesh. But I said that of course he had hurt me, but not in a way which betrayed what I felt; I spoke as he had spoken, as if my being hurt was something that could be thought of casually three months after the beginning of such an encounter.

He said: 'Anna, it occurs to me—surely I can't be so bad—if I can imagine how one ought to be, if I can imagine really loving someone, really coming through for someone ... then it's a kind of blueprint for the future, isn't it?'

Well these words moved me, because it seems to me half of what we do, or try to be, amounts to blueprints for the future that we try to imagine; and so we ended this conversation, with every appearance of comradeship.

But I sat, in a kind of cold fog, and I thought: What has happened to men that they can talk like this to women? For weeks and weeks Nelson has been involving me in himself—

495

and he has been using all his charm, his warmth, his experience of involving women, and using them particularly when I've been angry, or he knows he has said something particularly frightening. And then he turns casually and says: Have I hurt you? For it seems to me such an abrogation of everything that a man is, that when I think of what it means I feel sick and lost (like being in a cold fog somewhere), things lose their meaning, and even the words I use then, become echo-like, become a parody of meaning.

It was after the time he rang me to ask: Have I hurt you? that I dreamed and recognised it as the joy-in-destruction. The dream was a telephone conversation between me and Nelson. Yet he was in the same room. His outward guise was the responsible, warm-feeling man. Yet as he spoke his smile changed and I recognised the sudden unmotivated spite. I felt the knife turn in my flesh, between my ribs, the edges of the knife grinding sharp against the bone. I could not speak, because the danger, the destruction, came from someone I was close to, someone I liked. Then I began to speak into the telephone receiver, and on my own face I could feel the beginning of the smile, the smile of joyful spite. I even made a few dancing steps, the head-jerking, almost doll-like stiff dance of the animated vase. I remember thinking in the dream: So now I am the evil vase; next I'll be the old man-dwarf; then the hunch-backed old woman. Then what? Then Nelson's voice down the receiver into my ear: Then the witch, then the young witch. I woke, hearing the words ring out with a terrible spiteful gleeful joy: 'The witch, and then the young witch!'

I have been very depressed. I have depended a great deal on that personality—Janet's mother. I continually ask myself—how extraordinary, that when inside I am flat, nervous, dead, that I can still, for Janet, be calm, responsible, alive?

I haven't had the dream again. But two days ago I met a man at Molly's house. A man from Ceylon. He made overtures, and I rejected them. I was afraid of being rejected, of another failure. Now I am ashamed. I am becoming a coward. I am frightened because my first impulse, when a

496

man strikes the sexual note, is to run, run anywhere, out of the way of hurt.

[A heavy black line across the page.]

De Silva from Ceylon. He was a friend of Molly's. I met him years ago at her house. He came to London some years ago and earned his living as a journalist, but rather poorly. He married an English woman. He impressed one at a party by his sarcastic cool manner; he made witty remarks about people, cruel, but curiously detached. Remembering him, I see him standing away from a group of people, looking on, smiling. He lived with his wife the bed-sitting-room, spaghetti-life of the literary fringes. They had one small child. Unable to earn a living here, he decided to return to Ceylon. His wife was unwilling: he is the younger son of a high-class family, very snobbish, who resented his marrying a white woman. He persuaded his wife to go back with him. His family would not take his wife in, so he found a room for her and spent his time half with her and the child and the other half with the family. She wanted to return to England, but he said it would be all right, and talked her into having another baby, which she did not want. No sooner was this second child born than he took flight.

I suddenly had a telephone call from him, asking for Molly, who was away. He said he was in England because 'he had won a bet in Bombay, as a result of which he had a free ticket to England.' Later I heard this was untrue: he had gone to Bombay on a journalistic assignment where, on an impulse, he had borrowed money and flown to London. He had hoped that Molly, from whom he had borrowed money in the past, would take him on. No Molly, so he tried Anna. I said I had no money to lend at that time, which was true, but because he said he was out of touch with things, asked him to dinner and invited some friends to meet him. He didn't come, but telephoned a week later, abject, childish, apologetic, saying he was too depressed to meet people, 'couldn't remember my telephone number on the evening of the dinner.' Then I met him at Molly's, who had come back.

497

He was his usual cool, detached, witty self. He had got a journalist's job, spoke with affection of his wife who was 'coming to join him, probably next week.' That was the night he invited me and I ran away. With good reason. But my fear was not from judgement, it was running away from any man, and that was why when he telephoned me next day I asked him to supper. I saw from how he ate that he wasn't eating enough. He had forgotten he had said that his wife was coming 'probably next week,' and now said 'she didn't want to leave Ceylon, she was very happy.' He said this in a detached way, as if he were listening to what he said. Up to this point we had been rather gay and friendly. But the mention of his wife struck a new note, I could feel it. He kept giving me cool, speculative and hostile glances. The hostility was not to do with me. We went into my big room. He was walking around it, alert, his head on one side, as it were *listening*, giving me the quick impersonal interested glances. Then he sat down, and said: 'Anna I want to tell you something that happened to me. No, just sit and listen. I want to tell you and I want you to just sit and listen and not say anything.'

I sat and listened out of the passivity that now frightens me, because I know I should have said *no*, and at just that point. Because there was hostility and aggression in it—not personal at all. But the atmosphere was full of it. He told me this story, remote, detached, smiling, watching my face.

A few nights before he had made himself high on marihuana. Then he walked into the street, somewhere in Mayfair—'you know Anna, the atmosphere of wealth and corruption, you can smell it. It attracts me. I walk there sometimes and I smell corruption, it excites me.' He saw a girl on the pavement, and walked straight up to her and said: 'I think you're beautiful, will you sleep with me?' He couldn't have done this, he said, unless he was high on alcohol or on marihuana. 'I didn't think she was beautiful, but she had beautiful clothes, and as soon as I had said it, I thought she was beautiful. She said, quite simply, yes.' I asked, was she a prostitute? He said, with a calm impatience (as if he'd been expecting me to ask just that question and even willed it): 'I

498

don't know. It doesn't matter.' I was struck by the way he said: It doesn't matter. Cool, deadly—he was saying: What does it matter about anyone else, I'm talking about me. She said to him: 'I think you're handsome, I'd like to sleep with you.' And of course he is a handsome man, with alert, vigorous, glossy good looks. But cold good looks. He said to her: 'I want to do something. I'm going to make love to you, as if I were desperately in love with you. But you mustn't respond to me. You must just give me sex, and you must ignore what I say. Do you promise?' She said, laughing: 'Yes, I promise.' They went to his room. 'This was the most interesting night of my life, Anna. Yes, I swear it, do you believe me? Yes, you must believe me. Because I behaved as if I loved her, as if I loved her desperately. And I even believed I did. Because—you must understand this, Anna, loving her was just for that night, the most wonderful thing you can imagine. And so I told her that I loved her, I was like a man desperately in love. But she kept falling out of her role. Every ten minutes I could see her face change and she responded to me like a woman who is loved. And then I had to stop the game and say: No, that's not what you promised. I love you, but you know I don't mean it. But I did mean it. For that night I adored her. I have never been so in love. But she kept spoiling it by responding. And so I had to send her away, because she kept being in love with me.'

'Was she angry?' I asked. (Because I felt angry, listening, and I knew he wanted me to be angry.)

'Yes. She was very angry. She called me all kinds of names. But it didn't matter to me. She called me sadist and cruel—everything like that. But it didn't matter to me. We had made the pact, she agreed, and then she spoiled everything for me. I wanted to be able to love a woman once in my life without having to give something back in return. But of course it doesn't matter. I'm telling you this because it doesn't matter. Do you understand that Anna?'

'Did you ever see her again?'

'No, of course not. I went back to the street where I picked her up, though I knew I wouldn't see her. I hoped she was a prostitute, but I knew she wasn't, because she told me

499

she wasn't. She was a girl who worked in one of the coffee bars. She said she wanted to fall in love.'

Later on in the evening he told me the following story: he has a close friend, the painter B. B. is married, the marriage has never been sexually satisfactory. (He said: 'Of course the marriage has never been sexually satisfactory, and the words, sexually satisfactory sounded like a clinical term.) B. lives in the country. A woman from the village comes in every day to clean the house. For something like a year B. slept with this woman, every morning, on the kitchen floor, while his wife was upstairs. De Silva went down to visit B. but B. was away. So was his wife. De Silva used the house waiting for them to come back and the cleaning woman came in every day as usual. She told De Silva that she had been sleeping with B. for a year, that she loved B. 'but of course, I'm not good enough for him, it's only because his wife isn't good for him.' 'Isn't that charming, Anna? That phrase, his wife isn't good for him—it's not our language, it's not the language of our kind.' 'Speak for yourself,' I said, but he put his head on one side, and said: 'No, I liked that—the warmth of it. And so I made love to her too. On the kitchen floor on a sort of home-made rug they have there, just as B. did. I wanted to because B. had. I don't know why. And of course, it didn't matter to me.' And then B.'s wife came back. She came back to get the house ready for B. She found De Silva there. She was pleased to see De Silva, because he was her husband's friend and 'she tries to please her husband out of bed because she doesn't care about him in bed.' De Silva spent the whole evening trying to find out if she knew about her husband's love-making with the cleaning woman. 'Then I realised she didn't know so I said: "Of course, your husband's affair with the cleaning woman doesn't mean anything, you shouldn't mind." She blew up. She went frantic with jealousy and hate. Can you understand that, Anna? She kept saying: He has been sleeping with that woman every morning on the kitchen floor. That was the phrase she kept saying: He's been sleeping with her on the kitchen floor while I was reading up-stairs.' So De Silva did everything to pacify B.'s wife, as he put it, and then B. came back. 'I told B. what I'd done and he forgave me. His wife said she'd leave him. I think she's going to leave him. Because he slept with the cleaning woman "on the kitchen floor." '

I asked: 'What did you do it for?' (Listening, I felt an extraordinary cold, a listless terror. I was passive in a sort of terror.)

'Why? Why do you ask? What does it matter? I wanted to see what would happen, that's all.'

As he spoke he smiled. It was a reminiscent, rather sly, enjoyable, interested smile. I recognised the smile—it was the essence of my dream, it was the smile from the figure in my dream. I wanted to run out of the room. And yet I was thinking: This quality, this intellectual 'I wanted to see what was going to happen,' 'I want to see what will happen next,' is something loose in the air, it is in so many people one meets, it is in me. It is part of what we all are. It is the other face of: It doesn't matter, it didn't matter to me—the phrase that kept ringing through what De Silva said.

De Silva and I spent the night together. Why? Because it didn't matter to me. Its mattering to me, the possibility of its mattering to me was pushed well away into a distance. It belonged to the Anna who was normal, who was walking away somewhere on a horizon of white sand, whom I could see but could not touch.

For me, the night was deadly, like his interested, detached smile. He was cool, detached, abstracted. It didn't matter to him. Yet at moments he suddenly relapsed into an abject mother-needing child. I minded these moments more than the cool detachment and the curiosity. For I kept thinking stubbornly: Of course it's him, not me. For men create these things, they create us. In the morning, remembering how I clung, how I always cling on to this, I felt foolish. Because why should it be true?

In the morning, I gave him breakfast. I felt cold and detached. Blasted—I felt as if there was no life or warmth left in me. I felt as if he had drained life out of me. But we were perfectly friendly. I felt friendly and detached from him. Just as he left, he said he would telephone me and I said that I would not sleep with him again. His face changed suddenly into a vicious anger; and I saw his face as it must have been when the girl he picked up in the street responded to his saying that he loved her. That was how he looked when she responded—angry and vicious. But I had not expected it. Then the mask of smiling detachment came back, and he said: 'Why not?' I said: 'Because you don't care a damn whether you sleep with me or not.' I had expected him to say: 'But you don't care either,' which I would have accepted. But suddenly he cracked into the pathetic child of the moments in the night, and he said: 'But I do, indeed I do.' He was positively on the point of beating his breast to prove it—he stopped his clenched hand on the way to his breast, I saw him. And again I felt the atmosphere of the dream of the fog—meaninglessness, the emptiness of emotion.

I said: 'No, you don't. But we'll go on as friends.' He went right downstairs, without a word. That afternoon he rang me up. He told me two or three cool, amused, malicious stories about people we know in common. I knew something else was coming, because I felt apprehension, but I couldn't imagine what. Then he remarked, abstractedly almost indifferent: 'I want you to let a friend of mine sleep in your upstairs room tonight. You know, the one just above your room where you sleep.'

'But it's Janet's room,' I said. I couldn't understand what he was really saying.

'But you could move her out—but it doesn't matter. Any room. Upstairs. I'll bring her this evening about ten o'clock.'

'You want to bring a woman friend to my flat to stay the night?' I was so stupid that I didn't know what he meant. But I was angry, so I should have understood.

'Yes,' he said, detached. Then in the abstracted cool voice: 'Well, it doesn't matter anyway.' And he rang off.

I stood thinking. Then I understood, because of my anger, so I rang him back. I said: 'Do you mean that you want to bring a woman into my flat so that you can sleep with her?'

'Yes. Not a friend of mine. I was going to take a prostitute off the station and bring her. I wanted to sleep with her just above your room so that you could hear us.'

502

I couldn't say anything. Then he asked: 'Anna, are you angry?'

I said: 'You wouldn't have thought of it at all if you hadn't wanted to make me angry.'

And then he let out a cry like a child, 'Anna, Anna, I'm sorry, forgive me.' He began wailing and crying. I believe he was standing there beating his chest with the hand that did not hold the receiver, or banging his head against the wall— at any rate, I could hear irregular thumps that might have been either. And I knew quite well that he had planned all this from the beginning, right from the moment when he telephoned me about bringing the woman to my flat, so that he could end by beating his breast or thumping his head against the wall, and that was the point of it all. So I rang off.

Then I got two letters. The first one cool, malicious, impertinent—but above all, irrelevant, it was off the point, a letter that might have been written after a dozen different situations, each of them quite unlike. And that was the point of the letter—its inconsequence. And then another letter, two days later, the hysterical wail of a child. The second letter upset me more than the first.

I have dreamed of De Silva twice. He is, incarnate, the principle of joy-in-giving-pain. He was in my dream without disguise, just as he is in life, smiling, malicious, detached, interested.

Molly telephoned me yesterday. She has heard that he has abandoned his wife without money, with the two children. His family, the rich upper-class family, have taken them all in. Molly: 'The point of all this is of course that he talked his wife into having the second child, which she didn't want, just to make sure of nailing her fast and leave him free. Then he buggered off to England where I suppose he expected me to smooth his brow. And the awful thing is, if I hadn't been away at the crucial moment, I would, I'd have taken the whole thing at its face value: poor Cingalese intellectual unable to earn a living, has to leave his wife and two children to come to the well-paid intellectual marts of London. What fools we are, perpetually, eternally, and we never learn, and I know quite well that next time it happens I'll have learned nothing.'

I met B., who I've known for some time now, in the street by accident. Went to have coffee with him. He spoke warmly of De Silva. He said he had persuaded De Silva 'to be kinder to his wife.' He said that he, B., would put up half the money for a monthly allowance for De Silva's wife, if De Silva would promise the other half. 'And does he pay the other half?' I asked. 'Well, of course he won't,' said B., his charming intelligent face full of apology, not merely for De Silva, but for the entire universe. 'And where is De Silva?' I asked, already knowing the answer. 'He's going to come and live in the village next to me. There's a woman he's fond of. Actually the woman who comes to clean my house every morning. She'll go on cleaning our house though, I'm glad about that. She's very nice.'

'I'm glad,' I said.

'Yes, I'm so fond of him.'

FREE WOMEN: 4

FREE WOMEN

■ FREE WOMEN: 4 ■

Anna and Molly influence Tommy, for the better.
Marion leaves Richard. Anna does not feel herself

ANNA was waiting for Richard and Molly. It was rather late, getting on for eleven. The curtains in the tall white room were drawn, the notebooks pushed out of sight, a tray with drinks and sandwiches already waiting. Anna sat loose in a chair, in a lethargy of moral exhaustion. She had now understood that she was not in control of what she did. Also, earlier that evening she had caught sight of Ronnie in a dressing-gown through Ivor's half-open door. It seemed that he had simply moved back in, and now it was up to her to throw them both out. She had caught herself thinking: What does it matter? And even that she and Janet should pack their things and move out and leave the flat to Ivor and Ronnie, anything to avoid fighting. That this idea was not far off lunacy did not surprise her, for she had decided she was very likely mad. Nothing she thought pleased her; for some days she had been observing ideas and images pass through her mind, unconnected with any emotion, and did not recognise them as her own.

Richard had said he would pick Molly up from her theatre where she was currently playing the part of a deliciously frivolous widow trying to choose between four new husbands, each one more attractive than the next. There was to be a conference. Three weeks before, Marion, kept late by Tommy, had slept upstairs in the empty flat once inhabited by Anna and Janet. Next day Tommy had informed his mother that Marion needed a *pied-à-terre* in London. She would of course pay the full rent for the flat, though she

507

intended to use it occasionally. Since then Marion had been to her home only once, to pick up clothes. She was living upstairs, and had in fact quietly left Richard and her children. Yet she did not seem to know she had, for every morning there was a fluttering expostulating scene in Molly's kitchen, where Marion exclaimed that she was really so naughty to have been kept so late the night before, but that she would go home and look after everything today—'yes, really, I promise, Molly'—as if Molly were the person to whom she was responsible. Molly had telephoned Richard, demanding that he should do something. But he refused. He had hired a house-keeper for form's sake; and his secretary Jean was practically installed already. He was delighted Marion had gone.

Then something else happened. Tommy, who had not left the shelter of his home since leaving the hospital, went with Marion to a political meeting to do with African independence. Afterwards there was a spontaneous demonstration in the street outside the London headquarters of the country in question. Marion and Tommy had followed the crowd, mostly students. There was skirmishing with the police. Tommy did not carry a white stick, there was no outward sign that he was blind. He did not 'move along' when told to do so, and was arrested. Marion, who had been separated from him for a few moments by the crowd, threw herself on the policeman, shrieking hysterically. They were taken to the police station with a dozen others. Next morning they were fined. The newspapers prominently displayed a story about the 'wife of a well-known city financier.' And now Richard telephoned Molly, who, in her turn, refused to help him. 'You wouldn't lift a finger about Marion, you only care now because the newspapers are on the trail and might find out about Jean.' So Richard telephoned Anna.

During this conversation Anna watched herself standing holding the telephone receiver, a small brittle smile on her face, while Richard and she exchanged the phrases of their hostility. She felt as if she were being willed to do this; as if no word that either she or Richard used could have been any different; and as if what they were saying was the exchange of maniacs.

He was incoherently angry: 'It's an absolute farce. Plotted it, that's what you've done, to get your own back. African independence, what a farce! Spontaneous demonstration. You've sicked the communists on to Marion and she's so innocent she doesn't recognise one when she sees one. It's all because you and Molly want to make a fool out of me.'

'But of course that's all it is, dear Richard.'

'It's your idea of a joke, company director's wife turned red.'

'Of course.'

'And I'm going to see that you're exposed.'

Anna was thinking: the reason why this is so frightening is that if this weren't England, Richard's anger would mean people losing their jobs, or going to prison, or being shot. Here he's just a man in a bad temper, but he's a reflection of something so terrible . . . and I stand here making feeble sarcasms.

She said, sarcastically: 'My dear Richard, neither Marion nor Tommy planned this. They just drifted along with the crowd.'

'Drifted along! Who do you think you are fooling?'

'As it happens I was there. Didn't you know that demonstrations at this particular moment are in fact spontaneous? The C.P.'s lost whatever grip it had on young people, and the Labour Party's too respectable to organise this sort of thing. So what happens is, groups of young people go and express themselves about Africa or war and so on.'

'I might have known you were there.'

'No, you needn't have known. Because it was an accident. I was coming home from the theatre, and I saw a crowd of students rushing along the street. I got off the bus and went along to have a look. I didn't know Marion and Tommy were there until I saw it in the newspapers.'

'So what do you intend to do about it?'

'I don't intend to do anything about it. You can deal with the red menace yourself.'

And Anna put down the receiver, knowing that this was

509

not the end, and that in fact she would do something about it, because some kind of logic was working that would force her to.

Molly telephoned, in a state of collapse, soon after: 'Anna, you've got to see Tommy and try and make him see sense.'

'Have you tried?'

'That's what's so odd. I can't even try. I keep telling myself—I can't go on living like a guest in my own house with Marion and Tommy taking it over. Why should I? But then something odd happens, I work myself up to go and face them—but you can't *face* Marion, she isn't there. And I find myself thinking: Well why not? What does it matter? Who cares? I find myself shrugging my shoulders. I come in from the theatre and I sneak upstairs in my own home so as not to disturb Marion and Tommy, feeling rather guilty to be there at all. Do you understand that?'

'Yes, unfortunately I do.'

'Yes. But what frightens me is this—if you actually describe the situation in words—you know, my husband's second wife moving into my house because she can't live without my son, etc.—it's not merely *odd*, it's—but of course, that's got nothing to do with anything. Do you know what I was thinking yesterday, Anna? I was sitting upstairs, quiet as a mouse, so as not to disturb Marion and Tommy and thinking I'd simply pack a bag and wander off somewhere and leave them to it, and I thought that the generation after us are going to take one look at us, and get married at eighteen, forbid divorces, and go in for strict moral codes and all that, because the chaos otherwise is just too terrifying . . .' Here Molly's voice wavered, and she ended quickly: 'Please see them Anna, you've got to, because I simply can't cope with anything.'

Anna put on her coat, picked up her bag, was ready to 'cope.' She had no idea at all of what to say, or even what she thought. She was standing in the middle of her room, empty as a paper bag, ready to walk over to Marion, to Tommy, and say—what? She thought of Richard, of his conventional thwarted anger; of Molly, all her courage drained into listless weeping; of Marion gone beyond pain into a cool hysteria; of

510

Tommy—but she could only see him, see the blinded stubborn face, she could feel a kind of force coming from him, but she could not put a name to it.

Suddenly she giggled. Anna heard the giggle: yes, that was how Tommy giggled that night he came to see me before he tried to kill himself. How odd, I've never heard myself laugh like that before.

What has happened to that person inside Tommy who giggled like that? He's gone completely—I suppose Tommy killed him when the bullet went through his head. How strange I should let out that bright meaningless giggle! What am I going to say to Tommy? I don't even know what's happening.

What's it all about? I have to walk up to Marion and Tommy and say: You must stop this pretence of caring about African nationalism, you both know quite well it's nonsense?

Anna giggled again, at the meaninglessness of it.

Well, what would Tom Mathlong say? She imagined herself sitting across the table in a café with Tom Mathlong telling him about Marion and Tommy. He would listen and say: 'Anna, you tell me these two people have chosen to work for African liberation? And why should I care about their motives?' But then he would laugh. Yes. Anna could hear his laugh, deep, full, shaken out of his stomach. Yes. He would put his hands on his knees and laugh, then shake his head and say: 'My dear Anna, I wish we had your problems.'

Anna, hearing the laugh, felt better. She hastily picked up various bits of paper suggested to her by thinking of Tom Mathlong; she stuffed them into her bag and ran down into the street and along to Molly's house. She thought as she went of the demonstration Marion and Tommy had been arrested at. The demonstration was not at all like the orderly political demonstrations of the communist party in the old days; or like a Labour Party meeting. No, it was fluid, experimental—people were doing things without knowing why. The stream of young people had flowed down the street to the headquarters like water. No one directed or controlled them. Then the flood of people around the building, shouting slogans almost tentatively, as if listening to hear how they would sound. Then the arrival of the police. And the police were hesitant and tentative too. They didn't know what to expect. Anna, standing to one side, had watched: under the restless, fluid movement of people and police was an inner pattern or motif. About a dozen or twenty young men, all with the same look on their faces—a set, stern, dedicated look, were moving in such a way as to deliberately taunt and provoke the police. They would rush past a policeman, or up to him, so close that a helmet was tipped forward or an arm jogged, apparently accidentally. They would dodge off, then come back. The policemen were watching this group of young men. One by one, they were arrested; because they were behaving in such a way that they would have to be arrested. And at the moment of arrest each face wore a look of satisfaction, of achievement. There was a moment of private struggle—the policeman using as much brutality as he dared; and on his face a sudden look of cruelty.

Meanwhile the masses of students who had not come to pursue their private need to challenge and be punished by authority continued to chant slogans, to test out their political voices, and their relationship with the police was a different one altogether, there was no bond between them and the police.

And what look had Tommy's face worn when he had been arrested? Anna knew without having seen it.

When she opened the door of Tommy's room he was alone and he asked at once: 'Is that Anna?'

Anna stopped herself from saying: How did you know? and asked: 'Where's Marion?'

He said, stiff and suspicious: 'She's upstairs.' He might have said aloud: 'I don't want you to see her.' His dark blank eyes were fixed on Anna, almost centred on her, so that she felt exposed, so heavy was that dark stare. Yet it was not quite centered; the Anna whom he was forbidding or warning was very slightly to her left. Anna felt, with a touch of hysteria, that she was being forced to move left, into his direct line of vision, or no-vision. Anna said: 'I'll go up, no please don't bother.' For he had half-raised himself, in a movement to stop her. She shut the door and went straight up the stairs to the flat she had lived in with Janet. She was thinking that she had left Tommy because she had no connection with him, had nothing to say; that she was going to see Marion, to whom she had nothing to say.

The stairs were narrow and dark. Anna's head lifted out of the well of dark into the white painted cleanliness of a tiny landing. Through the door she saw Marion, bent over a newspaper. She greeted Anna with a gay social smile. 'Look!' she cried, thrusting the paper triumphantly at Anna. There was a photograph of Marion, and the words: "It's absolutely sickening the way the poor Africans are being treated.' And so on. The comment was malicious, but apparently Marion couldn't see that it was. She read over Anna's shoulder, smiling, giving naughty little hunches to her shoulders, almost wriggling with guilty delight. 'My mother and my sisters are absolutely furious, they are absolutely beside themselves.'

'I can imagine,' said Anna, drily. She heard her dry critical little voice, saw Marion wince away from it. Anna sat in the white-covered armchair. Marion sat on the bed. She looked like a great girl, this untidy handsome matron. She looked winsome and coquettish.

Anna thought: I'm here, presumably, to make Marion face reality. What is her reality? An awful honesty lit by liquor. Why shouldn't she be like this, why shouldn't she spend the rest of her life giggling and tipping policemen's helmets and conspiring with Tommy?

'It's lovely to see you, Anna,' said Marion, after waiting for Anna to say something. 'Would you like some tea?'

'No,' said Anna, rousing herself. But it was too late. Marion was already out of the room and in the little kitchen next door. Anna followed her.

'Such a lovely little flat, how I love it, how lucky you were to live here, I wouldn't have been able to tear myself away.'

Anna looked at it, the charming little flat, with its low ceilings, its neat gleaming windows. Everything was white, bright, fresh. Every object in it caused her pain, because these small smiling rooms had held hers and Michael's love,

513

four years of Janet's childhood, her growing friendship with Molly. Anna leaned against a wall and looked at Marion, whose eyes were glazed with hysteria while she acted the role of a tripping hostess, and behind the hysteria was a mortal terror that Anna was going to send her home and away from this white refuge from responsibility.

Anna switched off; something inside her went dead, or moved apart from what was happening. She became a shell. She stood there, looking at words like love, friendship, duty, responsibility, and knew them to be all lies. She felt herself shrug. And as Marion saw the shrug real terror claimed her face and she said: 'Anna!' It was an appeal.

Anna faced Marion with a smile, which she knew to be empty, and thought well, it doesn't matter in the slightest. She went back into the other room and sat down, empty.

Soon Marion came in with the tea-tray. She looked guilty and defiant, because of the Anna she had expected to face her. She began with a great fussing of teaspoons and teacups, to put off the Anna that was not there; then she sighed, she pushed away the tea-tray, and her face went soft.

She said: 'I know Richard and Molly told you to come and talk to me.'

Anna sat silent. She felt she would sit silent forever. And then she knew she was going to begin talking. She thought: I wonder what I'm going to say? And I wonder who the person is who will say it? How odd, to sit here, waiting to hear what one will say. She said, almost dreamily: 'Marion, do you remember Mr Mathlong?' (She thought: I'm going to talk about Tom Mathlong, am I, how odd!)

'Who's Mr Mathlong?'

'The African leader. You remember, you came to see me about him.'

'Oh yes, the name slipped away from me for the moment.'

'I was thinking about him this morning.'

'Oh were you?'

'Yes. I was.' (Anna's voice continued calm and detached. She listened to it.)

Marion had begun to look conscious and distressed. She

was tugging at a strand of loose hair, winding it around her forefinger.

'When he was here two years ago, he was very depressed. He had spent weeks trying to see the Colonial Secretary, and being snubbed. He had a pretty good idea he'd be in prison very soon. He's a very intelligent man, Marion.'

'Yes, I'm sure he is.' Marion's smile at Anna was quick and involuntary, as if to say: Yes, you're being clever, I know what you're getting at.

'On Sunday he rang me up and said he was tired and he needed a rest. So I took him down to Greenwich on the river boat. On the way back he was very silent. He sat in the boat smiling. He was looking at the banks. You know, Marion, it's very impressive, coming back from Greenwich, the solid mass of London? The County Council Building? And the enormous commercial buildings. And the wharves and the ships and the docks. And then Westminster ...' (Anna was talking, softly, still interested to find out what she was going to say next.) 'Everything's been there for centuries. I asked him what he was thinking. He said: I don't get discouraged by the white settlers. I wasn't discouraged when I was in prison last time—history's on the side of our people. But this afternoon I feel the weight of the British empire on me like a gravestone. He said: Do you realise how many generations it takes to make a society where buses run on time? Where business letters get answered efficiently? Where you can trust your ministers not to take bribes? We were passing Westminster and I remember thinking that very few of those politicians could have half his qualities—because he's a sort of saint, Marion ...'

Anna's voice cracked. She heard it and thought: Now I know what's happening. I'm hysterical. I've gone right over into Marion's and Tommy's hysteria. I've got no control at all over what I'm doing. She was thinking: I use a word like saint—I never use it when I'm myself. I don't know what it means. Her voice continued, higher, rather shrill: 'Yes, he is a saint. An ascetic, but not a neurotic one. I said to him it was very sad to think of African independence being turned into a question of punctual buses and neatly typed business letters. He said it might be sad, but that was how his country would be judged.'

Anna had begun to cry. She sat crying, watching herself cry. Marion watched her, leaning forward, bright-eyed, curious, full of disbelief. Anna controlled her tears and went on: 'We got off at Westminster. We walked past Parliament. He said—I suppose he was thinking of those little politicians inside it—"I shouldn't have been a politician at all. In a national liberation movement all kinds of men get involved almost by accident, like leaves being sucked into a dust-devil." Then he thought that over for a moment, and he said: "I think it's quite likely that after we get our independence I'll find myself in prison again. I'm the wrong type for the first few years of a revolution. I'm uncomfortable making popular speeches. I'm happier writing analytical articles." Then we went into a place to have some tea and he said: "One way and another I expect to spend a good deal of my life in prison." That's what he said!'

Anna's voice cracked again. She was thinking: Good Lord, if I were sitting here watching myself I'd feel quite sick at all this sentimentality. Well, I am making myself sick. She said aloud, her voice shaking: 'We shouldn't make what he stands for look cheap.' She was thinking: I'm making what he stands for look cheap in every word I say.

Marion said: 'He sounds marvellous. But they can't all be like that.'

'Of course not. There's his friend—he's bombastic and rabble-rousing and he drinks and whores around. He'll probably be the first Prime Minister—he has all the qualities—the common touch, you know.'

Marion laughed. Anna laughed. The laughter was overloud and uncontrolled.

'There's another,' went on Anna. (Who? she thought. Surely I'm not going to talk about Charlie Themba?) 'He's a trade union leader, called Charlie Themba. He's violent and passionate and quarrelsome and loyal and—well recently he cracked up.'

'Cracked up?' said Marion, suddenly. 'What do you mean?'

Anna thought: Yes, I had been meaning to talk about

516

Charlie all the time. In fact that's probably who I've been leading up to all this time.

'Broke down, then. But do you know Marion, what's really odd is, no one recognised the beginning of his breakdown? Because the politics out there—they're violent and full of intrigue and jealousies and spite—rather like Elizabethan England . . .' Anna stopped. Marion was frowning with annoyance. 'Marion did you know you look angry?'

'Do I?'

'Yes, it's because it's one thing to think *poor things* and another to allow that African politics could have any resemblance at all to English politics—even such a long time ago.'

Marion blushed, then she laughed. 'Go on about him,' she said.

'Well Charlie started to quarrel with Tom Mathlong who was his closest friend, and then all his other friends, accusing them of intriguing against him. Then he began writing bitter letters to people like me, here. We didn't see what we should have seen. Then suddenly I got a letter—I brought it with me. Would you like to see it?'

Marion held out her hand. Anna put the letter into it. Anna was thinking: When I put this letter into my bag I wasn't conscious why . . . The letter was a carbon copy. It had been sent to several people. *Dear Anna* was written in rough pencil at the top.

'Dear Anna, in my last letter I told you of the intrigues against me and the enemies who are plotting my life. My former friends have turned against me and they tell the people in speeches in my territory that I am the enemy of Congress and their enemy. Meanwhile I am ill and I am writing to ask you to send me clean food for I fear the poisoner's hand. I am ill, for my wife I have found to be in the pay of the police and the Governor himself. She is a very bad woman who I must divorce. Two unlawful arrests have been made on me, and I must suffer them since I am without help. I am alone in my house. Eyes watch me through the roof and the walls. I am being fed on many types of dangerous foods from human flesh (dead human flesh) to reptiles, including crocodiles. The crocodile will have its revenge. At

517

night I see its eyes shining at me, and its snout comes at me through the walls. Hasten to help me. With fraternal greetings, Charlie Themba.'

Marion let the hand that held the letter fall by her side. She sat silent. Then she sighed. She got up, sleep-walker-wise, handed Anna the letter, and sat down again, smoothing the skirt under her, and folding her hands. She remarked, almost dreamily: 'Anna, I was awake all last night. I can't go back to Richard. I can't.'

'What about the children?'

'Yes, I know. But what's awful is, I don't care. We have children because we love a man. Well, I think so. You say it isn't true for you, but it's true for me. I hate Richard. I really do. I think I must have hated him for years without knowing it.' Marion slowly got up, with the same sleep-walker's motion. Her eyes were searching the room for liquor. A small bottle of whisky stood on top of a pile of books. She half-filled a glass, and sat down holding the glass, sipping. 'So why shouldn't I stay here with Tommy? Why shouldn't I?'

'But Marion, this is Molly's house . . .'

At this moment, a sound from the foot of the stairs. Tommy was coming up. Anna saw how Marion's body jerked into self-possession. She put down the whisky glass and wiped her mouth quickly with a handkerchief. She had forgotten herself in the thought: Those slippery stairs, but I mustn't go to help him.

Slowly the firm, blind feet came up the stairs. They halted on the landing while Tommy turned himself, feeling at the walls. Then he came in. This room being unfamiliar to him, he halted with his hand on the edge of the door, then he turned his dark blind muzzle to the centre of the room, let go the door and walked forward.

'More to the left,' said Marion.

He steered himself to the left, took one step too many, bumped his knee on the edge of the bed, turned himself around fast to stop himself falling, and sat, with another bump. Now he looked enquiringly around the room.

'I'm here,' said Anna.

'I'm here,' said Marion.

He said to Marion: 'I think it's time you started cooking supper. Otherwise there won't be time before the meeting.'

'We're going to the big meeting tonight,' said Marion to Anna, gay and guilty. She met Anna's eyes, grimaced, and looked away. And at that moment Anna saw, or rather felt, that whatever she had been expected to 'say' to Marion and Tommy, she had said. Now Marion remarked to Tommy: 'Anna thinks we are going about things the wrong way.'

Tommy turned his face towards Anna. His full stubborn lips worked together. It was a new movement—his lips fumbled over each other, as if all the uncertainty he refused to show in his blindness emerged here. His mouth, formerly the visible signature of his dark, set will, always controlled, now seemed the only uncontrolled thing about him, for he was unconscious that he sat and worked his mouth. In the clear shallow light of the little room, he sat alert on the bed, very young, very pale, a defenceless boy, with a vulnerable and pathetic mouth.

'Why?' he asked. 'Why?'

'The thing is,' said Anna, hearing her voice again come humorous and dry, all the hysteria gone out of it, 'the thing is, London's full of students rushing about bashing policemen. But you two are in a fine position to study everything and become experts.'

'I thought you'd come here to take Marion away from me,' Tommy said, quick and querulous, on a note no one had heard from him since his blindness. 'Why should she go back to my father? Are you going to make her go back?'

Anna said: 'Look, why don't you two go away for a holiday for a bit? It'd give Marion time to think out what to do. And it would give you a chance to try your wings outside this house, Tommy.'

Marion said: 'I don't have to think. I'm not going back. What's the use? I don't know what I ought to do with my life, but I know I'm finished if I go back to Richard.' Her eyes welled tears, and she got up and escaped to the kitchen. Tommy listened with a turn of his head to her departure, listened, apparently with the straining muscles of his neck, to her movements in the kitchen.

'You've been very good for Marion,' Anna said, in a low voice.

'Have I?' he said, pathetically eager to hear it.

'The thing is—you've got to stand by her. It's not so easy when a twenty-year-old marriage breaks up—it's nearly as old as you are.' She got up. 'And I don't think you ought to be so hard on us all,' she said, in a quick low voice, which to her surprise sounded like a plea. She was thinking: I don't feel that, why do I say it? He was smiling, conscious, rueful, blushing. His smile was directed somewhere just past her left shoulder. She moved into the line of his gaze. She thought: Anything I say now will be heard by the old Tommy, but she could not think of what to say.

Tommy said: 'I know what you're thinking, Anna.'

'What?'

'Somewhere at the back of your mind you're thinking: I'm nothing but a bloody welfare worker, what a waste of time!'

Anna laughed with relief; he was teasing her.

'Something like that,' she said.

'Yes, I knew you were,' he said, with triumph. 'Well Anna, I've been thinking a lot about that sort of thing, since I tried to shoot myself, and I've come to the conclusion that you're wrong. I think people need other people to be kind to them.'

'You may very well be right.'

'Yes. No one really believes all the big things are any use.'

'No one?' said Anna drily, thinking of the demonstration at which Tommy had assisted.

'Isn't Marion reading you the newspapers any more?' she enquired.

He smiled, as dry as she, and said: 'Yes, I know what you mean, but all the same it's true. Do you know what people really want? Everyone, I mean. Everybody in the world is thinking: I wish there was just one other person I could really talk to, who could really understand me, who'd be kind to me. That's what people really want, if they're telling the truth.'

'Well, Tommy . . .'

'Oh yes, I know you're thinking my brain was damaged by

520

the accident, and perhaps it was, sometimes I think so my-self, but that's what I believe is true.'

'That isn't why I've been wondering if—you've changed. It's because of the way you treat your mother.'

Anna saw the blood come up into his face—then he lowered it, and sat silent. He made a gesture with his hand which said: All right, but leave me alone. Anna said good-bye and went out, passing Marion, who had her back turned.

Anna went home, slowly. She did not know what happened between the three of them, or why it had happened, or, indeed, what they could expect next. But she knew some barrier had gone down and that now everything would be changed.

She lay down for a while; attended to Janet when she returned from school; caught the glimpse of Ronnie which told her she could expect a battle of wills later, and then sat waiting for Molly and Richard.

When she heard the two coming up the stairs, she steeled herself for the inevitable bickering, but in the event it was unnecessary. They entered almost like friends. Molly had clearly set herself not to be aggravating. Also, she hadn't had time to make herself up after the theatre, so the vivid quality in her that always irritated Richard was absent.

They sat down. Anna poured drinks. 'I've seen them,' she reported. 'And I think everything is going to be all right.'

'And how did you achieve this miraculous change?' enquired Richard, the words, but not the tone, sarcastic.

'I don't know.'

Silence, and Molly and Richard looked at each other.

'I really don't know. But Marion says she won't come back to you. I think she means it. And I've suggested they go off somewhere for a holiday.'

'But I've been saying that for months,' said Richard.

'I think if you offered Tommy and Marion a trip to one of your things somewhere, and suggest they investigate condi-tions, they'd go.'

'It really astounds me,' said Richard, 'the way you two come out with ideas I suggested long ago as if they were brilliant new suggestions.'

'Things have changed,' said Anna.

'You don't explain why,' said Richard.

Anna hesitated, then said to Molly, not to Richard: 'It was very odd. I went up there, with not an idea in my head of what to say. Then I got all hysterical just like they are, and I even cried. It worked. Do you understand it?'

Molly thought, then nodded.

'Well I don't understand it,' said Richard, 'but I don't care. What happens next?'

'You should go and see Marion and fix things up—and don't nag at her, Richard.'

'I don't nag at her, she nags at me,' said Richard, aggrieved.

'And I think you should talk to Tommy tonight Molly. I've got a feeling he might be ready to talk.'

'In that case I'll go now, before he goes to bed.'

Molly got up, and Richard with her.

'I owe you my thanks, Anna,' said Richard.

Molly laughed. 'Back to normal hostilities next time, I'm sure, but it's a pleasure, all this politeness, just for once.'

Richard laughed—unwillingly, but it was a laugh; he took Molly's arm, and the two went off down the stairs.

Anna went upstairs to Janet, and sat by the sleeping child in the darkness. She felt the usual surge of protective love for Janet, but tonight she examined this emotion critically: I know no one who isn't incomplete and tormented and fighting, the best one can say of anyone is that they fight—but I touch Janet and immediately I feel: Well, it will be different for her. Why should it be? It won't be. I'm sending her out into such a battle, but that isn't what I feel when I watch her sleeping.

Anna, rested and restored, left Janet's room, shut the door, and stood on the landing in the dark. Now was the moment to face Ivor. She knocked on the door, opened it a few inches and said into the dark: 'Ivor, you've got to go. You've got to leave here tomorrow.' A silence, then a slow and almost good-humoured voice: 'I must say that I see your point, Anna.'

'Thank you, I hoped that you would.'

522

She shut the door and went downstairs. How easy! she thought. Why did I imagine it would be difficult? Then she had a clear mental picture of Ivor coming up the stairs with a bunch of flowers. Of course, she thought, tomorrow he would try to get round her, he would come up the stairs with a bunch of flowers in his hand, humouring her.

She was so certain this would happen that at lunch-time she was waiting, when he climbed the stairs holding a big bunch of flowers, and the weary smile of a man determined to humour a woman.

'To the nicest landlady in the world,' he murmured.

Anna took the flowers, hesitated, then hit him across the face with them. She was trembling with anger.

He stood smiling, his face averted in the parody of a man suffering unjust punishment.

'Well well,' he murmured. 'Well well well.'

'Get out,' said Anna. She had never in her life been angry like this.

He went upstairs and in a few moments she heard the noises of his packing. Soon he came down, a suitcase in each hand. His possessions. All he had in the world. Oh how sad, this poor young man, all his possessions locked in a couple of suitcases.

He laid the rent he owed—five back weeks, for he was bad about money, on the table. Anna noted, with interest, that she had to suppress an impulse to give it back to him.

Meanwhile he stood, weary with disgust: this money-grubbing woman, well what can one expect?

But he must have taken the money out of the bank or borrowed it that morning, which meant that he had expected her to stay firm, in spite of the flowers. He must have said: There's a chance I'll get round her with flowers, I'll try it, it's worth risking five shillings on it.

THE NOTEBOOKS

[The black notebook now abandoned its original intention to be divided into two parts, The Source, and Money. Its pages were covered with newspaper cuttings pasted in and dated, covering the years 1955, 56, 57. Every one of these news items referred to violence, death, rioting, hatred, in some part of Africa. There was only one entry in Anna's handwriting, dated September 1956:]

Last night I dreamed that a television film was to be made about the group of people at the Mashopi Hotel. There was a script ready, written by someone else. The director kept assuring me: 'You'll be pleased when you see the script, it's exactly what you would have written yourself.' But for one reason or another I never saw the script. I went to the rehearsals for the television film. The 'set' was under the gum-trees beside the railway lines outside the Mashopi Hotel. I was pleased that the director had got the atmosphere so well. Then I saw that the 'set' was in fact the real thing: he had somehow transported the whole cast to Central Africa, and was filming the story under the gum-trees with even such details as the smell of wine rising off white dust, the smell of eucalyptus in hot sunlight. Then I saw the cameras come wheeling in to make the film. They reminded me of guns, in the way they pointed and swung over the group waiting to start their play. The play started. I began to feel uneasy. Then I understood that the director's choice of shots or of timing was changing the 'story.' What would emerge on the completed film would be something quite different from what I remembered. I was powerless to stop the director and the cameramen. So I stood to one side and watched the group (among whom was Anna, myself, but not as I remembered her). They were speaking lines of dialogue I did not remember, their relationships were altogether different. I was filled with anxiety. When it was all over, and the cast began drifting off, to drink in the Mashopi Hotel bar, and the cameramen (who I now saw were all black, all the technicians were black) were wheeling off their cameras and dismantling them (for they were also machine guns). I said to the director: 'Why did you change my story?' I saw he did not understand what I meant. I had imagined he had done it on purpose, had decided my story was no good. He looked rather hurt, certainly surprised. He said: 'But Anna, you saw those people there, didn't you? You saw what I saw? They spoke those words, didn't they? I only filmed what was there.' I did not know what to say, for I realised that he was right, that what I 'remembered' was probably untrue. He said, upset because I was: 'Come and have a drink, Anna. Don't you see, it doesn't matter what we film, provided we film something.'

I shall close this notebook. If I were asked by Mother Sugar to 'name' this dream, I would say it was about total sterility. And besides, since I dreamed it, I have been unable to remember how Maryrose moved her eyes, or how Paul laughed. It's all gone.

[There was a double black line across the page, marking the end of the notebook.]

[The red notebook, like the black notebook, had been taken over by newspaper cuttings, for the years 1956 and 1957. These referred to events in Europe, the Soviet Union, China, the United States. Like the cuttings on Africa in the same period, they were about, for the most part, violence. Anna had underlined the word 'freedom' whenever it occurred, in red pencil. Where the cuttings ceased, she had added up the red lines, making a total of 679 references to the word freedom. The only entry in her own handwriting for this period was the following:]

Yesterday Jimmy came to see me. He has just come back from a visit to the Soviet Union with a teachers' delegation. Told me this story. Harry Mathews, a teacher, dropped his job to fight in Spain. Was wounded, ten months in hospital with a fractured leg. During this time thought over Spain—communist dirty work, etc., read a lot, became suspicious of Stalin. Usual in-fight—C.P. then expulsion, joined the Trotskyists. Quarrelled with them, left them. Unable to fight in the war, because of his crippled leg, he trained to teach backward children. 'It goes without saying that for Harry there is no such thing as a stupid child, only unfortunate children.' Harry lived through the war in a small spartan room near King's Cross, performing more than one act of heroism, rescuing people from bombed and burning buildings, etc. 'He was quite a legend in the area, but of course at the moment when people started looking for the limping hero who had saved the child or poor old woman Harry was nowhere to be found, because it goes without saying he would despise himself if he took credit for heroic deeds.' At the end of the war Jimmy, back from Burma, went to see his old friend Harry, but they quarrelled. 'I was a hundred per cent Party member, and there was Harry, a dirty Trot, so there were high words and we parted forever. But I was fond of the silly sod, so I used to make a point of finding out what happened to him.' Harry had two lives. His outward life was all self-sacrifice and devotion. He not only worked in a school for backward children, and with great success, but he used to invite children of the area (a poor one) into his flat for classes every evening. He taught them literature, made them read, coached them for examinations. He was teaching, one way or another, for eighteen hours a day. 'It goes without saying that he regards sleep as a waste of time, he trained himself to sleep four hours a night.' He lived in this one room until the widow of an airforce pilot fell in love with him and transferred him to her flat, where he had two rooms. She had three children. He treated her with kindness, but if her life was now dedicated to him, his was to his children, in the school and off the street. That was his outer life. Meanwhile he learned Russian. Meanwhile he collected books, pamphlets, newspaper cuttings, about the Soviet Union. Meanwhile he built up for himself a picture of the real history of the Soviet Union, or rather of the Russian Communist Party, from 1900 onwards.

A friend of Jimmy's visited Harry, about 1950, and told Jimmy about him. 'He used to dress in a sort of bush shirt, or tunic, and sandals, with a military hair-cut. He never smiled. A portrait of Lenin on the wall—well that certainly goes without saying. A smaller one of Trotsky. The widow hovering respectfully in the background. Kids rushing in and out from the street. And Harry, talking about the Soviet Union. He spoke Russian fluently by then, and knew the inside history of every minor squabble or intrigue, let alone the big blood-baths, from the year dot. And what was all this in aid of? Anna, you'd never guess.' 'Of course I can,' I said. 'He was preparing himself for the day.' 'Of course. Right first time. The poor lunatic had it all worked out—the day would come when the comrades in Russia would all suddenly and at the same moment see the light. They'd say: "We've lost our road, we've missed the right path, our horizons are unclear. But over there in St Pancras, London, England, is Comrade Harry, who knows it all. We'll invite him over and ask his advice." ' Time passed. Things got worse and worse, but from Harry's point of view, better and better. With every new scandal from the Soviet Union, it seems that Harry's morale rose. The piles of newspapers rose to the ceiling in Harry's rooms and overflowed into the widow's rooms. He was speaking Russian like a native. Stalin died—Harry nodded and thought: It won't be long now. And then the Twentieth Congress: Good, but not good enough. And then Harry meets Jimmy on the street. Ancient political enemies, they frown and stiffen. Then they nod, and smile. Then Harry takes Jimmy back to the widow's flat. They have tea. Jimmy says: 'There's a delegation to the Soviet Union, I'm organising it, like to come?' Harry is suddenly illuminated. 'Imagine it, Anna, there I sat, like a clot, thinking: Well, the poor Trot's got his heart in the right place after all, he's still got a soft spot for our Alma Mater. But all the time he was thinking: My day has come. He kept asking me who had suggested his name, and it was obviously important to him and so I didn't say the idea had only just that moment crossed my mind. Little did I realise that he believed that "the Party itself," and all the way from Moscow at that, was summoning him to help them out. So anyway, to cut a long story short, off we all go to Moscow, thirty happy British teachers. And the happiest, poor Harry, who has documents and papers stuffed into every pocket of his military tunic. We arrive in Moscow, and he has a dedicated and expectant air. He is kind to the rest of us, but we charitably put it down to the fact that he despises us for our comparatively frivolous lives but is determined not to show it. Besides, most of us are ex-Stalinists, and there is no denying that more than one ex-Stalinist has a twinge or two, meeting the Trots these days. However. The delegation proceeds on its flowery way of visits to factories, schools, Palaces of Culture, and the University, not to mention speeches and banquets. And there is Harry, in his tunic, with his gammy leg, and his revolutionary sternness, the living incarnation of Lenin, only those foolish Russians never recognised him. They adored him of course for his high seriousness, but more than once they enquired why Harry wore such bizarre clothes, and even, as I recall, if he had a secret sorrow. Meanwhile, our old friendship had been restored and we used to chat about this and that in our rooms at night. I noticed he was looking at me increasingly bewildered. I noticed he was getting agitated. And still I had no idea what was going through his mind. Well, on the last night of our visit, we were supposed to go off and banquet with some teachers' organisation but Harry wouldn't come. He said he didn't feel well. I went to see him, when I got back, and there he was, sitting in a chair by the window, his gammy leg stuck out in front of him. He rose to meet me, positively radiant, then he saw it was only me, and it was a blow, I could see that. Then he cross-examined me and found out that he had been invited on to the delegation only because I had thought of it when I saw him in the street. I could have kicked myself for telling him. I swear, Anna, at the moment when it began to dawn on me, I wished I had made up some story about "Khrushchev himself," etc.

He kept saying: "Jimmy, you must tell me the truth, *you* invited me, it was just your idea?" over and over again. It was really terrible. Well, suddenly the interpreter came in to see if we had everything for the night and to say good-bye, because we wouldn't see her in the morning. She was a girl of about twenty or twenty-two, an absolute honey-pot, with long yellow plaits and grey eyes. I swear that every man on the delegation was in love with her. She was dropping with exhaustion, because it's no joke, nannying thirty British teachers for two weeks all round those palaces and schools. But suddenly Harry saw his chance. He pulled out a chair, and said: "Comrade Olga, sit down please." Brooking no argument. I knew what was going to happen, because he was unloading theses and documents from all over his person and arranging them on the table. I tried to stop him but he simply nodded at the door. When Harry nods at the door, one goes out. Well, I went to my room and sat and smoked, waiting. That was about one in the morning. We were due to get up at six so as to be driven to the airport at seven. At six Olga came in, white with exhaustion, and definitely at a loss. Yes, that's the phrase, at a loss. She said to me. "I have come to tell you that I think you must look after your friend Harry, I think he is not well, he is over-excited." Well, I told Olga all about his Spanish war record, and his acts of heroism, and I invented two or three extra ones, and she said: "Yes, it is easy to see he is a very fine man." Then she nearly split her face yawning and she went off to bed, because she had to start work on another delegation of peace-loving churchmen from Scotland next day. And then Harry came in. He was gaunt as a ghost and dead with emotion. The whole basis of his life had collapsed. He told me what had happened, while I kept trying to hurry him up, because we had to be leaving for the airport and neither of us had even changed since the night before . . .'

Harry had apparently unloaded papers and cuttings on to the table and then began a lecture on the history of the Russian Communist Party, starting from the days of *Iskra*. Olga sat opposite, suppressing her yawns, smiling and full of charm and preserving the civic politeness that is owed to progressive guests from abroad. At one point she asked if he were a historian, but he replied: 'No, I am a socialist, like yourself comrade.' He took her through years of intrigues, and heroism and intellectual battles, missing nothing. At about three in the morning she had said: 'Will you excuse me a moment, comrade?' She went out, and he had sat thinking that she had gone for the police, and now he would be arrested and 'sent to Siberia.' When Jimmy asked him how he felt about vanishing into Siberia, possibly for good, Harry had replied that: 'For such a moment as this, no price is too high.' Because of course he'd forgotten by now that he was addressing Olga the interpreter, the pretty twenty-year-old blonde whose father had been killed in the war, who looked after a widowed mother, and intended to marry a journalist from *Pravda* next spring. By that time he was addressing History itself. He waited for the police, quite limp with ecstatic acceptance, but when Olga came back it was with two glasses of tea she had ordered from the restaurant. 'The service is beyond words appalling Anna, so I can imagine that he was sitting there waiting for the handcuffs for some time.' Olga sat down, pushing his glass of tea across to him, and said: 'Please go on, I am sorry I interrupted you.' Soon after she went to sleep. Harry had just reached the point where Stalin had arranged for the assassination of Trotsky in Mexico. Apparently Harry sat there, cut off in the middle of a sentence, looking at Olga, her gleaming plaits slipping forward over her slumped shoulders, her head fallen sideways. Then he pushed his papers together, and put them away. Then he very gently woke her, apologising for boring her. She was overcome with shame at her bad manners, but explained that while she enjoyed her work, as interpreter for one delegation after another, it was hard work, 'And besides, my mother is an invalid and I have to do the housework when I get home at nights.' She clasped his hand, and said: 'I will make you a promise. I promise you that when our Party Historians have re-written the history of our Communist Party in accordance with the revisions made necessary by the distortions imposed during the era of Comrade Stalin, I promise you that I will read it.' Apparently Harry had been overcome by her embarrassment because of her lack of manners. They spent some minutes reassuring each other. Then Olga went off to see Jimmy to say that his friend was over-excited.

I asked Jimmy what happened next. 'I don't know. We had to get dressed and packed in a hurry, then we flew back. Harry was silent and rather ill-looking but that's all. He made a point of thanking me for getting him on to the delegation: a very valuable experience, he said it was. I went over to see him last week. He's married the widow at last and she's pregnant, I don't know what that proves, if anything.'

[Here a double black line marked the end of the red notebook.]

[The yellow notebook continued:]

*1 A SHORT STORY

A woman, starved for love, meets a man rather younger than herself, younger perhaps in emotional experience than in years; or perhaps in the depth of his emotional experience. She deludes herself about the nature of the man; for him, another love affair merely.

*2 A SHORT STORY

A man uses grown-up language, the language of emotionally grown people, to gain a woman. She slowly understands that this language comes from an idea in his head, it has nothing to do with his emotions; in fact he is an adolescent boy emotionally. Yet, knowing this, she cannot prevent herself being moved and won by the language.

531

*3 A SHORT STORY

Saw in the review of a book recently: 'One of those unfortunate affairs—women, even the nicest of them, tend to fall in love with men quite unworthy of them.' This review, of course, written by a man. The truth is that when 'nice women' fall in love with 'unworthy men' it is always either because these men have 'named' them, or because they have an ambiguous uncreated quality impossible to the 'good' or 'nice' men. The normal, the good men, are finished and completed and without potentialities. The story to be about my friend Annie in Central Africa, a 'nice woman' married to a 'nice man.' He was a civil servant, solid, responsible, and he wrote bad poetry in secret. She fell in love with a hard-drinking womanising miner. Not an organised miner, the manager, or clerk, or owner. He moved from small mine to small mine that were always precarious, on the point of making a fortune or of failing. He left a mine when it failed or was sold to a big combine. I was with the two of them one evening. He was just in from some mine in the bush three hundred miles off. There she was, rather fat, flushed, a pretty girl buried in a matron. He looked over at her and said: 'Annie, you were born to be the wife of a pirate.' I remember how we laughed, because it was ludicrous, pirates in that suburban little room in the city; pirates and the nice kind husband and Annie, the good wife, so guilty because of this affair, more of the imagination than the flesh, with the roving miner. Yet I remember when he said it, how gratefully she looked at him. He drank himself to death, years later. I got a letter from her, after years of silence: 'You remember X? He died. You'll understand me—the meaning of my life has gone.' This story, translated into English terms, should be the nice suburban wife in love with a hopeless coffee-bar bum, who says he is going to write, and perhaps does, one day, but that isn't the point. This story to be written from the point of view of the entirely responsible and decent husband, unable to understand the attraction of this bum.

*4 A SHORT STORY

A healthy woman, in love with a man. She finds herself becoming ill, with symptoms she has never had in her life. She slowly understands that this illness is not hers, she understands the man is ill. She understands the nature of the illness, not from him, how he acts or what he says, but from how his illness is reflected in herself.

*5 A SHORT STORY

A woman who has fallen in love, against her will. She is happy. And yet, in the middle of the night, she wakes. He starts up, as if in danger. He says: No, no, no. Then, consciousness and control. He slowly lays himself down again, in silence. She wants to say: What is it you are saying *No* to? For she is filled with fear. She does not say it. She sinks back to sleep, and weeps in her sleep. She wakes; he is still awake. She says, anxiously, Is that your heart beating? He, sullen: No, it's yours.

*6 A SHORT STORY

A man and a woman, in a love affair. She, for hunger of love, he for refuge. One afternoon he says, very carefully: 'I have to go and see—' But she knows it is an excuse, while she listens to a long, detailed explanation, for she is full of dismay. She says, 'Of course. Of course.' He says, with a sudden loud young laugh, very aggressive: 'You are very permissive,' and she says: 'What do you mean, permissive? I'm not your keeper, don't make me into an American woman.' He comes into her bed, very late, and she turns to him, just awake. She feels his arms about her, cautious, measured. She understands he doesn't want to make love to her. His penis is limp, though (and this annoys her, the naivety of it) moving himself against her thighs. She says, sharp: 'I'm sleepy.' He stops moving. She feels bad, because he might feel hurt. Suddenly she realises he is very big. She is dismayed because he wants her just because she has refused. Yet she is in love, and she turns to him. When the sex is over, she knows that for him it has meant accomplishing something. She says sharply, out of instinctive knowledge, not knowing she was going to say it: 'You've just been making love to someone else.' He says quickly: 'How did you know?' And then, just as if he has not said, how did you know, he says: 'I haven't. You're imagining it.' Then, because of her tense miserable silence, he says, sullen: 'I didn't think it would matter. You have to understand, I don't take it seriously.' This last remark makes her feel diminished and destroyed, as if she does not exist as a woman.

*7 A SHORT STORY

A wandering man happens to land in the house of a woman whom he likes and whom he needs. He is a man with a long experience of women needing love. Usually he limits himself. But this time, the words he uses, the emotions he allows himself, are ambiguous, because he needs her kindness for a time. He makes love to her, but for him the sex is no worse or better than what he has experienced a hundred times before. He realises that his need for temporary refuge has trapped him into what he most dreads: a woman saying, I love you. He cuts it. Says good-bye, formally, on the level of a friendship ending. Goes. Writes in his diary: Left London. Anna reproachful. She hated me. Well, so be it. And another entry, months later, which could read either: Anna married, good. Or: Anna committed suicide. Pity, a nice woman.

*8 A SHORT STORY

A woman artist—painter, writer, doesn't matter which, lives alone. But her whole life is oriented around an absent man for whom she is waiting. Her flat too big, for instance.

Her mind is filled with shapes of the man who will enter her life, meanwhile she ceases to paint or to write. Yet in her mind she is still 'an artist.' Finally a man enters her life, some kind of artist, but one who has not yet crystallised as one. Her personality as 'an artist' goes into his, he feeds off it, works from it, as if she were a dynamo that fed energy into him. Finally he emerges, a real artist, fulfilled; the artist in her dead. The moment when she is no longer an artist, he leaves her, he needs the woman who has this quality, so that he can create.

*9 A SHORT NOVEL

An American 'ex-red' comes to London. No money, no friends. Black-listed in the film and television worlds. The American colony in London, or rather, the American 'ex-red' colony, know him as the man who started criticising Stalinist attitudes in the communist party three or four years before they had the courage to do it. He goes to them for help, feeling that as he has been justified by events, they will forget their hostility. But their attitudes to him are still what they were when they were still dutiful party members or fellow-travellers. He is still a renegade, this in spite of the fact that their attitudes have changed, and they are now beating their breasts because they didn't break with the party earlier. A rumour starts among them, a man who was formerly a dogmatic non-critical communist, but now hysterically breast-beating, that this new American is an agent of the F.B.I. The colony accepts this rumour as fact, refuse him friendship and help. While they are ostracising this man, they are talking self-righteously about the secret police in Russia, and the behaviour of the anti-American activity committees and the informers, ex-reds. The new American commits suicide. Then they all sit around remembering incidents from the political past, finding reasons to dislike him, to drown their guilt.

*10

A man or a woman who has, because of some mental

condition, lost a sense of time. A film, obviously, marvellous what one could do with it. Well I'd never have a chance to write it, so there's no point thinking about it. But I can't help thinking about it. A man whose 'sense of reality' has gone; and because of it, has a deeper sense of reality than 'normal' people. Today Dave said, quite casually: 'That man of yours, Michael, the fact that he's turning you down, you shouldn't let it affect *you*. Who are *you* if you can be broken up by someone being fool enough not to take you on?' He spoke as if Michael were still in the process of 'turning me down' instead of its being years old. And of course he was talking about himself. He was, for a moment, Michael. My sense of reality shivered and broke. But something very clear was there, all the same, a sort of illumination, though it would be hard to say what. (This art of comment belongs to the blue notebook, not this one.)

*11 A SHORT NOVEL

Two people together, in any kind of relationship—mother, son; father, daughter; lovers; it doesn't matter. One of them acutely neurotic. The neurotic hands on his or her state to the other, who takes it over, leaving the sick one well, the well one sick. I remember Mother Sugar telling me a story about a patient. A young man had come to see her convinced he was in desperate psychological trouble. She could find nothing wrong with him. She asked him to send along his father to her. One by one all the family, five of them, arrived in her consulting room. She found them all normal. Then the mother came. She, apparently 'normal,' was in fact extremely neurotic, but maintaining her balance by passing it on to her family, particularly to the youngest son. Eventually Mother Sugar treated the mother, though there was terrible trouble getting her to come for treatment. And the young man who had come in the first place found the pressure lifting off him. I remember her saying: Yes, often it's the most 'normal' member of a family or a group who is really sick, but simply because they have strong personalities, they survive, because other, weaker personalities, express their illness for them. (This sort of comment belongs to the blue notebook. I must keep them separate.)

*12 A SHORT STORY

A husband, unfaithful to his wife, not because he is in love with another woman, but in order to assert his independence of the married state, comes back from sleeping with the other woman, with every intention of being discreet, but 'accidentally' does something to give the show away. This 'accident,' scent or lipstick or forgetting to wash off the smell of sex, is in fact why he did it in the first place, though he doesn't know it. He needed to say to his wife: 'I'm not going to belong to you.'

*13 A SHORT NOVEL, TO BE CALLED 'THE MAN WHO IS FREE OF WOMEN.'

A man of about fifty, a bachelor, or perhaps was married for a short time, his wife died, or he got divorced. If an American, he is divorced, but if English, he has this wife tucked away somewhere, he might even live with her or share a house, but without real emotional contact. At fifty, he has had a couple of dozen affairs, three or four serious. These serious affairs were with women who hoped to marry him, they lingered on, in what were really marriages without formal ties, he broke the affairs off at the point where he had to marry them. At fifty he is dry, anxious about his sexuality, has five or six women friends, all ex-mistresses, now married. He is a cuckoo in half a dozen families, the old family friend. He is like a child, dependent on women, gets vaguer and more inefficient, is always ringing up some woman to do something for him. Outwardly a dapper, ironic intelligent man, making an impression on younger women for a week or so. He has these affairs with girls or much younger women, then returns to the older women who fulfil the function of kindly nannies or nursemaids.

*14 A SHORT NOVEL

A man and a woman, married or in a long relationship, secretly read each other's diaries in which (and it is a point of honour with them both) their thoughts about each other are recorded with the utmost frankness. Both know that the other is reading what he/she writes, but for a while objectivity is maintained. Then, slowly, they begin writing falsely, first unconsciously; then consciously, so as to influence the other. The position is reached where each keeps two diaries, one for private use, and locked up; and the second for the other to read. Then one of them makes a slip of the tongue, or a mistake, and the other accuses him/her of having found the secret diary. A terrible quarrel which drives them apart forever, not because of the original diaries—'but we both knew we were reading *those* diaries, that doesn't count, how can you be so dishonest as to read my private diary!'

*15 A SHORT STORY

An American man, English woman. She, in all her attitudes, emotions, expects to be possessed and taken. He, in all his attitudes and emotions, expects to be taken. Regards himself as an instrument to be used, by her, for her pleasure. Emotional deadlock. Then they discuss it: the discussion, on sexual emotional attitudes turns into a comparison of the two different societies.

*16 A SHORT STORY

Man and a woman, both sexually proud and experienced, seldom meeting others as experienced. Suddenly both afflicted by dislike for the other, an emotion which, when examined (and they are nothing if not self-examiners), turns out to be dislike for themselves. They have found their mirrors, take a good look, grimace, leave each other. When they meet it is with a wry sort of acknowledgement, become good friends on this basis, after a time this wry ironical friendship turns into love. But love is barred to them because of the first stark experience, without emotion.

*17 A SHORT NOVEL

Two rakes, male and female, together. Their concourse has the following ironical rhythm. He takes her, she wary from experience, but she slowly succumbs emotionally. At the moment when she emotionally gives herself to him, his emotions cut off, he loses desire for her. She, hurt and miserable. Turns to another man. But at this point, the first man finds her desirable again. But whereas he is excited by the knowledge she has been sleeping with someone else, she is frozen up because he is excited, not by her, but the fact she has been with someone else. But slowly, she succumbs to him emotionally. And just at the moment when it is at its best for her, he freezes up again, takes another woman, she another man, and so on.

*18 A SHORT STORY

Same theme as Chekhov's *The Darling*. But this time the woman doesn't change to suit different men, one after another; she changes in response to one man who is a psychological chameleon, so that in the course of a day she can be half a dozen different personalities, either in opposition to or in harmony with him.

*19 THE ROMANTIC TOUGH SCHOOL OF WRITING

The fellows were out Saturday-nighting true-hearted, the

539

wild-hearted Saturday-night gang of true friends, Buddy, Dave and Mike. Snowing. Snow-cold. The cold of cities in the daddy of cities, New York. But true to us. Buddy, the ape-shouldered, stood apart and stared. He scratched his crotch. Buddy the dreamer, pitch-black-eyed, sombrely staring, he would often masturbate in front of us, unconscious, pure, a curious purity. And now he stood with the snow crumb white on his sad bent shoulders. Dave tackled him low, Dave and Buddy sprawled together in the innocent snow, Buddy winded. Dave drove his fist into Buddy's belly, oh true love of true friends, mensch playing together under the cold cliffs of Manhattan on a true Saturday night. Buddy passed out cold. 'I love this son-of-a-bitch,' Dave said, while Buddy sprawled, lost to us and to the sadness of the city. I, Mike, Mike-the-lone-walker, stood apart, the burden of knowing on me, eighteen-years-old and lonely, watching my true buddies, Dave and Buddy. Buddy came to. Saliva flecked his near-dead lips and flew off into the saliva-white snowbank. He sat up, gasping, saw Dave there, arms around his kneecaps, staring at him, love in his Bronx-sad eyes. Left side of hairy fist to chin, he hit and Dave now fell flat out, out in the death-cold snow. Laughing Buddy, Buddy sat laughing, waiting in his turn. Man, what a maniac. 'Whatta you going to do, Buddy?' I said, Mike-the-lone-walker but loving his true friends. 'Ha ha ha, d'you see the expression on his face?' he said and rolled breathless, holding his crotch. 'Didja see that?' Dave gasped, life coming to him, rolled, groaned, sat up. Dave and Buddy fought then, true-fought, laughing with joy, till, laughing, fell apart in the snow. I, Mike, winged-with-words Mike, stood sorrowing with joy. 'Hey I love this bastard,' gasped Dave, throwing a punch to Buddy's midriff and Buddy, fore-arm stopping it said: 'Jeez, I love him.' But I heard the sweet music of heels on the frost-cold pavement, and I said: 'Hey, fellas.' We stood waiting. She came, Rosie, from her dark tenement bedroom, on her sweet-tapping heels. 'Hey, fellas,' says Rosie, sweet-smiling. We stood watching. Sad now, watching the proud-fleshed Rosie, swivelling on her true sex down the pavement, twitching her

540

round-ball butt, which jerked a message of hope to our hearts. Then Buddy, our buddy Buddy, moved apart, hesitant, sad-eyed, to our sad eyes: 'I love her, fellas.' Two friends were left then. Two-fisted Dave and winged-with-words Mike. We stood then, watching our friend Buddy, fated with life, nod and move on after Rosie, his pure heart beating to the tune of her sweet heels. The wings of mystic time beat down on us then, white with snowflakes, time that would whirl us all after our Rosies to death and the framehouse funeral. Tragic and beautiful to see our Buddy, move on out into the immemorial dance of fated snow-flakes, the dry rime rhyming on his collar. And the love that went out from us to him then was fantastic, true-volumed, sad-faced and innocent of the purposes of time, but true and in fact serious. We loved him as we turned, two friends left, our adolescent top coats flapping around our pure legs. On then, Dave and I, I-Mike, sad, because the intimation-bird of tragedy had touched our pearly souls, he-Dave and I-Mike, on then, goofy with life. Dave scratched his crotch, slow, owl-scratching pure Dave. 'Jeez, Mike,' he said, 'you'll write it someday, for us all.' He stammered, inarticulate, not-winged-with-words, 'You'll write it, hey feller? And how our souls were ruined here on the snow-white Manhattan pavement, the capitalist-money-mammon hound-of-hell hot on our heels?' 'Gee, Dave, I love you,' I said then, my boy's soul twisted with love. I hit him then, square to the jaw-bone, stammering with love-for-the-world, love-for-my-friends, for the Daves and the Mikes and the Buddies. Down he went and I then, Mike, then cradled him, baby, I-love-you, friendship in the jungle city, friendship of young youth. Pure. And the winds of time were blowing, snow-fated, on our loving pure shoulders.

If I've gone back to pastiche, then it's time to stop.

[The yellow notebook ended here with a double black line.]

People have heard the room upstairs is empty, they ring me up about it. I've been saying I don't want to let it, but I am short of money. Two business girls came round, they heard from Ivor I had a room. But then I realised I didn't want girls. Janet and myself, and then two girls, a flat full of women, I didn't want it. Then some men. Two of them instantly set up the atmosphere: you and me in this flat alone, so I sent them off. Three were in need of mothering, wrecks and waifs, I knew I'd be put in the position of looking after them before a week was out. So then I decided not to let rooms any more. I'll take a job, move to a smaller flat, anything. Meanwhile Janet's been asking questions: It's a pity Ivor had to leave, I hope we'll get someone as nice as him again, and so on. Then out of the blue she said she wanted to go to boarding-school. Her friend from the day school is going. I asked why and she said she wanted other girls to play with. Instantly I felt sad and rejected, then angry with myself that I did. Told her I'd think it over—money, the practical side. But what I really wanted to think over was Janet's character, what would suit her. I've often thought that if she hadn't been my daughter (I don't mean genetically, but my daughter because she's been brought up by me) she would have been the most conventional child imaginable. And that is what she is, despite a surface of originality. Despite the influence of Molly's house, despite my long affair with Michael, and his disappearance, despite the fact that she's the product of what is known as a 'broken marriage,' when I look at her I see no more than a charming, conventionally intelligent little girl, destined by nature for an unproblematical life. I nearly wrote: 'I hope so.' Why? I have no time for people who haven't experimented with themselves, deliberately tried the frontiers, yet when it's a question of one's own child, one can't bear the thought of all that for them. When she said: 'I want to go to boarding-school' with the petulant charm she is using now, trying her wings as a woman, what she was really saying to me was: 'I want to be ordinary and normal.' She was saying: 'I want to get out of the complicated atmosphere.' I think it is because she must be aware of my increasing depression. It is true that with her I banish the Anna who is listless and frightened. But she must feel that Anna is there. And of course, the reason why I don't want her to go is that she is my normality. I have to be, with her, simple, responsible, affectionate, and so she anchors me in what is normal in myself. When she goes to school . . .

Today she asked again: 'When am I going to boarding-school, I want to go with Mary.' (Her friend.)

I told her we would have to leave this big flat, get a smaller one, and that I must get a job. Not immediately however. For the third time a film company has bought the rights of *Frontiers of War*, but it won't come to anything. Well I hope not, anyway. I wouldn't have sold the rights if I'd believed the film would be made. The money will keep us, living simply, even with Janet at boarding-school.

I've been investigating progressive schools.

Told Janet about them, she said: 'I want to go to an ordinary boarding-school.' I said, 'There is nothing ordinary about a conventional English girls' boarding-school, they are unique in the world.' She said: 'You know quite well what I mean. And besides, Mary is going.'

Janet will be leaving in a few days. Today Molly rang up and said there was an American in town looking for a room. I said I didn't want to let rooms. She said: 'But you're in that enormous flat all by yourself, you don't have to see him.' I persisted, and then she said, 'Well I think it's just anti-social. What's happened to you Anna?' The *what's happened to you* hit me. Because of course it's anti-social, and I don't care. She said: 'Have a heart, he's an American lefty, he's got no money, he's been black-listed, and there you are in a flat with all those empty rooms.' I said: 'If he's an American on the loose in Europe, he'll be writing the American epic novel and he'll be in psychoanalysis and he'll have one of those awful American marriages and I'll have to listen to his troubles —I mean problems.' But Molly didn't laugh, she said: 'If you don't look out you'll be like the other people who've left the Party. I met Tom yesterday, he left the Party over Hungary.

He used to be a sort of unofficial soul-daddy for dozens of people. He's changed into something else. I heard he'd suddenly doubled the rent of the rooms he lets in his house, and he's stopped being a teacher, he's taken a job in an advertising agency. I rang him up to ask what the hell he thought he was doing, and he said: "I've been taken for a sucker long enough." So you'd better be careful Anna.'

So I said the American could come, provided I didn't have to see him, and then Molly said: 'He's not bad, I've met him, awfully brash and opinionated, but then they all are.' I said: 'I don't think they're brash, that's a stereotype from the past, the Americans these days are cool and shut off, they've got glass or ice between themselves and the rest of the world.' 'Oh if you say so,' Molly said, 'but I'm busy.'

Afterwards I thought of what I'd said, it was interesting because I hadn't known I'd thought it until I said it. But it's true. Yes. They can be brash and noisy, but more often full of good humour, yes that's their characteristic, good humour. And underneath the hysteria, the fear of involvement. I've been sitting and thinking about the Americans I've known. A lot of them now. I remember the week-end I spent with F., a friend of Nelson's. At first, I was relieved, I thought: A normal man at last, thank God. Then I understood, everything was from his head. He was 'good in bed.' Consciously, positively dutifully 'a man.' But no warmth. Everything measured out. The wife 'back home' whom he patronised with every word he said (but really he was afraid of her—he was afraid not of her but of the obligations to society she represented). And the careful non-committal affairs. Exactly the right amount of warmth measured out—everything worked out, for such and such a relationship, so much emotion. Yes, that's their quality, something measured, shrewd and cool. Of course, emotion is a trap, it delivers you into the hands of society, that's why people are measuring it out.

I put myself back into the state of mind I was in when I went to Mother Sugar. I can't feel, I said. I don't care about anyone in the world except Janet. Seven years ago now?—something like that. When I left her I said: You've taught me to cry, thank you for nothing, you've given me back feeling, and it's too painful.

How old-fashioned of me to seek a witch-doctor to be taught to feel. Because now I think of it, I see that people everywhere are trying not to feel. Cool, cool, cool, that's the word. That's the banner. From America first, but now us. I think of the groups of young people, political and social around London, Tommy's friends, the new socialists—that's what they have in common, a quality of measured emotion, coolness.

In a world as terrible as this, limit emotion. How odd I didn't see it before.

And against this instinctive retreat into no-feeling, as a protection against pain, Mother Sugar—I remember saying to her in exasperation: 'If I said to you that the H bomb has fallen and obliterated half of Europe, you'd click with your tongue, tck, tck, and then, if I was weeping and wailing, you'd invite me, with an admonitory frown or a gesture, to remember, or take into account some emotion I was wilfully excluding. What emotion? Why, joy, of course. Consider, my child, you'd say, or imply, the creative aspects of destruction! Consider the creative implications of the power locked in the atom! Allow your mind to rest on those first blades of tentative green grass that will poke into the light out of the lava in a million years time!' She smiled, of course. Then the smile changed and became dry, there was one of the moments, outside the analyst-patient relationship that I waited for. She said: 'My dear Anna, it is possible after all that in order to keep ourselves sane we will have to learn to rely on those blades of grass springing in a million years?'

But it isn't only the terror everywhere, and the fear of being conscious of it, that freezes people. It's more than that. People know they are in a society dead or dying. They are refusing emotion because at the end of every emotion are property, money, power. They work and despise their work, and so freeze themselves. They love but know that it's a half-love or a twisted love, and so they freeze themselves.

It is possible that in order to keep love, feeling, tenderness alive, it will be necessary to feel these emotions ambiguously,

545

even for what is false and debased, or for what is still an idea, a shadow in the willed imagination only . . . or if what we feel is pain, then we must feel it, acknowledging that the alternative is death. Better anything than the shrewd, the calculated, the non-committal, the refusal of giving for fear of the consequences . . . . I can hear Janet coming up the stairs.

Janet went to school today. Uniform is optional, and she chose to wear it. Extraordinary that my child should want a uniform. I can't remember a time in my life when I wouldn't have felt uncomfortable in one. Paradox: when I was a communist, it was not in the service of uniformed man, but the opposite. The uniform is an ugly sage-green tunic with a yellowish-brown blouse. It is cut to make a girl of Janet's age, twelve, as ugly as possible. Also there is an ugly round hard dark green hat. The greens of the hat and the tunic are ugly together. Yet she is delighted. The uniform was chosen by the head-mistress, whom I interviewed—an admirable old Englishwoman, scholarly, dry, intelligent. I should imagine that the woman in her died before she was twenty, she probably killed her off. It occurs to me that in sending Janet to her, I am providing Janet with a father-figure? But oddly enough, I was certainly trusting Janet to oppose her, by refusing, for instance, to wear the ugly uniform. But Janet doesn't want to oppose anything.

The young girl's quality, the petulant, indulged-child's charm, which she put on like a pretty dress about a year ago, vanished the moment she put the uniform on. On the station platform she was a nice, bright little girl in a hideous uniform, among a herd of such young girls, her young breasts hidden, all charm vanquished, her manner practical. And, seeing her, I mourned for a dark, lively, dark-eyed, slight young girl, alive with new sexuality, alert with the instinctive knowledge of her power. And at the same time I noticed I had a truly cruel thought: my poor child, if you are going to grow up in a society full of Ivors and Ronnies, full of frightened men who measure out emotions like weighed groceries, then you'll do well to model yourself on Miss Street, the head-mistress. I was feeling, because that charming young girl had been put out of sight, as if something infinitely precious and vulnerable had been saved from hurt. And there was a triumphant malice in it, directed against men: All right, so you don't value us?—then we'll save ourselves against the time when you do again. I ought to have been ashamed of the spite, of the malice, but I was not, there was too much pleasure in it.

The American, Mr Green, was coming today, so I got his room ready. He telephoned to say he was invited to spend a day in the country, could he come tomorrow. Many careful apologies. Was annoyed, had made arrangements that I had to change. Later Molly telephoned to say that her friend Jane told her that she, Jane, had spent the day with Mr Green 'showing him Soho.' I was angry. Then Molly said: 'Tommy met Mr Green and didn't like him, he said he was unorganised, that's a mark in Mr Green's favour, don't you think? Tommy never approves of anyone who isn't just so. Don't you think that's odd? Ever such a socialist he is, and all his friends, and they're all as respectable and petit-bourgeois as—they've only got to meet someone with a bit of life in them, and they start drawing their moral skirts aside. And of course that ghastly wife of Tommy's is worse than anybody. She complained that Mr Green was nothing but a bum, because he doesn't have a regular job. Can you beat it? That girl'd do beautifully as the wife of a provincial businessman with slightly liberal leanings that he uses to shock his Tory friends. And she's my daughter-in-law. She's writing a great tome about the Chartists and she puts aside two pounds a week as a nest-egg against her old age. Anyway, if Tommy and that little bitch don't like Mr Green, it means you probably will, so virtue won't have to be its own reward.' Well, I laughed at all this, and then I thought that if I could laugh I couldn't be in such a bad state as I thought. Mother Sugar once told me it had taken her six months to get a depressed patient to laugh. Yet there's no doubt that Janet's going, leaving me alone in this big flat, has made me worse. I am listless and idle. I keep thinking of Mother Sugar, but in a new way, as if the idea of her can save me. From what? I don't want to be saved. Because Janet's going has reminded me of something else—time, how time can be, when one hasn't got pressure on one. I haven't moved, at ease, in time, since Janet was born. Having a child means being conscious of the clock, never being free of something that has to be done at a certain moment ahead. An Anna is coming to life that died when Janet was born. I was sitting on the floor this afternoon, watching the sky darken, an inhabitant of a world where one can say, the quality of light means it must be evening, instead of: in exactly an hour I must put on the vegetables, and I suddenly went back into a state of mind I'd forgotten, something from my childhood. I used at night to sit up in bed and play what I called 'the game.' First I created the room I sat in, object by object, 'naming' everything, bed, chair, curtains, till it was whole in my mind, then move out of the room, creating the house, then out of the house, slowly creating the street, then rise into the air, looking down on London, at the enormous sprawling wastes of London, but holding at the same time the room and the house and the street in my mind, and then England, the shape of England in Britain, then the little group of islands lying against the continent, then slowly, slowly, I would create the world, continent by continent, ocean by ocean (but the point of 'the game' was to create this vastness while holding the bedroom, the house, the street in their littleness in my mind at the same time), until the point was reached where I moved out into space, and watched the world, a sunlit ball in the sky, turning and rolling beneath me. Then, having reached that point, with the stars around me, and the little earth turning underneath me, I'd try to imagine at the same time, a drop of water, swarming with life, or a green leaf. Sometimes I could reach what I wanted, a simultaneous knowledge of vastness and of smallness. Or I would concentrate on a single creature, a small coloured fish in a pool, or a single flower, or a moth, and try to create, to 'name' the being of the flower, the moth, the fish, slowly creating around it the forest, or the sea-pool, or the space of blowing night air that tilted my wings. And then, out, suddenly, from the smallness into space.

It was easy when I was a child. It seems to me now that I must have lived for years in a state of exhilaration, because of 'the game.' But now it is very hard. This afternoon I was exhausted after a few moments. Yet I did succeed, just for a few seconds, to watch the earth turn beneath me, while the sunlight deepened on the belly of Asia and Europe fell into darkness.

Saul Green came to see the room and to leave his things. I took him straight up to the room, he gave one glance at it and said: 'Fine, fine.' This was so offhand I asked if he expected to leave again soon. He gave me a quick wary look, which I already knew to be characteristic, and began long, careful explanations, in the same tone he had used for his apologies about the day in the country. Reminded, I said: 'I believe you spent the day exploring Soho with Jane Bond.' He looked startled, then offended—but quite extraordinarily offended, as if he'd been caught out in some crime, then his face changed, it became wary and careful, and he started off on a long explanation about changed plans, etc., and the explanation was even more extraordinary, since it was clearly all untrue. Suddenly I got bored, and said that I had only asked about the room because I intended to move to another flat, so if he planned a long stay, he should look for somewhere else. He said it was Fine, it was Fine. It seemed as if he wasn't listening, and that he hadn't seen the room at all. But he came out after me, leaving his bags. Then I said my land-lady's piece, about there being 'no restrictions,' making it a joke, but he didn't understand, so I had to spell it out, that if he wanted girls in his room I didn't mind. Was surprised by his laugh—loud, abrupt, offended. He said he was glad I assumed he was a normal young man; this was so American, the automatic reaction one is used to when virility is in question, so I didn't make the joke I had been going to, about the previous occupant of the room. Altogether I felt everything to be jarring, discordant, so I went down to the kitchen, leaving him to follow if he wanted. I had made coffee, and he came into the kitchen on his way out so I offered him a cup. He hesitated. He was examining me. I have never in my life been subjected to as brutal a sexual inspection as that one. There was no humour in it, no warmth, just the stockman's comparison-making. It was so frank that I said: 'I hope I pass,' but he gave his abrupt

549

offended laugh again and said: 'Fine, fine'—in other words, he was either unconscious he had been making a list of my vital statistics, or he was too prudish to acknowledge it. So I left it, and we had coffee. I was uncomfortable with him, I didn't know why, something in his manner. And there is something upsetting about his appearance, as if one instinctively expects to find something when one looks at him that one doesn't find. He is fair, his hair is close-cut, like a fair glistening brush. He is not tall, though I kept thinking of him as tall, and then checking again and seeing he was not. It's because his clothes are all too big for him, they hang around him. One would expect him to be that fair, rather stocky, broad-shouldered American type, with the greenish-grey eyes, the square face. I kept looking, I realise now, expecting to see this man, and seeing a slight, unco-ordinated man with clothes hanging loose from broad shoulders, and then being caught and held by his eyes. His eyes are cool grey-green, and never off guard. That is the most striking thing about him, he is never for one second off guard. I asked one or two questions out of the fellow-feeling of 'A socialist from America' but I gave it up, because he turned aside my questions. For something to say, I asked why he wore his clothes so big, and he looked startled, as if he were surprised I had noticed it, and then evasive, and said he had lost a lot of weight, he was normally a couple of stones heavier. I asked if he'd been ill, and again he was offended, suggesting by his manner that pressure was being put on him or that he was being spied on. For a while we sat in silence, while I wished he would go, since it seemed impossible to say anything at all that he wouldn't resent. Then I said something about Molly, whom he hadn't mentioned. I was surprised how he seemed to change. Some kind of intelligence switched on suddenly, I don't know how else to put it: his attention focused, and I was struck by how he spoke of her, extraordinarily acute about her character and situation. I realised there was no other man I had met, with the exception of Michael, capable of such quick insight into a woman. It struck me that he was 'naming' her on a level that would please her if she heard it . . .

[From this point on in the diary, or chronicle, Anna had marked certain points in it with asterisks, and numbered the asterisks.]

. . . and this made me curious, envious rather, so I said something (*1) about myself and so he spoke of me. Rather, he lectured me. It was like being lectured by a fair-minded pedant, on the dangers and pitfalls and rewards of a woman living alone, etc. It occurred to me, giving me the most curious feeling of dislocation, of disbelief, that this was the same man, who ten minutes before had given me such a cold and almost hostile sexual inspection; yet in what he was saying now there was nothing of that quality, and nothing, either, of the half-veiled curiosity, the sudden moment of lip-licking expectation one is used to. On the contrary, I could not remember any other man talking with this simplicity, frankness and comradeship about the sort of life I, and women like me, live. I laughed at one point, because I was being 'named' on such a high level (*2), yet lectured as if I were a small girl, instead of being several years older than he. It struck me as odd that he did not hear my laugh, it wasn't a question of being offended by it, or waiting until I stopped laughing, or asking why I was laughing, he simply went on talking, as if he had forgotten I was there. I had the most uncomfortable feeling that I literally didn't exist for Saul any longer, and I was glad to bring the thing to an end, which I had to do because I was expecting a man from the company who wants to buy *Frontiers of War*. When he came I decided not to sell the rights of the novel. They do want to make the film, I think, so what is the use of standing out all these years simply to give in now, just because for the first time I'm running short of money. So I told him I wouldn't sell. He assumed I had sold it to someone else, was unable to believe that a writer existed who wouldn't sell, at a high enough price. He kept raising the price, absurdly, I kept refusing, it was all farcical, I began to laugh—it reminded me of the moment I laughed and Saul didn't hear: he didn't know why I was laughing and kept looking at me as if I, the real Anna who was laughing, didn't exist for him. And when he went off, it was with dislike on both sides. Anyway, to go back to Saul, when I told him I was expecting someone to come, I was struck by how he scrambled up, as if he were being thrown out, yes, really, as if I'd thrown him out, instead of just saying I was expecting a man on business. Then he controlled the scrambling defensive movement, and nodded, very cool and withdrawn, and went straight downstairs. When he had gone I felt bad, the whole encounter full of jarrings and discordancies, and I decided I had made a mistake about letting him come to my flat. But later I told Saul about my not wanting to sell the novel for a film, and rather defensively, because I am used to being treated as if I were foolish, and he took it for granted I was right. He said the reason he finally left his job in Hollywood was because there wasn't anybody left in it who was capable of believing that a writer would refuse money rather than have a bad film made. He talks like all these people who have worked in Hollywood—with a sort of grim, incredulous despair that anything so corrupt can actually exist. Then he said something that struck me: 'We've got to make stands all the time. Yeah, O.K., we make stands on false positions sometimes, but the point is to make the stand at all. I've the advantage over you on one point . . .' (I was struck, this time uncomfortably, by the sullenness of I've the advantage over you on one point, as if we were in some sort of a contest or battle) '. . . and that is, the pressures that have been put on me to give in have been much more direct and obvious than the pressures in this country.' I said, knowing what he meant, but wanting to hear him define it: 'Give in to what?' 'If you don't know, I can't tell you.' 'Oh, but I do know.' 'I think you do. I hope you do.' And then, with the touch of sullenness: 'Believe me, that's one thing I learned in that hell-hole—the people who aren't prepared to take a stand somewhere, and sometimes on bad issues, won't make a stand, they sell out. And don't say: *Sell out to what?* If it were easy to say exactly what, we wouldn't all have to make stands on bad issues sometimes. We shouldn't be afraid to be naïve and foolish, that's the one thing we should none of us be afraid of . . .' He began lecturing me again. I liked being lectured. I liked what he said. And yet as he talked, again unaware of me—I swear he had forgotten I was there—I was looking at him, from the safety of his having forgotten me, and I saw his pose, standing with his back to the window in a way that was like a caricature of that young American we see in the films—sexy he-man, all balls and strenuous erection. He stood lounging, his thumbs hitched through his belt, fingers loose, but pointing as it were to his genitals—the pose that always amuses me when I see it on the films, because it goes with the young, unused, boyish American face—the boyish, disarming face, and the he-man's pose. And Saul stood lecturing me about the pressures of society to conform, while he used the sexy pose. It was unconscious but it was directed at me, and it was so crude I began to be annoyed. There were two different languages being spoken to me at the same time. Then I noticed he looked different. Earlier I had kept looking at him, uneasy, because of how I was expecting to see something different from what he was, and seeing the thin bony man in loose hanging clothes. He was wearing clothes that fitted him. They looked new. I realised he must have gone out and bought new clothes. He wore new neat blue jeans, tight-fitting, and a close dark blue sweater. He looked slight, with the fitting new clothes, and yet he still looked wrong, the shoulders being too broad, and the jutting bones of his hips. I broke into the monologue, and asked if he had bought new clothes simply because I had said what I had that morning. He frowned, and replied stiffly, after a pause, that he didn't want to look a hick—'Any more than I have to.' I felt uncomfortable again, and said: 'Hadn't anyone told you before that your clothes were hanging on you?' He said nothing, it was as if I hadn't spoken, his eyes were abstracted. I said: 'If no one told you, well, your mirror must have.' He laughed gruffly, and said: 'Lady, I don't enjoy looking into mirrors these days, I used to think of myself as a good-looking boy.' He intensified the sexy, lounging pose as he said these words. I could see him as he was when his flesh fitted his bone-structure: broad, solid, a strong fair-coloured man glistening with health, with cool greyish eyes, shrewdly measuring. But the new neat clothes intensified the discordancy in his appearance; he looked all wrong. I realised he looked ill, there was an unhealthy whiteness in his face. And yet still he lounged, not looking at me, Anna; but directing sexual challenge at me. I thought how odd that this was the same man who was capable of such real perception about women, such a simple warmth in the form of the words he used. I nearly challenged him in his turn, saying something like: What the hell do you mean by using that grown-up language to me, and then standing there like a heroic cowboy with invisible revolvers stuck all over your hips? But there was a great space between him and me, he started talking again, lecturing. Anyway I said I was tired and went off to bed.

Spent today playing 'the game.' Towards afternoon reached the point of relaxed comprehension I was aiming for. It seems to me that if I can achieve some sort of self-discipline, instead of aimless reading, aimless thinking, I can defeat my depression. Very bad for me, Janet's not being here, no need to get up in the morning, no outer shape to my life. Must give it an inner shape. If 'the game' doesn't work, I'll get a job. I must anyway, for financial reasons. (Find myself not eating, watching pennies, I hate the idea of working so much.) I'll find some sort of welfare work—it's what I'm good at. Very silent here today. No sign of Saul Green. Molly rang late—says that Jane Bond has 'taken a fall over' Mr Green. She added that she thought that any woman who got involved with Mr Green was out of her senses. (A warning?) (*3) 'That's a man to go to bed with for one night and be damned sure you lose his telephone number afterwards. If we were still the sort of women, that is, who went to bed with a man for one night. Ah well, those were the days . . .'

This morning I woke up feeling as I never have before. My neck was tense and stiff. I was conscious of my breathing—had to force myself to breathe deeply. Above all, my stomach pained me, or rather, the region under my diaphragm. It was as if my muscles there were clenched into a knot. And I was filled with a kind of undirected apprehension. It was this feeling that finally made me dismiss self-

554

diagnosis of indigestion, having caught cold in my neck, etc. I rang Molly and asked her if she had any sort of book with medical symptoms in it, and if so, would she read me a description of an anxiety state. It was in this way I discovered I am suffering from an anxiety state—I told her it was to verify some description in a novel I'd read. Then I sat down to find out why I have an anxiety state. I am not worried about money, being short of money has never in my life upset me, I'm not afraid of being poor, and anyway one can always earn it if one sets one's mind to it. I'm not worried about Janet. I can see no reason at all why I should be anxious. 'Naming' the state I am in as an anxiety state lessened it for a while, but tonight (*4) it is very bad. Extraordinary.

Today the telephone rang very early—Jane Bond for Saul Green. Knocked on his door, no answer. Several times he hasn't been in at all, all night. Was going to tell her that he hadn't been in, but it occurred to me that wasn't tactful, if she has really 'taken a fall' over him. Knocked at the door again, looked in. He was there. Struck by how he slept, in a tight curve under neat bedclothes. Called him, but no answer. Went close, put my hand on his shoulder, no response. Suddenly frightened—he was so still that for the second I thought he was dead, there was such a quality of absolute stillness. What I could see of his face paper-white. Like fine slightly crinkled paper. Tried to turn him over. Very cold to the touch—could feel the cold striking up into my hands. I felt terror. I can feel, even now, on the palms of my hands, the cold heavy quality of his flesh through his pyjamas. Then he woke—but suddenly. He simultaneously put his arms up round my neck, in a frightened child's gesture, and was sitting up, his legs already swinging over the edge of the bed. He looked terrified. I said: 'For goodness sake, it's only Jane Bond on the telephone.' He stared—it took a long half minute for the words to get through to him, and I repeated them. Then he stumbled to the telephone. He said: 'Yeah. Yeah, no'—very abrupt. I went past him down the stairs. The thing had upset me. I could feel the deadly coldness on my palms. And then his arms around my neck speaking a language different from anything he was when awake. I called up to him to come and have some coffee. Repeated it several times. He came down, very quiet, very pale, on guard. Gave him coffee. I said: 'You sleep very heavily.' He said: 'What? Yeah.' Then he made a half-remark about the coffee, tailed off. He was not hearing what I said. His eyes were at the same time concentrated and wary and absent. I don't think he saw me. He sat stirring his coffee. Then he began talking, and I swear it was at random, he might have chosen any other subject. He was talking about how to bring up a small girl. He was very intelligent about it all, and very academic. He talked and talked—I said something, but he did not know that I had. He talked—I found myself absent-minded, then with my attention half on what he said, realised I was listening for the word *I* in what he said. I, I, I, I, I—I began to feel as if the word I was being shot at me like bullets from a machine gun. For a moment I fancied that his mouth, moving fast and mobile, was a gun of some kind. I broke in, he didn't hear, I broke in again, saying: 'You're very well-educated about children, have you been married?' He started, his mouth was slightly open, he stared. Then the loud, abrupt young laugh: 'Married? Who are you kidding?' It offended me, it was so clearly a warning to me. This man, warning me, a woman, about marriage, was quite a different person from the man compulsively talking, compulsively spinning out intelligent words (but punctuated every second by the word *I*) about how to bring up a small girl to be 'a real woman,' and quite different again from the man who had undressed me with his eyes on the first day. I felt my stomach clench, and for the first time I understood that my anxiety state was due to Saul Green. I pushed aside my empty coffee cup, and said it was time for my bath. I'd forgotten how he reacts, as if he's been hit or kicked, when one says one has something else to do. For he again scrambled off his chair as if he had been ordered. This time I said: 'Saul, for the Lord's sake, relax.' An instinctive movement towards flight, which he controlled. The moment of his self-control was a visible physical struggle with himself in which all his muscles were involved. Then he gave me a charming shrewd smile and said: 'You're right, I guess I'm not the most relaxed person in the world.' I was still in my dressing-gown, and had to pass him to the bathroom. As I went past he instinctively assumed the 'mensch-pose,' thumbs hooked in his belt, fingers arrowing down, the consciously sardonic stare of the rake. I said: 'I'm sorry I'm not dressed like Marlene Dietrich on her way to the back room.' The offended loud young laugh. I gave it up and went to have a bath. Lay in the bath, clenched up with every sort of apprehension, but watching the symptoms of an 'anxiety state' with detachment. It was as if a stranger, afflicted with symptoms I had never experienced, had taken possession of my body. Then I tidied the place up and sat on the floor in my room, and tried 'the game.' I failed. It then occurred to me I was going to fall in love with Saul Green. I remember how I first ridiculed the idea, then examined it, then accepted it: more than accepted it—fought for it, as for something that was my due. Saul was in all day upstairs. Jane Bond telephoned twice, once when I was in the kitchen and could hear. He was telling her, in his careful detailed way, that he couldn't go to dinner at her place because ... then a long story about a trip to Richmond. I went to supper with Molly. We neither of us mentioned Saul in relation to me, from which I understood that I was already in love with Saul, and that the man-woman loyalty, stronger than the loyalty of friendship, had already imposed itself. Molly went out of her way to tell me about Saul's conquests in London, and there was now no doubt she was warning me, but there was also possessiveness in it. As for me, with every woman she mentioned he had impressed, a calm, secretly triumphant determination grew, and this feeling was related to the rake's pose, thumbs in his belt, and the cool sardonic stare, not at all to the man who had 'named' me. When I got back, he was on the stairs, could have been deliberate. Invited him to coffee. He made a wistful remark about my being lucky, with friends and a settled life, referring to my having had supper with Molly. I said we hadn't invited him because he said he had an engagement. He said quickly: 'How do you know?' 'Because I heard you tell Jane so on the telephone.' The defensive startled stare—couldn't have said more clearly, What's it to do with you? I was angry and said: 'If you want to have private

557

telephone conversations all you have to do is lift the telephone into your bedroom and shut the door.' 'I'll do that,' he said, grim. Again the jarring and unpleasantness, the moment I really do not know how to cope with. I began asking questions about his life in America, and persisted through the barrier of evasions. At one point I said: 'Do you realise that you never answer a question directly—what's the matter?' He replied, after a pause, that he was not yet used to Europe, in the States no one ever asked if someone had been a communist.

I said it was a pity to come all the way to Europe and use the defences of America. He said I was right, but that it was hard for him to adjust, and we began talking about politics. He's the familiar mixture of bitterness, sadness, and a determination to keep some sort of balance that we all are. I went to bed deciding that to fall in love with this man would be stupid. I was lying in bed examining the phrase 'in love' as if it were the name of a disease I could choose not to have.

He has a way of being about at the time I am making coffee or tea, he goes up the stairs, very stiff, with a stiff nod. At such times he exudes loneliness, isolation, I can feel the loneliness, like a coldness around him. I formally ask him to join me, he formally accepts. This evening, sitting opposite me, he said: 'I have a friend back home. Just before I left to come to Europe he said to me that he was tired of affairs, of getting laid. It gets very dry and meaningless.' I laughed and said: 'Since your friend is so well-read, he must know this is a common condition, after too many affairs.' He said, quickly: 'How do you know he is well-read?' The familiar jarring moment: first, because it was so obvious he was talking about himself, and at first I thought he was being ironical. Then, because he jerked into himself, all suspicion and caution, as over the incident with the telephone. But worst of all because he didn't say: 'How did you know I was well-read?' but '*he* was well-read,' and yet it was clearly himself. He even, after the quick warning stare at me, looked away as if staring at someone else, at *him*. By now I recognise these moments not by the pattern of words, or even looks, but by the sudden tightening of my stomach into apprehension. First I feel the sick anxiety, the tension, then I quickly re-hear something we've said, or think over an incident and I realise there's been the jar, the shock, like a crack in a substance through which something else pours through. The something else is terrifying, hostile to me.

I said nothing after the exchange about the well-read friend. I was thinking that the contrast between his cool analytical intelligence and the moments of gaucherie (I used the word gaucherie to conceal from myself what was frightening) are incredible. Literally, so that for the space of a breath I am silent. Always, after such moments, when I am afraid, there is compassion, and I think of when he put his arms up to me, the lonely child, in his sleep.

Later he came back to the 'friend.' Just as if he had not mentioned him before. I had the feeling he had forgotten talking about him, only half an hour before. I said: 'This friend of yours—' (and again he looked into the centre of the room, away from us both, at the friend) '—does he intend to give up *getting laid,* or is it just another little impulse toward self-experiment?'

I had heard the emphasis I had put on the words getting laid, and realised why I was sounding irritable. I said: 'Whenever you talk about sex or love you say: he got laid, I got laid or they got laid (male).' He gave his abrupt laugh, but not comprehending, so I said: 'Always in the passive.' He said, quick: 'What do you mean?'

'It gives me the most extraordinary uneasy feeling, listening to you—surely *I* get laid, *she* gets laid, they (female) get laid, but surely you, as a man, don't get laid, you lay.'

He said slowly, 'Lady, you sure know how to make me feel a hick.' But it was the parody of a crude American saying: You sure know how to make me feel a hick.

His eyes gleamed with hostility. And I was full of hostility. Something I've been feeling for days boiled up. I said: 'The other day you were talking about how you fought, with your American friends, about the way language degraded sex— you described yourself as the original puritan, Saul Galahad to the defence, but you talk about getting laid, you never say a woman, you say a broad, a lay, a baby, a doll, a bird, you

559

talk about butts and boobs, every time you mention a woman I see her either as a sort of window-dresser's dummy or as a heap of dismembered parts, breasts, or legs or buttocks.'

I was angry, of course, but felt ridiculous, which made me angrier, and I said: 'I suppose that's what you'd call being a square, but I'm damned if I see how a man can have a healthy attitude to sex if he can't talk about anything but butts and babies being stacked or packed and so on and so on. No wonder the bloody Americans are all in trouble about their bloody sex lives.'

After a while he said, very dry: 'It's the first time in my life I've been accused of being anti-feminist. It'd interest you to know that I'm the only American male I know who doesn't accuse American women of all the sexual sins in the calendar. Do you imagine I don't know that men blame women for their inadequacies?'

Well, and of course that softened me, stopped my anger. We talked about politics. For on this subject we don't disagree. It's like being back in the Party, but when a communist meant holding high standards, fighting for something. He was kicked out of the Party for being 'prematurely anti-Stalinist.' Then he was black-listed in Hollywood for being a red. It's one of the classic, already archetypal stories of our time, but the difference between him and the others is that he isn't bitter or soured.

I was able for the first time to joke with him, so that his laugh wasn't defensive. He wears his new blue jeans, new blue sweater, sneakers. I told him he should be ashamed to wear the uniform of American non-conformism; he said he wasn't adult enough yet to join the tiny minority of human beings who didn't need a uniform.

I am hopelessly in love with this man.

I wrote the last sentence three days ago, but I didn't realise it was three days until I worked it out. I'm in love and so time has gone. Two nights ago we talked late, while the tensions built up. I wanted to laugh, because it's always funny, two people manoeuvring, so to speak, before sex; at the same time I felt a reluctance, precisely because I was in love; and I swear that either one of us might have broken the current, and said good night. At last he came and put his arms around me and said: 'We're both lonely people, let's be good to each other.' I noted there was a touch of sullenness as he said it, but chose not to hear it (*5). I'd forgotten what making love with a real man is like. And I'd forgotten what it was like to lie in the arms of a man one loves. I'd forgotten what it was like to be in love like this, so that a step on the stair makes one's heart beat, and the warmth of his shoulder against my palm is all the joy there is in life.

That was a week ago. I can say nothing about it except that I was happy. (*6) I am so happy, so happy. I find myself sitting in my room, watching the sunlight on the floor, and I'm in the state that I reach after hours and hours of concentration with 'the game'—a calm and delightful ecstasy, a oneness with everything, so that a flower in a vase is oneself, and the slow stretch of a muscle is the confident energy that drives the universe. (*7) And Saul is relaxed, a different person from the man who walked into my flat, tense and suspicious, and my state of apprehension is gone, the sick person who inhabited my body for (*8) a while has vanished.

I read the last paragraph as if it were written about someone else. The night after I wrote it, Saul did not come down into my room to sleep. There was no explanation, he simply did not come. He nodded, cool and stiff, and went upstairs. I lay awake and thought of how, when a woman begins making love with a new man, a creature is born in her, of emotional and sexual responses, that grows in its own laws, its own logic. That creature in me was snubbed by Saul's quietly going up to bed, so that I could see it quiver, and then fold itself up and begin to shrink. Next morning, we had coffee, and I looked across the table at him (he was extraordinary white and tense-looking) and I realised that if I said to him, Why didn't you come to my room last night, why didn't you make some kind of explanation for not coming, he would frown and go hostile.

Later that day he came into my room and made love to me. It wasn't real love-making. He had decided he would

561

make love. The creature inside me who is the woman in love was not implicated, refused to be lied to.

Last evening he said: 'I have to go and see ...' a long complicated story followed. I said: 'Of course.' But he went on with the story, and I got annoyed. I knew what it was all about, of course, but I didn't want to know and that in spite of the fact that I had written the truth in the yellow diary. Then he said, sullen and hostile: 'You are very permissive, aren't you?' He had said it yesterday, and I wrote in the yellow notebook. I said aloud, suddenly: *'No.'* A blind look came over his face. And I remembered that I knew the blind look, I'd seen it before and not wanted to. The word permissive is so alien to me, it's got nothing to do with me. He came into my bed late, and I knew he had just come from sleeping with another woman. I said: 'You've slept with another woman, haven't you?' He stiffened and said, sullen: 'No.' But I didn't say anything and he said: 'But it doesn't mean anything, does it?' What was strange was, that the man who had said No, defending his freedom, and the man who said, pleading, It doesn't mean anything, were two men. I couldn't connect them. I was silent, in the grip of apprehension again, and then a third man said, brotherly and affectionate: 'Go to sleep now.'

I went to sleep, in obedience to this third friendly man, conscious of two other Annas, separate from the obedient child—Anna, the snubbed woman in love, cold and miserable in some corner of myself, and a curious detached sardonic Anna, looking on and saying: 'Well, well!'

I slept lightly, with terrible dreams. The dream that kept recurring was myself with the old dwarfed malicious man. In my dream I even nodded a sort of recognition—so there you are, I knew you'd turn up some time. He had a great protruding penis sticking out through his clothes, it menaced me, was dangerous, because I knew the old man hated me and wanted to hurt me. I woke myself up, tried to calm myself. Saul lay against me, a weight of inert dense cold flesh. He was lying on his back, but even asleep his pose was defensive. In the dim early morning light I could see his face, defensive. I was aware of a sharp sour smell. I thought: It can't be

Saul, he is too fastidious; then I could smell the sourness coming off the flesh of his neck, and I knew it was the smell of fear. He was afraid. In his sleep he was locked in fear, and he began to whimper, like a child afraid. I knew he was ill (though during the week of being happy I had refused to know it) and I felt full of love and compassion and I began rubbing his shoulders and neck into warmth. Towards morning he gets very cold, the cold was coming out of him, with the smell of his being afraid. When he was warmed, I put myself back to sleep, and instantly I was the old man, the old man had become me, but I was also the old woman, so that I was sexless. I was also spiteful and destructive. When I woke, Saul was again cold in my arms, a weight of cold. I had to warm myself out of the terror of the dream before I could warm him. I was saying to myself: I've been the malicious old man, and the spiteful old woman, or both together, so now what next? Meanwhile the light had come into the room, a greyish light, and I could see Saul. His flesh which, had he been well, would have been the warm dun-coloured flesh of his type of man—the broad strong fair man, strongly fleshed, was yellowish, loose on the big bones of his face. Suddenly he woke, afraid, out of a dream, and sat up, defensive, looking for enemies. Then he saw me and smiled: I could see how his smile would be on the broad, brown face of Saul Green, healthy. But his smile was yellow and terrified. He made love to me, out of fear. Fear of being alone. It was not the counterfeit love the woman-in-love, that instinctive creature, repudiated, but it was love from fear, and the Anna who was afraid responded; we were two frightened creatures, loving through terror. And my brain was on guard, fearful.

For a week he didn't come near me, again, no explanations, nothing, he was a stranger who came in, nodded, went upstairs. For a week I watched the female creature shrink, then grow angry, grow jealous. It was a terrible, spiteful jealousy I didn't recognise in myself. I went upstairs to Saul and said: 'What sort of man is It who makes love to a woman with every appearance of enjoying the process for days on end, and then switches off without so much as a

563

polite lie?' The loud aggressive laugh. Then he said: 'What sort of a man, you ask? You may very well ask.' I said: 'I suppose you are writing that great American novel, young hero in search of an identity.' 'Right,' he said. 'But I'm not prepared to take that tone of voice from inhabitants of the old world who for some reason I don't understand never have a moment's doubt about their identity.' He was hard, laughing, hostile; I was also hard, and laughing. I said, enjoying the cold moment of pure hostility: 'Well good luck, but don't use me in your experiments.' And went downstairs. A few minutes later he came down, no longer a kind of spiritual tomahawk, but kindly and responsible. He said: 'Anna, you are looking for a man in your life, and you're right, you deserve one, but.' 'But?' 'You're looking for happiness. It's a word that never meant anything to me until I watched you manufacturing it like molasses out of this situation. God knows how anyone, even a woman, could make happiness out of this set-up, but.' 'But?' 'This is me, Saul Green, and I'm not happy, and I never have been.' 'So I'm making use of you.' 'That's right.' 'Fair exchange, for your making use of me.' His face changed, he looked startled. 'Forgive me for mentioning it,' I said, 'but surely it must have crossed your mind that you are?'

He laughed, a real laugh, not the hostile laugh.

Then we went to drink coffee, and we talked about politics or rather about America. His America is cold and cruel. He talked of Hollywood, of the writers who were 'red,' who fell into a conformity of being 'red' under pressure from McCarthy, of the writers who became respectable and fell into a conformity of anti-communism. Of the men who informed on their friends to the inquisatorial committees. (*9) He speaks of this with a sort of detached amused anger. Told a story about his boss, who had called him into the office to ask if he was a member of the Communist Party. Saul wasn't a member then, had in fact been expelled from the Party some time before, but he refused to answer. The boss, full of regrets, then said that Saul must resign. Saul resigned. Met this man at a party a few weeks later, and he began to weep and accuse himself. 'You're my friend, Saul, I like to think of you as my friend.' This note I've heard in a dozen stories from Saul, from Nelson, from others. While he talked I felt in myself an emotion which disquiets me, the sharp angry pressure of contempt for Saul's boss, for the 'red' writers who took refuge in conforming communism, for the informers. I said to Saul: 'It's all very well, but what we are saying, our attitude, stems from an assumption that people can be expected to be courageous enough to stand up for their individual thinking.' He raised his head, sharp and challenging. Usually, when he talks, he talks blind, his eyes blank, he is talking to himself. Only when his whole personality swung into line behind his cool grey eyes did I realise how used I have got to this way of his—talking to himself, hardly conscious of me. He said: 'What do you mean?' I realised it was the first time I had thought all this so clearly, having him here makes me think clearly, because so much of our experience is similar, and yet we're so different as people. I said: 'Look, take us, there isn't one of us who hasn't done this thing, saying one thing publicly and another privately, one thing to one's friends, another to the enemy. There isn't one of us who hasn't succumbed to the pressure, fear of being thought a traitor. I remember at least a dozen times when I thought: The reason why I'm terrified to say that, or even think that, is because I'm frightened of being thought a traitor to the Party.' He was staring at me, his eyes hard, with a sort of sneer. I know that sneer, it's 'the revolutionary sneer,' and everyone of us has used it some time, and that's why I didn't challenge it but went on: 'So what I'm saying is that precisely the kind of person in our time who by definition might have been expected to be fearless, outspoken, truthful, has turned out to be sycophantic, lying, cynical, either from fear of torture, or of prison, or fear of being thought a traitor.' He barked out, an automatic bark: 'Middle-class talk, that's what that is. Well your origins are showing at the moment, aren't they?' I was stopped short for a moment. Because nothing he had ever said to me, no tone he had ever used, could have prepared me for that remark: it was a weapon from the armoury, jeering and sneering, and it took me by surprise. I said: 'That isn't the point.' He said, in

565

the same tone: 'The fanciest bit of red-baiting I've heard in a long time.' 'But your criticisms of your old Party friends I suppose are just dispassionate comment?' He did not reply, he was frowning. I said: 'We know, from looking at America, that an entire intelligentsia can be bullied into routine anti-communist attitudes.' Suddenly he remarked: 'That's why I love this country, it couldn't happen here.' Again the feeling of jar, of shock. Because what he said was sentimental, stock from the liberal cupboard, just as the other remarks were stock from the red cupboard. I said: 'During the cold war, when the communist hue and cry was at its height, the intellectuals here were the same. Yes, I know everyone's forgotten about it, now everyone's shocked at McCarthy, but at the same time, our intellectuals were playing it all down, saying things were not as bad as they seemed. Just as their opposite numbers were doing in the States. Our liberals were mostly defending, either openly or by implication, the anti-American activity committees. A leading editor could write a hysterical letter to the gutter press saying if only he'd known that X and Y, who were old friends of his, were spies, he'd have gone straight to M.I.5 with information about them. No one thought the worse of him. And all the literary societies and organisations were engaged in the most primitive sort of anti-communism—what they said, or a great deal of it, was quite true, of course, but the point is, they were simply saying what might have been found any day in the gutter press, no attempt to really understand anything, they were in full cry, a pack of barking dogs. And so I know quite well that if the heat had been turned on even a little harder, we'd have had our intellectuals packing anti-British activity committees, and meanwhile, we, the reds, were lying black is white.'

'Well?'

'Well, judging from what we've seen happening in the last thirty years, in the democracies, let alone the dictatorships, the number of people in a society really prepared to stand against a current, really ready to fight for the truth at all costs is so small that . . .'

He suddenly said: 'Excuse me,' and walked out with his stiff blind walk.

566

I sat in the kitchen and thought over what I'd just said. I and all the people I knew well, some of them fine people, had been sunk inside the communist conformity and lied to themselves or to others. And the 'liberal' or 'free' intellectuals could be and had been swung into witch-hunts of one kind or another very easily. Very few people really care about freedom, about liberty, about the truth, very few. Very few people have guts, the kind of guts on which a real democracy has to depend. Without people with that sort of guts a free society dies or cannot be born.

I sat there, discouraged and depressed. Because in all of us brought up in a Western democracy there is this built-in belief that freedom and liberty will strengthen, will survive pressures, and the belief seems to survive any evidence against it. This belief is probably in itself a danger. Sitting there I had a vision of the world with nations, systems, economic blocks, hardening and consolidating; a world where it would become increasingly ludicrous even to talk about freedom, or the individual conscience. I know that this sort of vision has been written about, it's something one has read, but for a moment it wasn't words, ideas, but something I felt, in the substance of my flesh and nerves, as true.

Saul came back down the stairs, dressed. He was now what I call 'himself,' and he said simply, with a kind of whimsical humour: 'I'm sorry I walked out, but I couldn't take what you were saying.'

I said: 'Every line of thought I pursue these days turns out to be bleak and depressing. Perhaps I can't take it either.'

He came over to me and put his arms around me. He said: 'We are comforting each other. What for, I wonder?' Then, with his arms around me still: 'We've got to remember that people with our kind of experience are bound to be depressed and unhopeful.'

'Or perhaps it's precisely people with our kind of experience who are most likely to know the truth, because we know what we've been capable of ourselves?'

I offered him lunch, and now we talked about his childhood. A classically bad childhood, broken home, etc. After lunch he went upstairs saying he wanted to work. Almost immediately he came down, and leaned against the door frame, remarking: 'I used to be able to work for hours at a stretch, now I can't work for more than an hour without a break.'

I felt the jar again. Now, having thought it all out, it is quite clear, but then I was confused. For he was talking as if he had worked for an hour instead of perhaps five minutes. He stood there, lounging, restless. Then he said: 'I've a friend back home whose parents separated when he was a kid. Do you think it might have affected him?'

For a moment I couldn't answer, because 'the friend' was so obviously himself. But he'd been talking about his parents not ten minutes before.

I said: 'Yes, I'm sure your parents' splitting up has affected you.'

He jerked himself up, his face closed into suspicion, and he said: 'How did you know?'

(*10) I said: 'You've got a bad memory, you told me about your parents a few minutes ago.'

He stood, alert, watchful, thinking. His face was sharp with suspicious thought. Then he said in a scramble of words: 'Oh, I was thinking about my friend, that's all . . .' He turned and went upstairs.

I sat, confused, fitting things together. He had genuinely forgotten he had told me. And I remembered half a dozen occasions in the last few days—he had told me something, and then mentioned it a few minutes later again as if it were a new subject. Yesterday, for instance, he said: 'Do you remember when I first came here?' speaking as if had been here many months. And another time he said: 'That time we went to the Indian restaurant,' when we'd been there that day for lunch.

I went into the big room and shut my door. We have an understanding that when my door is shut, I'm not to be disturbed. Sometimes, with my door shut, I hear him walking up and down overhead, or coming halfway down the stairs, and it's as if a pressure is on me to open the door, and I do. But today I shut the door fast, and sat on my bed and tried to think. I was sweating lightly, and my hands were cold, and

I couldn't breathe properly. I was clenched with anxiety, and saying over and over again: This isn't my anxiety state, it isn't mine—didn't help at all. (*11) I lay on the floor on my back with a cushion under my head, relaxed my limbs and played 'the game.' Or tried to. No use, for I could hear Saul upstairs, prowling around. Every movement he made went through me. I thought I should get out of the house, see someone. Who? I knew I couldn't discuss Saul with Molly. I telephoned her nevertheless, and she asked casually: 'How's Saul?' and I said: 'Fine.' She remarked she had seen Jane Bond, who is 'in a real state over him.' I hadn't thought of Jane Bond for some days, so I talked quickly of something, and lay down on the floor again. Last night Saul had said: 'I must take a little walk or I won't be able to sleep.' He had been gone about three hours. Jane Bond lives about half an hour away walking, ten minutes by bus. Yes, he had telephoned someone before he left. That meant, he had arranged with Jane, from my home, to meet her to make love, gone over, made love, come back, got into my bed, slept. No, we didn't make love last night. Because, unconsciously, I was defending myself against the pain of knowledge. (Yet with my intelligence I don't care, it's the creature inside me who cares, who is jealous, who sulks and wants to hurt back.)

He knocked, said through the door, 'Don't want to disturb you, I'm going for a little walk.' Without knowing I was going to do this, I went to the door, opened it—he had already started off down the stairs, and asked: 'Are you going to see Jane Bond?' He stiffened, then slowly turned and faced me. 'No, I'm going for a walk.'

I didn't say anything, because I was thinking it was not possible he should lie, when I asked him directly. I should have asked: 'Did you see Jane Bond last night?' I realise now I didn't because I was afraid he would say no.

I made some bright and unimportant remark, and turned away, shutting the door. I couldn't think or even move. I was ill. I kept saying to myself: He's got to go, he's got to leave here. But I knew I couldn't ask him to go, so I kept saying to myself: Then you must try to detach yourself.

When he came back, I knew I'd been waiting for his step

for hours. It was nearly dark by then. He called a loud over-friendly greeting to me and went straight into the bathroom. (*12) I sat there thinking: It's simply not possible that this man should come straight back from Jane Bond and then go and wash off sex, knowing that I must know what he was doing. It's not possible. And yet I knew it was possible. I sat screwing myself up to say: Saul have you been sleeping with Jane Bond?

When he came in I said it. He gave his loud, crude laugh, and said: 'No, I haven't.' Then he looked at me closely and came over and put his arms around me. He did so simply and warmly that I immediately succumbed. He said, very friendly: 'Now Anna, you're much too sensitive about everything. Take things easy.' He caressed me a little and then said: 'I think you ought to try and understand something—we're very different people. And another thing, the way you were living here before I came wasn't good for you. It's all right, I'm here.' With this he laid me down on the bed and began soothing me, as if I were ill. And in fact I was. My mind was churning and my stomach churned. I couldn't think, because the man who was being so gentle was the same man who made me ill. Later he said: 'And now make me supper, it'll be good for you. God help you, but you're a real domestic woman, you ought to be married to a nice settled husband somewhere.' Then, sullen, (*13) 'God help me, I always seem to pick them.' I made him supper.

This morning, early, the telephone rang. I answered it and it was Jane Bond. I woke Saul, told him, left the room and went to the bathroom, where I made a lot of noise, running water, etc. When I came back he was back in bed, curled up, half asleep. I was expecting him to tell me what Jane had said or wanted, but he didn't mention the telephone call. I was angry again. Yet the whole of last night was warm and affectionate, he had turned to me like a lover in his sleep, kissing and touching me, and even using my name, so it was meant for me. I didn't know what to feel. After breakfast he said he had to go out. He made a long, detailed explanation of having to see some man in the film industry. I knew, because of the wooden obstinate look on his face, and because of the unnecessary complication of the explanations, that he was going to see Jane Bond, he had made an arrangement to see her when she telephoned him. As soon as he left I went up to his room. Everything extremely neat and tidy. Then I began to look among his papers. I remember thinking, without any shock at myself, but as if it were my right, because he lied, that this was the first time in my life I had read another person's letters or private papers. I was angry and sick but very methodical. I found a stack of letters rubber-banded together in one corner, from a girl in America. They had been lovers. She complained he hadn't written. Then another stack of letters from a girl in Paris—again, complaints that he hadn't written. I put the letters back, not carefully, but anyhow, and looked for something else. Then I found stacks of diaries. (*14) I remember thinking it was odd that his diaries ran chronologically, not all split up like mine are. I leafed through some of the earlier ones, not reading them, but getting an impression, an unending list of new places, different jobs, an endless list of girls' names. And as a thread through the diversity of place-names, women's names, details of loneliness, detachment, isolation. I sat there on his bed, trying to marry the two images, the man I knew, and the man pictured here, who is totally self-pitying, cold, calculating, emotionless. Then I remembered that when I read my notebooks I didn't recognise myself. Something strange happens when one writes about oneself. That is, one's self direct, not one's self projected. The result is cold, pitiless, judging. Or if not judging, then there's no life in it—yes, that's it, it's lifeless. I realise, in writing this, I'm back at the point in the black notebook where I wrote about Willi. If Saul said, about his diaries, or, summing his younger self up from his later self: I was a swine, the way I treated women. Or: I'm right to treat women the way I do. Or: I'm simply writing a record of what happened, I'm not making moral judgements about myself—well, whatever he said, it would be irrelevant. Because what is left out of his diaries is vitality, life, charm. 'Willi allowed his spectacles to glitter across the room and said ...' 'Saul, standing four-square and solid, grinning slightly—grinning derisively at his own seducer's pose, drawled: Come'n baby, let's fuck, I like your style.' I went on reading entries, first appalled by the cold ruthlessness of them; then translating them, from knowing Saul, into life. So I found myself continually shifting mood, from anger, a woman's anger, into the delight one feels at whatever is alive, the delight of recognition.

Then the delight vanished as I came across an entry which frightened me, because I had already written it, out of some other kind of knowledge, in my yellow notebook. It frightens me that when I'm writing I seem to have some awful second sight, or something like it, an intuition of some kind; a kind of intelligence is at work that is much too painful to use in ordinary life; one couldn't live at all if one used it for living. Three entries: 'Must get out of Detroit, I've got from it all I need. Mavis making trouble. I was crazy for her a week ago, now nothing. Strange.' Then: 'Mavis came to my apartment last night. I had Joan with me. Had to go out into the hall and send Mavis away.' Then: 'Got a letter from Jake in Detroit. Mavis cut her wrists with a razor. They got her to hospital in time. Pity, a nice girl.' There were no more references to Mavis. I was angry, with the cold, vindictive anger of the sex war; so angry I simply switched off my imagination. I left the mass of diaries. They would have taken weeks to read and I wasn't interested. I was curious now to know what he had written about me. I found the date he had come to this flat. 'Saw Anna Wulf. If I'm going to stick around London, it'll do. Mary offered me a room, but I saw trouble there. She's a good lay, but that's all. Anna doesn't attract me. A good thing in the circumstances. Mary made a scene. Jane at the party. We danced, practically fucked on the dance floor. Small, slight, boyish—took her home. Fucked all night—oh boy!' 'Today, talking to Anna, can't remember anything I said, I don't think she noticed anything.' No entries for some days. Then: 'Funny thing, I like Anna better than anyone, but I don't enjoy sleeping with her. Perhaps time to move on? Jane making trouble. Well screw these dames, *literally!*' 'Anna making trouble about Jane. Well too bad for her.' 'Broke with Jane. Pity, she's the best lay I've had in this bloody country. Marguerite in the coffee bar.' 'Jane telephoned. Making trouble about Anna. Don't want trouble with Anna. Date with Marguerite.'

That was today, so when he went off it was to Marguerite and not to Jane. I am shocked at myself because I am not shocked at reading someone's private papers. On the contrary, I'm full of a triumphant ugly joy because I've caught him out.

(*15) The entry, I don't enjoy sleeping with Anna, cut me so deep I couldn't breathe for a few moments. Worse, I didn't understand it. Worse, I lost faith, for a few minutes, in the judgement of the female creature who responds, or does not, according to whether Saul is making love out of conviction or not. She can't be lied to. For a moment I imagined she had been deluding herself. I was ashamed that I cared more for his not wanting to sleep with me, since at the best I would be 'a good lay' than his liking me. I put away the diaries, but carelessly, out of a kind of contempt, as I had put away the letters, and came downstairs to write this. But I'm too confused to write sensibly.

I've just been up to have another look at the diary—he wrote 'I don't like sleeping with her' in the week that he didn't come downstairs. Since then, he's been making love as a man does when he's attracted to a woman. I don't understand it, I don't understand anything.

Yesterday I forced myself to challenge him: 'Are you ill, and if so in what way?' He said, and I'd almost expected this: 'How do you know?' I even laughed. He said, carefully: 'I think if you're in trouble you should put it under your belt and not afflict other people with it.' He said this seriously, the responsible man. I said: 'But in fact you're doing just that. What's wrong?' I feel as if I were caught in a sort of psychological fog. He said seriously: 'I was hoping that I didn't put it on you.' 'I'm not complaining,' I said. 'But I think that it's no good locking things up, you should get them into the open.'

He said, suddenly abrasive and hostile: 'You sound like a bloody psycho-analyst.'

I was thinking how, in any conversation, he can be five or six different people; I even waited for the responsible person to come back. He did, and said: 'I'm not in any too good a shape, that's true. I'm sorry if it's shown. I'll try to do better.' I said: 'It's not a question of doing better.'

He turned the conversation determinedly; there was a hunted, wounded look on his face; he was a man defending himself.

I rang up Dr Paynter, and I said I wanted to know what was wrong with someone who had no sense of time, and seemed to be several different people. He replied: 'I don't diagnose over telephones.' I said: 'Oh come off it.' He said: 'My dear Anna, I think you'd better make an appointment.' 'It's not for me,' I said. 'It's a friend,' but there was a silence. Then he said: 'Please don't be alarmed, you'd be surprised how many charming people are walking our streets, the mere ghosts of themselves. Do make an appointment.' 'What's the cause of it?' 'Well, I'd say, hazarding a guess, and not saying a word too much, it's all due to the times we live in.' 'Thanks,' I said. 'And no appointment?' 'No.' 'That's very bad, Anna, that's spiritual pride, if you're several different people whose bootstraps are you going to pull yourself up on?' 'I'll convey your message to the right quarter,' I said.

I went to Saul and said: 'I've telephoned my doctor and he thinks I'm ill. I told him I had a *friend*—you see?' Saul looked sharp and hunted, but he grinned. 'He says I should make an appointment, but that I shouldn't be in any way alarmed at being several different people at once with no sense of time.'

'Is that how I strike you?'

'Well, yes.'

'Thanks. I expect he's right, at that.'

He said to me today, 'Why should I waste money on a psychiatrist when I get treatment from you, free?' It was said savagely, with triumph. I said to him it was unfair to use me in this role. He said, with the same triumphant hate: 'English woman! Fair! Everyone makes use of each other. You make use of me to create a Hollywood dream of happiness, and in return I'm going to use your experience of the witch-doctors.' A moment after we were making love. When we quarrel, we hate each other, then sex comes out of

574

the hate. It's a hard violent sex, like nothing I've known before, nothing (*16) to do with the creature who is the woman-in-love. She disowns it completely.

Today he criticised me in bed for a movement, and I realised he was comparing me with someone. I remarked that there were different schools in love-making, and we came from two different schools. We were hating each other, but all this was quite good-humoured. For he began thinking about it, and then he roared with laughter. 'Love,' he said, sentimental as a schoolboy, 'is international.' 'Screwing,' I said, 'is a matter of national styles. No Englishman would make love like you. I am referring of course to the ones that do make love.' He began making up a pop-song—'I'll like your national style if you'll like mine.'

The walls of this flat close in on us. Day after day we're alone here. I'm conscious that we are both mad. He says, with a yell of laughter: 'Yeah, I'm crazy, it's taken me all my short life to recognise it, and now what? Suppose I prefer being crazy, what then?'

Meanwhile my anxiety is permanent, I've forgotten what it is like to wake up normally; yet I watch this state I'm in, and even think: Well, I'll never suffer from my own anxiety state, so I might just as well experience someone else's while I get the chance.

Sometimes I try to play 'the game.' Sometimes I write in this and the yellow notebook. Or I watch the light change on the floor, so that a grain of dirt or a knot in the wood magnify and symbolise themselves. Upstairs Saul walks up and down, up and down, or there are long periods of silence. Both silence and the sound of feet reverberate along my nerves. When he leaves the flat 'to go for a little walk' my nerves seem to stretch out and follow him, as if tied to him.

Today he came in and I knew by instinct he had been sleeping with someone. I challenged him, not out of being hurt, but because we are two antagonists, and he said: 'No, what makes you think that?' Then his face became greedy, cunning, furtive, and he said: 'I'll produce an alibi if you like.' I laughed, although I was angry, and the fact that I laughed restored me. I am mad, obsessed with a cold jealousy

575

which I have never experienced before. I am the sort of woman who reads private letters and diaries; yet when I laugh, I am cured. He didn't like my laughing, for he said: 'Prisoners learn to talk a certain language.' And I said: 'If I've never been a jailor before, and if I've now become one, perhaps it is because you need one.'

His face cleared, he sat down on my bed, and he said, with the simplicity he can switch into from one moment to the next: 'The trouble is, when we took each other on, you took fidelity for granted, and I didn't. I've never been faithful to anyone. It didn't arise.'

'Liar,' I said. 'You mean, when a woman began to care about you, or found you out, you simply moved on to the next.'

He gave his frank young laugh, instead of the hostile young laugh and said: 'And perhaps there's something in that, too.'

I was on the point of saying, Then move on. I was wondering why I didn't, what sort of personal logic I was following, through him. During the flash of a second, when I almost said: Then move on, he gave me a quick, frightened glance, and said: 'You should have told me that it mattered to you.'

I said: 'Then I'm telling you now that it matters to me.'

'O.K.,' he said, carefully, after a pause. His face had the furtive cunning look. I knew perfectly well what he was thinking.

Today he went out for a couple of hours, after a telephone call, and I went straight upstairs to read the recent entries in his diary. 'Anna's jealousy is driving me mad. Saw Marguerite. Went home with her. A nice kid. Marguerite cold to me. Met Dorothy at her house. I'll sneak out when Anna goes to visit Janet next week. When the cat's away!'

I read this with cold triumph.

And yet, in spite of this, there are hours of affectionate friendliness, while we talk and talk. And we make love. We sleep together every night, and it's a marvellous deep sleep. Then the friendliness switches to hate in the middle of a sentence. Sometimes the flat is an oasis of loving affection, then suddenly it's a battleground, even the walls vibrate with hate, we circle around each other like two animals, the things we say to each other are so terrible that thinking about them afterwards I am shocked. And yet we are quite capable of saying these things, listening to what we've said, and then bursting out into laughter so that we laugh and roll on the floor.

I went down to see Janet. All the way I was miserable because I knew Saul was making love to Dorothy, whoever she was. I was unable to shake this off when with Janet. She seems happy—remote from me, a little school-girl, absorbed in her friends. Coming back in the train, I thought again how strange it is—for twelve years, every minute of every day has been organised around Janet, my time-table has been her needs. And yet she goes to school, and that's that. I instantly revert to an Anna who never gave birth to Janet. I remember Molly saying the same thing: Tommy went for a holiday with some friends when he was sixteen, and she spent days walking around the house astonished at herself. 'I feel as if I'd never had a child at all,' she kept saying.

Getting near my flat, the tension in my stomach increased. By the time I reached the house I was sick. I went straight to the bathroom to be sick. I've never in my life been sick from nervous tension. Then I called upstairs. Saul was in. He came down, cheerful. Hi! How was it, etc. As I looked at him, his face changed into furtive caution, with triumph behind it, and I could see myself, cold and malicious. He said: 'Why are you looking at me like that?' Then: 'What are you trying to find out?'

I went into my big room. The—what are you trying to find out, was a new note in the exchange, a step downwards into a new depth of spite. Pure waves of hatred had come from him as he said it. I sat on my bed and tried to think. I realised the hatred had made me physically frightened. What do I know about mental sickness? Nothing at all. Yet an instinct told me there was no need to be frightened.

He came after me into the room and sat on the bottom of the bed, humming a jazz tune and watching me. He said: 'I've bought you some jazz records. Jazz'll relax you.'

I said: 'Good.'

He said: 'You're such a bloody Englishwoman, aren't you?' This was sullen and disliking.

I said: 'If you don't like me, then go.'

He gave me a quick startled look and walked out. I waited for him to come back, knowing how he would be. He was calm, quiet, brotherly, affectionate. He put a record on my record-player. I examined the records, early Armstrong and Bessie Smith. We sat quiet and listened and he watched me.

Then he said: 'Well?'

I said: 'All that music is good-humoured and warm and accepting.'

'Well?'

'It's got nothing to do with us, we aren't like that.'

'Lady, my character was formed by Armstrong, Bechet and Bessie Smith.'

'Then something has happened to it since.'

'What has happened to it is what has happened to America.' Then he said, sullen: 'I suppose you are going to turn out to have a natural talent for jazz too, it just needed that.'

'Why do you have to be so competitive about everything?'

'Because I'm an American. It's a competitive country.'

I saw that the quiet brother had gone, the hatred was back. I said: 'I think it would be better if we separated for tonight, sometimes you're too much for me.'

He was startled. Then his face controlled itself—when this happens, the defensive, ill face literally seems to take itself in hand. He said quietly, with a friendly laugh: 'Don't blame you. I'm too much for myself.'

He went out. A few minutes later, when I was in bed, he came down, walked up to the bed and said, smiling: 'Move over.'

I said, 'I don't want to fight.'

He said: 'We can't help ourselves.'

'Don't you think it's odd, the issue we choose to fight over? I don't give a damn who you sleep with, and you're not a man who punishes women sexually. So obviously we are fighting about something else. What?'

'An interesting experience, being crazy.'

578

'Quite so, an interesting experience.'

'Why say it like that?'

'In a year's time, we'll both look back and say: So that's what we were like then, what a fascinating experience.'

'What's wrong with that?'

'Megalomaniacs, that's what our lot are. You say I am what I am because the United States is such and such politically. I am the United States. And I say, I am the position of women in our time.'

'We're probably both right.'

We went to sleep, friendly. But sleep changed us both. When I woke he was lying on his side, watching me with a hard smile. He said: 'What were you dreaming about?' I said, 'Nothing,' and then I remembered. I had had the terrible dream, but the malicious irresponsible principle was embodied in Saul. Throughout a long nightmare it had taunted me, laughing. It had held me tight by the arms, so I couldn't move, and said: 'I'm going to hurt you. I enjoy it.'

The memory was so bad I got out of bed and away from him, and went to the kitchen to make coffee. He came in, dressed, about an hour later, his face like a fist. 'I'm going out,' he said. He hung around a little, waiting for me to say something, then slowly went down the stairs, looking back for me to stop him. I lay on my back on the floor and played early Armstrong, and envied the easy, blithe, good-humouredly-mocking world that music came from. He came in, four or five hours later, and his face was vivid with vindictive triumph. He said: 'Why don't you say something?' I said: 'There's nothing to say.' 'Why don't you fight back?'

'Do you realise how often you ask why I don't fight back? If you want to be punished for something find somebody else.'

And then the extraordinary change, when I say something and he thinks it over. He said, interested: 'Do I need to be punished? Hmmmm, interesting.' He sat on the foot of my bed, plucking at his chin, frowning. He remarked: 'I don't think I like myself very much at the moment. And I don't like you either.'

'And I don't like you and I don't like me. But we're neither of us really like this at all, so why bother disliking us?'

His face changed again. He said, cunning: 'I suppose you think you know what I've been doing.'

I said nothing, and he got up, and walked fast round the room, giving me quick fierce glances all the time: 'You'll never know, will you, there's no way you'll ever know.' My saying nothing was not a determination not to quarrel, or to keep self-control, but an equally cold weapon in the battle. After a long enough silence: 'I know what you've been doing, you've been screwing Dorothy.'

He said quickly: 'How do you know?' And then, just as if he hadn't said it: 'Ask me no questions and I'll tell you no lies.'

'I'm not asking questions, I read your diary.'

He stopped in his striding walk around the room, and stood looking down at me. His face, which I watched with a cold interest, showed fear, then rage, then furtive triumph. He said: 'I wasn't screwing Dorothy.'

'Then it was someone else.'

He began shouting, flapping his hands in the air, his jaw grinding over the words: 'You spy on me, you're the most jealous woman I've ever known. I haven't touched a woman since I've been here and for a red-blooded American boy like me, that's something.'

I said, malicious: 'I'm glad you're red-blooded.'

He shouted: 'I'm a mensch. I'm not a woman's pet, to be locked up.' He went on shouting, and I recognised the feeling I'd had the day before, of descending another step into will-lessness. I, I, I, I, I, he shouted, but everything disconnected, a vague, spattering boastfulness, and I felt as if I were being spattered by machine-gun bullets. It went on and on, I, I, I, I, I, and I stopped listening, and then I realised he had become silent, and was looking at me with anxiety. 'What's wrong with you?' he said. He came over, knelt beside me, turned my face to his, and said: 'For Christ sake's, you must understand sex isn't important to me, it just isn't important.'

580

I said: 'You mean sex is important but who you have it with isn't.'

He carried me to the bed, gentle and compassionate. He said, self-disgusted: 'I'm very good at picking up the pieces when I've knocked a woman flat.'

'Why do you have to knock a woman flat?'

'I don't know. Until you made me conscious of it, I didn't know it.'

'I wish you'd hire yourself a witch-doctor. I keep saying it, I keep saying it, you'll crack us both up.'

I began to cry, I felt as I had in the dream the night before, held fast by the arms while he laughed and hurt me. Meanwhile he was kind and gentle. Then I knew suddenly that the whole thing, this cycle of bullying and tenderness, was for this moment when he could comfort me. I got off the bed, furious at being patronised and at myself for allowing it, and got a cigarette.

He said, sullen: 'I may knock you down, but you don't stay down long.'

'Lucky for you, you can have the pleasure of doing it again and again.'

He said, thoughtful, positively abstracted, looking at himself from a distance: 'But tell me, why?'

I shouted at him: 'Like all Americans you've got mother-trouble. You've fixed on me for your mother. You have to outwit me all the time, it's important that I should be outwitted. It's important to lie and be believed. Then, when I get hurt, your murderous feelings for me, for the mother, frighten you, so that you have to comfort and soothe me . . .' I was screaming in hysteria. 'I'm bored with the whole thing. I'm bored with nursery talk. I feel nauseated with the banality of it all . . .' I stopped and looked at him. His face was the face of a child who has been smacked. 'And now you're feeling pleasure because you've provoked me into screaming at you. Why aren't you angry? You ought to be—I'm naming you, Saul Green, and I'm naming you on such a low level that you ought to be angry. You should be ashamed, at the age of thirty-three, to be sitting there taking this kind of banal over-simplification from me.' When I stopped, I was

581

exhausted. I was inside a shell of anxious tension that I could positively smell, like a stale fog of nervous exhaustion.

'Go on,' he said.

'That's the last bit of free interpretation you're going to get from me.'

'Come here.'

I had to go. He pulled me down beside him, laughing. He made love to me. I responded, to the fierce coldness of it. It was easy to respond to the coldness, because it could not hurt me, like tenderness. Then I felt myself grow unresponsive. Because I felt this, I knew, before I thought it, that there was something new here, he was not making love to me. I said to myself, incredulously: He's making love to someone else. He switched his voice, and began talking in a deep South accent, half-laughing, aggressive: 'Well, ma'am, you certainly are a lay, yes you certainly are that, I'll tell the world.' Touched me differently, he was not touching me. He ran his hand over my hips and buttocks and said: 'A good strong woman's shape, I'll say.' I said: 'You're getting us mixed up, I'm the thin one.'

Shock. Literally, I saw him come out of the personality he had been. He rolled over on his back, his hand over his eyes, gasping a little. He was very white. Then he said, not in the Southern accent, but in his own, but the rake's voice, as he had said: I'm a full-blooded American boy, 'Baby, you should take me easy, like good whisky.'

'Then that defines you,' I said.

Shock again. He fought to come out of that personality, gasped, made himself breathe slowly, then said normally: 'What's wrong with me?'

'You mean, what's wrong with us. We're both mad. We're inside a cocoon of madness.'

'You!' This was sullen. 'You're the sanest bloody woman I've ever known.'

'Not at the moment.'

We lay a long time, silent. He was gently stroking my arm. The sound of lorries along the street below was loud. With the gentle caress on my arm, I could feel the tension leave me. All the madness and the hate had gone. And then another of the long, slowly darkening afternoons, cut off from the world, and the long, dark night. The flat is like a ship floating on a dark sea, it seems to float, isolated from life, self-contained. We played the new records, and made love, and the two people, Saul and Anna, who were mad, were somewhere else, in another room somewhere.

(*17) We have had a week of being happy. The telephone has not rung. No one has been. We have been alone. But it's over now, a switch has been turned in him, and so I sit and write. I see I've written—happiness. That's enough. It's no use his saying, you manufacture happiness like molasses. During the week I had no desire to come near this table with the notebooks. There was nothing to say.

Today we got up late, and played records and made love. Then he went upstairs to his room. He came down, his face like a hatchet, and I looked at it and knew the switch had been turned. He strode around the room and said: 'I'm restless, I'm restless.' It was full of antagonism, so I said: 'Then go out.' 'If I go out, you'll accuse me of sleeping with someone.' 'Because that's what you want me to do.' 'Well I'm going.' 'Go then.' He stood looking at me, full of hate, and I felt the muscles of my stomach tighten, and the cloud of anxiety settle down like a dark fog. I watched the week of being happy slide away. I was thinking: In a month Janet will be home and this Anna will cease to exist. If I know I can switch off this helpless sufferer because it is necessary for Janet, then I can do it now. Why don't I? Because I don't want to, that's why. Something has to be played out, some pattern has to be worked through ... He felt I had withdrawn from him, and he became anxious and said: 'Why should I go if I don't want to?' 'Then don't go,' I said. 'I'll go and work,' he said, abrupt, with a frown. He went out. In a few minutes he came down and leant against the door. I had not moved. I was sitting on the floor waiting for him because I knew he would come down. It was getting dark, the big room full of shadows, the sky turning colour. I had sat watching the sky fill with colour as the dark came into the streets, and without trying I had gone into the detachment of 'the game.' I was part of the terrible city and the millions of people, and

583

I was simultaneously sitting on the floor and above the city, looking down at it. When Saul came in, he said, leaning against the door frame, accusing: 'I've never been like this before, so tied to a woman I can't even go for a walk without feeling guilty.' His tone was remote from how I felt, so I said: 'You've been here for a week, without my asking you. You wanted to. Now your mood has changed. Why should my mood change too?' He said carefully: 'A week's a long time.' I realised from how he said it, that until I used the words, a week, he had not known how many days had passed. I was curious to know how long he thought it was, but was afraid to ask. He was standing frowning, looking at me sideways, plucking at his lips as if they were a musical instrument. He said, after a pause, his face twisted into cunning: 'But it was only the day before yesterday that I saw that film.' I knew what he was doing: he wanted to pretend that the week was two days, partly to see if I was convinced it had been a week, and partly because he hated the idea he had given any woman a week of himself. It was getting dark in the room, and he was peering to see my face. The light from the sky made his grey eyes shine, his square blond head glisten. He looked like an alert threatening animal. I said: 'You saw the film a week ago.'

He said, cold: 'If you say so, I've got to believe you.' Then he leaped over at me, and grabbed my shoulders and shook me: 'I hate you for being normal, I hate you for it. You're a normal human being. What right have you to that? I suddenly understood that you remember everything, you probably remember everything I've ever said. You remember everything that's happened to you, it's intolerable.' His fingers dug into my shoulders and his face was alive with hatred.

I said: 'Yes, I do remember everything.'

But not in triumph. I was aware of myself as he saw me, a woman inexplicably in command of events, because she could look back and see a smile, a movement, gestures; hear words, explanations—a woman inside time. I disliked the solemnity, the pompousness of that upright little custodian of the truth. When he said: 'It's like being a prisoner, living with someone who knows what you said last week, or can say: three days ago you did so and so,' I could feel a prisoner with him, because I longed to be free of my own ordering, commenting memory. I felt my sense of identity fade. My stomach clenched and my back began to hurt.

He said: 'Come here'—moving away and gesturing towards the bed. I obediently followed. I could not have refused. He said, through his teeth: 'Come on, come on,' or rather, 'come'n, come'n.' I realised he had gone back some years, he was probably about twenty then. I said No, because I did not want that violent young male animal. His face flared into grinning derisive cruelty, and he said: 'You're saying no. That's right baby, you should say no more often. I like it.'

He began stroking my neck and I said No. I was nearly crying. At the sight of my tears his voice changed into a triumphant tenderness, and he kissed the tears, like a connoisseur, and said: 'Come'n baby, come'n.' The sex was cold, an act of hatred, hateful. The female creature who had been expanding, growing, purring, for a week, bolted into a corner and shuddered. And the Anna who had been capable of enjoying, with the antagonist, combative sex, was limp, not fighting. It was quick and ugly, and he said: 'Bloody Englishwomen, no good in bed.' But I was freed forever by being hurt by him in this way, and I said: 'It's my fault. I knew it wouldn't be any good. I hate it when you're cruel.'

He flung himself over on his face and lay still, thinking. He muttered: 'Someone said that to me, just recently. Who? When?'

'One of your other women said you were cruel, did she?'

'Who? I'm not cruel. I've never been cruel. Am I cruel?'

The person speaking then was the good person. I didn't know what to say, fearful of driving him away and bringing the other back. He said: 'What shall I do, Anna?'

I said: 'Why don't you go to a witch-doctor?'

And at that, as if the switch had been turned on, he gave his loud triumphing laugh, and said: 'You want to drive me into the loony bin? Why should I pay for an analyst when I've got you? You've got to pay the fee for being a healthy normal person. You're not the first person to tell me to get to a headshrinker. Well I'm not going to be dictated to by

585

anyone.' He leaped off the bed and shouted: 'I am I, Saul Green, I am what I am what I am. I ...' The shouting, automatic I, I, I speech began, but suddenly stopped, or rather halted, ready to go on: he stood, mouth open, in silence, said: 'I, I mean I . . .' the scattered last shots of gun-fire, then remarked normally: 'I'm getting out, I've got to get out of here.' He went out, jumping up the stairs in a frenzy of energy. I heard him opening drawers and crashing them shut. I thought: Perhaps he's leaving here altogether? But in a few moments he was down, and knocked on my door. I began to laugh, thinking this was a sort of humorous apology, the knock. I said, 'Come in, Mr Green,' and he came in, and said, with a polite formal dislike: 'I've decided I want to take a walk, I'm getting stale, being shut in this flat.'

I realised that while he was up in his room, what had happened in the last few minutes had changed in his mind. I said: 'All right, it's a perfect evening for a walk.'

He said, with boyish candour, enthusiasm: 'Gee, but you're right.' He went down the stairs like a prisoner escaping. I lay for a long time, hearing my heart thump, feeling my stomach churn. Then I came to write this. Yet, of the happiness, the normality, the laughter, not a word will be written. In five or ten years time, reading this, it will be a record of two people, crazy and cruel.

Last night, when I had finished writing, I took out the whisky and poured myself half a glassful. I sat taking small mouthfuls, drinking deliberately so that the liquor would slide down and hit the tension below my diaphragm, stun it into painlessness. I thought: If I stayed with Saul, I could easily become a drunkard. I thought: How conventional we are: the fact that I've lost my will, have spells of being a jealous maniac, that I'm capable of malicious driving joy in outwitting a man who is sick, none of this shocks me as much as the thought: You might become an alcoholic. Yet being an alcoholic is nothing, compared to the rest. I drank Scotch, and thought of Saul. I imagined him leaving this flat to telephone, from downstairs, one of the women. Jealousy drove through every vein in my body, like a poison, altering my breathing, making my eyes hurt. Then I imagined him stumbling through the city, ill, and I was frightened, thinking I shouldn't have let him go, although I couldn't have stopped him. I sat for a long time, worrying about his being ill. Then I thought of the other woman and the jealousy started to work again in my blood. I hated him. I remembered the cold tone of his diaries and hated him for it. I went upstairs, telling myself I should not, but knowing I would, and looked in his current diary. It was lying carelessly exposed. I wondered if he had written something for me to see, there were no entries for the last week, but under today's date: Am a prisoner. Am slowly going mad with frustration.

I watched the spiteful anger flash through me.

I thought, sanely, for a moment that during that week he had been relaxed and happy as he was capable of being, so why did I react to that entry with hurt? But I was hurt and miserable, as if the entry cancelled out the week for both of us. I went downstairs and thought of Saul with a woman. I sat watching myself thinking of Saul with a woman. I thought: He's right to hate me and to prefer other women, I'm hateful. And I began to think longingly of this other woman out there, kind and generous and strong enough to give him what he needed without asking for anything in return.

I remember Mother Sugar and how she 'taught' me about the obsessions of jealousy being part homosexuality. But the lesson at the time seemed rather academic, nothing to do with me, Anna. I wondered if I wanted to make love with that woman he was with now.

Then there was a moment of knowledge. I understood I'd gone (*18) right inside his craziness: he was looking for this wise, kind, all-mother figure, who is also sexual playmate and sister; and because I had become part of him, this is what I was looking for too, both for myself, because I needed her, and because I wanted to become her. I understood I could no longer separate myself from Saul, and that frightened me more than I have been frightened. For with my intelligence I knew that this man was repeating a pattern over and over again: courting a woman with his intelligence and sympathy, claiming her emotionally; then, when she began to claim in return, running away. And the better a woman was, the sooner he would begin to run. I knew this with my intelligence, and yet I sat there in my dark room, looking at the hazed wet brilliance of the purple London night sky, longing with my whole being for that mythical woman, longing to be her, but for Saul's sake.

I found I was lying on the floor, unable to breathe because of the tension in my stomach. I went to the kitchen and drank more whisky, until the anxiety eased a little. I went back to the big room, and tried to get back to myself by seeing Anna, a tiny unimportant figure in the ugly old flat in an ugly decaying house, with the wastes of dark London around her. I could not. I was desperately ashamed, being locked in Anna's, an unimportant little animal's, terrors. I kept saying to myself: Out there is the world, and I care so little that I haven't even read the newspapers for a week. I fetched the week's newspapers, and spread them around me on the floor. During the week things had developed—a war here, a dispute there. It was like missing several instalments of a serial on the films but being able to deduce what had happened in them from inner logic of the story. I felt bored and stale, knowing that, without having read the newspapers at all, I could have made a pretty good guess, from political experience, at what had happened in that week. The feeling of banality, the disgust of banality, mingled with my fear; and then suddenly I moved forward into a new knowledge, a new understanding; and this knowledge came out of Anna's, the frightened little animal's, sitting on the floor, cowering. It was 'the game,' but it came out of terror. I was invaded by terror, the terror of nightmares, I was experiencing the fear of war as one does in nightmares, not the intellectual balancing of probabilities, possibilities, but knowing, with my nerves and imagination, the fear of war. What I was reading in the newspapers strewn all round me became real, not an abstract intellectual fear. There was a kind of shifting of the balances of my brain, of the way I had been thinking, the same kind of realignment as when, a few days before, words like democracy, liberty, freedom, had faded under pressure of a new sort of understanding of the real movement of the world towards dark, hardening power. I *knew*, but of course the word, written, cannot convey the quality of this knowing, that whatever already is has its logic and its force, that the great armouries of the world have their inner force, and that my terror, the real nerve-terror of the nightmare, was part of the force. I felt this, like a vision, in a new kind of knowing. And I knew that the cruelty and the spite and the I, I, I, I of Saul and of Anna were part of the logic of war; and I knew how strong these emotions were, in a way that would never leave me, would become part of how I saw the world.

But now, writing it, and reading what I've written, there's nothing there, just words on paper. I can't communicate, even to myself when I read it back, the knowledge of destruction as a force. I was lying limp on the floor last night, feeling like a vision the power of destruction, feeling it so strongly that it will stay with me for the rest of my life, but the knowledge isn't in the words I write down now.

Thinking how war would explode, chaos would follow, I was cold and sweating with fear, and then I thought of Janet, the delightful rather conventional little girl at her girls' school, and I was angry, so angry that anyone anywhere could harm her, that I stood upright, able to fight off the terror. I was exhausted, the terror had gone away from me, to be contained in lines of print in newspapers. I was limp with exhaustion, and no longer needing to hurt Saul. I undressed and got into bed and I was sane. I realised the relief Saul must feel, when the hands of madness let go his throat and he thinks: It's gone for a time.

I lay thinking of him, warm and detached, strong.

Then I heard his step outside, furtive, and at once my switch was turned, I felt a surge of fear and anxiety. I didn't want him to come in, or rather I didn't want the owner of the furtive listening feet to come in. He stood for a time outside my door listening. I don't know what time it was, but judging from the light in the sky, it was early morning. I heard him tiptoe very, very carefully upstairs. I hated him. I was appalled that I could hate him so soon. I lay, hoping he would come down. Then I crept upstairs to his room. I opened his door, and from the dim light from the window I saw him

589

curled up neat and tidy under the blankets. My heart wrenched with pity. I slipped into bed beside him, and he turned and grabbed me close. I knew he had been stumbling about the streets, ill and lonely, from the way he held me.

This morning I left him sleeping and made coffee and tidied the flat, and made myself read the newspapers. I don't know *who* will come down the stairs. I sit here, reading the newspapers, but no longer with the nerves of knowledge, only with my intelligence, and I think how I, Anna Wulf, sit here waiting, not knowing who is going to come down the stairs, the gentle brotherly affectionate man, who knows me, Anna; or a furtive and cunning child; or a madman full of hate.

That was three days ago. These last three days I have been inside madness. When he came downstairs he looked very ill; his eyes were sharp bright wary animals inside circles of brownish bruised flesh; his mouth was tight, like a weapon. He had a jaunty soldier air, and I knew all his energies were absorbed in simply holding himself together. All his different personalities were fused in the being who fought only for survival. He gave me repeated glances of appeal, of which he was not aware. This was only a creature at the limits of itself. In response to the need of this creature, I felt myself tense and ready to take stress. The papers were lying on the table. When he came in I had pushed them away, feeling the terror I had been in the night before was too near, too dangerous to him, although I didn't feel it myself at that moment. He drank coffee and began talking about politics, glancing at the pile of papers. This was compulsive talking, not the I, I, I talking of his triumphant accusation and defiance of the world, but talking to hold himself together. He talked, talked, his eyes not implicated with what he was saying.

If I had tape-recordings of such times, it would be a record of jumbling phrases, jargon, disconnected remarks. That morning it was a political record, a hotchpotch of political jargon. I sat and listened as the stream of parrot-phrases went past, and I labelled them: communist, anti-communist, liberal, socialist. I was able to isolate them: Communist, American, 1954. Communist, English, 1956. Trotskyist, American, early 19-fifties. Premature anti-Stalinist, 1954.

Liberal, American, 1956. And so on. I was thinking, If I were really a psychoanalyst, I'd be able to use this stream of gibberish, catch at something in it, focus him, for he is a profoundly political man, and that is where he is at his most serious. So I asked him a question. I could see how something in him was checked. He started, came to himself, gasped, his eyes cleared, he saw me. I repeated the question, about the collapse of the socialist political tradition in America. I wondered if it were right, to check this flow of words, since it was being used to hold himself together, to stop himself collapsing. Then, and it was as if a piece of machinery, a crane perhaps, accepted a great strain, I saw his body tense and concentrate and he began speaking. I say *he*, taking for granted that I can pinpoint a personality. That there is a *he* who is the real man. Why should I assume that one of the persons he is is more himself than the others? But I do. When he spoke then it was the man who thought, judged, communicated, heard what I said, accepted responsibility.

We began discussing the state of the left in Europe, the fragmentation of socialist movements everywhere. We had of course discussed all this before, often; but never so calmly and clearly. I remember thinking it was strange that we were able to be so detachedly intelligent when we were both sick with tension and anxiety. And I thought that we were talking about political movements, the development or defeat of this socialist movement or that, whereas last night I had known, finally, that the truth for our time was war, the immanence of war. And I was wondering if it was a mistake to talk about this at all, the conclusions we reached were so depressing, it was precisely this depression that had helped to make him ill. But it was too late, and it was a relief to have the real person there opposite me, instead of the gabbling parrot. And then I made some remark, I forget what, and his whole frame quivered as he went into a different gear, how else can I put it?—he took a shock somewhere inside himself and switched back into another personality, this time he was the pure, socialist, working-class boy, a boy, not a man, and the stream of slogans started again, and his whole body jerked and gesticulated in abuse of me, for he was abusing a middle-class liberal. I sat there and thought how odd, that while I knew it was not 'him' talking at that moment, and that his abuse was mechanical and out of an earlier personality, yet it hurt me and made me angry, and I could feel my back start to ache and my stomach clench in response to it. To get away from the reaction I went into my big room, and he followed me shouting: 'You can't take it, you can't take it, bloody Englishwoman.' I took him by his shoulders and shook him. I shook him back into himself. He gasped, breathed deeply, put his head down on my shoulder for a moment, then staggered to my bed and collapsed on it, face down.

I stood by the window, looking out, trying to calm myself by thinking of Janet. But she seemed remote from me. The sunlight—it was a pale winter sun, was remote. What went on in the street was remote from me, the people passing were not people, they were marionettes. I felt a change inside me, a sliding lurch away from myself, and I knew this change to be another step down into chaos. I touched the stuff of the red curtain, and the feel of it on my fingers was dead and slippery, slimy. I saw this substance, processed by machinery, dead stuff, to hang like dead skin, or a lifeless corpse at my windows. I touched the plant in a pot on the window sill. Often when I touch the leaves of the plant, I feel a kinship with the working roots, the breathing leaves, but now it seemed unpleasant, like a little hostile animal or a dwarf, imprisoned in the earthenware pot and hating me for imprisoning it. So I tried to summon up younger, stronger Annas, the schoolgirl in London and the daughter of my father, but I could see these Annas only as apart from me. So I thought of the corner of a field in Africa. I made myself stand on a whitish glitter of sand, with the sun on my face, but I could no longer feel the heat of that sun. I thought of my friend Mr Mathlong, but he, too, was remote. I stood there, trying to reach the consciousness of a hot yellow sun, trying to summon Mr Mathlong, and suddenly I was not Mr Mathlong at all, but the mad Charlie Themba. I became him. It was very easy to be Charlie Themba. It was as if he stood there slightly to one side of me, but part of me, his small spiky dark figure, his small, intelligent, hotly indignant face looking at me. Then he melted into me. I was in a hut, in the Northern Province, and my wife was my enemy, and my colleagues on the Congress, formerly my friends, were trying to poison me, and somewhere out in the reeds a crocodile lay dead, killed with a poisoned spear, and my wife, bought by my enemies, was about to feed me crocodile flesh, and when it touched my lips I would die, because of the furious enmity of my outraged ancestors. I could smell the cold decaying flesh of the crocodile, and I looked through the door of the hut and saw the dead crocodile, rocking slightly on warm decaying water, in the reeds of the river, and then I saw the eyes of my wife peering through the reeds that made my hut, judging to see if she could safely enter. She came bending through the hut door, her skirts held to one side with the sly lying hand I hated, and in the other hand a tin plate where shreds of stinking flesh lay ready for me to eat.

Then in front of my eyes I saw the letter written by this man to me and I snapped out of the nightmare as if I had walked out of a photograph. I was standing at my window, sweating with terror because of being Charlie Themba, mad and paranoic, the man hated by the white men and disowned by his comrades. I stood there, limp with cold exhaustion, and tried to summon Mr Mathlong. But while I could see him, clearly, walking rather stooped across a sunlit space of dust from one tin-roofed shanty to another, smiling courteously, with his unfailing gentle, rather amused smile, he was separated from me. I clutched on to the window curtains, to stop myself falling, and felt the cold slipperiness of the curtains between my fingers like dead flesh and I shut my eyes. My eyes shut, I understood through waves of sickness that I was Anna Wulf, once Anna Freeman, standing at the window of an old ugly flat in London, and that behind me on the bed was Saul Green, wandering American. But I don't know how long I was there. I came to myself like coming out of a dream, not knowing what room one is going to wake in. I realised that, like Saul, I no longer had a sense of time. I looked at the cold whitish sky, and the cold distorted sun, and turned carefully to look into the room. It was rather dark in the room, and the gas fire made a warm glow on the floor. Saul

593

lay very still. I walked very carefully across the floor, which seemed to heave and bulge under me, and I bent over to look at Saul. He was asleep, and the cold seemed to come out of him. I lay down beside him, fitting myself to the curve of his back. He did not move. Then, suddenly, I was sane, and I understood what it meant when I said, I am Anna Wulf and this is Saul Green and I have a child named Janet. I tightened my hold on him, and he turned, abrupt, his arm up to ward off a blow, and saw me. His face was dead white, the bones of his face sticking out through thin skin, his eyes a sick lustreless grey. He flung his head on to my breasts and I held him. He slept again and I tried to feel time. But time had gone out of me. I lay with the cold weight of this man against me, as if ice lay against me, and I tried to make my flesh warm enough to warm his. But his cold crept into me, so I gently shoved and pushed him under the blankets and we lay under warm fibres and slowly the cold went away and his flesh warmed against mine. Now I was thinking about my experience of being Charlie Themba. I could no longer remember it, as I could no longer 'remember' how I had understood that war was working in us all, towards fruition. I was, in other words, sane again. But the word sane meant nothing, as the word mad meant nothing. I was oppressed by a knowledge of immensity, feeling the weight of hugeness, but not as when I play 'the game,' only in its aspect of meaninglessness. I cowered, and I could see no reason why I should be mad or sane. And, looking past Saul's head, everything in the room seemed sly and threatening and cheap and meaningless, and even now I could feel the slippery dead curtains between my fingers.

I slept and I dreamed the dream. This time there was no disguise anywhere. I was the malicious male-female dwarf figure, the principle of joy-in-destruction; and Saul was my counterpart, male-female, my brother and my sister, and we were dancing in some open place, under enormous white buildings, which were filled with hideous, menacing, black machinery which held destruction. But in the dream, he and I, or she and I, were friendly, we were not hostile, we were together in spiteful malice. There was a terrible yearning nostalgia in the dream, the longing for death. We came together and kissed, in love. It was terrible, and even in the dream I knew it. Because I recognised in the dream those other dreams we all have, when the essence of love, of tenderness, is concentrated into a kiss or a caress, but now it was the caress of two half-human creatures, celebrating destruction.

There was a terrible joy in the dream. When I woke up the room was dark, the glow of the fire very red, the great white ceiling filled with restful shadow, and I was filled with joy and peace. I wondered how such a terrible dream could leave me rested, and then I remembered Mother Sugar, and thought that perhaps for the first time I had dreamed the dream 'positively'—though what that means I don't know.

Saul had not moved. I was stiff and moved my shoulders, and he woke up, frightened, and called out: 'Anna!' as if I were in another room or another country. I said: 'I'm here.' His prick was big. We made love. In the love-making was the warmth of the love-making of the dream. Then he sat up and said: 'Jesus, what time is it?' and I said: 'Five or six, I suppose,' and he said: 'Christ, I can't sleep my life away like this,' and rushed out of the room.

I lay on the bed, happy. Being happy, the joy that filled me then was stronger than all the misery and the madness in the world, or so I felt it. But then happiness began to leak away, and I lay and I thought: What is this thing we need so much? (By we, meaning women.) And what is it worth? I had it with Michael, but it meant nothing to him, for if it did, he wouldn't have left me. And now I have it with Saul, grabbing at it as if it were a glass of water and I were thirsty. But think about it, and it vanishes. I did not want to think about it. If I did there would be nothing between me and the little dwarf-plant in the pot on the window sill, between me and the slippery horror of the curtains, or even the crocodile waiting in the reeds.

I lay on the bed in the dark, listening to Saul crashing and banging over my head, and I was already betrayed. Because Saul had forgotten the 'happiness.' By the act of going upstairs, he had put a gulf between himself and happiness.

595

But I saw this not merely as denying Anna, but as denying life itself. I thought that somewhere here is a fearful trap for women, but I don't yet understand what it is. For there is no doubt of the new note women strike, the note of being betrayed. It's in the books they write, in how they speak, everywhere, all the time. It is a solemn, self-pitying organ note. It is in me, Anna betrayed, Anna unloved, Anna whose happiness is denied, and who says, not: Why do you deny me, but why do you deny life?

When Saul came back he stood efficient and aggressive, his eyes narrowed, and he said: 'I'm going out.' And I said: 'All right.' He went out, the prisoner escaping.

I lay where I was, exhausted with the effort of not caring that he had to be the escaping prisoner. My emotions had switched off, but my mind ran on, making images, like a film. I was checking the images, or scenes, as they went past, for I was able to recognise them as fantasies common to a certain kind of person now, out of common stock, shared by millions of people. I saw an Algerian soldier stretched on a torture bed; and I was also him, wondering how long I could hold out. I saw a communist in a communist jail, but the jail was certainly in Moscow, but this time the torture was intellectual, this time the holding out was a fight inside the terms of Marxist dialectic. The end-point of this scene was where the communist prisoner admitted, but after days of argument, that he took his stand on individual conscience, that moment when a human being says: 'No, that I can't do.' At which point the communist jailor merely smiled, there was no need to say, Then you have confessed yourself to be at fault. Then I saw the soldier in Cuba, the soldier in Algeria, rifle in hand, on guard. Then the British conscript, pressed into war in Egypt, killed for futility. Then a student in Budapest, throwing a home-made bomb at a great black Russian tank. Then a peasant, somewhere in China, marching in a procession millions strong.

These pictures flicked in front of my eyes. I thought that five years ago the pictures would have been different, and that in five years they would be different again; but that now

596

they were what bound people, of a certain kind, unknown to each other as individuals, together.

When the images stopped creating themselves, I checked them again, named them. It occurred to me that Mr Mathlong had not presented himself. I thought that a few hours ago I had actually been the mad Mr Themba, and with no conscious effort on my part. I said to myself I would be Mr Mathlong, I would make myself be this figure. I set the stage in every possible way. I tried to imagine myself, a black man in white-occupied territory, humiliated in his human dignity. I tried to imagine him, at mission school, and then studying in England. I tried to create him, and I failed totally. I tried to make him stand in my room, a courteous, ironical figure, but I failed. I told myself I had failed because this figure, unlike all the others, had a quality of detachment. He was the man who performed actions, played roles, that he believed to be necessary for the good of others, even while he preserved an ironic doubt about the results of his actions. It seemed to me that this particular kind of detachment was something we needed very badly in this time, but that very few people had it, and it was certainly a long way from me.

I fell asleep. When I woke it was getting on for morning. I could see my ceiling lying pale and stagnant, disturbed by lights from the street, and the sky was a full purple, wet with a wintry moonlight. My body cried out with being alone because Saul was not there. I did not sleep again. I was dissolved in the hateful emotion, the woman-betrayed. I lay with my teeth clenched, refusing to think, knowing that everything I thought would come out of the solemn wet emotion. Then I heard Saul come in, he came in silent and furtive and went straight upstairs. This time I didn't go up. I knew that this meant he would resent me in the morning, because his guilt, his need to betray, needed the constant reassurance of my going to him.

When he came down it was late, nearly lunch-time, and I knew this was the man who hated me. He said, very cold: 'Why do you let me sleep so late?' I said: 'Why should I have to tell you what time to get up?' He said: 'I have to go out to lunch. It's a business lunch.' I knew from how he said it it was not a business lunch, and that he had said the words in that way so that I should know it was not.

I felt very ill again, and I went into my room and set out the notebooks. He came in and stood by the door, looking at me. He said: 'I suppose you're writing a record of my crimes!' He sounded pleased that I was. I was putting away three of the notebooks. He said: 'Why do you have four notebooks?' I said: 'Obviously, because it's been necessary to split myself up, but from now on I shall be using one only.' I was interested to hear myself say this, because until then I hadn't known it. He was standing in the door, holding on to the frame of the doorway with both hands. His eyes were narrowed at me in pure hate. I saw the white door with its old-fashioned unnecessary mouldings, very clear. I thought how the mouldings on the door recall a Greek temple, that's where they come from, the pillars of a Greek temple; and how they in turn recall an Egyptian temple, and how that in turn recalls the bundle of reeds and the crocodile. There he stood, the American, clutching this history in both hands for fear he would fall, hating me, the jailor. I said, as I had said before: 'Don't you think it's extraordinary that we are both people whose personalities, whatever that word may mean, are large enough to include all sorts of things, politics and literature and art, but now that we're mad everything concentrates down to one small thing, that I don't want you to go off and sleep with someone else, and that you must lie to me about it?' For a moment he was himself, thinking about this, and then he faded away or dissolved and the furtive antagonist said: 'You're not going to trap me that way, don't you think it.' He went upstairs, and when he came down again, a few minutes later, he said cheerfully: 'Gee, I'll be late if I don't go. See you later baby.'

He went off, taking me with him. I could feel part of myself leaving the house with him. I knew how he went. He stumbled down the stairs, stood a moment before facing the street, then walked carefully, with the defensive walk of Americans, the walk of people ready to defend themselves, until he saw a bench, or perhaps a step somewhere and sat on it. He had left the devils behind him in my flat, and for a moment he was free. But I could feel the cold of loneliness coming from him. The cold of loneliness was all around me.

I looked at this notebook, thinking that if I could write in it Anna would come back, but I could not make my hand go out to take up the pen. I telephoned Molly. When she answered I realised I could not communicate what was happening to me, I could not talk to her. Her voice, cheerful and practical as always, sounded like the quacking of a strange bird, and I heard my own voice, cheerful and empty.

She said: 'How's your American?' and I said: 'Fine.' I said: 'How's Tommy?' She said: 'He's just signed up to do a series of lectures all over the country about the life of the coal-miner, you know, the Life of the Coal-miner.' I said: 'Good.' She said: 'Quite so. He is simultaneously talking about going to fight with either the F.L.N. in Algeria or in Cuba. I had a bunch of them here last night, and they're all talking of going off, it doesn't matter which revolution, provided it is a revolution.' I said: 'His wife wouldn't like that.' 'No, that's what I said to Tommy, when he confronted me, all aggressive, suggesting I would stop him. It's not me, it's your sensible little wife, I said. You have my blessing, I said, any revolution anywhere regardless, because obviously none of us can stand the lives we are leading. He said I was being very negative. Later he rang me up to say unfortunately he could not go off to fight just at this time, because he was going to do the series of lectures on The Life of the Coal-miner. Anna, is it only me? I feel as if I'm living inside a sort of improbable farce.' 'No, it isn't only you.' 'I know, and that makes it even worse.'

I put down the instrument. The floor between me and the bed was bulging and heaving. The walls seemed to bulge inwards, then float out and away into space. For a moment I stood in space, the walls gone, as if I stood above ruined buildings. I knew I had to get to the bed, so I walked carefully over the heaving floor towards it, and lay down. But I, Anna, was not there. Then I fell asleep, although I knew as I drifted off this was not an ordinary sleep. I could see Anna's body lying on the bed. And into the room, one after another, came people I knew who stood at the foot of the bed, and seemed

599

to try and fit themselves into Anna's body. I stood to one side, watching, interested to see who would come into the room next. Maryrose came, a pretty blonde girl, smiling politely. Then George Hounslow, and Mrs Boothby, and Jimmy. These people stopped, looked at Anna, and moved on. I stood to one side, wondering: Which of them will she accept? Then I was conscious of danger, for Paul came in, who was dead, and I saw his grave whimsical smile as he bent over her. Then he dissolved into her, and I, screaming with fear, fought my way through a crowd of indifferent ghosts to the bed, to Anna, to myself. I fought to re-enter her. I was fighting against cold, a terrible cold. My hands and legs were stiff with cold, and Anna was cold because she was filled with the dead Paul. I could see his cool grave smile on Anna's face. After a struggle, which was for my life, I slipped back into myself and lay cold, cold. In my sleep I was in Mashopi again, but now the ghosts were ordered around me, like stars in their proper places, and Paul was a ghost among them. We sat under the eucalyptus trees in the dusty moonlight, with the smell of sweet spilt wine in our nostrils and the lights of the hotel shone across the road. It was an ordinary dream, and I knew that I had been delivered from disintegration because I could dream it. The dream faded in a lying pain of nostalgia. I said to myself in my sleep, hold yourself together, you can do it if you get to the blue notebook and write. I felt the inertia of my hand, which was cold and unable to reach out for the pen. But instead of a pen I held a gun in my hand. And I was not Anna, but a soldier. I could feel the uniform on me, but one I didn't know. I was standing in a cool night somewhere, with groups of soldiers moving quietly behind me around the business of getting a meal. I could hear the clink of metal on metal, rifles being stacked together. Somewhere before me was the enemy. But I didn't know who the enemy was, what my cause was. I saw my skin was dark. At first I thought I was an African or a Negro. Then I saw dark glistening hair on my bronze forearm which held a rifle on which moonlight glinted. I understood I was on a hillside in Algeria, I was an Algerian soldier and I was fighting the French. Yet Anna's brain was working in this man's head, and she was thinking: Yes I shall kill, I shall even torture because I have to, but without belief. Because it is no longer possible to organise and to fight and to kill without knowing that new tyranny arises from it. Yet one has to fight and organise. Then Anna's brain went out like a candle flame. I was the Algerian, believing, full of the courage of belief. Terror came into the dream because again Anna was threatened with total disintegration. Terror brought me out of the dream, and I was no longer the sentry, standing guard in the moonlight with the groups of his comrades moving quietly behind him over the fires of the evening meal. I bounded off the dry, sun-smelling soil of Algeria and I was in the air. This was the flying dream, and it was a long time since I had dreamed it, and I was almost crying with joy because I was flying again. The essence of the flying dream is joy, joy in light, free movement. I was high in the air above the Mediterranean, and I knew I could go anywhere. I willed to go east. I wanted to go to Asia, I wanted to visit the peasant. I was flying immensely high, with the mountains and seas beneath me, treading the air down easily with my feet. I passed over great mountains and below me was China. I said in my dream: I am here because I want to be a peasant with other peasants. I came low over a village, and saw peasants working in the fields. They had a quality of stern purpose which attracted me to them. I willed my feet to let me descend gently to the earth. The joy of the dream was more intense than I have experienced, and it was the joy of freedom. I came down to the ancient earth of China, and a peasant woman stood at the door of her hut. I walked towards her, and just as Paul had stood, bending, by the sleeping Anna a short time before, needing to become her, so I stood by the peasant woman, needing to enter her, to be her. It was easy to become her. She was a young woman, and she was pregnant, but already made old by work. Then I realised that Anna's brain was in her still, and I was thinking mechanical thoughts which I classified as 'progressive and liberal.' That she was such and such, formed by this movement, that war, this experience, I was 'naming' her, from an alien personality. Then Anna's brain, as it had done on the hillside in Algeria, began to flicker and to wane. And I said: 'Don't let terror of dissolution frighten you away this time, hold on.' But the terror was too strong. It drove me out of the peasant woman, and I stood to one side of her, watching her walk across a field to join a group of men and women working. They wore uniforms. But now terror had destroyed the joy, and my feet would no longer tread down the air. I trod down and down, frantic, trying to climb up and over the black mountains which separated me from Europe, which now, from where I stood, seemed a tiny meaningless fringe on the great continent, like a disease I was going to re-enter. But I could not fly, I could not leave the plain where the peasants worked, and fear of being trapped there woke me. I woke into the late afternoon, the room full of dark, the traffic roaring up from the street below. I woke a person who had been changed by the experience of being other people. I did not care about Anna, I did not like being her. It was with a weary sense of duty I became Anna, like putting on a soiled dress.

And then I got up and switched on the lights, and heard movements upstairs, which meant Saul had come back. As soon as I heard him my stomach clenched up, and I was back inside sick Anna who had no will.

I called up to him and he called down. His voice being cheerful, my apprehension went. Then he came down, and it returned, for he had on his face a consciously whimsical smile, and I wondered, which role is he playing? He sat on my bed and he took my hand and looked at it with a consciously whimsical admiration. I knew then, that he was comparing it with the hand of a woman he had just left, or a woman he wanted me to believe he had just left. He remarked: 'Perhaps I like your nail varnish better after all.' I said: 'But I'm not wearing nail varnish.' He said: 'Well, if you were I'd probably like it better.' He kept turning my hand over, looking at it with amused surprise, watching me to see how I took the amused surprise. I took my hand away. He said: 'I suppose you're going to ask me where I've been.' I said nothing. He said: 'Ask me no questions and I'll tell you no lies.' I said nothing. I felt as if sucked into a quicksand, or pushed on to a conveyor belt that would carry me into grinding machinery. I walked away from him to the window. Outside was a dark glistening rain and the roofs were wet and dark. The cold struck on the window panes.

He came after me, put his arms around me and held me. He was smiling, a man conscious of his power with women, seeing himself in this role. He wore his tight blue sweater and the sleeves were rolled up. I saw the light hair glistening on his forearms. He looked down into my eyes and said: 'I swear I'm not lying. I swear. I swear. I haven't had another woman. I swear.' His voice was full of dramatic intensity, and his eyes were focused in a parody of intensity.

I did not believe him, but the Anna in his arms believed him, even while I watched the two of us playing out these roles, incredulous that we were capable of such melodrama. Then he kissed me. At the moment I responded he broke away, and he said as he had said before, with his characteristic sullenness at such moments: 'Why don't you fight me? Why don't you fight?' I kept replying: 'Why should I fight? Why do you have to fight?' And I had said this before, we had done all this before. Then he led me by the hand to the bed and made love to me. I was interested to see who he was making love to, for I knew it was not me. It appeared that this other woman needed a great deal of admonition and encouragement in love and is childish. For he was making love to a childish woman and she had flat breasts and very beautiful hands. Suddenly he said: 'Yes, and we'll make a baby, you're right.' When it was finished he rolled away, gasping, and exclaimed: 'By Christ, that would be the end, a child, you'd really finish me.' I said: 'It wasn't me who offered to give you a child, this is Anna.' He jerked his head up to look at me, and he dropped his head back and laughed, and said: 'So it is. It is Anna.'

I went to the bathroom and was very sick, and when I came back I said: 'I've got to go to sleep.' I turned away from him and went to sleep, to get away from him.

But I went towards him, in sleep. It was a night of dreams. I was playing roles, one after another, against Saul, who was playing roles. It was like being in a play, whose words kept changing, as if a playwright had written the same play again and again, but slightly different each time. We played against each other every man-woman role imaginable. As each cycle of the dream came to an end, I said: 'Well, I've experienced that, have I, well it was time that I did.' It was like living a hundred lives. I was astonished at how many of the female roles I have not played in life, have refused to play, or were not offered to me. Even in my sleep I knew I was being condemned to play them now because I had refused them in life.

In the morning I woke beside Saul. He was cold, and I had to warm him. I was myself, and strong. I came straight to the trestle table and laid out this notebook. I wrote for a long time before he woke. He must have been awake and watching me for some time before I saw him. He said: 'Instead of making a record of my sins in your diary, why don't you write another novel?'

I said: 'I could give you a dozen reasons why not, I could speak on the subject for several hours, but the real reason is that I have a writer's block. That's all. And it's the first time I've admitted it.'

'Perhaps,' he said, his head on one side, smiling with affection. I saw the affection and it warmed me. Then, as I smiled back, his smile cut off, his face went sullen, and he said with energy: 'Anyway, knowing you are here spinning out all these words, it drives me crazy.'

'Anyone could tell us two writers shouldn't be together. Or rather, that a competitive American shouldn't be with a woman who has written a book.'

'That's right,' he said, 'It's a challenge to my sexual superiority, and that isn't a joke.'

'I know it isn't. But please don't give me any more of your pompous socialist lectures about the equality of men and women.'

'I shall probably give you pompous lectures because I enjoy it. But I won't believe in them myself. The truth is, I resent you for having written a book which was a success. And I've come to the conclusion I've always been a hypo-

604

crite, and in fact I enjoy a society where women are second-class citizens, I enjoy being boss and being flattered.'

'Good,' I said. 'Because in a society where not one man in ten thousand begins to understand the ways in which women are second-class citizens, we have to rely for company on the men who are at least not hypocrites.'

'And now we've settled that, you can make me some coffee, because that is your role in life.'

'It will be a pleasure,' I said, and we had breakfast in good humour, liking each other.

After breakfast I took my shopping basket and walked along the Earl's Court Road. I enjoyed buying food and groceries, and enjoyed knowing that I would cook for him later. Yet I was also sad, knowing it would not last long. I thought: He'll be gone soon, and then it will be over, the pleasure of looking after a man. I was ready to come home, yet I stood at the corner of a street in a thin grey rain, among poking umbrellas and pushing bodies, and wondered why I was waiting there. Then I walked across the street into a stationer's shop, and went to a counter loaded with notebooks. There were notebooks there similar to these four I have. Yet they were not what I wanted. I saw a large thick book, rather expensive, and opened it, and it had good thick white paper, unlined. The paper was pleasant to touch, a little rough, but silky. It had a heavy cover, of dull gold. I had never seen a similar notebook, and I asked the assistant what it was manufactured for, and she said that an American customer had ordered it to be especially made for him, but had not come back for it. He had paid a deposit, so it wasn't as expensive as I expected it to be. Even so, it was expensive, but I wanted it, and I brought it home with me. It gives me pleasure to touch it and look at it, but I don't know what I want it for.

Saul came into my room, prowling around and around, restless, and he saw the new notebook, and pounced on it. 'Oh this is pretty,' he said. 'What is it for?' 'I don't know yet.' 'Then I want it,' he said. I nearly said: 'All right, have it,' watching in myself a need to give spouting like water from a whale. I was annoyed at myself, because I wanted it, yet so nearly gave it to him. I knew this need to comply was part of the sadistic-masochistic cycle we are in. I said: 'No, you can't have it.' It cost me a great deal to say it—I even stammered. He took the book up and said, laughing: 'Gimme, gimme, gimme.' I said: 'No.' He had expected me to give it, because he had made a joke of the gimme, gimme; and now he stood glancing at me sideways, and murmuring, not laughing at all, gimme, gimme, gimme, in a child's voice. He had become a child. I saw how the new personality, or rather, the old one, entered him like an animal entering a thicket. His body curved and crouched, became a weapon; his face, which when he is 'himself,' is good-humoured, shrewd, sceptical, was the face of a little murderer. He whipped around, holding the book, ready to run for the door; (*19) and I saw him clearly, the slum kid, member of a gang of slum kids, lifting something from a shop counter, or running from the police. I said: 'No, you can't have it,' as I would have done to a child, and he came to himself, slowly, all the tension going out of him; and he laid the book down, good-humoured again, even grateful. I thought how odd it was, that he should need the authority of someone who could say no, and yet it was my life he had drifted into, I who find it so hard to say no. Because now I had said no, and he laid the book down, every line of him expressing the deprived child who had had something he very badly wanted denied to him, I felt stricken. I wanted to say: Take it, for God's sake, it's not important. But now I couldn't say it, and I was frightened at how quickly this unimportant thing, the new pretty book, had become part of the fight.

He stood for a while, by the door, forlorn; while I watched him straighten himself, and saw how a thousand times in his childhood he had straightened himself, stiffened his shoulders, and 'put it under his belt,' as he had told me everyone must do when they had trouble.

Then he said: 'Well, I'll go up and work.' He went slowly upstairs, but did not work, for I heard him prowling about upstairs. The tension started again, though for a few hours I had been free of it. I watched the hands of pain lay hold of my stomach and fingers of pain jab into the muscles of my neck and the small of my back. Sick Anna came back and inhabited me. I know it was the prowling footsteps upstairs that had summoned her. I put on an Armstrong record, but the naïve good-humour of the music was too remote. I changed it for Mulligan, but the self-pity of that was the voice of the illness in my flat, so I switched off the music and thought: Janet will be home soon, and I must stop this, I must stop.

It's been a dark cold day, not even a winter's gleam of sun; and now it's raining outside. The curtains are drawn and both paraffin stoves are lit. Now the room is dark, and on the ceiling two gently-flickering patterns of gold-red light from the heaters, and the gas fire is a red glow whose fierceness has no power to penetrate the cold further than a few inches from the bars of the fire.

I have been sitting looking at the new pretty notebook, handling it and admiring it. Saul has scribbled in the front of it in pencil without my seeing the old schoolboy's curse:

> Whoever he be who looks in this
> He shall be cursed,
> That is my wish.
> Saul Green, *his* book. (! ! !)

It made me laugh, so that I nearly went upstairs and gave it to him. But I will not, I will not, I will not. I'll pack away the blue notebook with the others. I'll pack away the four notebooks. I'll start a new notebook, all of myself in one book.

[Here the blue notebook ended with a heavy double black line.]

THE GOLDEN NOTEBOOK

THE GOLDEN NOTEBOOK

Whoever he be who looks in this
He shall be cursed,
That is my wish.
Saul Green, *his* book. (! ! !)

It is so dark in this flat, so dark, it is as if darkness were the shape of cold. I went through the flat turning on light everywhere, the dark retreated to outside the windows, a cold shape trying to press its way in. But when I turned on the light in my big room, I knew this was wrong, light was foreign to it, so I let the dark come back, controlled by the two paraffin heaters and the glow from the gas fire. I lay down, and thought of the little earth, half of it in cold dark, swinging in immense spaces of darkness. Soon after I lay down Saul came and lay beside me. 'This is an extraordinary room,' he said, 'it's like a world.' His arm under my neck was warm and strong, and we made love. He slept, and when he woke he was warm, not full of the deathly cold which frightens me. Then he remarked: 'Well *now* perhaps I can work.' The egoism was so direct, like mine when I need something, that I began to laugh. He laughed, and we couldn't stop. We rolled on the bed laughing and then on the floor. Then he jumped up off the floor, saying in a prissy English voice: 'This won't do, it won't do at all,' and went out, still laughing.

The devils had gone out of the flat. That is how I thought, sitting on my bed naked, warmed by the heat from the three fires. The devils. As if the fear, the terror, the anxiety were not inside me, inside Saul, but some force from outside which chose its moments to come and go. I thought like that, lying to myself; because I needed that moment of pure happiness—

611

me, Anna, sitting naked on the bed, my breasts pressing between my naked arms, and the smell of sex and sweat. It seemed to me that the warm strength of my body's happiness was enough to drive away all the fear in the world. Then the feet began again upstairs, moving, driven, from place to place above my head, like armies moving. My stomach clenched. I watched my happiness leak away. I was all at once in a new state of being, one foreign to me. I realised my body was distasteful to me. This has never happened to me before; and I even said to myself: Hullo, this is new, this is something I have read about. I remembered Nelson telling me how sometimes he looked at his wife's body and hated it for its femaleness; he hated it because of the hair in the armpits and around the crotch. Sometimes, he said, he saw his wife as a sort of spider, all clutching arms and legs around a hairy central devouring mouth. I sat on my bed and I looked at my thin white legs and my thin white arms, and at my breasts. My wet sticky centre seemed disgusting, and when I saw my breasts all I could think of was how they were when they were full of milk, and instead of this being pleasurable, it was revolting. This feeling of being alien to my own body caused my head to swim, until I anchored myself, clutching out for something, to the thought that what I was experiencing was not *my* thought at all. I was experiencing, imaginatively, for the first time, the emotions of a homosexual. For the first time the homosexual literature of disgust made sense to me. I realised how much homosexual feeling there is floating loose everywhere, and in people who would never recognise the word as theirs.

The sound of feet had stopped upstairs. I could not move, I was gripped by my disgust. Then I knew that Saul would come downstairs and say something that echoed what I was thinking; this knowledge was so clear that I simply sat and waited, in a fug of stale self-disgust, waiting to hear how this disgust would sound when said aloud in his voice, my voice. He came down and stood in the doorway, and he said: 'Jesus, Anna, what are you doing there, sitting naked?' And I said, my voice detached and clinical: 'Saul do you realise we've got to the point where we influence each other's moods even when we are in different rooms?' It was too dark in my room to see his face, but the shape of his body, standing alert by the door, expressed a need to fly, to run from Anna sitting naked and repulsive on the bed. He said in the scandalised voice of a boy: 'Put some clothes on.' I said: 'Did you hear what I said?' For he had not. He said: 'Anna, I told you, don't sit there like that.' I said: 'What do you think this thing is that makes people like us have to experience everything? We're driven by something to be as many different things or people as possible.' He heard this, and said: 'I don't know. I don't have to try, it's what I am.' I said: 'I'm not trying. I'm being driven. Do you suppose that people who lived earlier were tormented by what they had not experienced? Or is it only us?' He said, sullen: 'Lady, I don't know, and I don't care, I just wish I were delivered from it.' Then he said, friendly, not out of disgust: 'Anna, do you realise how damned cold it is? You'll be ill if you don't put on clothes. I'm going out.' He went. As his feet went down the stairs, my mood of self-disgust went with him. I sat and luxuriated in my body. Even a small dry wrinkling of skin on the inside of my thigh, the beginning of being old, gave me pleasure. I was thinking: Yes, that's as it should be, I've been so happy in my life, I shan't care about being old. But even as I said it, the security leaked away again. I was back in disgust. I stood in the centre of the big room, naked, letting the heat strike me from the three points of heat, and I knew, and it was an illumination—one of those things one has always known, but never really understood before—that all sanity depends on this: that it should be a delight to feel the roughness of a carpet under smooth soles, a delight to feel heat strike the skin, a delight to stand upright, knowing the bones are moving easily under flesh. If this goes, then the conviction of life goes too. But I could feel none of this. The texture of the carpet was abhorrent to me, a dead processed thing; my body was a thin, meagre, spiky sort of vegetable, like an unsunned plant; and when I touched the hair on my head it was dead. I felt the floor bulge up under me. The walls were losing their density. I knew I was moving down into a new dimension, further away from sanity than I had ever been. I knew I had to get to the bed fast. I could not walk, so I let myself down on my hands and knees and crawled to the bed and lay on it, covering myself. But I was defenceless. Lying there I remembered the Anna who can dream at will, control time, move easily and is at home in the underworld of sleep. But I was not that Anna. The areas of light on the ceiling had become great watchful eyes, the eyes of an animal watching me. It was a tiger, lying sprawled over the ceiling, and I was a child *knowing* that there was a tiger in the room, even while my brain told me there was not. Beyond the triple-windowed wall a cold wind blew, striking the panes and making them shudder, and the winter's light thinned the curtains. They were not curtains they were shreds of stinking sour flesh left by the animal. I realised I was inside a cage into which the animal could leap when it wished. I was ill with the smell of dead flesh, the reek of the tiger and with fear. And, while my stomach swayed, I fell asleep.

It was the kind of sleep I have known only when ill: very light, as if lying just under water, with real sleep in bottomless layers beneath me. And so all the time I was conscious of lying on the bed, and conscious of sleeping, and thinking extraordinarily clearly. Yet it was not the same as when I stood, in a dream, to one side and saw Anna sleeping, watching other personalities bend over to invade her. I was myself, yet knowing what I thought and dreamed, so there was a personality apart from the Anna who lay asleep; yet who that person is I do not know. It was a person concerned to prevent the disintegration of Anna.

As I lay on the surface of the dream-water, and began very slowly to submerge, this person said: 'Anna, you are betraying everything you believe in; you are sunk in subjectivity, yourself, your own needs.' But the Anna who wanted to slip under the dark water would not answer. The disinterested person said: 'You've always thought of yourself as a strong person. Yet that man is a thousand times more courageous than you are—he has had to fight this for years, but after a few weeks of it, you are ready to give in altogether.' But the sleeping Anna was already just under the surface of the water, rocking on it, wanting to go down into the black depths under her. The admonishing person said: 'Fight. Fight. Fight.' I lay rocking under the water, and the voice was silent, and then I knew the depths of water under me had become dangerous, full of monsters and crocodiles and things I could scarcely imagine, they were so old and so tyrannous. Yet their danger was what pulled me down, I wanted the danger. Then, through the deafening water, I heard the voice say: 'Fight. Fight.' I saw that the water was not deep at all, but only a thin sour layer of water at the bottom of a filthy cage. Above me, over the top of the cage, sprawled the tiger. The voice said: 'Anna, you know how to fly. Fly.' So I slowly crawled, like a drunk woman, to my knees in the filthy thin water, then stood up and tried to fly, treading down the stale air with my feet. It was so difficult that I almost fainted, the air was too thin, it wouldn't hold me. But I remembered how I had flown before, and so with a very great effort, fighting with every down-pushing step, I rose and clutched the top bars of the cage, over which the tiger lay sprawled. The smell of fetid breath suffocated me. But I pulled myself up through the bars and stood by the tiger. It lay still, blinking greenish eyes at me. Above me was still the roof of the building and I had to push down the air with my feet and tread up through it. Again I fought and struggled, and slowly I rose up and the roof vanished. The tiger lay sprawled at ease on a small ineffective cage, blinking its eyes, one paw stretched out and touching my foot. I knew I had nothing to fear from the tiger. It was a beautiful glossy animal lying stretched out in a warm moonlight. I said to the tiger: 'That's your cage.' It did not move, but yawned, showing white rows of teeth. Then there was a noise of men coming for the tiger. It was going to be caught and caged. I said: 'Run, quickly.' The tiger got up, stood lashing its tail, moving its head this way and that. It stank of fear now. Hearing the clamour of the men's voices and their running feet, it slashed with its paw at my forearm in a blind terror. I saw the blood running down my arm. The tiger leaped right down from the roof, alighting on the pavement, and it ran off into the shadows along the railings of the houses. I began to cry, filled with sorrow, because I knew the men would

615

catch and cage the tiger. Then I saw my arm was not hurt at all, it had already healed. I wept with pity, saying: The tiger is Saul, I don't want him to be caught, I want him to be running wild through the world. Then the dream, or the sleep, became quite thin, close to waking, yet not quite waking. I said to myself: I must write a play about Anna and Saul and the tiger. The part of my mind concerned with this play went on working, thinking about it, like a child moving bricks about a floor—a child, moreover, who has been forbidden to play, because she knew it was an evasion, making patterns of Anna and Saul and the tiger was an excuse not to think; the patterns of what Anna and Saul would do and say were shapes of pain, the 'story' of the play would be shaped by pain, and that was an evasion. Meanwhile, with the part of my mind which, I knew, was the disinterested personality who had saved me from disintegration, I began to control my sleep. This controlling person insisted that I must put aside the play about the tiger, must stop playing with the bricks. He said that instead of doing what I always do, making up stories about life, so as not to look at it straight, I should go back and look at scenes from my life. This looking back had a remarkable quality about it, like a shepherd counting sheep, or the rehearsal for a play, a quality of checking up, touching for reassurance. It was the same act as when I was a child and had bad nightmares every night: before I slept each night I lay awake, remembering everything in the day that had a quality of fear hidden in it; which might become part of a nightmare. I had to 'name' the frightening things, over and over, in a terrible litany; like a sort of disinfection by the conscious mind before I slept. But now, asleep, it was not making past events harmless, by naming them, but *making sure they were still there*. Yet I know that having made sure they were still there, I would have to 'name' them in a different way, and that was why the controlling personality was forcing me back. I revisited, first, the group under the eucalyptus trees at the Mashopi station in a wine-smelling moonlight, the patterns of leaves dark on white sand. But the terrible falsity of nostalgia had gone out of it; it was emotionless, and like a speeded-up film. Yet I had to watch

George Hounslow come stooping his broad shoulders up from the black lorry standing by the glinting railway lines under the stars, to look with his fearful hunger at Maryrose and at me; and to hear Willi hum tunelessly in my ear the bars from Brecht's opera; and to see Paul bend slightly towards us with his mocking courtesy, before he smiled and went off up to the block of bedrooms near the tumbling granite boulders. And then, following him, we were walking along the sandy track. He was standing waiting for us, facing us, smiling with a cool triumph, looking not at us, the group sauntering towards him in hot sunlight, but past us, towards the Mashopi Hotel. One after another we, too, stopped and turned to look. The hotel building seemed to have exploded in a dancing whirling cloud of white petals or wings, millions of white butterflies had chosen the building to alight on. It looked like a white flower opening slowly, under the deep steamy blue sky. Then a feeling of menace came into us, and we knew we had suffered a trick of sight, had been deluded. We were looking at the explosion of a hydrogen bomb, and a white flower unfolded under the blue sky in such a perfection of puffs, folds and eddying shapes that we could not move, although we knew we were menaced by it. It was unbelievably beautiful, the shape of death; and we stood watching in silence, until the silence was slowly invaded by a rustling, crawling, grating sound, and looking down we saw the grasshoppers, their gross tumbling fecundity inches deep, all around us. The invisible projectionist who was running this film now snapped the scene off, as if saying: 'That's enough, you know it's still there.' And immediately he began running a new part of the film. It was running slowly, because there was a technical hitch of some kind and several times he (the invisible projectionist) turned back the film so as to go through it again. The trouble was that the film was not clear, it had been shot badly. Two men, who were the same, yet separate, seemed to be fighting, in a silent duel of wills to be in the film. One was Paul Tanner, the man from the working-class, who had become a doctor, and whose quality of dry critical irony was what had sustained him in his struggle, the quality, however, which had fought with, and slowly defeated the idealism in him. The other was Michael, the refugee from Europe. When these two figures finally merged, a new person was created. I could see the moment, it was as if the shape of a human being, a mould already created to contain the personality of Michael, or Paul Tanner, swelled out and altered, as if a sculptor working from inside his material was changing the shape of his statue by pressing his own shoulders, his own thighs, against the substance that had been Paul, been Michael. This new person was larger in build, with the heroic quality of a statue, but above all, I could feel his strength. Then he spoke, and I could hear the thin sound of the real voice before it was swallowed or absorbed by the new strong voice: 'But my dear Anna, we are not the failures we think we are. We spend our lives fighting to get people very slightly less stupid than we are to accept truths that the great men have always known. They have always known, they have known for ten thousand years, that to lock a human being into solitary confinement can make a madman of him or an animal. They have always known that a poor man is frightened of the police and his landlord is a slave. They have always known that frightened people are cruel. They have always known that violence breeds violence. And we know it. But do the great masses of the world know it? No. It is our job to tell them. Because the great men can't be bothered. Their imaginations are already occupied with how to colonise Venus; they are already creating in their minds visions of a society full of free and noble human beings. Meanwhile, human beings are ten thousand years behind them, imprisoned in fear. The great men can't be bothered. And they are right. Because they know we are here, the boulder-pushers. They know we will go on pushing the boulder up the lower slopes of an immensely high mountain, while they stand on the top of the mountain, already free. All our lives, you and I, we will use all our energies, all our talents, into pushing that boulder another inch up the mountain. And they rely on us and they are right; and that is why we are not useless after all.' This voice faded; but already the film had changed. Now it was perfunctory. Scene after scene flicked on, then off; I knew this brief 'visiting' of the past was

618

so that I should be reminded I had still to work on it. Paul Tanner and Ella, Michael and Anna, Julia and Ella, Molly and Anna, Mother Sugar, Tommy, Richard, Dr West—these people appeared briefly, distorted with speed, and vanished again, and then the film broke off, or rather ran down, with a jarring dislocation. And the projectionist, in the silence that followed, remarked (and it was in a voice that struck me, because it was a new voice, rather jaunty, practical, jeering, a commonsensical voice): 'And what makes you think that the emphasis you have put on it is the correct emphasis?' The word *correct* had an echoing parodic twang. It was a jeer at the Marxist jargon-word *correct*. It also had a primness, like that of a schoolteacher. No sooner did I hear the word, correct, than I was attacked by a feeling of nausea, and I knew that feeling well—it was the nausea of being under strain, of trying to expand one's limits beyond what has been possible. Feeling sick, I listened to the voice saying: 'And what makes you think that the emphasis you have put on it is correct?' while he, the projectionist, began running the film through again, or rather, the films, for there were several, and I was able, as they flicked past me on the screen, to isolate and 'name' them. The Mashopi film; the film about Paul and Ella; the film about Michael and Anna; the film about Ella and Julia; the film about Anna and Molly. They were all, so I saw now, conventionally, well-made films, as if they had been done in a studio; then I saw the titles: these films, which were everything I hated most, had been directed by me. The projectionist kept running these films very fast, and then pausing on the credits, and I could hear his jeering laugh at *Directed by Anna Wulf*. Then he would run another few scenes, every scene glossy with untruth, false and stupid. I shouted at the projectionist: 'But they aren't mine, I didn't make them.' At which the projectionist, almost bored with confidence, let the scenes vanish, and he waited for me to prove him wrong. And now it was terrible, because I was faced with the burden of re-creating order out of the chaos that my life had become. Time had gone, and my memory did not exist, and I was unable to distinguish between what I had invented and what I had known, and I knew that what I had invented was all false. It was a whirl, an orderless dance, like the dance of the white butterflies in a shimmer of heat over the damp sandy vlei. The projectionist was still waiting, sardonic. What he was thinking got into my mind. He was thinking that the material had been ordered by me to fit what I knew, and that was why it was all false. Suddenly he said aloud: 'How would June Boothby see that time? I bet you can't do June Boothby.' At which my mind slipped into a gear foreign to me, and I began writing a story about June Boothby. I was unable to stop the flow of words, and I was in tears of frustration as I wrote in the style of the most insipid coy woman's magazine; but what was frightening was that the insipidity was due to a very slight alteration of my own style, a word here and there only: 'June, a just-sixteen-year-old, lay on the chaise lounge of the verandah, looking past the luxuriant foliage of the golden shower to the road. She knew something was going to happen. When her mother came into the room behind her and said: June, come and help me with the hotel dinner—June did not move. And her mother, after a pause, went out of the room without speaking. June was convinced that her mother *knew*, too. She thought: Dear Mum, you know how I feel. Then it happened. A lorry drew up in front of the hotel beside the petrol pumps, and *he* got out. June, without hurrying, sighed and stood up. Then, as if impelled by an outer power, she left the house and walked, on the path which her mother had used a few moments before, towards the hotel. The young man standing beside the petrol pumps seemed to be conscious of her approach. He turned. Their eyes met . . .' I heard the projectionist laughing. He was delighted because I could not prevent these words emerging, he was sadistically delighted. 'I told you,' he said, his hand already lifted to start the film again. 'I told you you couldn't do it.' I woke into the stuffy dark of the room, illuminated in three places by glowing fire. I was exhausted by the dreaming. Instantly I knew I had woken because Saul was in the flat. I could hear no movement but I could feel his presence. I even knew just where he was, standing a little beyond the door on the landing. I could see him, in a tense indecisive pose, plucking at his lips, wondering

620

whether to come in. I called: 'Saul, I'm awake.' He came in, and said in a jaunty false voice: 'Hi, I thought you were asleep.' I knew who had been the projectionist in my dream. I said: 'Do you know, you've become a sort of inner conscience or critic. I've just dreamed of you like that.' He gave me a long, cool, shrewd look, then said: 'If I've become your conscience, then it's a joke, you're certainly mine.' I said: 'Saul, we're very bad for each other.' He was on the point of saying: 'I may be bad for you, but you're good for me—' because on to his face came the consciously whimsical but arrogant look that was the mask that went with those words. I stopped him by saying: 'You're going to have to break it. I ought to, but I'm not strong enough. I realise you're much stronger than I am. I thought it was the other way around.'

I watched anger, dislike, suspicion, move over his face. He was watching me sideways, eyes narrowed. I knew that now he was going to fight, out of the personality that would hate me for taking something away from him. I also knew that when he was 'himself,' he would think about what I had said, and being responsible, he would, in fact, do what I asked.

Meanwhile he said, sullen: 'So you're kicking me out.'

I said: 'That's not what I said'—speaking to the responsible man.

He said: 'I don't toe your particular line so you're going to kick me out.'

Without knowing I was going to do it, I sat up and shrieked at him: 'For Christ's sake, stop it, stop it, stop it, stop it.' He ducked back, instinctively. I knew that for him a woman shrieking in hysteria meant that he would be hit. I thought how odd it was we two should be together at all, so close we should have become each other, for I had never hit anyone in my life. He even moved to the end of the bed, and sat ready to run off from a woman shrieking and hitting. I said, not shrieking, but crying: 'Can't you see that this is a cycle, we go around and around?' His face was dark with hostility, I knew he was going to fight against going. I turned away from him, wrestled down the sickness in my stomach, and said: 'Anyway, you'll go by yourself when Janet comes back.'

I hadn't known I was going to say it, or that I thought it. I lay thinking about it. Of course it was true.

'What do you mean?' he asked, interested, not hostile.

'If I had had a son, you'd have stayed. You'd have identified with him. At least for a time, till you worked yourself through that. But since I've got a girl you'll go because you'll see us as two women, two enemies.' He slowly nodded. I said: 'How odd, I'm always afflicted by feelings of doom, fate, inevitability. But it was chance I had a girl and not a boy. Just pure chance. So it's chance you'll leave. My life will be changed, completely, because of it.' I felt easier, less caged, holding on to chance. I said: 'How strange, having a baby is where women feel they are entering into some sort of inevitable destiny. But right in the heart of where we feel most bound is something that's just chance.' He was watching me, sideways, unhostile, with affection. I said: 'After all, no one in the world could make my having had a girl and not a boy into anything but chance. Imagine Saul, if I'd had a boy, we'd have had what you Yanks call a relationship. A long relationship. It might have turned into anything, who knows?'

He said quietly: 'Anna, do I really give you such a bad time?'

I said, with precisely his brand of sullenness—borrowed from him at a moment when he was not using it, so to speak, for now he was gentle and humorous: 'I haven't done time with the witch-doctors not to know that no one does anything to me, I do it to myself.'

'Leaving the witch-doctors out,' he said, putting his hand on my shoulder. He was smiling, concerned for me. For that moment he was all there, the good person. Yet already I could see behind his face the black power; it was coming back into his eyes. He was fighting with himself. I recognised that fight as the fight I had had while sleeping, to refuse entrance to alien personalities wanting to invade me. His fight got so bad he sat, eyes shut, sweat on his forehead. I took his hand, and he clutched at it, and he said: 'O.K. Anna, O.K. O.K. Don't worry. Trust me.' We sat on the bed, clutching at each other's hands. He wiped the sweat off his forehead, then kissed me, and said: 'Put on some jazz.'

I put on some early Armstrong. I sat on the floor. The great room was a world, with its glow of caged fire, and its shadows. Saul was lying on the bed, listening to the jazz, a look of pure contentment on his face.

Just then I couldn't 'remember' sick Anna. I knew she was there in the wings, waiting to walk on, when some button was touched—but that was all. We were silent a long time. I wondered, when we began to talk, which two people would be talking. I was thinking that if there were a tape recorder of the hours and hours of talk in that room, the talk and the fighting and the arguing and the sickness, it would be a record of a hundred different people living now, in various parts of the world, talking and crying out and questioning. I sat and wondered what person would start crying out when I began talking, and I said:

'I've been thinking.' This is already a joke when one of us says, 'I've been thinking.' He laughed and said: 'So you've been thinking.'

'If a person can be invaded by a personality who isn't theirs, why can't people—I mean people in the mass—be invaded by alien personalities.'

He lay, popping his lips to the jazz, plucking at an imaginary guitar. He didn't reply, merely grimaced, saying: I am listening.

'The joint is, comrade . . .' I stopped, hearing how I used the word, as we all do now, with an ironical nostalgia. I was thinking that it was first cousin to the jeering voice of the projectionist—it was an aspect of disbelief and destruction.

Saul said, laying aside his imaginary guitar: 'Well comrade, if you're saying that the masses are infected with emotions from outside, then I'm delighted, comrade, that you're holding fast to your socialist principles in spite of everything.'

He had used the words comrade and masses ironically, but now his voice switched to bitterness: 'So all we have to do, comrade, is to arrange that the masses are filled, like so many empty containers, with good useful pure kindly peaceful emotions, just the way we are.' He spoke well beyond

623

irony, not quite in the voice of the projectionist, but not far off it either.

I remarked: 'That's the sort of thing I say, that kind of mocking, but you hardly ever do.'

'As I crack up out of that 100 per cent revolutionary, I notice I crack up into aspects of everything I hate. That's because I've never lived with my eye on becoming what is known as mature. I've spent all my life, until recently, preparing myself for the moment when someone says: "Pick up that rifle"; or, "run that collective farm"; or, "organise that picket line." I always believed I'd be dead by the time I was thirty.'

'All young men believe they are going to be dead by the time they're thirty. They can't stand the compromise of ageing. And who am I to say they're not right?'

'I'm not *all* men. I'm Saul Green. No wonder I had to leave America. There's no one left who speaks my kind of language. What happened to them all—I used to know plenty once. We were all world-changers. Now I drive across my country, looking up my old friends, and they're all married or successful and having drunken private conversations with themselves because American *values* stink.'

I laughed because of the sullen way he said married. He looked up to see why I laughed, and he said: 'Oh yes, yes, I mean it. I'd walk into the fine new flat of an old friend, and I'd say: "Hey, what the hell do you mean by doing this job, you know it stinks, you know you're destroying yourself?" And he'd say: "But what about my wife and kids?" I'd say: "Is it true what I heard—that you'd turned informer on your old friends?" And he'd swallow another quick drink and say: "But Saul, there's my wife and the kids." Jesus, yes. And so I hate the wife and the kiddies, and I'm right to hate them. Yes, all right, laugh, what could be funnier than my kind of idealism—it's so old hat, it's so naïve! There's one thing you can't say to anyone any more, so it seems: You know in your heart of hearts you shouldn't be living like this. So, why do you? No, you can't say it, you're a prig ... what's the use of saying it, some kind of guts have gone out of people. I should have gone to Cuba earlier this year and joined Castro, and been killed.'

'Obviously not, since you didn't go.'

'Determination enters again, in spite of the chance you were saluting a moment ago.'

'If you really want to be killed, there are a dozen revolutions around you can get killed in.'

'I'm not fitted to live life as she is organised for us. Do you know what Anna? I'd give anything to go back to when I was in the gang of idealist kids on the street corner, believing we could change everything. That's the only time in my life I've been happy. Yes, all right, I know what you're going to say.'

So I said nothing. He lifted his head to look at me, and said: 'But obviously I want you to say it.'

So I said: 'All American men look back and hanker after when they were in the group of young men before they had pressure on them to be successful or get married. Whenever I meet an American man, I wait for the moment when his face really lights up—it's when he's talking about the group of buddies.'

'Thanks,' he said, sullen. 'That buttons up the strongest emotion I've ever felt and disposes of it.'

'That's what's wrong with us all. All our strongest emotions are buttoned up, one after another. For some reason, they're irrelevant to the time we live in. What's my strongest need—being with one man, love, all that. I've a real talent for it.' I heard my voice sullen, as his was, a moment before. I got up and went to the telephone.

'What are you doing?'

I rang Molly's number, and I said: 'I'm ringing Molly. She'll say: How's your American? I'll say: I'm having an affair with him. An affair—that's the word. I always did love that word, so sophisticated and debonair! Well, and she'll say: That's not the most sensible thing you ever did in your life? I'll say no. That'll button this one up. I want to hear her say it.' I stood listening to the telephone ringing in Molly's flat. 'I say now about five years of my life—that was when I loved a man who loved me. But of course I was very naïve in those days. Period. *That's* buttoned up. I say: Then I went

625

through a time when I was looking for men who would hurt me. I needed it. Period. *That's* buttoned up.' The telephone went on ringing. 'I was a communist for a time. On the whole, a mistake. A useful experience though, and one can never have too many of those. Period. That's buttoned up.' There was no reply from Molly's house, so I put my receiver down. 'So she'll have to say it another time,' I said.

'But it won't be true,' he said.

'Possibly not. But I'd like to hear it, all the same.'

A pause. 'What's going to happen to me, Anna?'

I said, listening to hear what I would say, to find out what I thought: 'You're going to fight your way through what you are in now. You'll become a very gentle, wise, kind man who people will come to when they need to be told that—they're crazy in a good cause.'

'Jesus, Anna!'

'You sound as if I'd insulted you!'

'Our old friend maturity again! Well, I'm not going to be bullied by *that* one.'

'Oh, but ripeness is all, surely?'

'No, it is not!'

'But my poor Saul, there's no help for you, you're heading straight for it. What about all those marvellous people we know, aged about fifty or sixty? Well, there *are* a few of them . . . marvellous, mature, wise people. *Real* people, the phrase is, radiating serenity. And how did they get to be that way? Well, *we* know, don't we? Every bloody one of them's got a history of emotional crime, oh the sad bleeding corpses that litter the road to maturity of the wise, serene man or woman of fifty-odd! You simply don't get to be wise, mature, etc., unless you've been a raving cannibal for thirty years or so.'

'I'm going right on being a cannibal.' He was laughing, but sullen.

'Oh no you're not. I can recognise a candidate for middle-aged serenity and ripeness a mile off. At thirty they are fighting mad, spitting fire and defiance and cutting sexual swathes in all directions. And I can see you now, Saul Green, living all strong and isolated from hand to mouth in some cold-water flat somewhere, sipping judiciously from time to

626

time at some fine old Scotch. Yes, I can see you, you'll have filled yourself out to your proper shape again. You'll be one of those tough, square, solid middle-aged men, like a shabbying brown bear, your golden crew-cut greying judiciously at the temples. And you'll probably have taken to spectacles, too. And you'll have taken up silence, it might even come naturally by then. I can even see a neat blond temperately-greying beard. They'll say: Know Saul Green? Now there's a man! What strength! What calm! What serenity! Mind you, from time to time one of the corpses will let out a small self-pitying bleat—*remember me?*'

'The corpses, I would have you know, are one and all on my side, and if you don't understand that, you understand nothing.'

'Oh I understand it, but it doesn't make it less depressing, the way the victims are always so willing to contribute their flesh and blood.'

'Depressing! I'm good for people, Anna. I wake them up and shake them and push them on their proper way.'

'Nonsense. The people who are oh so willing to be victims are those who've given up being cannibals themselves, they're not tough or ruthless enough for the golden road to maturity and the ever-so-wise shrug. They know they've given up. What they are really saying is: *I've* given up, but I'll be happy to contribute my flesh and blood to you.'

'Crunch, crunch, crunch,' he said, his face clenched up so that his blond eyebrows met in a hard line across his brow, and his teeth showed, grinning angrily.

'Crunch, crunch, crunch,' I said.

'You, I take it, not being a cannibal?'

'Oh yes indeed. But I've dished out aid and comfort too, from time to time. No, I'm not for sainthood, I'm going to be a boulder-pusher.'

'What's that?'

'There's a great black mountain. It's human stupidity. There are a group of people who push a boulder up the mountain. When they've got a few feet up, there's a war, or the wrong sort of revolution, and the boulder rolls down—not to the bottom, it always manages to end a few inches higher than

627

when it started. So the group of people put their shoulders to the boulder and start pushing again. Meanwhile, at the top of the mountain stand a few great men. Sometimes they look down and nod and say: Good, the boulder-pushers are still on duty. But meanwhile we are meditating about the nature of space, or what it will be like when the world is full of people who don't hate and fear and murder.'

'Hmm. Well I want to be one of the great men on top of the mountain.'

'Bad luck for both of us, we are both boulder-pushers.'

'And suddenly he leaped up and off the bed, like a black steel spring snapping, and stood, the hatred behind his eyes, as sudden as if switched on, and said: 'Oh no, you don't, oh no, I'm not going to . . . I'm not . . . I, I, I.' I thought, Well, so *he's* back, is he. I went to the kitchen, got a bottle of Scotch, came back, lay on the floor, and drank the Scotch, while he talked. I lay on the floor, looking at the patterns of gold light on the ceiling, hearing the irregular pattering of big rain outside, and felt the tension lay hands on my stomach. Sick Anna was back. I, I, I, I, like a machine-gun ejaculating regularly. I was listening and not listening, as if to a speech I had written someone else was delivering. Yes, that was me, that was everyone, the I. I. I. I am. I am. I am going to. I won't be. I shall. I want. I. He was walking around the room like an animal, a talking animal, his movements violent and charged with energy a hard force that spat out I, Saul, Saul, I, I want. His green eyes were fixed, not seeing, his mouth, like a spoon or a spade or a machine-gun, shot out, spewed out, hot aggressive language, words like bullets. 'I'm not going to be destroyed by you. By anyone. I'm not going to be shut up, caged, tamed, told be quiet keep your place do as you're told I'm not . . . I'm saying what I think, I don't buy your world.' I could feel the violence of his black power attack every nerve in me. I felt my stomach muscles churning, my back muscles tense as wires. I lay with the bottle of Scotch in my hand, sipping it steadily, feeling the drunkenness take hold, listening, listening . . . I realised I had been lying there a long time, hours perhaps, while Saul stalked and shouted. Once or twice I said something, threw words against his stream of talk, and it was if a machine, tuned or set by a mechanic to stop briefly at a sound from outside, stopped, checked itself mechanically, mouth, or metal opening already in position to ejaculate the next stream of I I I I I I. I once got up, not really seen by him, for he was not seeing me, except as an enemy he had to shout down, and I put on Armstrong, partly for myself, clutching close as a comforter the pure genial music, and I said: 'Listen Saul, listen.' He frowned slightly, his brows twitching, and said mechanically: 'Yeah? What?' Then I I I I I I, I'm going to show you all with your morality and your love and your laws, I I I I. So I took off the Armstrong, and put on his music, cool and cerebral, the detached music for men who refuse the madness and the passion, and for a moment he stopped, then sat, as if the muscles of his thighs had been cut, he sat, his head on his breast, eyes shut, listening to the soft machine-gun drumming of Hamilton, the drumming that filled the room as his words had, then he said, in his own voice: 'My God, what we've lost, what we've lost, what we've lost, how can we ever get back to it, how can we get back to it again? And then, as if this had not happened, I could see how the muscles of his thighs tensed and jerked him up and I switched off the machine, since he was not listening, except to his own words, I I I, and lay down again and listened to the words spattering against the walls and ricochetting everywhere, I I I, the naked ego. I was so sick, I was clenched up into a ball of painful muscles, while the bullets flew and spattered, and for a moment I blacked out and revisited my nightmare where I knew, but really knew, how war waited, me running down the emptied street of white dirtied buildings in a silent city but filled with human beings silent with waiting, while somewhere close the small, ugly container of death exploded, soft, soft, it exploded into the waiting silence, spread death, crumbling the buildings, breaking the substance of life, disintegrating the structure of flesh, while I screamed, soundless, no one hearing, just as all the other human beings in the silent buildings screamed, no one hearing. When I came out of the blackout, Saul was standing against the wall, pressing against it with his back, the muscles of his thighs and back gripping the wall, looking at me. He had seen me. He was back again, for the first time in hours. His face was white, blood-drained, his eyes grey and strained and full of horror because I was lying there screwed up with pain. He said, in his own voice: 'Anna, for God's sake, don't look like that,' but then a hesitation, and back came the madman, for now it was not only I I I I, but I against women. Women the jailors, the consciences, the voice of society, and he was directing a pure stream of hatred against me, for being a woman. And now the whisky had weakened me and soddened me, and I felt in myself the weak soft sodden emotion, the woman betrayed. Oh boohoo, you don't love me, you don't love, men don't love women any more. Oh boohoo, and my dainty pink-tipped forefinger pointed at my white, pink-tipped betrayed bosom, and I began to weep weak, sodden whisky-diluted tears on behalf of womankind. As I wept I saw his prick stand up under his jeans, and I got wet, and I thought, derisive, oh so now he's going to love me, he's going to love poor betrayed Anna and her wounded white bosom. Then he said in the scandalised little voice of a schoolboy, a prig, 'Anna, you're drunk, get off the floor.' And I said, 'I won't,' weeping, luxuriating in the weakness. So he dragged me up, scandalised and lustful, and came into me, very big but like a schoolboy, making love to his first woman, too quick, full of shame and heat. And then I said, being unsatisfied: 'Now be your age,' using his language, and he said, scandalised: 'Anna you're drunk, now sleep it off.' So he covered me and kissed me, went tiptoeing out, like a guilty schoolboy proud of his first lay, and I saw him, I saw Saul Green, the good American boy, sentimental and ashamed, having laid his first woman. And I lay and I laughed, and I laughed. Then I slept and woke laughing. I don't know what I had been dreaming, but I woke out of pure light-heartedness, and then I saw he was beside me.

He was cold, so I held him in my arms, full of happiness. I knew, because of the quality of my happiness, that I must have been flying easily and joyfully in my sleep, and that meant I would not always be sick Anna. But when he woke he was exhausted from the hours of I I I I, and his face was yellow and agonised, and when we got out of bed we were both exhausted, and we drank coffee and read the newspapers silent, unable to say anything, in the big, brightly coloured kitchen. He said: 'I ought to work.' But we knew we would not; and we went back to bed, too tired to move, and I even wished the Saul back from the night before, full of black murderous energy, it was so frightening to be so exhausted. Then he said: 'I can't lie here.' And I said: 'No.' But we didn't move. Then he got, or crawled, out of bed. And I thought: How is he going to get himself out of here, he's got to get steam up to do it. And though the tension in my stomach told me, I was even interested to see. He said, challenging: 'I'm going for a walk.' I said: 'All right.' He gave me a furtive look and went out to dress and then came back. He said: 'Why don't you stop me?' And I said: 'Because I don't want to.' And he said: 'If you knew where I was going, you'd stop me.' And I said, hearing my voice harden: 'Oh, I know you're going to a woman.' And he said: 'Well, you'll never know, will you?'

'No, and it doesn't matter.'

He had been standing at the door, but now came into the room, hesitating. He had an air of being interested.

I remembered De Silva's: 'I wanted to see what would happen.'

Saul wanted to see what would happen. And so did I. I could feel in myself, stronger than anything else, a spiteful, positively joyous interest—as if he, Saul and I were two unknown quantities, two forces anonymous, without personality. It was as if the room held two totally malignant beings who, if the other suddenly fell dead or began screaming with pain, would say: 'Well, so that's it, is it?'

'It doesn't matter,' he said, now sullen, but in a kind of tentative sullenness, a rehearsal for sullenness, or a repetition of it too old for conviction. 'It doesn't matter, you say, but you watch every movement I make like a spy.'

I said, in a jaunty jolly voice, accompanying it with a laugh, like a weak ebbing gasp (a laugh I've heard from women under acute stress and which I was copying): 'I'm a spy because you make me one.' He stood silent, but looked as if he were listening, as if the words he must say next would

631

be fed to him from a play-back: 'I'm not going to be corralled by any dame in the world. I've never been yet and I never shall.'

The 'I've never been yet and I never shall' came out in a hastening rush, as if a record had been speeded up.

And I said, in the same murderously jolly malicious voice: 'If you mean by being corralled, that your woman should know every move you make, then you're corralled now.'

And I heard myself letting out the expiring, weak, yet triumphant laugh.

'That's what you think,' he said, malignant.

'That's what I know.'

The dialogue had run itself out, and now we looked at each other, interested, and I said: 'Well we'll never have to say that again.' And he said, interested: 'I should hope not.' With which he went out, in a rush, driven by the energy from this exchange.

I stood and thought: I can find out the truth by going upstairs and looking at his diary. But I knew I would not, and that I never would again. All that was finished. But I was very ill. I went to the kitchen for coffee, but measured myself a small measure of Scotch. I looked at the kitchen, very bright, very clean. Then vertigo attacked me. The colours were too bright, as if they were hot. And I became conscious of all the faults of the kitchen which usually gives me pleasure—a crack in glistening white enamel, dust on a rail, the paint beginning to discolour. I was overwhelmed with a feeling of cheapness and nastiness. The kitchen should all be painted again, but nothing would change the flat's being so old and the walls decaying in a decaying house. I switched off the lights in the kitchen and came back into this room. But soon it seemed as bad as the kitchen. The red curtains had an ominous yet tawdry gleam, and the white of the walls was tarnished. I found I was walking around and around the room, staring at the walls, curtains, the door, repelled by the physical substance of which the room was made, while colours attacked me by their hot unreality. I was looking at

632

the room as I might look at the face of someone I know very well, for the marks of strain or tension. At my own, or Saul's for instance, knowing what is behind my neat, composed little face, what is behind Saul's broad, open, blond face, that looks ill, admittedly, but who would guess, who had not experienced it, the explosion of possibilities that deploy through his mind? Or at the face of a woman on a train, when I can see from a tense brow or a knot of pain that a world of disorder lies hidden there and marvel at the power of human beings to hold themselves together under pressure. My big room, like the kitchen, had become, not the comfortable shell which held me, but an insistent attack on my attention from a hundred different points, as if a hundred enemies were waiting for my attention to be deflected so that they might creep up behind me and attack me. A door-knob that needed polishing, a trace of dust across white paint, a yellowish streak where the red of the curtains had faded, the table where my old notebooks lie concealed—these assaulted me, claimed me, with hot waves of rocking nausea. I knew I had to get to the bed, and again I had to crawl across the floor to reach it. I lay on the bed and I knew before I fell asleep that the projectionist was in wait for me.

I also knew what I was going to be told. Knowing was an 'illumination.' During the last weeks of craziness and time-lessness I've had these moments of 'knowing' one after the other, yet there is no way of putting this sort of knowledge into words. Yet these moments have been so powerful, like the rapid illuminations of a dream that remain with one waking, that what I have learned will be part of how I experience life until I die. Words. Words. I play with words, hoping that some combination, even a chance combination, will say what I want. Perhaps better with music? But music attacks my inner ear like an antagonist, it's not my world. The fact is, the real experience can't be described. I think, bitterly, that a row of asterisks, like an old-fashioned novel, might be better. Or a symbol of some kind, a circle perhaps, or a square. Anything at all, but not words. The people who have been there, in the place in themselves where words, patterns, order, dissolve, will know what I mean and

633

the others won't. But once having been there, there's a
terrible irony, a terrible shrug of the shoulders, and it's not a
question of fighting it, or disowning it, or of right or wrong,
but simply knowing it is there, always. It's a question of
bowing to it, so to speak, with a kind of courtesy, as to an
ancient enemy: All right, I know you are there, but we have
to preserve the forms, don't we? And perhaps the condition
of your existing at all is precisely that we preserve the forms,
create the patterns—have you thought of that?

So all I can say is that before going to sleep I 'understood'
why I had to sleep, and what the projectionist would say, and
what I would have to learn. Though I knew it already; so
that the dreaming itself already had the quality of words
spoken after the event, or a summing-up, for emphasis' sake,
of something learned.

As soon as the dream came on, the projectionist said, in
Saul's voice, very practical: 'And now we'll just run through
them again.' I was embarrassed, because I was afraid I'd see
the same set of films I had seen before—glossy and unreal.
But this time, while they were the same films, they had
another quality, which in the dream I named 'realistic'; they
had a rough, crude, rather jerky quality of an early Russian or
German film. Patches of the film slowed down for long, long
stretches while I watched, absorbed, details I had not had
time to notice in life. The projectionist kept saying, when I
had got some point he wanted me to get: 'That's it lady, that's
it.' And because of his directing me, I watched even more
emphasis, or to which the pattern of my life had given
emphasis, were now slipping past, fast and unimportant. The
group under the gum-trees, for instance, or Ella lying in the
grass with Paul, or Ella writing novels, or Ella wanting death
in the aeroplane, or the pigeons falling to Paul's rifle—all
these had gone, been absorbed, had given place to what was
really important. So that I watched, for an immense time,
noting every movement, how Mrs Boothby stood in the
kitchen of the hotel at Mashopi, her stout buttocks projecting
like a shelf under the pressure of her corsets, patches of
sweat dark under her armpits, her face flushed with distress,
while she cut cold meat off various joints of animal and fowl,

and listened to the young cruel voices and crueller laughter through a thin wall. Or I heard Willi's humming, just behind my ear, the tuneless, desperately lonely humming; or watched him in slow motion, over and over again, so that I could never forget it, look long and hurt at me when I flirted with Paul. Or I saw Mr Boothby, the portly man behind the bar, look at his daughter with her young man. I saw his envious, but un-bitter gaze at this youth, before he turned away his eyes, and stretched out his hand to take an empty glass and fill it. And I saw Mr Lattimer, drinking in the bar, carefully not-looking at Mr Boothby, while he listened to his beautiful red-haired wife's laughter. I saw him, again and again, bend down, shaky with drunkenness, to stroke the feathery red dog, stroking it, stroking it. 'Get it?' said the projectionist, and ran another scene. I saw Paul Tanner coming home in the early morning, brisk and efficient with guilt, saw him meet his wife's eyes, as she stood in front of him in a flowered apron, rather embarrassed and pleading, while the children ate their breakfast before going off to school. Then he turned, frowning, and went upstairs to lift a clean shirt down from a shelf. 'Get it?' said the projectionist. Then the film went very fast, it flicked fast, like a dream, on faces I've seen once in the street, and have forgotten, on the slow movement of an arm, on the movement of a pair of eyes, all saying the same thing—the film was now beyond my experience, beyond Ella's, beyond the noteboks, because there was a fusion; and instead of seeing separate scenes, people, faces, movements, glances, they were all together. The film became immensely slow again, it became a series of moments where a peasant's hand bent to drop seed into earth, or a rock stood glistening while water slowly wore it down, or a man stood on a dry hillside in the moonlight, stood eternally, his rifle ready on his arm. Or a woman lay awake in darkness, saying No, I won't kill myself, I won't, I won't.

The projectionist now being silent, I called to him, It's enough, and he didn't answer, so I leaned out my own hand to switch off the machine. Still asleep, I read the words off a page I had written: That was about courage, but not the sort of courage I have ever understood. It's a small painful sort of courage which is at the root of every life, because injustice and cruelty is at the root of life. And the reason why I have only given my attention to the heroic or the beautiful or the intelligent is because I won't accept that injustice and the cruelty, and so won't accept the small endurance that is bigger than anything.

I looked at these words which I had written, and of which I felt critical; and then I took them to Mother Sugar. I said to her: 'We're back at the blade of grass again, that will press up through the bits of rusted steel a thousand years after the bombs have exploded and the world's crust has melted. Because the force of will in the blade of grass is the same as the small painful endurance. Is that it?' (I was smiling sardonically in my dream, wary of a trap.)

'And so?' she said.

'But the point is, I don't think I'm prepared to give all that much reverence to that damned blade of grass, even now.'

At which she smiled, sitting in her chair four-square and upright, rather bad-tempered because of my slowness, because I so invariably missed the point. Yes, she looked like an impatient housewife who has mislaid something or who is going to be out with her time-table.

Then I woke into a late afternoon, the room cold and dark. I was depressed; I was entirely the white female bosom shot full of cruel male arrows. I was aching with the need for Saul, and I wanted to abuse him and rail at him and call him names. Then of course he would say: Oh poor Anna, I'm sorry, then we would make love.

A short story: or a short novel: comic and ironic: A woman, appalled by her capacity for surrendering herself to a man, determines to free herself. She determinedly takes two lovers, sleeping with them on alternate nights—the moment of freedom being when she would be able to say to herself that she has enjoyed them both equally. The two men become instinctively aware of each other's existence; one, jealous, falls in love with her seriously; the other becomes cool and guarded. In spite of all her determination, she cannot prevent herself loving the man who has fallen in love with her; freezing up with the man who is guarded. Nevertheless, although she is in despair that she is as 'unfree' as ever, she announces to both men that she has now become thoroughly emancipated, she has at last achieved the ideal of full sexual and emotional pleasure with two men at once. The cool and guarded man is interested to hear it, makes detached and intelligent remarks about female emancipation. The man she is in fact in love with, hurt and appalled, leaves her. She is left with the man she does not love and who does not love her, exchanging intelligent psychological conversation.

The idea for this story intrigued me, and I began thinking how it should be written. How, for instance, would it change if I used Ella instead of myself? I had not thought about Ella for some time, and I realised that of course she had changed in the interval; she would have become more defensive, for instance. I saw her with her hair altered—she would be tying it back again, looking severe; she would be wearing different clothes. I was watching Ella moving about my room; and then I began imagining how she would be with Saul—much more intelligent, I think, than I, cooler, for instance. After a while I realised I was doing what I had done before, creating 'the third'—the woman altogether better than I was. For I could positively mark the point where Ella left reality, left how she would, in fact, behave because of her nature; and move into a large generosity of personality impossible to her. But I didn't dislike this new person I was creating; I was thinking that quite possibly these marvellous, generous things we walk side by side with in our imaginations could come in existence, simply because we need them, because we imagine them. Then I began to laugh because of the distance between what I was imagining and what in fact I was, let alone what Ella was.

I heard Saul's feet coming up the stairs, and I was interested to know who would come in. As soon as I saw him, although he looked ill and tired, I knew the devils would not be in my room that day; and perhaps never again, because I also knew what he planned to say.

He sat on the edge of my bed and said: 'It's funny that

637

you should have been laughing. I was thinking about you while I was walking around.'

I saw how he had been walking through the streets, walking through the chaos of his imagination, clutching at ideas or sets of words to save him. I said: 'Well, what were you thinking?'—waiting for the pedagogue to speak.

'Why are you laughing?'

'Because you've been rushing about a crazy city, making sets of moral axioms to save us both with, like mottoes out of Christmas crackers.'

He said drily: 'It's a pity you know me so well. I thought I was going to astonish you with my self-control and brilliance. Yes, I suppose mottoes out of Christmas crackers is just.'

'Well, let's have them.'

'In the first place, you don't laugh enough Anna. I've been thinking. Girls laugh. Old women laugh. Women of your age don't laugh, you're all too damned occupied with the serious business of living.'

'But I was in fact laughing my head off—I was laughing about free women.' I told him the plot of my short story, he sat listening, smiling wryly. Then he said: 'That's not what I meant, I meant really laughing.'

'I'll put it on my agenda.'

'No, don't say it like that. Listen Anna, if we don't believe the things we put on our agendas will come true for us, then there's no hope for us. We're going to be saved by what we seriously put on our agendas.'

'We've got to believe in our blueprints?'

'We've got to believe in our beautiful impossible blueprints.'

'Right. What next?'

'Secondly, you can't go on like this, you've got to start writing again.'

'Obviously if I could, I would.'

'No, Anna, that's not good enough. Why don't you write that short story you've just told me about? No, I don't want all that hokum you usually give me—tell me, in one simple sentence, why not. You can call it Christmas cracker mottoes if you like, but while I was walking about I was thinking that if you could simplify it in your mind, boil it all down to something, then you could take a good long look at it and beat it.'

I began to laugh, but he said: 'No, Anna, you're going to really crack up unless you do.'

'Very well then. I can't write that short story or any other, because at that moment I sit down to write, someone comes into the room, looks over my shoulders, and stops me.'

'Who? Do you know?'

'Of course I know. It could be a Chinese peasant. Or one of Castro's guerrilla fighters. Or an Algerian fighting in the F.L.N. Or Mr Mathlong. They stand here in the room and they say, why aren't you doing something about us, instead of wasting your time scribbling?'

'You know very well that's not what any of them would say.'

'No. But *you* know quite well what I mean. I know you do. It's the curse of all of us.'

'Yes, I do know. But Anna, I'm going to force you into writing. Take up a piece of paper and a pencil.'

I laid a sheet of clean paper on the table, picked up a pencil and waited.

'It doesn't matter if you fail. Why are you so arrogant? Just begin.'

My mind went blank in a sort of panic. I laid down the pencil. I saw him staring at me, willing me, forcing me—I picked up the pencil again.

'I'm going to give you the first sentence then. There are the two women you are, Anna. Write down: The two women were alone in the London flat.'

'You want me to begin a novel with The two women were alone in the London flat?'

'Why say it like that? Write it, Anna.'

I wrote it.

'You're going to write that book, you're going to write it, you're going to finish it.'

I said: 'Why is it so important to you that I should?'

'Ah,' he said, in self-mocking despair. 'A good question. Well, because if you can do it, then I can.'

639

'You want me to give you the first sentence of your novel?'

'Let's hear it.'

'On a dry hillside in Algeria, the soldier watched the moonlight glinting on his rifle.'

He smiled. 'I could write that, you couldn't.'

'Then write it.'

'On condition you give me your new notebook.'

'Why?'

'I need it. That's all.'

'All right.'

'I'm going to have to leave, Anna, you know that?'

'Yes.'

'Then cook for me. I never thought I'd say to a woman, cook for me. I regard the fact that I can say it at all as a small step towards what they refer to as being mature.'

I cooked and we slept. This morning I woke first and his face, sleeping, was ill and thin. I thought it was impossible he should go, I couldn't let him, he was in no state to go.

He woke, and I was fighting the desire to say: You can't go. I must look after you. I'll do anything if only you'll say you'll stay with me.

I knew he was fighting his own weakness. I was wondering what would have happened if, all those weeks ago, he had not put up his arms around my neck unconsciously, in his sleep. I wanted, then, for him to put his arms up around my neck. I lay, fighting not to touch him, as he was fighting not to appeal to me, and I was thinking how extraordinary that an act of kindness, of pity, could be such a betrayal. My brain blacked out with exhaustion, and while it did, the pain of pity took me over and I cradled him in my arms, knowing it was a betrayal. He clung to me, immediately, for a second of genuine closeness. Then, at once, my falseness created his, for he murmured, in a child's voice: 'Ise a good boy,' not as he had ever whispered to his own mother, for those words could never have been his, they were out of literature. And he murmured them mawkishly, in parody. But not quite. Yet as I looked down at him, I saw his sharp ill face show first the sentimental falseness that went with the words; then a grimace of pain; then, seeing me look down, in horror, his grey eyes narrowed into a pure hating challenge, and we looked at each other helpless with our mutual shame and humiliation. Then his face relaxed. For a few seconds he slept, blacked out, as I had blacked out the moment before, just before I had bent to put my arms around him. Then he jerked himself out of sleep, all tenseness and fight, jerked himself out of my arms, glancing alert and efficient around the room for enemies, then stood up; all in one movement, so fast did these reactions follow each other.

He said: 'We can't either of us ever go lower than that.'

I said: 'No.'

'Well *that's* played out,' he said.

'Buttoned up and finished,' I said.

He went up to pack his few things into his bag and cases.

He came down again soon and leaned against the door of my big room. He was Saul Green. I saw Saul Green, the man who had walked into my flat some weeks before. He was wearing the new close-fitting clothes that he had bought to clothe his thinness. He was a neat, smallish man with over-big shoulders and the bones of a too-thin face standing out, insisting that this was a stocky, strong-fleshed body, that this would again be a strong, broad-shouldered man when he had worked through his illness into health. I could see standing beside the small, thin, fair man, with his soft brush of blond hair, his sick yellow face, a strong sturdy brown-fleshed man, like a shadow that would absorb the body that cast it. Meanwhile he looked stripped for action, pared down, light on his feet, wary. He stood, thumbs hooked in his belt, fingers arrowing down (but now it was like a gallant parody of a rake's stance) and he was sardonically challenging, his cool grey eyes on guard, but friendly enough. I felt towards him as if he were my brother, as if, like a brother, it wouldn't matter how we strayed from each other, how far apart we were, we would always be flesh of one flesh, and think each other's thoughts.

He said: 'Write the first sentence for me in the book.'

'You want me to write it for you?'

'Yes, write it down.'

'Why?'

'You're part of the team.'

'I don't feel that. I hate teams.'

'You think about it then. There are a few of us around in the world, we rely on each other even though we don't know each other's names. But we rely on each other all the time. We're a team, we're the ones who haven't given in, who'll go on fighting. I tell you, Anna, sometimes I pick up a book and I say: Well, so you've written it first, have you? Good for you. O.K., then I won't have to write it.'

'All right, I'll write your first sentence for you.'

'Good. Write it, and I'll come back and get the book and say good-bye and I'll be on my way.'

'Where are you going?'

'You know quite well I don't know.'

'Sometime you're going to have to know.'

'All right, all right, but I'm not mature yet, have you forgotten?'

'Perhaps you'd better go back to America.'

'Why not? Love's the same the world over.'

I laughed, and I went to the pretty new notebook, while he went off downstairs, and I wrote: 'On a dry hillside in Algeria, a soldier watched the moonlight glinting on his rifle.'

[Here Anna's handwriting ended, the golden notebook continued in Saul Green's handwriting, a short novel about the Algerian soldier. This soldier was a farmer who was aware that what he felt about life was not what he was expected to feel. By whom? By an invisible *they*, who might be God, or the State, or Law, or Order. He was captured, tortured by the French, escaped, rejoined the F.L.N., and found himself torturing, under orders to do so, French prisoners. He knew that he should feel something about this that he did not in fact feel. He discussed his state of mind late one night with one of the French prisoners whom he had tortured. The French prisoner was a young intellectual, a student of philosophy. This young man (the two men were talking secretly in the prisoner's cell) complained that he was in an intellectual prison-house. He recognised, had recognised

642

for years, that he never had a thought, or an emotion, that didn't instantly fall into pigeon-holes, one marked 'Marx' and one marked 'Freud.' His thoughts and emotions were like marbles rolling into predetermined slots, he complained. The young Algerian soldier found this interesting, he didn't find that at all, he said, what troubled him—though of course it didn't really trouble him, and he felt it should—was that nothing he thought or felt was what was expected of him. The Algerian soldier said he envied the Frenchman—or rather, he felt he *ought* to be envying him. While the French student said he envied the Algerian from the bottom of his heart: he wished that just once, just once in his life, he felt or thought something that was his own, spontaneous, undirected, not willed on him by Grandfathers Freud and Marx. The voices of the two young men had risen more than was wise, particularly that of the French student, crying out against his situation. The Commanding Officer came in, found the Algerian talking, like a brother, with the prisoner he was supposed to be guarding. The Algerian soldier said: 'Sir, I did what I was ordered: I tortured this man. You did not tell me I should not talk with him.' The Commanding Officer decided that his man was some sort of a spy, probably recruited while he had been a prisoner. He ordered him to be shot. The Algerian soldier and the French student were shot together, on the hillside, with the rising sun in their faces, side by side, the next morning.]

[This short novel was later published and did rather well.]

■ FREE WOMEN: 5 ■

■ FREE WOMEN: 5 ■

Molly gets married and Anna has an affair

WHEN Janet first asked her mother if she could go to boarding-school, Anna was reluctant. She hated everything boarding-schools stood for. Having made enquiries about various 'progressive' schools, she talked to Janet again; but meanwhile the little girl had brought home a friend of hers, already at a conventional boarding-school, to help persuade her mother. The two children, bright-eyed and apprehensive that Anna might refuse, chattered about uniforms, dormitories, school outings and so on; and Anna understood that a 'progressive' school was just what Janet did not want. She was saying, in fact, 'I want to be ordinary, I don't want to be like you.' She had taken a look at the world of disorder, experiment, where people lived from day to day, like balls perpetually jigging on the top of jets of prancing water; keeping themselves open for any new feeling or adventure, and had decided it was not for her. Anna said: 'Janet, do you realise how different it will be from anything you've ever known? It means going for walks in crocodiles, like soldiers, and looking like everyone else, and doing things regularly at certain times. If you're not careful you're going to come out of it like a processed pea, just like everyone else.' 'Yes, I know,' said the thirteen-year-old, smiling. The smile said: I know you hate all that, but why should I? 'It will be a conflict for you.' 'I don't think it will,' said Janet, suddenly sullen, reacting away from the idea that she could ever accept her mother's way of life enough to be in conflict over it.

Anna understood, when Janet had gone to school, how much she had depended on the discipline which having a child had enforced on her—getting up at a certain time in the

647

morning, going to bed soon enough not to be tired because of having to get up early, arranging regular meals, organising her moods so as not to upset the child.

She was alone in the enormous flat. She should move to a smaller one. She did not want to let rooms again, the idea of another experience like the one with Ronnie and Ivor frightened her. And it frightened her that it frightened her—what was happening to her, that she shrank from the complications of people, shrank from being involved? It was a betrayal of what she felt she ought to be. She compromised: she would stay in the flat another year; she would let a room; she would look around for a suitable job.

Everything seemed to have changed. Janet was gone. Marion and Tommy, paid for by Richard, went off to Sicily, taking with them a large number of books on Africa. They intended to visit Dolci, to find out if they could, as Marion put it, 'be of any help to the poor thing. Do you know Anna, I keep a photograph of him on my desk all the time?'

Molly was also alone in an empty house, having lost her son to her ex-husband's second wife. She invited Richard's sons to stay with her. Richard was delighted, although he still blamed Molly's life for his son's blindness. Molly entertained the boys while Richard went to Canada with his secretary to arrange the financing of three new steel mills. This trip was something like a honeymoon, since Marion had now agreed to a divorce.

Anna discovered she was spending most of her time doing nothing at all; and decided the remedy for her condition was a man. She prescribed this for herself like a medicine.

She was telephoned by a friend of Molly's she had no time for, because she was busy with Richard's sons. This man was Nelson, an American script-writer whom she had met at Molly's, and sometimes had dinner with.

When he rang Anna he said: 'I must warn you against seeing me at all. I'm in danger of finding my wife impossible for the third time.'

At dinner they talked mostly about politics. 'The difference between a red in Europe and a red in America is that in Europe a red is a communist; but in America he is a man who has never taken out a Party card out of caution or cowardice. In Europe you have communists and fellow-travellers. In America you have communists and ex-reds. I—and I insist on the difference, was a red. I don't want to get into any more trouble than I am in already. Well now I've defined my position, will you take me home with you tonight?'

Anna was thinking: There's only one real sin, and that is to persuade oneself that the second-best is anything but the second-best. What's the use of always hankering after Michael?

So she spent the night with Nelson. He was, as she soon understood, in bad sexual trouble; she conspired with him, out of chivalry, in pretending there was nothing seriously wrong. They parted in the morning with friendship. Then she found herself weeping, in a low helpless depression. She told herself that the cure for this was not to sit alone, but to ring up one of her men friends. She did nothing of the sort, she was unable to face seeing anyone, let alone another 'affair.'

Anna found that she was spending her time in a curious way. She had always read newspapers, journals, magazines in large quantities; she suffered from the vice of her kind, that she *had* to know what was going on everywhere. But now, having woken late, and drunk coffee, she would sit on the floor of the big room, surrounded by half a dozen daily newspapers, a dozen weekly journals, reading them, slowly, over and over again. She was trying to fit things together. Whereas, before, her reading had been to form a picture of what was taking place all over the world, now a form of order familiar to her had disappeared. It seemed as if her mind had become an area of differing balances, she was balancing facts, events, against each other. It was not a question of a sequence of events, with their probable consequences. It was as if she, Anna, were a central point of awareness, being attacked by a million unco-ordinated facts, and the central point would disappear if she proved unable to weigh and balance the facts, take them all into account. Thus, she would find herself staring at the statement: 'The ignition hazard from the thermal radiation of 10 M.T. surface burst will extend over a circle of about 25 miles in radius. A fire circle of 25 miles radius encompasses an area of 1,900 square miles and if the weapon detonates near the intended aiming point, will include the most densely populated sections of the target complex which means that under certain clear atmospheric conditions everyone and everything within this tremendous area would probably be subject to a grave thermal hazard and many consumed in the holocaust,'— and now it was not the words that were terrible but that she could not make what they said match imaginatively with: 'I am a person who continually destroys the possibilities of a future because of the numbers of alternative viewpoints I can focus on the present.' So that she would stare at these two sets of words, until the words themselves seemed to detach themselves from the page and slide away, as if they had detached themselves from their own meaning. Yet the meaning remained, unconfirmed by the words, and probably more terrible (though she did not know why) because the words had failed to confine it. And so, having been defeated by these two sets of words, she would put them aside and turn her attention to another set: 'It is too little realised in Europe that there is no *status quo* in Africa as it is at present ordered.' 'Formality, I think (not, as Mr Smith suggests, a neo-neo-romanticism), may be the coming mode.' So that she was spending hours sitting on the floor, all her attention focused on selected fragments of print. Soon a new activity began. She carefully cut out the patches of print from newspapers and journals and stuck them on the walls with drawing-pins. The white walls of the big room were covered all over with large and small cuttings from papers. She walked carefully around the walls, looking at the statements pinned there. When she ran out of drawing-pins, she told herself it was stupid to go on with a meaningless occupation; yet she put on a coat, went down to the street, and bought two boxes of drawing-pins and methodically attached the still unanchored fragments of print to the walls. But the newspapers piled up, landing on her door-mat every morning in a great thick pack of print, and every morning she sat, fighting to order this new supply of material—and going out to buy more drawing-pins.

650

It occurred to her that she was going mad. This was 'the breakdown' she had foreseen; the 'cracking-up.' Yet it did not seem to her that she was even slightly mad; but rather that people who were not as obsessed as she was with the inchoate world mirrored in the newspapers were all out of touch with an awful necessity. Yet she knew she was mad. And while she could not prevent herself from the careful obsessed business of reading masses of print, and cutting out pieces, and pinning them all over her walls, she knew that on the day Janet came home from school, she would become Anna, Anna the responsible, and the obsession would go away. She knew that Janet's mother being sane and responsible was far more important than the necessity of understanding the world; and one thing depended on the other. The world would never get itself understood, be ordered by words, be 'named,' unless Janet's mother remained a woman who was able to be responsible.

The knowledge that Janet would be home in a month nagged at Anna inside her obsession with newspaper facts. It turned her towards the four notebooks which she had neglected ever since Tommy's accident. She turned the pages of these books over and over, but had no connection with them. She knew that some sort of guilt, which she did not understand, cut her off from them. The guilt was of course connected with Tommy. She did not know, would never know, if Tommy's attempt at suicide was triggered off by reading her notebooks; or, if this were true, whether there was something in particular which had upset him; or whether she was in fact arrogant. 'It's arrogant, Anna; it's irresponsible.' Yes, he had said that; but beyond knowing she had let him down, that she had not been able to give him something he needed, she did not understand what had happened.

One afternoon she went to sleep and dreamed. She knew it was a dream she had often had before, in one form or another. She had two children. One was Janet, plump and glossy with health. The other was Tommy, a small baby, and she was starving him. Her breasts were empty, because Janet had had all the milk in them; and so Tommy was thin and puny, dwindling before her eyes from starvation. He vanished altogether, in a tiny coil of pale bony staring flesh, before she woke, which she did in a fever of anxiety, self-division and guilt. Yet, awake, she could see no reason why she should have dreamed of Tommy being starved by her. And besides, she knew that in other dreams of this cycle, the 'starved' figure might be anyone, perhaps someone she had passed in the street whose face had haunted her. Yet there was no doubt she felt responsible for this half-glimpsed person, for why otherwise should she dream of having failed him—or her?

After this dream, she went feverishly back to work, cutting out news items, fastening them to the wall.

That evening, sitting on the floor, playing jazz, desperate because of her inability to 'make sense' out of the bits of print, she felt a new sensation, like a hallucination, a new and hitherto not understood picture of the world. This understanding was altogether terrible; a reality different from anything she had known before as reality, and it came from a country of feeling she had never visited. It was not being 'depressed'; or being 'unhappy'; of feeling 'discouraged'; the essence of the experience was that such words, like joy or happiness, were meaningless. Coming around from this illumination—which was timeless; so that Anna did not know how long it had lasted, she knew she had had an experience for which there were no words—it was beyond the region where words could be made to have sense.

Yet she again stood before the notebooks, letting her hand with the stylo in it (which looked, with its fragile entrails showing, like a sea-animal, a sea-horse) wait above first one, then another, to let the nature of the 'illumination' decide for itself where it should be written; but the four notebooks, with their various sub-divisions and categories, remained as they were, and Anna laid down her pen.

She tried various passages of music, some jazz, some bits of Bach, some Stravinsky, thinking that perhaps music might say what words could not; but this was one of the times, increasingly frequent, when music seemed to irritate her, seemed to attack the membranes of her inner ear, which repulsed sounds as if they were enemies.

She said to herself: I don't know why I still find it so hard to accept that words are faulty and by their very nature inaccurate. If I thought they were capable of expressing the truth I wouldn't keep journals which I refuse to let anyone see—except, of course, Tommy.

That night she hardly slept; she lay awake re-thinking thoughts already so familiar to her she was bored even by their approach—political thoughts, the patterns of action in our time. It was a descent into banality; because as usual she concluded that any act she might make would be without faith, that is, without faith in 'good' and 'bad,' but simply a sort of provisional act, hoping it might turn out well, but with no more than that hope. Yet from this attitude of mind she might very well find herself making decisions that would cost her her life, or her freedom.

She woke very early, and soon found herself standing in the middle of the kitchen, her hands full of bits of newspaper and drawing-pins, the walls of her big room being entirely covered as far as she could reach, with clippings. She was shocked into laying aside the new clippings, and the bundles of journals and papers. She was thinking: but there's no sensible reason why I should be shocked by starting on a second room, when I wasn't shocked by covering the whole of the first room—or at least, not shocked enough to stop.

Nevertheless, she was encouraged because she would stick up no more fragments of print, offering unassimilable information. She stood in the middle of the big room, telling herself to strip the walls. But she was unable to. She was again moving from point to point, around the room, matching statement with statement, one set of words with another.

While she was doing this, the telephone rang. It was a friend of Molly's. An American left-winger needed a room for a few days. Anna joked that if he was an American he would be writing an epic novel, be in psychoanalysis, and in the process of divorcing his second wife; but said he could have a room. He telephoned later to say he would be over that afternoon at five. Anna dressed to receive him, realising that she had not dressed, except to go out and buy odd bits of food and drawing-pins, for several weeks. Just before five he telephoned again to say he couldn't come, he had to see his agent. Anna was struck by the careful detail he put into his account of the appointment with the agent. A few minutes later Molly's friend rang again to say that Milt (the American) was coming over to a party at her place, and would Anna like to come too? Anna was annoyed, shrugged off the annoyance; refused the invitation, put on her dressing-gown again, and returned to the floor, surrounded by newspapers.

Late that night the bell rang. Anna opened the door, saw the American. He apologised for not telephoning; she apologised for not being dressed.

He was young, about thirty, she judged; with close young brown hair, like healthy fur, a lean intelligent face, bespectacled. He was the shrewd, competent, intelligent American. She knew him well, 'naming' him a hundred times more sophisticated than his English equivalent, by which she meant that he was the inhabitant of a country of desperation still uncharted by Europe.

He began to apologise, as they climbed the stairs, for going to his agent; but she interrupted by asking if he had enjoyed the party. He gave an abrupt laugh, and said: 'Well, you've caught me out.' 'You could always have said that you wanted to go to a party,' she said.

They were in the kitchen, examining each other, smiling. Anna was thinking: A woman without a man cannot meet a man, any man, of any age, without thinking, even if it's for a half-second, Perhaps this is *the* man. That's the reason I was annoyed because he lied about the party. How boring it all is, these ever-so-expected emotions.

She said: 'Would you like to see the room?'

He stood with his hand on the back of a yellow-painted kitchen chair, supporting himself because he had had too much to drink at the party, and said: 'Yes, I would.'

But he did not move. She said: 'You have the advantage of me—I'm sober. But there are some things I must say. First, I do know that all Americans are not rich, the rent is low.' He smiled. 'Second, you're writing the epic American novel and ...' 'Wrong, I haven't started yet.' 'Also, you are in psycho-analysis because you have problems.' 'Wrong again, I went to a headshrinker once and decided I could do better for myself.' 'Well that's a good thing, it will be possible to talk to you at least.'

'What are you being so defensive about?'

'I should have said aggressive, myself,' said Anna, laughing She noted, with interest, that she might just as easily have wept.

He said: 'I dropped in at this unseemly hour because I want to sleep here tonight. I've been at the Y, which in every city I've been in is my least favourite place. I've taken the liberty of bringing my case, which I have with transparent cunning left outside the door.'

'Then bring it in,' said Anna.

He went downstairs to fetch the case. Anna went into the big room to fetch linen for his bed. She went in without thinking; but when she heard him close behind her, she froze as she understood just how that room must look. The floor was billowing with newspapers and journals; the walls were papered with cuttings; the bed was unmade. She turned to him with sheets and pillowcases, saying: 'If you could make your own bed . . .' But he was already in the room, examining it from behind shrewdly focused lenses. Then he sat on her trestle table where the notebooks lay, swinging his legs. He looked at her (she saw herself, in a faded red gown, her hair lying in straight black wisps around an unmade-up face) at the walls and at the floor and at the bed. Then he said, in a mock-shocked voice: 'Gee.' But his face showed concern.

'They said you were a left-winger,' said Anna, in appeal; interested that this was what she instinctively said in explanation of the state of affairs.

'Vintage, post-war.'

'I'm waiting for you to say: I and the other three socialists in the States are going to . . .'

'The other *four*.' He approached a wall as if he were stalking it, took off his glasses to look at its papering (revealing eyes that swam with myopia) and said again: 'Gee.'

He carefully fitted back his spectacles, and said: 'I once knew a man who was a first-rate newspaper correspondent. If

655

you very naturally want to know what his relation to me was, he was my father-figure. A red. Then one thing and another caught up with him, yeah, that's one way of describing it, and now and for the last three years he's been sitting in a cold-water flat in New York, with the windows draped, reading the newspapers. He's got newspapers stacked to the ceiling. The floor space has dwindled to let's say, at a conservative estimate, two square yards. It was a big flat before the newspapers took over.'

'My mania has only lasted a few weeks.'

'I feel it's my duty to say, it's something that can set in and take over—to wit, my poor friend. He's called Hank, by the way.'

'Naturally.'

'A good man. Sad to see, someone going that way.'

'Luckily I have a daughter coming home from school next month, by which time I'll be normal.'

'It might go underground,' he said, sitting on the table and swinging his lanky legs.

Anna began switching covers up on the bed.

'Is that for my benefit?'

'Who else?'

'Unmade beds are my specialty.' He approached her silently as she bent over the bed, and she said: 'I've had all I can take of cold and efficient sex.'

He returned to the table, and remarked: 'Haven't we all? What's happened to all that warm and committed sex we read about in books?'

'It's gone underground,' said Anna.

'Besides, I'm not even efficient.'

'Haven't you ever had it at all?' said Anna, making a point.

She turned, the bed made. They smiled at each other, ironic.

'I *love* my *wife*.'

Anna laughed.

'Yeah. That's why I'm divorcing her. Or she's divorcing me.'

'Well a man loved me once—I mean, *really*.'

656

'And so?'

'And so he ditched me.'

'Understandable. Love is too difficult.'

'And sex too cold.'

'You mean, you've been chaste ever since?'

'Hardly.'

'I thought not.'

'All the same.'

'Having made our positions clear, can we go to bed? I'm a bit lit, and I'm sleepy. And I can't sleep alone.'

The *I can't sleep alone* was said with the cold ruthlessness of someone in extremity. Anna was startled, then came out of herself to really examine him. He sat smiling on her table, a man holding himself together in desperation.

'I can still sleep alone,' said Anna.

'Then from the advantage of your position you can be generous.'

'It's all very well.'

'Anna, I need it. When someone needs something you give it to them.'

She said nothing.

'I shall ask nothing, make no demands and go away when I'm told.'

'Oh quite,' said Anna. She was suddenly angry; she was shaking with anger. 'None of you ask for anything—except everything, but just for so long as you need it.'

'It's the times we live in,' he said.

Anna laughed. Her anger went away. His laugh was sudden, loud, relieved.

'Where did you spend last night?'

'With your friend Betty.'

'She's not my friend. She's the friend of a friend.'

'I spent three nights with her. After the second she told me she loved me and would leave her husband for me.'

'Very square.'

'You wouldn't do a thing like that, would you?'

'I might very well. Any woman would who liked a man.'

'But Anna, you must *see* . . .'

'Oh, I see very well.'

657

'Then I needn't make up my bed?'

Anna began to cry. He came over to her, sat beside her, put his arm around her. 'It's a crazy thing,' he said. 'Moving about the world—I've been moving about the world, did they tell you?—you open a door, and behind it you find someone in trouble. Every time you open a door, there's someone there in pieces.'

'Perhaps you choose your doors.'

'Even so, there have been an astonishing number of doors which—don't cry Anna. That is, not unless you enjoy it, and you don't look as if you do.'

Anna let herself fall back on the pillows, and lay silent. He sat hunched up, near her, plucking at his lips, rueful, intelligent, determined.

'What makes you think that on the morning of the second day I won't say: I want you to stay with me.'

He said carefully, 'You're too intelligent.'

Anna said, resenting the carefulness: 'That will be my epitaph. Here lies Anna Wulf, who was always too intelligent. She let them go.'

'You could do worse, you could keep them, like some I might mention.'

'I suppose so.'

'I'm going to put my pyjamas on and come back in.'

Anna, alone, took off her dressing-gown, hesitated between a night-gown and pyjamas, and chose the night-gown, knowing by instinct he would prefer pyjamas—a sort of gesture of self-definition as it were.

He came in, dressing-gowned, bespectacled. He waved to her as she lay in bed. Then he went to a wall and began stripping off the bits of newsprint. 'A small service,' he said, 'but one I feel that is overdue already.' Anna heard the small tearing of newsprint, a small tapping, as drawing-pins scattered to the floor. She lay, arms under her head, listening. She felt protected and cared for. She lifted her head every few minutes to see how he was progressing. White walls slowly became revealed. The job took a long time, over an hour.

At last he said: 'Well, that's fixed. Another soul for sanity.'

He then stretched out his arms to gather in acres of soiled newsprint, heaping newspapers under the trestle table.

'What are those books? Another novel?'

'No. I wrote a novel once though.'

'I read it.'

'Did you like it?'

'No.'

'No?' Anna was excited. 'Oh, good.'

'Mere*tricious*. That's the word I'd use, if asked.'

'I'm going to ask you to stay on the second morning, I can feel it coming on.'

'But what are these salutarily-bound books?' He began turning the covers back.

'I don't want you to read them.'

'Why not?' he said, reading them.

'Only one person read them. He tried to kill himself, failed, blinded himself, and has now turned into what he tried to kill himself to prevent.'

'Sad.'

Anna lifted his head to see him. He had on his face a deliberately owlish smile.

'You mean, it's all your fault?'

'Not necessarily.'

'Well I'm not a potential suicide. I would say I'm more of a feeder on women, a sucker of other people's vitality, but I'm not a suicide.'

'There's no need to boast about it.'

A pause. Then he said: 'Well yes, as it happens, and having thought out the thing from all *angles*, I'd say it was something to state. Which I'm doing. I'm not boasting. I'm stating. I'm defining. At least I know it. That means I can beat it. You'd be surprised the number of people I know who are killing themselves, or who feed off other people, but they don't know it.'

'No, I wouldn't be surprised.'

'No. But I know it, I know what I do, and that's why I shall beat it.'

Anna heard the dull flap, flap, as the lids of her notebooks closed. She heard the young, cheerful shrewd voice: 'What have you been trying to do? Cage the *truth*? Verity and so forth?'

'Something like that. But it's no good.'

'No good either, to let that vulture guilt get at you, no good at all.' Anna laughed. He began to sing, in a sort of pop-song:

> The vulture guilt,
> Feeds on you and me,
> Don't let that old vulture guilt get you,
> Don't let him be . . .

He went to her record-player, examined her records, put on Brubeck. He said: 'Home from home. I left the States all hot for new experience, but everywhere I find the music I left behind me.' He sat, a solemn cheerful owl in his spectacles, jerking his shoulders and pursing his lips to the jazz. 'There is no doubt,' he said, 'it gives one a sense of continuity, yes, that's the word, a *de*finite sense of continuity, moving from city to city to the same music, and behind every door, a nut like oneself.'

'I'm only temporarily a nut,' said Anna.

'Oh yes. But you've been there. That's enough.' He came to the bed, took off his dressing-gown, got into it, like a brother, friendly and casual.

'Aren't you interested to know why I'm in such bad shape?' he asked after a pause.

'No.'

'I'm going to tell you anyway. I can't sleep with women I like.'

'Banal,' said Anna.

'Oh I agree. Banal to the point of tautology and tedium.'

'And rather sad for me.'

'Sad for me too, surely?'

'Do you know how I feel now?'

'Yes. Believe me, Anna, I know, and I'm sorry. I'm not a square.' A pause. He said: 'You were thinking: And how about me?'

'Oddly enough, yes.'

660

'Want me to screw you? I could, at that.'

'No.'

'No, I thought you wouldn't and you're right.'

'All the same.'

'How'd you like it, being me? The woman I like best in the world is my wife. The last time I screwed her was on our honeymoon. After that, the curtain came down. Three years later, she got sore and said Enough. Do you blame her? Do I? But she likes me better than anyone in the world. The last three nights I spent with your friend's friend Betty. I don't like her, but I do like a certain little wriggle of her ass.'

'Oh don't.'

'You mean you've heard all this before?'

'In one way and another, yes.'

'Yeah, we all have. Shall I go into the sociological—yes, that's the word, the sociological reasons for it?'

'No, I know them.'

'I thought you did. Well. Yes, well. But I'm going to beat it. I told you, I'm a great believer in the mind. I'd put it like that—with your permission? I'm a great believer in knowing what's wrong, admitting it, and saying: I'm going to beat it.'

'Good,' said Anna, 'so am I.'

'Anna, I like you. And thanks for letting me stay. I go nuts sleeping alone.' And then, after a pause: 'You're lucky to have that kid.'

'I know it. That's why I'm sane and you're nuts.'

'Yes. My wife doesn't want a kid. At least, she does. But she said to me: Milt, she said, I'm not going to have a kid with a man who can only get a hard on for me when he's drunk.'

'Using those words?' said Anna, resentful.

'No, doll. No, baby. Saying: I'm not going to have a baby with a man who doesn't love me.'

'How simple minded,' said Anna, full of bitterness.

'Not in that tone of voice, Anna. Or I'll have to go.'

'You don't think there's something slightly extraordinary about a state of affairs where a man walks into a woman's flat and says: I've got to share your bed because I fall into space if I sleep alone, but I can't make love to you because if I do I'll hate you?'

'Any more extraordinary than certain other phenomena we might mention?'

'No,' said Anna judiciously. 'No.' She added: 'Thank you for taking that nonsense off my walls. Thank you. Another few days and I really would have gone round the bend.'

'It's a pleasure. I'm a flop, Anna, at the moment of speaking, I don't need you to tell me, but there's one thing I'm good at, seeing someone in trouble and knowing what strong measures to take.'

They went to sleep.

In the morning she felt him deadly cold in her arms, a weight of terrible cold, like holding death. She slowly rubbed him warm and awake. Warm, awake, and grateful, he came into her. But by then she was already armed against him, she could not prevent herself from being tense, she could not relax.

'There you are,' he said afterwards, 'I knew it. Wasn't I right?'

'Yes, you were. But there's something about a man with a whacking great erection that it's hard to resist.'

'All the same, you should have. Because now we're going to have to spend a lot of energy on not disliking each other.'

'But I don't dislike you.' They were very fond of each other, sad, and friendly and close, like people who had been married to each other for twenty years.

He was there five days with her, sleeping in her bed at night.

On the sixth day, she said, 'Milt I want you to stay with me.' She said it in parody, a kind of angry self-punishing parody, and he said, smiling and rueful: 'Yeah, I know it's time to move on. It's time I moved on. But why do I have to, why do I have to?'

'Because I want you to stay.'

'Why can't you take it? Why not?' His spectacles glinted anxiously, his mouth was carefully amused, but he was pale, and his forehead glinted with sweat. 'You've got to take us on, you've got to, don't you know that? Don't you see it's all

662

much worse for us than it is for you? I know you are bitter for yourselves and you're right, but if you can't take us on now, and see us through it . . .'

'And the same to you,' said Anna.

'No. Because you're tougher, you're kinder, you're in a position to take it.'

'You'll find another well-tempered woman in the next city.'

'If I'm lucky.'

'And I hope you are.'

'Yes, I know you do. I know it. And thank you . . . Anna, I'm going to beat it. You've every reason to think that I won't. But I shall. I know I shall.'

'Then good luck,' said Anna, smiling.

Before he left, they stood in the kitchen, both near tears, reluctant to make the break.

'You aren't going to give in, Anna?'

'Why not?'

'It would be a pity.'

'And besides, you might want to drop in again some time for a night or two.'

'All right. You are entitled to say that.'

'But next time I'll be occupied. For one thing, I'm getting a job.'

'Oh don't tell me, let me guess. You're going to do social work? You're going to—let me think it out for myself—you're going to be a psychiatric social worker or teach school or something like that?'

'Something like that.'

'We all come to it.'

'You, however, will be saved from it because of your epic novel.'

'Unkind, Anna, unkind.'

'I don't feel kind. I'd like to shout and scream and break everything down.'

'As I was saying, that's the dark secret of our time, no one mentions it, but every time one opens a door one is greeted by a shrill, desperate and inaudible scream.'

'Well thanks anyhow for pulling me out—of what I was in.'

'Any time.'

They kissed. He jumped lightly down the stairs, his suitcase in his hand, turning at the bottom to say: 'You should have said—I'll write.'

'But we won't.'

'No, but let's preserve the forms, the *forms* at least of ...' He was gone, with a wave of his hand.

When Janet came home she found Anna in the process of finding another, smaller flat, and getting a job.

Molly had telephoned Anna, to say she was getting married. The two women met in Molly's kitchen, where Molly was preparing them salad and omelettes.

'Who is he?'

'You don't know him. He's what we used to refer to as a progressive businessman. You know, the poor Jewish boy from the East End who got rich and salved his conscience by giving money to the communist party. Now they just give money to progressive causes.'

'Oh he's got money?'

'Quantities. And a house in Hampstead.' Molly turned her back to her friend, while Anna digested this.

'What are you going to do with this house?'

'Can't you guess?' Molly turned, the briskness of her former irony back in her voice. Her smile was wry and gallant.

'You don't mean that Marion and Tommy are going to take it?'

'What else? Haven't you seen them?'

'No, nor Richard.'

'Well. Tommy's all set to follow in Richard's footsteps. He's already installed, and taking things over, and Richard's slowly going to ease out and settle down with Jean.'

'You mean, he's all happy and content?'

'Well I saw him with a pretty bit last week in the street, but don't let's jump to conclusions.'

'No, don't let's.'

'Tommy is very definite about not being all reactionary and unprogressive like Richard. He says the world is going to be

664

changed by the efforts of progressive big business and putting pressure on Government departments.'

'Well he, at least, is in tune with our times.'

'Please don't, Anna.'

'Well, how's Marion?'

'She's bought a dress shop in Knightsbridge. She's going to sell good clothes—you know, *good* clothes as distinct from smart clothes? She's already surrounded by a gaggle of little queers who exploit her, and she adores them and she giggles a lot and drinks just a *little* too much, and thinks they are ever such fun.'

Molly's hands lay on her lap, fitted together at the finger-tips, exercising malicious no-comment.

'*Well*.'

'And how about your American?'

'Well I had an affair with him.'

'Not the most sensible thing you ever did, I should have thought.'

Anna laughed.

'What's funny?'

'Getting married to a man who has a house in Hampstead is going to make you very remote from the emotional rat-race.'

'Yes, thank God.'

'I'm going to take a job.'

'You mean, you're not going to write?'

'No.'

Molly turned away, and flipped omelettes on to plates, filling a basket with bread. She determinedly said nothing.

'Do you remember Dr. North?' said Anna.

'Of course.'

'He's starting a sort of marriage welfare centre—half-official, half-private. He says three-quarters of the people who come to him with aches and pains are in fact in trouble with their marriages. Or lack of marriages.'

'And you're going to dish out good advice.'

'Something like that. And I'm going to join the Labour Party and teach a night class twice a week for delinquent kids.'

'So we're both going to be integrated with British life at its roots.'

'I was carefully avoiding that tone.'

'You're right—it's just the idea of you doing matrimonial welfare work.'

'I'm very good at other people's marriages.'

'Oh, quite so. Well perhaps you'll find me in that chair opposite you one of these days.'

'I doubt it.'

'Me too. There's nothing like knowing the exact dimensions of the bed you're going to fit yourself into.' Annoyed with herself, Molly's hands made an irritated gesture, and she grimaced and said: 'You're a bad influence on me, Anna. I was perfectly resigned to it all until you came in. Actually I think we'll get on very well.'

'I don't see why not,' said Anna.

A small silence. 'It's all very odd, isn't it Anna?'

'Very.'

Shortly after, Anna said she had to get back to Janet, who would have returned by now from the cinema, where she had been with a friend.

The two women kissed and separated.